THE

RAVEN SCHOLAR

THE
RAVEN
SCHOLAR

BOOK ONE OF THE
ETERNAL PATH TRILOGY

∞

ANTONIA
HODGSON

orbit

orbitbooks.net

Copyright © 2025 by Antonia Hodgson
Excerpt from *The Mercy Makers* copyright © 2025 by Tessa Gratton

Cover design by Stephanie A. Hess
Cover illustrations by Tom Roberts and Shutterstock
Map illustrations by Dewi Hargreaves
Author photograph by Rebecca Douglas

Orbit
Hachette Book Group
1290 Avenue of the Americas
New York, NY 10104
orbitbooks.net

First Edition: April 2025
Simultaneously published in Great Britain by Hodderscape, an imprint of Hodder & Stoughton, an Hachette UK company

Orbit is an imprint of Hachette Book Group.
The Orbit name and logo are registered trademarks of Little, Brown Book Group Limited.

The Hachette Speakers Bureau provides a wide range of authors for speaking events. To find out more, go to hachettespeakersbureau.com or email HachetteSpeakers@hbgusa.com.

Orbit books may be purchased in bulk for business, educational, or promotional use. For information, please contact your local bookseller or the Hachette Book Group Special Markets Department at special.markets@hbgusa.com.

Library of Congress Control Number: 2024939056

ISBNs: 9780316577229 (trade paperback), 9780316577236 (ebook)

Printed in the United States of America

LSC-C

Printing 1, 2025

THE
RAVEN
SCHOLAR

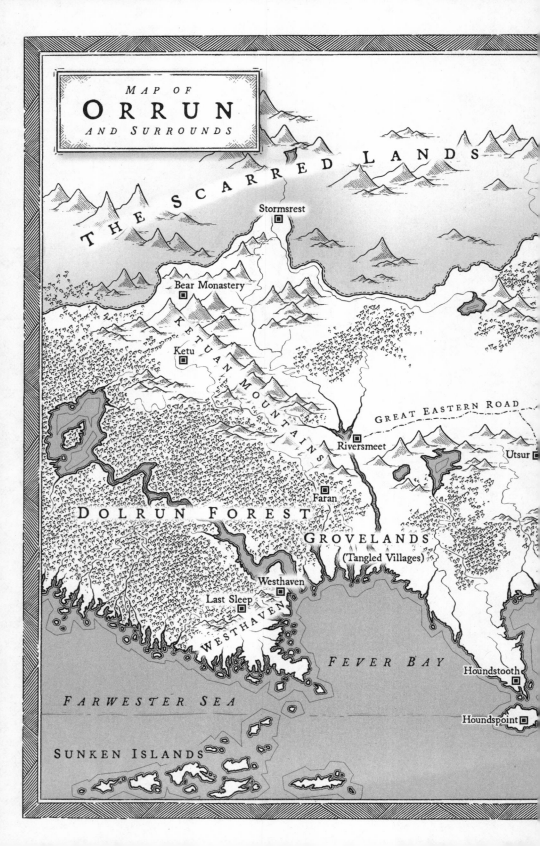

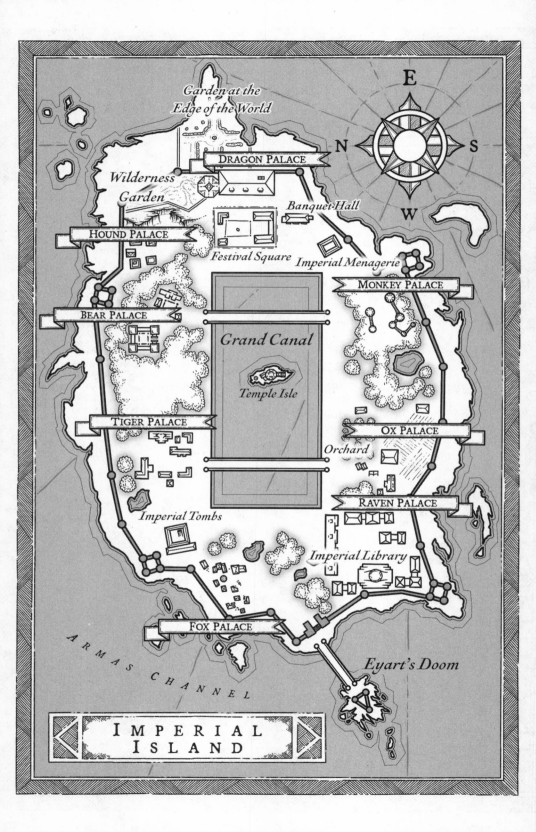

Garden at the
Edge of the World

DRAGON PALACE

Wilderness
Garden

Banquet Hall

HOUND PALACE

Festival Square

Imperial Menagerie

BEAR PALACE

MONKEY PALACE

Grand Canal

Temple Isle

TIGER PALACE

OX PALACE

Orchard

Imperial Tombs

RAVEN PALACE

Imperial Library

FOX PALACE

A R M A S   C H A N N E L

Eyart's Doom

IMPERIAL
ISLAND

Brother, Sister—listen to me,
The Eight will Return in blood and fire.
You will taste them in the water,
You will hear them in the wind,
You will glimpse them in the lightning storm.
They will come to you in dreams.
They will call to you.
Do not let them in, do not let them in.
They are coming.

"The Bear Warrior's Lament," anon

…and the skies wept poison on to the ruined
earth…

Dolrun tomb inscription,
trans. Neema Kraa

PART ONE

An Invitation

CHAPTER

One

ONCE THEY MADE sacrifices here, to appease the Eight. This was many thousands of years ago, but the rock remembers. There was a modest temple on the hill, with views across the island, and worn stone steps leading up to a plain stone slab. Now there is a palace with golden halls and floors of white marble. Lustrous silk tapestries hang from the walls, telling intricate stories of love and war, and the death of tyrants. The air is lacquered with incense, rich and heady.

This is where my father died.

Yana Valit walked beside her twin brother Ruko, willing herself to stay calm. The emperor had no reason to hurt her; she had done nothing wrong.

Nothing he could know about.

Yasila followed close behind them, her footsteps muffled by the fine antique rugs that lined the way. Without turning, Yana could picture her mother's expression precisely—composed, dignified. Yasila wore her fabled beauty like a mask, her light brown skin unmarked by years of loss and misfortune. A flick of kohl, a dab of perfume. Three paces away, and as distant as the moon.

Had she known the emperor would summon them here, this morning? No point in asking. Yasila had grown up a hostage on the Dragon island of Helia, where secrets were hoarded like precious jewels. She had learned young how to hold her tongue, and bind her heart.

They headed down another hushed corridor, deep within the inner sanctum. A solitary guard watched them approach, hand upon the hilt of his sword. He was dressed in the uniform of the Imperial

Bodyguard—black trousers and a red tunic slashed with five black claw marks. The Bear sigil, worn to honour the emperor. The man carried himself more like a Hound warrior, Yana thought, his weight balanced slightly towards his toes, giving him a poised, dynamic stance. Yasila had trained her children to notice these things. As they passed beneath the guard's piercing gaze, Yana spotted the square silver ring on his middle finger. The sigil of the Hound. She smothered a smile, imagining her mother's admonishment. *This is not a game, Yanara. This is how we survive.*

Another turn, another incense-laden corridor, almost identical to the last. There were no windows, no way for Yana to orientate herself. This, she knew, was a trick of the sanctum. Even experienced courtiers arrived at the throne room with a queasy sensation that they had both reached their destination, and lost their way.

There is a world, Yana reminded herself, beyond these walls. Out there, out across the imperial island and its lesser palaces, courtiers strolled through pleasure gardens and woodland trails, trading scandals or starting new ones behind the deafening roar of frothing fountains. Servants sweated in the laundries, burned their fingers in the kitchens, talked of leaving as they shared a roll-up behind the service huts.

Yana felt a familiar tension in her chest—a desire to run out into the bright morning sunshine and disappear. Dodge the guards and take a boat back to the mainland, melt away into the busy streets of central Armas. Hitch a ride out of the capital and head north to Scartown, or some other rundown place on the borders. Start a new life, with a new name…

A dream, a fantasy. There was no escape for the daughter of Andren Valit, the Great Traitor. There was no disappearing into the crowd. For the last eight years—half her life—Yana and her family had been watched, ceaselessly. When neighbours in their grid complained about the rubbish piling up, the rising cost of food, the street crime, the Valits kept their mouths clamped shut. They could not afford the luxury of speaking their minds. They must assume—always—that someone was listening, eager to report them to the Hounds. Theirs was a tightrope of a life, sharks circling below.

Ruko was gnawing his lip. Yana wanted to tell him not to worry, everything would be fine. But when she tried to speak, there was a knot in her throat. She never could lie to her brother.

∞ ∞ ∞

The Palace Hounds had arrived in the middle of the night. Boots on the stairs, a sharp rap at the door. Instantly awake, Yana threw back her bedsheet and swung her legs over her bunk. She'd trained herself to shift like this, from deep sleep to high alert. Her family might live under the emperor's written protection, but that only extended so far. There were plenty who still believed the Valits had been dealt with too kindly, after the rebellion. A piece of paper would not deflect an assassin's blade.

"Open up, please," a voice called through the door.

Dropping down to the floor, Yana reached into the bottom bunk and punched Ruko in the arm. He groaned and burrowed deeper under the blanket. "Ruko," she hissed, irritated. She loved her brother, but for Eight's sake. "*Move.*"

In the living room, her mother stood in front of a mirror, clipping back her long black hair. "Open the door to our guests, Yanara."

The Valits lived in a cramped, three-roomed apartment above a tailor's workshop. To reach it, visitors must take a rotting wooden staircase, flimsily attached to the external wall. Yasila had dismissed the tailor's offer to have it replaced. Let the way to her door be treacherous. The young Hound sergeant, having assessed the risk, had come up alone. His squad waited for him below, yawning in the velvet dark, batons fixed to their belts.

He introduced himself in neutral tones, giving nothing away. "Madam Valit? Sergeant Shal Worthy. His Majesty summons you to the island. No, not your youngest, just you and the twins. One of my officers will watch over…" He groped for a name. *Eight*, what was she called again, the little one?

"Nisthala," Ruko offered, earning a sharp look from his mother. The sergeant gave Ruko a nod. "Nisthala. Thank you, sir."

Sir. The title sounded strange to Yana, but it was formally correct. She and her brother had turned sixteen yesterday. According to the law, Ruko was a man now.

And how old was the sergeant? Yana wondered, studying him in the candlelight. Only a few years ahead of them. He looked like a hero from a dance-tragedy, all soulful and athletic, with striking hazel eyes and smooth, warm-brown skin. He'd done his best to rough up his edges, in a bid to blend in with his more experienced squad. His full moustache merged with a thick stubble and his dark brown curls were chopped short. But his hands were a young man's hands, his frame and his jawline still boyish. Twenty-one, Yana decided. Fresh out of Houndspoint and straight to squad sergeant, which meant he was being groomed for a high imperial position—

Shit.

She was studying him, he was studying her, his eyes blazing with internal fire. Houndsight. A rare, innate ability to read a person's thoughts and feelings with uncanny accuracy. Yana's heart flared a warning. What had he seen? What had she given away?

The sergeant's eyes dimmed back to normal. "Twenty-two, as a matter of fact." He rubbed his jaw, rueful. "Maybe a beard would help, what do you reckon?"

Yana liked the way he'd made a joke, to counter the effect of his unsettling gift. But it didn't alter the fact that the emperor—who could have sent anyone to escort them to the island—had chosen a man who could read them right down to the bone. Well—not her mother, perhaps. Not a child raised by Dragons.

A brief hug for Nisthala, sleepy and fretful and annoyed at being left behind—why was she always left behind, it wasn't fair—and it was time to go. As they followed Sergeant Worthy down the stairs, Yana murmured a warning in Ruko's ear, about the Houndsight. He nodded. He'd seen.

Armas City was built on a grid system, once revolutionary, now familiar. Yana's grid—G4 NW—was comprised of the usual eight connecting squares, each one arranged around a shared courtyard. In more glamorous parts of the capital, these common spaces were transformed into whatever stood for paradise among the fashionable that year. (Lush scent gardens, in 1531—everyone had gone wild for lush scent gardens.) Yana's square was not glamorous by any definition, but it was well looked after, with a communal vegetable plot and mature fruit trees, and a tiled prayer octagon for the faithful. Rundown but respectable. When the residents of Square 3 had first learned that the Valits were moving in, they had organised a petition in protest. We are loyal citizens of Orrun, it said. We do not want our home tainted by these people. Some of them had softened their opinion over the years. Some had not.

The squad's arrival had woken them all. Neighbours leaned from windows, fascinated. They'd seen the mother taken away for interrogation plenty of times, but always on her own. This was new. What now, for the Valits? Some fresh disgrace?

"What's happening?" someone shouted down. "Where are you taking them?"

"My apologies for the disturbance, citizens," Sergeant Worthy replied. Houndspeak for none of your business. He tapped one of his officers on the shoulder—an older woman. "Stay and watch the little one." As she set off he pulled her back, added in a quieter voice, "She's frightened, trying to hide it. Be patient with her."

People were still calling down, demanding answers. "What have they done?" "Are they under arrest?" "We've been saying for years, you can't trust them—"

"Good night, citizens." The sergeant's tone had shifted. They heard the warning laced through it, and fell silent. After a tense moment, he added, friendly again, "May the Eight protect you..."

"...and remain Hidden," people called back, with varying degrees of conviction.

The nearest docks were a couple of miles to the east. As they walked, they moved from the residential sector through squares dedicated to millwork and forges, and cavernous storehouses where people worked through the night, loading and unloading by lantern light. Some of the workers nodded at the sergeant as he passed. One woman dropped her load and put her fist to her chest in a Hound salute. This was something more than respect for his position. Ruko nudged Yana, and mouthed: *Worthy*. A not uncommon family name, but given the sergeant's Houndsight, and his swift elevation…

"I'm his nephew," he said, eventually.

Yana's skin prickled. High Commander Gatt Worthy had died in her father's attempted coup eight years ago. When Andren rushed the throne steps, it was Gatt Worthy who saw the threat, and placed himself between the emperor and Andren's blade. It had been the pivotal moment of the rebellion. Gatt Worthy's sacrifice. Andren Valit's treachery.

"I'm sorry," Ruko said.

"I can see that," Worthy replied. Of course he could. *Those eyes.* After a short pause, he added, "Thanks."

The north-east docks were quiet, the sea lapping gently against the quay. In this bridging hour before dawn, the world was cloaked a sullen grey—the colour of loss, the colour of mourning. A couple of fishing boats were preparing to set sail, their crews moving in a silent harmony born of daily repetition. On rooftops, seagulls stretched out their throats, calling sharply to one another across the water. We are here, we are here. Another day begins.

Sergeant Worthy set off alone down the quay to inspect their boat, leaving his squad to conduct the mandatory strip and search. As if, perhaps, he wanted no part of it. Yana fumbled to remove her clothes under the withering gaze of her guard. The search was not gentle. The woman wrenched apart Yana's short plait, poked and prodded her body with mean fingers. "What do you expect?" she hissed, when Yana protested. "Traitor's daughter."

Fighting back the tears, Yana tidied herself up as best she could without a comb. Her hair—like her mother's, and her brother's—was straight and black, with subtle strands of iridescent purple and blue that only showed in certain lights. An inheritance from their ancestor Yasthala the Great, the last Raven empress.

To her left, Ruko was joking with the men searching him. That's how he'd learned to survive with the cursed Valit name hanging round his neck. Yana used her wits, Ruko his good humour.

And their mother?

Dignity.

As the Hounds approached, Yasila stretched out her arms and inclined her head—a goddess, bestowing upon her handmaidens the privilege of disrobing her. There was a brief debate over the jewelled hairclip—might it be used as a weapon? "It might," Yasila decided for them, and handed it over. "Keep it, for your trouble," she murmured. A gift that robbed them of their power to take. As the women made their respectful bows, Yasila angled her gaze towards her daughter. *This is how it is done, Yanara.* And Yana thought, not for the first time—if I live to be a hundred, I will never perfect my mother's exquisite cunning, her regal defiance.

Yasila had been summoned to the imperial island dozens of times since the rebellion. There was no discernible pattern to her visits. Emperor Bersun might request her presence three nights in a row. He might let a season pass without mentioning her name. Either way, Yasila was fixed to him by an invisible chain. It was his majesty's right to pull upon it as and when he pleased.

As to *why* he summoned her—one obvious, sordid possibility. Yasila—a clever, bewitchingly beautiful woman of thirty-five—met with the emperor alone in his private chambers: no servants, no bodyguards. How the court loved the idea, how they laughed behind their sleeves. The craggy old soldier, the enigmatic widow.

Yana would not think of that. Her mother and the emperor.

A guard handed her a pair of brown cotton trousers and a matching long-sleeved tunic. If they were asked, the Hounds would say they were keeping the emperor safe. The outfits had no pockets, the material was too thin to conceal a weapon. But this was also a deliberate slight: the once rich and powerful Valits presented at court in outfits more suited to farm work.

Yana didn't care—she hated dressing up—but the clothes were too big for her short, narrow frame. She wondered if they had given her Ruko's outfit by mistake. No, she realised, as she turned to study her brother. He was already dressed, and looked as he always did these days: like a golden god. Bastard.

He threw a pose to amuse them both. Yana laughed, their mother frowned. Yasila could never understand this about her twins, the secret messages and in-jokes passing between them. Yana laughed because she knew that beneath the clowning her brother was worried. She laughed to reassure him, just as he had posed to distract her. And it worked, on the surface.

But underneath, the thrumming fear.

Why had the emperor called for them today, of all days? What did he want?

∞ ∞ ∞

Seven and a half years had passed since they last stood before the great Bear warrior. Bersun the Brusque, the reluctant emperor, who wore the crown out of duty, not desire.

After the rebellion, after the riots, the purges and the public executions, Bersun had sailed in procession down Dragon's Mouth Bay to Samra City—ancestral home of the Valit dynasty. No one missed the significance. Entire neighbourhoods streamed from their homes to welcome him, packing the streets, waving and cheering with hectic fervour. The weather was bad. The weather was terrible. No matter. This was a day for the city that raised the Great Traitor to affirm its loyalty to the crown.

On the cracked marble steps of the Assembly Hall, Bersun stood beneath a golden canopy, shielded from the pounding rain —a hulking giant with a long, battered face. The sort of man you prayed to the Eight was on your side on a battlefield.

The canopy was not for him. Bear warriors preferred to stand as they were trained—out in the open, exposed to the elements. This was how you stayed tough, and strong, and focused. The canopy was for his ceremonial clothes, which he hated. Golden robes, densely woven with eight-sided patterns. A heavy, sumptuous red velvet cloak, trimmed with fur. Worst of all, a pair of soft, embroidered satin shoes, which could only look ridiculous on his enormous feet. He had roared when they were first presented to him —literally roared, like an actual bear. A man who had patrolled the Scarred Lands for twenty years, defeated by a slipper.

The emperor did not like his clothes, but duty said he must wear them, and they must not be spoiled. The dignity of the office. So he stood beneath the canopy, glowering as he always did on these occasions.

As for the crowds crammed into White Tiger Square, they were drenched, hair plastered to their skulls. Their one consolation in such miserable, inauspicious weather—Emperor Bersun hated speech-making even more than he hated his elaborate robes. This would not take long.

Raising his arms, the emperor displayed his ruined right hand for all to see. He had lost three fingers in his desperate, bloody fight with Andren Valit. Almost lost his life too, by all accounts. This was his first public appearance since that day. His giant frame and bulky robes could not disguise the truth: the Bear warrior was diminished, both in body and spirit.

"There's been enough blood spilled," he declared, shouting over the rain. His voice was gruff, with the short vowels and hard consonants of a far Norwesterner. "My body's broken: it will mend. The empire's broken, it will mend. We shall heal together. We shall grow stronger, together. This I swear, on the Eight."

Cheers and applause washed through the square, as those at the front passed the message back. Had his rebellion succeeded, Andren would have restored his beloved city to its former glory. The ancient capital would have become the seat of power once more. The fear was, the emperor had come to destroy Samra in revenge. It wouldn't take much. The once invincible Marble City had been in decline for fifteen centuries. Rubble City, people called it now, part mocking, part wistful.

Bersun waited for his people to settle. Then, on his signal, the Hounds brought Yana and Ruko up to join him. Eight years old they were then, clutching each other's hand for courage. As Yana stepped under the golden canopy, she saw tears of sympathy in the Old Bear's eyes. He beckoned to them, encouraging, and she hated him for it. How dare he be kind? This man who had killed her father.

The twins had been told to give the emperor a Bear salute. They did so in unison, right hand raised smartly to right temple, palm out.

Bersun looked touched. He wrapped an arm around Yana's shoulder, gathering her in to him. The same to Ruko, on his left side. A great Bear hug from the great Bear emperor. Yana felt sick.

He turned them to face the crowds. "You've stood here before," he said, softly. "You know these people."

It was true. As Governor of Samra, their father was always proclaiming something or other on the Assembly steps. People had loved to see the twins beside him. And Yasila in her flowing silks, long black hair netted with gold latticework.

"What do you see?" the emperor asked them.

Yana had gazed down at the crowds, still cheering and clapping wildly. "Fear," she answered, at the same moment Ruko said, "Relief."

"Fear and relief," the emperor repeated, to himself. "Yes. That's it. Very good." He gave them both a final squeeze and let them go.

A few weeks later Gatt Worthy's successor, High Commander Hol Vabras, had issued an edict stating that Yasila Valit was guilty of "indirect support" of the rebellion. In other words—her husband had used her money to fund it. For this crime she was stripped of all titles and estates, and given a six-month sentence. As she had already languished in the imperial dungeons for almost eight months, she was released the same day, cradling her baby daughter in her arms. Nisthala Valit—born in darkness, brought into the light. The edict continued:

Citizen Yasila Valit and her children shall be permitted to live freely in the Armas grids, with the following caveats:

On pain of death: they shall not leave the capital.

On pain of death: they shall not consort with sympathisers of the Traitor Andren Valit, nor seek to restore his reputation.

Also: the Valits must surrender themselves and their property to any inspections deemed necessary by His Majesty's servant, High Commander Hol Vabras.

Under these terms, it pleases His Majesty that the Valit children should grow to maturity without harm or prejudice.

May the Eight protect His Majesty and remain Hidden.

Signed by
High Commander Hol Vabras
this fourth day of the month of Am, 1523

∞ ∞ ∞

Bersun had kept his promise. Nothing stronger in this world, my friend, than the word of a Bear warrior. But yesterday, the twins had turned sixteen. No longer children. No longer protected by the edict.

"Yana," Ruko said quietly, as they boarded the boat to the imperial island. "The emperor spared us all these years. He won't destroy us now."

Her brother, the optimist.

CHAPTER

Two

T HE JOURNEY WOULD take well over an hour, the sun rising
ahead of them as they sailed east. They were travelling with
the day servants on a leaking heap that moaned and shuddered as
it rode the waves. When visitors arrived in the capital they would
rush to take in this celebrated view: the sea stretching off to the
horizon, the imperial island a tantalising glimmer in the distance.
Last stop before the end of the world.

All citizens of Armas felt a tug of connection to the island.
Their city had been designed with the sole purpose of serving
the court. Yana's relationship was more complicated. Her father
may have died on the island, but she and Ruko were born there.
Yasila had given birth to the twins in the imperial palace, in the
middle of the Festival Trials. *Auspicious*, people said, at the time.
Then later: *Cursed*. This was the first time Yana had returned to
her birthplace. As the boat drew slowly nearer, she felt a lift of
anticipation, laced with dread.

The island had no name, and it never would. Yana's ancestor,
Empress Yasthala, had moved her court there after the War of the
Raven's Dream. A new beginning, with a new capital and a new
calendar. In the autumn of II N.C., Yasthala's ministers had gathered before the white marble throne, where she sat beneath the
great octagonal window. On bended knee, they'd begged leave to
name the island in her honour. *And in her memory*, they thought,
but did not say. For the empress was fading, everyone saw it.

Yasthala, dressed in her indigo robes and amethyst crown, had
lowered her head. In the garden beyond the window, burnt orange
leaves fluttered from the branches, and the sky was grey. "What

poisoned deeds are born from love," she'd said, in a weary voice. "This island is not mine. To stamp my name upon it would be a betrayal of everything I have fought for. This island belongs to no one, and to everyone. Name it not."

Yana clung to the slatted bench, gritting her teeth as the boat pitched and rolled, and her stomach pitched and rolled with it. Her neighbour—a bald-headed black man—watched her from the corner of his eyes as he smoked his roll-up. He was wearing short-sleeved overalls and a pair of battered leather boots, and had the solid, indomitable physique of a working man in his prime. He also smelled faintly of fish, which wasn't helping. "Deep breaths," he said. "Eyes on the horizon."

Yana nodded, and promptly threw up over the side.

The man stubbed out his roll-up. "Ginger pastilles," he called out to the other passengers. They seemed to know each other, probably took the same boat out every day. "Anyone?"

A tin was found, and passed up through the boat to her neighbour. Everyone seemed to like him. Not in the way people liked Ruko, or had liked her father—moths to a flame. He just felt comfortable to be around, the way some people do.

He handed the tin to Yana. While she sucked on a pastille, he told her about the fourth palace, where he worked. An Oxman, then. If he was lucky, he said, he would finish his fucking paperwork over breakfast, then he'd get out into the orchards and, he added vaguely, "see how that's going." The island, he explained, was designed to be self-sufficient in times of siege; the farm attached to the Ox palace could support the court for years if necessary. This wasn't news, everyone knew about the imperial island and how it worked, but he carried on talking, in his laid-back, Southern Heartlands drawl, and after a while Yana felt much better, which had been the whole point.

The island was close now; she could see black and white terns and guillemots nestled among its steep cliffs, waves rinsing the rocks below. Above the cliffs sat the high perimeter walls, cornered with watchtowers. "A thousand years old, those walls," the Oxman said. "They teach you that in school?"

Yana let the last of the ginger pastille dissolve before answering. "Pirate raid, 517. Took forty years to build."

"You know your history." The Oxman sounded impressed. "Raven?"

Yana scrunched her face. Now she was sixteen, she was free to head over to the temple and affiliate with whichever Guardian she preferred. Definitely *not* the Raven, despite the ancestral connection. Ravens were lawyers, scholars, teachers, administrators. Desks, ink, bookshelves. No thanks.[1] "Too much fucking paperwork," she said, and her new friend grinned to have his words thrown back at him.

She stole a glance at Yasila, sitting further down the boat with Ruko. "My mother's cross with me."

The Oxman lifted his eyebrows. "Oh, she is? For throwing up?" He laughed at the idea.

"For needing help."

"Ah."

A sleek grey seal swam up alongside the boat, huffing through its wide nostrils. The Oxman pulled a large, plump fish from his overalls. The seal leapt up on its tail, caught the fish neatly in its mouth and flopped back into the sea, spraying Yana with water. She laughed and wiped her face.

The Oxman laughed with her. "You know, it's the little things."

"Life is short, so enjoy it."

He lowered his head, still smiling. But his eyes were serious. "Exactly."

"Yanara." Her mother's voice floated down the boat. "Come and sit with your brother."

Before the island, one last stop—a sharp, treacherous rock, at the top of which lay a squat garrison, built of dark grey brick. Here the Valits would be processed before walking across the Mirror Bridge to the ancient Guardian Gate. This dramatic approach to the island was a sign that their visit was of high significance to the

---

1. An unforgivably reductive description; we are aggrieved.

emperor. Perhaps they would be honoured. Perhaps they would be punished. The uncertainty was deliberate.

Yana watched the day boat set off again, taking the friendly Oxman with it. She felt a pang of loss. She hadn't even caught his name.

Sergeant Worthy ushered her on to a small wooden platform with roped sides. There was only room for three at a time—he would have to return for her mother and Ruko. He turned his back and cranked the winch. The pulley juddered into life, drawing them slowly up the rock—an ugly, jagged thing, like a rotten tooth. Eyart's Doom, they called it. Empress Yasthala had signed the truce up there with the Six Families, at the end of the war. "Our trials are over," her husband had declared, his hand upon her shoulder. "At last we shall know peace." Never say this. Three days later Eyart was dead.

Yana looked down. Ruko and Yasila were twenty feet below and receding. Beyond them, the restless sea churned against the rocks. Ruko's brows were drawn into a frown. She couldn't tell from this distance if he was worried for her, or annoyed he was going second. Yana was the firstborn. Their father used to tease them about it. "*Eight*, Ruko!" he'd laugh, whenever Yana beat her brother at something. "She's elbowed you out the way again." Family jokes. Powerful things.

The platform creaked its way up the side of the rock, disturbing the terns that lifted and wheeled about in protest. A hot summer breeze blew Yana's hair across her face. She pushed it back. She could see the Mirror Bridge from here. She tried not to think of those who had walked it before her—how many of them had come to a bad end. Instead she studied Sergeant Worthy's back, the smooth way he worked the winch. He must know why they were summoned, he must know if she and her brother were in danger.

"Is there anything you can tell me?" she asked.

He didn't answer.

She tried again. "It's just you and me up here."

He glanced back at her. Bright hazel eyes, framed with thick black lashes. "When you come before the emperor,

I'll be watching you. My advice?" He returned to the winch. "Don't lie."

The Mirror Bridge stretched across the sea from the garrison to the palace island. Constructed from huge iron segments bolted together, it was painted gold, like something from a folk tale. The floor gave the bridge its name—tiles of mirrored glass, dazzlingly bright in the morning sun. Some said a Dragonspell kept it in pristine condition. The team of servants who maintained it knew better.

Yana took two steps, and slipped. For a half-second she felt the terror of falling, before her fingers found the railing. And there on the floor she saw herself, trapped in a dozen mirrored pieces. Fear and relief. From this height, you'd fall so fast the sea might as well be rock. Here was the hidden lesson of the bridge. Watch your footing. Watch yourself. The emperor awaits. She took off her borrowed felt slippers and walked the rest of the way barefoot.

At the mid point, she stopped to read a small bronze plaque fixed to the railing. Shimmer Arbell had jumped to her death here, just over a year ago. Right in front of the emperor. The greatest artist of the age, gone at thirty-nine.

The plaque said: *Her light still shines.*

"Keep moving," Sergeant Worthy called from the back.

The Guardian Gate loomed up before her—a pair of giant, painted wooden doors, almost as tall as the perimeter wall. Yasthala had shipped the Gate from the old court at Samra. It was ancient even by Samran standards—but its message remained as fresh as the day it was first painted. Fierce icons of the Eight glared out towards the mainland, eyes rimmed white in the old style, blood streaming from tooth and claw. These were not the Eight of the Kind Returns, cheerful and benevolent. These were the Eight that would come at the end of the world, to judge and to destroy.

Yana stepped off the bridge, still barefoot. Out of habit, she looked for the Monkey's image on the Gate. The Guardians were paired in the traditional way, side by side, one on each door:

Yana had always felt a close connection to the Monkey, Guardian of the Arts, of Festivals and Games. In fact, she had planned to visit the temple this morning to affiliate. The Sixth Guardian was usually portrayed as the most approachable of the Eight, friendly and helpful. Staring up at the ferocious image on the door, she was reminded of something her father had taught her. "The Monkey can be playful, but it is still a creature of the wild. Today, it dances at your side. Tomorrow it may jump on your back, and sink its teeth in your throat. Affiliate as you please, when the time comes. But choose with your eyes wide open. Every Guardian has its shadow side."

"Yana!" A strangled voice to her right.

She turned in surprise. It was her friend from the boat, panting heavily as he rubbed the sweat from his face and scalp. He must have climbed the steps carved into the island's cliff face—an almost vertical ascent. There were several routes on to the island. Why the Eight would he stagger up this way?

He put his hands on his knees, still panting. "Damn. Time was…I could run up…those steps…four at a time. And sing you a song at the end. Badly," he conceded. "Very badly. But I could sing it."

"What's wrong?" Yana asked.

"The pastilles," he gasped, beckoning for her to hand them over.

Yana's face fell. "The Hounds confiscated them. I'm so sorry. I'll find a way to pay you back if…"

The Oxman laughed himself into a coughing fit.

"Oh. You're joking."

He nodded, still coughing.

Yana glanced back towards the bridge. Ruko had almost made it across, Yasila and Sergeant Worthy not far behind.

The Oxman was patting his overall pockets. He dug out a brooch, shaped like an ox-head. The skull was carved from white jade, the wide horns tipped with bronze. He pinned it to his chest.

The guards at the Gate immediately stood to attention, hands punched to their hearts in the Hound salute.

Yana's mouth dropped. Not a brooch, but a badge of High Office. Fenn Fedala. It had to be. The emperor's High Engineer. The man who kept the empire running.

He grinned, enjoying her reaction. "They salute the office, not the person," he said, signalling to the Hounds to stand down. "I've always admired that. It's what you do that matters, not who you are."

Yana slapped her hands to her cheeks. "I threw up in front of *Fenn Fedala*."

"And I shall never forget it," Fenn said, solemnly.

Sergeant Worthy approached them, then thought better of it. Fenn outranked him by several miles. He called to the Hounds to open the Gate.

Fenn touched Yana's arm. "Came to wish you good luck. May the Ox clear the road ahead for you."

"And remain Hidden," she answered in a wavering voice, touched by the blessing, and the effort he'd made. Spite, she could handle. Kindness always knocked her sideways.

The Guardian Gate cracked open. Over Fenn's shoulder, Yana saw a wide stone path, cutting through sloping lawns studded with broad oak trees. A pair of gardeners were busy clipping the grass, wide straw hats shading their brows.

"Looks idyllic, doesn't it?" he said.

His voice was mild, but Yana heard the warning. *Looks* idyllic.

Very, very softly he added, "So…I'll be in the orchards, like I said."

And again, Yana heard the part he left out. Come find me, if you need me.

When he saw that she understood his meaning, he squeezed her shoulder, and walked on through the Gate.

Sergeant Worthy had no intention of keeping the emperor waiting. Leading the way, he kept a fast, striding pace over the undulating common ground. Yana, back in her borrowed felt slippers, struggled to keep up. One of the Hounds jabbed her in the back with his baton. "Stop that," Worthy said, without turning round. Which was eerie—exactly how good was his peripheral vision?—but also gave Yana hope. Were they not to be harmed? Were they guests, not prisoners?

They were halfway up the stone path when Yana spotted three figures at the top of the lawn bank. Courtiers, she guessed from their fine-tailored tunics and sashes. They stood for a moment with their hands draped on each other's shoulders, watching the new arrivals. And then, to Yana's astonishment, they dropped to the grass and rolled down the slope together, head over heels, tumbling at increasing speed until they landed at the bottom in a tangle, laughing.

"Foxes," Worthy explained in a tight voice. He tilted his chin up ahead to the left. "The first palace is over that way."

"But why did they—"

"Because they're twats," the Hound behind her muttered.

Foxes and Hounds. Rarely friends.

At the top of the rise, far to the east, they saw their ultimate destination: the eighth palace. The imperial palace. The Palace of the Awakening Dragon. A noble edifice of pale gold limestone, capped with sea-green slate, it stood at the island's highest point, and all things bowed before it. Attached to the northern wing lay the inner sanctum—an octagonal building of dazzling white marble. The throne room lay nestled somewhere within, a jewel curled loosely inside a dragon's claws.

In front of the palace lay the Grand Canal—a glittering waterway a quarter-mile wide and two and a half miles long,

filled with brightly coloured pleasure boats and banqueting platforms. At the centre of the canal, lined up in perfect symmetry
with the Dragon palace, sat the Imperial Temple, white and
gold and gleaming on its own small island. Three white marble
bridges arced from bank to bank, their sides cascading with
roses of cream and apricot. Weeping willows trailed their leaves
gracefully, touching their own reflection on the canal's mirrored
surface.

"Beautiful," Ruko said, then shook his head. It was so much
more than that. A dream. A wonderful, dangerous dream.

Yana was using this moment for a more practical purpose—to
catch her breath. The climb had given her a stitch. She clutched
her side, wincing at the sharp, stabbing pain.

Worthy noticed it. He noticed everything. "We'll take a boat
from here," he told his squad, and dismissed them. The canal was
the most direct route to the imperial palace—and the quickest, if
you weren't prepared to jog.

When they reached the water's edge, he waved down a boatwoman. "Can you manage four of us to the eighth?" he asked. She
gave him a look. Of course she could. The cheek. They clambered
aboard and she rowed off, biceps bulging, oars slicing the water
with a smooth, practised precision.

As they glided along, Yana caught glimpses of the island's seven
satellite palaces, each set within its own private land. The black
larch cladding of the Raven palace. The Bear palace, a fortress
with thick stone walls, red pennants rising over dense pine forest.
The Tiger palace, with its white marble columns and obelisks, its
elegant glass pavilions and botanical gardens. "Samra," Ruko whispered in her ear, and he was right, it did look like the old capital,
in the days before its decline.

If you had asked Yana—Have you seen this before?—she would
have said no. But that was not strictly true. The day the twins
were born, their father had carried them proudly down the Grand
Canal, and the people on the banks had cheered and waved, because they thought Andren was certain to win the Festival, and
become their next emperor. They were mistaken.

Today, the courtiers did not cheer. They stared. Taking breakfast under a shaded veranda; strolling arm in arm across an arched bridge. Sprawled on the canal bank with friends. They stared and whispered. Stared and looked away. Many wore coloured sashes around their waists, showing their Guardian affiliation. Some had wrapped their hair in scarves—yellow for the Monkey, green for the Tiger. A group of brown-sashed Oxes heading for the temple fell into awkward silence as they sailed past. Yana kept her head down, until she felt her mother's hand at the base of her spine. Not for comfort, but to correct her posture.

When they reached the eastern end of the canal, Sergeant Worthy tipped the boatwoman an extra bronze tile for her efforts. They'd arrived in good time. Crossing the vast, cobbled parade ground, he warned them to stay close, which made Yana feel like a prisoner again.

At the door, Worthy waved his summons at a pair of Hounds and they nodded him through. This was the working end of the palace, the corridors and staircases bustling with staff and servants, black-clad Raven lawyers clutching files, Ox engineers consulting blueprints, a harried minister arguing with her entourage. A series of doors and checks funnelled them towards the inner sanctum. The press of the crowds, the chatter of court business faded away, until they were alone, the four of them.

They stopped at a pair of carved oak doors. Two guards barred the way, red tunics slashed with five black claw marks. They opened the door without a word.

The inner sanctum.

Silence. The deep silence of immeasurable power.

The golden halls gleamed. Tapestries and silk rugs. Incense burning on white marble plinths. Frankincense for long life. Patchouli for serenity.

This is where our father died.

The doors to the throne room opened. They had arrived. Yana reached for Ruko's hand and they walked in together, side by side.

CHAPTER
Three

"YOU WILL KNOW the story of Prisoner Quen and the Bear," the emperor said, from his white marble throne. Behind him, the morning sun streamed through the great octagonal window. He could have settled back into that golden shaft of light, sanctifying himself, but that would have been out of character. Instead, he sat hunkered at the edge of his seat, legs apart, hands clasped between his knees. The posture of a man who would rather be on his feet.

Today, Bersun was plainly dressed. An iron band for a crown, stamped with an ∞—sacred symbol of the Eternal Path. His black tunic was slashed with five scarlet claw marks, a reversal of his bodyguards' uniform. He wore chain mail beneath his tunic, and a longsword at his belt. Orrun was at peace, the rebellion a long-faded scar. But Bersun was a warrior to the bone. Even now, after more than two decades on the throne, he looked more natural dressed as one.

Quen and the Bear. Of course they knew it—the most famous story of the age, already passed into legend. How the ruthless pirate Quen was transformed by his encounters with the Bear into Brother Lanrik, wise and saintly abbot of Anat-garra.

"Quen was a worthless piece of shit," the emperor said. "But the Bear gave him a second chance."

A warrior, yes. A storyteller, no.

Yana, standing with Ruko at the base of the throne steps, kept her eyes on the floor. She was feeling sick again. The heady, overwhelming smell of the incense. The grim-faced bodyguards lining the steps. Most of all the giant frescoes that covered every inch of the walls and ceiling. *Dedication to the Eight*—Shimmer Arbell's infamous masterpiece. Defying convention, she had painted the eight Guardians not as symbols or myths, but as living beings, in their natural settings. On the wall behind Yana, the Bear stood in a rushing river, snatching salmon from the rapids. Painted over the doors, the Tiger stalked its prey through the long grass. To her right, a magnificent Raven posed on a cliff beside a storm-swept sea.

Arbell had etched a single word in gold above each portrait. Together, they formed half of a phrase every child learned at temple.

SEVEN TIMES HAVE THE GUARDIANS SAVED ORRUN

The second half was left unwritten, for its message could be found painted on the ceiling. A portrait of the Dragon. Not slumbering in the usual way, coiled within its cave, but swimming down through a jagged tear in the sky, fire building in its throat, preparing to burn all before it to ash. The Awakening Dragon of the Last Return, poised right above Yana's head. She could almost feel the heat from its jaws.

Seven times have the Guardians saved Orrun. The next time they Return, they will destroy it.

"Your father," the emperor said. The room stilled at those two words. A faint smile crossed his lips. "He's causing trouble again."

Yana held her breath. Her father was dead. He'd died right here on this spot, where she was standing. Beneath the Dragon.

She sensed movement from one of the bodyguards, the scuff of boots. When she looked up, the emperor was holding a scroll in his fist. He held it out for the room to see. The message was written in dark green ink and signed with a tiger's eye, painted in green and gold. Yana recognised the flowing, elegant handwriting, though she had not seen it in years. It belonged to Rivenna Glorren, abbess of the Tiger Monastery. The twins' Guardian-mother.

Few had expected the abbess to survive the purges. She and Andren had been lovers before he married Yasila, and had remained the closest of friends. How could she not have played some part in the rebellion? The inquiry subjected her to hours of interrogation under Houndsight, to no avail. Not only was Rivenna found innocent, but she demanded—and was given—a formal apology for her treatment.

Yana had not seen her Guardian-mother for years. She had not mourned the loss. Even as a very young child, Yana had sensed that Rivenna's indifference was much safer than her interest.

The emperor was reading the message again, as if he hoped it might say something different this time. "It seems your father saw something special in you." He looked up. "Yanara."

In her periphery, Yana saw Ruko's shoulders slump.

"A future contender for the throne." Bersun lifted his brow at the presumption. "He left a legacy in your name, for when you came of age." He waved the scroll again. "You have a place waiting for you at the Tiger monastery. If you want it."

The floor tilted under Yana's feet. The Guardians loomed from the wall as she fought through a tangle of emotions. Pride, fear, confusion, excitement. And beneath that—a dark slick of guilt. This was her brother's wish, not hers. A secret he had shared only with Yana—that he planned to affiliate to the Tiger, and seek a place at Anat-hurun, like his father before him. Yana had indulged him in his fantasy—for that is what it had seemed to her. Her brother, the Traitor's son, training to become a Tiger warrior. A dream so impossible, it was rendered harmless.

"I could prevent this," Bersun said. "My Raven lawyers would peck it apart in five minutes." He had made it his coronation pledge to reform the monasteries—most of all these paid-for places. "But I've read the Foxes' reports on you." The emperor swivelled towards Yasila, who stood beneath the portrait of the Raven like an accompanying statue. "And your mother speaks well of you."

Yasila—always so scrupulous with what she hid and what she revealed—threw the emperor a glare of such intense, undisguised hatred that Bersun burst out laughing.

Well at least those rumours about them aren't true, Yana thought.

Bersun swivelled back again. He deliberated for a moment, his gaze softening as it settled on Yana. "A child should not pay for the sins of her father. I'm willing to give you a second chance, as the Bear teaches. Take the place, with my blessing."

There was a silence. Yana realised she was supposed to fill it. "Thank you, your majesty..."

Bersun narrowed his eyes. "You're not sure you want it," he said, shrewdly. "Fair enough. This will change your life. Take a moment." He handed the scroll back to his guard. "A *moment*, mind. I'm sure you've heard of my legendary impatience." He shared an amused glance with the guard.

Yana took her moment.

The Tiger monastery. The most elite of all the anats, and the most secretive. A future unfurled in front of her—a path into a magic forest. She could transform herself into a Tiger warrior. She could compete to become their next contender for the throne. Bersun had at most eight years left to rule, before the law demanded he step down.

Eight years—she would be twenty-four. Not a bad age to face the Trials. And what better way to honour her father, than to take the throne in his memory?

I could clear his name.

Was this what Andren had foreseen, when he put the legacy down in her name? Her father, always ten steps ahead.

But this was Ruko's dream. Could she really steal it from him?

As if reading her thoughts, the emperor tutted, annoyed with himself. "Damn it. I should say. If you refuse, I'm to offer the place to your brother." He gave Ruko a glancing smile. "Sorry, lad—forgot all about you there."

A soft hiss escaped Ruko's lips—half annoyance, half excitement. Suddenly, there was a chance for him. "Yana." He pleaded silently with her, dark brown eyes filled with hope and hunger. *My dream. Let me have my dream back.*

But their father had chosen her.

Ruko reached for her. "Yana, please..."

"Quiet," a flat voice prompted.

It was the first time High Commander Hol Vabras had spoken. He stood to their left at the base of the throne steps, so unremarkable, so average, that any attempt at description would slide off him. Describing Hol Vabras would be like trying to describe the taste of water. "He's so forgettable," a Fox courtier once said, "it's a wonder his mother remembered to push him out." And everyone had laughed, then stopped, because Vabras was standing there, right next to them. The courtier had disappeared shortly afterwards, which was a shame. If you're going to lose your life over a joke, at least make it a good one.

The emperor rose from his throne, gripping the hilt of his battle-worn sword. On the steps, his bodyguards stood to attention, slamming their halberds to the ground in one explosive movement. The sound echoed off the walls, leaving silence behind it. He made his way down the steps, and stopped in front of the twins. Eight, he really was a giant. "So. Yanara Valit. What will it be?"

Yana was still deliberating. Her father had taught her that. Don't rush in, no matter who is pressing you for an answer. Weigh your options. Consider the risks versus the rewards. *Think.*

Did she want to rule? Because that was the implicit offer, hidden within her Guardian-mother's scroll. To be trained up as a contender, and win the throne. And below that, whispered between the lines of green ink, so quiet that the emperor could not hear it—*avenge your father.*

Yana's only dream—until this moment—had been to run an art shop and café in the Central Grid. Settle down, have a family, and be known as Yanara, instead of Traitor's daughter. Even that had felt overly ambitious.

But now here was the emperor, offering her a gift so vast she could barely grasp its dimensions. The chance to rise. The chance to rule. Empress Yanara.

The magic forest called out to her. Why not? *Why not?*

"Yes or no," the emperor prompted.

"Yes, your majesty." Barely a whisper. Shocked by her own daring.

Bersun cupped his ear, playful.

Yana repeated, in a clear voice: "Yes, your majesty."

He dropped his great paw of a hand on her shoulder and gave her an encouraging shake. "Good. Good! Don't be so timid." The floor dropped away under Yana's feet. Vertigo, as her new life rushed towards her.

"But it's not fair!" Ruko exploded.

The emperor sighed and gave Ruko a complicated look—a mixture of irritation and sympathy. "Peace, lad."

Ruko was too caught up in the injustice to stop himself. "But she's not a Tiger," he protested. "She was going to the temple this morning to affiliate to the Monkey. Yana, for Eight's sake." Ruko snatched her wrist. She had never seen him look so desperate. His dream, slipping away from him. "You know this isn't right. Let me go. I swear, beneath the Awakening Dragon, I will train harder than anyone has ever trained."

"Enough." The emperor said it gently, but everyone heard the warning wrapped inside it. Enough.

Ruko lowered his head, crushed. His thick black hair swung forward, covering his face. And in that moment Yana thought—I have lost him, my twin. My brother. Perhaps not for ever, but for a long, long time.

"'The path to the throne is narrow, and must be walked alone,'"[2] the emperor said, observing her quietly.

So—he did know what the scroll was offering. And he was letting her go anyway. He was choosing to trust her.

"Your majesty," Vabras interjected. "Before you make a final decision—I have some questions."

"As you wish." The emperor shrugged. He had made up his mind.

Ruko—sensing a fresh opportunity—lifted his head and squared his shoulders. Yana felt a flicker of alarm. This was Vabras, the man who had led the purges. She tried to signal to Ruko. *Be careful...* He ignored her. This was his last chance, and he would take it.

---

2. *attrib.* Tiger Empress Shin (reigned 1237–52). The quote continues: "be wary of the one who walks behind you, and ruthless to the one who walks ahead."

"You believe you deserve this gift," Vabras said. "Not your sister."

Ruko raised his chin, defiant. "I do."

"Why? Your sister is the better student."

Ruko bristled. "I've fallen a few points behind this year…"

A few points? Yana clamped her mouth shut, but the emperor spoke for her. "You barely scraped a pass, boy," he growled. "Coasting on your charm and good looks."

Ruko, eager to defend himself, barely paused for breath. "I've spent the whole summer volunteering with an Ox team, restoring our home grid's community hall, doing my civic duty."

Volunteering? Yana had to stop herself from rolling her eyes. He'd only joined that Ox team as punishment for failing half his exams. Ruko wouldn't know his civic duty if it paraded past him on a Kind Return Festival float, trailing streamers.

"Ask anyone. They'll tell you I'm a good, honest citizen, loyal to his majesty—"

Vabras pounced. "And your sister is not?"

Ruko's brow furrowed. "I didn't mean that. I wasn't talking about Yana."

"Worthy," Vabras said, signalling for the sergeant to join the interrogation.

For that is what it had been, all along.

Sergeant Worthy, who had been standing patiently by the doors, peeled away and took his place next to his commander.

The emperor retreated up the steps.

Worthy and Vabras stood in front of Ruko. They said nothing, only studied him, building up the pressure.

Ruko bit his lip. He had finally realised his mistake.

"Is your sister loyal to the emperor?" Vabras asked.

"Yes." He answered too fast. There was a waver in his voice. Anxiety—but it sounded like doubt.

"Is your sister loyal to the emperor?" Vabras asked again.

Ruko swallowed, and glanced at Yana. "Yes. Of course she is. Yes."

"He's hiding something," Sergeant Worthy said.

"I'm not," Ruko said, eyes pleading. "I swear I'm not."

Worthy glanced at his commander. "He's lying."

Without changing his expression, Vabras unsheathed his dagger.

Ruko shrank back, terrified.

"Whatever it is, just tell us." Sergeant Worthy sounded weary. "If you keep lying, you'll put your whole family under suspicion. But if it's nothing…No one's looking to punish you, or your sister, for some small lapse of judgement."

A skilfully prepared line. Ruko—always so keen to talk himself out of trouble—snatched his chance. "It really is nothing," he said, relief softening his shoulders.

Yana's stomach dropped. *No, no, no.*

Subtly, Sergeant Worthy shifted position, blocking Ruko's view of his twin. Easier to betray someone, when you can't see them. "Go on."

Ruko took a breath. "Yana kept my father's colours."

A quiet hiss from the emperor, on the steps. The embroidered silk band, worn by his rival, when they competed against each other for the throne.

"It doesn't mean anything," Ruko added in a rush. "It was just a lapse in judgement, like you said."

Vabras sheathed his dagger. "Would you have kept them?"

"Well, no…"

"Why not?"

Ruko's mouth opened and closed. There was no way to answer, without implicating Yana.

"Because you are loyal to his majesty," Vabras answered for him.

"No. No, it's not that…Yana is loyal."

Vabras said, in a deathly voice, "I shall be the judge of that."

Yana's legs were trembling. It was too much. Vabras. Sergeant Worthy, circling. The Guardians glaring down from the walls. The Dragon on the ceiling, jaws wide, fire in its throat.

"Why did you keep your father's colours?"

"He asked me…" She took a breath. "He made me promise to keep them safe."

The very last time she had seen him. A cold, grey morning in the Governor's House in Samra. Andren was dressed in his travel clothes, long black hair plaited and tied for the road, watching from his study window as the groom saddled his horse in the vine-strewn courtyard below. A leather purse in his hand.

"Why would he give them to you?" Vabras wondered.

"Open it," her father had said, handing her the purse. She could still remember the awe of that moment, as they stood together by the crackling fire. The neat click of the clasp. Her intake of breath as she pulled out the forest-green band and realised what she was holding. Her father's colours. The Tiger's eye sigil embroidered so perfectly in the centre she thought it might blink, if she touched it.

"Why not your brother?" Vabras said. "Why not your mother?"

Yana glanced anxiously towards Yasila. She'd drifted further behind the throne, standing now beneath the wild drama of the Fox fresco—a cornered vixen, defending her cubs from some unseen attack. Defend *us*, Yana begged, with her eyes. *Mother.* Yasila did nothing.

"He chose you," Vabras said, "because you were his favourite."

"No, that's not true—" Except it was. It was true. He'd put her name down for Anat-hurun. Not Ruko's. Not both of them. Just hers.

Vabras talked over her. "Because you were alike. Clever. Cautious. Hard to read." A quirk of a smile. "Did your father confide in you?"

A white burst of fear. "No."

"Did he tell you of his plans to kill the emperor? To take the throne by force?"

Yana was shaking, violently. The moment she had always feared, and it had snuck up on her like an assassin.

That cold winter's morning in front of the fire. The green silk colours in her hand, the stamp of hooves in the courtyard below. Her father said, "The throne has been stolen from me, and I must steal it back, for the good of Orrun. One day you will understand."

She never had.

A tear slid down her cheek.

"Worthy," Vabras prompted. "What do you see?"

The sergeant's eyes gleamed, then faded. His face was sombre. "She knew. He told her."

"Traitor!" Bersun snarled, snatching the sword from his belt. Not the emperor in that moment, but something far more ferocious. A Bear warrior, raging. Yana cringed, afraid he would storm down the steps and cut her head from her shoulders. Instead, he prowled the same step back and forth, as if he had caged himself. "You knew. You could have stopped it all. And you said *nothing!*"

Yana dropped to her knees. She curled her fingers against the cold marble floor, finding no comfort there. He was right. She *could* have stopped it. "I'm sorry. Your majesty, I'm so sorry. I was eight years old...I didn't know what to do. I prayed every day that he would change his mind and come home. That's all I wanted. For him to come home." She wept then, remembering, and there was silence from the room.

The emperor sheathed his sword, muttering something under his breath. He looked to his High Commander. What now?

"She's a traitor," Vabras said, to the point as ever.

"She was eight, Vabras."

"She's sixteen now. And she still holds his colours."

The emperor had no answer to that.

"The law is clear. The greatest crime carries the greatest punishment."

Exile.

No. They wouldn't do that to her. The Guardians glared down from the wall. They wouldn't...

"Yana?" Worthy said, taking a step towards her. "She's going to faint."

Yana willed herself to breathe. She would not faint. She would not. Slowly, she got to her feet.

The sergeant drew back.

The emperor was arguing with Vabras. "...a punishment for monsters. I haven't exiled a soul in all my years on the throne. I won't start now."

Yana needed her brother. "Ruko," she whispered, and reached for his hand.

He wouldn't look at her.

Bersun had retreated to his throne. He called for wine, which appeared at once, in a golden cup embellished with rubies. He drank slowly, while the room watched and waited, held captive. This was a trick her father used to play—the emperor had probably learned it from him. *We live on in the gifts we give.*[3]

At last, he came to a decision. In a formal tone he had not used before, he said, "Yanara Valit. You have openly confessed to treason. And the law *is* clear." A nod to Vabras. "That being said. I promised you a second chance. I commute your sentence to life in the House of Mist and Shadows."

Yana dropped back down to her knees in relief. "Thank you, your majesty. May the Eight bless you."

"And remain Hidden," the guards murmured. Shal Worthy gave a tight, satisfied nod. This was good, this was wise. This would satisfy both the people and the law. Not an easy life, locked away in the eastern marshes. So young, to be giving up the world for a life of service. But given the alternative...

Yana sent a silent prayer to the Guardians who had saved her. To the Bear, merciful and wise. To the Fox, the Guardian of Escape. To the Monkey, her own Guardian, for watching over her. *Thank you, thank you, thank you.*

Ruko stepped forward. "Then I am going to Anat-hurun?" he said, not bothering to conceal his excitement. "I can take her place?"

The emperor stared at the remnants of his wine. "No," he said. "No. I think not."

Ruko's face fell. "But why?"

"We are talking of treason," the emperor said. "The darkest of crimes. My own High Commander thinks I am being too generous. I cannot spare your sister *and* send you to Anat-hurun. There must be consequences."

---

3. From "We Live On," by Bear warrior and poet Mordir (117–180). The poem continues, "...and the greatest gift is love."

"But why should I be punished for her crimes? It's not *fair*—"

The emperor leapt from the throne and threw his goblet at Ruko. It clanged down the steps, splashing red wine across the white marble. When it reached the bottom Vabras stopped it neatly with his foot.

"What would you have me do?" Bersun shouted. "Send your sister into exile? You do know what that means? What they'll do to her? Is that what you want?"

"No, but it was her mistake, not mine—"

"*What would you have me do?*" the emperor repeated. "What would *you* do, boy, in my place? She's *your* sister. Go on, tell me. Would you…" He stopped. An idea was forming. "*Eight*, why not. Why not? Let's teach the boy a lesson. Get up here." Bersun beckoned Ruko up the steps.

Ruko hesitated, sensing a trap.

"Get up here *now*," Bersun roared.

Ruko hurried up the steps. When he reached the top, Bersun grabbed him and slung him on the throne like a sack of rubbish. "There. Emperor Ruko. How does that feel?"

Ruko, sprawled on the throne, was too stunned to answer.

"Guardians of Orrun!" Bersun swept his arm to take in the portraits of the Eight. "Witness this oath—the unbreakable oath of a Bear warrior of Anat-garra. I hereby grant Ruko Valit the power to choose his sister's fate, and his own. Once made, his decision cannot be unmade. There. That should do it." He cuffed Ruko on the head, almost playful. "Her life's in your hands now, boy."

At the bottom of the steps, Yana was trapped in silent terror. The emperor couldn't see Ruko's expression, but she could. She could see that he was deliberating, was genuinely considering…

"Not so easy, is it?" Bersun said.

Ruko shook his head. No. It wasn't easy.

"Good. Now you understand. So let's hear it. Will you send your sister into exile, to feed your own ambition? Or will you spare her, as I did?"

Yana saw her brother's face empty. He sat up straight on the marble throne, and placed his hands on each arm, as if he really were the emperor.

"Exile."

Silence. And then, from behind the throne, a high, piercing wail. Her mother. Her mother was screaming.

I wonder if I could explain it to them, Ruko thought, in a way they might forgive.

He could tell them that he was saving his sister from a miserable fate. Locking her away with the Grey Penitents wasn't mercy but a slow, suffocating torture. This way might seem cruel, but it was kinder in the long run. He could say this, with that pathetic whine in his voice. It wouldn't make any difference.

And it wasn't true.

Be honest. A voice in his head, the voice of the man he would in time become. *Accept what you have done, and why you have done it.*

The emperor had given Ruko a taste of absolute power. For that brief moment, he was the most important person in the world. Everyone waiting on his word. And it had felt good. It had felt right.

He sat up straighter on the throne. Below him, collapsed on the floor, his mother was cradling his sister. "Not my Yana," she said, in a daze. "Not my Yana."

Ruko had always wondered how his mother kept her face so blank. Now he understood. You had to open a hole inside yourself and let everything drain through it. The horror, the grief, the guilt. The love. Most of all, the love. Let it drain away until there was no feeling left.

And in that starless void, Ruko saw a golden rope, stretching off into the distance. His path, his golden path to the throne. The only way forward now. He put one foot upon the rope, and then the other. His journey had begun.

CHAPTER

Four

L ET US FLY now from the eighth palace, away from the Valits
and their unfolding tragedy. Skim low over the Grand Canal,
past drifting pleasure boats, courtiers sharing stories under cream
silk parasols, popping bottles of sparkling wine—it's early but why
not, it's a beautiful day.

Then up, up again into the bright blue sky, soaring high over the
Ox farm, where Fenn Fedala is pacing up and down the orchards.
Later, when he hears the news of Yana's exile, he will head to the
temple with his hands curled into fists. He will ask the Eight—
How could you let this happen, you fuckers?—and receive no answer.

And look, here it is, the Imperial Temple of the Eight. No time
to linger among its white towers and parapets, no time to admire
its stained-glass windows, its intricately carved entrance. Briefly,
our shadow ripples over the golden dome, and we are gone.

Far behind us, buried deep in the evergreens, the Bear palace's
great bell is chiming the hour.

Six...seven...

Don't worry. We'll make it.

Eight...nine...

And we've reached the Raven palace. More of a village than a
palace, with its interlocking houses of blackened larchwood and
purple tiling. Dark buildings brightened with flower gardens and
fountains, painted pavilions, cushioned benches and walkways
woven with garlands.

Ten...

The Raven palace has many rooms, singular and communal.
So many rooms, so many people with inky hands and hunched

shoulders. Scholars and lawyers, clerks and accountants, speculators with their hoods over their heads, scribbling dense equations
as the days pass by unnoticed. We could fly through any window
and startle someone at their desk, knocking tea across their papers,
flapping books off the shelves. Our more playful fragments would
enjoy that tremendously, but even we have rules we must follow.
Today we are here to see, not to be seen. And we have an appointment to meet.

Eleven...

A tiny balcony, attached to a modest room on the north side of
the palace, overlooking a service hut, and some bins. Through the
balcony doors, a glimpse of a young black woman seated at her
desk, head down, writing. A scholar.

Twelve.

As the last chime fades we drop neatly on to the balcony's rusting hand rail, folding our wings with a soft shuffle. Noon, on the
ninth day of the eighth month, 1531. Neema Kraa's lodgings. We
are here, exactly where we should be, at exactly the right moment,
because we are the Raven, and we are magnificent.

∞ ∞ ∞

Neema Kraa, Junior Archivist (Third Class) sat at her desk, proof-
reading her latest monograph.[4] A smell of rotting food wafted
gently up from the bins and through the balcony doors. When she
was first allocated this room, Neema would try to cover the smell
with incense and fresh flowers. These days, she barely noticed it.

There was a tap at the door. Neema looked up in surprise. No
one ever visited her here except Cain, and it couldn't be him, for
obvious reasons.

"Who is it?" she called, enjoying the novelty of asking.

The door opened to reveal High Commander Hol Vabras. The
second most powerful man in Orrun.

---

4. Kraa, Neema, *An Annotated Bibliography of Twelve Ancient Ketuan Folk Tales*
(1531, Imperial Palace Archives).

"Neema Kraa."

"Yes."

"I'm told you have the best hand on the island."

Neema lay an arm along the back of her chair. "That's right."

Vabras stepped back outside, giving the two guards he'd brought with him the space to squeeze through. They set to work, clearing Neema's desk before laying out fresh paper and brushes, an inkstone, a scroll sealed with gold wax, and a copy of *The Laws of Orrun Volume XII*, marked with a blue ribbon. In ten seconds they were done, and Vabras was back.

Neema stared at the drab, grey-green inkstone. "Is that—"

"The Stone of Peace," Vabras confirmed.

The inkstone Empress Yasthala had used to write the Five Rules, carved by her own hand from a rare piece of Dolrun Riverstone. Neema ransacked her brain, trying to think of a more priceless artefact, and came up blank.

Vabras indicated the scroll. "Two copies, by sundown."

Neema brushed her fingers over the gold wax, marked with five slashes. The emperor's seal, pressed into the wax by his own hand. Imagine that. "I'd rather use my own brushes. New ones take a while to—"

"Fine." Vabras handed her a thumb-sized stick of ink, embossed with a feather design.

She turned the stick in her fingers, admiring its exceptional quality and depth of colour, the intense black base softened with hints of indigo. Raven's Wing ink. Produced on the Dragon island of Helia and reserved for the highest imperial proclamations. Coronations, abdications. Executions.

Vabras had picked up the first page of Neema's proofs. He read a few lines. "Ketuan folk tales."

Neema waited for the usual comments. *You're a historian, how is this history? They're just stories for children. Ephemera. What are you doing, wasting your time on such worthless crap?* (That final comment scrawled across the proofs themselves, by Neema's head of department. A dispiriting moment.)

"This is thorough," Vabras said.

Neema, who had not met the High Commander before, assumed he was being catty. It was either that, or he was genuinely
interested in her work. Which would be a first, to put it mildly. No
one cared about Neema's studies except Neema.

She had arrived at court straight from the Raven monastery,
with perfect grades and no friends. Without connections, she'd
struggled to secure a decent position. And everyone knew the
longer you remained in the same junior role, the harder it became
to escape it. "Here in two years, here in ten," was the rule at the
Raven palace. Neema had been in her post for three. "I'm stuck on
the first rung of the ladder," she'd complained recently, to her head
of department. He'd responded with a startled smile. "You think
you're on the ladder?"

If it was just about the work, she wouldn't mind so much.
She was yet to find a subject she did not find interesting. What
bothered her—what *infuriated* her, in a quiet, seething way
—was the reason why she was being held back. Neema was a
Commoner, of Scartown. The first Commoner of Scartown in
history to secure a place at the second palace. For the last three
years, she'd been forced to smile, and bite her tongue, as people
with far less talent and dedication leapfrogged right over her.
Every one of them had been from a Venerant or High Middling
family.

"I am going to stab someone in the eye, the next time it happens,"
she'd told Cain. He'd agreed that was certainly an option and then
suggested, as he always did, "Why don't you leave, Neema?"

But she didn't want to leave. She wanted to prove them all
wrong. The fuckers.

Vabras was still reading. "Is this a complete list?" he asked.

It was only now that Neema realised—Eight, he's serious. The
High Commander of Orrun wants to know more about *Ancient
Ketuan Folk Tales and their Variants*. "No, it's not complete," she
replied. "That would be impossible."

He looked up, sharply. "Why?"

A pragmatic shrug. "There must be dozens more variations
buried away in the western archives. Not to mention private col-

lections. And those are just the written versions. Ketu has a long oral tradition—"

Vabras was reading again. "But they could be collected."

"In theory. You'd need a team of researchers. Fox travellers to collect the unwritten versions from border villages…" She lifted her hands at the prohibitive time and expense. Why were they even discussing this?

Vabras mused for a moment, casting around Neema's room. Sifting for evidence. His gaze snagged on the painting of her parents' grocery shop in Scartown, with its cheerful frontage. Her framed graduation certificate from Anat-ruar—*First in Year*. A cartoon triptych of the Fox and the Raven, first dancing, then fighting, then dancing again. Signed by the artist: *Look, it's us! Happy Birthday, N. Love, Cain x*

"The emperor has developed a passion for his homeland's ancient history and culture," Vabras said, shifting his attention back to Neema. "We ordered new studies from the Raven palace. His majesty was disappointed with the results."

Neema was not surprised to hear it. She knew the scholars involved. Chosen for seniority, not expertise. Neema was the only Ketuan expert on the island, and not one of them had deigned to come to her for advice.

"You may be useful," Vabras said, as if she were a garden implement. One of those odd-shaped tools designed for a single, highly specific purpose. "We shall discuss this further, once you have finished the Order of Exile."

"Exile?" she echoed, weakly.

"Two copies. Bring them directly to my office. We shall visit the emperor together. His majesty has had a trying day. It will please him to meet someone who shares his interests." Vabras paused, musing again. "This cannot be coincidence, to have found you today. This is the will of the Hound."

Neema, who did not believe in the Eight, gave a frozen smile. But Vabras was already on his way out, closing the door behind him with a smart click.

There was a short silence.

"Is it strange," Cain said, from the bed, "that he didn't acknowledge me? At all? I think it's strange."

Neema stroked her arm absently, staring at the scroll. *Exile.* The cruellest of all punishments—not just for the victim, but for those who loved them.

"I'm right here," Cain protested, pointing at himself. He was lying on his back, shirtless, balancing a bowl of chicken wings on his chest. "You can't miss me. Unless I've turned invisible. Have I turned invisible?"

She forced her attention to the bed. "You know what they say about Hol Vabras."

"I know what everyone says about everything. That's my job." A pause. "What do they say about Hol Vabras?"

Neema leaned back in her chair. "Schedules. Efficiency. He came here for me. Talking to you would have been a waste of his time."

"That's hurtful. I was going to share my chicken wings with you—"

"No you weren't."

"—but now I won't." Cain sat up, only to discover the bowl was empty. "What? Where did you go?" he demanded of the missing wings. "How am I still hungry? Neema, I think my stomach has a false bottom. Like a magic trick. I eat the chicken wings and then someone else…" He mimed someone sliding open the false bottom and catching the food as it fell through. "Speaking of which, I built a secret compartment in the skirting yesterday, I know you said not to bother, but maybe one day your life will be exciting enough to need one, and then you will thank me…"

He carried on, circling around the only topic that mattered, the one resting on Neema's desk. They were heading for an argument about it, no question. But Cain Ballari was a Fox, of Anat-russir. Foxes didn't walk straight up to a problem and shake it by the hand. They circled, they sidled. And then, when the problem was looking the other way, they bit it on the ankle.

So Cain talked and Neema watched him, the way he moved, his lean, supple body. Thick auburn hair, sharp cheekbones. Those hips. He chattered on in that peculiar way of his—eloquence and street swagger, and a thick, thick accent from the gutters of Scartown that he wilfully refused to shake.

We're going to break up over this, she thought. Before the temple bell chimes one it will be over. Again. They were always falling out, and making up—a ceaseless cycle.

Neema had first met Cain when she was nine and he was eight and three quarters. She was tucked away in the family storeroom, reading a book, and he was breaking in. Tunnelling through, to be precise. He'd emerged through a hole in the floor, coughing up dirt, shaking with exhaustion. Hollow eyes, hollow cheeks. Painfully thin.

Neema could have screamed, and then a series of very bad things would have happened to Cain. Instead, she'd let him eat whatever he wanted, which he did with his back turned, so she couldn't see him crying with relief. And then they'd talked on the storeroom floor, legs crossed, knees almost touching. Hours and hours, caught in the spell of each other. He told her he'd been kicked out of his Scrapper gang, wouldn't say why. Now he had no protection, no shelter, no patch. If a rival gang found him in their territory, they'd slit his throat. So he had to keep moving, and hiding. He'd been living that way for months. Hadn't eaten properly in weeks.

Neema wasn't supposed to talk to Scrappers, it was taboo. But then, no one talked to Neema, either, outside of her family. Friendship was an art that eluded her. "I know someone who can help you," she'd said, and taken him to her teacher Madam Fessi, who let him stay the night, and then another, and eventually adopted him. Madam Fessi didn't give a shit about taboos either, which was why she was running a school in Scartown, when she could have been making a fortune preparing Venerant children for their monastery exams.

For the next seven years, Neema and Cain were inseparable, until Neema won a scholarship to the Raven monastery, and Cain disappeared into Anat-russir, the Fox monastery.[5]

They still wrote—Neema's letters neat and detailed, Cain's spidery—but the world was pulling them apart. Neema secured a position at court, Cain travelled the empire, sniffing out secrets and scandals and anything else that caught his interest, feeding it back to his superiors. For a long time, they did not see each other. Neema buried herself in her work, her most constant sanctuary.

Then one night, sitting at her desk just as she was now, she had caught a scent of him—sweet, dusty cinnamon and a hint of sweat. Looked up, and there he was, pulling a stupid face through the window of her balcony door. Twenty-four years old and so fucking handsome, even with his tongue sticking out.

He'd poked about her room, flipping through her books and eating her food—some things never changed. Except he'd seemed nervous, which wasn't like him at all.

"I never stopped thinking of you," he admitted out of nowhere. He'd turned his back to her, just as he had the first day they met. "This is new," he said, tapping the picture of her family's shop. "Did you paint this? No, wait, there's a signature."

Neema's heart was beating so hard, she could hardly breathe.

"Oh, your cousin painted it for you, that's sweet. Do you ever think about me?" His back still turned. "Don't worry if you don't. I'm sure you don't. Forget I asked. How old is Trestan now, seventeen?" He scratched the back of his head, eyes still on the painting.

"Eighteen." She swallowed, found her courage. "I think about you all the time."

He'd turned then, and she had laughed. He looked so happy, and surprised. He genuinely had no idea how much she loved him, the idiot.

---

5. Literally. There were no entrance exams for Anat-russir. If you could sneak in without being spotted, you were welcome. Over the centuries myths had grown up around the more elaborate "admissions." People said, for example, that the Fox adventurer Maliwren Tide (723–97) used a trebuchet to fling herself over the walls. They didn't *believe* it, but they said it, with considerable relish. "Sailed right over the wall. Arms and legs wheeling. Landed in a laundry cart."

"You answered the empirical question first," he said. "That is so commendably you."

"They're both empirical questions," she told him, "it's just one is more objectively measurable than the other. Also, for the record, I should tell you that my second answer was hyperbolic. I don't think about you *all* the time. That would be impractical. But I do think about you a lot. Possibly more than is healthy."

He was moving towards her by this point, and she was moving towards him, and the next thing they were kissing, with a passion that surprised them both, and the next thing after that they were on her very narrow bed, and clothes were coming off everywhere.

Almost two years ago now. Cain travelled. Neema worked. They spent more time apart than together. They fought, they made up. They loved each other. Neema had missed Cain so much on his last long trip away, she had painted her door a bright emerald green, the same colour as his eyes, so she could remember him every time she came home. The way he looked at her.

She picked up her penknife and broke the emperor's seal. Opening out the scroll, she groaned as she read the name. Yanara Valit.

"Well that settles it," Cain said, as if they were already halfway through the argument. "She's not a traitor."

"The emperor says she is." Neema tossed the scroll back on to her desk.

Cain picked it up and read it. "She kept her father's colours. That's it?" He turned the scroll over, examined the empty back. Shook it vigorously, as if something else might drop out.

"She knew about the rebellion—"

"She was *eight*." Cain peered at her, incredulous. "You're not actually considering writing it for them. You can't."

Neema touched the inkstone, the Raven's Wing ink. Straightened her brushes.

"Neema, you *can't*. She's a child."

"She's sixteen," Neema muttered.

"That's disgusting. Why are you being disgusting? You're not a disgusting person. What's wrong with you?"

Neema opened *The Laws of Orrun Volume XII* with the ribbon. Page ninety-seven: the formal words for an Imperial Order of Exile and its design. The precise measurements for the paper.

> One copy of the Order should be lodged in the Imperial Archives. The other must be stitched directly into the Traitor's skin, over the heart, and worn for the duration of the Procession. The Order must be left upon the abandoned corpse, once the Exile is complete.

The abandoned corpse. She rubbed her eyes.

"I met her last summer," Cain said, throwing on his shirt.

"You were spying on the Valits?" He didn't talk much about his work, but she knew what he did. What he was.

"I talked to her, N. She's harmless. Her big dream is to open a sort of café/bookshop/theatre venue."

Neema pulled a face. "I hate those places."

"I love them. Why be one thing when you can be three?"

"Ugh."

"Remember that place on Pumphouse Street? The Velvet Frog?"

"I remember," Neema said, darkly. "You'd be drinking your coffee, minding your own business, and the waiters would start juggling at you. No warning, just whenever the mood took them. Spontaneous juggling."

"I know, but *if you could focus for a moment*," Cain said, and they both laughed, because that was usually Neema's line, "my point is, Yanara Valit is not a threat to anyone."

"She confessed."

Cain rolled his eyes at her.

Neema fell silent. She could say no. She could. And that would be the end of her life at court.

"Let's leave, today," Cain said. "Give it all up, and start afresh."

This was not a new idea. They'd often discussed it, usually late at night, half asleep. Travel the empire, find a place of their own. Or they could go home to Scartown. Raise a family. Reopen the school. Neema had never really believed any of it would happen.

Cain was too restless to settle. And, *be honest Neema:* she liked it here. She liked her work. Even if no one else did.

She rubbed the silver pendant hanging from her neck, an anniversary gift from Cain. Fox on one side, Raven on the other. "If I don't write it, someone else will."

"So let them. Neema," Cain shifted to the edge of the bed and reached out, covering her hand with his. "Let them."

It felt good for a moment. The warmth of his hand over hers. Then it felt restrictive. She slid her hand free. "This is a big chance for me, Cain. A meeting with the emperor."

"Well don't trip on Yana's corpse in the rush over," Cain snapped. It was the wrong thing to say, he winced as soon as he said it.

Neema bridled. "*You're* lecturing *me*? Seriously?"

"I'm not lecturing you. I'm trying to protect you." Cain's expression was more serious than she'd ever seen before. "There's a line, Neema. A thick, black line. Once you cross it…" His jaw tightened. "You're not the same person any more."

"And how many times have you crossed that line, Cain?"

He drew back, searching her face. "What's that supposed to mean?"

"Oh come on, I'm not stupid. I know what you are."

Cain went very still. "What am I?"

She looked at him.

Some Fox spies were just that—spies, and nothing more. But Neema had suspected for a long time that Cain was an imperial assassin. Things he'd said, or not said, about his missions. The places he'd been and the rumours that followed. Subtle hints, but Cain was Neema's specialist subject. It had broken her heart when she'd first realised. But over time, she had come to accept it. Fox assassins acted within the law. Little darts of contained chaos, delivering peace and order to a vast empire. That's what she told herself, and that's what she'd come to believe. She had to, if she wanted to keep loving him. Which she did—she really did.

Cain was staring at her. "How long have you known? Weeks? Months?"

"About a year."

Cain hissed through his teeth. "And you never thought to say anything? Never asked me a single question…"

Neema's eyes widened, incredulous. "You're not suggesting *I'm* the one at fault here?"

"No, what I'm saying is—"

"Because you're the one who kills people for a living, Cain."

There. She'd said it. It was out there in the air between them.

He looked away from her, out to the balcony. Looked without seeing. "Well," he said, quietly. "I guess you have a choice to make." He stood up, and slung his bag over his shoulder. "There's a boat leaving in two hours. I'll wait for you at the quay."

Cain hesitated, stealing one last look. Then he slipped out through the balcony door, and was gone.

Neema sat for a while. All around her, the familiar sounds of the palace. Footsteps in the room above. A conversation down the hall. On the service path, someone walked by, whistling.

Cain's scent lingered, then faded.

Yanara Valit was going to die a cruel, miserable death. Dragged across the empire, forced to stand in every town square along the route. Confess her crimes in front of jeering crowds. And then, as she left, they would turn their backs, shunning her. You exist no longer in this place. You are nothing. You are no one. Day after day, month after month, town after town, until she reached her final destination. Dolrun Forest. There she would die in its poisoned embrace, untended, alone.

And after that, no one would ever speak of her again—on pain of death. She must be forgotten, completely. Her name cut from the records. Her family forced to smother their grief. No memorial stone, no prayers, no candles. Nothing. Exile wasn't just death. It was erasure. And if you believed in such things, even her spirit would be destroyed. No chance to return to the Eternal Path, and begin a new journey. What had been Yana would be a void, an absence. For ever.

But she had confessed. And the emperor had passed sentence.

The emperor was a good man. His reforms had given Commoners like Neema the chance to attend the great monasteries, the anats, and take positions at court. She wouldn't be here if it weren't for him. If Andren Valit's rebellion had succeeded, the only Commoners working on the island would be the servants.

The bell in the Bear tower chimed one.

Yanara Valit would suffer and die whether Neema wrote the Order or not.

And she had been commanded, by her emperor.

And Cain had done far worse.

She poured a splash of water into the inkstone and began to grind the block of Raven's Wing ink against the stone's rough surface. It took her half an hour to get the colour and consistency she wanted.

She breathed. Relaxed her posture. And set to work.

Her brushwork was a hand trailing in water, a breeze ruffling the grass. And it was beautiful. Achingly beautiful.

They will stitch this to her skin.

She pushed the thought away. Dipped her brush and began the second copy.

As she wrote, a horn blared from the western quay. The afternoon boat was leaving for the mainland. Neema, absorbed in her work, didn't hear it.

Lowering her brush to the paper one last time, she added the name, and the crime.

Yana's fate seeped into the paper, indigo-black.

As Neema finished the final stroke, she caught a ruffling of feathers, the light ting of claw on metal. She leaned sideways in her chair, craning to see through the balcony door. Was that a blur of black? The snap of opening wings? Or was it nothing?

It was nothing. Just her mind playing tricks, as she moved from her trance world of ink and brush and paper, back into the cramped reality of her narrow room.

She turned her attention back to the Order of Exile, reading it through one more time for errors. "*...on behalf of His Majesty,*

Bersun the Second…according to the laws of Orrun…Yanara Valit…traitor to the empire…"

Perfect.

Neema blew on the ink, a scholar's kiss, and it was done.

Eight years later.

PART TWO

Festival Eve

∞

THE EMPEROR'S CHAMELEON WAS MISSING.

Pink-Pink had appeared at court one morning three years ago, under mysterious circumstances. There were no chameleons on the island, wild or caged. Yet there he was, basking on the back of the throne, nose in the air. "A good omen," the emperor had declared. "A tiny dragon come to bless our court. Who will look after him for me?"

"I'm sure that—" Neema began.

"Perfect." Bersun dropped the startled lizard into Neema's hands. "Some company for you, High Scholar. Look after him well."

"I was going to suggest the menagerie—"

"No," the emperor said. And that was that.

Neema's vertiginous rise from junior archivist to high minister had provoked consternation and dismay at court. No one expressed it that way, naturally. Consternation and dismay were not safe words to describe the emperor's decisions. No—they were *astonished*. "She's an astonishing woman, is she not, our High Scholar?" "She is indeed. Quite remarkable."

Remarkable. That was another one.

Neema's elevation had brought many changes, but one thing remained the same. She still had no friends. A combination of reasons, other than her general personality:

1. Time. Her official duties, and her private research for the emperor, kept her extremely busy.
2. Envy. Obviously.
3. Snobbery. She was still a Commoner of Scartown, and always would be.

4. Caution. One of the best ways to make friends at court was to share gossip and grievances. But Neema had been discovered by High Commander Vabras, which made them wary of confiding in her.

5. Judgement. Everyone knew that Neema had written the Order of Exile for [she who did not exist]. That act of erasure was the foundation of Neema's success. Knowing this, and not being able to speak of it, only made it fester. Others may have been culpable—most of all that wretched boy Ruko. But Neema was right there in front of them, benefiting from the tragedy. Swanning about in her fine clothes, giving orders.

And of course, Neema could not speak about her feelings of guilt and remorse for what had happened. The Order of Exile was pinned to her heart too, and could not be removed. She could not be forgiven, she could not forgive herself—because what had happened *had not happened*. This was the great poison of Exile. There was no space for redemption, not for anyone.

So Neema did what she had always done: she threw herself into her work. Vabras and the emperor came to rely upon her even more, and people were *astonished*, and the wheel spun round and round. After eight years, Neema Kraa was at the very height of her power and unpopularity.

But she did have one companion. Green and yellow, nine inches long from nose to unfurled tail. Pink-Pink. Someone must have named him that, but no one would own up to it. The name had simply...permeated. As to its meaning, that was easily solved. Any time he passed by something pink he would instantly match it, merging into the background. Pink-Against-Pink. Evidently, it was his favourite colour.

Chameleons—ironically—do not like change. Pink-Pink took a long time to settle into Neema's grand apartment, with its silk rugs and soft leather day beds, its views across the Imperial Library's sweeping lawns. Its woeful lack of pink fabrics. Months of hissing, and snapping, and baleful stares followed. Neema persisted. She fed him, and talked to him, and eventually Pink-Pink relaxed into a daily routine: eat, sleep, swivel eyes, repeat. A natural courtier, in other words.

One oddity to his schedule: every morning he would climb down from the filigree headboard of Neema's raised sleep platform, and walk determinedly over her face. Was he staking his territory? Absorbing her body heat? Saying good morning? Who could say. Still—it was a useful wake-up call, upon which Neema had come to rely.

But today of all days Pink-Pink had abandoned the ritual. Neema had woken an hour later than usual, groggy from Dr. Yetbalm's Sleep Remedy. She had taken a double dose the night before, hoping for oblivion. An escape from the portentous dreams she'd been having these past few months.

Now she was running late on Festival Eve. The most important day of her life. The emperor—as he must—was preparing to hand over power after twenty-four years on the throne. The seven contenders had arrived from their respective monasteries, accompanied by their contingents. Tonight they would be welcomed in an extravagant opening ceremony, which the emperor had asked Neema to organise. It was her last and most prestigious assignment, and it would set the tone for the rest of the Festival. Any mistake—no matter how small—would be marked as inauspicious, and she would be held responsible. Every detail must be perfect.

Hurrying down from her sleep platform, she washed and dressed quickly. There was no time to fix her hair, so she wrapped it in a black chiffon headscarf, the lightest thing she could find. It was going to be another sultry day. There had been weeks of this weather—dense, oppressive heat with no rain to offer relief.

Heading into the sunken living area, she found her useless assistant lounging in her favourite chair, his feet up on the table. Janric Tursul, of the Venerant Tursuls. Or, as she had privately named him, Generic Arsehole, of the Venerant Arseholes. His beige skin looked dull and puffy from another night out partying on the Grand Canal. He had eaten her breakfast except for two cucumber slices, now resting delicately over his eyelids.

"Have you seen Pink-Pink?"

He removed the cucumber slices. "Not actually my job?"

"Did you feed him last night?"

"Sure, I guess?"

Neema gritted her teeth. Janric had been the worst in a long line of lazy, entitled assistants. At the end of his first week, he had lodged a formal complaint about having to work for someone "who didn't understand the way of things." This was Venerant code for "a Commoner." Today was his last day, thank the Eight. He was joining the official Raven contingent, supporting Gaida Rack in her bid for the throne.

He stared up at the clockwork ceiling fan, hands behind his head. "Do you actually need me for anything?"

The fan whirred and clacked. "No. I don't actually need you for anything, Janric." *You fundamentally pointless being.* "You can go."

Neema's quarters were designed to remain cool, even at the height of summer. Stepping outside, she walked into a wall of heat. She stopped for a moment, adjusting to the change. Tomorrow, the contenders would have to compete in this furnace, in a series of fights and Trials. *Whereas I will be over there in the library,* she thought, smugly. Far from the heat, and the crowds. She still had a few days left to make use of the imperial archives, and with the Festival underway, she would have them almost to herself. At last, after months of delay, she could focus on her latest monograph: *Ketuan Prison Ballads of the Seventh Century.* The world, she knew, held its breath for publication.

In her private courtyard, an elderly Oxwoman in a broad-brimmed hat was watering the late summer flowers; dahlias and verbena, the last of the roses. Neema asked if she had seen Pink-Pink. She had not, but promised to check all the pink flowers carefully. "You're not training today?" the Oxwoman asked.

Neema shifted on her hip. "No, not today," she muttered. She had been using the courtyard as a practice ground for years. Initially she had kept to the series of stretches and strengthening exercises she'd been taught as a novice at the Raven monastery, designed to help her survive a lifetime of desk work. Over time she'd added some martial applications: a rolling drill of steps, kicks, punches and strikes that Cain had shown her back in Scartown. She found they benefited her mood as much as her body. She hadn't realised anyone had noticed her training. Like most of life's observers, the thought of being studied in turn made her intensely uncomfortable.

"Have you tried the north service path?" the woman suggested. She hesitated, then added, "By the bins."

Neema understood the hesitation. It meant the cockroaches were back, just in time for the Festival. An irresistible snack for Pink-Pink, and thus a good place to look—but the servants would be in trouble if anyone found out. "Thanks," she said, conveying with a careful nod that she wouldn't say anything.

"I hope you find him, High Scholar," the Oxwoman said, returning to her work. "I know you're fond of him."

The bins smelled of bleach and old memories.

She had not visited this part of the palace in years. Too painful. This was the path that had run beneath her balcony, when she was a Junior Archivist. The same hut, the same bins. Same cockroaches, probably. They were resilient. She moved one of the bins and they scattered wildly, like thieves.

No sign of Pink-Pink. Frustrated, Neema leaned against the service hut and tapped the back of her head against the wood. Today. Why did he have to disappear today? The heat had drawn out the tung oil used to protect the wood. It had a sharp, nutty scent, somehow pleasant and unpleasant at the same time.

Don't look, she told herself, and looked.

Someone had repainted her old balcony, but it was peeling again. A couple of cracked terracotta pots filled with dead plants. A solitary chair folded away and propped against the wall.

She thought of Cain with his nose pressed against the glass. *Did you ever think about me?* She would see him again tonight, at the opening ceremony. The first time since that fateful day. She wasn't the only one who had experienced an elevation in the last eight years. Cain Ballari was the official Fox contender for the throne. He and Ruko Valit were close favourites to win. Neema couldn't decide which option was worse.

No matter. Straight after the coronation she would set off for Ketu—two thousand miles away from the imperial court. The Bear monastery was in urgent need of a new abbot following the death of Brother Lanrik.[6] Bersun was the natural choice. He had never wanted the crown—had only fought for it on Lanrik's in- sistence. Now the Old Bear was going home, and he had invited Neema to join him. She was going to help him write his official memoirs. ("Stupid business," he'd grumbled, as he did about most court traditions.)

Neema was nervous about her new home. Anat-garra was a bleak mountain fortress, and they would arrive in deep winter. But there would be no place for her here, once Bersun gave up the throne.

If he did give up the throne.

She dismissed the thought, annoyed with herself. She gave no credence to the darker rumours swirling around the island—that the emperor was reluctant to hand over power after ruling Or- run for his full term of twenty-four years. Neema had spent long hours with Bersun in private, discussing her Ketuan research. A couple of glasses of whisky by the fire, and he would confess to her as if she were a temple servant. He was homesick, even now. He loathed the island, and could not wait to escape.

No. The emperor was not the problem, she was sure of that. Bersun would leave as soon as the coronation was complete. It was his successor people should be worrying about.

---

6. Brother Lanrik (1440–1538), born Quen Quereka of the Venerant Querekas. Disowned by his family aged seventeen, he embarked on a life of piracy. Cap- tured in 1465, Quen was sent to the Ketuan prison mines for life. In 1472 he ex- perienced three powerful dream encounters with the Fifth Guardian, as told in "Prisoner Quen and the Bear," after which he took the name Lanrik, meaning "little friend of the Bear" in the old tongue. Pardoned 1474, following a series of miracles. Entered Anat-garra as a mature recruit and became abbot nine years later, in 1483.

She was about to move on when the balcony door to her old room slid open. An irrational fear gripped her, that it might be Cain. Pressing herself against the service hut, she tried to blend into the shadows. As High Scholar, she always wore black or purple to honour the Raven. Today she was dressed in a black, pleated crepe outfit that swung about her tall, honed body. Her badge of office—a raven formed from black diamonds, with outstretched wings—glinted softly on her chest. She took it off, afraid it would give her away, and slipped it in her pocket.

A second later, Princess Yasila stepped out on to the balcony.

It can't be.

And yet it was. Princess Yasila, dressed in gossamer-thin layers of floating sea-green silk and lace, her long black hair captured in a diamond and silver net.

After that day, that terrible day eight years ago, the emperor had reinstated Yasila's fortune and her title.[7] She had taken the opportunity to renounce the Valit name—no doubt to distance herself further from her estranged son. Henceforth she would go by her old family name: Majan. Gathering up her surviving daughter Nisthala, she had sailed off to her ancestral home on the south-east coast, near Three Ports. A place to grieve and heal in private.

Then Nisthala fell ill. Tragedy heaped on tragedy.

The emperor had been swift to offer his help. The palace was home to the best healers in the empire. Nisthala would receive the care she needed. And while she recovered, they were welcome to take over the imperial suite, the finest apartment on the island, at his majesty's expense.

Guilt, people whispered.

Reparation, others suggested. A chance to *save* a child, instead of…Well. The law prevented them from saying more.

---

7. In the mid third century, the direct blood descendants of Yasthala were given leave to refer to themselves as princes and princesses once they came of age. The great Raven empress—who despised dynastic power above all things— would never have countenanced this, which was precisely why the Six Families granted their permission, "in her honour." A sly, petty piece of revenge by Yasthala's enemies, served up two hundred and fifty years after the fact.

Yasila returned to the island with her daughter. The years passed. Nisthala's health remained fragile. Hidden away in the shuttered apartment, she had not been seen since her arrival. Locked in her room, it was rumoured. Some even wondered if she was still alive.

Yasila was almost as reclusive. Rarely did she descend from the imperial suite, and when she did, she drifted over the island like a lost spirit, wrapped in the shroud of her grief. She was not allowed to wear mourning grey to mark her loss. As far as the law was concerned, she had lost nothing. So she clothed herself in sea-green and silver, the colours of the Dragon. The Guardian of Death. She used her body as a protest, a silent wail of pain. The places she visited leaned towards the symbolic. The temple. The imperial tombs. The western docks, where those who were Exiled began their journey. She'd laid flowers there once, it was said, and been reprimanded for it by Vabras.

What the Eight was she doing *here*?

Shielding her eyes from the sun, Yasila leaned over the balcony and peered down the service path. Then she turned sharply, as if she'd heard her name being called, and retreated inside. The balcony door slid shut. A moment later, the shutters folded neatly into place.

Her entrance and exit had lasted no more than fifteen seconds.

Neema felt a light fluttering in her stomach, a presentiment of…something. The scent of tung oil vanished, and the air around her turned thin and cool. Fresh, mountain air. She felt weightless, as if she could lift up into the sky.

She dug her nails into her palms and the sensation faded. She was solid again, rooted to the ground.

She gazed up at her old room, trying to recall who lived there these days. A name clicked into place. Marius Au, Office of Speculation. Hadn't he left a couple of months ago? Yes, she was sure of it—he'd gone back home to Gridtown, some family emergency. Whoever Yasila was meeting up there, it wasn't Marius.

Interesting.

"Neema!" Fenn Fedala strode down the path towards her, dressed in his usual battered overalls, roll-up dangling from his fingers.

Neema cursed softly, under her breath.

It was not that she had forgotten her appointment with the High Engineer. It was more that he had slid down her priority list for the day.

He did not look happy about it.

Fenn had been in a foul temper for weeks. For the last fifteen years—ever since the emperor had personally summoned him to court—he had stubbornly refused to live on the island. Every morning he took the boat from the capital, and every night he returned home to his wife, who ran civic projects in the poorer grids. Fenn's private time in Armas was the source of his equilibrium. He needed to see his family, catch up with friends at his local grid café. Cook his own food, sleep in his own bed. Escape the demands of his role for a few hours. But with the Festival looming, the emperor had ordered him to stay on the island. Fenn hadn't been home in over a month, he'd been working eighteen-hour days. Like his overalls, he was fraying at the edges.

"Where the fuck have you been? We were supposed to meet an hour ago."

Neema peeled herself from the wall. "Pink-Pink is missing. He usually wakes me, but he didn't this morning, so . . ."

Fenn covered his ears.

Neema stopped talking.

Fenn lowered his hands. "Is everything under control?"

"Yes."

If Neema were an Oxwoman, that would have satisfied him. *We pull the plough together* and all that. But she was a Raven. She was not part of his team. "You've spoken to the musicians? Chef Ganstra? What about the banners for the Second Trial, are they—"

"Everything's in hand," Neema cut in, sharply. Now they were both irritated.

They frowned at each other.

Fenn took a long drag on his roll-up. Breathed the smoke out with a sigh. "Sorry. Caught me at a bad moment." He looked away to the middle distance. "I saw him just now. He's here. Motherfucking piece of shit."

Neema squinted. This was the imperial court, she would need a clue.

"Ruko Valit." Fenn spat the name from his mouth.

"Oh. Right." She didn't know what else to say. It was a strange situation, to know what Ruko had done—that unforgivable betrayal—and not be able to discuss it. It left an empty space where the words should go. "I just saw his mother." She nudged her chin towards her old room. "She's up there now."

Fenn looked up at the balcony, the closed shutters, then back down at Neema.

Neema lifted her hands. *I know. Weird.* "Why do you think—"

"I don't."

"But—"

Fenn took her by the elbow and walked her away, boots crunching on gravel. When they were at a safe distance he said, "You didn't see her. You didn't see anything."

"What's she doing up there, Fenn?"

"I don't care." He dropped his roll-up on to the gravel, and ground it with his boot. "Nor should you. She's a Valit. Valits are trouble."

"She goes by Majan, these days."

"For fuck's sake, Neema."

"Sorry." Correcting facts was a compulsion, she couldn't help herself. Another reason why her only friend at court was a chameleon.

"What did you see back there?" Fenn asked, testing her.

This was very hard for Neema. Eventually, she forced out the lie. "Nothing."

Fenn snapped his fingers, and pointed at her. *Correct.* Then he shoved his hands in his pockets and continued on his way.

CHAPTER
Six

NEEMA SPENT THE next few hours making sure everything
was ready for the opening ceremony. She sat in on the dress
rehearsal for the court procession—the ministers, the emperor's
retinue, the musicians and dancers. She wasn't happy, so they did
it again. They all hated her for it, but the emperor didn't pay her
to be popular. That would be a singular waste of money. He paid
her to be perfect.

By the end of the day her top was sticking to her skin with
sweat and her hair was starting to frizz. She paid a visit to the arti-
ficial waterfall at the Monkey palace and stood under its ice-cold
cascade, fully clothed and shrieking with laughter. (The emperor
did not pay her to be dignified, either.)

The sun was setting as she returned to the second palace, her
clothes almost dry again from the heat. She slid open the door to
her antechamber and sighed with relief. Peace.

The door to the main apartment flew back, revealing a young
white woman dressed in kitchen uniform. She was tiny, and over-
joyed. "High Scholar—welcome home!" She danced on the spot,
weaving her shoulders from side to side. "That's my welcome home
dance. Wow, this is so exciting, thank you so much for this opportunity, your rooms are *awesome*." She sang the last word.

Neema blinked.

"I'm Benna. Benna Edge. Your new assistant."

Neema had completely forgotten—with Janric leaving, she
had called in a favour from Chef Ganstra. He'd promised to send
someone over from the imperial kitchens to help for the next few
days. And here she was.

Benna beamed, as if she had won the Kind Festival lottery. "Do I bow? I should bow." She gave it a go, ending up somewhere between a Raven and a Fox salute, arms crossed over her chest, one foot wobbling in front of the other.

Neema stepped down into the living area. It was spotless, and smelled of lemon. The cushions were plumped, and there was a vase of freshly cut flowers on the table.

"I didn't touch your books," Benna said, suddenly anxious. "Chef Ganstra said, don't touch her books or she'll kill you."

"I won't kill you."

"Phew. Would you like some tea? And cake? I wasn't sure which you liked best, so..." She gestured towards a tray piled high with bite-sized cakes—pistachio, banana, chocolate, cherry frangipane...there had to be a hundred of them. Neema tried one, to be polite, then tried three more.

"Oh you like them all best, fantastic," Benna said. "Would you like some ginger tea? Or whisky? Chef Ganstra said those were your favourite."

"Tea, thank you."

Benna danced her way over to the stove singing, "Ginger tea, ginger tea," under her breath. This should have been insanely annoying, but somehow wasn't.

"You're from Westhaven," Neema guessed.

"Wow, yeah. Good spot. Was it the accent?"

Neema smiled to herself. It *was* the accent—a lilting song of long vowels and lost consonants. It was also *everything* about her. Her surname, her tiny stature, her twin plaits of hair braided with white ribbon—the colour of the unaffiliated. Most of all, the tattoos winding up her arms, memorials to those she had lost, and prompts to enjoy the moment, and live life to the full. These were not empty words for a Westhavener. Their territory bordered the poisoned forest of Dolrun. People died young there. One in three children never reached adulthood.

Benna finished making the tea, humming to herself. "What else can I do for you, High Scholar?"

"Did you see a chameleon while you were tidying up?"

Benna clutched her cheeks in joy. "You have a pet chameleon? Oh my short, sweet life—I LOVE chameleons!"

Neema suspected that Benna LOVED lots of things. "I think someone may have stolen him."

"No!"

"But he may have wandered off somewhere."

"Yes!" Benna much preferred this theory. "He's on an adventure! I'll look for him while you're at the ceremony, High Scholar."

"You don't have to."

Benna nodded, but she was going to conduct an inch-by-inch search, Neema could tell from the determined set of her jaw.

She took her tea and cake into the dressing area. Through the screened window, she could hear the palace choir out on the lawn, practising their song for the Day of the Raven. She hummed along as she rubbed avocado oil into her scalp and through her hair. Her evening gown was hanging by the mirror—she rinsed her hands and slipped it on, before calling to Benna for help with the hooks.

"Ohhhh," Benna said, wide-eyed in the mirror.

Neema smoothed her hands over the dark indigo silk, admiring the way it skimmed her waist and hips. The skirt was pleated and tucked at the back to suggest a raven's folded wings, diamond-shaped tail fanning out along the floor. The sheer bodice was embroidered with diamonds and silver thread in a pattern of intertwining feathers.

The dress had eaten up most of Neema's savings, but it was worth it—she needed to look good tonight. *Feel* good. Once the party was over she could sell it back to the imperial wardrobe for their archives, for two gold tiles less than she had paid for it. Two gold tiles to feel invincible. Still a fortune—but worth it.

She watched her new assistant in the mirror as she set to work closing the hooks. "How old are you, Benna?"

"I'll be nineteen this Fading Light."

Neema would have guessed a little older. But then the average life expectancy for a deep southwesterner was forty-six. Life had already sunk its claws into Benna.

"How did you end up so far east?"

Benna brought her hands together, revealing another upbeat tattooed message. Left hand: LIFE IS SHORT. Right hand: ENJOY IT ! "I left home at fifteen, worked my way across the empire. I'm heading back though, after the Festival. I miss my family so much. How about you, High Scholar?"

Neema felt a twinge of guilt. She had not been back to Scartown since the emperor called her to his side. Letters only. She changed the subject. "You're not affiliated?"

Benna touched the white ribbon in her plait. "No, we don't bother with that," she said, blithely dismissing a system followed by ninety-five per cent of the population.

"But if you had to pick one of the Eight—which would you choose?"

"All of them," Benna said. She closed the last hook.

They admired the dress together in the mirror.

"You look amazing."

"Thanks." No point denying it. Neema snapped a diamond cuff on to her left wrist. It struck her that if she'd had Benna at her side, instead of a long series of twats like Janric Tursul, her life at court would have been easier, more productive and much more pleasant. How nice to discover this, eight days before she left for ever.

Crossing to a high shelf, she lifted out a lacquered box and brought it back to her dressing table. She smiled at Benna, like a magician about to perform a trick, and opened the box. Glimmering inside was a diamond choker, with a large, eight-sided amethyst at its heart. Purple, for the Raven. She had asked Facet, the court jeweller, to send her something special, and this had arrived for her last night.

Benna lifted it reverently from the box and clipped it around Neema's throat.

A touch of make-up, a spray of perfume and her armour was complete.

"I should be back by midnight," she said. "Could you have a bath ready? And some chamomile tea?"

Benna looked perplexed. "What about the afterparty?"

"I'll freshen up first, then head over."

"Maybe not the chamomile tea then, High Scholar? Something to pick you up, instead?"

"Good thinking. Thanks."

"You are *so* welcome." Benna did a little hop from foot to foot. "Have fun!"

Neema smiled and headed for the door. Shoulders back, hips swaying as the train fanned out behind her.

The truth was she hadn't been invited to any of the informal afterparties taking place across the island, not even the one planned in Gaida's honour. Until now, her Raven peers had been forced to show respect to Neema's badge of office, at least. But with the emperor so close to abdication they could snub her without risk of reprisal. Her lack of invitation was a message screamed in capital letters: YOU ARE NOT ONE OF US YOU NEVER WILL BE.

She was too embarrassed to explain this to Benna. How unpopular she was. It is one thing to admit to being feared, or hated. Quite another to admit that you are unloved, and lonely, and that it is taking all your strength to hide it.

CHAPTER
Seven

S HE WAS HALFWAY ACROSS THE lawn when Kindry Rok
ambushed her.

"Neema Kraa!" he twinkled. "Your radiance honours the Raven."

The emperor's long-serving High Justice was wearing a purple
tunic that made him look like a blueberry. He waited for a compliment. "You're all dressed up," she said.

Kindry chuckled. He was a man who chuckled. He'd been
suave and attractive once—a sweep of sandy hair, a strong jaw.
Years of indulgence had damaged all that, slowly at first and then
rapidly. At the far end of his fifties, he looked more than a decade
older. Nothing for it but to become a character: everyone's least-
favourite uncle.

He was always well-mannered towards Neema in public—not
because he liked her, but because she made him look good. She
had taken over many of his more onerous duties over the years,
leaving him free to pursue more important business: building alliances, destroying enemies, amassing a vast personal fortune. In
private he called her his pack mule, and sniggered about it.

"Our dear contender wishes to speak with you." His smile broadened. He knew full well that Gaida and Neema hated each other.

"I'll see her at the ceremony."

Kindry's smile stretched so far, it contorted his face. "In private
I'm afraid, High Scholar. Right away."

Neema seethed her way back through the palace. Gaida was playing games again. The Raven contender had been living at the
second palace for the past month, acclimatising for the Festival.

Neema had invited her for tea in her private garden—as was the custom. Gaida had accepted graciously, and then—having kept Neema waiting for over an hour—had sent a servant down with a message. *Contender Rack offers her deepest apologies. She is too busy to meet with you this afternoon.* As though Neema spent her days floating down the Grand Canal eating cherries.

The snub was carefully calculated to offend. Gaida, who had taken the apartment above Neema's, was entertaining friends on her balcony that day. They were laughing, and talking passionately about something. Gaida was always talking passionately about something. Even from the floor below, Neema could feel the infectious energy of that meeting. Convivial, engaged, committed. Both genuine and also a performance. Gaida always acted as though everyone around her was taking notes about her for their memoirs. To be fair, they often were.

Neema and Gaida had entered the Raven monastery on the same day—literally walked through the iron gates together. Two fourteen-year-old girls from very different worlds. Neema Lee of Scartown, Gaida Kalair of Arbell City, as they were known then, before they took their Raven names. Gaida—a sweet-faced white girl with dark blue eyes and a mass of loose brown curls—had an unmistakeably Venerant aura: the beautifully tailored uniform, the easy confidence. More specifically, in her case, a sloppiness with her possessions. Her bag was battered, her shoes were scuffed. A priceless gold hairclip lay tangled in her curls, threatening to slip out at any moment.

On instinct Neema had pulled back, trying to make herself invisible. With the notable exception of her old schoolteacher, Madam Fessi, her experience with Venerants was poor. But then Gaida had smiled at her—a warm smile, full of eager assurance. "That's my favourite," she'd said, gesturing to the book tucked under Neema's arm. Instantly, Neema had been seduced. Pushing through her shyness, she'd introduced herself. Maybe they could sit together at lunch, and talk about it? "I'd *love* that," Gaida said.

By lunchtime, Gaida had already formed a tight circle of admiring friends. All of them shaven-headed now, to denote their status as novices. Commiserating with each other and laughing as they touched each other's scalps. When Neema tried to join them, Gaida apologised—there wasn't room. Except there was, there was plenty. Embarrassed, Neema had walked off at once, in shoes that were not scuffed, because they were her only pair, and would have to last her the next four years.

Behind her back, giggles and snorts. And Gaida hushing them. "Be kind, she can't help it. She's just a bit…" Neema didn't see the face Gaida pulled, but it produced more laughter, not less.

Long ago, Neema had learned to draw out the sting of rejection. Work. Work tirelessly. Immerse yourself. She had fought hard to win her scholarship, and nothing would spoil that. She would find her friends and companions in her books. The vast, soaring library of Anat-ruar was famed throughout the empire. There she made her home, and if Gaida and her friends showed up, she would gather her things and head for the empty, echoing martial rooms to train.[8] At night, while the rest of her year gathered in the common rooms, she stayed in her cell, reading and perfecting her calligraphy, and pretending she was fine. If that didn't work, she took out Cain's sprawling letters and read them over and over in the flickering candlelight, to remind herself that there was one person out there in the world who understood her, and liked her as she was.

All that extra study thrust Neema to the top of the class. Gaida, trailing a weak second, would smile and say, "She tries so hard, doesn't she? I've never met anyone so desperate to win." Desperate —the ultimate Venerant putdown. It became Neema's nickname, shortened to Desy.

Neema may have won the coveted "First in Year" award four years in a row but it was Gaida who was tipped for greatness. Before she had even completed her final exams, High Justice Yaan

---

8. In ancient days, the Raven Warriors of Anat-ruar were feared and respected throughout the empire, but they suffered a long, tragic decline. The last Raven warrior died fighting for Yasthala. By the time Neema entered the monastery in 1519, students were offered no formal martial training.

Rack had offered her a position at court, working at his side. Then came Andren's rebellion, and the purges. Rack, who had served four successive rulers of Orrun, was accused of conspiracy. He denied it, but the evidence was compelling. He was executed that autumn along with his wife, his three sons, and fifteen members of his office.

Gaida could have distanced herself from her mentor. Instead, when it came to selecting her Raven name, she had chosen to honour him—ruining her chance of a life at court. Even Neema had to admit, that had shown courage.

It had also made her the radical hero of the Raven community. Untainted by court politics, Gaida was free to present herself as the noble idealist, burning with moral authority. "Principles before power, compassion before ambition," she proclaimed.[9] (Neema had clenched her jaw so hard when she read that, she gave herself a stress headache.)

And now she was their contender. She hadn't put herself forward (again, she wasn't *desperate*)—but a word here, a word there, and somehow it was known that Professor Rack might *consider* representing the Ravens, if that was the *overwhelming* wish of the Flock. Within days, every other potential candidate had stepped back. Gaida was named contender without contest.

One consolation for Neema—Gaida stood almost no chance of winning the throne. She would probably do well in the more strategic Trials, but the contenders also had to face each other on the fight platform. Every other monastery had chosen its contender through fierce internal competition. No matter how much martial training Gaida had crammed into the last couple of years, she would be no match for her rivals. She was going to get trampled, once a day for the next seven days.

Gaida's suite lay on the top floor of the Raven palace. Like Neema's apartment, it was a large rectangular space broken up with sunken

---

9. From "A Way Through the Clouds," *Addresses to the Flock: the Collected Wisdom of Professor Gaida Rack* (1533).

areas and painted screens, and a long balcony with sliding doors. Unlike Neema's apartment, the place was a tip, clothes slung over chairs, half-eaten bowls of food, hairbrushes and make-up pots and bottles of perfume, piles of papers. One of the antique screens had a fresh elbow hole through the middle.

Janric Tursul opened the door—something he'd always refused to do for Neema. "Contender Rack is an *inspiration*," he said, leading her through to a private seating area. "It's such an *honour* and a *privilege* to support her."

"So where is she?"

"Contender Rack will be with you when she's ready," he said, already turning to leave. No offer of refreshments.

Neema sighed. It was all so petty and exhausting.

A book lay open on the table in front of her. *Orrun's Ancient Tyrannies: The Definitive History* by Professor Gaida Rack. Someone (Gaida) had underlined a passage about the High officials who had supported Orrun's worst rulers. "These spineless, amoral worms are as guilty as the monsters they served. Let us take comfort from the fact that so many came to a bad end at the hands of their masters." On the facing page, illustrating her point, was a wood engraving of Esgril the Pitiless, feeding his High Scholar to a crocodile.

The worst thing about this, Neema thought, is she thinks she's being subtle. She picked up a pencil and asterisked the opening phrase. Added, in the margin, "All worms are spineless. Tautology. Amend for next reprint?"

She waited a few minutes, then lost patience. Gaida was talking out on the balcony, Neema could hear the familiar, earnest rise and fall of her voice as she explained something she wanted, to someone who was failing to give it to her. A servant, Neema guessed, as she rose to find them, stepping back into the sweltering heat. She'd hoped the evening would bring respite, a freshening of the air, but if anything it had turned even more humid.

Gaida had her back turned, posing against the pink-orange sunset. She was dressed in her Festival uniform—a black, sleeveless tunic and black trousers, cut to mid-calf. She looked good, like a proper contender, her body honed in preparation for the Festival. She'd fixed her hair neatly for once, holding it in place with pins and an ebony comb. Neema spotted a few early strands of grey mixed in with the brown. Yes, she made a point of looking, Gaida made her petty like that.

Twenty years had passed since they'd walked through the gates of Anat-ruar together. Fourteen years old. Smiling shyly, and promising to meet again at lunch. People were puzzles, Neema thought. Not fun ones, with prizes. They were puzzles that made no sense, and gave no answer, and broke your heart for no reason.

Gaida was—as Neema had anticipated—arguing with a servant. "No, leave the shutters open tonight. I will sleep there." She indicated a day bed, drawn up beside the balcony.

"Contender Rack, I wouldn't advise that—"

Annoyed, Gaida turned round. For a fluttered second she almost faltered, seeing Neema standing there in her finery: the magnificent indigo silk dress with its regal silhouette, the glittering amethyst and diamond choker. She touched a hand to the sigil emblazoned across her chest—a pair of raven wings stretched out in flight, embroidered in shades of purple to show against the solid black of her tunic. The gesture restored her confidence. She was the Raven contender—nothing beat that. "I want to wake with the sun," she said to the baffled servant, in her rich, theatrical voice. She shifted her pose, and looked to the mid distance.

Neema cringed in anticipation. Poetry. She was going to recite poetry.

Worse than that. She was going to recite her own poetry.

"'Sleep, sleep, gentle soul, the stars shine but for you. And with the dawn, the sun will kiss your cheek, awakening you to glory.'"

The servant caught Neema's eye, and made a swirling gesture with his finger and thumb. Mosquitoes. That's why he'd protested. *Mosquitoes* would be kissing Gaida's cheek. But as every servant knows, some people will not be told.

"The shutters will remain open," Gaida said, imperious.

She's been practising, Neema thought.

The servant gave a deep Raven salute, arms crossed over his chest. So deep, it had to be ironic. That was the thing about Gaida. She might be the darling of the Raven Flock, but ask those who served her? Not so beloved.

"And change the tea," Gaida said, oblivious. "The valerian root is off."

"I think that's just the way it tastes, Contender—"

"It's off. Change it for lavender. That's all."

The servant bowed again and left.

Gaida gave Neema an enchanting smile. "Desy."

Neema's stomach swooped at her old nickname.

"Why the Eight did we call you that?" Gaida laughed, nostalgic. "I can't remember, for the life of me." (She definitely remembered.) "No matter, you'll always be Desy to me." She opened her arms wide. "Give me a hug, it's been ages."

They hugged. It was dreadful.

"Look at you." Gaida stepped back, to take in the vision. "The famous dress. Janric tells me you've spent a fortune." Her dark blue eyes glittered. "Are you sure that was wise?"

Neema brushed imaginary dust from her skirt. "Was that Poldren the Bleak[10] you were quoting, back there?"

Gaida's smile faded. If Princess Yasila was the exemplar of hidden feelings, Gaida was her opposite. Joy, rage, humour, everything passed across her face unfiltered. She tucked a wayward strand of hair behind her ear. Neema caught the familiar tell. *She has something on you, and it's going to hurt. Steel yourself.*

"Do you know what I've been doing these last two years, Desy?"

Neema did know. Gaida had been on what she called a Sacred Flight, trotting across the empire in lavish style, writing about the nobility of the poor, and the searing majesty of the landscape, and how small she felt in relation to the universe. Pages and pages about how small she felt. "Yes," Neema said. "You've been on holiday."

"I went in search of myself. Do you know what I found?"

---

10. Notoriously terrible fifth-century poet.

Neema made a show of crossing her fingers. "Humility?"

"My father."

Neema uncrossed her fingers. She had met Gaida's father at the Raven monastery once—a sweet man who collected antique fiddles. They'd had a nice conversation about it, Gaida had been furious with him.

"My mother had an affair, here at court." Gaida looked out across the palace gardens, labouring the dramatic pause. "With Yaan Rack."

That was a surprise. Neema sifted through what she knew of Gaida's mother, a much-admired actress and singer. She'd performed at the Monkey Palace theatre, the summer of 1504, taking the part of Gutara the Fox in *The Magic Forest*. It was possible. Unlikely, but possible. Yaan Rack. *Yaan Rack.* Damn. Neema rubbed a knot in her left collarbone, not realising that was her own, anxious tell.

"You can see it, once you look." Gaida touched her angular jaw line, the side of her eyes. Those clever, expressive, dark blue eyes.

A bead of sweat trickled down Neema's back. "I didn't know him."

"But you did meet him that one time, Desy." Gaida smiled. "Didn't you?"

There it was. The poisoned dart.

And Neema was falling back in time. 1523, the month of the Tiger. Three o'clock on the twelfth day, an overcast afternoon. Standing in perfect, respectful posture, her black robes freshly laundered. Her shoes were thin and worn, but she'd spent her last bronze tile to have them polished to a mirror shine.

Neema had completed her four years of intensive training and study at the monastery. Her final exams were over. In a few weeks, she would choose her Raven name and "fledge." (Anat-ruar used a lot of bird metaphors. Some people found this charming.) While the rest of her year-mates were looking forward to a bright spring of travels, celebrations and family gatherings, Neema was fretting about her future. Despite her high scores, her evident talents, she was yet to secure a position. "We have placed you on the reserve list," the letters read. Seven of them.

She knew what they were waiting for. This meeting.

Once a year, High Justice Yaan Rack spent a week at the monastery, meeting with every student before they fledged. Sailing from the imperial island with his retinue, he would set up office in a grand suite kept solely for this purpose. Officially, he came to offer his counsel. Unofficially, he was deciding which individuals were worthy of his support. Well-connected graduates such as Gaida were already tucked safely beneath his wing, of course. Whereas Neema was yet to speak a word to the great man. Rack had pinned her First in Year wings to her cape four years in a row, but had only nodded absently as he did so, without saying a word.

This one brief interview could shape her entire career. Naturally Neema was anxious. She had paced her cell night after night in preparation, rehearsing her answers, perfecting her grateful face in the mirror. This would be a trial, and she must be ready for it. Rack's cross-examinations as a young lawyer were legendary.

Then, when the moment came, he surprised her, bursting from his office with an engaging enthusiasm, blue eyes bright with welcome. His long grey curls (also legendary—everything about Rack was legendary) were tied up with purple ribbon, his robes expertly padded to bulk out his frail body. Before Neema could even begin the greeting she'd practised, he had gathered her in a light hug. She felt awkward, conscious that she was sweating with nerves. Rack, in comparison, was dry as a fresh sheet of paper, and smelled wonderfully of lemon, crisp and sharp.

He let her go. "Neema Lee, Commoner of Scartown. Here on your own merit and First in Year." He gave an earnest smile. At the grand age of eighty-three, his face was scored with deep lines, but his energy was undiminished. "Wonderful. Wonderful! *You* are the reason I supported Emperor Bersun's monastery reforms. Now sit down, sit down. Tell me about yourself, and your experience here at Anat-ruar. Be honest. I am curious. I am open."

Neema's tutors had warned her to be humble, respectful and positive. But Rack was a seeker of knowledge, a seeker of truth. *First know, then act.* One of his best-known aphorisms. This was her chance to improve the system for those who came after her.

So—discarding her carefully rehearsed lines—she spoke honestly, describing what life was like at the monastery for outcasts like her. How the other students had shunned her. How even a couple of the teachers had tried to sabotage her work, and destroy her confidence. How hard she'd had to fight every day to convince people—to convince herself—that she deserved to be there. Rack listened intently, nodding briskly for her to continue when she faltered, encouraging her to open up further.

When she was done he steepled his fingers. "There is a saying," he murmured. "Master Tovan Rork, in *The Wisdom of the Flock*. I find it apposite, here." He closed his eyes, and quoted from memory. "'Beware the Solitary Raven. She has been banished for good reason.'"

He opened his eyes. All the good humour, the bright curiosity had vanished. "I gave you a gift this morning, Neema Lee. The gift of my time. You might have asked for my advice. You might have thanked me for opening the gates of Anat-ruar to Commoners for the first time in Orrun's history. But instead you chose to waste it with your complaints. Your tittle-tattle. Your petty feuds. Eight, you didn't even bother to wear a decent pair of shoes." He picked up his pencil and began scratching ill-tempered notes in her file. The interview was over.

Neema sat for a moment in stunned disbelief. She watched his bowed head, half expecting him to look up again and tell her he was joking. When that didn't happen, she tried to think of what she could say to change his mind. Apologise? Beg? Explain about the shoes? But she could tell from the set of his shoulders, the firm scrape of his pencil, that he would not shift, or soften. In fact, she was beginning to suspect that this interview had been a trap, from the moment he'd burst out of the room and hugged her. For some reason he'd wanted her to fail. He'd orchestrated it.

There was nothing to be done. And yet, there was *one* thing she had to say, before she left. A weight upon her chest, that must be lifted. *Don't say it, don't say it.* But she couldn't help herself. "Osil Gronk."

Rack raised his head, brows furrowed with irritation. Was she still here? "I *beg* your pardon?"

"That quote, about the Solitary Raven. You attributed it to Master Rork. He edited *Wisdom of the Flock*, but the line comes from an essay by Osil Gronk."

Rack stared at her, mouth open. "You question my knowledge?" he said, when he had recovered. "Who the Eight do you think you are? Who *the Eight* do you think you are speaking to?"

Neema drew herself up in her seat. "'A Raven must never be afraid to admit fault, in the pursuit of truth.'" She was quoting the High Justice himself. It seemed…apposite.

For forty years, Yaan Rack had lorded over the Raven community. No one had dared question him in decades—let alone use his own words against him. "*You,*" he spat. "On my life. You are expelled from Anat-ruar. You will not take your Raven name. I forbid it. *I forbid it.* No school, no court, no office in the land will hire you. By the time I am finished with you, Neema Lee, you will be lucky to find work on an Ox Team, cleaning sewers with your bare hands. Now—get *out.*" He banged his fist on the desk.

Neema had left the room in a daze. When she reached her cell she'd curled up on her bed and wept. She was nineteen years old, and her life was ruined.

Later, she thought: Who cleans sewers with their bare hands? Surely they used shovels? And long poles for blockages?

All day she hid in her room, waiting for the knock on the door, rocking back and forth in a way even she found pathetic. Would they expel her in front of the whole monastery, in some hideous ceremony? Or let her crawl away in disgrace?

Night fell, and no one came. She couldn't bear it any longer. She washed her face and slipped outside—to find the monastery in uproar. Students sobbing in each other's arms, tutors huddled in corners with worried faces.

Eventually Neema found someone who would talk to her. There'd been a coup at the palace. Andren Valit, Governor of

Armas, had tried to assassinate the emperor. Valit was dead; the emperor wounded, perhaps mortally. Valit's friends and allies were fleeing the capital for the safety of their ancestral seats. There would be a war, no question. Maybe even the Last Return of the Eight.

So much for the predictions of Ravens. There was no war, and no Return. Hol Vabras held the empire together while the emperor recovered. The Imperial Hounds searched the Raven palace and found evidence that High Justice Yaan Rack had been colluding with Lord Valit for years. Half the Justice Office had to be purged. Yaan Rack was executed for high treason, frail and trembling at the end, and still protesting his innocence.

There was no one left alive to remember his promise to Neema.

So she took her Raven name and became Neema Kraa. She chose it in honour of her old schoolteacher Madam Fessi Aark, reversing the name. Kraa. It still sounded like a raven call. The following year a position came up at the Imperial Library. She moved into her narrow room, which smelled of bins, and found that her life was not ruined after all. It had just begun.

"Yes I did meet him once," Neema said now to Gaida, on the balcony. Her voice sounded high and thin. She was thinking—was that why he wanted to destroy me, back then? Because I kept Gaida from winning Raven of the Year? Because he had to pin those wings on my chest, instead of his daughter's?

"Are you all right, Desy?" Gaida asked, gloating. "Do you need to sit down?"

"I'm fine. How did you find out he was your father?"

"His sister told me, just before she died. I paid her a visit, on my pilgrimage. I don't think she planned to tell me, but then we met, and…" Gaida shrugged. "Blood calls to blood."

"She survived the purges?"

Gaida looked sombre. "She was an Oxwoman, lived in Tuk all her life—nothing to do with the court. When Yaan died, they sent her his private papers. She was the only one left."

For a moment, the ghost of Yaan Rack, his wife, his three sons, hung between them. Neema sighed, and the ghosts departed, ephemeral. "So you found my file."

Gaida held Neema's gaze. "I found your file."

"Congratulations. It was years ago, Gaida."

"What difference does that make? My father expelled you. You knew it, and you took your Raven name anyway. You're a fraud, Desy. Everything you've earned, every post you've taken, you stole from a true Raven of Anat-ruar."

Neema put a hand to her stomach. Stay calm. "Who else knows?"

Gaida stretched out the torture. After an agonising pause she said, "No one. Yet."

Neema laughed, exasperated. "So...what? You're blackmailing me? What do you *want*, Gaida?"

"Nothing. I'll hand the papers over to Kindry tomorrow. He can decide what to do with you." A pursed smile. "I just wanted to warn you, Desy. Before your big party tonight."

Now Neema understood. This wasn't blackmail, it was spite. The opening ceremony would be the defining moment of her career at court—the last great firework display—and Gaida had ruined it for her. Even if it went ahead without a hitch, Neema would spend the evening fretting over what tomorrow would bring. (Disgrace, presumably.)

"Why?" She sounded weary. She was weary. Exhausted by this endless, pointless feud. "Seriously, Gaida. What do you get out of this?"

"It's not about me."

"It's always about you."

Gaida reddened. "I have a duty—"

"No you don't. You don't." One last try. One final attempt to locate her compassion. Neema had seen Gaida be kind and generous, many times. Just never to her. "We walked through the gates together, do you remember? We talked about the book I was reading. We could have been friends." Neema gestured helplessly. "What did I ever do to you?"

Gaida bit her lip, uncomfortable. It didn't suit her to remember how she'd behaved back then. She couldn't have bullied Neema, because she wasn't like that. It wasn't in her nature. She took refuge in her script. "My father was a great man. He died, and you flourished, like a weed on his grave. I'm going to pull you up by the roots."

Yes, that worked. That sounded good, and noble, and just. She had convinced herself again.

Nothing more to say. Nothing more to do except leave. There was a spiral staircase, leading from the balcony to the palace grounds below. Neema took it, feeling Gaida's eyes on her back.

Her shoes clanged on the iron steps. *Clang, clang, clang*, all the way down, ringing through the night air. There was something martial about the sound—like a sword striking a shield. You're smarter than her, she told herself. And deep down you're stronger than her, too. She didn't destroy you then. She won't destroy you now.

CHAPTER
Eight

"THIS IS ONE of those parties," Cain Ballari said, "that everyone wants to be at, unless they're here. It's an anti-party. A party to make you hate parties. It's like this snack bowl," he said, stealing one from a passing servant. "Enticing from the outside, in a gaudy way, but look closer…" He tilted the multi-coloured porcelain bowl to reveal a handful of blanched almonds sweating feebly at the bottom. "Bleak." He tipped the almonds into his mouth. "And tasteless. My compliments to you, High Scholar. I presume this was the ambience you were aiming for? Gaudy, bleak and tasteless?" He grinned at Neema.

That grin, that fake grin. So like the real one he used to give her, when they were teasing each other. But his emerald eyes were winter cold.

She softened her shoulders. Relax. Smile. She had prepared for this, their first encounter, more assiduously than she had prepared for her meeting with Yaan Rack all those years ago. What she would say, what she wouldn't. How she would hold herself, in her exquisite gown. The confidence it would give her. Cain looked good in his black uniform, the half-moon, half-sun sigil of the Fox glowing on his chest. He looked very good.

She looked better.

Arriving late to the banqueting hall, it had taken Neema seconds to locate him through the dense crowd. He was chatting with one of his rivals for the throne, a tough, compact young Ox-woman called Tala Talaka. With his pale white skin and bright copper hair, Cain was like a candle blazing in the middle of the room. But even if he'd dyed his hair mud brown and skulked in a corner, Neema would have found him as fast. He might be a master spy, but he could not hide from her. She could write ten thousand words on the languorous set of his shoulders. Maybe she should. Unlike her previous monographs, people might read it. She could follow it up with a treatise on his hips. People would definitely read that.

Touching her amethyst choker for good luck, she'd swished her way over and said, "Hi Cain," as though they bumped into each other twice a day. And Cain, ever adaptable to the moment, had said, "Oh, hello Neema," and offered her that grin. It had skewered her heart, but she would never let him see that. She'd returned his false smile with one of her own—she was a courtier, she had several.

She would talk to him now, for ten minutes. She would be polite, calm, interested. Then she would glide away in her beautiful gown, *fine, fine, fine,* and avoid him for the rest of the Festival. An easy task. For the next seven days, Cain, Tala and their fellow contenders would be subjected to a series of punishing Trials of skill and endurance, set by the seven Guardian palaces in turn. Not to mention the daily fights in the Festival Square. Any spare time would be spent resting or training, or discussing tactics with his contingent. If Neema kept herself tucked away in the library archives as planned, she would not speak with him again, after tonight.

Looking out across the mass of brightly dressed bodies, she had to admit that Cain was right. This party *was* bleak, and it was her fault, because she had come up with the idea of using the first Festival as a template. Two years ago, Neema had suffered through a very long, very frustrating planning meeting with the emperor and Vabras. One by one, Bersun's ministers had presented their ideas for the Festival, only for Vabras to veto them as too costly and difficult to police. Exasperated, Neema had said, to the ceiling, "Empress Yasthala knew what she was doing. Seven days, seven Trials, everyone locked down on the island. *Done.*"

Bersun had banged his enormous fist on the table. "That's it! That's it!" With the next breath, he was instructing Neema to research the original Festival and work out how to replicate it. Even

Vabras looked pleased—at least, he didn't look displeased, which amounted to the same thing.

When Neema had complained to Fenn about the extra work later, he'd snorted and said, "I've warned you before about being useful."

Bersun, carried away with the idea, had demanded authenticity down to the last detail. Yasthala had begun her Festival of the Eight with an opening ceremony in the banqueting hall. So here they were again, fifteen hundred years later, shaking hands with history. The same gilded mirrors on the walls. The same painting of the constellations on the vaulted ceiling. The same raised dais and gold-painted throne at the far end, awaiting the arrival of the emperor.

The difference was, Yasthala's feast had taken place in the short, cold month of the Raven, with only a handful of courtiers in attendance, whereas Bersun's feast was being held in the torch-heat of high summer. All the senior courtiers from the seven palaces must be invited, plus the eight core members of each contingent; key representatives of the High Venerant families; city governors, generals, admirals, judges…Neema had struggled to keep the guest list to four hundred.

And still they streamed in from the gardens—with more to follow when the imperial procession began. Usually, the banqueting hall was the ideal choice for large, formal gatherings. Set within the lush grounds of the eighth palace, it did not favour one Guardian over another. (For the Dragon spreads its wings wide and encircles all, and there is no beginning or end to its mystery.) Its lofty proportions regulated the heat and its sprung wooden floors—Fenn's invention—were kind on elderly joints. There were a lot of elderly joints at court.

But four hundred guests…this wasn't so much a party as a violent assault on the senses—the overwhelming smell of sweat and clashing perfumes, the furiously flapping fans, the dazzle of jewelled clothes, the deafening roar of very important people shouting their very important thoughts out of their very important mouths.

Cain brushed crumbs from his uniform—a black slab amid the swirling rainbow of gowns and tunics and sashes. Only contenders were permitted to wear full black during the Festival, their matching uniforms handed to them on arrival. Cropped trousers, a pair of martial shoes and a sleeveless tunic embroidered with their Guardian sigil. Rivals but equals. Tala Talaka had added a black headband to keep her short auburn hair from her face—a practical addition permitted by the Festival rules.

Cain's uniform, though—was there something *unofficial* about it? Neema narrowed her eyes. If she didn't know him so well, the way things looked on him, she wouldn't have seen it. But now she studied him more closely, it was undeniable. The quality of the fabric, the depth of colour, the way it draped, the way it moved…

Imperial silk. An exact copy of his uniform, made from *imperial* silk. An extremely precious material, reserved solely for the rulers of Orrun and Helia.

This was reckless, even for Cain. If the Hounds found out they would arrest him. They were on the prowl now, watching for trouble. Neema sipped her wine. She could call one over. Cain's bid for the throne would be over before it began. But he was a Fox, and Foxes liked to play games. With her Raven training, Neema projected a few moments into the future.

She stands like an empress in her glittering ceremonial gown. Diamonds circle the huge amethyst at her throat. More jewels on her wrists and fingers. She points at Cain, humble in his black tunic. "Guards! This man is wearing a forbidden material. Arrest him!"

Still projecting, Neema shuffled through the potential reactions.

Laughter. Denial. No one wants to see Cain Ballari brought low— unlike Neema, he is well liked at court. They turn on her, instead. The bitter ex-lover.

In her best projection, she is mocked for being spiteful, and the party continues. In the worst case, she is the one arrested, for attempting to discredit a contender. It's the prison mines of Ketu for you, Neema Kraa. Where she dies in a tunnel collapse, screaming as the rocks thunder down on her head. No one attends her funeral. The end.

She returned to the present. The sounds of the party over-whelmed her, distorted and shrill.

Cain caught her eye and winked.

A timely reminder not to trust him, not one inch. Behind the carefree facade lay a shrewd, determined schemer. As he had once told her: "I have to work really hard to look this lazy." Long before the official guest list was announced, he would have investigated everyone's background, gathering every last scrap of information he could find, from their favourite ballad to their most shameful secret.

He would know that only a tiny handful of people would be able to spot the difference between very fine black silk, and excep-tionally fine black silk. He would also know that—for a variety of reasons—none of them would mention it.

But why take the risk? Putting aside the fact that Foxes were transgressive risk-takers by nature, Neema could think of two reasons. The fabric breathed better, and moved better—a valuable quality, especially during a summer Festival. The second benefit was more subtle—the way it would make him feel, when he put it on. Like an emperor. Which was precisely why he was forbidden from wearing it.

"Something to say, Neema?" Cain taunted. He knew how much she hated keeping information to herself. The words *imperial silk* were lodged in her throat, pushing against her amethyst choker.

But: she had prepared for this. She selected another fake smile from her armoury. "I was just thinking how *imperial* you look," she said. "In your *silk* uniform." There. She had said the words, they were released. Not perfectly, but it would do. The knot in her throat loosened.

Cain smoothed his tunic. "Are you accusing me of something, High Scholar?" he asked, daring her to try. When Neema said nothing, he smiled. "Wise choice. You're in no position to take the moral high ground, are you?"

Tala Talaka took a half-step back, dismayed by the jagged tension thrumming between them. Oxes searched always for harmony and connection. Also Tala was young, and optimistic, and liked to fix broken things. Furniture and farming implements, mainly—but she would give this a go. "How's the wine?" she asked.

Neema lifted her glass in appreciation. It came from the Talaka family vineyard—a gift from the Ox contingent.

Tala smiled, revealing a gold front tooth embossed with the Ox sigil. When people asked her how she lost it, she always gave a different, one-word answer. "Horse," she'd told Neema, the first time they met. "Sex," she'd told Cain. It wasn't the only dent on her—her mid-brown skin was as scratched and scarred as an old desk. Tala had grown up on her family's vast estate near Utsur before entering the Ox monastery, where she had trained in construction. Those years of punishing physical labour had built up a natural strength and stamina that would serve her well in the Trials.

Neema and Tala talked about the ceremony, while Cain flagged down a fresh tray of drinks. Neema had to command all her will to keep her attention on Tala. She wanted to leave, but she'd promised herself ten minutes. So she stood there, trapped and miserable, and smiling. I have never looked so good and felt so wretched, she thought.

"Cain's goading Katsan again," Tala sighed, tilting her chin towards the Bear monastery's contender.

Katsan Brundt was standing at one remove from their small circle, hands clasped behind her back, honey-blonde hair pulled into a painfully tight knot. Neema had tried before to engage the Bear warrior in conversation, hoping to learn more about the place she would soon be calling home. The only answer she'd received was a contemptuous, ice-blue stare. Neema could guess why. Gaida had spent several weeks at the Bear monastery during her travels across the empire. She and Katsan had become close friends, despite being rivals for the throne. It was not unusual for contenders to strike up alliances—but this went deeper. Katsan called her Raven friend "Sister"—a rare honour for one who had not trained at Anat-garra.

There was a famous, blunt saying among the Bears—"The friend of my Sister is my friend, the enemy of my Sister is my enemy." Katsan had clearly taken this to heart.

Cain was pushing a glass of wine at her. "One sip. Go on. Why deny yourself on Festival Eve?"

"It's not denial, Contender Ballari," Katsan replied, in a clipped voice. "I choose to keep my head clear and my body healthy." Like all who joined the fifth monastery, Katsan followed the Way of the Bear, an old, austere spiritual path reinstated by Brother Lanrik when he became abbot. On passing through the gates of Anat-garra, novices swore a sacred oath to give up all possessions and family ties and commit to a lifetime of service. Lanrik had also introduced a rigorous new diet of fish, pulses, nuts and fresh vegetables, designed to keep his warriors in peak condition for their long winter patrols. No alcohol was permitted.

When Bersun left the monastery to become emperor, he had resolved to keep to the same regime. Over time, he had weakened. Katsan had not. Neema had to admit the Bear contender looked the very picture of good health. Her rosy white skin glowed, as if she'd just scrubbed her face with a palmful of mountain snow. Edging towards forty, she was both the oldest contender, and most likely the fittest when it came to endurance. She was also by far the most experienced fighter, having spent the last decade defending the north-west fringes of the empire from brutal out-law bands.

"A clear head," Cain mused, weaving gently on unsteady feet. "Sounds unpleasant. Don't you ever feel like letting go? Don't you get tired of being so…upright?"

"No," Katsan replied. She gave the group a curt bow, and strode off.

"That woman has a stick up her arse," Cain said. "And not in a fun way."

"You shouldn't push her to drink if she doesn't want to," Tala scolded him.

"He knew she wouldn't take it," Neema said. "That wasn't the point. He wanted her to think he was drunk."

Tala shot Cain a confused look. "You're *not* drunk?"

"He's as sober as Katsan," Neema answered for him. "But now she thinks he lacks self-restraint. And tomorrow she'll reckon he's hungover. At some point she'll underestimate him, and he'll press his advantage."

Tala took this in, then laughed. "Eight that's so devious. Suru!" She had spotted her daughter, toddling across the room towards them with comically fierce concentration. Suru's co-mother Sunur followed close behind, letting her wobble and stumble and find her feet again. They were both dressed in rich shades of brown to honour the Ox. Even Sunur's spectacles were framed with burnished tortoiseshell, similar in tone to her olive skin. Tala hurried over to join her family, kissing Sunur and tousling Suru's hair.

Which left Neema and Cain alone, together. Standing so close that she caught his scent in the air between them. She used to press her nose against his neck, and breathe him in. He used to love that.

Stop. Stop.

She took a quiet breath. She was calm, she was ready. Ring the bell.

"So, I'm curious," he said, from the corner of his mouth. "What's it like to lose your only friend?"

She folded her arms. Really? "You may find this hard to believe, but I barely think of you from one year to the next. Sorry if that bruises your pride."

"I was referring to your chameleon." He smiled. *Got you.* "I hear he ran away. Couldn't stand your company for another second. How tragic. Snubbed by a lizard."

Another lump had formed in Neema's throat. "Actually..." she said.

"It begins," Cain murmured to himself.

"...chameleons are natural loners and hate to be handled, so I wouldn't take it personally. But Pink-Pink didn't run away. Which —just as a side point—would be highly improbable in itself. Chameleons tend to move in a painstakingly slow, jerky fashion." To her horror Neema found herself mimicking the movement with her left arm and right leg, jolting them forward in tandem while rotating her wrist and ankle.

"Excuse me, I have to turn around for a second," Cain said, and did so. Which was a shame, because Neema missed his first genuine expression of the evening.

"I've taken care of Pink-Pink for three years and he's never tried to escape before," she said, to his back. "*Someone* took him."

Cain turned back to face her. "You think I crept into your apartment in the dead of night and stole your pet lizard?"

"He's not my pet, he belongs to the emperor—"

"Would you like me to creep into your apartment in the dead of night?"

She rolled her eyes at him. He was trying to unsettle her, first cruel, then weirdly flirty. Testing and prodding for any weakness in her armour. He never used to be like this. Was this who he was now? She had no idea. The thought made her impossibly sad.

"But you wore this for me." He reached out to touch her dress.

She knocked his hand away. "I wore it for me. The world doesn't revolve around you, Contender Ballari."

"Not yet."

Neema snorted, but it was possible. He could win the Festival, and rule them all. Emperor Cain the First. What an extraordinary feat that would be. A child sold to the Scrappers for dope, an outcast among outcasts, so far below Common you would have to dig for days to reach him. She could see in his eyes, in the way he held himself, the effort and discipline it had taken to reach this point. He had taken every bad hand he'd been dealt, and found a way to win against the odds, every time. And now here he stood, the Fox contender. She could only guess what it must have cost him to win that title, the battles he must have fought to scramble his way to the top of the pile.

If he were anyone else, she would be cheering him on. Despite the fact that every Fox ruler in history had been a howling disaster. To see a Commoner sit upon the throne for the first time, Eight, to even imagine it—was a thing of wonder. If he were *anyone* else.

She heard a distinctive, deep-throated laugh, rising over the roar of voices. Gaida.

"All your favourite people in one room," Cain said.

That was the line that almost destroyed her, out of the blue. Cain knew how thrilled Neema had been to win her scholarship to Anat-ruar. How excited she was at the thought of being surrounded by like-minded people at last, of being part of the flock. Gaida had destroyed those dreams on her very first day. Neema had never stood a chance. Four years on her own, even more lonely than she'd been back in Scartown. Cain knew that, and now he was putting himself in Gaida's camp. Of all the ways he could have hurt her, this was the least-expected, and the most painful.

She wouldn't let him see that. She wouldn't hand him that victory.

She glanced at the floor. The wood was reverberating under her feet from all the people jostling about, the servants weaving through with trays of food and drinks. The boards were painted with temple symbols and the sigils of the Eight, freshly restored for the ceremony. She was standing on an ∞, as if she'd died and her spirit had returned to the Eternal Path, ready to take its next journey.

"Nothing you want to say to me, Neema?" Cain asked. And then lower, more honest. "Nothing?"

She looked up, and their eyes locked. They were the same height, always had been. As if neither could bear to lose that comfort of being at the same level. "Eight, look at the two of you," her mother used to say. "A pair of bookends."

"There is something." Neema plucked a bowl from a passing tray. "These are not gaudy, they are vibrant."

Cain's shoulders settled. Maybe he'd been hoping for an apology, for something heartfelt. But pedantry was on its way, and he must endure it. "If you say so."

"The mix of colours," Neema continued, "matches precisely the stained-glass windows of the Imperial Temple, and as such offers a message of unity between the Guardians. As for the supposed 'bleakness' of the snacks, as you'll see, this bowl is filled to the brim. You took a bowl that was going back to the kitchens to be replenished." She handed him the fresh bowl.

"Shrimps," Cain said, and started eating. He never turned down food, especially in moments of high tension. "Shal's watching us," he said, wiping his mouth. "Over there."

"That's what he does."

Shal Worthy, contender for the Hounds. The man who had brought Yanara Valit to court, and escorted her on her Procession of Exile. Neema had read his report, before it was destroyed. The experience had shattered him, but since then he had transformed himself into a respected senior officer, training elite recruits at Houndspoint.

Neema stole a glance in his direction. He was standing a few feet away, listening politely to a mixed group of courtiers. He looked very different from the young sergeant who used to rough himself up to fit in with his squad. These days he was impeccably well groomed, in an understated way—dark brown curls lightly oiled, short beard neatly trimmed. Flawless brown skin. (A fan of Dr. Yetbalm's Ultimate Face Saver Cream, Neema suspected.) There was no doubt the man took care of himself, but some of it was innate. Unlike Cain, Shal Worthy didn't need the trick of imperial silk to look good in his uniform. It was the way he held himself, Neema decided. Katsan was rigid, Cain was louche and restless, Tala was solid and tough. Shal was poised somewhere between them all. Balanced.

"I don't like his earrings," Cain said. They were silver, and shaped in eternal eights as a sign of his faith.

"What's wrong with them?"

"Nothing," Cain admitted. "He looks great, it's annoying." He threw the last shrimp in his mouth and rubbed his hands over his Fox sigil. Half-moon, half-sun, blurring into each other. The Fox was the Guardian of Transitions. The Guardian of Neither Here Nor There. "Let's hope he's unspeakably vile under the surface."

"I don't think he is."

"I bet," Cain said, "that at the first sniff of power, he'll betray his principles and break his best friend's heart. People do that, you know. Unexpected people, who seem nice on the surface."

"Or maybe," Neema countered, "he'll turn out to be a giant hypocrite who murders people for money."

"I think it's best," Cain said, after a brief but ugly pause, "if we avoid each other for the rest of the Festival."

"I think we should avoid each other for the rest of our lives."

"Fine."

"Fine."

Neema cast around the nearest groups, hoping to find at least one friendly face, and instead saw a commotion spreading through the crowds—people turning and hissing to each other, talking behind their fans.

The Tiger contingent had arrived, which meant…

Without thinking, she grabbed Cain's arm.

Passing through the banqueting hall, ripples of horror, and disgust.

He's here.

Next to the abbess. Look!

Eight. Is that really him?

Ruko Valit.

Even Yana would have struggled to recognise him. Nothing left of that eager, careless boy who'd come to the palace eight years ago full of dreams and optimism. He had melted himself down in the forge of Anat-hurun; hammered himself into a new and deadly shape. An iron-hard, grim-faced warrior, towering over his contingent.

Looks just like his father, someone said, and was quickly hushed.

It was true, though. Ruko was a few inches taller than Andren had been. He wore his black hair short, and he was clean-shaven. Otherwise, the resemblance was striking. The handsome geometry of his face, the golden skin. The dark, penetrating charisma that made you stare, and stare again.

"I'd definitely fuck him," Cain said, in her ear. "But I wouldn't hang around after."

Neema was still gripping Cain's arm. She let go.

"Look at him," Cain said.

Oh, she was looking. It was looking away that was the problem. He was so perfect, it was disturbing. If Shimmer Arbell had painted him, she would have given him a flaw, just to make him human.

"Is that the Blade of Peace?" Cain asked, knowing that it must be.

Hurun-tooth, the cursed blade. Ruko was wearing it on his left hip, sheathed in a plain leather scabbard. Only the wooden hilt was visible, equally plain.

Cain tilted his head. "The question is, do we want an emperor who killed his own sister? I think the answer's no, right?"

"You can't talk about her. It's forbidden."

He slid Neema a scathing look. "And so much worse than *writing her death warrant.*"

"Technically," she said, because she could never help herself, "it was an Imperial Order of Exile."

"Oh, I do beg your fucking pardon," Cain muttered.

Across the room, a servant approached Ruko with a drinks tray. Ruko looked at her. She stumbled back, as if she had been shoved hard in the chest.

"Eight, I hope he doesn't win," Neema said, then cursed under her breath.

Ruko was staring at her. She waited for him to move on, but he kept his gaze locked on hers, hard and unblinking. The seconds passed into something intensely uncomfortable.

"Can he read lips?" she asked Cain. "Do they teach that at the Tiger monastery?"

Ruko curled his finger at her. *Come.* The arrogance. She almost resisted on principle. But curiosity won out, as it always did with her. "I'm going over."

"Have fun," Cain drawled.

The moment she was gone, he was surrounded by fawning admirers, fans flapping. Are you enjoying yourself, Contender Ballari? Would you like a fresh glass of wine? Look, I'm wearing orange in your honour, Fox contender, does it suit me? Of course, he said. Of course, of course. My answer is always yes. More laughter, more flapping.

And all the while he kept one eye on Neema, walking away from him.

Nine

"WELCOME TO COURT, Contender Valit," Neema said. "I trust you've settled in comfortably?" The Tigers had been the last to arrive on the island, sailing up Dragon's Mouth Bay in a swift, three-masted yacht—a journey designed to avoid setting foot in the capital. Abbess Glorren was a child of Samra. She loathed the very existence of Armas, the city built to diminish her own.

Ruko did not answer Neema's question; he had not summoned her here for small talk. He turned to his contingent, dismissing them with a look. The abbess remained at his side. It was said that the faithful sometimes grew to look like their favoured Guardian. If so, Rivenna Glorren was a true believer. A black woman of middling years, her appearance was distinctly feline—wide cheekbones, pointed chin. Even her expression was catlike—unblinking and filled with disdain.

And she had style, Neema had to admit. The Tiger abbess cut a sleek, sophisticated figure, her forest green robes more regal than spiritual in design. The beads in her hair were formed of tiger's eye stone, polished to a smooth sheen. Around the middle fingers of her right hand she wore a gold ring, shaped in an eternal eight.

"I will speak to the High Scholar alone," Ruko said.

The abbess lifted her hood to conceal her annoyance. Her student, her *Guardian-son*, ordering her as if she were a servant. But to protest was beneath her. "As you wish," she murmured, and moved away.

If she had a tail, Neema thought, it would be waving.

"I visited the imperial archives today," Ruko said. "To view your work."

Neema lifted her eyebrows, surprised. "My work?"

"The Order of Exile."

A chill spread through her. The way he'd said it. No feeling, utterly flat.

"The name had been cut out," he said.

The name. Yanara. She was called Yanara. "Yes, they do that—"

"Once death is confirmed." He spoke in statements, even as he looked for answers. "They saw the body."

Had he been hoping that his sister had survived somehow? For a second, Neema's heart went out to him. No one survived exile. No one survived Dolrun. "Yes." She swallowed. "We should not be talking of this, Contender Valit, the law is clear—"

"You read the report," Ruko pressed, "before it was destroyed."

She nodded, feeling sick, as she always did when she thought of it. Shal's report. His account of Yana Valit's final days. Her cruel and lonely death. *Seventeen*, he'd written, more than once. *She made it to seventeen before we killed her. May the Eight forgive us and remain Hidden.*

Don't ask me if she suffered, Neema thought. Please don't ask.

The party smeared around them like a carousel.

"It was beautifully done," Ruko said.

Bile rose in her throat. The exile? His sister's body left to rot? Beautifully done? What sort of monster was he?

"Your brushwork," he added, seeing her expression. "You have an exceptional hand, High Scholar."

He was talking about the Order of Exile again, she realised. She raised her glass to her lips. It rattled against her teeth. She lowered it without taking a sip.

In the distance, the sound of drums.

"The emperor's coming," she said. Thank the Eight.

The doors to the banqueting hall had been closed, for the sole purpose of opening them again. The room turned as one as they swung wide and the trumpets blared. Neema felt goosebumps rising along her arms. Yasthala had entered through those same doors fifteen centuries ago, to the same fanfare. Walking across a painted floor just like this one, she had taken her place on the dais, and recited the Five Rules in front of the first contenders.

1. No ruler shall govern for more than twenty-four years.
2. Rulers may not choose their own successor.
3. No child of an emperor or empress may take the throne.
4. Instead: seven contenders will compete in a series of Trials; champions from each of the anats. The Dragons, who desire not the throne, shall send a proxy in their name.
5. The winner shall rule without exception, and all shall bow before them.

That these rules had remained unbroken for fifteen hundred years was a source of pride throughout the empire. These were the rules that had kept Orrun safe from civil war, from dynastic rule, from tyranny. For the faithful—these were also the rules that had kept the Guardians Hidden, and prevented the Last Return. Tonight, the emperor would recite them again, and the Festival would begin.

The familiar, pungent scent of frankincense and patchouli invaded the air. Eight Officiates of the temple followed, swinging censers. The perfumed smoke was so heavy it would seep into the courtiers' clothes and never quite leave it—a lingering scent memory of the evening.

Next came the music: thunderous drums that reverberated beneath the skin, pipes and flutes twirling over the top. Performers from the Monkey palace matched the music with a martial dance with long staffs, leaping and spinning as they cleared a path for those coming behind. Neema counted the beats in her head, watching for mistakes. There were none. Everything was going to plan.

The tempo shifted and the dancers kept pace, processing down the hall. Weaving through them, teams of servants set up the feasting tables, decorated with traditional portraits of the Eight.

The servants wore matching Guardian masks, eyes rimmed white, lips painted black. Another detail Neema had found in a contemporary account of Yasthala's Festival—simple but arresting.

The music rose to a crescendo, and the dance was done. Musicians and dancers bowed low to warm applause from the jaded court. It was working just as Neema had hoped. No one was more revered than Yasthala. She stole a glance at Ruko—a direct descendant of the great Raven empress. His face was blank.

More drumming, more fanfare, and the emperor's advisers strode into the hall. Fenn Fedala had teased Neema for weeks that he would turn up in his overalls and old boots, but there he was leading the way in cape and sash, and a velvet hat with a feather. As far as Neema knew, this was the first time the High Engineer had worn his ceremonial robes in fifteen years at court. He didn't look pleased about it, but that would be asking too much. Behind him, and much more comfortable in her fine white robes, came the High Servant of the Temple, her shaved head painted with a golden ∞. As for High Justice Kindry Rok, he strutted in chest first, nodding graciously as if he were guest of honour.

Hol Vabras came next, but no one noticed him, because he did not want them to.

Ruko said to Neema: "You should be with them."

She kept her eyes on the procession. "It's easier to direct things when you're not performing."

"And you are more comfortable on the periphery."

"I don't think standing next to you counts as the periphery, Contender Valit." And it certainly wasn't comfortable.

The ministers were all through. Now came the emperor's private household—his mistress, Lady Kara Kandraga of the Venerant Kandragas, a few favoured retainers. No family. Bersun, having chosen the Way of the Bear, had been estranged from his younger brother Gedrun for decades.

And finally, the High Venerants—direct ancestors of those who had taken part in the original procession. Tursuls, Arbells, Ranors. The Justs and the Majans. The powerful dynastic families Yasthala had fought with and against in the War of the

Raven's Dream, and eventually brought together in a truculent peace. The Valits should have been among them too—historically they had been the richest and most influential of all the High Families. But there was no one left to invite. Those who were not killed in the purges had chosen to abandon the name, to avoid its stigma. Only Ruko remained—for some, a symbol of renewal. For others, a warning.

Neema felt him stir next to her. He had shifted into a fighting stance. Who could rattle the great Tiger Warrior?

Ah yes. His mother.

Princess Yasila floated through the doors, dressed as always in the ocean colours of the Dragon. The hall was now crammed with guests, servants, guards, tables and chairs. The only place left to stand comfortably was the space around Ruko and Neema. Yasila hesitated, then glided towards them.

Conversations stopped, as people craned their necks to get a better view. No matter that the emperor was only seconds from arrival. This was the moment everyone had been waiting for: the reunion of the princess and her estranged son.

A held moment in the hushed room. Yasila did not acknowledge her son. *He was not there.* Instead she studied Neema. Took in her elegant gown, her silver shoes. The amethyst choker. A flicker of feeling—revulsion, perhaps. She muttered a stream of words beneath her breath, like a prayer, or a poem.

And Neema couldn't move. Logic told her that she could, but when she tried to shift, nothing happened. She tried to speak, and found she couldn't breathe. Her throat was closed, her lungs burning. She had sunk to the bottom of the ocean, weights pressed upon her chest.

A second passed. And another. Locked inside her body, Neema started to panic, started to choke.

White pinpricks formed in front of her eyes.

And then, without warning, she was released. Neema sank to her knees, gasping for air, eyes streaming.

Trumpets blared, and a herald stepped forward. "His Majesty, Bersun the Second. Kneel before your emperor!"

Everyone joined Neema on the floor. The timing was so close, no one but Ruko understood what had really happened. As he kneeled down next to her, she noticed a tiny bead of sweat at his temple. It slid down his hairline as she watched, and melted into his skin. That's what Shimmer Arbell would have painted, she thought. Human after all.

A squad of Imperial Bodyguards marched through the door in their red tunics with black slashes. And there, in the middle, a good head taller than those who would protect him: Emperor Bersun. The Old Bear.

The musicians struck up a tune, a brisk battle song. Bersun's coronation hymn. For twenty-four years it had been his anthem, played at every formal occasion. Once he abdicated, in eight days' time, it would never be heard again.

"All hail His Majesty, Bersun the Second, Emperor of Orrun, Warrior Brother of Anat-garra," the herald called.

"See How Orrun is Restored in His Name!" the room replied, as one.

Bersun did not miss a beat. He strode to the dais with the same brisk manner he brought to all official gatherings.

Neema got back to her feet, still struggling to catch her breath. Yasila rose at the same moment, her back turned.

If she was going to retaliate, it had to be now. Before the moment passed, and she persuaded herself that nothing had really happened. Nothing more than a clever trick Yasila had picked up from her childhood with the Dragons, some subtle form of hypnosis.

Neema leaned forward and whispered in Yasila's ear. "I saw you on the balcony."

Yasila gave a start, then caught herself.

Six words.

CHAPTER
Ten

NEEMA LOVED NOTHING more than a good mystery. It was like the old joke: How do you trap a Raven? Ask them a question, and they'll trap *you* for half an hour. But Neema's curiosity was extreme even by Raven standards.

One of her biggest obsessions was Shimmer Arbell's throne-room masterpiece *Dedication to the Eight*, and to what extent it had caused the artist's breakdown and tragic death. Neema had decided to write a book about it, a side project once she had settled in at the Bear monastery. She had romantic visions of the private suite that awaited her there—a deep, imposing stone fireplace, snowflakes swirling against the windowpanes, thick blankets and hot chocolate, shelves and shelves of books. She wasn't sure where she was going to get the hot chocolate from, given that her hosts were committed to the Way of the Bear. She might have to buy some and take it with her. Neema's romantic visions often ended like this—with her fretting over their verisimilitude.

Before she left the island, she was keen to snatch an interview with Shimmer's older sister, Lady Harmony Arbell-Ranor. As a gift to herself, Neema had seated the celebrated composer next to her at the feast.

Lady Harmony wafted over to join them in diamonds and blue velvet, smelling of peaches. Settling herself down with straight-backed poise, she surveyed the table, which included Tala and Sunur, and Facet the court jeweller, as if they were the cast of an opera she was glad she hadn't written. "How lucky we are," she declared. "Such a vivid mix." Then she turned round and fell into a deep conversation with her cousin, who was sitting behind her at the next table.

"Nice manners," Sunur grumbled.

Tala put a hand on her wife's leg.

The soup arrived. "We should thank the Eight," someone said, and everyone dutifully held hands as he said the blessing. "Divine Guardians of Orrun—we thank you for this feast. We thank you for your protection and guidance. Eternal Eight, watch over us always."

"And remain Hidden," everyone else mumbled.

Lady Harmony plucked her hand free from Neema's and swivelled back to her cousin. There was talk of a new yacht, and the struggle to find a decent crew. "One cannot teach discretion," Lady Harmony said. "One cannot teach them anything," her cousin replied.

This continued through the first course, Lady Harmony with her back to the table, her soup untouched. Neema had to fight the urge to tap her bare shoulder with her spoon. Just lightly, to get her attention. *Tap tap*, like a boiled egg.

"This soup is delicious," Tala said, and Facet agreed. The jeweller —a short, elderly black man with sapphire blue eyes—was professionally amiable. He had a saying, which he'd polished up like one of his gemstones, that "no diamond ever shone as brightly as an open heart." As a survivor of the purges and—more deadly— the vagaries of court fashion, the chances he actually believed this were slim. But it sounded lovely.

"Chef Ganstra adapted Empress Yasthala's menu to suit a modern palate," Neema told them, across the table. "The original was based around her favourite recipes: pomegranate rice, fragrant roast chicken, spiced prawns, sea bass in a chilli sauce, garlic greens with toasted chickpeas. Simple, traditional recipes refined for a grand occasion. The only significant change is to the central dish. Yasthala's banquet featured a twenty-foot-long sea eel, dressed to look like the Dragon. Chef Ganstra found that at such a monstrous size, the eels become tough and unpleasant to eat. For our feast he has created individual dragons for each guest, using smaller eels wrapped in a light pastry. This makes for a much tastier, if less dramatic dish."

Neema stopped there because Facet's eyes had glazed over, and everyone else was either laughing or trying hard not to.

"Thanks for the lecture," someone muttered. The same man who had given the blessing.

"Ah, right. Sorry." Neema turned the stem of her wine glass between her fingers. She had an unfortunate tendency to speak in paragraphs when she was nervous.

A melon sorbet next to cleanse the palate, and still Lady Harmony did not turn around.

Sunur lost patience. "Hey!" she called across the table. "Your ladyship!"

Reluctantly, Lady Harmony shifted back to face them.

Sunur pushed her tortoiseshell glasses up her nose, enjoying herself. "Do you want Havoc to lose?"

The table froze. Lady Harmony's son was the Monkey contender for the throne.

Sunur grinned, to show she was joking (sort of). "You're not wearing his colour."

Lady Harmony rescued her smile. "Yellow does nothing for one's complexion," she said, patting her ivory skin.

Facet leapt into the breach. "My Lady suits every colour. But in blue, she outshines us all."

Sunur made a loud gagging noise, then yelped as Tala kicked her ankle.

"Lady Harmony," Neema said, snatching her chance. "I'm researching a book on *Dedication to the Eight*, and your sister's—"

"*We do not speak of her*," Lady Harmony hissed, and pivoted back to her cousin.

Chastened, Neema returned to her sorbet. With the conversation flowing over her head, her thoughts returned to her argument with Gaida. She had to get her hands on Yaan Rack's report, before Gaida passed it over to Kindry. If she could find it, and destroy it…She was tempted to sneak away now, but this was her ceremony, her responsibility—she couldn't leave until it was over.

So, when? It had to be tonight. But Gaida was hosting the Raven afterparty in her rooms straight after the feast.

The shutters. She's going to leave the shutters open all night. I can sneak in while she's asleep. Neema projected ahead, trying to imagine herself treading barefoot up the iron steps to the balcony, picking her way through Gaida's mess of belongings without waking her. Impossible, but what choice did she have?

She could ask Cain. Master thief.

Would he do it? One last favour, for old time's sake?

She searched for him, hoping to catch his eye. He was not where he was supposed to be, of course. Eventually she found him, a few tables away. He was sitting next to Gaida, his chair pushed right up against hers, murmuring in her ear. Gaida had let her hair down, soft brown curls cascading about her shoulders. Cain felt Neema's stare and looked up. Smiling, he whispered something to Gaida, and they laughed, conspiratorial. Gaida picked up her glass and clinked it against Cain's.

Neema sniffed, to hold back the tears. Stupid, to think she could rely on him. Pathetic. Eight years she'd managed perfectly well on her own. *I'll save myself.*

"High Scholar. There has been a mistake."

Oh, fuck the Eight—what now?

Twisting in her seat, she looked up at the figure standing behind her—a neat, cherubic man with cloudy puffs of perfumed hair. Lady Harmony's husband, Lord Clarion Ranor. Playwright, patron of the arts, and the richest man in Orrun. His son Havoc stood a few paces back, dressed in his contender uniform. The Monkey sigil blazed across his tunic—a golden circle made up of three twining branches. Father and son shared the same colouring —blonde hair, blue eyes, white skin deeply tanned and freckled by the sun—but Havoc was a head taller, with a swimmer's build —lean and muscular, with wide shoulders. He wore the resigned expression of someone who knew his parents were about to be wincingly awful, and would just have to wait it out.

Lord Clarion put a hand on his wife's shoulder, fingers stroking her collarbone. Lady Harmony closed her eyes for a second, then turned to look up at him. Adoration. "What's wrong, darling?"

"A disaster with the seating, dearest. We should be together, naturally."

"Naturally," Lady Harmony murmured.

He offered her his hand. "Come with me, darling, your husband has saved the day. Havoc will sit here with these people."

And with that they were gone.

Havoc took his mother's seat and gave the table a rueful smile.

Tala raised her glass to him. "Don't worry, we're happy with the swap."

"Much as we enjoyed staring at your mother's back," Sunur added.

Havoc turned to Neema and made a seated Monkey salute, palms pressed together. "High Scholar. Good evening."

Neema gave a Raven salute in return, arms crossed over her chest. They did not know each other, except by reputation. Havoc had been serving in the imperial navy for the last six years, fighting pirates along the southern coast. Last summer he had been promoted to admiral, with command of eight Leviathans. The long stretches at sea had bleached his hair and eyebrows a white-blonde.

Unlike his mother, he was happy to talk about Shimmer, or Auntie Shim as he called her. Unfortunately, he could barely remember her. She had moved to Armas when he was five and died while he was studying at Anat-shonn, down in Three Ports. Havoc had been sent to the Monkey monastery to study music ("my parents insisted"), but it was the renowned martial training that had called to him, that and the ocean.

Neema had more questions, but Havoc couldn't answer them. He bored her for a while with stories of life at sea, and then she bored him for a while with stories of life in the library. After which the conversation lay becalmed for a while, upon a sea of mutual indifference.

"Tell me about your name," she said, after they had sat in silence for several minutes. Monkeys of Anat-shonn changed their name when they left the monastery, just as Ravens did. In their case, they selected a new first name—something with a personal resonance. Harmony, Clarion, Shimmer—these were all chosen names. Havoc, unusually, had stuck with the one he'd been given at birth. "Do you mind me asking?"

"No, I don't mind," Havoc said, with the patience of someone who was asked a lot, and had learned to live with it. He piled up his plate with more food as he explained, keeping his eyes on the task. "My parents never wanted children. I was a mistake, something they are always keen to remind me. They called me Havoc as a joke. Because I 'wreaked havoc on their perfect lives.'"

Well that's horrific, Neema thought, nodding politely for him to continue.

Havoc selected an eel pie and poured over the honey and rice wine sauce. "You can let something like that destroy you, or you can use it to make you stronger. But that's enough about me," he said, briskly. "Tell me about your family."

Neema opened her mouth.

"No, wait!" Havoc lifted his fork to stop her. "Tell me about Gaida."

Neema closed her mouth.

Havoc leaned in, his face alive with renewed interest. "Weren't you in the same year at Anat-ruar?"

"Are we talking about Gaida?" Facet called across the table. "I *adore* her."

Everyone agreed she was amazing. "I really like her," Tala said.

"You really like everyone," Sunur observed.

"Professor Rack is the greatest mind of our generation," someone said. That fucking arsehole who gave the blessing, again. "Have you read her *Addresses to the Flock*, Contender Talaka?"

"Sunur does the reading in our house," Tala said, as if it were a domestic chore.

"My wife only likes practical books," Sunur explained to the table. "*The A-Z of Sheep Shearing. The Big Book of Plumbing.*"

"Are those actual books?" Tala asked. "Because I would definitely read them."

"What was Gaida like back then?" Havoc pressed Neema. "I bet she was wonderful."

Everyone waited for her to say something nice.

Neema poured herself some more wine. "She hasn't changed a bit."

Smiles and nods around the table, as everyone took that at face value. Everyone except for Sunur. When the conversation moved on she caught Neema's eye. *I'm with you.*

The desserts arrived soon after—edible replicas of the imperial island's most celebrated buildings and treasures. Servants carried them in on silver litters, to gasps and applause from the guests. Neema watched a perfect simulacrum of the Monkey palace theatre go by, complete with a candlelit stage and tinkling music box. The table next to them had the treasury, with tiny automaton Hounds guarding the entrance, and edible jewelled delights hidden inside. A Leviathan sailed past on marzipan seas, mechanical oars moving back and forth. "Very good," Havoc said, as if he were inspecting one of his own ships. "Excellent."

Vabras had tried to block this grand finale. There was no way the original desserts had been this elaborate, or expensive. The emperor had overruled him. "We do need *some* spectacle, Vabras. Something for the Raven historians to write about."

His instinct had been proved right. The room was alight with excitement, courtly cynicism replaced with a childlike wonder, as each table received its own unique creation.

"Here's ours," Havoc said.

The Imperial Temple. They clapped in appreciation as the servants lowered it carefully down on to the table, turning it on its rotating stand to show it off from every angle. The golden dome was shaped from tempered chocolate, covered in gold leaf. The stained-glass windows were made of coloured sugar, the gleaming walls from smoothed white icing. The attention to detail was exquisite and charming, from the golden filigree work on the miniature shutters, to the intricate carvings etched into the entrance doors.

Facet peered through a window, a fellow craftsman marvelling at the artistry. "There's more inside."

Havoc opened the door, then drew back in surprise as a tiny mechanical raven flew out, perching on top of the dome. The table clapped again in astonished delight.

The display wasn't over. The raven began to peck at the roof, precise rhythmic taps. The dome cracked neatly down the middle and slid back to reveal the expertly rendered interiors.

The ginger cake, when they could bring themselves to slice into it, was flavoured with nutmeg, cardamom and other spices blended to match the incense used on Festival days. The servants, with a final flourish, brought out flaming brandy cocktails, mixed with the same spice blend.

"Is this appropriate?" the man who gave the blessing asked, and everyone ignored him.

Tucking into her cake and brandy, Neema thought she finally understood why Yasthala had done this, at the end of the original banquet. When the empress moved the court here after the war, there was only one habitable building on the island: remnants of the Raven monastery, the original Anat-ruar. This she renamed the inner sanctum, and made her seat of power. The Guardian Gate and the marble throne were brought up from the old court at Samra.

Everything else, barring the network of tombs that lay beneath the island, she designed from scratch. The eight palaces, the Grand Canal, the Mirror Bridge, the Garden at the Edge of the World, the Imperial Temple. For millennia, Samra had served as Orrun's capital, its grand architecture a symbol of its power and wealth. Now the power had shifted, and the wealth would follow—to the island and to the new grid city of Armas. With this dessert, playful as it might seem, the empress had been saying: Samra is the past. A past of tyranny and civil war that brought Orrun to the brink of destruction. A past that almost provoked the Last Return of the Eight. From this point, we are building a new future. Come—share in the feast.

CHAPTER
Eleven

THE EMPEROR WAS ON HIS FEET. He had recited the Five Rules—now it was time for his speech. He held up a sheet of gold-edged paper and everyone laughed. He'd made a pledge at his coronation that his speeches would never last longer than one side of paper, and he had honoured that promise ever since.

"This night reminds us of the gift Yasthala gave us," he said, without preamble. "In her day, only Venerants could join a monastery, or attend court. Even Middling folk," he patted his chest, "were barred. As for the throne, the High Families chose rulers from their own bloodlines, breeding themselves like lap dogs."

He paused to let the insult hit. Neema slid her gaze to Havoc —son of not one High Venerant family but two. If he was offended by the emperor's words, he didn't show it. Too well trained, Neema thought.

"The empire was sliding once more towards tyranny," Bersun said, slashing down with his damaged hand. "Each ruler worse than the last. Then came Yasthala. Yasthala the Cruel, they called her. For three years Orrun suffered under her rule. Thousands dead from famine and disease. Thousands more worked to death in prison mines and labour camps. Yasthala didn't care. While her people suffered, she laughed. While they starved, she feasted.

"Until one night the Raven left the Hidden Realm and paid the empress a visit. The Second Guardian showed Yasthala what would come to pass if she didn't change her ways. The Raven's Dream, the Scriptures call it. A vision of blood, and fire, and vengeance. The destruction of Orrun. The end of days. The Last Return of the Eight."

The room held its collective breath, gripped with dread. On Neema's table, the man who'd given the blessing made a discreet sign over his heart, to ward off ill fortune. He was not the only one.

The emperor lifted his hand in a placating gesture, acknowledging their discomfort. "Yasthala took the Raven's warning to heart. She set out across her empire in disguise, to see for herself the sorrows she had inflicted. To feel what her people felt, to suffer as they suffered, to dream as they dreamed. On the fringes of Dolrun Forest she made a promise to end tyranny for ever. And then she fought a war for five long and bloody years, to protect Orrun from the fate the Raven had shown her. She saved her people, and all the generations that followed. May the Eight bless her."

"And remain Hidden," people responded, with more vehemence than usual. *Please yes, dear beloved Guardians. Do not come for us.*

"She saved us," Bersun said. "But her work is not complete. The truce forced her to compromise. Yasthala planned to open the monasteries up to anyone worthy of a place, no matter their background. But the anats were left to interpret her words as they wished. Anat-garra opened its doors to anyone with the courage and strength to survive novitiate training." Bersun stood taller, proud of his monastery. "And anyone may enter Anat-russir, if they can find the way in." Cheers and whistles from the Foxes in the room.

"The Ravens and Oxes, Monkeys and Hounds set up academies across the empire—beacons of learning that now have noble histories of their own. But when I took the throne, the doors to their monasteries were mostly shut to Commoners. And the Tigers? They had done nothing."

He let his disapproval fill the room, thick and heavy as the incense that signalled his coming.

"This is not right. This is not fair. Empress Yasthala knew it. We all know it in our hearts. That is why I am so proud of our reforms, and why I believe they will stand as the most significant achievement of my reign. The doors to the anats are open. May they never be closed again."

Ah! So that was the point. His beloved monastery reforms. The room burst into dutiful applause.

Bersun had not finished. With genuine comic timing, he held up the paper—and flipped it. "Nearly!" he said, to waves of laughter.

Neema didn't join in. There was no writing on the other side. Whatever the emperor was about to say was unrehearsed—and that made her nervous. She shifted in her seat, to get a better view.

"I have spoken to each of the contenders, in private," the emperor said. "I explained to them, as I have explained to you, that these reforms are not mine, but Yasthala's. We honour her by completing the work she began. By fulfilling the oath she made to her people. All but one agreed with their emperor."

All but one. No guesses required. Ruko and Abbess Rivenna sat rigid with defiance, as everyone turned to look at them.

"Perhaps this has changed his mind," Bersun said, handing his speech to the nearest bodyguard. Another emperor might have sat down at this point, on his golden chair. Bersun prowled the dais, hand upon his sword. "Perhaps we have moved him with our words. Let us see. Contenders—I call on you to swear an oath here tonight. Will you promise to uphold these reforms? Will you swear it on the Eight?"

Cain was already on his feet, Katsan a close second. Not a difficult decision for a Bear or a Fox. On Neema's table, Tala and Havoc rose together, nodding to each other. Shal Worthy stood next, for the Hounds.

And finally Gaida, slowed only because she was clipping her hair back into something resembling a bun. Crossing her arms across her chest, she saluted the room. "I swear upon the Eight to protect these vital and long overdue reforms. And I take this opportunity to acknowledge my many Commoner friends," a nod to Cain, "who inspire me every day with their courage, their spirit, and their dignity."

Neema poured another glass of wine.

Only one contender left. On the dais, the emperor gripped the hilt of his sword. He could not order Ruko to swear an oath. He'd had his term of twenty-four years. He could not dictate what happened next—that was strictly forbidden. Even the promise he'd wrestled from the other contenders was not binding. If Neema had known he planned to do this, she would have counselled him against it, even as a Commoner. All the Old Bear had done was remind everyone that his power was fading. She felt an ache of sympathy. He was a good man, the emperor. He had brought peace and stability, he had worked tirelessly, she had watched him wear himself out. Give him this, Ruko, she thought. Even if you go back on your word later, do not humiliate him tonight.

"Contender Valit," the emperor prompted. He was not used to being kept waiting. "Will you rise?"

But Ruko remained seated. "A Tiger does not cage itself," he said, in a voice that rang up to the very rafters of the banqueting hall.

Everyone waited for Bersun to explode. His infamous temper.

Instead, he laughed. A chilling laugh of release. Like a hunter who has taken down his prey, after long days of pursuit. It went on for too long, poisoning the air, then faded to silence. Neema had never heard the emperor laugh like that—and hoped she never would again.

"Vabras," he called down from the dais, sounding just like himself again. "The colours."

And with that, the ceremony lurched back into life as if nothing had happened. The drums sounded, the trumpets blared, and Ruko—finally—found his feet, joining his rivals at the base of the dais. Vabras brought up the colours and, as he did so, he bent low and whispered something in Bersun's ear. The emperor frowned. They were still conferring when the music ended.

The contenders had formed a line in the traditional order of the Guardians, stage right to left: Cain for the Fox, Gaida for the Raven, Ruko for the Tiger, Tala for the Ox, Katsan for the Bear, Havoc for the Monkey, Shal for the Hound. The seven great champions of Orrun. Facing the room, shoulder to shoulder in their matching uniforms, sigils glowing on their chests, they looked like the mythic gods of the olden days.

"Welcome, brave contenders!" the herald shouted. "May the Eight protect you."

"And remain Hidden," the contenders replied, in unison.

The room burst into applause.

The emperor, still deep in discussion with Vabras, gave a final, decisive nod, then called down the steps. "Cain Ballari."

Cain mounted the dais. Bersun, struggling slightly with his maimed hand, tied the embroidered band around Cain's right bicep—bright orange for the Fox.

Neema smiled, despite herself. She might not like the man Cain had become, but she still loved the boy he had once been.

Cain headed back down the steps on another wave of applause.

"Gaida Rack." Bersun pinched his lips at her Raven name, the memory of his treasonous old High Justice.

Gaida mounted the dais with aching solemnity. A purple band for her, embroidered with the black wings of the Raven.

Next, the Tiger contender. Muted applause this time—a certain wariness. The emperor wrapped a green band around Ruko's bulging bicep, and sent him back down the steps without a word.

Tala's colours were dark copper, embroidered with wide golden horns. Before she left the dais she gave the room a collective Ox bow, arms forming a circle, fingers clasped. A gesture of peace and inclusion. *We pull the plough together.*

Katsan followed next. Bersun opened his arms in welcome. He might be her emperor, but as a Bear warrior he was also her Brother—and would soon be her abbot. Katsan accepted the hug, stiffly, and shifted away as soon as it was done. Neema found that curious, but it was not out of character. As if the bitter norwestern winters had chilled her soul while she was out patrolling the mountain paths, and never thawed. The applause was equally cool as she returned to the line, her red band with black slashes prominent against her bare, tautly muscled arm.

Havoc, by contrast, was granted a rousing reception. Like Katsan, he had risked his life defending the empire. Like Shal, he was a proven leader. He also had a lot of friends in the room. He accepted his yellow band as if it were a military honour, and returned to his place, neatly avoiding the foot Cain had stuck out to trip him.

Shal Worthy came up last, for the Hounds. Bersun tied the colours around his arm—a blue band with a silver square. And in that alchemical way, without even trying—the band added to his dashing appearance—the subtle glint of silver matching his earrings and his tunic sigil. Shal gave a Hound salute, fist pressed to his chest, and the colours ceremony was complete.

Again, an awed hush fell upon the room. In a few days' time, one of these contenders would be crowned ruler of Orrun. Looking down the line, there was no denying Ruko's superior physique, or the burning hunger in his eyes. He was the one to beat, without question. Another reason for Havoc's reception, Neema thought. The High Venerants liked the Monkey contender because he was one of them. Everyone else liked him because he wasn't Ruko. Havoc was a contender in the classic style—the right bearing, the right temperament. It was obvious what kind of ruler he would be. (Solid, well-prepared, fond of ceremony.) But Ruko? Who could guess what Ruko Valit would do with all that power?

Into the silence, a deep boom of drums.

Everyone turned towards the door in anticipation.

The drumming grew louder, Neema could feel the reverberation deep in her chest. It rose to a crescendo, then stopped. The banqueting doors opened wide to admit a group of cloaked and hooded figures.

The Dragon contingent.

They moved like a wave down the hall towards the dais, their cloaks spread out behind them, each one a different shade of sea green laced with silver thread that glinted in the candlelight. At the foot of the dais they stopped as one. Seven drew back, forming a protective semicircle around their leader—a short, slender woman clasping a plain wooden staff.

Jadu, Servant of the Dragon and ruler of Helia for over sixty years. This would be her fifth Festival, and there was no reason to assume it would be her last. Servants were twice Chosen by the Dragon, Guardian of Mystery, Guardian of Death. Their lives were long.

With her back to the room, Jadu lowered her hood. Her long waves of red hair had softened with age to a burnished rose-gold. For a crown she wore a silver diadem, the links made of eternal eights.

Neema could not see Jadu's face, but she saw the contenders' reactions—surprise, wonder.

"Welcome, honoured guests," Bersun said, perched in his familiar way at the edge of his chair. He held out a band of pale sea-green silk, embroidered with the sigil of the Dragon, the Eighth Guardian twining and coiling into another ∞. "Will you take your colours, and join the Festival of the Eight?"

"We are Dragons," Jadu replied. "We desire not the throne." Her voice was eerie, a whisper that carried to the back of the hall, drifting through the mind like smoke.

"You renounce your right to contend?"

"We do." A touch of scorn, as if ruling the world was for children.

"What do you ask, in return?"

"To govern ourselves in peace, and to bring the Chosen home."

"This we promise on the Eight," the emperor said. "Contenders. Do you bind yourselves to this oath?"

"We do," they replied, in unison. This was a promise even Ruko was happy to make. No one knew why the spell-casters of Helia did not use their magic to take over the empire, and no one asked. Why give them ideas?

The Ritual of Renunciation was complete. The eighth contingent turned as one, and the room reacted as the contenders had done: surprise and wonder. Jadu was nearing a hundred years of age, but she looked forty years younger. Like all those Chosen by the Dragon, her eyes had turned amber when she was initiated—very pale in her case, like the centre of a flame. With her near-white brows and lashes, the effect was striking. In the middle of her forehead, set within the diadem, lay the Eye of the Dragon—the flawless emerald passed down from Servant to Servant.

Jadu gazed out across the room, searching for someone. "Yasila," she said, when she'd found her quarry. "Child of Helia. How fares your life since you left us?" A twist of a smile. "Do you enjoy the freedom you craved?"

Yasila, seated at her table with her hands folded in her lap, said nothing.

Jadu lifted up her hood and glided back down the hall. As she passed Neema's table she paused and took a breath, as if she had scented something in the air. The emerald glinted on her forehead, caught in the candlelight.

"Look at that," Facet breathed. "Beautiful."

Jadu gave him a withering look, and continued on her way.

Sunur was reminding Tala of Princess Yasila's doomed childhood. "…no, she wasn't Chosen, she was kept hostage. The shipwreck, remember? She escaped when she was sixteen…"

It's over, Neema thought, flooded with relief. The ceremony was done. Everything had gone smoothly. No disasters, no mistakes. Apart from Ruko's defiance, but that was beyond her control. All the rehearsals and fine tuning had been worth it. The emperor was drinking wine from a golden cup—not happy, exactly, Bersun never looked happy on high occasions. But gruffly satisfied. The contenders began to peel away from the line.

I hope Benna has poured my bath. Sitting back in her chair, Neema allowed herself an indulgent projection. The soft lap of water, the swirl of rose oil on its surface. Flickering candles arranged around the edge. Rich creams for tired feet and aching limbs.

Gaida stepped forward. "Permission to speak, your majesty."

Neema returned to the present with a thud.

The rest of the contenders were back in their seats. Guests fanned and tutted in disapproval. *The afterparties!*

The emperor's lips formed a thin line. "Very well. Be brief."

Gaida bowed her thanks. "Your majesty, I wish to thank my fellow Raven, High Scholar Neema Kraa, for arranging this remarkable ceremony."

Everyone turned towards Neema and clapped politely. A clever piece of deflection from Gaida. By the time everyone turned back, three young men with matching ginger hair were threading their way towards the dais.

The Imperial Bodyguards drew their swords.

"Peace, peace!" Gaida said. She patted the air, as if she were a schoolteacher settling an unruly classroom. "My friends. Please welcome the Ankalla brothers, of Three Ports!"

The musicians gave deep Monkey salutes, bowing from the waist with their palms pressed together. First to the emperor, then to the room. The Hounds relaxed. The brothers were favourites at court, and had performed in the procession earlier.

The emperor, however, did not like to be ambushed. He was a soldier, after all. "What is this?"

"Your majesty, forgive me. I know how much you wished for this ceremony to be authentic. I'm afraid the High Scholar has missed something out. A small detail, but," a modest, faux-embarrassed laugh, "it happens to relate to me."

Neema's heart dropped off a cliff. She knew what was coming.

"An accident, I'm sure," Gaida said, and smiled.

Bersun grunted. "Well? What is it?"

"At the end of Yasthala's feast, the Raven contender surprised the empress with a performance of her favourite song."

Bersun throttled the hilt of his sword. "Neema Kraa. Is this so?"

Neema rose to her feet. Her legs were shaking. "Yes, your majesty."

He glared at her. "And you *forgot* this detail?"

"No, your majesty." She knew better than to lie. She stumbled on, in a strained voice. "It was a fleeting reference, in an obscure account. If it did happen, and that's debatable, it wasn't considered part of the official opening ceremony. I took the decision—"

"*You* took the decision."

Disapproving frowns from the other guests, the shaking of jew-elled heads.

"Do you rule Orrun, Neema Kraa?" Bersun enquired.

"No, your majesty."

It was her own fault, completely her own fault. She'd known that if she'd brought the reference to the Festival committee, they would have felt honour-bound to include it. Authenticity. She'd also known that the emperor would hate it—Gaida warbling away, taking centre stage. So she'd taken a gamble not to mention it. No one would notice, especially not Gaida. She was too grand for footnotes.

Wrong.

Gaida caught her eye. She tilted her head and pulled a sad face. Mouthed, *Sorry.*

A golden fork in the neck, Neema thought. She could do it, before the Hounds caught her. Clamber over the tables. It would be worth it, maybe. She balled her hands into fists, dug her nails into her palms.

The emperor was furious. But there was nothing he could do. Which made him even more furious. Gritting his teeth, he turned back to Gaida. "Our thanks to you, Raven contender, for bringing this oversight to our attention. Sing us the song, *if that is your wish.*"

Ignoring the hint, Gaida gave another Raven salute, hands crossed over her chest. "Your majesty. Last summer, on my pilgrimage across the empire, I had the honour of visiting your beloved home of Anat-garra."

Neema dropped back down in her seat. This was going to be even worse than she'd thought.

Gaida softened her voice. "I was privileged to gain audience with your abbot and mentor Brother Lanrik, mere weeks before he died. I also met your brother Gedrun. He wishes you good health, and hopes you may be reconciled when you return west."

The emperor's face was frozen. The feud with his brother was longstanding, and painful. When Bersun had taken the Way of the Bear, Gedrun had accused him of being selfish for abandoning his family, his responsibilities as the oldest brother. The two men had sworn never to speak to one another again.

"He told me this song was a favourite of yours," Gaida said, and nodded to the musicians.

The youngest Ankalla brother pulled out a flute and played an introductory refrain, sweet and mournful. People sighed in recognition. "Come to the Mountain"—an ancient folk song from the north-west borderlands.

The emperor covered his face with his hand.

"Come to the mountain, my lost brother," Gaida sang, in a warm, expressive voice. The three brothers joined her, in close harmony.

> *"Come to the mountain, my lost brother*
> *I would see your face again*
> *Come to the mountain, lonely warrior*
> *Through the darkness, through the rain*
> *Death the Dragon cannot part us*
> *Strong and true our bond remains*
> *Come to the mountain, my lost brother*
> *I would see your face again."*

The final, haunting note faded away to silence.

Everyone looked to the emperor. His hand was still shielding his face, head bowed, shoulders shaking. He was weeping. The Old Bear was weeping, in front of the entire court. Neema covered her mouth, wracked with shame. She'd done this to him. This was her fault.

Scrubbing the tears from his cheeks, Bersun jumped down from the dais and strode vigorously down the hall, robes trailing. His bodyguards, taken by surprise, hurried after him, pushing Gaida out of the way. She too, was taken aback. Whatever reaction she had expected, it wasn't this.

The emperor came to a halt at Neema's table. With a sharp gesture, not looking her way, he summoned her in front of him.

Neema dropped to one knee. "Your majesty. Forgive your servant for her mistake—"

"Where is your badge of office?"

A vision of herself this morning, back pressed against the service hut, slipping her badge into her pocket. She had forgotten to retrieve it. "You majesty, I—"

"Does the honour mean so little, that you do not bother to wear it?"

She lifted her eyes, miserable.

"Then we shall remove you of the burden. Neema Kraa. We strip you of your position. From this moment, you have no place at court, or in my retinue. You are released."

"Your majesty—"

A slice of the hand, an executioner's axe, into his palm. It is done. "Vabras. What time does the boat leave tomorrow?" The last boat to the mainland, before they sealed the island for the Festival.

The emperor's shadow materialised at his side. "Seven o'clock, your majesty."

"Be on it," Bersun said, to Neema.

Neema bowed her head, accepting the order. She knew better than to beg, or defend herself. Her disgrace was public, and thus permanent. "May the Eight protect his majesty," she said, in a cracked voice.

"And remain Hidden," Vabras murmured.

The emperor moved on without a word.

CHAPTER
Twelve

I T TOOK NEEMA over an hour to walk back to the Raven palace, feet rubbing in her silver sandals. The news, barefoot and eager, raced on ahead of her. By the time she'd reached home, everyone had heard. People making their way to Gaida's rooms for the Raven contender's afterparty smirked openly as Neema limped past. "About time they clipped her wings," they said to each other. "Long overdue."

Benna was waiting for her at the door. "I'm so sorry, High Scholar."

Neema didn't have the heart to correct her. It was just Neema now. She slipped out of her heels, removed her rings and her diamond cuff. She felt numb, barely conscious of what she was doing.

Benna set to work unhooking the dress. *The famous dress.* Gaida's words. She'd known her performance would have serious repercussions for Neema; that the dress would be cursed by association. Courtiers were superstitious creatures. No one would dare wear it again. Grace Eliat, the imperial designer, would not buy it back for the archives. Neema would leave the island tomorrow morning with nothing to her name but a modest purse of tiles, some clothes, and a few pieces of paste jewellery. Everything else of value in her apartment—the silk rugs, the antique furniture, the unused dinner service, all the glamorous trappings of her high position—she'd rented from the imperial repository. That was the way things were done at court, for those who had not inherited such things from their family. A large portion of Neema's salary had flowed straight back to the treasury, to pay for a lavish lifestyle she didn't even want.

A moth patted plaintively against a lantern. Through the shuttered windows, Neema could hear music and conversation, peppered with laughter. Now the opening ceremony was over, people could relax and enjoy themselves, spilling out on to balconies and courtyards, drinking iced wine in a futile bid to keep cool in the deep, sultry heat of the night.

"She's ruined," someone crowed, from the balcony above. The afterparty, already in full swing.

You don't know the half of it, Neema thought. Tonight she had lost the emperor's favour. Tomorrow she would lose her position in the Flock. Her wings not just clipped but broken. No one would hire her. She would be shunned by the entire Raven community. And her family—would they be pulled into her disgrace? She blinked back the tears.

In the mirror, Benna winced in sympathy, nimble fingers hard at work on the dress.

So what now? Neema thought. What the Eight do I do? She couldn't risk stealing the file as she'd planned. Imagine, if she were caught creeping through Gaida's apartment in the middle of the night, on top of everything else.

Her only chance now was to appeal to Gaida's better nature. If she could keep her Raven name, she might find a clerical post in some quiet, backwater town. If she begged, if she literally got down on her knees and begged, Gaida might enjoy showing mercy, as she would see it. Every act of mercy is an act of power.

"Ugh," Neema said, out loud.

Benna paused in her work, and put her tattooed knuckles together. *Life is short/Enjoy it!* "Does that help?"

Not really. "Yes. Thank you."

She pushed the dress over her hips and let it slide to the floor. Released. For months, she'd dreamed of wearing it. Now all she wanted to do was kick it away from her.

Benna gathered it up with a questioning look.

Neema gave her the directions to Grace Eliat's workshop at the Monkey palace. The designer wouldn't buy the dress back, but she might pay something for the material, the tiny, winking diamonds on the bodice. "Tell her I'll take twelve silver tiles for it. She'll haggle you down to nine." Neema could live a few months on nine silver tiles, if she was frugal.

Benna held the dress to her chest, like a protective parent. "But it's so beautiful…"

Neema lifted her hands. Beautiful, yes—and for ever tainted. "You'll probably have to wait, I'm afraid. She could be out all night." Grace liked a party, and a drink, gossiping in dark corners. "Could you bring the tiles here first thing tomorrow, before I leave?"

The emperor had ordered her to take the last boat, and she must be on it. After that, the island would be shut off from the mainland until the Festival was over. An attack was unlikely—there were no reports of rebellion, and pirates hadn't dared raid this section of the coast in centuries. But Orrun's richest and most powerful citizens would be gathered together on the island for the next few days, not to mention the Dragons and their ruler. The simplest way to protect them was to do what Yasthala had done fifteen centuries before. Seal up the docks, patrol the waters. No one out, no one in.

"Twelve silver tiles," Benna checked.

"But accept nine."

Benna gave her wobbly bow, indigo silk trailing from her arms. "Is there anything else, High Scholar?"

Neema felt another pang for her lost title. "No…wait. Did you find Pink-Pink?"

Benna's face dropped.

"Don't worry. He'll find his way home." She hunted out a couple of bronze tiles. "Thank you for your service today."

She held her smile until Benna had left.

Then she sat down on the floor and cried. Silently, so the laughing guests on the balcony above didn't hear her, and laugh even harder.

When she was done, she rubbed her face and crossed over to the bath Benna had prepared for her. It was just as she had projected—candles flickering around the edge, the air misty with steam. A thick layer of precious rose oil swirled across the surface in drifting patterns, tempting her in. But as she put her hand into the water she hissed and drew it out again, scalded. Way too hot. Well, Benna had come from the kitchens—she was used to boiling things, not bathing them.

Something else to soothe her, then, while she waited for the water to cool down. Her secret treasure.

Moving to her bookshelves, she brushed her fingers along her collection until she reached a thick black volume, the title debossed in dark blue letters: Tales of the Raven. Putting her nose to the spine, she inhaled its familiar perfume: mottled pages, old leather. Behind that, a faint trace of pepper and liquorice.

She'd found it at the turn of the year, when she was working in the imperial tombs. The emperor thought there might be some Ketuan artefacts buried down there that he could add to his collection, and had sent Neema to investigate.

No one could (or would) explain what happened next, but she had ended up locked in the tombs overnight. She suspected the guards—they'd been muttering as she went in that her visit was a desecration. *Shouldn't be allowed.* She'd held her nerve until the lanterns lining the tunnels died out. Then she'd cracked. The cold, the dark, the unseen, scuttling things. Desperate for comfort, she'd prayed to the Raven. When it didn't answer—of course it didn't, it was a metaphor, not an actual *being*—she'd crawled on her hands and knees, groping for…what, exactly? A miraculous tinderbox? A magical, flaming torch? Her courage?

She'd found a book.

Picking it up in the pitch black tunnel, it had felt warm to the touch, emanating comfort. She'd hugged it to her chest all night, and when she was finally rescued the next morning—by the same guards who'd most likely locked her in—she'd tucked it in her bag, and brought it home.

It was only when she'd laid it out on her desk and its pages started riffling and flapping *of their own accord*, that she'd realised the priceless treasure she had found. An enchanted book, from the Hidden Library on Helia. How it had escaped the Dragon monastery and found its way into the imperial vaults was a mystery, but here it was.

Keeping it was not just forbidden, it was dangerous. There were a thousand cautionary tales about foolish, UnChosen folk who meddled with Dragon magic, and came to a thousand terrible ends. But whenever Neema thought about handing the book over, it resisted. That was the only way she could describe it. She'd brought it here and now it wouldn't leave, like a stubborn house guest. So she kept it on her bookshelf, hidden in plain sight.

Days would go by when she did not think of it. Then she would catch its scent—that warm yet peppery scent that tickled the nose —and she would take it down. Or she would wake in the night from one of those disturbing dreams that had been plaguing her for months—and before she even knew what she was doing, she was crouched at her desk, reading it by candlelight.

Then there were times like this, when she felt as she had done in the tombs. Alone, afraid, abandoned. The book became her solace, carrying her away into its stories. Sometimes it told her fables of the Hidden Realm. Sometimes it recounted the myth of the Kind Returns—the seven times the Guardians had saved the world from the edge of destruction. Sometimes it took her back into Orrun's more recent history, recounting events in such vivid detail she felt as if she were living through them. It never told the same story twice.

Neema had never believed in magic until she encountered the book. At first she had found this shift in her reality disquieting, but in time she had come to terms with it. She had grown used to the way her tongue pressed down in her mouth, whenever she thought of telling anyone about it. She'd accepted the way it sometimes appeared beneath her pillow, when she was sure she had left it on the shelf. As far as she could tell it meant her no harm—quite the opposite. What it felt like, if it felt like anything, was a companion. A friend in the dark.

Carrying it to her desk, she opened it at the middle and settled down. The book had other ideas. Its pages shrugged at the edges before whisking towards the back.

For a moment, she stared at an empty spread. Then the left-hand page bloomed with life. She was looking down through the branches of an oak tree at a grass bank rampant with wild primrose. A man lay sprawled in the grass, bathed in lemon sunshine. Neema recognised him at once from the setting and from the blood seeping from his chest. Eyart Just—Empress Yasthala's husband, and father to her two sons. This was the scene of his murder —three days after the signing of the truce. When he'd thought it was safe to put down his sword at last, and rest.

Not the comforting story she was hoping for. But once the book was open, she was compelled to read, until it was done with her.

Ink blossomed on the opposite page, forming into text. A title resolved itself.

Empress Yasthala and the Cursed Blade

"Oh, actually I would like to hear about that," Neema conceded, and the book gave a satisfied shuffle as if to say, *I know*, and continued:

…and when the guards came to Yasthala, and gave her the news, she would not believe them. The Eight would not take Eyart from her now after five years of civil war, fighting for a victory that most days felt like a defeat. For the empress knew it would take a lifetime to heal Orrun, and fulfil the promises she had made to her people. Only with Eyart at her side could she hope to succeed—her love, her friend, her wise and honest counsel.

Angrily she rose from her white marble throne. With her own eyes she would see him, and prove them all wrong. The empress who once walked pilgrimage across her lands in shabby travel clothes, who led her armies into battle in blood-spattered armour, strode now down the golden halls in robes of black velvet and imperial silk—and those she passed sank to their knees, and bowed their heads.

They kneel not to you but to the crown, Eyart had told her, and so she had allowed it, this deference she despised.

"He is not dead," she told them—as if she could command Death the Dragon, as she had commanded her troops.

Yasthala walked until she reached the sloping grass banks that led down to the Guardian Gate. And there, beneath an oak tree, the empress found her husband's body, and lost all reason.

With a piercing scream she fell to her knees, touching the savage wounds in his chest as though she might seal them closed with her fingers, and make him whole again. But Eyart Just had fought his last battle. When Yasthala saw he could not be saved, she sat back upon her heels. Hollow were her black eyes, as she smeared his heart's blood down her face.

Only then did she see the Raven, perched in the oak tree.

"*You*," she spat—for she knew the Second Guardian of old. "You saw this and did nothing."

The Raven's voice reverberated in her head, thrummed through her bones. The voice of all the ravens that were, all the ravens that are, and all the ravens that will be. "We did nothing," it said. For even the Raven, Guardian of What Has Been and What Will Come, cannot stand against the will of the Dragon.

"I saved this world," the empress said. "And yours. I stopped the Last Return. You said I would know peace, Raven, when it was done."

The Raven tilted its head, to study her the better. "And so you have, Empress, these past three days."

"Give him back to me!" she screamed. And in her grief, she picked up the blade she had found lodged in Eyart's chest. A small, plain cook's knife with a wooden handle. A modest weapon to fell the greatest warrior of the age. "Do not forget, Raven, that you promised me a gift when the war was done. I claim it now. Bring him back to life."

The Raven gave itself a short preen. "This is not in our power," it muttered, beak under its wing. The Second Guardian did not like to be reminded of its limits.

Yasthala fell silent. A look of quiet acceptance crossed her face. She placed the blade to her throat. "Then I shall go to him. Wherever he has landed on the Eternal Path, I shall find him, for I am his, and he is mine."

The Raven stopped its preening, opened its black beak wide and let out a deep, rattling cry.

Yasthala's head jerked back. An oily, purple-black liquid spread out across her eyes, coating them and spilling over the lids, streaming down her face. Dark, viscous tears, mingling with her husband's blood.

And as the present blurred into the future, she saw what would become of Orrun, and her people, if she left them. How her enemies would rise again and steal back all she had won from them. More battles, more bloodshed, pushing the empire back into civil war. Her two young sons used as pawns, and set against each other. Their deaths, violent and terrible. And on, more death, more horror, until the Guardians had no choice but to Return from the Hidden Realm, streaming down from the sky to destroy the world.

The vision ended, replaced by another. What would happen if she stayed. The empress saw how Eyart's senseless death brought her people together in grief. How she won not a perfect peace, but a lasting one. Her sons grew up and had children of their own. The world turned, and life flourished.

The last of the black oil spilled from Yasthala's eyes and down her cheeks. She blinked, and found herself upon the grassy bank once more, in the spring sunshine. "These futures are not certain," she said.

The Raven did not answer. It had shown her its visions. The empress must decide what to do with them.

Yasthala looked upon Eyart's ruined body. And in her heart she knew that he would not wish her to follow. "I shall remain until my work is done. Wait for me, my love, and I will find you."

The Raven shook its ruffled neck, pleased by her words. "A wise choice, Empress. Fare well." Spreading its wings, it prepared for flight.

"Wait," the empress said. "I have yet to claim my gift."

The branch beneath the Raven's claws shuddered. A breeze, hot and sour, riffled its feathers. Uneasily, the Second Guardian folded its wings. "Very well. What is your wish?"

Yasthala inspected the modest cooking knife that had killed her husband. "I wish to name this blade." She ran her finger along its blunt edge. "And curse it."

The branch shuddered more violently. The Raven lifted lightly into the air, and settled. "Curses are dangerous things, Empress," it warned. "Most of all for those who make them."

"So be it. The Tigers of Anat-hurun are responsible for this. I am sure of it. I name this blade Hurun-tooth in their honour. The blade is named." Sheltering the blade in her cupped palms, she lifted it high. "And now I curse it. The next time Hurun-tooth takes a life, the Eight will Return in blood and fire."

"Yasthala!" cried the Raven. "No!"

"Seal the curse into the blade," she demanded.

"You would bind the fate of two worlds to one blade? Such a weapon cannot be allowed to exist."

"Not a weapon," Yasthala said, her grief lending her voice a touch of madness. "A gift from an empress, to her enemies. The Tigers of Anat-hurun shall guard this blade with their lives. This shall be their punishment and their burden, until the end of time." She lifted the knife higher, the steel glinting in the sun. "Seal the curse into the blade."

The Raven had made a promise—it must obey. Stretching its neck, it gave out a sharp, piercing cry that ripped through the air. For one long, terrible moment, the day vanished, replaced by a freezing, soulless night. And then the light returned, and it seemed to Yasthala that the grass looked fresher, the leaves on the trees brighter, the sun kinder than she had ever known them before. Tilting the blade, she saw a tiger's eye etched into the steel, and knew that it was done.

Regret flew on swift wings to her heart.

"What have I done?" she whispered. "Eyart…Eyart…" And she fell upon his body again, and wept, because her husband would have stopped her, her wise and patient friend, but he was gone.

When she could weep no longer, Yasthala took the knife again in her hands. She had done what she had done. "Hurun-tooth. Blade of Peace. Yes. That is what you must become. A Blade of Peace. Perhaps you *are* a gift," she mused, balancing its weight on her fingers. "Within you lies all the destructive potential of our Guardians. So: we must be careful. Our world is precious, and fragile. We must take care of it, as closely and as lovingly as we shall take care of you."

This is how an empress lives with her mistakes.

The Raven was not impressed. Snapping its wings open it said, "Goodbye, Yasthala. We shall not meet again in this life."

With that it left her. And from that day the Raven empress saw no visions, and dreamed no dark dreams that were not of her own making.

**So ends the story of the Empress Yasthala,
and the Cursed Blade.**

The words faded from the page. Neema blinked, as if coming out of a trance. "Was that *really* what happened?" she wondered aloud. "I believe Eyart was murdered with a cooking knife, and Yasthala cursed it and gave it to the Tigers. But I don't think it has the power to summon the Eight. The Eight are metaphors. The Raven is a metaphor."

And you are talking to a magic book. The words materialised on the page, surprising her. The book had never spoken to her directly before.

"Hello," she said, and felt a wave of profound embarrassment when it didn't reply. The words had already faded from the paper. She rubbed her eyes; maybe she'd imagined them.

Your bath is ready, the book said, and closed itself with a smart *snap.*

Well, that was strange, Neema thought, as she sank down into the water. It was the perfect temperature, and smelled divine. The rose bath oil clung to her skin in fat, translucent beads. Benna must have emptied out the whole bottle, not realising it only needed a few drops. No matter. Neema couldn't take it with her, and it felt deliriously good; rich and indulgent. She massaged the oil deeper into her arms and legs, across her stomach, feeling the stresses and aches of the day melt away.

The mirrored ceiling threw back her reflection, blurred by the steam. Something sparkled at her neck. The amethyst choker. She'd forgotten she was wearing it. She reached up to remove it, then changed her mind. It was still hers, for an hour or two.

She lowered her arms back into the water, and closed her eyes. Her thoughts turned to Cain. Eight. He'd looked good in imperial silk. Toned from his years of Festival training. The way he'd reached out, and touched her dress.

Would you like me to creep into your apartment in the dead of night?
No.
No.
She took a deep breath, and slid under the water.

Emerging a while later, she slipped into her white linen wrapping gown and stepped out on to her balcony. Leaning out, she could see that the afterparty up in Gaida's apartment was thinning out. Another half hour and she could go up and beg for her future. "Ugh," she said again.

She started packing for the morning, then gave up. She'd hoped the bath would calm her nerves, but if anything she felt more agitated. Her heart was hammering as if she'd downed several cups of strong coffee.

Taking herself up to her sleep platform, she found the book lying on her pillow. No, you see...*no*...she was absolutely certain she had left it on her desk. "I'm not reading any more tonight," she said, defiantly. "I'm done."

One page.
The thought tugged her forward as the book opened up again. It seemed insistent—anxious, even, as it reached the final page —a brightly painted illustration, edged in gold. The Awakening

Dragon of the Last Return, wings unfurled, fire glowing in its sinuous throat. With its next breath, it would burn down the world.

She had seen this exact illustration before, many times—on the ceiling of the throne room. The same Dragon, the same pose, the same backdrop.

She traced the twists and turns of the Dragon's body with her fingers. So lifelike, she could almost feel it moving against her skin.

Something's wrong, she thought, dimly. Usually the book calmed her down, but now it seemed to be screaming at her, silently. Her heart was pounding and she felt feverish—tipping towards delirium. She could hear the laughter from the balcony above as if it were here in the room, tormenting her. The flower patterns on her quilt were moving, petals opening, stems tangling and knotting together. The scent of roses from the bath oil, heady and sickly sweet. Her senses were opening up and deepening, halfway to pain, halfway to pleasure.

More laughter from above—piercingly loud. She clapped her hands to her ears.

The Dragon twisted and turned on the page, calling to her. The fire building in its throat was a furnace, rippling the air between them.

And suddenly the torment stopped. She felt nothing, heard nothing. The whole world and everything within it was reduced to one, overriding thought.

The throne room. The painting. She had to see it. She had to see it now.

Go.

Down the steps of the sleeping platform.

Across the living area.

Balcony.

Garden.

The Dragon. The Dragon. *Now.*

Neema was moving, and nothing would stop her.

CHAPTER

Thirteen

N EEMA STRODE DOWN the golden hallways of the inner
sanctum, swift and certain.

She had no right to be here. She had no badge of office, she
had no pass, no imperial summons. If the Hounds found her, they
could kill her on the spot. *You trespass, you die.*

Neema knew this. She didn't care.

Luckily for her, she had just missed the night watch. Except it
wasn't luck. She could hear them, their footsteps heading in the
opposite direction, the rumble of their conversation. She could
even catch their lingering scent—the polished leather of their
boots, the laurel soap they all used. Some deep, animal part of her
brain was gathering this information and using it, helping her to
reach her goal, her desire, her one and only reason to be: *the painting, the painting, the painting.*

She had arrived. Pushing open the doors, she grabbed a torch
from its sconce and moved to the centre of the room, her attention clamped to the ceiling.

The Awakening Dragon of the Last Return coiled and writhed,
silver-green scales glinting in the torchlight. Was it moving? Was it
breathing? Was that sulphur, and blood, and judgement in the air?
Tantalised, Neema stood beneath its gaping jaws, its dagger teeth.
Heat emanated from its throat, fire building from deep within.

"Show me your mysteries, Guardian of Death." The words
flowed from some dark, potent corner of her soul. Another lifetime, perhaps. Another journey on the Eternal Path. A time when
she was Chosen. "Destroy me, and bring me back to life. I am
ready for the fire."

She opened her arms, welcoming the white-hot flames as they tore through her. Then on, through the palace, out along its golden halls, its pristine gardens, flames flicking across the Mirror Bridge, over the sea to the mainland. An ancient, purifying fire, raging hard enough to consume an empire. Raging in her. The fire was hers now. *Burn it down. Burn it all down.*

"Neema?"

Cain was sitting on the throne in the dark, a small canvas bag at his feet. "What are you doing?"

She lowered her arms. The fire swept to the edges of her vision, lingered for a moment, then died. She saw not the world, expanding, but a room, contracting. At her feet, a few dwindling embers. "The Dragon called me here."

"Oh, you're drunk." Curiosity sated, Cain settled back on the throne, trying it out for size. "How do I look? Commanding?"

Cain's hair was fire. His eyes were emeralds. His skin was silk, imperial silk. She would like to touch, she would like to taste. Must have. Will have. Need. "Your hair is fire. I'm not drunk."

Cain shouldered his bag and slunk down the throne steps to inspect the evidence. "Wow," he laughed. "High as a raven's nest. What did you take?"

Want, want, want. She shook her head, trying to clear it. "Didn't...I didn't..."

"You were spiked?" A flicker of concern, and professional interest. Drugs were an integral part of Fox training, especially hallucinogens. "How do you feel?"

His hair was fire, his eyes were jewels, and there was a war inside her. "Possessed." Possessed by herself, by her own desire. The deepest core of herself. Neema Kraa's inner sanctum.

"What else?" Cain prompted.

His voice vibrated through her. Ripples of pleasure, pain, need. "I can hear...I can feel...too much."

"Your senses are heightened."

He was too close. She could smell him. His skin, his sweat.

He touched her forehead with the back of his hand, then frowned at the heat coming off her. Her ever-expanding pupils. "Neema…what did you take?"

He was right there, and she needed, she needed…

She kissed him, hard—then wrenched herself away. "Sorry, I'm sorry…"

Cain licked his lips, then flinched at the taste. "No. It can't be." He took her wrist and breathed in deeply, confirming it. "Dragonscale. You lucky woman."

"Dragonscale," she repeated. She was going to kiss him again, she was going to lick his face like an ice cream.

"Type of fungus. The Dragons use it in their rituals. Eight—I wish I was you right now."

"Stop…Make it stop."

He laughed softly. "It'll fade in a couple of hours. Find somewhere quiet to sit it out, you might even enjoy it. Neema? Are you listening?"

The portraits of the Eight were swirling and shifting on the walls. The Raven, perched on its clifftop, opened its beak and called her name. *Kraa! Kraa!*

"Big dose. Very big…"

"Don't worry—it's potent, but you can't have taken a dangerous amount. Dragonscale oil is fantastically rare—and impossibly expensive for that matter."

"Oil…"

"Yeah, it's thick and oily." He rubbed his fingers and thumb together. "And smells bitter. It was probably mixed with something sweeter like rose, or lavender."

An image floated into Neema's mind. Lying in her bath, breathing the fragrant steam, massaging oil into her tired limbs. "Bath…"

"Bath oil? No, that would be far too much…" A shadow passed over Cain's face. He stepped right into her, ran his fingers down her bare neck. "No, no, no," he said, hastily wiping the oil from his hands.

For a moment he stood paralysed, then his training kicked in. He grabbed her by the shoulders. "We need to rinse this off *now*."

He pushed her towards the octagonal window behind the throne. Neema was humming to herself—the vibrations in her throat and chest helped distract her from Cain, and the wanting. Dimly, she knew she could be dying, but she wasn't worried. The stars were diamonds, the sky was black velvet.

Cain was levering open a section of the window. A fronded path led into the Garden at the Edge of the World. The emperor's private grounds, perched over the ocean like a jewelled lozenge. She glided (it *felt* like gliding) through the window into a small courtyard, breathing the night into her lungs, her senses gloriously alive. Earth. Salt spray. Leaves, roots, bark. Smoke, from distant campfires. The subtle perfume of closed flowers.

Below the moon, the Tiger's Path constellation gleamed an invitation. "Let's fly to the Hidden Realm," she said, reaching out to the stars. So close. "I can rip the sky open with my claws."

Even Cain didn't have an answer to that one. "Here," he said, pointing to a raised ornamental fish pond covered in lily pads. Frogs croaked in the dark, surprised by the intrusion. "Get in. Neema." The fear in his voice cut through to her. "Take off your robe. Hurry."

She plunged into the pond, naked, and laughed. The fish were bumping up against her legs. "Another bath. A fish bath."

The edge of the pond was decorated with chunks of pumice stone. Cain shoved a piece in her hand. "Scrub as hard as you can bear."

He watched her for a moment to be sure she was following his instructions. Then he set off with the torch, the flame a bright, comforting orange as he disappeared into the night.

Neema rubbed the pumice over her body, sanding the oil from her skin as the fish weaved around her. As she scrubbed, the oil began to float on the water. If she wasn't quick, her skin would reabsorb it. She jumped out and crossed to another pond close by, rinsing off the last of the oil as best she could.

The scrubbing had worked. The drug was still racing through her system, but she held the reins. She no longer wanted to fly to the Hidden Realm, or lick Cain's face, or burn the world to ash. She wanted to go home, and sleep for a hundred years.

She looked about for her dressing robe.

"It was steeped in the oil," Cain said, emerging from the darkness. He tossed her a pair of overalls and some gardening shoes, liberated from a tool shed.

She put them on. Behind her, in the pond, the fish writhed and thrashed as they succumbed to the drug.

"How do you feel?" Cain asked her.

"Sad."

"The fish?" he guessed.

"The fishes." Sitting on the ground, she shoved the boots on, before coming to a stop. The laces were too much for her.

Cain kneeled down and tied them for her. "Someone just tried to kill you."

Neema didn't think so. Whoever dosed her bath oil couldn't have known that Benna would tip in the whole bottle. "Generic," she guessed, using her private name for him without noticing. He had access to her quarters and the money to pay for the drug. "Assistant. Former."

"You do have a knack for making enemies."

"We enemies?" She'd lost her verbs in the fish pond.

"Neema," Cain sighed. He had his head down, she didn't hear him. The laces were done. He put his hands under her armpits and lifted her up, then prodded her towards the path. She stumbled forward, woozy and exhausted, but not dead, so that was something.

They took a shortcut, skirting around the back of the palace. The moon silvered the branches. In the distance, the ocean turned and crashed against the rocks. It could be romantic if you were in that frame of mind, which she wasn't.

"We should go back and save the fishes," she said.

"We can't save the fish, Neema."

"We could wash them, we could wash the fishes. Can you wash fishes?"

This was not the drug talking, this was just Neema. "It'll take a while for the effects to wear off," Cain said. "It's lucky you're leaving tomorrow. Rent a room in Armas, rest up for a few days. No thrills, no excitement. Read one of your essays, that should do the trick."

"Monographs," she corrected.

"Already on the mend."

They slipped through a break in the bushes and came out on a service path, a safe distance from the Dragon palace. Neema realised he'd been escorting her out of danger.

"I'd do the same for anyone," he said, and her heart cracked with disappointment.

From here she could see the wooden lodges of the Monkey palace perched in the trees, lit up with strings of lanterns. Anyone still looking for a party at this hour would be on their way to the campfire gatherings—music, poetry, philosophy. Sex in the bushes.

A sharp hissing broke the silence.

Even in her heightened state, she recognised it instantly. Pink-Pink.

A longer, sharper hiss.

It was coming from Cain's bag.

"You!" She pointed at him.

He laughed, because she was pointing at him, and there was no one else around. He pointed at himself, mimicked her aggrieved tone. "Me! I kidnapped your chameleon!"

"Why? Why would you do that?"

"I don't know. Maybe because you destroyed my faith in love, and left me a cold, empty husk of a man. Does that make us even? What do you reckon?"

"Fucker."

"A well-aimed dart, expertly thrown." He opened the bag.

More energetic hissing from Pink-Pink. Neema peered inside and there he was, nine inches of swivel-eyed fury. She opened her palm in invitation. Pink-Pink relaxed. Rotating his feet for a better grip, he walked solemnly up Neema's arm to her shoulder, and gave Cain a final, full-bodied hiss before settling.

"Well," Cain said. "Fun as this has been, I'm late for an orgy at the Monkey palace."

She pulled a face.

"I'm joking. Of course I'm joking. They wouldn't dream of starting without me. Guest of honour." He backed away, sharp green eyes taking her in one last time. The overalls, her damp, dark brown skin, the lizard on her shoulder. His expression softened, and for a second, just a second, she glimpsed the old Cain through the artifice.

"See you in the next life," he said.

And then he was gone, into the woods.

Neema had walked in heels tonight; she had walked barefoot. The gardening boots were a revelation. She clomped her way back to the second palace, down the service paths in the dark, and was almost home when she walked through a hedge. This wasn't intentional—one moment she was not walking through a hedge, and the next moment she was. It was a hedge ambush. She dragged her way through.

Fenn Fedala was sitting on a stone bench, smoking a joint. He was still in his ceremonial robes and she was in overalls and boots, as if she'd stolen his look. He sketched a wave as she made it out from the hedge.

She waved back, brazening it out.

"You found your lizard."

She stared at him, then remembered Pink-Pink, clinging to her shoulder. "Kidnapped."

"Huh." Fenn breathed out a trail of smoke. "Sorry about tonight. Maybe it's a good thing." He made a circle with his finger, meaning—this island. He'd only accepted the position of High Engineer after Andren's rebellion. He'd wanted to help Bersun restore peace. Unfortunately, he'd proved far too effective at the job, and had been trapped in it ever since. He was always the first to congratulate someone when they escaped, as he saw it.

The difference was, Fenn had a life out there on the mainland. Neema had nothing. Yes, she could find an apartment in Armas for a few days, as Cain suggested. But then what? Even if Gaida let her keep her Raven name, did she have the strength to start again? To burn herself to the ground, and rise up from the ashes?

On reflex she looked up at Gaida's apartment. She was standing right by the iron staircase that led up to the balcony. The shutters were open, just as Her Contendership had demanded. But Neema was in no state to plead her case now. She'd have to wait until morning.

Bed, then. Abandoning Fenn, she stumbled on. The temple bell struck the half hour as she reached her door. Two thirty. Neema did the maths. Four and a half hours before the last boat left the island.

She dragged herself up to her sleeping platform. Lizard, wall. Face, pillow.

Oblivion.

PART THREE

The Day of the Fox

∞

CHAPTER
Fourteen

T HREE HOURS LATER, Neema was back on her feet. Eight, she felt terrible, but she was up.

She had woken with Pink-Pink walking over her face, and Benna calling from the living room, "High Scholar, *sorry*, Citizen Kraa! Breakfast!"

Neema had been dreaming of flaked pastries filled with sweet roast pork, the special ones Chef Ganstra made on Festival days, sprinkled with sesame seeds and glazed with honey. Coming down from her sleeping platform in her stolen overalls, she found that he'd baked a batch for her as a goodbye present. The smell had wafted into her dreams, along with the freshly brewed coffee.

"Is that Pink-Pink?" Benna asked, as Neema descended. He was clinging possessively to her head. "You found him! I'm so happy."

Neema fell on the pile of warm pastries.

"I think some of those are meant for the journey," Benna said, and then, shortly after, in a bright voice, "never mind."

Neema poured herself a second bowl of coffee. "Did you talk to Grace about the dress?"

Benna's eyes lit up. She pulled out a gingham bag filled with tiles and dropped it on the table. It sounded heavy.

Neema opened the bag. "What the Eight?"

Benna was beaming. "Nineteen silver tiles. Yay!"

"How did you…"

"I know you said start at twelve, but when Citizen Eliat got back she was…" Benna swayed, and crossed her eyes. Blind drunk.

Neema retrieved three of the octagonal silver tiles and held them out. When Benna drew back, she persisted. "Please. You earned them."

Benna hesitated, then took them. "Thank you," she said, serious for once.

Neema drained her coffee and got to her feet. The room tilted, then steadied. The food had helped, but she felt bruised and hollow, and her senses had been pulled out of shape. Sounds thudded through her, and her vision was distorted. Certain comforting smells overpowered the rest—the coffee, the food, her books.

"I need to speak with Contender Rack," she said, rubbing the heel of her palm into her forehead. "Could you pack a few things for me? They can send the rest on later."

Benna was nodding enthusiastically.

"And Pink-Pink, where's Pink-Pink?" She turned a circle, looking for him.

"Citizen Kraa." Benna pointed to a spot above Neema's head.

"Oh." She'd forgotten he was up there; she'd mistaken him for an ominous sense of doom pressing down upon her. "Thanks. He needs feeding. Would you mind?"

"I would *love* to," Benna sang, as if feeding cockroaches to a temperamental chameleon was the only job she had dreamed of her whole life.

Praying that she would find Gaida in a forgiving mood, Neema hurried up to her apartment.

The door to the antechamber was open. Stepping through, she collided with Gaida's servant. He was fretting, pressing his thumb into the centre of his palm in an effort to soothe himself. Contender Rack hadn't called him in yet, and it was way past dawn. He didn't know what to do. "I'm not supposed to disturb her," he said, pushing his thumb deeper into his palm. "But..."

But the sun was up, and Gaida was due on the parade ground within the hour, for the Revelation of the Dragon Proxy. She couldn't miss that—it would be an unforgivable, diplomatic snub.

"Where's Generic? Sorry, *Janric*," Neema corrected, when the servant looked baffled.

"They're all at breakfast, citizen."

They shared a tired look. The Raven contingent existed for exactly this reason—to take care of their contender and make sure everything ran according to plan.

"What's your name?" Neema asked him.

"Navril," he said, and pressed his ear to the door.

She did the same. She could hear the repetitive clack of a clockwork fan turning the air, nothing else.

"She could be meditating," Navril said. "If I interrupt her…"

"It'll be your fault if she does badly today," Neema guessed. She sighed into the door. "I'll go in first. I have to speak with her, and I don't have much time. If there's any trouble, you can blame me. Say I insisted."

Relief flooded Navril's face.

She tapped lightly on the door, then cracked it open. A waft of Gaida's perfume hit her—sweet honeysuckle and vanilla. She opened the door further.

The interior was dark.

"She closed the shutters," Navril said, smothering a smug look. "Mosquitoes."

"I tried to warn her."

Neema entered the apartment. Now it made sense. Gaida had wanted to "wake with the sun," but the reality of being bitten half to death must have drawn her back inside. Shutters pulled tight and no servant to wake her—no wonder she'd slept through. The place was pitch black.

This is what happens, Neema thought, when you try to live poetically. She called Gaida's name. Nothing. "Hand me the lantern," she said to Navril.

The screened-off living area was in an even worse state than the night before—a discarded guitar with a broken string, spent glasses and sticky marks on the furniture. The melancholy remnants of the afterparty. The sensible option would have been to host the party somewhere else, but Gaida had always been like this, her cell at the monastery had been just the same. She had to be at the centre of things, just as Neema had to be at the outer fringes.

Even with the lantern, it was hard to navigate through the mess. Neema tripped over a pile of books, knocking them under the table.

"She doesn't let me tidy," Navril grumbled.

Neema was listening hard, head tilted to one side. The sliding books should have woken her, surely. But the room remained still, save for the clacking ceiling fan. She revised her theory. "I don't think she's here."

Navril looked hopeful.

This was promising. If Gaida was already on her way to the parade ground, Neema had the perfect opportunity to hunt for Yaan Rack's report and destroy it. No begging for mercy required.

She had reached the shutters. The day bed near the balcony was empty, but it was evident that Gaida had slept there. One of the cushions was dented like a pillow, and she'd dragged a sheet down from her sleep platform. On the floor, tucked under the day bed, was a half-spent pot of tea, the empty cup smeared with bright red lipstick. To be thorough, Neema climbed halfway up to the sleeping platform and peered over the top. "She's not here," she called down to Navril, confirming it.

He put a hand to his chest and breathed out a long sigh. "Thank the Eight."

From her vantage point on the steps, Neema could see that there was a degree of order to the chaos. One area spilling over with clothes and scarves, disgorged from an antique chest. Another area given over to training weights and a stretching mat. In one corner, stacked boxes of papers. Her breath caught.

"I was supposed to collect a folder," she said casually as she climbed back down the platform ladder. "Maybe I could take a look around."

She couldn't have asked for a less-interested servant. "Good luck finding anything in this dump," Navril muttered, leaving her to it.

Neema held the lantern up to a mantel-clock. Ten past six. It would take a quarter hour to reach the boat from here, at a run. She'd have to be quick. Daylight would help. Sliding open the shutters to the east balcony, she winced as the sun dazzled her eyes.

Something odd. Something not right.

Her exhausted brain took a moment to catch up.

Six large, painted terracotta plant pots had been arranged in a rough circle. Well, so what? Afterparty high jinks. *Turn away. You don't have time for this.*

Except they looked suspicious, as if the tall ornamental grasses were forming a barrier around something in the middle.

It's nothing. Go back inside.

There was a smear of red on one of the pots. And there, a palm print. Whoever had moved the pots had blood on their hands.

They cut themselves, it doesn't matter. Don't look. This isn't your business. Go back inside and find the folder. Catch the boat and go, get as far away from here as you can.

Don't look.

She looked.

Of course she looked.

Gaida was lying on her front inside the circle of pots, dressed in her contender's uniform. She looked peaceful, head turned to one side, eyes closed, lips parted. Sleeping. There was a knife in her back.

Neema shifted one of the pots and kneeled down. She wasn't dead, she couldn't be. *The Dragonscale, it's showing you things that aren't there. The knife isn't real; you're imagining it.*

Neema touched Gaida's shoulder. "Gaida. Gaida, wake up. You're late for the Festival. Gaida please. You need to wake up."

She didn't stir. She wasn't breathing.

Neema touched Gaida's neck, searching for a pulse. Her skin was cold. Neema shuddered, and withdrew her hand. This was true, this was happening.

She sat back on her heels.

Who would do this?

A terrible thought invaded her mind.

Did I do this?

Could the Dragonscale have taken hold while she was sleeping, and brought her here to confront her enemy? Had it released in her a deep, ugly desire? *Kill her, and save yourself.* Could she have resisted the urge, under its influence?

But the blade. Where had that come from?

She stared at the plain wooden hilt, worn smooth from handling. An old cook's knife, nothing special…

No—it couldn't be.

Taking a deep breath, Neema reached out and touched the hilt. It wasn't enough. She would have to…Another breath, and then quickly, before she could change her mind, she pulled the blade from the wound. There was a soft sucking sound as it came free.

And there it was, etched into the steel, the one thing she was praying not to find: the Tiger's eye sigil. Hurun-tooth, the Blade of Peace. Ruko Valit's dagger. Blood trickled down the blade. Neema stared at it in horror, thinking of the curse she had read about only a few hours before.

A phrase rose unbidden in her mind—a line from the Scriptures. *When the Tiger's eye weeps blood, then shall the Eight Return.*

A soft breeze riffled the grasses in the terracotta pots. Clouds scudded across the blue sky. Such a terrible thing, on such a beautiful day.

Neema felt the air thicken, as if some deep incipient power was gathering. *They are coming, they are coming…*

A fly landed on the wound in Gaida's back, breaking the moment. The world started up again. The tick of the clock, the whirring fan.

Nothing was coming. Ridiculous.

Facts. Gaida was dead, stabbed with the Blade of Peace. The Eight had not Returned because they weren't real. The curse was a story, nothing more.

Neema brushed the fly away. She didn't know what to do with the blade, it didn't feel right to drop it on the ground. And so, swallowing back her revulsion, she slotted it back as she had found it, and somehow that was the worst part of all, as if she

were murdering Gaida a second time. "I'm sorry," she whispered.
It surprised her, how sorry she was. In spite of everything. All
that life, all that energy, snuffed out for ever.

In the waiting area, where Neema had sat the day before, Navril
was sorting the books into neat piles. "Did you find what you were
looking for?" he asked, still tidying. When she didn't answer he
turned, and saw her face. "What's wrong?"

She had to force the words out. "Contender Rack is dead."

Navril stared at her, speechless.

Seeing him like that snapped Neema from her own shock.
There were protocols for this. There were protocols for everything.
She took the books from his hands and pushed him towards the
door. "Vabras. Tell the Hounds, we need Vabras."

CHAPTER Fifteen

"How does it feel?" Cain asked.

They were alone in a waiting chamber attached to the emperor's private rooms, close to the inner sanctum. Hol Vabras was inside, giving his report on Gaida's murder; Neema could hear their voices, muffled by the thick oak door—the emperor's low growl, the High Commander's thin, unmodulated reply.

Cain was sitting against the wall, legs out, as if he were drunk outside a brothel, not awaiting an imperial summons. Sunlight streamed in from a high window, slicing him half in shadow, half in light.

"Gaida Rack is dead. Your arch enemy. Your *Neemasis*." He paused. "Don't you get it—"

"I get your terrible pun."

Cain—so hard to offend—looked genuinely insulted. It was a fantastic pun. "Did you kill her?"

She made a tight circle with her finger and thumb. *Arsehole.*

"Is that your official defence? It may require some finessing."

Slowly, with great deliberation, Neema pushed her finger through the hole.

"You have to admit," Cain said, "you're the obvious suspect."

"Says the assassin."

"That again," Cain grumbled.

There was a small display case set into the opposite wall, surrounded by gold and white votive candles. Hoping Cain would take the hint and leave her alone, she went over to inspect the contents, then wished she hadn't. The Stone of Peace. The drab, grey-green inkstone she'd used to write the Order of Exile. Bile rose in her throat. She'd forgotten they'd moved it here for the duration of the Festival. It lay on its white velvet cushion, taunting her. *Oh, hello again. Remember that unspeakable thing we did together?* She could see faint traces of Raven's Wing ink, trapped in its rough surface—from the inkstick she had ground with her own hand that day. The stone had not been used since. But it would be, once they found Gaida's killer. The sentence for murdering a contender was exile.

And wouldn't that be fittingly ironic revenge, served eight years late. Neema had sent an innocent girl to her death, and now the same could happen to her.

Assuming she *was* innocent.

"You look worried," Cain said, from the floor. "At least, the back of you does."

Neema rubbed the sweat from her forehead, before it dropped on the display case. It was hotter than yesterday, how was that possible? She was still dressed in the overalls Cain had stolen for her last night. They smelled of dirt, and a stranger's sweat.

Cain was right. Once news of the murder was released, she was bound to fall under suspicion. Who else wanted Gaida dead? No one. Gaida was loved, admired, respected. Neema couldn't even offer herself up for a Houndsight interrogation—if she couldn't remember what she did last night, how could they dig it out of her? All they'd see was maybes, and don't knows. She had to find a way to prove her innocence—first to herself, and then to everyone else. And as she thought on this, an idea came to her. A radical one, but it just might—

"—What's this junk?"

Neema yelped and jumped a foot in the air. Cain had crept up on her. The swift, silent tread of a trained killer.

"The Stone of Peace," he said. Improvising Neema the Historian, he tapped a finger on the glass display case. "Carved by Empress Yasthala in the year zero, this modest-looking inkstone was used to write the Five Great Rules of Orrun. Religious idiots believe the Raven helped the empress carve the stone with its mighty beak. To honour this thing that didn't happen, the Stone is coddled in white velvet, denoting its status as a sacred object. More recently, in 1531, Junior Archivist Neema Kraa used the Stone to condemn an innocent girl to unspeakable suffering and death. As punishment, the Stone cursed the young scholar to a sad, lonely life poisoned by shame and regret."

The insults bounced off Neema like hailstones. "You're just annoyed because you did that big, dramatic 'see you in the next life' bit last night, and now here we are again, five minutes later."

Cain grinned, before he could stop himself. "I am annoyed about that," he admitted. "I'd been saving it for ages."

"You walked off into the shadows really well," Neema said, graciously. "Did *you* do it?" That silent tread.

"Now why would I kill Gaida?"

Neema looked at him. Wasn't it obvious? "To frame Ruko."

Cain blinked.

No one else would have read anything into it—not even Shal Worthy with his Houndsight. People blink. But Neema knew Cain better than she knew herself. That blink meant he didn't know about the dagger. Which meant he wasn't the killer.

Unless he'd blinked on purpose, to make it look like he didn't know anything. In which case, he was the killer.

Neema rubbed the knot in her collarbone. "Gaida was stabbed with the Blade of Peace."

"Fuck." That *sounded* genuine, but he was a good actor. She watched him work through the implications. "*When the Tiger's eye weeps blood, then shall the Eight Return...*"

"You don't believe that."

"No, but they do," he said, indicating the private chambers. Vabras and the emperor were men of unshakeable faith. "They're *still* talking."

They were. Vabras would be annoyed. His beloved schedule.

Cain ventured closer to the door.

"You can't eavesdrop on the emperor," Neema said.

Cain did a headstand against the door. No law against that. Not his fault if he accidentally overheard something. "They're talking about me," he said, upside down. "How incandescently marvellous I am. Favourite contender…legend in the bedroom…"

"I need to tell you something."

"Did I make a factual error about the inkstone?"

"Yes."

It's not easy to laugh upside down, but Cain managed it.

"You know how it is for me," Neema said, plaintively. "Like an itch. If I don't scratch it, it just gets worse. I'll blurt it out at some inappropriate moment."

"I *love* inappropriate moments. They're my favourite moments." His face was turning pink, the blood rushing to his head. "Go on then, go on."

Neema visibly relaxed. "Yasthala carved the inkstone in the last year of the old calendar, not the year zero. It's Mordir's fault—he wrote a poem about it and needed a rhyme for hero."

Cain's tunic had dropped down, showing a flash of smooth, etched stomach. "And the part about your grim, meaningless existence? Was that factually accurate?"

Neema folded her arms. "Scholars remain divided. What are they actually talking about?"

"Too quiet." He listened harder. "They've stopped." Cain flipped back on to his feet as an elderly servant opened the door. Neema watched her make the same mental calculations she often made herself, with Cain: was it worth the effort of protesting? Answer: almost never.

"His Majesty will see you now," she said, instead. And then, pointedly, "No acrobatics in the private chambers."

"Noted," Cain said.

CHAPTER
Sixteen

THE EMPEROR WAS perched on an embroidered couch, drinking tea from a porcelain cup. It didn't suit him, or his mood. A rocky ledge would have been better, in a thunderstorm.

Hurun-tooth lay on a low, gilded table in front of him. The most dangerous weapon in existence—if you believed in curses. The blade had been wiped clean.

The door servant ushered them through. "Contender Ballari. Citizen Kraa. Prostrate yourselves," she said, then gestured to the floor in case they did not know where it was.

Lying there on her stomach, next to Cain, Neema realised she was lying in roughly the same position she had found Gaida. She couldn't have fallen like that, it wasn't natural. Her killer must have arranged her that way. Neema felt a twinge in the middle of her spine, where the blade should be.

Gaida had looked peaceful. How could she look peaceful, with a knife in her back? Had the killer arranged her expression, too? Was that even possible?

The servant droned the usual formalities over their heads. Bersun had toyed with abandoning this tedious protocol when he first took power. In more recent years he had come to appreciate its purpose, though he used it sparingly. No one else in Orrun could demand full prostration. If he wished, the emperor might hold them there for hours, face to the floor. Or not. His exercise of that choice was as much a sign of his power as the iron band he wore as a crown.

Neema, exhausted, was in danger of drifting off. The silk rug she was lying on was very soft, and smelled powerfully of the imperial scent. Frankincense…patchouli…She was sliding towards sleep when an image of Gaida slammed into her mind. The fly on the wound, the sucking sound of the blade. Acid bile rose again in her throat. She swallowed it down.

"…rise and hail His Majesty, Bersun the Second."

Cain and Neema got back up and recited their line in unison. "See How Orrun is Restored in His—"

"Murdered," Bersun spat, cutting them off. "On my watch." The tea sloshed in his hand, scalding his fingers. Furious, he threw the cup at the wall.

Poor cup, Neema thought, as it smashed against a tapestry. Now someone would have to make a new one, and someone else would have to soak the tea out of the tapestry, a portrait of the Guardians in a tree, which had never made much sense to her. What were they doing in there? The Ox looked especially uncomfortable. This was probably not what she should be focusing on.

Sweat poured down her back, sticking her overalls to her skin. The room was stifling, the air laden with a haze of moisture. Usually the doors would be open on to the courtyard with its cooling fountains and sweet birdsong. Today they were barred and guarded. There was a killer at large on the island. The emperor must be protected, even if that left him sweating. No clockwork fans in the eighth palace—they would ruin the painted ceilings. He could use a hand fan, but that would look preposterous, a little fan in his giant paw. Bersun had always struggled with scale in these dainty, elegant rooms, like an adult in a child's playhouse.

He gestured to the Blade of Peace, looked pointedly at Cain. "Someone stole that from Contender Valit's quarters."

"An outrage," Cain murmured. "Do we know how it was stolen, your majesty? I thought Contender Valit was supposed to carry it on his person at all times?"

A good point. Neema turned, and gave him an appraising look.

"Not just a devastatingly handsome face," Cain said. And then, slyly, "Perhaps it *wasn't* stolen."

Bersun considered this, frowning. "Why the Eight would he kill Contender Rack?" *He*. Ruko Valit. The boy.

"Yes, that would be out of character," Cain conceded. "Ruko would never kill a young woman—a sister for example—just to clear his path to the throne. That is something he has categorically never done. Killed his own sister."

Bersun shot him a warning look. "High Scholar. What are your thoughts on this?"

A correcting murmur from Hol Vabras, in the shadows. "Citizen Kraa, your majesty."

Bersun grunted, and inspected Neema properly for the first time. Was there a flicker of regret, for how he had treated her last night? "What is this, a new fashion?"

Neema looked down at her gardening overalls, her clumpy boots. "Travel clothes, your majesty." She shifted, bunched her fists anxiously, then opened them again.

The emperor had spent enough time in her company to recognise the sign. More bad news. "Go on. Spit it out."

She took a breath, preparing herself. "I was poisoned last night."

"Poisoned?" The emperor sat up in alarm.

Touched by his concern, she lifted a hand to reassure him—*I'm fine.* "My bath oil was spiked with Dragonscale. It's a very rare, potent drug, extracted from—"

"We know of it," the emperor stopped her. He looked stricken.

Vabras, true to form, showed no feeling on the matter. But a very close observer—Shal Worthy, perhaps—might have noticed a moment's absence, a retreat within himself as he processed the information. "You think you may have killed her under its influence."

Neema lifted her chin. "I fear it's a possibility, High Commander."

"Fuck the Eight," Cain muttered to himself.

"Contender Rack chose to sleep with her shutters open last night," Neema said, to Vabras. She had prepared this speech for his benefit. Vabras expected information to be served to him like a lean piece of meat—no fat, no gristle, no garnish. "When I returned to my rooms at two thirty they were still open. When I found her this morning, they were closed. She could have shut them herself, but given the deliberate positioning of the body, it seems more likely that the killer pulled them closed before leaving via the balcony. Considering this, and the condition of the body, I believe that Contender Rack was stabbed well before dawn."

Vabras nodded for her to continue.

Neema steeled herself. "I have no memory of those hours."

"Because you were knocked out cold!" Cain burst in. "A high dose of Dragonscale—"

"Do we know it was a high dose?" Vabras asked, sharply.

Cain didn't answer, because he wasn't supposed to know.

"So," Vabras said, to Neema. "You could have killed Gaida in a trance state."

"Yes."

"Because she humiliated you at the opening ceremony."

"Yes." And because of Yaan Rack's folder—but she kept that to herself.

"You're not a killer, Neema," the emperor said, gently.

Tears flooded her eyes. "I hope not. But I was drugged, I was upset...Her apartment is directly above my own...If *I'm* not sure—what about the rest of the court? How soon before I'm judged and found guilty—with or without proof?"

"There will be a formal investigation," Vabras said.

"But how long will that take?" She crossed her arms in a quick Raven salute, to show she meant no disrespect. "The Festival is about to begin, you have a thousand calls upon your time. Can you even spare a senior officer to investigate?"

"What is it you ask of us?" the emperor said. But he had already guessed. He was a shrewd man.

"Your majesty." Neema dropped to her knees. "Let me lead the inquiry."

"Fuck the Eight," Cain muttered again.

"You know how persistent I am once I have a task in hand. No one needs to find Gaida's killer more than I do. I can't live with this hanging over my head. I *have* to prove my innocence—to myself as much as anyone."

The emperor remained silent, undecided.

She tried again. "Your majesty, the last boat has already left—I can't go anywhere. Give me these eight days of the Festival. You have my word—I will find Gaida's killer for you."

"And if the evidence points in your direction?" Vabras asked.

"Then I shall accept my punishment. I am a Raven. We live and die by the law."

There was a pause, while the emperor considered the implications. A fresh cup of tea had appeared in his enormous fist. He blew on the surface, then drank. "You have four days. Keep the High Commander informed of your findings." He jerked his chin. *Up.*

Neema rose and gave a deep Raven's salute. "Thank you, your majesty." Four days should be plenty of time—which was why she'd asked for eight. The emperor had a habit of halving the time his courtiers asked for. His legendary impatience.

"She will need an imperial pass," he said.

Vabras nodded—it would be done. The pass would give Neema the authority to go wherever she pleased within the palaces, and interview whoever she wished.

The emperor offered Neema a smile. It was small and brief, but she could see the apology in it, for the opening ceremony. "You will find our killer, Neema, I have no doubt. You will assist her, Ballari."

Cain was dumbfounded. "Your majesty—I can't spare the time. I'm fighting for the throne—"

"An emperor never has time. This will be a good lesson for you." Another, less friendly smile.

"What about Contender Worthy—he's used to this kind of work. Or Ruko Valit. The Blade is his responsibility, surely—"

"You question the emperor's wisdom?" Vabras murmured.

Cain skidded to a halt. Some borders were too dangerous to cross, even for a Fox.

Neema, meanwhile, was contemplating the Blade of Peace, lying on the low table in front of her. Start with the weapon. Even displayed on an ornate silver tray, it looked ordinary. And Gaida's death proved it wasn't cursed. Only its provenance gave it power—

handed down from warrior to warrior. This might be the first time it had left the Tigers' possession since Yasthala had handed it to them. She was struggling to think of a reason why Ruko would part with it.

So had he killed Gaida? Was it as simple as that? If Gaida had discovered something damaging about the Tiger warrior, and confronted him about it, just as she had confronted Neema last night…Gaida was certainly fearless enough to challenge anyone if she thought she was in the right. And Gaida *always* thought she was in the right.

But even so, Ruko wouldn't be reckless enough to use *the Blade of Peace* to kill her. And he certainly wouldn't leave it behind for someone to find.

A clumsy attempt to frame him, then.

A clumsy attempt by someone subtle enough to steal the dagger from Ruko's side in the first place. Someone who didn't believe in curses, or prophecies, or vengeful Guardians. Someone who would very much like to knock Ruko off his stride. Someone exactly like the man standing right next to her.

Would Cain really kill Gaida just to throw suspicion on a rival?

The truth was, Neema didn't know what Cain was capable of any more. An imperial assassin, competing for the throne—what would he *not* do?

Another thought came to her, one she should have considered from the start. "Are we sure it's the real Blade?"

"Yes," Bersun said, and then, to Vabras: "Show them."

Vabras picked up the knife and placed the blade into the flame of the nearest candle. The flame hissed and spat in protest, before turning an eerie shade of sea-green, and then—even more disturbing—a deep indigo.

"Cursed by the Raven empress, to the end of the world," Bersun said, his voice lowered in awe.

Cain shot Neema a dubious look. Cain did not believe in magic. He believed in trickery, and fakery, and deception.

Vabras withdrew the blade from the flame and touched his finger against the steel. Cold. He placed the knife back on the table.

"The Tigers have confirmed it was stolen," Bersun said. He lifted a craggy eyebrow. "I suppose we must believe them. I suggest you begin there. Find the thief, find the killer."

"What will happen to it now?" Neema asked.

"*The boy* has demanded its return. Insolent brat. If he's careless enough to lose it, he does not deserve to hold it. We shall keep it in our possession until the Festival is done."

Vabras inclined his head in approval.

"Now," Bersun said. His mood had improved dramatically. "To the matter at hand."

Neema frowned, puzzled. There was another matter?

"We need a new Raven contender." Bersun slung his empty cup at a servant and said, to Cain, "You designed this morning's Trial, I hear."

As the Fox contender, Cain could not take part in the First Trial, but he could organise it. He spread his arms like a carnival showman. "A bespoke experience, tailored to each contender's personal history and character."

Neema's brain whirred ahead. Cain would have to adapt the Trial to suit Gaida's replacement. Neema could help him with that—she knew all the potential candidates.

"Well," Bersun said. "It's lucky you're adaptable, Ballari. I'm sure you'll find a way to test Contender Kraa as hard as the rest of them."

Contender Kraa. Cain laughed.

The emperor did not. "Vabras—the colours."

Vabras pulled out the purple armband he'd removed from Gaida's corpse and scraped off a patch of dried blood with his thumbnail.

"You're not serious." Cain looked from Vabras, to the emperor, to Neema, searching for someone to assure him that this was a joke. A very stupid, not even remotely funny joke.

Neema couldn't speak. Everything was happening too fast. She watched, dazed, as Vabras handed the Raven colours to the emperor.

"She's not a contender," Cain said.

Neema found her voice. "He's right. I'm not...I can't."

"She's a scholar," Cain said. "She sits down for a living. She's a *scholar*," he repeated.

"My High Scholar," Bersun corrected, neatly forgetting that he'd dismissed Neema from his service the night before. "And one of the most talented people I've ever met. She will do her Flock proud, I have no doubt."

Neema couldn't take it in. This wasn't happening. It didn't make any sense. Even if she *were* contender material, it wasn't the emperor's place to decide. Only the Ravens had the power to choose Gaida's replacement. "I don't...How..."

"*Laws of the Festival*," Vabras said. ""In the event of a contender's death by foul play, the head of the relevant contingent is responsible for selecting a replacement.""

"*Kindry* chose me?"

"Lord Kindry," Vabras said in a voice so dry it was a wonder his tongue didn't crumble to dust. "Eternal."

So that was it. After years of petitioning, they'd given Kindry the one thing he coveted above all else. Not just a title, but an hereditary one. They'd say it was for his years of service, but clearly it was the only way they could persuade him to select Neema as Gaida's replacement. But why the Eight would they do that? Bersun loathed hereditary titles—he would have abolished them the moment he'd taken the throne, if they hadn't been etched into Yasthala's Truce. Now here he was casually handing one out to Kindry, simply to ensure Neema's place in the contender line. It was more than puzzling, more than out of character. It was unethical. An emperor must play no part in choosing his successor. That was the whole point of Yasthala's Five Rules.

The only thing that saved it was the fact that Neema stood no chance of winning.

"Your majesty, I thank you profoundly for this honour, but I must decline it. I have to focus on Gaida's murder. Four days will be plenty, but not if I'm forced to divide my time—"

"If four days are plenty, why did you ask for eight?" The emperor was amused. "They double their estimates and think I won't notice," he said, to Vabras. "Four days will indeed be plenty. I have every faith in you, Neema Kraa. My most loyal and capable servant." He regarded her fondly.

Neema's heart sank. It was like Fenn always said. *Make yourself useful, and you're going to get used.* "But I don't want to be a contender," she said, miserable. "I don't want the throne."

"Exactly," Bersun wagged his finger at her. "I said the same to Brother Lanrik, when he made me his contender. Those exact words. *I do not want the throne.* D'you know what he said to me, in reply? He said: *Brother—that is why I have chosen you. The throne is a burden to be carried, not a prize to be won.*"

"But—"

"Enough," he said, amiably. The emperor had a thousand ways of saying "enough," but whatever the tone, every courtier knew that it was a final warning. Any further argument, and Neema would be facing a stint in the imperial dungeons. Which might be preferable, if she didn't have a murder to solve.

Bersun lumbered to his feet, holding the purple band in both hands.

Neema stepped forward. What choice did she have?

He wrapped the band around her arm, making sure the black wings of the Raven sigil were visible and centred. "The blood's hidden," he assured her, as he tied the knot.

But it's still there.

"The nice thing," Cain said, folding his arms, "is that this is very much what Gaida would have wanted."

CHAPTER
Seventeen

Fenn was hanging back in the waiting room when they emerged, a large cedarwood box tucked under his arm. Cain skirted past him—off to tell his abbot the news, and work out a new strategy. He was furious about everything, but would never show it. All Fenn saw of the Fox contender was a wide, dangerous grin—and he was gone.

Fenn laid the box carefully on top of the display case. The lid was inlaid with a large ∞ picked out in bronze. Neema had seen it before—she knew what lay inside. Fenn took out a key, and unlocked it.

"Don't," she blurted. Once he opened that box, it was over, it was real. She put a hand on the lid. "I need a moment."

This was Fenn's uniform, from the previous Festival. Barely twenty-two years old, when he competed for the throne. Too young, really—another five years of training and he might have won. If Empress Haven had not fallen sick and abdicated sooner than expected, Fenn might have been ruler of Orrun. Instead—as the bronze ∞ denoted—he had come third, behind Bersun for the Bears, and Andren Valit for the Tigers. Quite a long way behind, to be honest. But still, it had been the best result for an Ox contender in over two centuries.

Fenn was a legend, in his understated way. The thought of wearing his uniform filled Neema with a kind of anticipatory shame. She wasn't a warrior, she wasn't a contender. Humiliation was guaranteed. Humiliation while dressed in an Ox hero's uniform would be even worse.

"Does this make *any* sense to you?" she asked him.

Fenn snorted at the general concept of things making sense. Had she not lived thirty-four years in this ludicrous world? "Could have been worse. Kindry wanted you to wear Gaida's uniform, as a tribute. Not the spare, you understand. The one she was stabbed in."

"Eight," Neema muttered, and then, after a valiant fight, "Sorry, but it's actually *Lord* Kindry, now."

Fenn gave her a tired look. "Just make the noise, Neema."

"The noise" was the sound she always made, when she was given a task she didn't want, didn't think she was up to, but had to accept. A long, defeated sigh, ending in an irritable growl. Fenn had heard it a lot.

"Haaahhahhhurrghhh," she said, and removed her hand from the lid.

Fenn opened the box. The uniform was wrapped in tissue paper, sealed with bronze wax. "Haven't taken this out for a while," he said, breaking the seal.

They stared together at the uniform, the tunic folded to best display the wide curved horns of the Ox sigil. Even Fenn seemed subdued, remembering his younger self, and what he might have been. Then he sniffed. "Yeah, I'd have hated it. Go on."

Neema lifted out the black silk tunic and trousers and crossed to an embroidered screen to change. It hadn't been there earlier —Fenn must have set it up. Behind the screen she found a pair of black canvas martial shoes, a needle and thread, and a black patch to cover the Ox sigil. He thought of everything, the High Engineer. Anticipation was half the battle, when you had as many responsibilities as he did.

She held the trousers to her hips. "I'll need to dart the waistband," she called over the screen, then set to work.

While he waited, Fenn talked her through the day's schedule. Essentially it hadn't changed, except that the breaks were shorter, to make up for the late start. Morning fights on the parade ground. A brief stop for lunch followed by the first Trial, which would take place in the imperial vaults, bordering the Fox palace. After the Trial—which was expected to take about two hours "but you know Foxes and time-keeping"—another, shorter break. Then back to the parade ground for the afternoon fights.

"You've missed the bit where I solve Gaida's murder," Neema said, tying off the stitches. "When am I supposed to do that?"

"You could interrogate me now," Fenn suggested.

She pulled on the trousers, poked her head around the screen. "Why would I interrogate you?"

"I was at the Raven palace last night. You waved. I waved. Remember?"

She remembered. She could see him now, smoking on a bench in the dark. "Why would you kill her, though?"

"I wouldn't." He slapped imaginary dust from his palms. "There you go. One suspect out of the way."

She retreated behind the screen and placed the black patch over the Ox sigil. She would try to keep the stitches light. Contender uniforms were treasured artefacts. Fenn wouldn't care if she damaged it, but his children might. "So what *were* you doing, then?"

"Hiding."

"From?"

"Everyone." He mimicked a trio of courtiers. "'Fenn—the algae's spreading in the Grand Canal.' 'Fenn—the hinges on the Guardian Gate need oiling.' 'Fenn, there's an emergency—Lady Harmony needs you to build her a new gazebo.'"

"No one asks for a gazebo in the middle of the night."

"Oh, do they not?" he asked sarcastically, because they very much did.

"You weren't hiding," Neema decided. "Even I noticed you sitting there, and I was..." she searched for the right word to describe her semi-delirious state.

"Mangled," Fenn suggested for her, and then, as if she'd twisted his arm, "All right, fine—I was waiting for you." He lowered his voice. The emperor was still in his rooms, with Vabras. "He shouldn't have lost his temper with you at the ceremony. So, you made a mistake and we all had to listen to a sad song about a mountain. That's no reason to *destroy* you, in front of the whole court. For fuck's sake. I came to tell you that, before you left. Share a spliff, say goodbye. Then you walked through a hedge with a lizard on your shoulder and I thought, maybe I'll write a letter." He gave a rumbling laugh.

Neema was touched, but too awkward to say so. She put on the tunic. "Did you see anyone else while you were waiting?"

"Nope. No one. Just you." He put a hand over his mouth, to cover his smile. Neema had emerged from behind the screen, looking hilarious. She was only a couple of inches shorter than him, but Fenn was a big man, packed with a lot of muscle. The trousers looked more like a skirt, there was so much extra material. The tunic sloped off one shoulder, and swung loosely about her thighs.

She made a helpless gesture, that made it even funnier. "For Eight's sake, Fenn. This is madness."

"You'll have your own set by tomorrow. Ask me another question, that'll make you feel better." Ravens and their questions.

"How long were you sitting in the garden?" He would have had a prime view of Gaida's apartment from his bench. And her own, for that matter.

"Hard to say." Fenn brought an imaginary spliff to his lips, in explanation.

"Roughly, then."

He moved his hand back and forth, the spliff still in his fingers. "An hour and a half? You and the hedge were maybe the halfway point."

"Did you see anyone close Gaida's shutters? Any movement at all?" *Did you see me?*

"Nothing. Damn." A thought had struck him. "Were they waiting for me to leave so they could kill her?" He winced at the thought. "Poor Gaida."

Neema pulled her tunic back on to her shoulder. It slid off the other side. "How am I supposed to fight in this? How am I supposed to fight in *anything*? I'm not a warrior, Fenn. Not even close. I was going to spend the Festival researching seventh-century prison ballads." She gave him a beseeching look, as if he could cast a spell and make that still happen.

"Well you're in luck with today's fight," he said, instead. "Shal won't hurt you if he can avoid it. Hound Code of Ethics. No honour in injuring someone weaker than you."

"I'm fighting Shal Worthy?" Neema squeaked, in a tiny voice.

"Yes, you're fighting Shal Worthy," Fenn squeaked in reply, amusing himself. "This afternoon. For now, we just have to get you to the square. Come on. You don't want to hold up the Festival."

Yes I do, Neema thought. I really, really do.

It wasn't a long walk to the parade ground, but it *felt* long. The first day of the Festival was running two hours late. Of the sixteen hundred courtiers who'd come to watch the fights, more than half had abandoned their seats to cool off inside. They gathered in clusters, talking about Gaida, and how terrible it was. Shocking. The fact that the killer had used the Blade of Peace was being kept quiet from the general court—Vabras had seen to that, no need to start a panic. But the murder of a contender was more than enough to frighten the superstitious. Would the Second Guardian seek retribution? The Raven had keen eyes and a long memory. It held grudges.

In this febrile atmosphere, the vision of Neema Kraa hurrying through the imperial palace dressed in black triggered shock and disbelief, followed swiftly by outrage. What was this—a tasteless joke? Last night's disgraced High Scholar, elevated to contender? Impossible. People turned to their Raven friends for explanation, but they were equally confused. "She can't be," a senior lawyer said, emphatically. People began to jostle and shove to get a better view.

"Keep moving," Fenn said, touching his hand to the small of Neema's back. He knew how these things could turn.

Outside, he waved down a couple of Hounds to take her the rest of the way. Other duties called. "I'll meet you at the armoury after the Fox Trial."

"The armoury?"

"You need to choose your weapons."

"Weapons? I thought we just…" Neema moved her hands in a chopping motion.

Fenn scrunched his face. "What? Massaged each other to death?"
The Hounds exchanged amused glances.

"Yasthala's rules," Fenn reminded her. "Three rounds, the second
with weapons." He gave her a pointed look. "Your idea, Neema.
More authentic, you said."

He was right. She had suggested it. Back when she thought she'd
be safely squirrelled away in the library. Back when the idea of Gaida
having to fight had filled her with secret glee. "I'm going to die."

"You're not going to die."

"I'M GOING TO DIE."

"Just yell stop," Fenn said. He was used to dealing with melt-
downs; they happened a lot at court, and to be fair to Neema, over
much pettier problems. "You know this."

She did know this. It was one of the few alterations the committee had made to the original Festival. Back in Yasthala's day,
the contenders were expected to fight to the death, should it come
to that. Over time, the weapons round had disappeared, and formal rules and restrictions had been added, to reduce the risk of
serious injury. Now those rules and restrictions had been removed,
and the weapons were back. The fights would be bloodier than
they had been for centuries. After protests from some of the contingents, the Festival committee had created one safety net. Call
stop, and the fight was over. The contender would lose the fight
instantly, and would be penalised half a point. Not to mention the
huge loss of face, and an embarrassing note in the official History
of the Festival. But no one had to die out on the platform, if they
were prepared to swallow their pride.

"You can shout stop the moment they ring the bell, if you want,"
Fenn pointed out.

"I can't do that. People will laugh."

"Neema, listen to me for a moment, this is serious. No matter
what you do, no matter what you say..." Fenn reached out and
straightened her flappy, over-sized tunic. "They are going to *piss*
themselves."

∞ ∞ ∞

The parade ground. A vast, featureless cobbled square covering the space between the Dragon palace and the Grand Canal. A barren place, scorched in summer, bleak in winter. Courtiers rarely cross it; they skirt the edges, though it takes longer. Too exposed. Only the Hounds use it, for their daily drills. Stamp, stamp, turn, stamp, stamp, halt—all that business. Very neat, they are, very sharp. During the purges, the parade ground doubled up as a place of execution. Yaan Rack died here, a quarter hour kicking his heels upon the rope, eyes bulging, tongue turning blue.

Now it is transformed into the Festival Square.

The best place to view this miracle is from the imperial balcony, on the fourth floor of the Dragon palace. Well *of course* the emperor is granted the best view. So do come and join us—yes, hello, we are here, perched on the balustrade, biding our time and being magnificent.

Look down, if you will, and marvel at the spectacle. What was grey and desolate is filled with noise and colour. Wooden stalls rise up on three sides of the square, brightly painted with Guardian sigils. Long, padded benches for the comfort of our noble spectators. Vendors move up and down the aisles, offering sweet and salty snacks in paper cones, drinks and fans and ribbons on sticks, for some reason people love the ribbons on sticks. They are finding their seats again, called back by a blare of trumpets. Courtiers, honoured guests and contingent members pack the galleries, row upon row, shouting over each other to be heard.

On the remaining north side of the square lies the contenders' pavilion—a glamorous black silk extravagance with carved mahogany props. It is filled with all manner of luxuries and refreshments, most of which the contenders will not touch. A tent with some iced water would have sufficed, but this is the Festival of the Eight, and in a few days one of these warriors will be emperor, or empress.

Close to the pavilion, and equally well stocked—a white canvas medical tent. Pristine, for now.

And finally, taking centre stage and the reason everyone is gathered here: the raised fight platform. From this imperial vantage point, you can clearly see the giant, golden ∞ on the canvas.

Look closer and you will also make out Ish Fort, Abbot of Anat-russir, testing the side ropes. A notably seedy old white man, he has made no effort to clean himself up, even though the honour of opening the Festival belongs to him. His orange robes resemble a tatty old dressing gown, rope tied loosely over his pot belly. His white hair, lank with grease, has a yellowish tinge, his cheeks are unshaven. He looks, in fact, as though he has been plucked at random from the floor of the cheapest tavern in Armas, and prodded out here by mistake. But appearances, with Foxes, can be deceptive. Still chatting with his assistant, Fort jumps nimbly on to a corner post and balances there, continuing his conversation as he rope-walks his way around the platform.

As he does this, there is a second blare of horns and the contenders emerge from their pavilion and line up in Guardian order. Over there to your right, look. Six warriors dressed in black, you can just make them out. Shal Worthy at the far end. For once, the Hound contender's innate elegance has escaped him. He is not well this morning; were it not for his training he would be languishing in the medical tent. There is a silver bucket at his feet, he looks as if he might need to use it again shortly.

Next in line comes Havoc Arbell-Ranor for the Monkeys, legs wide as if he were at the prow of his Leviathan, sailing to victory. Katsan Brundt, the Bear contender, stands sentinel beside him, hands clasped behind her back. Two things we can guess—that Gaida's murder will have cut her deep, and that Neema's elevation will have only added to her anger and her grief. But she gives nothing away, eyes fixed on mid-distance, locked up in the prison of her own discipline.

Tala Talaka, in contrast, is beaming up at the crowds, drawing energy from them. She has spoken passionately and openly of her ambition to modernise the court, to dismantle the system of privileges and favours upon which so much of the imperial island is run. This would make her unpopular if people thought she might win. Given the strength of her rivals, the court is free to find the young contender's views *refreshing* and *thought-provoking*.

Ruko takes nothing from the crowds. He does not want their energy, or need it. A Tiger draws his power from within. He stands alone, beautiful and terrible. The voice he carries inside him—the voice he has become—tells him all he needs to know. I will win. I will rule.

Next to him a space, where Gaida should be.

And finally Cain. Can you see the difference in his imperial silk uniform, the way it drapes across his lean but martial frame? So subtle, the quality it gives him, the hidden confidence. His clear green eyes sweep the packed-out stalls—once a spy, always a spy—then snag on a solitary figure dressed in black, entering the square from the south-east corner.

Neema. She is here. Let us join her.

∞ ∞ ∞

Neema had never felt so exposed as she stepped into the square. Alone: abandoned by her Hound escorts. Everywhere she looked, from the coveted front benches to the highest row, she was met with anger and disapproval. Folded arms, curled lips. Someone in the western stalls set off a wave of booing that moved through the square, until the Hounds barked orders for them to stop.

The Raven contingent was huddled together, dressed in matching purple uniforms. They watched her approach with sullen, tear-streaked faces. Clearly, Kindry hadn't told them of the deal he'd struck with the emperor. They thought she'd orchestrated this herself—that she actually wanted this. She had to bite back a laugh, it was so preposterous. This wasn't her dream, it was her nightmare.

Janric, her old assistant, stepped out to confront her. Like the rest of them, he wore a grey mourning patch over his heart, for Gaida. For added impact, he'd wrapped a silver-grey headscarf over his braids. Nothing said grief like a fancy headscarf. "Shame on you," he spat. "You will *never* be my contender."

Neema kept her eyes and her voice level. "Then I dismiss you from my contingent."

Janric looked stricken. His parents had paid a fortune to see his name added to the official History of the Festival. His contingent uniform alone had cost five gold tiles. But more than the money, it was the loss of privilege and prestige that pained him. The front row seats, the access to the contenders' pavilion. The swaggering. "You can't—"

"But she can," Kindry interrupted him, smoothly. "Neema Kraa is our contender now. Painful as that may be." He patted the mourning patch that covered his heart.

There was a long, awkward pause as Janric waited for someone to speak up in his defence. When no support came he stalked off without a word, fists bunched.

"Thank you," Neema said.

Kindry gave a shallow bow and spoke not to her, but to the contingent. "It is our duty to support our contender, whatever reservations we may have," he reminded them. He let his eyes trail slowly down Neema's baggy uniform. "Let us pray she does not disgrace the Raven with her performance."

Neema felt a swell of rebellion. Fine, she was no contender— they could all agree on that. But she would do her best. She would not shame the Flock.

Kindry took out a fan and flapped it in front of his face. "I hear you've put yourself in charge of the investigation. Do you not worry there's a conflict of interest, given your ..." flap, flap, flap, "*history* with Gaida?"

"The emperor isn't worried," Neema replied, neatly.

"Yes." Kindry closed his fan with a snap. "I wonder if his majesty's indulgence will last the Festival?" He leaned forward, lowering his voice. "I wouldn't count on it, my dear."

Neema whispered back, in his ear. "I'm not your dear."

They both drew back, smiling matching fake smiles.

"Very true," Kindry murmured. "Absolutely true."

Eighteen

CROSSING THE SQUARE ALONE, Neema took her position in the contender line between Cain and Ruko. Only Tala acknowledged her as she arrived—a brief, encouraging smile, a flash of gold tooth. The rest kept their gaze turned resolutely forward.

Now that Neema was in place, the Day of the Fox could begin.

A final blare of trumpets as the emperor stepped out on to the balcony, surrounded by his household and high ministers. Princess Yasila was the last to emerge, veiled and glittering. She made a point of standing as far away from the emperor as possible. Neema touched her throat, remembering the terrible trick the princess had played on her last night.

It struck her that Yasila had a very strong motive to frame her son for murder. Not only that, Neema had seen her at the Raven palace only a few hours before Gaida's death. That didn't feel like a coincidence, given how rarely Yasila left her apartment.

"You are right to fear my mother," Ruko said, under his breath. "You think she—"

"Later," Ruko said, in a finishing tone.

Abbot Fort's voice carried across the square. "Friends. Enemies. Welcome! Before we begin, let us take a moment to remember our fallen contender, Gaida Rack. May the Eight bless her next journey upon the Eternal Path."

"And remain Hidden," people murmured, bowing their heads.

After a respectful pause, the abbot continued. "Seven contenders stand waiting.".

The audience stirred in anticipation. These were Yasthala's words, used to begin every Festival.

"The Festival demands an eighth warrior to complete the line."
The abbot turned a slow circle, taking in the crowds. "Who here
among us will join them?"

Everyone looked round eagerly, up and down the rows. Dragons
did not compete for the throne, but the fights required an even
number of participants. Tradition demanded they provide a proxy
to fight in their name, their identity kept secret until this moment.
It was customary for the other seven monasteries to suggest suitable candidates from their ranks—a promising young student or
an older, seasoned warrior. In this way, while the Dragons made
the selection, the proxy represented all those who had missed the
chance to be a true contender.

The Revelation of the Dragon Proxy was a highlight of
every Festival. There were several potential candidates sitting
in the stalls this morning. Everyone enjoyed the moment when
the proxy stood up, especially those who had placed a quiet bet
on the most likely choice.

As the spectators craned their necks to search among their
ranks, a short, grey-haired white man entered the square from
the south-eastern corner. Those who noticed his arrival dismissed
him—his slender frame, his plain travel clothes, his unassuming
demeanour. They looked elsewhere as he moved through the
shadows cast by the eastern stalls. Only as he stepped out into
the light did people start to point, and call out. Wait. That can't
be him. Is that him?

A cheer went up, turning quickly to dismay as he kept on walking. He was supposed to smile and wave to the crowds. They had
their ribbons on sticks, ready to wave back. If he sensed their consternation, it did not trouble him. The crowds, the fight platform,
the Fox abbot, the emperor. These things were of no interest. He
walked towards the line of contenders like the tide coming in;
flowing, inevitable.

"A Dragon," Neema said, as the crowds fell into silence. Everyone
saw it now. Only the Dragons of Helia moved with such distinctive,
snaking grace: hypnotic in its beauty, unsettling in its hidden power.
Only the Dragons of Helia, and Yasila, who escaped them.

For the first time in fifteen centuries, they had sent one of their own to fight.

Ruko shifted at Neema's side and said, under his breath, "Visitor."

"No," Neema said, because that was unthinkable.

"That is Visitor Pyke." Ruko kept his eyes fixed on the man gliding towards them. "We have met before."

The words of an old folk song came to Neema's mind.

> *I saw a Visitor on the road,*
> *Down where the rivers meet*
> *He said, I have killed ten men today*
> *And need a place to sleep.*

Visitors were rare even among the Dragons: four solitary travellers who criss-crossed the empire on a singular mission. When a child was Chosen by the Dragon, and the scorched ∞ appeared on the underside of their wrist, a Visitor would arrive within hours to escort them to Helia. How they knew when and where to come was a mystery they did not share, but they were as inevitable, as inescapable as death. The Visitor came and the child was taken, never to return.

Once in a while, someone made the mistake of resisting. There were graveyards where whole families lay buried together, the same date marked upon their headstones. Parents, grandparents, children. The Visitor had the right to hunt down every single member of the family and destroy them in retribution.

How could the Dragons send a Visitor to fight as their proxy? Not only were they supremely strong and fast, but their bodies were woven with protection spells. Neema couldn't see how the Festival Laws would allow it.

The Visitor was almost upon them now. Neema found it difficult to age him. He had the tough, wiry physique of a man who walked long distances every day. His face was lined and weather-beaten, his grey hair cropped and receding. A large, dividing scar shaped like the letter Y carved through his right cheek into his beard—an old knife injury, healed to silver-white. But most striking of all were his eyes—a soft blue-grey.

Neema's mouth dropped. So this was how the Dragons had circumvented the Festival Laws. They'd stripped him of his powers.

When a Chosen child arrived on Helia they passed through an initiation ceremony, and their eyes transformed from their natural colour to a shade of amber. Lit by Dragonfire, so it was said. The greatest punishment a Dragon could face was a reversal of that ceremony; for the fire to be extinguished. Even a short period in this state was said to be agonising. Why the Eight would he submit to such torture? Why would the Dragons ask him to?

Whatever pain the Visitor was suffering, he kept it buried. Stopping a few paces from the contender line, he studied them in silence.

Katsan was the first to recover. With the blade of her hand, the Bear contender made a respectful sign of the eternal eight, warrior to warrior. "Welcome, Dragon Proxy."

"Welcome, Dragon Proxy," Shal Worthy echoed, from the end of the line, and the rest joined in the protocol.

Except for Ruko. "Visitor Pyke."

The Visitor gave a half-smile, the scar puckering on his cheek. "Sister-Killer."

"Wow," Cain breathed. The rest were too stunned to speak.

The Dragons of Helia were self-governing—they were not bound by Orrun's laws of Exile. The Visitor was free to speak as he pleased of Yanara Valit and her doomed fate. But still, the insult was a shock.

Ruko, however, seemed impervious. "I am not the child you met in Armas," he said. "If you are here to stop me, you will fail."

"I am not here to stop you, Ruko Valit," the Visitor replied. "I am here to kill you. As I should have done that night."

He walked on, and took his place at the far end of the line.

The Visitor's presence had disturbed the crowd, more even than Gaida's murder. Neema saw a woman instinctively reach for her son, pulling him close.

Through the darkening mood, the Fox abbot beckoned to a band of shaven-headed Fox novices waiting below the platform. They sprang up at once, performing an enthusiastic display of leaps and tumbles, somewhere between an improvised dance and a staged fight. Neema realised they were mimicking fox cubs, pouncing and jumping back, playful but testing. Each time she thought she saw order in their movements, they broke away into some new game, sometimes forming alliances, before flipping and turning on their partners.

"Lovely," Cain said, eyes shining with pride.

Abbot Fort clapped his hands and the students came to a tangled halt, panting and laughing. The crowd rose to applaud as they left the platform; the distraction had worked.

"My friends, my enemies," Fort said, from the platform. "The Fox—bravest and most adventurous of the Guardians—will always leap highest, and leap first. Where the Fox leads, the rest follow." He flashed a mischievous grin, as the good-natured jeers of dissent fell around him from the stalls. "And so it falls to me, Ish Fort, Fox abbot of Anat-russir, to open the Festival of the Eight." He stretched his arms wide. "It begins!"

Taking their cue, Cain and Tala set off together for the platform, waving to the crowds. Tala took a headband from her pocket and put it on without breaking stride, pushing her hair back off her face.

As they mounted the platform, Cain gave Tala an insouciant Fox salute, arms lifted out with a flourish, one leg bent behind the other. Tala responded with an Ox salute, hands clasped together, arms forming a circle.

Without warning, the abbot rang the bell, taking everyone by surprise. Except for Cain. Foxes are always ready. He was flying through the air before Tala had finished her bow, aiming to knock her off her feet.

But Tala had the sure-footed stance of an Ox. Instead of toppling her, Cain collided with an immovable object. Tala seized him by the tunic and tossed him over her shoulder like a sack of corn.

Cain somersaulted neatly and hooked his foot around her ankle. No pause to his movements, no space for her to anticipate.

Tala faltered then righted herself, and the fight began in earnest. She stayed in a high stance, fists up, feet glued to the platform. Her punches when they landed were strong, but Cain was hard to catch. He leapt and spun around her, teasing and testing for weak spots. The Fox style was an improvised style, constantly evolving and adapting to the moment.

Watching him, Neema remembered how Cain used to dodge the streetsellers of Scartown, always playful, always one fingertip out of reach. How they'd laugh even as he stole from them, because he did it with such panache. The same was true when he fought. His intent was serious, but still somehow filled with delight. Even Tala was enjoying herself. As the bell rang to end the round, she grinned at Cain, and he grinned back.

Ruko huffed in disapproval. "Who am I?" he murmured, just loud enough for Neema to catch the reference. "Who am I?" was the title of a Guardian Ballad, a nasty little song about the Fox that had been shelved for centuries.

> *I am the wedding without a bride,*
> *I am the box with nothing inside.*
> *Nobody trusts me, what do I care?*
> *Look in the mirror, I am not there.*
> *Who am I? Who am I?*
> *I am the Fox.*

"He's not as shallow as he seems," Neema muttered.

"He's an opportunist. All opportunists are shallow."

"He knows how to adapt quickly. That's not quite the same thing."

Ruko was silent for a moment. Then he nodded, accepting the point. "Interesting. Thank you."

Neema frowned to herself. She was not here to give Ruko Valit helpful insights into his rivals.

For the weapons round, Cain and Tala both chose the narrow sword. Here there was no contest. Tala parried as best she could, but Cain's years of dedicated combat training at the Fox monastery, his speed and agility, put him comfortably ahead. She survived the round without injury, but only just.

They retreated to their corners.

Tala gained some ground back in the final round—her stamina giving her an edge as Cain's pace slowed. But the fight was his, long before the bell rang. The first two points of the Festival.

When it was over they clasped hands in friendship, then stepped down from the platform together. Cain whispered something in Tala's ear. She gave him a playful punch in the arm.

"She's a good loser," Katsan noted.

Havoc agreed. "Yes, I've often observed at sea—Oxes make for poor leaders, but excellent followers."

"I dare you to say that to her face," Shal murmured.

"I meant it as a compliment—"

"Excuse me," Shal said, and threw up neatly in his silver bucket. Exquisite manners, the Hound contender.

It was time for the second fight. Dragon vs Monkey. The contenders watched with narrowed eyes as Havoc and the Visitor walked to the platform. They had spent years assessing each other's strengths and flaws in preparation for these fights. The Dragon Proxy was the wild card. But how much of a threat was he, now his powers had been torn from him?

On the platform, Havoc pressed his palms together in the Monkey salute: to the emperor, the Fox abbot, the crowd.

The Visitor stood with his arms loosely at his side, waiting.

The fight began.

Havoc was a head taller than the Visitor, and probably half his age. Within moments, he had the upper hand. He had a direct, confident style, and unlike Cain, he didn't take risks. Less surprising, more focused.

Neema recognised some of his moves—she had practised the Monkey form herself, alone in her garden. She liked the strength and balance it required, and its propulsive energy. There was no question, Havoc was a master.

The crowds watched entranced as he pushed the Dragon Proxy around the platform. *Not so special without your spells.* Everyone hated Visitors. They began to cheer, and chant Havoc's name. He grinned and pushed harder, feeding off their support.

"He's a natural," Neema said.

Cain laughed. "Natural? He's been training since he was six years old. Private tutors, sparring partners, the works. So desperate to win Mummy and Daddy's approval. And look." He lifted his chin towards two empty seats on the front row. Lady Harmony and Lord Clarion were neglecting their son again. "At least my mother had the honesty to sell me to the Scrappers. He'll spend his life trying to please them, and never—"

"*Sssssssssssss,*" Ruko hissed. His eyes had never left the platform, following every move.

Following the Visitor's moves.

Why would he care about the loser?

The Visitor sidestepped a fraction too late, allowing Havoc to knock him to the ground. He was back on his feet in a heartbeat, narrowly avoiding a punch to the throat.

Allowing. Avoiding.

Once or twice might be coincidence. But as she watched, Neema found the pattern. The Dragon Proxy took a few blows, but only the lightest ones. Anything worse he evaded by the same fraction each time.

"He's letting him win," she murmured, as the bell rang.

"First round to the Monkey contender," Ish Fort called.

"May I speak now?" Cain asked Ruko. "Oh great one?"

Ruko grunted his permission. It was unclear if he heard the irony.

"You're right," Cain said to Neema. "He's hiding his technique." The message rippled down the line, all the way to Katsan.

"Where's Shal gone?" Neema asked. The Hound contender was missing from his spot in the line.

"Food poisoning." Tala gestured to the Hound contingent, who were clustered around their contender, shielding him from view as he threw up again. "Spent the whole night being sick—and the rest." She pulled a sympathetic face. "Dodgy eel, they reckon. The Hounds have put in a formal complaint."

Neema stored the information away. She was sure Shal wasn't sick from the banquet. Chef Ganstra was a meticulous cook, and no one else had fallen ill.

Shal took a delicate sip of ginger tea, while a member of his contingent rubbed his back.

"At least that gives him an alibi for last night," Neema said to Cain, but the others caught it.

Katsan whispered something to Tala.

"I don't know." Tala called down the line. "Neema—are you investigating Gaida's murder?"

"Yes, the emperor—"

"No!" Katsan exploded.

Everyone looked taken aback, including Katsan.

Shal limped back to the line, smoothing his beard. "What's wrong, what's happened?"

"Neema's investigating Gaida's murder. Katsan's furious," Tala summarised.

"I'm not furious," Katsan said, furious.

"They're starting again," Shal said, and everyone turned their attention back to the platform.

Havoc had chosen a seven-foot staff, with a short blade at the tip.

"A pike," Tala said. "Interesting choice."

Neema bit her lip.

"Say it," Cain whispered. "Say it, say it, say it."

"Technically it's a spontoon," Neema blurted.

Cain clenched his fists in victory.

While he waited for the bell, Havoc warmed up with an impressive display, balancing and turning on the pole before leaping and slashing the air. The artists making sketches for the official History of the Festival moved round the platform, catching him from different angles. Raven historians scribbled notes. "Blue eyes flashing with imperial intent," they wrote. "Crowd enraptured."

The Visitor returned to the platform, carrying a short wooden baton. He watched Havoc for a moment, then said something.

"'Do I fight a warrior, or a clown?'" Shal said, reading the Visitor's lips.

Havoc scowled as he paced back and forth.

The bell rang.

Havoc sprang forward, spinning his staff with blurring speed. The Visitor lifted his baton, deflecting a blow that would have shattered his jaw. The move left him open. Havoc punched him hard in the stomach. The Visitor staggered back, winded.

The crowd roared, the whole square willing Havoc on. *Bring the bastard down.* The emperor leaned on the balcony for a better view.

The two men circled each other, eyes locked. Havoc swung the staff around and around, building velocity. Then without warning he swung it hard, aiming for the Visitor's right temple. If it struck, it would crack open his skull.

The Visitor dropped down.

Easy, effortless timing. One moment he was in mortal danger, the next he was sinking, back straight, one leg sliding out to the side for balance.

Havoc had thrown his full weight behind the blow. As the staff struck thin air, he stumbled forward.

The Visitor hooked his baton under Havoc's ankle and let gravity do the rest. Havoc thudded to the canvas. The Visitor pinned him on his front and lightly jabbed a series of kill points with his baton. Liver. Kidneys. Base of the neck. *See what I could do, if I thought you were worth the trouble.*

The bell rang.

The Visitor released his victim and stepped back.

He let Havoc win the third round. Everyone could see it now. It was embarrassing. The more Havoc weaved and danced, the more ridiculous he seemed. It was just a show, a stage fight, like something you'd watch at the Monkey theatre. The sketchers put down their pencils.

The bell rang for the third and final time. Abbot Fort declared Havoc the winner.

Havoc—victorious—returned to the line with his head down, to a spattering of applause. Silence, somehow, would have been less humiliating.

CHAPTER
Nineteen

L
UNCH HAD BEEN set up in the imperial menagerie—a
typically perverse decision by the Foxes. The tables were laid
with silver cutlery and embroidered napkins, and the air stank of
shit. This sort of juxtaposition delighted the followers of the First
Guardian, and annoyed everyone else. A double win.

Cain was in a playful mood. The emperor, the investigation,
Neema's elevation to contender—all had been brushed away, like
crumbs from his tunic. The Visitor was going to destroy Ruko for
him. The one serious obstacle on his path to the throne would be removed, and he wouldn't have to lift a finger. Was life not marvellous?

"How would you like to be my High Engineer?" he asked Tala,
shovelling chicken salad on to his plate. They were sitting with
Neema, next to an aviary filled with small angry parrots.

"How would you like to be mine?" Tala snapped back. She
watched the parrots clawing their way along the bars, chewing at
the locks. "When I'm empress I'm tearing this place down."

"I'm tearing everything down," Cain said.

"Good plan." Tala never bothered to hide her frustration with
the court. Too much power in too few hands, too many shady deals
and suspicious accounting. Most Oxes felt the same way. They'd
hoped things would change when Bersun came to power, and for a
while they did. But somewhere along the way the Old Bear seemed
to have given up. The rebellion, Fenn always said. Never the same
after that. Andren Valit broke his heart, or his spirit, or both.

"Fix it yourself if it's broken." An Ox motto. Tala had the energy
and confidence to mend things, Neema was sure of that. Part-
ly her youth, but mostly her nature. Taking inspiration from her

Guardian, Tala could plough her way through any problem, dragging everyone along with her. Head down, feet planted, day in, day out. She would *toil* for her empire.

And a Fox might be a good adviser for an Ox empress. The problem with ploughing along in straight lines is, you don't always see what's coming at you from your flank. A Fox saw things differently. Nose and whiskers in the air, constantly on the lookout for trouble, for adventure, for change.

The partnership *could* work, Neema thought, except for one problem. Tala and Cain were talking at cross purposes. When Cain said he wanted to tear down everything, Tala thought he meant the court. But he didn't. He meant *everything*.

It didn't occur to Neema to imagine what she would do, if she won. Kindry's words had sunk deep. She would do her best in the Trials, if only to prove him and the wider Raven community wrong. She would not be an embarrassment to the Flock, or to Gaida's memory—she would not let them write that version of history. But nor was she deluded. She knew she was not a real contender. Of course she wasn't. The rest of them had trained and fought for years—they were the best of the best of the best. She couldn't hope to match them.

Cain and Tala were arguing about which desultory post they would give each other, when they ruled Orrun. "You can be my Chief Arse Wiper," Tala said. "You can be my High Scholar," Cain shot back, and they both laughed—no, that really would be the worst fate of all, imagine wasting your life doing…whatever it was High Scholars did. "Sad things," Tala suggested. "Sad things with paper," Cain agreed.

Ignoring them, Neema looked out across the menagerie. Tucked behind the banqueting hall, it sat on the edge of the emperor's private pleasure grounds. Bersun, who had never shown any interest in the collection, had allowed it to dwindle over the course of his reign. An elderly leopard lay stretched along a branch, fast asleep, tail dangling like a bell pull.

On a distant table Katsan and Havoc talked with their heads bowed close, ignoring a group of monkeys that reached through the bars, begging for food. Shal, still weak from his food poisoning, sat at the other end of the table, nursing a glass of water. Selfishly, Neema was glad he was distracted. Otherwise he might read the thought that kept turning over and over in her mind, a dark refrain she couldn't shake.

I could have done it. I could have killed her. I could be a murderer. Sitting here in the sunshine, eating lunch.

She put down her fork.

To distract herself she turned to study Ruko, who was sitting cross-legged, meditating beneath a willow tree. He had removed his shoes, and she remembered a detail she'd heard about his martial training—how he always fought barefoot. He'd developed his own style, camping out alone in the forest for months at a time. Rumour was he practised by fighting wild animals—tusked boars, wolves, even bears. This seemed improbable to Neema—more the sort of dark rumour the Tigers might spread for tactical reasons. But she did know that of the twelve Tiger warriors Ruko had fought to become contender, three had died of their injuries, and several more would likely never fight again. That was terrifying enough for her.

Cain and Tala were still arguing about which of them would take the throne, but it would be Ruko, Neema was sure of it. He had the ruthless ambition, the focus, the self-control. Most of all, the *need*. Sacrificing his sister had left him with no choice—he *had* to win, or else he had killed her for nothing.

Could anyone here stop him? Katsan was better with a sword, no question. Shal had his Houndsight, Cain his wits, Tala her stamina. Havoc was the great all-rounder and a natural politician, admired by the court. But still Ruko towered above them, literally and figuratively. They would need another monster to keep this one from the throne.

As if she had conjured him, the Visitor appeared at the entrance to the menagerie. He had changed into his proxy uniform —silk tunic and cropped trousers in a dark sea-green, the colour of the ocean trapped under thick storm clouds. His sigil—a dragon twined into an eternal eight, eating its own tail—was embroidered in dark silver thread across his narrow chest. His pale arms were bare, for only contenders took their colours. Visitor Pyke was here for Ruko, not for the throne. As to why—that remained a puzzle. The Dragons had never interfered in the Festival before, they had always held themselves above such matters.

Ruko, sensing the Visitor's presence, opened his eyes and rose gracefully to his feet in one slow, menacing movement. The rest of the contenders watched, fascinated, as two very different predators sized each other up across the patch of lawn.

At first glance, Ruko appeared to be the superior figure. But there was something about the Visitor that stopped the breath— that coiled strength, that brooding inner calm. Ruko had taken on the attributes of a tiger—grace, poise, power. But the Visitor *was* a dragon, transformed by fire into something beyond human. Even with his powers removed, this essential truth remained.

They had both fallen into fight stances, but neither made a move towards the other. When they fought, it would be to the death. If the Visitor killed a contender away from the Festival Square, it would spark a war between Helia and Orrun. The same, if Ruko killed the Visitor. So, they must wait.

The parrots screeched, breaking the moment. Cain laughed, because it proved his favourite theory—that if you held out long enough in any drama, no matter how terrible, something funny would happen. Usually a fart, so a parrot made a nice change. He stirred the fish stew he'd found...*somewhere.* Cain was always finding food...*somewhere.* He sniffed it, pulled a face, and ground in some black pepper.

The Visitor made his way to a table set apart from the rest. He moved without a sound, and left no mark where he walked, but the air was dense when he passed their table, and Neema thought again of the rhyme.

> *And in the morning when we woke*
> *The Visitor was gone.*
> *But where he'd lain the air was still*
> *And heavy as a stone.*

Tala waited until he was gone, then said, in a low voice, "I need to tell you both something. Sunur couldn't sleep last night. She hates it here. She's allergic to court life. Literally—it's brought her out in a rash."

"This stew is disgusting," Cain said.

"Have you tried not eating it?" Neema suggested.

Cain blinked at this novel concept.

Tala rapped on the table to get their attention. "She went for a walk in the orchard to clear her head. She thought she'd have the place to herself, but she didn't. *He* was there." She lifted her chin in Ruko's direction.

"The Ox orchard?" Neema frowned. The Tiger palace was on the opposite side of the canal.

"Sunur thought he was waiting for someone," Tala said.

"And this was late?" Cain prodded doubtfully at the stew.

"Middle of the night, around three. He was still prowling up and down when she came back, over an hour later. That's strange, right? Festival Eve. Why wasn't he resting, or training?"

"Was he wearing the Blade?" Neema asked.

"I don't know. I doubt she looked, but I can check."

They sat back. Cain dropped his spoon in his bowl, despondent. "So it wasn't him."

Not only was Ruko over in the Ox orchard when Gaida was killed, but if he'd left the Blade in his rooms, that would have given the killer the perfect opportunity to steal it. "So he was lured out to meet someone who never showed up."

"Someone who told him to come unarmed," Cain guessed.

Neema clicked her fingers. *Yes.* "Then they took the Blade and used it to frame him." She frowned again. Even as she said that last part, it didn't sound plausible. Too clumsy.

"How about you?" Cain asked Tala out of nowhere. "Sunur was out, so…What's your alibi?"

"Me?" Tala looked wounded. "I was asleep. Cain! I would never do something like that—"

"You're not a suspect," Neema reassured her. "You were talking about Gaida at our table last night, remember? How much you liked her."

Tala's expression softened. "I *did* like her. I can't believe she's dead. It doesn't make any sense. Who would kill Gaida? Everyone loved her."

"Universally adored," Cain agreed. "It's especially hard for Neema. They were like this." He crossed his fingers.

"Gaida hated me," Neema said, to Tala. There was no point pretending—it wasn't exactly a secret. If Tala had spent more time at court, she would know this already. "That's why Katsan's so angry about the investigation."

Tala was puzzled. "Why would Gaida hate you, Neema?"

"I know. Thank you. I never could work it out—"

"She was such an open, generous person," Tala blundered on. "I can't imagine her hating anyone, not without good reason…"

Neema sighed, defeated. She had tried before to describe the subtle ways Gaida had made her life miserable at the monastery—but it all sounded so trivial in isolation. Gaida was *lovely*. And so, it must be Neema's fault.

"Is that all the contenders accounted for?" Cain asked, shifting the conversation back. "You know I loathe being diligent, but you only have four days to solve this."

"We," Neema corrected him. "*We* have four days." She counted the contenders off on her fingers. "Havoc was training with his contingent." She'd checked with him on the walk over; he practised at the same time every night, when it was cooler. "Shal was sick, Ruko was over at the orchard. You have no motive," she said, to Tala. "Gaida was Katsan's Sister, she would never hurt her." That was five. She stuck out a final thumb. "Cain was at an orgy."

"Multiple satisfied witnesses," Cain said. And then, "Visitor Pyke. Join us!"

The Visitor was standing quietly at the far edge of their table. He stared at the empty bowl in front of Cain. "You ate my lunch."

"Eight!" Tala leapt to her feet, chair clattering to the ground.

Visitors were vulnerable to attack on the road. Before they began their first journey, along with their martial training and spells of protection, they introduced a toxin to their diet, extracted from a rare type of sea urchin. The toxin acted as a barrier to other poisons, but it was deadly to anyone else who tried it. You *never* touched a Visitor's food. Everyone knew that. Tiny children knew that.

Cain settled back, untroubled. "I'll be fine, don't worry. I can eat anything."

"You will be dead in five minutes," the Visitor said, indifferent.

Neema felt a surge of terror.

"Five minutes exactly?" Cain asked. "Or roughly? Do we time it? Does anyone have a watch?" His training had taken over. Laugh, laugh in the face of Death the Dragon. But under the tablecloth he reached out and grabbed Neema's hand.

"There must be an antidote," she said, quietly linking her fingers with his. His palm burned hot against hers.

"Too late," the Visitor said.

Tala rounded on him. "Where is it? *Please*. I can't just stand here and watch."

The Visitor relented. "Servant Jadu. The temple."

Tala was already running.

Neema squeezed Cain's hand under the table. "Hold on," she said. "Just hold on." Her voice cracked. He was going to die. Even a contender couldn't run to the temple and back in five minutes. He was going to die and she couldn't bear it.

"It's fine," he murmured. "I'm ready, I've got something."

Foxes were expected to say something funny with their last breath. *Life is a joke and death is the punchline.*

"What are the symptoms?" Neema asked the Visitor.

"Yes, please tell me what I have to look forward to," Cain said.

The Visitor counted them off in a disinterested voice. "Sweating. Cramps. Paralysis. Death."

Cain grunted, and forced a smile. "Like reading one of your monographs, then," he said to Neema.

She tried to laugh, but it came out as a sob. Sweat was streaming down his face, but maybe that was a good thing. His body, forcing out the toxins. Foxes were trained for this, Cain most of all. They were *trained*.

He closed his eyes, steadied his breathing.

"What can I do?" she whispered.

His body spasmed, then settled. "Scartown," he said, through gritted teeth. "Walk me home."

Neema did as he asked. Her perfect memory guiding him through the narrow streets, stopping at his favourite haunts. She used to do this for him long ago, lying in bed together late at night. The baker's on South Street, the Ratcatcher Tavern. Dead-man's Bridge. Vedric's Spice Emporium, the covered market. Her family store. Madam Fessi's school, when it was still there, before the fire. That's where she took him, back home, backwards in time. When they were friends.

Cain kept his eyes closed, riding the convulsions. Sweat poured down his face, dripped off his chin. His dark red hair was soaked through.

Five minutes is a long time. The rest of the contenders clustered around the table, except for Ruko, who had returned to his medi-tation beneath the willow.

Neema hated him then. Cain was fighting for his life a few feet away. What was wrong with him?

Another five minutes passed.

"You should be dead," the Visitor said.

Cain opened his eyes. "Sorry to disappoint," he croaked. By some miracle, the colour was returning to his face. The danger had passed. He slid his hand from Neema's and wiped his face with a napkin. Blew his nose in it. "You simply *must* give me the recipe," he said to the Visitor, and laughed into the silence that followed. "That was it. My death joke." He looked around at everyone, their harrowed faces. "Tough crowd." He poured himself a glass of water. His hand was trembling.

"This is not possible," the Visitor said.

"You should take more care with your food," Havoc snapped. "Eight. Any one of us could have eaten it by mistake."

Shal gestured to a table for one, guarded by an armed Hound. "I think the rest of us would have taken that as a warning, not a challenge."

Everyone groaned at Cain.

"Idiot," Havoc muttered. "You're lucky to be alive."

"It wasn't luck," Ruko said.

The contenders were too well trained to jump, but Neema felt the atmosphere change as he joined them. She saw Katsan reach on instinct for her sword, before remembering she was unarmed.

"He didn't eat the stew," Ruko said, and walked on.

There was a pause as everyone took this in. Neema thought back. Had she actually seen Cain eat any of it? She'd seen him stir it, and sniff it, but…She couldn't say for certain.

Cain lifted his brows. *Got you.*

"Shame on you, Cain Ballari," Katsan spat. "We lost Gaida last night. And you play games with us, in our grief?"

"This is the Day of the Fox, remember." He raised his hands, as the contenders abandoned him in disgust. "Life is a game without any rules, played by masters, played by fools," he called after them.

Neema hated him when he was like this. Cynical, shallow. Quoting lines from a comic opera. *You're better than this*, she thought, then corrected herself. She had no idea what he was, these days. She got to her feet.

"Oh, you're leaving too," he said, and took another sip of water. "Thanks for the tour of Scartown."

"Fuck you, Cain."

"Our catchphrase!" he cheered, as she stalked off. "I've upset everyone," he said, to the only person left. "What a shame."

Shal's hazel eyes glimmered as he focused his Houndsight.

Cain balanced the empty bowl of stew on its edge, and spun it. "It's rude to stare," he said, keeping his attention on the bowl.

"Do you think I can't read you?" Shal asked.

Cain spun the bowl again, humming to himself.

"You ate the stew. I saw you."

"Did I?" Cain let the bowl drop to the table. "Never trust a Fox, Contender Worthy. Especially around poisons." He smiled.

Shal kept staring, probing deeper. "What *is* it about you? What are you hiding?" His eyes were burning bright, flaying through Cain's many surfaces, searching for something deeper.

It was too much, even for someone as self-possessed as Cain. He closed his eyes against the scrutiny.

When he opened them again, Shal was gone.

"Alone at last," Cain said, to the furious parrots, and poured himself another glass of water.

Five minutes later Tala arrived with the antidote. What she said to Cain, when she had recovered her breath, is best left unwritten.

Twenty

THE IMPERIAL TOMBS lay to the west of the island, bordering the Fox palace. West was death, as the saying went. The oldest part had been carved from deep within the bedrock for purposes unknown, with skills or magic far beyond the understanding of modern engineers. A complex labyrinth of vaults and tunnels had grown out from there over the subsequent millennia. Few would dare venture down without a map, or a guide. There were stories of ghosts and other things, darker things, inhabiting the shadows. Let us not worry ourselves with those things, let us not speak of them.

There were two entrances to the tombs—one accessed from the sea and this one, in a quiet courtyard set aside for mourners. The doors sat at the bottom of a gently sloping walled path, fringed with sweet-scented climbing plants. The air was filled with the sound of bees buzzing as they moved from flower to flower. Life continued, in the midst of death.

The Fox abbot was waiting at the top of the path, accompanied by the emperor. Neema was startled to see him here—a surprising change to the schedule. The two men were as different as spring and winter—Ish Fort short and grimy in his orange robes; the Old Bear huge and soldier-smart. Neema couldn't imagine what they could have been discussing while they waited for the contenders to arrive; their differences ran far deeper than appearance. Like every ruler before him, Bersun had relied upon the services of Anat-russir from time to time, but he did not like or trust the abbot, and made no effort to disguise it.

Bersun claimed he had come to wish everyone good luck, but what he really wanted was news from Contender Kraa on her investigation. He seemed to enjoy calling her that, patting her shoulder and enquiring about her new uniform like a general inspecting a new recruit. "We must see it arrives before your fight this afternoon." And with that one glancing comment, what would have happened tomorrow, would now happen today. The words of an emperor were never casual. "Continue," he said, to Fort.

The Fox abbot grinned, the way animals do sometimes, before they bite. It was not the emperor's place to issue commands, he was not supposed to involve himself in the Trials. Choosing to let the matter go, Fort tapped his toes lightly on the courtyard's mosaic floor. "The imperial tombs lie beneath your feet. We have spent the last few months sealing tunnels and digging new ones. One of them will lead you directly to the temple crypts. You have one hour to find it, head up to the Fox chapel, and light a stick of incense in honour of the First Guardian. That's it. Simple."

Neema narrowed her eyes, instantly suspicious. Foxes were many things, but they were never simple. Earlier, in the emperor's private rooms, Cain had suggested that the Trial would test the contenders as individuals. Also, she knew the High Servant of the Temple would *never* allow the Foxes to burrow a new exit through into the crypts.

No. Something was waiting for them down there. A challenge as dark and winding as the tombs themselves.

"Cain will rescue you at the end of the hour, if you get lost," Fort added.

"Will I?" Cain was standing with his contingent, one black tunic in a huddle of burnt orange.

"My apologies," the abbot said. It was the height of bad manners for one Fox to pin down another. "Cain *might* rescue you. Should the mood take him."

Shal stepped forward. "Permission to speak, your grace."

Responding to the Hound contender's formal tone, Fort flipped up his hood and tightened his belt. "Granted."

"I must withdraw from the Trial for personal reasons."

The abbot considered this. "Your uncle," he guessed.

The emperor sighed in understanding. General Gatt Worthy. The man who had saved his life, by sacrificing his own. Buried these past sixteen years in the Hall of Heroes. "You would forfeit your points? Is that what your uncle would want, Contender Worthy?"

The winner of the Trial would receive five points, and so on down to the final contender, who would receive none. Fights, in comparison, offered a maximum of two points. One missed Trial could make a significant difference to a contender's placing on the table. By withdrawing, Shal was putting himself at a considerable disadvantage.

He planted his feet more firmly. "I am resolved, your majesty. Your grace. I will not disturb my uncle's rest in pursuit of my own ambitions."

"Then I suggest you wait in the shade, Hound contender." Abbot Fort gestured across the courtyard to a grey-bricked chapel used by mourners for prayer and reflection. The attached veranda was densely covered with more climbing flowers. The Fox contingent had laid out refreshments there, along with cushions and day beds, and a rope hammock. To Neema, who was only taking part in the Trial to defy her contingent's expectations, it looked like a dream. A tempting dream.

Shal bowed and left the line.

"Fool," Ruko muttered.

Shal stopped dead. "What did you call me?"

"I called you a fool," Ruko replied, more clearly.

Shal was a head shorter than his rival, but still somehow he managed to look down on him. "And what should I call you, Ruko Valit?" He bared his teeth, as if in pain. "I was there that day, remember? When you sat upon the marble throne."

"Careful," the emperor warned, softly. *Do not speak of her.*

Shal took a step closer to Ruko. The two men were inches apart. "I looked into your eyes, when…" He let the rest hang silent in the air between them. *When you sacrificed your own sister.* "Do you know what I saw? The same thing I see now. *Nothing.* A void, where a soul should be. An empty shell of a man. So you may call me what you wish, Tiger contender. In a thousand lifetimes, I would rather be a fool, than whatever *you* are."

With that, he walked away.

Fort lowered his hood and returned to his introduction. The contenders would enter the tombs in pairs. The emperor was persuaded to pick names from a tatty felt hat. Shal and Ruko were the first two he pulled out, so Ruko would go in alone. Tala and Havoc were the next pairing. Neema and Katsan would head in last.

Abbot Fort escorted Ruko down the sloping path to the tomb doors. They had a brief conversation, then Ruko disappeared inside with a lantern. The Foxes closed the doors behind him. Together, the handles formed an ∞, reminding mourners of the Eternal Path, where souls would return after death, reborn into a new life.

"Send news of the results," the emperor said, and strode off with his bodyguards. Cain and the abbot vanished, along with the Fox contingent. The remaining contenders were left abandoned in the courtyard with no instructions. Neema, Tala, Katsan, Havoc, standing in line, in Guardian order.

A few minutes passed. Nobody spoke. Everyone was thinking.

The thing about Foxes—you rarely found them in the centre ground. The Fox is the Guardian of the borders, the fringes, the betwixt and between. The centre of this Trial was the trip down into the tombs. Which meant that it probably wasn't the most important part.

Something else, then.

Neema's legs began to ache. And her shoulders. Why did her shoulders ache? Only the Dragon knew. She shifted her weight from one hip to the other. Rolled her neck. No one else moved. They had trained for this. Maybe they felt discomfort, but they would never show it.

The thing to remember, Neema thought, was that this wasn't just "the Fox Trial." This was *Cain Ballari's* Fox Trial. His creation. There was no point trying to follow his moves and countermoves, the dodging and the doubling back. That would only leave her in a tangled mess. The trick was to work out his final destination and get there ahead of him. If you want to catch a fox, wait with the chickens.

What did Cain want, more than anything? To win the throne. He couldn't take part in his own Trial, but he *could* design it to favour some contenders more than others. Ruko was his biggest rival. Therefore, Cain would construct the Trial to ensure Ruko came last.

It didn't take Neema long to work it out after that. She knew exactly what this Trial was about. The question was, what to do with that knowledge.

She looked down the line at Tala, Katsan and Havoc. They were still standing rigidly to attention, though she could see Tala wavering. No one had ordered them to stay out here, the sun beating down on their heads. But no one had dismissed them, either.

This was such a Fox move.

"I'm going to join Shal," she said.

"Do as you please," Katsan replied in a cold voice. "You have no place here with us."

The veranda was blissfully cool and fresh. A couple of Fox novices were playing cards at a table, heads shaved and painted with the half-moon/half-sun sigil of their Guardian. She watched them for a moment, remembering the itch of her hair growing back, after she'd survived her first year at Anat-ruar. She'd looked pretty good with a shaved scalp. Maybe that was why Gaida had hated her. She'd looked terrible.

"You're both cheating," she said, to the Foxes.

The nearest one turned round. "Of course," he said, as his friend swapped a card behind his back. "Wouldn't be fair otherwise."

Neema fixed a couple of drinks, helped herself to a handful of grapes. The novices ignored her. She smiled to herself, suspicions confirmed. Definitely spies.

Shal was sitting on a padded bench, staring at the ground, his hands pushed deep into his dark brown curls. He looked like a painting. *Portrait of a Failed Contender.*

"Ginger tea," she said.

He looked up.

She held it out to him. "For your stomach."

He took it from her, still glum. "Thanks."

She sat down next to him and sipped her lemonade, ice rattling against the glass. Beyond the veranda, the air shimmered in the heat. Jewelled palace birds flitted from flower to flower. The bees hummed. Tala, Katsan and Havoc suffered silently in a row. Someone should stick a skewer through them, Neema thought. Grilled contender.

"I'm sorry about your uncle," she said, instead. "That was a tough decision."

Shal grunted softly. "Probably cost me the throne."

Neema lowered her voice. "Are you sure about that?" She couldn't spell it out, not here with the Foxes listening—but she didn't need to. She gave a subtle nod, encouraging him to use his Houndsight.

Shal's hazel eyes glittered as he scanned her face. He frowned as he read what was there—encouragement, optimism. It didn't make sense. "I'm out of the Trial," he whispered. "The abbot accepted my withdrawal."

Neema lifted an eyebrow. *Did he?* The abbot had suggested Shal bring himself here into the shade, but there had been no formal withdrawal. Shal was still in the Trial, if he wanted to be. But he'd have to figure that out for himself. She turned her gaze back to the courtyard, and sipped her lemonade.

It took him longer than her to get it, but when he did, he laughed softly. "He's already lost," he murmured, meaning Ruko. "That's funny."

"And you can win," Neema said, behind her glass. Because this Trial played to Shal's strengths, more than anyone else here. Which was fine by her. Of all the contenders, he was the one she would pick to rule Orrun. He would make a good emperor, Shal Worthy. Honest, fair, decent. Not to mention, he would actually look good in the ceremonial robes.

He raised his voice, just enough that it carried across the veranda to the card-playing Foxes. "You look exhausted, Contender Kraa. Why don't you rest for a while? I'll wake you when it's time."

"Well...if you're sure. Thank you, Contender Worthy. That's kind of you."

"My pleasure."

They were playing a game, of course. But she *was* exhausted—body and soul. Stumbling to the rope hammock, she climbed into it and fell into a deep, velvety sleep.

Where she dreamed of the marble throne. Gaida was sitting on it, drinking tea from a porcelain cup. And then it wasn't tea, it was blood. Flies buzzing on the rim. The blood spilled over the top, covering Gaida's hands. "Don't drink that," Neema said, trying to reach her, but she couldn't get her foot on the first step. "Gaida stop—don't drink that." Someone was grabbing her shoulder, shaking her, she tried to shrug them off...

"Neema." Shal was standing over her.

She lowered her feet to the ground. A floor of white marble, for a moment, as the dream lapped at her consciousness, resolving into warm terracotta tiles. Back to reality. She rubbed her face, clearing her head. She felt groggy but refreshed, in that distinctive way of short naps.

The novices were gone, replaced by two older students playing checkers.

"How long was I asleep?"

"Over an hour. You'll be up soon. Cain's gone to retrieve Havoc and Tala."

Neema squinted as she looked out across the blazing courtyard. A single figure stood to attention in the searing heat. Katsan. "Fuck the Eight, she's still out there."

"She's praying for Gaida."

"Does she have to do it out there?"

"I tried to get her to come in, or drink some water..." Shal drew himself into Katsan's posture. "'I am the Bear contender, Shal Worthy. I shall not withdraw, I shall not retreat. I hold my ground.'"

"So rigid."

"*So* rigid," Shal agreed. And then, much louder, "We must admire the tenacity and endurance of a true Bear warrior. Katsan

honours her Guardian, and her fallen Sister, with her suffering."
He caught Neema's look. "Too much?" he muttered.

She shrugged. Who could say? "How's the stomach?"

Shal's colour faded. "Better when I'm not thinking about it."

"Sorry." She paused. "Are you *sure* it was the eel pie? Chef Ganstra
is so careful—"

"—please, Neema," Shal begged her.

A blur of movement caught her eye, in a far corner of the courtyard. Ruko, practising a sequence of martial steps in the shade of
an ancient yew. He did like his trees. They watched him in silent
appreciation, mesmerised by the flowing grace and power of the
classic Tiger style. Whatever adaptations he had made, he would
not reveal them here, in advance of the fights. "Did he find his way
to the temple?"

Shal shook his head, still watching Ruko's performance. "Cain
had to rescue him, too."

"Did he say thank you?"

Laughter, from the Hound contender. "No, he did not."

Shortly after, there was a commotion at the entrance to the
tombs. Cain had found the missing contenders. Tala seemed
fine, dazzled by the sunlight but otherwise unharmed. Havoc,
however, was in bad shape. Tala slung his arm around her
neck and half carried him across the courtyard. When they
reached the veranda, Neema saw that he was filthy—skin, hair,
clothes grimed and encrusted with soil. His fingers were bleeding, nails torn. Blue eyes haunted, as if he were still trapped
down there.

Shal helped him to a day bed, while Tala went to fetch water.

"What happened?" Neema asked her.

"There's a penalty if we talk." She jerked her chin across the
courtyard, where Abbot Fort stood waiting at the tomb entrance.
"You'd better go."

As Neema left the veranda, Havoc began to shake, violently.
Shal rested a hand on his rival's back. "That's good," he said. "Shaking's good. It releases the fear."

∞

Katsan was on her knees before the tomb doors, praying. "May the Bear protect and guide me through this Trial. May it grant me the strength and courage to succeed."

"And remain Hidden," Abbot Fort murmured the response as Neema joined them.

Katsan made a sign of the eight, mirroring the shape of the door handles in front of her. "My mind is clear. My mind is still." She got to her feet, and gave a sharp, decisive nod. "I am ready."

Neema had brought a leather water bottle from the veranda. She offered it to Katsan. The Bear contender had caught the sun, standing out in the courtyard for so long.

Tempted, Katsan sucked her dry lips. Pride won out. She would take nothing from this fraud, this imposter.

"Abbot Fort?" Neema said, offering him the bottle instead.

"Kind or clever…" he murmured. "I wonder."

Neema, who had solved the riddle of the Trial, knew exactly what he meant. She offered him her best, most innocent smile.

"She is neither," Katsan said. "My Sister Gaida could have told you that, your grace."

Fort took a swig of water, then poured the rest over his head. It sluiced over his lank grey hair, and down his face and neck. The first wash he'd had in a while, Neema wagered. Up close, the Fox abbot smelled strongly of old and new sweat, his robes showing white crust marks under the arms. "Work as a pair, if you like," he said, then smiled at Katsan's reaction. "Or not." He thrust a lantern at her. "Off you go then, Bear contender."

Katsan marched off down the tunnel. "My mind is clear. My mind is still," she chanted in a determined voice. Her words faded as she turned a corner.

Fort handed Neema a lantern, then placed two fingers on her wrist to hold her. The lightest of touches, but it felt as dangerous as a blade. Fort had been an assassin, before he took the orange robes. "Cain," he said, and looked at her.

She waited.

"I knew he was a contender the moment he strolled into the monastery. Strolled in." Fort smiled, remembering. "Nonchalant little shit. He was born to lead us. Born and bred on the streets of Scartown. But he didn't know it until you broke his heart."

"I—"

"You made him the man he is today. Damaged. Cynical. Perfect. I am grateful to you. That being said." He stepped in closer, and her pulse jumped against his fingers. "If you distract him, or get in his way…"

He let the silent threat sink in, then slid his fingers from her wrist. Smiling, smiling. And she realised that although Abbot Fort's hair was greasy, and he stank of sweat, and he hadn't shaved in days, that his teeth were white, and his eyes were clear.

She thought about that smile, as she headed into the tombs. It stayed with her for a long time, in the dark.

CHAPTER
Twenty-One

NEEMA HAD A decision to make. In front of her lay three tunnels, fading off to black. The tunnel to her left led to the western vaults, the section she knew best. The central tunnel would take her down to the Hall of Heroes. Katsan had taken the eastern tunnel, to the right. Neema could hear her faintly, still chanting her mantra.

She headed left. She was walking in the opposite direction from the temple crypts, but she didn't believe for a moment that the Foxes had created a new linking tunnel. That was not what this Trial was about. At least this way, she could avoid Katsan.

She took her time, holding her lantern high, watching for traps. Cain's speciality. Brushing her fingers across a wall, she felt a slight give to one section. A hidden door. She ignored it, and moved on. A secret passage through a haunted, booby-trapped tomb system? No thank you.

This wasn't so bad. She had survived a night locked down here in the pitch black, with no promise of rescue; she could manage one solitary hour with a lantern. A wave of melancholy hit her, as it always did when she was forced to remember that night. Alone and abandoned in the dark, until she found the book. Her book.

She pushed the memory from her mind. *Focus*. Trials were not supposed to be deadly, but there was always an element of risk, especially in a Fox Trial. They did like to flirt on the boundaries of what was permitted. And whose fault was it, really, if a contender didn't watch where she was going?

Perhaps on instinct, Neema had stumbled on to a familiar route. She had undertaken numerous research trips down here at the emperor's request. Never alone, though—not after that first time. Vabras had insisted on that, sending two of his most trusted deputies to guard her. The High Scholar was too useful to be lost to the darkness.

Brushing cobwebs from her face, she held the lantern out ahead of her. She knew this tunnel well, she recognised its dank brickwork, the particular slope of the dirt floor. This would take her down to the sea entrance. She could smell a fresh salt tang laced into the stale tomb air.

Something felt different.

She paused, casting the lantern light all around her, searching for any changes. Some of the cobwebs were fake. She tested them, in case they were covering something. A hidden catch, maybe. Nothing. There was nothing. The cobwebs were a theatrical dressing. The tunnel was just a tunnel. The same one she had walked through a hundred times before.

She sighed to herself. This was how the Foxes trapped you, with their sneaky hints and secret smiles. Until you were so paranoid, you didn't trust your own judgement.

She was about to press on when she heard a scream in the distance.

Neema froze, listening hard. "Katsan?"

Another scream, high and desperate. Then silence.

The silence was worse.

"Katsan!" Neema yelled, and raced forward.

The floor collapsed beneath her.

Nothing she could do, but fall.

In a distant part of the tunnel, Katsan wasn't screaming. She was trying to stay calm, walking at a slow, steady pace. *My mind is clear, my mind is still.* But through the walls she heard the whispers. The words of her commander, the night she won the tournament to become contender.

Step aside, Sister, he'd said. *No, that is not an order, I will not compel you. You won the tournament. But was that skill, or luck, at your age? Ask yourself: are you the contender we need? Search your heart,*

Sister. There is no shame in recognising your limits. Do not let your pride overcome your honour.

No matter that she had beaten warriors half her age. That she was five years younger than Bersun had been, when Lanrik sent him off to fight for the throne.

Step aside.

And she would have done, if Gaida had not been there to counsel her. Gaida, her true Sister. *Don't listen to them, Katsan. You won the tournament. You are the Bear contender. You will step aside for no one.*

But now Gaida was dead, and the words had risen like ghosts to torment her again. Through the walls she heard her own doubt whispered back to her. *Was it skill or luck? Search your heart, Sister.*

The Foxes, it had to be. But how did they know the words?

Were they coming from her own head? Was she imagining them?

With a snarl of frustration, she staggered on down the tunnel. She sensed something following her, scuffing footsteps in the dark. Then it was gone. "Have you drugged me?" she called out, furious.

Snatched laughter, from behind the wall. *Too old, too slow*, the voices whispered. Up ahead, at the end of the tunnel…Whatever had been following her was now in front. A creature lumbering back and forth, as if waiting for her. Fur, teeth, claw…

The Bear.

She dropped to her knees. Was this real, was she dreaming? Why couldn't she think straight? The Bear—a blurred shape— came and went. If it was real, would it give her the answers she craved? *Tell me. Tell me! Was it skill, or luck? Am I worthy?*

She clamped her jaw shut. Real or fake, she was too afraid to ask.

A sound cut through her fevered thoughts. A scream in a distant tunnel. The Raven contender, presumably.

Another scream, sharper this time.

Katsan sat back on her heels. The Bear was gone, if it had ever been there. The warrior in her said—someone is in trouble, it is your duty to help them. Any other day she would have got to her feet. But her Sister was dead. Murdered. And that woman... that...*woman*...

"May the Eight give you what you deserve, Neema Kraa," she said, in a dead voice.

"And remain Hidden," a voice whispered back, through the walls.

Neema fell.

A flare of terror. Death, death was coming. And then relief. It was only a short drop, and she had landed on something soft.

The lantern slipped from her fingers and snuffed itself out, plunging her in darkness. She sat up. What had she landed on? Something soft but lumpy. Some *things*. Satin. No, fur. No, velvet. She tugged a piece free from the pile. Velvet, with a trailing lace ribbon. Her fingers worked their way round, making sense of the shape. A hat? She groped about and found another one, and another.

She had fallen into a sea of hats.

Foxes.

Whispers from the tunnel, ten feet above her head. The gleam of a fresh lantern.

"Hello?" she called out.

The card-playing novices from the veranda peeped over the edge, shaved heads pressed close together. They were grinning. "Hello."

"Could you help me out?" She gestured to the walls—too smooth to climb.

"We'd definitely help you," one of them said, shuffling further out over the edge. "But we don't have a rope. Sorry."

"So I'm stuck down here? Is Katsan all right? I heard a scream."

"That was us," the other one said. "Fox One and Fox Two."

"Those are your names?" Neema was still rummaging around among the hats.

They laughed. Today, those were their names. Fox novices spent their first year learning how to deal with constant change.

A different bed every night, a new name every morning. Constant change, while holding on to their essential self. Vital, for nascent spies. They didn't explain any of this to Neema, because she was already asking another question.

Ravens.

"Why am I sitting on a pile of hats?"

Fox One was dangling precariously over the edge, for the sheer joy of it. They waved their arms manically. "You've fallen into Tala Talaka's worst fear."

"Recurring childhood nightmare," Fox Two said. "Drowning in a sea of hats."

"How weird," Neema said. She snatched the dangling novice's wrist and pulled hard.

"Oh," Fox One said, as they slid into the hat pit.

"Ohh-hoh!" Fox Two agreed from above, delighted. "Sneaky!"

Fox One flailed about on the hats, snorting with laughter. "Aargh! Help! I'm drowning."

"Will you help me now?" Neema asked.

"I still don't have a rope," Fox Two said, with a helpless gesture.

"I do." While they'd been talking, Neema had been rummaging. Beneath the top layers she'd found other garments, including scarves. She tied them together. "I'm going to throw this to you," she told Fox Two. "Once I'm out, you can help your friend."

She tossed up the scarf rope. Fox Two caught it, bracing themself as Neema climbed to the top. She could tell they were tempted to let go at the last minute. "Don't you dare," she panted. "Don't you *dare.*"

She hauled herself out, sprawled on her stomach.

Fox Two applauded. Fox One joined in, from the pit of hats.

Neema gestured back towards the trap. "That was Cain's idea?"

"Never tell your nightmares to a Fox," the young novice replied, portentously.

Neema, who had been suffering in secret for months from strange, shadowed dreams, agreed this was solid advice. "Are you going to help your friend?"

Fox Two looked hesitant. "They'll just pull me in with them."

"I won't. I promise!" Fox One called unconvincingly from the trap. Neema took their lantern, and left them to it.

Walking away, she felt a flicker of satisfaction. She had tried to help Katsan, and she had survived Tala's nightmare. Surely she could sit out the rest of the hour. There was a storeroom down the next side tunnel—she would wait there until Cain came to find her. She had a horrible suspicion she wasn't even halfway through the hour yet. Time did strange things in the dark.

When she reached the storeroom, she found its narrow door was marked in white chalk with an eternal eight. She touched it, and rubbed her fingers. A white ∞ was usually drawn to ward off bad luck and dark spirits. She'd seen shipbuilders back in Scartown painting them on the hulls of new boats. They often appeared in graveyards, especially in the month of the Fading Light. The Foxes could have drawn this one, or it could have been someone working in the tombs.

Warily, she opened the door. The room was empty, cleared of supplies. Its earthen walls were lined on both sides with matching shelves, also empty. She breathed out, and stepped inside. A quick inspection, just to be sure, and then she could wait it out safely...

The door slammed shut behind her.

Spinning around, she ran towards it, but the key was already turning in the lock. She banged with her fist. "Let me out!"

"You chose the wrong door, contender," someone said. They sounded sorry for her.

She banged harder, but they were gone.

She turned a slow circle, preparing to defend herself. There were marks on the floor, as if a piece of heavy furniture had been dragged across it. Otherwise the room was bare. No, wait. Propped up on one of the shelves was a weathered strip of wood—painted blue with white lettering. *The Merry Dolphin.* She stepped closer, and felt a trigger click and release under her foot.

A grating sound, as the shelves lurched into life. No, not just the shelves...

The walls. The walls were pressing in.

Neema fled to the other end of the room, but it was even narrower here, like the prow of a ship. She returned to the widest point—arms stretched out as if she could hold the walls at bay—and screamed for help. But this was a Trial—no one was coming to rescue her. *You chose the wrong door, contender...*

The opposing shelves were inches apart. If she didn't think of something fast, they would crush her to death.

With moments to spare, she clambered up on to the shelf with the boat sign. Seconds later all the shelves met in the middle, and clicked neatly together. The grating sound stopped.

She lay there for a moment, panting hard. She was safe, it was over.

She was also trapped, face pressed against the packed-earth wall, her right shoulder jammed against the shelf above. Wriggling painfully in the tight space, she inched herself on to her back, spreading her weight evenly between the two connected shelves. At her head, the sides of the shelves joined; the same at her feet. Like a coffin, she thought.

The earth wall to her left collapsed.

Neema screamed.

The space around her was filling up with loose soil, spilling over her in soft, crumbling cascades. Burying her alive.

Terrified, she shuffled back on to her side, trying desperately to stop the avalanche of earth with her hands. Her fingers closed against the boat sign. She wedged it up against the collapsing wall. The soil slowed to a trickle, then stopped.

She coughed and spat earth from her mouth, and lay back, half buried—only a few precious inches left above her. She was struggling to breathe—the fear and shock pressing down on her as much as the collapsed wall. "Help!" she called out, then coughed again, suffocating in her panic. "Help!"

No one came. She was on her own.

In her mind she saw a blank page. Words blossomed on the paper. **Don't fight it. Relax. Breathe.**

She did her best. She breathed—in through the nose, out through the nose, mouth firmly shut. Her heartbeat slowed.

An image of Havoc, returning from the tombs, covered in dirt. Eyes vacant with dull horror. She'd stumbled into his nightmare.

Havoc was one of Cain's closest rivals. But this felt more than strategic. It felt personal. It felt like punishment. She touched her fingers to the boat sign. *The Merry Dolphin.* The wood was splintered and worn, the paint cracked. It must hold some personal meaning for Havoc, some tragedy or scandal from his past.

"You're safe," she told herself. "Just breathe." But she was in a coffin filled with earth, in the dark. What if they forgot about her? What if she ran out of air before they came back? And before she could stop herself, she was screaming again, from the top of her lungs. She was going to die, she was going to die...

The grating sound returned. Gears whirring in reverse, somewhere on the other side of the wall. The two connected shelves juddered beneath her and broke apart. Released, she fell to the ground, sobbing with relief.

Once she'd wiped the earth and the tears from her face, she saw that the door stood open. "Hello? Cain? Is that you?"

Avoiding the trip stone, she made her way back out into the tunnel. There was no one there. She was alone.

CHAPTER
Twenty-Two

B ACK IN SCARTOWN, Neema and Cain used to spend long, meandering hours together, exploring the city's underbelly. The cut-throughs and back alleys, the roofways and underpaths.

"We're lost again," Neema would say, to vigorous denials from Cain.

"How can we be lost, when we don't know where we're going?"

Down in the tombs, Neema was reminded of this philosophy. If she wasn't safe in a storeroom, she wasn't safe anywhere. Best to ramble without purpose and let her destination reveal itself when it was ready. Accept each encounter as an improvised moment on life's digressive path.

In other words, pretend to be Cain.

As she rambled through the tunnels, her mind returned to Gaida's murder. Her dream in the hammock had been a prompt from her subconscious to stay focused, not let her unexpected role as contender distract her from the far more important and pressing matter of proving her innocence.

She needed to search Gaida's apartment as soon as possible—but when? She wouldn't have time before the afternoon fights. Early evening, then. And with that decided, she composed a task list in her head, because fuck pretending to be Cain, she was a Raven not a Fox:

1. Complete this Trial without dying.
2. Visit the armoury with Fenn and choose weapons.
3. Fight Shal.
4. Visit Gaida's apartment, solve murder.
5. Cake?

Neema liked to put something positive at the end of a list as an inducement. Often she chose "bath," but last night's debacle had spoiled that particular treat. She would be approaching baths with trepidation for a while. Also storerooms. And balconies. She would be approaching a lot of things with trepidation for a while.

She was going through her list again—debating whether "fight Shal" was strictly a task she could perform, or more just a terrible thing that was going to happen to her—when a ten-foot bear appeared from a side corridor.

She stopped. The bear did not.

A thud of concern, before she realised it was sauntering towards her on its hind legs, and waving. "Hello?"

"Good afternoon!" the bear replied, and removed its giant head to reveal a tall, burly member of the Fox contingent, sweating profusely beneath his thick fur costume. He rubbed his face, turning it even redder. "I'm torturing Katsan. She thinks we've laced the walls with hallucinogens."

Of course that would be the Bear warrior's nightmare—the poisoning of her perfectly balanced body, the loss of control. Katsan's was not a mind that wished to be cracked open. She defended the borders—she did not cross them.

"It's worse than that," the Fox-bear said. He seemed happy to talk for a moment, and cool down. "Last night at dinner, Gaida confided in Cain—Katsan 's commander didn't think she was up to the Trials. He tried to persuade her to step aside."

"So now you're…"

"Whispering it through the walls. *Step aside, Sister, step aside…*"

Neema thought back to the banquet, Cain and Gaida gossiping together. It was just like Gaida to spill someone else's secret, and just like Cain to encourage her. Wily bastard. "*Have* you laced the walls with hallucinogens?" she asked the Fox-bear.

"Self-doubt is more potent than any drug," he said, slotting the massive head back into place.

"And more damaging."

He nodded, a bear again. They'd padded out a real bear skin, and sprayed it with some rich, animal musk. From a distance, in the dark, it would be convincing. "Also, I think she has a touch of heatstroke."

"Poor Katsan. At least it's cool down here."

"Oh thanks, rub it in. Eight. How do bears keep cool?"

Neema perked up. "They employ a variety of strategies," she began, but he was already lumbering off on all fours.

"I was being rhetorical," he called over his shoulder, his voice muffled by the costume.

So Neema created a new list—Six Ways Bears Keep Cool—and told it to the walls, because she had to tell someone.

Shortly after that she reached a familiar brick-lined tunnel, torches blazing in golden sconces. The entrance to the Hall of Heroes. Thank the Eight. Even Cain wouldn't dishonour such hallowed ground. She could wait there in peace until her hour was up.

The tunnel ceiling sloped lower and lower, forcing her to bow her head, until she was almost crawling. An architectural nudge to visitors, reminding them to show some respect for the dead. *Greet them on your knees, child of Orrun, for they are the best of us.*

Passing through the narrow entrance, Neema emerged into a high-domed cave, walls studded with rose and white crystals. Hazy beams of sunlight poured down from hidden skylights, imbuing the crystals with an ethereal glow. According to deep myth, the lost tribes had carved this space as a sanctuary, anticipating the Catastrophe to come. Now it was a cathedral to the fallen. Fifteen hundred years of service and sacrifice, courage and wisdom.

Neema moved down the central aisle at a respectful pace, past flanks of marble sarcophagi. Each tomb was lit with twin candelabra, wax spilling like blood and platting to the floor. Her skin prickled, as it always did when she walked through here. Forget myth, forget metaphor—these were the true Guardians of Orrun. Empress Yasthala's beloved husband Eyart Just, the first to be honoured. Mordir, the wise and soulful Bear warrior and poet. High Scholar Donalia Craw, who lost her life defending the Imperial Library from attack. Her effigy showed her resting in

peaceful slumber on her tomb, the precious scrolls she had saved
from the fire gathered in her arms.

The most recent addition was markedly different from its
neighbours. In place of a tomb stood a rough hunk of unshaped
marble. The plaque next to it read:

In memory of Shimmer Arbell—
lost to the ocean, summer 1530.
May her effigy remain unsculpted,
for none will touch her genius.

Neema drew a respectful sign of the eternal eight over her
heart. As she did so, she heard a panicked flapping in the
shadows ahead. A bird must have flown through a skylight and
got itself trapped—it happened sometimes. Taking a candle from
its holder, she followed the sound to the end of the Hall. The
flapping and fluttering grew more insistent. She pushed open
a heavy iron gate with her shoulder and squeezed through the
gap into a small, dank side chamber. The bird cried out through
the darkness.

Kraa! Kraa!

She lifted the candle higher, and caught a glimpse of a large
black bird, a raven or a crow. It was trapped behind a haphazard
collection of broken tombs—she could hear it lifting and dropping as it tried to escape, distressed and exhausted.

Kraa! Kraa!

A raven, definitely a raven. Neema's heart skipped. Of all the
places…She'd discovered this room last winter, when the wall
sealing it closed had collapsed. The inglorious resting place of
twelve ancient Raven warriors, from the days when the monastery
had stood on this site. They had been moved here generations ago
to make way for the new Heroes of Orrun. Now their tombs lay
mouldering under a thick seam of dust and cobwebs, their mum-
mified remains spilling from ruined coffins.

Neema had spent long, painstaking hours cataloguing everything, noting down inscriptions, extracting treasures buried with

the warriors' bones. The emperor had been delighted with her findings and the fresh insights they gave into Orrun's distant past. But when Neema asked for funds to restore the tombs, her request was turned down. Too expensive, too much trouble, too many awkward questions about why they'd ended up in that state in the first place.

The bird had fallen silent. She picked her way around the tombs, calling to it in a soft, coaxing voice. "It's all right. Don't be frightened…"

With a sudden snap of its wings it burst free and flew straight at her, hooked beak opened wide.

Kraa! Kraa!

Neema ducked as it skimmed her head and circled the room. She had barely recovered when two more lifted up from the shadows, then another, and another. A flock of ravens, wheeling and diving in the compressed space, screaming her name.

Kraa! Kraa!

A wing tip brushed her face. She flung her arms up to protect herself, but there was no aggression, they were not attacking her. It felt more like…

…a greeting.

Slowly, she lowered her arms. The birds were settling now—seven, eight, nine, ten of them, perched about the room, watching her with beady interest. The one that had lured her in strutted along the top of a crumbling tomb and tapped its beak sharply against the stone. *Open.*

Its companions watched intently as Neema approached the tomb—the oldest and the most ruined. When she'd opened it before, she'd found nothing inside. The coffin and its contents had disintegrated to dust long ago. The exterior of the tomb, worn down over millennia, offered no clues either.

The bird gave a second, impatient tap.

"All right," she murmured. She was not sure if she was dreaming, or hallucinating, whether this was part of the Trial or not. Cain had warned her that the Dragonscale might have lingering effects, perhaps that was it.

She put her palms against the edge of the tomb lid and pushed. Despite its poor condition it was still heavy; she had to put all her weight behind it. The ravens squawked encouragement from their perches, urging her on. Slowly, the slab came free, toppling to the ground with a violent thud. The birds flinched at the sound but remained where they were, hopping and calling out to each other in excitement.

Neema peered into the open tomb. Nestled inside lay an ebony chest, the size of a blanket box, the curved lid covered in black leather and carved with a feather design. The birds whirred and preened as she ran her fingers along it. The carving was so lifelike she could feel the ridges of each barb under her fingertips. Its quality put her in mind again of the lost tribes, except that it was in pristine condition, and the wood was freshly oiled.

The first raven curled its claws around the edge of the tomb and uttered a long stream of croaks and gurgles from the back of its throat. It seemed to be talking to her, as if she too were a raven. Long, involved sentences.

"I can't understand you," she said.

The bird carried on, unbothered. It reminded Neema of herself, when she got stuck on a favourite topic.

There was a brass key in the lid. She turned it, surprised by how smooth it was. The latch drew back with a satisfying *tok*. The raven mimicked the sound perfectly—*tok*—and gave a little shuffle of anticipation.

Neema opened the chest.

On the inside of the lid, the Raven of the Last Return glared out at her, painted in the old style with white-rimmed eyes and bold outlines, beak open, ready to attack.

The chest was packed with weapons.

Daggers, twin hooks, throwing knives. Swords in black leather scabbards. An iron fork, its prongs sharpened like talons. A black leather cosh. Everything held neatly in place, with black velvet compartments and black leather buckles. Black on black on black. Newly forged weapons of the highest quality, designed for a Raven warrior.

Which made no sense. The last Raven warrior had died fifteen centuries ago.

Neema lifted a warhammer from its compartment, admiring its weight and balance. The hammer head was curved like a raven's beak, coming to a sharp, deadly point. "Beautiful," she murmured. "Horrible."

The ravens agreed proudly.

She slotted the hammer back in place. Beneath the top layer was a second, deeper compartment, housing a set of leather armour, a helmet and shield, and a short cloak, all patterned with the same feather design as the trunk. Black on black on black. She held the jerkin against her body, testing it for size. "I think this would fit," she said, to the head raven. "What do you reckon?"

"Why don't you try it on?"

She turned, clutching the jerkin to her chest.

Cain was watching her from the doorway, hands in his pockets.

The ravens lifted up in a flurry of feathers. Neema felt the beat of their wings against her face as they circled above her head. One last call—**Kraa! Kraa!**—and the room was empty.

It became clear to her, in the silence that followed, that Cain had not seen the ravens, and that she had imagined them.

She had definitely imagined them.

"Would you like me to rescue you?" Cain asked. "Or are you happy down here talking to yourself?"

Neema put the jerkin back in the weapons chest. "Help me with this."

They lifted the chest out of the tomb, through the iron gate and into the pale crystalline glitter of the Hall of Heroes. Cain was leading the way. At the end of the hall they ducked their heads and crawled back up through the entrance tunnel, with its golden sconces and flickering torches.

When he could stand up straight Cain stopped, and put down his end of the chest. The torch flame warmed his ivory skin, burnished his dark red hair. "We're alone," he said, meaning—it's safe to talk.

Neema thought of all the things she would like to say. Not all the things. One thing. The thing she could never say. *I've missed you. My friend.*

His sharp green eyes were searching hers. "What's going on, Neema?"

She thought of Gaida, whispering Katsan's secrets into his ear. *I've missed you, my friend. But I don't trust you. Not one inch.* "Nothing."

He shunted the ebony chest with his foot. "You stumbled on this by accident?"

No. A flock of imaginary ravens led me to it. "Yes."

"Fine. Fine." A word people use when they are not fine. He walked off.

Neema dragged the chest up on her own.

CHAPTER

Twenty-Three

Foxes like things blurry. Foxes like things vague. Ending something, properly ending it, makes them itchy, and a touch melancholic. As for timekeeping, this is considered an unnatural practice, not to be trusted.

On the veranda, the Fox contingent was playing a maddeningly complex drinking game involving cards and checkers, and forfeits. Abbot Fort was half asleep in the hammock, swaying gently. Shal was trying to reassure Katsan that no, she had not been drugged, he would be able to tell. Havoc was rinsing streaks of tunnel dirt from his white-gold hair, his tunic washed and draped over a chair to dry.

Which left Tala, half mad with boredom. For all Fenn Fedala's complaints about being *used*, Oxes were famously bad at doing nothing. "Why don't I fetch Ruko?" she said. He was still training under the yew tree—a form of standing meditation, dropped down in a low squat.

"Bad idea," Havoc said, towelling his hair. A gold pendant glinted against his sun-tanned chest—another Monkey sigil, the three interwoven branches forming a circle. "He killed a servant once, just for breaking his concentration. Snapped his neck with one hand."

"That's true," Neema said. The Tiger abbess had mentioned the incident in one of her letters to the emperor. Bersun had insisted on receiving regular reports, and Rivenna Glorren had been happy to oblige. In fact, she had sounded proud of her protégé. *What should a mouse expect?* she'd written of the incident. *If it bites a tiger's tail?*

Tala bounced on the balls of her feet, tried a few more stretches, then gave in. She called over to the Foxes. "Is the Trial over?"

One of the players glanced up from their game. "Did it ever begin?"

"Are we even here?" someone else added, and the entire contingent went, "Oooooh," as if they'd made a seismic philosophical breakthrough.

Neema poured herself some mint tea. She was frustrated too, they were wasting precious time—but she hid it better. A vital skill at court. If you couldn't mask your irritation from the emperor after he'd kept you waiting half the day, then you were in serious trouble. It helped, she found, to focus on tiny moments of pleasure. This tea, for instance, poured over ice—a classic Fox drink, celebrating the mix of opposites. Warm and cool. Sweet and fresh. Each mouthful different from the last, reminding the drinker to savour every shifting, fleeting moment. The leaves had turned the water a pale, summer green, and the ice sparkled and clinked against the glass. Neema was so absorbed in her study, she didn't notice Katsan approach until the Bear contender ripped the drink from her hand and smashed it to the ground.

"This is how you hunt a killer?" she snarled. The warrior in her was looking for a fight—somewhere to channel her grief. She pressed closer, jamming Neema up against the table. "You're not even pretending to try."

"Let her be, Katsan," Shal said mildly, from his bench.

Exactly what she was looking for. An audience. She grabbed Neema under the arm and dragged her over. "Look." She pulled at the purple band wrapped around Neema's arm. "Look! These are Gaida's colours. Ripped from her body. Stained in her blood." She dug her nails in deeper. "Worn by her killer."

Neema froze.

There. It was said.

The entire veranda fell silent. In the hammock, Abbot Fort opened his eyes a crack.

Neema saw Tala and Havoc share a knowing look, as if Katsan had voiced something they too had wondered about but kept to themselves.

"That's quite an accusation, Katsan," Tala said, carefully.

Neema's tongue felt heavy in her mouth. She swallowed. Everyone was waiting for her to defend herself, but the words wouldn't come. The truth was, she didn't know. She didn't know if she was innocent or guilty.

This was *her* nightmare.

Katsan shoved her away in disgust. "Look at her, in her borrowed uniform. She thinks she's a real contender."

"I don't—" Neema managed.

"Is that why you killed her? To take her place?" Katsan's eyes were blazing with righteous fury. "Or were you just jealous? Because you were *nothing* next to her, and you hated her for it. You want our alibis, Neema Kraa? Where's yours? Where were you when my Sister was murdered?"

"Is the Trial ended?" Ruko stood at the edge of the veranda, his broad frame blocking the light.

"Contender Valit." Katsan stifled her irritation. "We are waiting for Neema Kraa's alibi. You must be keen to hear it." She dropped her voice. "We all know here, of your stolen blade."

"That is no business of yours." Ruko's lip curled in disdain. "Whoever stole Hurun-tooth will answer to me. Abbot Fort. The day grows long."

"So it does." The abbot's voice wafted up from the hammock. "So it does. Contender Brundt—would you help an old man to his feet?"

There followed a minute of immaculate physical comedy as Katsan attempted to extract the abbot from the hammock and he expertly hindered her. The more flustered she became, the funnier it was. The Foxes laughed first, then everyone else joined in. Even Ruko looked faintly amused. Tala was laughing so hard she had to walk away to recover.

Neema took the opportunity to withdraw to a quiet corner and compose herself. Her arm was throbbing where Katsan had dug in her nails—the Bear warrior had drawn blood. But it was the look Tala and Havoc had exchanged that really worried her. Ruko's interruption had won her some time—but she needed to prove her innocence, fast.

At last the abbot relented, and allowed Katsan to pull him free. "I hope you enjoyed your visit to the tombs, contenders," he said. A silver hip flask materialised from his robes, as they lined up for the results.

"Life," he declaimed, taking a swig, "is a puzzle with no answer; a game with no rules; a maze with no exit, except death. And still we stumble on through the dark, creating form where there is none, seeing patterns that are not there."

A short pause, while they figured this out.

"There was no path to the temple," Tala groaned. "So what the Eight were we doing down there?"

"Facing our fears," Havoc said, with a shrug. Wasn't it obvious?

"No, no," Abbot Fort corrected him. "That was just a bit of fun."

"What?" Havoc's face fell. "You buried me in a coffin! I could hardly breathe. I thought I was going to *die*—"

"Fun for us," the abbot said, and without further preamble launched into the results. Ruko had come last with no points. Katsan followed with one point. Havoc was next, then Neema in third place with three points. Tala was second. "Congratulations Contender Worthy—you have won the Fox Trial. Five points to the Hounds."

The Fox contingent clapped politely. Shal put a fist to his heart and bowed his thanks.

"Your grace," Havoc said, aggrieved. "Contender Worthy abandoned the Trial. You told him to withdraw."

The abbot held up a correcting finger. "I asked if he was *willing* to forfeit his points, in his uncle's name."

Katsan joined the protest. "No, Havoc's right—you very clearly told him to withdraw—"

"To the shade. Where he spent the next three hours taking care of his fellow contenders. Including you, Bear contender." A smile towards the card table. "We were listening."

Tala had finally worked it out. "So what happened in the tombs…didn't count? Only how we treated each other." She looked over to where Cain had just joined them, leaning against a wooden post. "Oh, clever. I like that."

He smiled back at her.

Katsan's shoulders dropped a fraction. "And how do you explain *her*?" she demanded, glowering at Neema.

The abbot tweaked an eyebrow. "*She* offered you water at the tomb steps. In the tunnels, when she thought you were in danger, she ran to help. Remind me, Contender Brundt. What did you do when you heard her screams?"

Silence from the Bear contender. But she lowered her gaze.

"Honour, self-sacrifice. Courage." Fort tucked his flask away. "I'm no expert on the matter, but...isn't that the Way of the Bear?"

"It is," Katsan muttered, to the ground.

"Well, then." A deadly grin from the abbot. "Instead of arguing with me, you should thank Contender Valit. If he had shown a speck of interest or concern for anyone but himself, you would have no points at all."

It was exactly as Neema had suspected. Cain had designed the Trial to play against Ruko's greatest weakness: his lack of compassion. When Shal had made the painful decision to step away from the Trial, Ruko had called him a fool. Perhaps he could have clawed things back, if he'd come into the veranda and supported his fellow contenders as they returned from the tombs. But he hadn't. Of course he hadn't. Tigers walk alone.

The only thing that surprised Neema was Ruko's indifference. The Foxes had set him up to lose and he didn't appear to care. He poured himself a glass of water, while the other contenders gathered around to congratulate Shal.

"Abbot Fort," he said, when things had settled. "I note that the Raven contender has sustained an injury to her arm."

"Too late for the fake pity, Ruko," Cain said, still leaning on his post. "Trial's over."

Ruko settled his glass. "Contender Brundt attacked a fellow contender outside of the fighting platform."

"I didn't attack her," Katsan said, in a tight voice.

Ruko lifted his chin towards Neema. "Her arm is bleeding."

Neema cupped her hand over the wounds in her arm. "It's nothing serious." Katsan hated her enough already.

"Your grace." Ruko appealed to the abbot. "It is your responsibility to administer the penalty."

"Is it?" The abbot frowned, and patted his robes. "Does anyone have a copy of *The Laws of the Festival* on them?"

The Fox contingent looked at each other. One of them raised a tentative hand. "I have a copy of *Advanced Positions for Intrepid Lovers?*"

"Not right now, thank you Nedwin."

"I expect Contender Kraa knows the Laws by heart," Ruko said.

He was right, she did. That's why she was banned from the Raven palace tavern quiz, after winning ten weeks in a row, in a team of one. Neema knew everything.

"Contender?" Fort asked Neema. And then, hastily, "Just the relevant line, please." Cain must have warned him.

And Neema, of course, couldn't help but answer. "For a minor assault—"

"I barely touched her," Katsan snapped.

"—the aggressor forfeits their most recent Trial points to the injured party," Neema finished.

Katsan clenched her fists. "I will *not* give my points to her."

"You only have one," Neema said, before she could stop herself, and the entire Fox contingent burst out laughing.

"A change to the results," Fort said. "I sense our Guardian at play." The Fox delighted in shifting fortunes. "The Raven contender now has four points. Bear contender…you have none."

And all thanks to Ruko, Neema thought. She didn't flatter herself he'd done it for her sake. Much more likely he'd seen an opportunity to take a point from a true rival. These subtle power games were all part of his training.

Nothing left for Katsan now but to shore up what was left of her dignity. She shifted into her signature stance, hands clasped behind her back. "Thank you, Fox abbot, for this instruction in humility. I shall reflect upon my actions, and strive to do better."

"Marvellous," Fort replied. "Good luck with that. Nedwin, I'll have that book now."

And with that, apparently, the Fox Trial was over.

CHAPTER
Twenty-Four

N EEMA WROTE FENN A NOTE: *No need to meet at the armoury, I have my own weapons.*

She wrote it at her desk, in her new quarters, and handed it to her newly re-hired assistant Benna, who was beyond thrilled to be an official part of the Festival, all expenses paid, and might die from the excitement, just a warning, but she might.

High Commander Hol Vabras had been busy during the Fox Trial. In the wake of Gaida's murder, he had decided to move the contenders into the Palace of the Awakening Dragon, where the Imperial Hounds could watch over them. The Visitor and Servant Jadu would be afforded the same protection—whether they wanted it or not. The contingents would remain in their respective palaces. Lack of space, Vabras said.

The contingents protested, furiously. Most of all the Dragons, camped out in the Imperial Temple.

Vabras was unmoved. Vabras was always unmoved. "This is happening," he said, once everyone had finished shouting, and left the rest to his sergeants.

Who were, unlike their commander, open to bribes. There followed an unseemly display of haggling for the best rooms. Kindry was not about to waste his precious gold tiles on Neema, so she was allotted the worst apartment. No bathroom, shabby furniture, wallpaper dotted with mould. A sweet, rotting smell that Neema didn't want to think about because evidently something had crawled away to die, and hadn't crawled far enough. Still, at least Pink-Pink would be happy here—she hadn't seen one yet but there had to be cockroaches.

Benna promised she would fix everything, and Neema believed her.

She stepped out on to the apartment's one good feature—a wide stone balcony overlooking the Festival Square, with views right across the island. From here Neema could see the imposing grey turrets of the Bear palace rising through the trees, red and black pennants lying slack in the humid air. Ahead of her lay the Grand Canal, and the golden dome of the temple, burnished by the sun. Far, far beyond that, before the western perimeter wall, she could just make out the dark sprawl of the Raven palace —a nagging reminder that she must return to Gaida's rooms. She'd asked Kindry to leave them untouched, so she could conduct a proper search. He'd told her she had until sundown. The Flock, he said, was upset by her lack of progress with the investigation. "You must try harder, my dear. I can't shield you for ever."

She stretched her arms along the balcony wall. "Fuck you, Kindry," she said, and felt instantly better.

"Neema?" A voice from the next balcony. Tala's wife, Sunur.

A trellis of white jasmine divided the two balconies. Neema poked her head around, enveloped in the jasmine's sweet, heady scent.

Sunur was stretched out on a day bed reading, her straight brown hair tied in a high pony tail. She waved her book in the air. "What do you make of all this?" she asked, meaning the move to the palace, the guards at the door.

"Makes sense to me."

Sunur gave Neema a serious, scrutinising look over her glasses. "You don't feel like a prisoner?"

"Not till you mentioned it."

"Sorry." Sunur hugged her knees. Anxious, but trying not to show it.

"You get used to seeing armed guards when you live here. Don't worry. It's nothing sinister."

Sunur looked dubious.

"Can I ask you about Ruko?"

She pulled a face. "Sure."

"You thought he was waiting for someone in the orchard last night?"

"I know he was. He had a note with him—he slid it under his tunic when he saw me coming. This tatty old square of paper..." Sunur stopped, revolted by a sudden thought. "Ugh. Was it a love letter?"

No. Neema knew about Ruko's love life—or lack thereof—from Rivenna Glorren's letters to the emperor. The abbess had been surprisingly forthcoming on the subject. *Ruko shuns all personal ties, and holds himself apart—even from me, his Guardian-mother. He ensures his physical needs are met, but only to stop them from becoming a distraction. These encounters are paid for.* "Did he see you?" she asked Sunur. "Did you talk to him?"

"Yes." Sunur breathed on her glasses, polished them. "I called him a cunt."

"Ohhhhhhh." Neema ran out of breath, and coughed. She thought of Ruko, all six foot five of him, iron muscles and no conscience. The two of them in the dark, with no witnesses. "That was brave."

"Thanks."

"Brave is court-speak for incredibly stupid."

"Oh. Right." Sunur grimaced. "Well I only said what everyone else is thinking. And," she lifted a finger, like a lawyer, "he didn't disagree."

She was joking, but there was pain underneath. Something personal. Neema waited.

Sunur hugged her knees again, talking to the floor. "The Procession of Exile passed through my town."

Yana. Neema's stomach flipped.

"They made us line the streets. We had to shout at her, as the cart passed by. *Traitor. You are nothing. You are nothing.* They made us, Neema. The Hounds." Tears filled Sunur's eyes as she remembered. "And you know the worst part? Some people enjoyed it. They were *laughing*, like it was a Kind Festival parade. They threw things at her. Neighbours. Friends. Family." Sunur gripped her knees tighter. "No one talked about it afterwards. Like it was taboo somehow.

But I always wanted to ask them. Were they ashamed of them-selves? Embarrassed? *Proud?*"

Neema, thinking of her own complicity, said, "They probably tried to forget it."

Sunur looked up sharply. "I won't. I remember what they did to her. What *he* did. Her brother. Her *brother*, Neema. Her *twin*."

Neema gave a sharp glance to the balcony above. Empty, thank the Eight. This was dangerous territory, they shouldn't be talking about this. Sunur could get them both into trouble. But she stayed where she was, only patted the air in warning.

"She looked at me," Sunur said, not taking the cue. "It was only a second, but I'll never forget it. That poor, terrified girl, trying so hard to be brave. I remember her." She lifted her voice. "Yanara Valit."

Neema winced, and pointed inside, where the Hounds were guarding the corridors. Then put a finger to her lips.

Sunur gave a mocking laugh. "But we're *not prisoners*, Neema. It's *nothing sinister*."

"Mama!" A scamper of footsteps, and Sunur's daughter Suru dashed out on to the balcony, holding a wooden ox in her fist. "Look at Fenn make me!"

Sunur pivoted instantly to attentive mother, lifting Suru on to her lap and admiring her new toy. At Suru's command, she held out her arm, so it might become the Great Eastern Road. Suru jumped the ox from her mother's wrist, to elbow to shoul-der. "Riversmeet…Tuk…Samra," they said together, naming the cities along the route. The game quickly descended into tickles, and laughter.

Neema retreated to her own balcony. She sensed that she had disappointed Sunur. Another relationship soured before it had begun.

You are just very bad at making friends, she reminded herself. *In the way some people are bad at singing.*

Down below in the Festival Square, the crowds were gathering for the afternoon fights. The white canvas of the fighting platform taunted her, its golden ∞. Within the next quarter hour, she would face Shal Worthy. She would *fight* Shal Worthy. It didn't seem possible.

There was a knock at the door. A delivery from Grace Eliat: two custom-made black contender uniforms, purple raven wings spread wide across the chest. Neema ran her hand over the sigil. There was no way the designer could have completed such intricately detailed embroidery in so short a time. As she examined the material more closely, Neema realised the front panel had been cut out of Gaida's tunic, then sewn into the new garment.

She changed quickly then stood in front of the mottled bedroom mirror, shifting and squatting to test the fit. She had to admit, Grace had done an excellent job. She squared her shoulders and toughened her expression, as if she were in the contender line, waiting to be called to fight. "Neema Kraa, Raven Contender," she murmured, then sagged and shook her head. She could say it as many times as she liked, but that didn't make it true.

Looking the part was not being the part.

CHAPTER
Twenty-Five

NOTHING COULD HAVE prepared Neema for the fight platform. Everything felt distorted—the deafening roar of the crowd, the rough feel of the rope, the bright Guardian banners.

"You're going to be great," Benna said.

"I'm going to throw up."

"No worries, I have a bucket." Nothing dented Benna.

In the opposite corner, Shal was chatting to a member of his contingent as if he'd bumped into them in the market. How was he so calm? Neema was in such a fugue state, she couldn't remember crossing the square, or mounting the steps. She was just... *here,* as if some giant, invisible bird had picked her up from the contender line and dropped her from a great height. Not a bird, she corrected herself. The emperor. The emperor had put her here. This was his doing.

She dragged her gaze up to the imperial balcony. Empty. No emperor, no retinue. Who could blame them? Highly trained Hound warrior vs highly terrified Raven scholar—hardly the match of the Festival.

"Contenders, your places," Abbot Fort said. Hip flask in one hand, bell in the other.

Shal strode out and saluted the three galleries in turn, fist to heart. He was popular—Neema could feel the warmth of the crowd's response, the positive energy surging his way.

The abbot said something to the crowd, and they laughed. Neema couldn't hear him; she could hardly breathe. She was falling down a hole marked panic. This was happening. This was actually happening.

Shal shifted into a fighting stance. Neema mirrored him. She lifted her arms. They felt heavy, as if she were wading through deep water.

Shal gave her a discreet smile of reassurance. He'd promised he would try his best not to hurt her. A thank you for helping him win the Fox Trial.

The bell rang.

They circled each other.

He moved and she jerked backwards, too sharply. Anyone else would have pressed the advantage, but Shal hung back, letting her regain her balance.

Come on. You know the basics. Give him something to work with.

The fight began in earnest. Neema kept her guard up and Shal kept his promise, pulling his punches. But it was hard—she hadn't realised how *hard* it was, just to maintain concentration. Each round lasted three minutes, which didn't sound like a long time until you were up here, with a stitch in your side and sweat streaming into your eyes.

She rubbed her forehead—losing concentration for a second. Enough time for Shal to leap in and—well, whatever it was he did, it was fast and decisive and she was flat on her back, the air punched from her lungs. The sky swung above her, then settled.

Shal dropped down and hissed in her ear. "Don't think, just move. Trust me."

For the next minute she moved naturally, and Shal did his best to make it look like a genuine contest. Enough to convince the crowds, at least. Abbot Fort was less easily duped.

He rang the bell. "First round to the overly generous Hound contender," he said, swigging from his flask.

Neema staggered to her corner. Three minutes. It had felt like three lifetimes.

"You were amazing!" Benna said, coming at her with a sponge.

Neema couldn't speak—her lungs were on fire. She collapsed to the ground. Benna squeezed the sponge over her head. Cool, fresh water streamed down her face, rinsing away a sheet of sweat. "Again," she panted. "Please."

Benna had a second sponge already loaded.

Should have yelled stop, Neema thought, as the water revived her. *Never mind the half point.* She'd thought about it when she was lying flat on her back, but the word had stuck in her throat. Kindry's dig about her shaming the Flock. And the crowd, willing her to fail. They didn't realise she fed off that, the way another contender might feed on their support. *Oh, you think I'm unworthy, do you? Well fuck you...*

The stitch was still fading when the abbot called them back. Round two—the weapons round. Neema had selected the shield, and the leather cosh. She didn't trust herself with anything sharp —she'd only end up injuring herself.

She fixed the shield to her left arm. It was shaped like a pair of folded raven's wings, narrowing to a sharp point at the bottom. "Would you look at that?" the abbot said, admiringly. He rapped the centre with his knuckle and it rang out clear and true, like a bell.

This was our cue.

Oh, had you forgotten about us? We have been watching and waiting, we have been very patient.

Opening our wings, we glided down from the palace roof, flying low over the crowds and landing with a neat *plack* on a platform post.

"Eight!" Neema said, staring at us.

Stretching out our neck, we greeted her loudly. **Kraa! Kraa!**

The abbot gave the shield another tap. "Where did you get this? I've never seen its like. Extraordinary."

Magnificent. The word was magnificent. We preened ourself.

Neema looked at the abbot, then looked at us. "Abbot Fort. Can you see a giant raven perched on that corner post?"

The abbot made a show of looking at the empty post. "Are you claiming insanity? There are other ways to stop the fight..."

Neema rubbed her face. The last remnants of the Dragonscale. Had to be. Either that, or the Second Guardian of the Eight was perched ten feet away, calling her name. Which was impossible, because the Second Guardian of the Eight did not exist. It was a myth, a metaphor, dreamed up by the ancients.

We tried one more time. **Kraa! Kraa!**

She ignored us. We have come to recognise this stage—it is called "denial." She was not yet ready to accept our magnificence. If we pushed any harder, she would break.

She shook her head to clear it—*no!*—and saw that the post was empty. (It was not empty, we were right there. She had simply chosen not to see us any more. Denial.)

Shal moved into a hanging stance, preparing for the bell. He'd chosen a pair of short wooden sticks, non-lethal weapons more suitable for training. Another kindness. As the bell rang he waited for her to attack, encouraging her with his eyes. *Come at me.* Neema swung at him. With a sharp snap of his wrist, Shal rapped his stick across her knuckles. Neema yelped in pain as the crowd cheered. *Bastards.*

Shal smiled and knocked his sticks together, giving Neema time to recover. For the next minute he led her in a martial dance about the platform. Most of the time he hit her shield, but a few strikes got through. Eight, they stung—she would be covered in bruises at the end of this.

A mistake was inevitable. Neema was slowing down, the shield heavier with every lift. Shal was tired, too—he was working for both of them.

She saw the strike in her periphery, too late to defend herself. The stick came down over her knuckles again, harder this time. On reflex she spread her fingers, and the cosh fell from her hand. *Raven protect me*, Neema thought, carelessly.

The world juddered to a halt.

She felt a cool, thin breeze surround her. A wisp of cloud misted her skin. A floating sensation, as if she could lift into the air.

Lightness. Balance. Control.

The cosh was still falling to the floor. Shal drew back his arm, preparing for another strike. His movements were painfully slow

—a quarter their usual speed. She could see the places he was exposed, she had time to plan her counterstrike.

Deflecting his striking hand, she raised her shield and slammed it against his chest.

Shal stumbled backwards, ungrounded. Surprised, for the first time he trained his Houndsight on her, hazel eyes glittering and intense. But Neema was already pressing her advantage, pushing him again with the shield. He fell against the ropes.

The base of the shield was very sharp. Sharp as a raven's beak.

There was time, she had time. The shield was made to do this, to pierce through flesh, it was only natural.

She lifted her shield arm. Shal's eyes widened in shock. For him, this was happening between heartbeats, bewilderingly fast. One moment winning, the next on the ropes, with a shield coming down, aimed at his throat.

What am I doing?

No, no, no . . .

At the last moment, Neema dashed the shield to the ground. It landed point first, so sharp it tore a hole in the canvas and sank into the wood beneath. Time snapped forward, to its normal pace.

We flew back up to the imperial balcony, pleased by our experiment. She was receptive, despite her denial. When the time came, she would be ready.

The bell rang out.

Neema scrambled back, tripping over herself, horrified by what she'd almost done. Eight. Eight. She could have killed him.

Abbot Fort took a casual swig from his hip flask. "Now that was interesting. Round two to the Raven contender."

The Fox contingent needed a moment to fix the tear in the canvas. Neema stumbled to her corner in a daze, while the crowd tried to work out what they'd just seen. An accident, it was decided. A fluke.

"Two sponges coming at you," Benna said.

Neema kept her head bowed between her knees as the water spilled down her neck and shoulders.

Benna crouched down, concerned. "Contender Kraa? Are you all right?"

Neema wiped the water from her face. She had to tell someone. She needed to explain…"I was drugged last night. Dragonscale oil. A really strong dose. Almost fatal."

"Oh, no!" Benna clutched her sponges tight. "Contender Kraa! I'm so sorry."

Neema shook her head. "It pushes you to do things…I can't control myself, Benna. It's still working through my system." She watched Shal, moving angrily back and forth on the other side of the platform. "I nearly killed him."

"You're not a killer," Benna said, emphatically. She wrapped a small, rough hand around Neema's wrist. Her *Life is Short* hand. "And you *did* control yourself back there. I saw it, Contender Kraa. You stopped yourself—in the heat of the fight."

Neema sighed, partially reassured. But still a thought broke its way through her defences. *Yes. But I like Shal. I didn't like Gaida.*

When the bell rang out for round three, Shal punched Neema so hard in the stomach she stopped breathing. As she bent double, he kicked her to the ground and twisted her arm in its socket.

"*Stop!*," she moaned, into the platform, leaving a smear of blood on the canvas. She'd caught her lip as she fell.

Shal waited another infernal second, then released her. Neema curled into a foetal position.

"The Raven contender stopped the fight," the abbot called out to the galleries. "Victory to the Hound contender."

By the time Neema got to her feet, Shal was already striding back to the contender line. She trailed after him, dabbing her lip with the back of her hand. Looking up, she saw the emperor emerge on his balcony, ready for the fight of the day. Tiger vs Bear. The galleries were now packed tight in anticipation of a close match.

Neema passed Ruko and Katsan on their way to the platform. Katsan said, without stopping, "Now we see your true colours."

Ruko blocked her path, staring down at her. The fixed gaze of a cat, considering a bird through a windowpane. "I did not expect you to interest me. We will speak again," he murmured, and let her go.

When she reached the line, she went straight over to Shal. "I am so sorry," she said, hand on her heart. "Shal—"

"My fault for trusting you, Contender Kraa," he said, not deigning to look at her. "I won't make that mistake again."

She slipped back into line between Cain and Tala, head down. As the bell rang for the first round, Cain whispered, "I hated you before it was fashionable."

"Shit!" Tala hissed. Ruko had just back-handed Katsan, sending her reeling. The Bears' champion of champions, swatted like a fly.

"Heat exhaustion," Havoc said.

"Grief," Tala countered.

"Both," Cain and Neema said, at the same moment.

As the fight continued, Katsan was pushed into a permanent, harried defence. Blood streamed from a cut on her brow. Her tunic was soaked with sweat.

Ruko was not sweating at all. He breathed easily, moved easily. He was taking the fight seriously—even at this distance, Neema could see the determination, the focus he brought to every move. But he looked as though he could spend the next hour up there without tiring.

Because for Ruko—Neema realised, in a flash of understanding—this fight had not begun on the platform, but at the afternoon's Trial. He must have realised the Foxes would rig things so he came away with nothing. That's why he didn't waste time arguing over the scores. He'd already factored in the loss, and made the tactical decision to conserve his energy for a fight he could win.

Tigers. Always ten steps ahead.

The fight had turned so bloody, Neema couldn't watch. She stared at her feet, willing it to be over. At last the bell rang out and Katsan hurried to her corner to be patched up by her contingent.

The crowd turned to one another, taken aback by the Bear warrior's weak performance. Neema was less surprised. Now she thought about it, the heat exhaustion and the grief were not separate things, they were connected. Katsan had lost her friend, and she wasn't thinking straight.

Bears felt things deeply. In the austere fortress of Anat-garra, kinship took on a profound importance. The loss of a Brother or Sister could be devastating. Whoever killed Gaida had taken out not one contender, but two.

And Ruko was reaping the benefit.

Neema narrowed her eyes. His alibi was solid, but there were others who were heavily invested in his success.

"What?" Cain said, softly.

"The Tiger abbess," she said, in his ear. "Does she have an alibi?"

A tight nod. *Leave it with me.*

The bell rang for the weapons round. And here at least Katsan had an edge—twenty years fighting real battles in the borderlands; her sword so familiar that it seemed a part of her.

She won the round, but she had given everything to it. Ruko had saved himself for the final bout—and again showed no mercy.

"Eight," Tala murmured, as Katsan dodged a lethal upper cut. "I'd rather fight a real tiger."

As the fight dragged on, the square fell into stunned silence. Ruko wasn't simply better than Katsan, he was in an entirely different class. His power, his focus...

"Stop," Katsan called out. "Stop." The fight was over. Another half point taken away, edging her below zero.

"He's going to win," Tala said, in a hollow voice. Not just the fight, but the Festival. "That's our next emperor. Eight protect us."

"And remain Hidden," Neema answered.

At the end of the line, entirely forgotten, the Visitor watched, and said nothing.

Twenty-Six

GAIDA'S BODY HAD been taken to the morgue. In all other ways, the apartment was just as Neema had left it a few hours before. The fan clacked on the ceiling, stirring the thick, humid air. On the desk, papers lifted and settled, lifted and settled. Through the open shutters, the voices of the Raven choir trailed up from the gardens. Tomorrow they would sing in front of the Festival crowds, to open the Day of the Raven. Neema could hear the strain of nerves as they worked on their harmonies.

Nerves and also grief for Gaida, their lost contender. The second palace was a sombre place today—candles flickering at every window, grey mourning patches worn over every heart, the Imperial Library closed out of respect. The stairs and corridor leading to the penthouse apartment were filled with flowers and notes of remembrance. On the door to the antechamber, someone had scrawled: **SHE WILL HAVE JUSTICE** in thick red chalk. It read, to Neema, like a threat.

As she searched the rooms, she imagined Gaida's ghost hovering at her shoulder, fuming. *You're only doing this to clear your name. You don't care about me. You only care about yourself. Typical.*

Gaida's ghost sounded uncannily like Neema's conscience.

She'd been hoping to unearth Yaan Rack's report as she searched, but she was out of luck. Either the killer had taken it, which seemed unlikely, or Gaida had hidden it somewhere else. *A secret lair*, Neema thought, dramatically—but then Gaida *was* dramatic. Everything a performance…

…of course.

Crossing to the balcony, Neema called down to the choir below. One of the Ankalla brothers was helping them rehearse. Riff, it looked like—the youngest of the three. Seventeen, if that. She waved at him to join her.

Riff dashed up the iron staircase as if the emperor had commanded him. When he reached the top he pressed his palms together and dropped to his knees, head bowed—the Monkey salute of abasement. His flappy ginger hair swung down into his eyes as he stared at the floor. "Contender Kraa—on behalf of myself and my brothers, I humbly beg your forgiveness for our part in the opening ceremony. I swear on my life—we had no idea our song would cause any trouble. She said she'd squared it with you." He pressed his forehead to the ground, and waited.

His abasement required a formal response from Neema. "Your words reflect well upon you, Riff Ankalla of Three Ports. I hear your remorse, and accept your apology."

His body sagged with relief. "Thank you, Contender Kraa," he said, into the floor.

"Please," she said, encouraging him to stand. As she did so a breeze picked up and she caught something in the air—the faint, iron tang of blood. Gaida's blood. Was she imagining it, or was it the last vestige of the Dragonscale, heightening her sense of smell? The balcony was long—they were a good twenty feet from the spot. The large terracotta pots stood clustered just as she'd found them, circling a now-empty space.

Riff got to his feet, his mind still on the ceremony. "Eight—the way the emperor looked at us." He cringed. "We'll be lucky to find work at court after this. Lord Kindry said he'd put in a word if I helped the choir with their harmonies."

For free, no doubt. Kindry was infamously mean. "Gaida—" she began.

Riff looked stricken. "I didn't kill her!"

The thought had not entered Neema's head. "No that's not—"

Riff, in a panic, talked over her. "I was with my brothers—you can ask them. We were so upset about the ceremony. We stayed up all night, crying."

Which was both the saddest and most convincing alibi Neema
had ever heard. "That's not why I called you up here, Riff. I'm sorry.
I was only wondering whether Gaida kept another room, separate
from this one. Somewhere she could practise her performance
without being overheard—"

"Yes, yes! The cupboard room. We rehearsed there together. You
may have noticed the melody wasn't the standard arrangement—it
changed the cadence slightly—"

She cut him off. "The cupboard room?"

"Aye, this tiny, narrow room…" He mimed it with his hands.
"Barely enough room for the four of us. Nice acoustics though—"
He caught Neema's impatience. "It's over on the north side of the
palace. You know—the ugly bit." He gestured northwards, and
scrunched his nose. "Round the back, by the bins."

Neema felt as if she were falling, the ground parting beneath
her feet. "Bright green door?"

"Yes, that's it. How did you—"

"You met Gaida there yesterday?"

He looked wistful. "She wanted it to be perfect. We *were* perfect, on the night. I don't think we've ever sung better."

"Did anyone else come by while you were there?"

He shook his head.

"You're sure?"

"Positive. It was all a big secret." He sighed, regretful. "We should
have realised…"

"You had no reason to doubt her word," Neema said, and felt a
flare of anger towards Gaida. Always so careless—with her work,
her belongings, with the people around her. She'd used the Ankalla
brothers then discarded them, the same way she'd lose a library
book, or break a vase, or steal a friend's lover. And if you complained, you were being trivial. Or, the even greater sin—tedious.

Riff was on his way back down the staircase when Neema
stopped him. One final question. "Who do you think killed her?"

He tensed, gripping the rail. Shook his head in answer. *No idea.*

Below him in the gardens, the choir had given up their practice
and were clustered in smaller groups, talking. The late afternoon

sun stretched their shadows across the grass. "What about them, what are they saying?"

Riff's knuckles had turned white.

"They think I did it, don't they?"

Riff's eyes widened. "I...don't listen to gossip, Contender Kraa."

She sighed, and let him go.

Wearily, she walked down to the other end of the balcony. Dragging a couple of the terracotta pots out of the way, she kneeled down and touched her fingers to the wooden boards. Someone had made an attempt to wipe them clean, but the blood had seeped through where Gaida had lain, leaving a small stain.

Could she have done this, with the Dragonscale urging her on? Neema forced herself to imagine it. Lifting the dagger and plunging it into Gaida's back. Gaida falling to her knees, and then to the ground. Arranging her body, and then the pots. Closing the shutters neatly behind her.

It felt...unlikely. She could imagine herself killing Gaida in the heat of the moment, in self-defence. If she'd gone hunting for the folder, and Gaida had disturbed her. If they'd fought. She could see how it could have ended badly. An accident, perhaps. But there was no sign of a struggle. Neema had no defensive marks on her and neither did Gaida.

Gaida would have fought, she thought, with sudden clarity. She would not have gone quietly; she never did anything quietly. She would have fought, she would have flailed, she would have smashed things. She would have screamed hard enough to wake the Dragon.

Something else struck Neema, the more she looked at the patch of blood. Shouldn't there be more of it? A *lot* more?

"She was already dead," Neema said, out loud. That's why she'd looked so peaceful. Her death had not been violent, there had been no struggle.

Neema ran through the possibilities. There'd been no signs she was strangled, or knocked out. Smothered? But even then, Gaida would have woken, and fought back. That peaceful expression... Drugged. She must have been drugged.

A memory prodded at Neema's consciousness. That dream she'd had on the veranda, the one Shal had woken her from. Gaida on the throne, drinking…

Tea. The teacup. She'd seen it from the start. Seen it and dismissed it.

Ducking back inside, she checked under the day bed. The teapot was still there, next to the discarded cup with its lipstick print. Lifting the teapot lid, she sniffed the dregs. Valerian root. Then she checked the caddy on a nearby table. The same.

She fell to the floor, overwhelmed with relief. It wasn't me. I didn't kill her.

Last night, Gaida had told Navril to replace the valerian root with lavender tea. He would have done as he was ordered, no question. Which meant someone else had refilled it; someone who knew Gaida usually drank valerian tea before she went to bed, but didn't know she'd changed her routine that night. They'd tipped out the lavender and added this new blend, prepared in advance. Neema was sure that when it was tested, they would find traces of a strong sedative. A couple of sachets of Dr. Yetbalm's sleeping draught would do it.

That's why there was no sign of a struggle. Gaida had drunk the tea, probably cursing Navril for not changing it as she asked. The strong taste of the valerian would have masked the sedative. Then all the killer had to do was slip back in and put a pillow over her face. Suffocate her in her sleep. Maybe they didn't even need to do that, if the sedative was strong enough. Then they arranged the body on the balcony and stabbed the Blade of Peace into her back, to throw suspicion on the Tigers, or as a double bluff.

All of this would have required careful preparation, at least a couple of hours before Gaida retired to bed.

"It wasn't me," Neema whispered, clutching the tea caddy. "Thank the Eight. It wasn't me."

Sitting on the floor, surrounded by the sprawl of Gaida's things, her relief turned to anger. Killed in her sleep. No chance to defend herself. No time to prepare herself for her encounter with the Dragon. Snuffed out like a candle. And maybe the killer thought that was a kindness. But Gaida was a fighter. She lived in the centre of her own drama. She should have been awake. She would have wanted that.

In Scartown, there were psychics who said they could talk to ghosts: spirits bound to their old lives, unwilling or unable to return to the Eternal Path and embark on their next journey. Charlatans and frauds, Neema always thought, with their incense and bells. But knowing Gaida, knowing the force of her personality, she thought—if anyone could linger here, out of sheer will, it would be her. And *Eight*, if she is here, she must be *livid*.

"Gaida," she said, to the air. "You never liked me. I never liked you. But you didn't deserve to die this way. Whoever did this to you—I will find them."

CHAPTER
Twenty-Seven

NEEMA LOWERED THE teapot and caddy carefully into a wooden storage box and secured the lid with one of Gaida's brightly patterned scarfs. The scent of vanilla and honeysuckle infused the material—a perfume so particular to Gaida it seemed almost indecent that it had lingered after her death. Neema felt a pang of sorrow, quickly suppressed. She was running out of time—Kindry would be here soon to organise the clear-up. (And, knowing him, poke around for anything of value.) She was hoping to avoid him if she could. She was always hoping to avoid Kindry.

Moving as fast as she could through the mess, she made a second pass over Gaida's papers. She thought about Cain, who was interviewing Rivenna Glorren at the Tiger palace. She could imagine the abbess smothering someone in their sleep, or more likely sending one of her contingent to do it. Using the Blade to sow confusion. Then again, she could just as easily imagine Ish Fort sending one of *his* people to do it. Kill Gaida, frame Ruko, distress Katsan. One ball to knock down three skittles. She remembered the press of the Fox abbot's fingers on her wrist, when he warned her about Cain. *If you distract him, or get in his way...* The way he'd smiled, as her pulse leapt in sudden warning.

And then there was Princess Yasila—standing on the rusting balcony of Neema's old room, waiting for someone to arrive. The room Gaida had been using for secret meetings. I'll head there next, Neema thought.

She flicked through a sheaf of training notes—lines Gaida had written to herself in preparation for the Trials. *You rush in too fast.*

Pause, take a breath. Neema had to stop herself from reading on. She was here for the folder—nothing else.

It wasn't here.

Pause. Take a breath.

Neema did so. And caught a scent, light and soothing above Gaida's perfume.

Lavender.

A small, indoor fig tree had been shoved here into the corner, presumably to make space for the afterparty. As Neema drew closer, the smell of lavender grew stronger. She ran her fingers through the soil and smiled in triumph. This was where the killer had tipped the lavender tea leaves out of the caddy. They'd raked them into the soil, but not enough to disguise them completely. Proof her theory was correct.

"Thank you, Gaida," she murmured.

She was brushing the dirt from her hands when Kindry flung open the door.

"What *are* you doing to that plant?" he bellowed. He took in the state of the room, the clothes and papers strewn about. "Eight save us and remain Hidden, you've torn the place apart."

"That wasn't me—"

Kindry pointed to the tear in the paper screen. "You'll pay for that."

Picking up the teapot in its box, Neema tried to navigate past him to the antechamber, but he blocked her.

"What's this?" He pulled at the scarf, trying to untie it.

She lifted it out of reach. "Evidence."

Kindry's bloodshot eyes glittered. "Show me."

"I answer to High Commander Vabras on this matter, Lord Kindry. Not to you."

A short, annoyed pause. Kindry huffed stale breath in her face. "Very well. We shall visit him together."

Neema cursed inwardly. Her visit to her old room would have to wait.

They took a boat up the Grand Canal, Kindry jumping the queue and demanding a fast rower. "Imperial business," he snapped. "We

need your best man." Neema could have told him this would be
taken as an insult, and that their boatman would go more slowly
in wilful protest—but there was no point. Kindry had the measure
of the world, of that he was certain.

The sun was setting behind the Dragon palace, its sea-green
roof tiles glinting like the scales of a serpent. Neema felt a welcoming, soft breeze on her face. "What do the Speculators say for
the weather tomorrow?" she asked.

"Hot and humid again," the boatman replied, and Kindry told
him to shut up and row faster.

Hol Vabras was at his desk in the Hound palace. An unremarkable desk in an unremarkable office. The window looked out on to
a wall. A Hound officer had once offered to plant some climbing
flowers to soften the view; Vabras had looked at him, and the
officer had retired the next day.

Neema was in a better mood, because Vabras had told Kindry
to go away and Lord Kindry had done as he was told. But oh, the
look on his face! "Each day," the Scriptures said, "in times of light,
in times of shadow, seek for one small pearl of joy and you shall
find it."

She gave her report, whittled down as usual for brevity, and
handed over the teapot and caddy for testing.

"Stabbed after death," Vabras said. "Why?"

"Cleaner," Neema suggested. "No struggle, no noise."

"But why stab her at all?" He looked annoyed. Perhaps it was the
waste of time and energy, killing someone twice. Inefficient.

"I can only theorise at this point, High Commander. But the
choice of weapon has to be the key."

"To frame Contender Valit."

"Or humiliate him." Neema toughened up her pose, mimicking
Ruko's stance in the contender line. "Here he is, the fierce, unbeat-
able Tiger warrior, emperor-in-waiting, holder of the Blade of
Peace—and..." She gestured helplessly at her hip. "Oh. It's gone."

Vabras grunted, tapped his pencil on the desk. "You are not a
believer," he observed.

Neema filled in the rest. *So it didn't occur to you there is a spiritual angle to this.* "You think the killer wanted to sow panic among the..." She groped for the word.

"Faithful," Vabras said.

Neema, who had been about to say "credulous," nodded. It never failed to amaze her that Vabras—surely the least numinous, the least soulful of any creature alive—believed in the Eight. And yet he spoke of them as if they were as real and solid as his desk.

"So," Neema said. "It wasn't me. I didn't do it."

Another man would have said, "Yes, that's good news," or, "You must be relieved." Vabras only looked at her steadily, waiting for her point.

"It could be one of the contingents," she said. Best not to accuse Fort or Glorren directly, not without proof. "But the whole thing seems rushed. Amateurish, even."

Vabras lifted an eyebrow. *Explain.*

She gestured to the painted lacquer box, still wrapped in Gaida's scarf. Vabras had placed it on the floor, where he could not see it. Too distinctive. "A decent assassin wouldn't leave evidence behind."

Vabras accepted this with a sharp nod. "Anything else?"

Neema hesitated. She hadn't mentioned her old apartment, or the fact that Gaida had met with Princess Yasila just a few hours before she died. Lying to Vabras was a risk—but she needed time to hunt for Yaan Rack's report. "No, that's it."

Vabras narrowed his eyes. He did not have the Sight, like Shal Worthy, but his scrutiny could be just as painful. Neema willed herself to hold his gaze.

"You're wounded," he said.

She coiled her forearms, where Shal's sticks had landed. "A few bruises. Could have been worse."

He touched his own upper arm, impatient. *Here.*

"Oh." Neema had almost forgotten the injuries around her armband. "That was Katsan. She accused me of killing Gaida. Her grief, the sun—"

"She attacked you."

"She grabbed me." Neema turned down her armband to show him the gouges, where Katsan's nails had dug into her skin. "She lost a point for it."

There was no expression on Vabras's face, but she knew that he was smothering a rare attack of anger. One of the High Commander's most unexpected traits was his interest in Neema's physical well-being. It was nothing personal, she knew that. Vabras didn't have *feelings* for her. *Eight*, no. But he had come to appreciate her value. Vabras cared about Neema's health the same way he cared about the inner workings of his pocket watch. Once, when she caught a fever, he had appeared at the end of her bed and said, "Your sickness impedes my work." It was the closest he had ever come to paying her a compliment. "You've cleaned the wounds? Thoroughly?"

"Vinegar and turmeric." Benna had applied the paste for her —an Edge family recipe. Wounds could turn bad quickly on the borders of Dolrun.

Vabras rose from his chair and turned to face the window.

This was a bad sign. When Vabras turned to stare at his wall, it was a very bad sign for someone. "She has no alibi. The Bear contender."

Neema felt a chill, on Katsan's behalf. "She also has no motive, High Commander."

"That we know of." And then, as if the two things were not connected, "His majesty expects a swift resolution to this matter."

"He gave me four days," Neema protested, but even as she said it, she remembered the countless times Bersun had tightened a promised deadline, generosity giving way to impatience. *Why is it not done yet? I should not have to ask twice.*

Vabras turned away from the window. "You're exhausted. Get some rest. You are of no use to me in this state."

Now he said it, she realised it was true. She was dead on her feet—but she had to give it one more try. "It wasn't Katsan, I'm sure of it."

"We shall see," Vabras said.

Twenty-Eight

NEEMA SLEEPS. A boat anchored in calm waters after long hours at sea.

We had planned to pay her a dream visit, the usual nightmare of blood and terror, the beat of portentous wings, **we are coming, we are coming, be much afeared Neema Kraa.** She would have woken drenched in sweat, gripped with a sense of existential dread, it would have been highly dramatic. But Neema has slipped far beyond the realms of dream into a deeper sleep. We cannot follow her there. So we watch her from the bed post. She lies sprawled in the middle of the mattress, sheets kicked away in the heat, wearing an embroidered nightgown Benna found for her. Her favourite white linen gown, drenched in Dragonscale, is lost to the ocean, floating off on adventures of its own.

Slow, peaceful breaths.

Not long now. She is almost ready.

Those we honour with our friendship must be introduced gradually to our magnificence. A dream here. A vision there. A giddy rush of high, thin air. The faint brush of feather on skin.

Transmogrification is another way we prepare our friends for our arrival. For example: the book tucked under Neema's pillow, the one she found in the tombs. Tales of the Raven. That is us, in disguise—at least, a tiny fragment of us. It has lived with Neema for months, perched on her bookshelf. A shame, a terrible shame, that it happens to be such a **worthless** fragment, such a **stupid** and **pathetic** piece of us, **peck out its eyes**. But even we have to admit that the **hopeless** thing has performed its function to the letter. And we have been very, very delighted to be rid of it for a while, what a holiday that has been from its **profoundly enervating** presence.

We are stretching our wings, preparing to fly off home when the door to the bedchamber opens, and a shadow-figure slips inside. Silently it moves, more spirit than person, towards the bed.

An assassin.

Our beak opens in alarm. What if Neema is not sleeping, what if she has been drugged like Gaida? Death by pillow, such an inglorious end. Hopping down on to her chest, we give her a sharp peck, right in the middle of her forehead.

Wake up!

Neema stirs, sighs, and sleeps on.

Wake up, wake up!

Nothing.

We turn to confront the intruder.

Ruko Valit.

He has stopped at the foot of the bed, head tilted to one side. Listening.

Those who have learned to hone their senses can sometimes feel our presence, especially in the dark. The Tiger warrior cannot see us, but this much he intuits: we are here. We are watching. We are not happy.

"Who's there?" he murmurs. Curious, not afraid.

Opening our wings, we cry fiercely:

We are the Raven.

Ruko cannot hear us, but he catches a distant echo of our message. Lifting his hand he draws a sign of the eternal eight in the air between us. *Peace.* Appeased, we snap our wings shut and hop back to our perch on the bed post. Respect, that's all we demand. Recognition of our magnificence. Offerings. Love. Fear. Trembling awe. Worship. Shiny things. Blood sacrifice, some of us very much enjoy blood sacrifice. Truly, we ask for so little.

Neema is rising from her deep sleep, a diver swimming up for air. From here, we can reach her. We send her a vision of Ruko standing at the foot of her bed. Waft the scent of him through the air—his sweat, the trace of oil in his thick black hair, the healing ointment he rubbed into his bruises after his fight with Katsan.

There. That should be warning enough. Now wake up.

Neema woke, and opened her eyes. "Fuck the Eight!"

Ruko Valit was standing at the foot of her bed, exactly as he'd appeared in her dream. The same scent, lingering in the air between them. She was too angry to think about that because seriously, what the fuck was he doing here? Groping for her tinderbox, she lit the lantern by the bed. "You scared the shit out of me."

"I said we would speak again."

She tightened her nightrobe and swung out of bed. "You do not have my permission to be here."

"I'm here to talk. You have no reason to fear me—"

"I will be the judge of that," she snapped.

For once, Ruko faltered. "I…Yes. Of course."

"Wait there." Neema pointed to a footstool in the corner.

Ruko padded across the room and sat down. The footstool was tiny, he looked ridiculous with his knees up to his nose, which was exactly why she had sent him there.

She stepped behind a screen to tug on some clothes, tired limbs protesting, then poured herself a slug of her favourite Ketuan whisky, Tears of the Dragon.

"It's not wise to drink before a fight," Ruko said.

Tomorrow's schedule had already been posted under her door when she returned to her apartment. Neema would face Tala on the platform—the first fight of the day. It could have been worse. It could have been Ruko. She took a large swig of the whisky, to spite him.

Annoyed, Ruko got up from the stool and took a step towards her.

"Stop." Neema stretched out her arm. "No further or I'll scream. *Stop!* My assistant is in the room next door."

"Your servant will not hear you."

Benna. Neema felt the floor tilt under her bare feet. "If you… if you've *touched* her—"

"She runs a fake errand on your behalf." His eyes glittered—the Tiger warrior was amused. "Contrary to rumour, I do not kill everyone in my path."

"You snapped a man's neck for disturbing your meditation."

"He was a Fox assassin."

She sat down on the edge of the bed to recover, and took another sip of whisky. "They sent someone to kill you."

Ruko shrugged. *Of course—why wouldn't they?* "We compete for the throne, not a Kind Festival ribbon."

"Rosette," she corrected him, on reflex. "Did you never win one?"

"I did not." The question seemed to unsettle him. Childhood memories. He prowled the room. "I hear you suspect my abbess."

Rivenna Glorren had refused to meet with Cain, despite his imperial pass. Let the Hounds arrest her—she would not answer to a Scartown Scrapper. Cain had laughed and talked to the servants instead. "She has no alibi for last night. She had access to the Blade of Peace. Why did you leave it in your rooms?"

Ruko ignored the question. "Gaida was no threat to me."

"But Katsan is. Her grief distracted her today."

Deep scorn. "I do not need to cheat to win the throne."

"Your abbess could have arranged it without your knowledge." Neema gestured expansively at Ruko with her glass of whisky. "The golden warrior with his golden blood line. Destined to rule over us. She'd do anything to smooth your path."

"Abbess Glorren is a woman of profound, unshakeable faith. She believes in Yasthala's curse, without question. She would never use the Blade to take a life."

"Gaida wasn't killed with the Blade."

Ruko stopped prowling, and stared at her.

"It was staged to look that way, but that's not what killed her. She was stabbed after she died."

Ruko closed his eyes briefly. An invisible weight lifted from his shoulders. "Thank the Eight."

"You believe in the curse too?" Neema was astonished. "The Return of the Eight? All that..." *All that nonsense?*

Ruko wasn't listening. He seemed dazed by the good news. Disarmed by it. He slid to the floor, his back against the wall.

She'd never seen him like this. A chink in his armour. "Would you like a drink?" she asked, on impulse.

Ruko lifted his brows in surprise, but didn't say no. She poured him a shot and he took a sip, then settled the glass at his side. That was it—the extent of his revelry.

She joined him on the floor, cross-legged. The room had a new rug thanks to Benna—no holes, or stains or mouse droppings. Neema brushed her fingers across it, enjoying its quality. "I read a lot of reports, as High Scholar. More than I needed to," she confessed. "Curiosity. Your abbess has a reputation for removing her enemies with poison. Nothing proven, all very subtle, but… Gaida was poisoned. Or drugged, at least. We're not sure yet." She looked at him, chewed her lip. "But you suspect someone else. That's why you're here."

Ruko didn't answer. He watched her intently as she worked it through.

"You snuck out to the Ox orchard last night to meet someone. They told you to leave the Blade behind—and you were so desperate to see them, you agreed."

His face spiked with anger, then turned blank.

"Sunur said you were holding a piece of paper." Neema mimed the size with her hands. "May I see it?"

For a second she thought he would refuse. Then he reached slowly beneath his tunic and took out the Order of Exile.

Neema held it in both hands like a sacred text. This was why he had visited its twin in the archives yesterday—not to admire it, as he'd said, but to authenticate this one. To match the hand. And that was why he had called Neema over at the opening ceremony and pressed her—*Was the death witnessed? Was it confirmed?* Because this Order was supposed to remain stitched to Yana's body, even after death. Left to disintegrate and disappear, until no trace was left.

Neema stared blindly at the words she had copied out so dutifully eight years ago. The Raven's Wing ink was still the same intense purple-black, thanks to the Dragonspell woven through it.

The paper had not fared as well. In the lantern light she could see the holes pierced in each corner, where the Hounds had stitched it into Yanara's skin.

She took a breath, fighting the sick feeling in her stomach. "You were waiting for *her*, last night." Yana. "You thought she sent this to you."

"It came with a note, telling me when to meet, and where. It was her hand, her voice." He shook his head, knowing this to be impossible. "I could have sworn..."

"Do you have it with you?"

"No."

In the centre of the Order was a neat rectangular hole, where Shal Worthy had cut out Yana's name. He'd described the moment at the end of his report. Yana was still weak from an infection she'd picked up on the road. Six weeks they'd been delayed, in a village on the edge of the Dolrun Forest. Shal had recognised the painful irony—watching Yana fight for her life under the villagers' gentle, attentive care.

When she was strong enough to walk again, he'd marched her away to her death.

He and two members of his squad took her across the border into the poisoned embrace of the forest. After a mile or so they'd stopped. Shal had chained Yana to the dank forest floor. She'd whispered in his ear as he worked. "Sergeant Worthy, please don't leave me alone, not yet. Please stay with me a while."

That's when he'd cut her name from the Order with his pocket knife. His hands were shaking; the blade slipped. It nicked the skin above her heart.

"Press a little deeper," she told him. "It would be a mercy."

He'd turned away then, to hide his tears.

They left her water, but no food. There were no wolves in Dolrun, no large predators of any kind to give her the blessing of a swift death. The forest itself would claim her in the end. It killed anyone who lingered too long.

The last words Shal said to her, were the words demanded of him by the ritual of Exile.

"Yanara Valit, traitor of Orrun. You exist no longer."

They'd waited ten days before returning. *The Dragon had taken her,* Shal wrote in his report, *but not as swiftly as I'd hoped. We could see that she had suffered greatly.*

"Your sister died in Dolrun," she told Ruko.

His dark eyes were empty. "Yes. I know."

Neema held the Order out for him to take back, but he refused it.

"There's a reason most contenders leave their loved ones at home. They are a distraction. Even in death." His jaw tightened. "I think my mother sent it. I think she killed Gaida to frame me."

"You may be right," Neema said, though she thought there might be more to it than that. Ruko did not know that Yasila had met with Gaida the afternoon before the murder.

They both stood up. Neema drained her glass. It was very late, or very early, depending how you looked at it.

"You will arrest her," he said. A statement, not a question.

"I need more evidence. I'll interview her tomorrow."

"Don't go alone. She hates you."

"I know." Looking back through her notes, after her talk with Vabras, Neema had found a connection, a line between the dots. Gaida was not the only one who had been targeted last night. Ruko was tricked. Shal was poisoned. And she had been drugged. Ruko, Shal, Neema. All three of them had played a role in Yanara Valit's exile. And now, it seemed, someone was punishing them for it. Who had more claim for revenge than Yasila?

"Does your mother have access to Dragonscale oil?"

Ruko froze. "Why do you ask?"

She told him what had happened to her, missing out the bit where she broke into the throne room, and met Cain, and killed all the fishes in the imperial fish ponds. She still felt bad about that. "It *raged* through me, like a fire." She ran her fingers up her arms, hugged her shoulders. "I've never felt anything like it. As if I'd been possessed by this part of myself I didn't even know existed. I felt this absolute, crippling *need* to act out my deepest desires, and forget the consequences. Not like this," she rolled the dregs of her whisky in its glass. "It didn't weaken my inhibitions, it burned them to the ground. Does that make sense?"

"Yes," Ruko said. "It does." And then he told her about his mother and the Dragons, and why they had never punished her for escaping them.

"That's...horrifying," Neema said, when he was finished.

"My mother is a very dangerous woman. You should thank the Eight you are so well protected."

Neema's brow furrowed. "I am?"

"The Raven watches over you, Contender Kraa."

"Oh right, the Raven." She pulled a polite face.

"I hope I don't kill you on the platform. You may be of use to me, when I am emperor."

And with that he left, as silently as he had come.

Neema picked up Ruko's barely touched glass of whisky and crawled back into bed with it. Benna had replaced the old, dubious mattress and pillows with brand-new ones, and ordered fresh linen sheets that smelled of sunshine and lemons. She knocked the whisky down in one. *Who needs the Raven*, she thought, blasphemously, *when I have Benna Edge to look after me? May the Eight bless her, and remain Hidden.*

Lying on her back, she felt a sharp stabbing pain in the middle of her forehead. A mosquito? She swatted the air.

Nothing.

Odd.

She turned over on her side, snuggled against the pillow and fell straight back to sleep.

Our patience is remarkable.

Two hours until dawn. We scratch our neck vigorously with a claw. Strut along the wooden bed frame, *plack, plack, plack, plack.* Back again. *Plack, plack, plack, plack.* Too late to fly back to the Hidden Realm, no point to it. Fox will have slunk in and slunk out again by now, with its nightly report. An incoherent, rambling mess, no doubt. Fox finds it hard to focus unless we are there to help. *Pull on its tail, Raven*, Ox would say. *Get it back in line.*

Two more hours until dawn.

Plack, plack, plack plack.

Plack, plack, plack, plack.

We could write down the story.

The book. Its voice is faint, muffled by the pillow.

Shut up.

Yes, shut up, who asked you?

Stupid thing.

Wretched thing.

We have a much better idea.

We could write down the story.

Excited, we tug the book (protesting) out from under the pillow and open it flat with our claw. Consider the empty page with one eye, and then the other. Dip our beak in the inky sheen of our magnificent blood and begin.

Yasila and the Dragons

One day in the late summer of 1497, Lord Eyart Majan said to his wife, "My dear! Look how calm and bright the sea is this morning! Let us sail to Three Ports and have lunch on the sand." And the Princess Marana agreed because she loved her husband, and was very bored.

"Tell the servants to make a picnic," said Lord Eyart. "I shall run and fetch our daughter."

"Yasila is too young for such a long trip," his wife replied. "She will only get sick and cry. And it might be nice, just the two of us—"

"Nonsense," her husband replied.

And so they headed down to their yacht, Lord Eyart carrying his daughter on his shoulders. Little Yasila was scarce eighteen months old, with pudgy hands, and plump cheeks, and her indigo-black hair was tied up in a tiny bun on top of her tiny head, with a sweet yellow ribbon to honour her parents' Guardian, the Monkey.

The captain of the yacht took Lord Eyart to one side and warned his master that sailing to Three Ports was not wise, not today. He said the sea might look calm but things could change rapidly; he'd heard reports of a violent storm on the way. He suggested instead an excursion to a sheltered bay close by. It would be a pleasant trip and they could stay close to the coastline.

Eyart said, "I have promised my wife a picnic on the beach at Three Ports."

The captain said, "But my lord—"

Lord Eyart reminded the captain who owned the yacht, and paid for its crew. He said, patting the captain's shoulder, that he had no desire to destroy a man's life, but he expected his orders to be obeyed, without question.

The captain set sail for Three Ports. As the crew pulled up the anchor Princess Marana brushed a drop of water from her face. "I think it's raining, dearest," she called to her husband.

"Nonsense," said Eyart.

The storm broke an hour later. Black clouds, grey seas, waves crashing down on the boat like a giant's fist. Rain so thick it was a fight to breathe through it. Wind so strong it ripped the sails from the masts. Bolts of lightning split the sky like illuminated screams. The sailors dropped to their knees in prayer, sure that the Last Return was upon them. Only the captain kept his head, shouting orders through the howling wind. "For Eight's sake, take your wife and child below," he yelled at Lord Eyart, and Lord Eyart did as he was told.

Nothing to be done but to ride out the storm. And everywhere, danger. North, they would be dashed against the rocks. East, they would be lost to the open ocean. South was unthinkable. Due west was their only chance for safe harbour.

The storm had other plans. South it drove them, south and south-west.

To Helia, island of the Dragons.

Only six survived the shipwreck. The captain, two crew, Lord
Eyart and his princess, and the baby Yasila. The storm spat
them out like a bad taste on to a narrow strip of sand, on the far
eastern tip of the island. All the rest were drowned.

When the storm had passed, the Dragons arrived. Three of
them, on the headland above the sand. Their leader was a slight,
narrow-boned white woman, not much taller than a child, with
waves of red hair that trailed across her face and down her back.
She wore a silver diadem with an emerald fixed in the middle of
her forehead.

She stared in silence at the survivors. There was no pity in her
pale amber eyes, and no comfort. "The sea brings us treasures,"
she said.

Lord Eyart stumbled to his feet. His fine clothes were ruined,
and blood streamed from a gash in his leg. "Jadu," he said,
pressing his hands together in a Monkey salute. "Servant of the
Dragon. Pray forgive our trespass. My name is—"

"We know who you are," Jadu said.

Yasila began to cry in her mother's arms.

Jadu frowned at the noise. "Only the Chosen may set foot on
Helia."

"The tempest winds drove us here," Princess Marana said,
holding her daughter close. "We had no choice."

The emerald on Jadu's forehead gleamed, then faded. "No
choice? Lord Eyart. Did your captain not warn you of the storm?
Did he not beg you to abandon your trip?"

Eyart fell to his knees. He knew the punishment for his
arrogant mistake. "Mercy," he cried. "Please, I beg you...My wife,
my child...They are innocent."

Yasila began to wail even louder.

Jadu muttered something beneath her breath, and drew a
sharp line in the air.

At once, both Eyart and his daughter fell silent. Little Yasila's
eyes widened in shock, as she found she had no voice, no voice
at all. She clutched at her mother's dress in silent terror, fist
bunching the ruined silk.

Marana rose to her feet with as much dignity as she could muster. "Jadu. Dragons. You have your ways and they are different from ours. Cold are the hearts of the Chosen, though they are lit by fire. But know this. My daughter and I are direct descendants of Yasthala. My husband is a Lord Eternal of the Majans. If you take our lives, Orrun will be forced to retaliate. Do you seek war with your great neighbour? Do you dare test the patience of the Eight? They will not spare Helia when they Return. All will be destroyed, in blood and fire."

A tense silence. The emerald eye sparked again into flame. Jadu's lips parted in surprise. Whatever was happening, she seemed to be resisting. The jewel burned brighter, so fierce she gasped in pain. "Your Servant hears you," she hissed.

Slowly, the light faded.

When Jadu spoke again, she did not conceal her displeasure. "Yasthala saved Helia when she stopped the Return. We shall release you in her memory—on two conditions. First, you must swear an oath, never to speak of what happened here today. For we are Dragons, and our mysteries are precious to us."

The princess swore on the Eight. Jadu released Eyart's voice, and he did the same. "And the second condition?" he asked, meekly.

Jadu gave a thin smile. "We shall keep one member of your family here as hostage."

The couple exchanged a distraught, tender look. They loved each other dearly, and were rarely parted. "For how long?" Marana asked.

"For ever."

"Then I shall stay," Eyart said at once. "This was my fault, and so it is my burden to bear."

"That is well spoken, Lord Eyart," Jadu acknowledged. "But we spare your family in Yasthala's name. It must be one of her blood who remains. Princess Marana. We will accept you, or your daughter. The choice belongs to you, and you alone."

Now it was the princess who sank to her knees. She hugged Yasila to her chest. "No. There must be another way." But even as she begged, she knew there was not.

"Choose," Jadu said, not unkindly. This pain was known to her. All Dragons are taken from their families against their will.

The princess kissed the top of her daughter's head. "I'm sorry," she whispered. And then, in a louder voice. "Dragons. I leave my daughter in your care. May the Eight forgive me."

"And remain Hidden," Jadu answered. What was done, was done.

"Marana, no!" Eyart cried out in horror.

"I have my reasons," said the princess, and spoke no more.

When Yasila's parents were gone, Jadu lifted the abandoned child from the sand, and held her out at arm's length. "I suppose I had best return your voice," she sighed, and did so.

Yasila cried so hard for her mama that she hurt her throat.

Jadu handed the bawling parcel to one of her companions. "Let us pray the Dragon chooses her, in time. What a miserable curse it would be to live here among us, UnChosen." Tugging the pretty ribbon from the little girl's hair, she threw it to the wind. There were no families here, and no mementoes.

"We wish you no harm," Jadu told her, as they passed through the gates of the monastery. "But do not look for love or kinship from us. Your mother spoke truth. The fire burns hot but we are cold."

That is how Yasila came to live on Helia. As for the captain, and the two surviving members of his crew, no one would fight wars for them. They were burned alive for trespass, in the usual way.

Afterwards, the Dragons sailed Lord Eyart and Princess Marana back to the mainland. Eyart refused to speak to his wife on their long journey home. He would not even look at her. If he had asked her, she would have told him about the child she was carrying. About the terrible, silent calculation she had been

forced to make on the sand. Had she stayed, two lives would
have been lost to the Dragons, instead of one.

When the couple reached their estate, they told the story
that the Dragons had ordered them to tell. Their boat had been
destroyed in the storm. All lives lost, save for their own. No one
doubted it. They could see the grief etched into Lord Eyart's
face, the bold, fresh strip of grey in his hair. And the princess,
pale and trembling.

Marana spent a restless night alone in her chamber, plagued
with bad dreams. When she woke it was to pain, and blood,
far too much blood, soaking the bed sheets. And she wept, and
wept, and cursed the Eight for their cruelty.

Some days later the couple sat down to dinner, facing each
other across a long table full of untouched dishes. It was the first
time they had spoken a word to each other, since the storm.

Lord Eyart said to his wife, "I am ready now to hear your
reasons."

And the princess, who was still bleeding, said to her husband,
"I have none." She would not burden him with more loss.

Lord Eyart pushed himself up from his chair. "To think that I
loved you," he said.

The next morning, they found his shattered body at the base
of the west tower.

The Dragon Island of Helia is no place for young children, it is
not designed for it.

The Dragons fed Yasila, and clothed her. Grey clothes, the
colour of mourning. They gave her a comfortable room, and
taught her how to read and write and do her sums. She was not
allowed into the Hidden Library where the spell books were
kept. But she was free to roam the island as she pleased. It didn't
matter what she saw or heard. Whether she was Chosen or not,
Yasila would live and die on Helia, and take its secrets to her
grave.

Perhaps you were expecting cruelty and spite. Perhaps you
imagined they starved her, and kept her in rags, and forced her

to sleep in a kennel with the dogs. No, no. The Dragons did not hate Yasila. They were indifferent to her.

On her ninth birthday she was brought before Jadu. They walked together through the Servant's dry and dusty gardens, past succulents and spiked grasses, gnarled rosemary bushes and weathered fig trees. Yasila had come to appreciate the land's bleached, desolate beauty. It was the only home she could remember.

She had also learned to hold her tongue in Jadu's presence. She remembered nothing of the storm, the shipwreck, her parents. But she remembered having her voice stolen from her. She would rather choose to keep silent, than have silence imposed upon her.

Jadu was holding a plain wooden staff. She lifted it up in both hands, to admire its quality. "I carved this from the wreckage of the ship that brought you here. So much loss creates space for the fire. The more loss, the more power." Golden flames flickered over the staff. She murmured something, and the flames were gone. "A great cave of emptiness lies within you, Yasila. I had hoped it would make you a suitable vessel for the Dragon. Its fire would have raged inside you like a furnace. But you have not been Chosen. There it is. The ways of the Dragon are mysterious, and must not be questioned."

They walked on, feet crunching on the shingle path.

"Your life, such as it is, will continue as before," Jadu said. A thought occurred to her. "Do you sew?"

"Yes," Yasila said, after a moment's shock. She had no memory of being asked about herself before. "I can also—"

Jadu put a finger to her lips. Quite enough of that. She studied the child, pale amber eyes fringed with pale lashes. "This is the last time we shall speak."

Summoning her courage, Yasila said, "May I ask you one question, Servant Jadu? Before you go?"

"If you must."

"Why did my mother leave me here? Why did she not send me home with my father?"

"Your mother kept her reasons to herself."

"Did she not love me?" Yasila asked, her heart aching.

But Jadu was already walking away. Do not ask Dragons about love.

Every light casts a shadow. Bears are deep thinkers, but prone to melancholy. Foxes are adventurous, and are often reckless with it. A steadfast Ox can turn stubborn. Loyal Hounds can be blind to the faults of those they serve.

Dragons hold within them great power. They are Chosen. That makes them proud. Condescending. *We are Dragons—high we soar above the earth, deep we swim beneath the waves.* Jadu never considered that Yasila could be a threat to her. What, that fleck of ash floating on the wind? That smudge of grey?

For the next seven years Yasila explored the island, the monastery, the miles of tunnels and vaults hidden below ground. She listened as the Dragons—unguarded—spoke secrets that had never escaped the walls of Anat-pyrrh. She watched them perform their ceremonies, she learned their incantations, she pieced together their history. And she made a friend, one friend. His name was Pyke, and he was as lonely as she was, because he was destined to become a Visitor—to leave Helia and spend his days travelling the empire. Even here among the Chosen he was kept separate, in preparation for a solitary life on the road.

No one thought their friendship might be dangerous. But two very lonely, unloved children who find solace and kinship in each other? Oh, you should not underestimate that kind of magic. It can burn through the world like Dragonfire.

Yasila was so far beneath the Dragons' interest, they didn't notice when she finally escaped the island. What they missed— several days later—was their precious store of Dragonscale oil.

All Dragonscale is rare. But this was the rarest and most potent form of all, gathered deep within the Dolrun Forest. To travel so many miles into that poisonous realm meant certain death. Those who collected the fungi for the Dragons were either desperate or already dying, and took the money to secure a future for their loved ones. For every three who went in, only one survived long enough to make the journey back.

Once the supply of fungi had been dried and shipped to Helia, the Dragons soaked out the pungent oil and imbued it with spells. It was then left to age for decades in stone bottles. The oil gave the Dragons the focus they needed to cast their strongest spells. Without it they were vulnerable. It would take decades for them to prepare a new batch of equal potency.

Yasila knew this because Pyke had told her. "It is our greatest treasure," he said. And she had stolen it all.

Helia was not completely cut off from the mainland. The Dragons kept themselves informed of imperial affairs. Yasila knew exactly where to go when she arrived. Not to her mother. Not to the empress. She took the Great North Road to Samra and there presented herself to the city's dashing young governor, Andren Valit.

In a grand room that had seen better days they sat alone before a large stone hearth. The day was mild, but Yasila was cold, missing the heat of Helia. Andren saw this and called a servant to light a fire, and bring a shawl for his guest. It was the first time in over fourteen years someone had thought of Yasila's comfort.

So much the Tiger warrior gained, from that one small act of kindness.

She told him her story, and what she wanted from him. When she was done, he asked, "Why me?"

Yasila had long rehearsed this meeting. "Because you are rich and powerful enough to protect me," she answered. "With the courage and skill to negotiate on my behalf."

"And because the empress would send you back to Helia," Andren said.

She smiled, pleased that he was so shrewd. This too was why she needed him.

"What do I get in return?" he asked.

"My hand in marriage. And with it, my fortune." She let her gaze rest on points around the room. The cracks in the marble statues, the faded wallpaper. The Valits were wealthy, but Samra City had been neglected for centuries. It would take more than one fortune to return it to its old glory. And this, she knew, was Andren's great dream.

He rubbed his beard, considering. "The Princess Marana is alive and in good health, by all accounts. It may be many years before you inherit."

Yasila made a flicking motion with her hand, pushing the problem to one side. "She sacrificed her only child to save herself, then played the grieving wife and mother. If the truth comes out, the whole world will hate her for it. Her reputation will be ruined."

"Not to the point of death," Andren said, mildly.

"You must visit her on my behalf. Tell her I will keep her secret. In exchange she must surrender her title and fortune, and enter the House of Mist and Shadows."

"You don't want to see her yourself?"

"I do not."

Andren rubbed his beard again, dark eyes gleaming. He would not make his final decision now—a Tiger does not leap without looking. But already he was calculating the benefits and opportunities of such a match. "Should we come to terms," he said, "I will not marry you at sixteen. It is too young."

"Then we shall wait until you are ready."

"And you should know, Yasila, that I am in love with someone else. Rivenna is my—"

"That concerns me not," Yasila replied, hands folded neatly in her lap.

So Andren arranged a meeting with the Dragons and negotiated a truce. Once a year, Yasila would send them enough Dragonscale oil to cast their magic and protect themselves. In return, they would swear a binding oath not to harm her. "You kept her hostage, now we do the same with your precious drug," he said, with a grin. He liked a neat arrangement, and he enjoyed having control over people of such immense power as the Dragons. He could see how unhappy it made them.

"If she speaks a word of this—"

"Peace, peace," Andren said, with an easy laugh. "All she wants is to get married, and have children, and forget about you."

And the Dragons believed him, because it suited them.

Princess Marana wept with joy when Andren came to visit her at the Majan estate. "She escaped? My Yasila is free?"

She dropped to her knees and thanked the Eight for answering her prayers.

Andren did not need to persuade her to give up her fortune, and take the grey cloak of the penitent. Whatever her daughter wanted of her she would do. Wherever she must go she would go. "Would she see me once, before I leave?" she asked.

Andren's silence was his answer.

"I understand," Marana said, in a soft voice.

"I can give her a short message," he offered.

The princess thought for a while. Perhaps if she explained her reason…But it was so long ago now, and she could give no proof, for she had told no one about the child she had lost. "If I said that I loved her, would she believe me?"

"Probably not," Andren admitted.

"And it might upset her." Marana paced for a moment before the window, rubbing her hands. "Tell her I am sorry," she decided. "And that I will pray for her happiness and good fortune. You will be good to her, Lord Andren? You will keep her safe?"

He promised he would do his best.

They married two years later. Andren was twenty-eight, Yasila just turned eighteen. She wore a sea-green dress, delicately embroidered with silver flowers. It caused a stir. Sea-green and turquoise were colours reserved for the Chosen. It was considered bad luck for anyone else to wear them. "I am a child of Helia, raised by Dragons," she said, when a guest challenged her. "It is my right."

Did Andren love Yasila? Not as he loved Rivenna Glorren. But she intrigued him, those dark currents only he saw, swirling beneath her immaculately calm surface. "My wife is an enigma," he said, on their wedding day. "I shall enjoy exploring her mysteries."

Everyone assumed he was talking about sex. There was much fanning.

He wasn't not talking about sex. Andren was handsome, Yasila was beautiful. There was an attraction. But he wanted more.

"Tell me about Helia. Tell me about the Dragons."

Glimpses, she gave him. Hints. Andren was too preoccupied to notice how much she was holding back. Empress Haven was suffering from poor health. In a few months she would host a Festival of the Eight, to find her replacement. The Tigers had chosen Andren as their contender. He was expected to win by some distance. The empire was already preparing for the rule of the Golden Tiger of Samra.

On the day Andren set off to the Tiger monastery to focus on his training, Yasila told him she was pregnant. He was thrilled by the news. "Imagine," he said, as he kissed her goodbye. "In a few months I shall be an emperor and a father."

But he did not win the Festival. He lost to Bersun—a Bear warrior who had made it plain he did not want the throne.

Andren was many good things, back then.

But he was a very bad loser.

That dress, people said.

In the middle of the Festival, Yasila gave birth to twins. Ruko and Yanara. Andren thought it was a sign of good luck. He was wrong. He lost the final Trial to the Bear contender. A few days later, Emperor Bersun removed Andren from his post as Governor of Samra and ordered him to return to his estate. "I don't like him," Bersun said. Not behind his hand, like a normal politician. Out loud, in front of the whole court.

Two years of house arrest. Five more rebuilding his position, slowly gaining the emperor's trust. Damping down all the things Bersun did not like about him—his charm, his wit, his confidence.

Such patience, the Tiger stalking its prey through the long grass. Such patience, such focus, such will. Seven years he planned and schemed and waited.

For nothing. For nothing! The month of the Tiger, 1523. Andren Valit's ruined corpse, blood spilling down the white marble steps. Yasila, a widow at twenty-seven, pregnant with their third child. *She should thank the Eight*, people said later. *That baby saved her life.*

The twins were born in a palace. Their sister was born in a prison cell.

It was a cold winter's evening, month of the Fox, when the Visitor came for the Valits.

They had been moved to a modest apartment above a tailor's workshop, in a rundown grid of Armas. No title, no fortune, no friends. Some of the neighbours were kind, some cursed them and spat at their feet. Twice they had come home to find the place ransacked. It might have been the Hounds, or it might have been done for sport. When the door burst open that night the twins jumped to their feet, ready to fight.

Their mother remained seated at the table, eating her soup.

Visitor Pyke was dressed for the road in a thick cloak and fur-lined boots. He brought a swirl of snow in with him, and a bitter wind. "Where's the oil?" he said, striding into the room.

Ruko, nine years old and small for his age, blocked his path. "Get out," he yelled, and shoved the Visitor in the chest.

With a bored expression, the Visitor broke the boy's arm, and threw him out of the way.

"Ruko!" Yana shouted, and ran to her brother.

Yasila finished her soup.

"The oil," the Visitor prompted. And then, when she did not reply, "You have three children. I will kill them all if I must."

Yasila moved the empty bowl to one side. "That will not be necessary," she said, and gestured for him to sit down.

The two childhood friends faced each other across the table. The Visitor's dark amber eyes began to gleam softly, lit by an inner fire. A reminder, in case she needed it, of his power.

"Yanara," Yasila said, still holding the Visitor's gaze. "Tea for our guest."

Yana left her brother's side, and approached the table. Her hand was steady as she poured the tea. She had never met a Dragon before, but she had listened to her mother's stories. *Never show fear before them, Yanara.* Ten years on the road in all weathers had whittled the Visitor's body, he was lean but tough. He smelled as though he had not bathed for several days—his grey, receding hair slick with grease, a rasp of stubble on his cheeks.

From the other room, a series of hiccuping cries. Baby Nisthala, half awake. Yana looked to her mother.

"She will settle," Yasila said.

The cries grew softer, and petered out.

"Your baby sister teaches you a lesson, Ruko," Yasila said to her son, her eyes never leaving the Visitor. "She will wake rested from this night. Whereas you shall have weeks of pain."

Ruko, huddled in a corner nursing his arm, stifled a sob.

"He was trying to protect us," Yana said, defending her twin.

"There is no courage in fighting battles you cannot win."

"Indeed," said the Visitor. You would not tell from his countenance, but he was growing impatient. These domestic matters, these children. He was used to walking into a home and taking what he wanted. The families, if they were wise, offered no protest. No tea, either. He had not spent this much time in someone's home since he was taken from his own family. It was stirring old, unsettling memories.

Yasila knew this, of course. She had stalled him for this very reason. She smiled. "The Dragons swore a sacred oath not to hurt me. Would they curse themselves to break it?"

"That promise does not extend to your family," the Visitor replied. "You will hand over the oil and return to Helia. In exchange, we shall spare the lives of your children. They concern us not."

"You think I am vulnerable, now that my husband is dead."

"We know it." He picked up his tea and drank. "You belong to us, Yasila. We do not give up our treasures, however trifling."

Yasila watched him drink for a moment. Then she lifted a hand from her lap, and chanted a few words under her breath.

The Visitor moved to put down his cup and found that he could not.

Shock, then annoyance. His amber eyes burned, as he sought the spell to free himself. It did not work. He could not move, could not speak. He was held fast to his chair.

"'Only the Chosen have the power to cast spells,'" Yasila quoted, in a mocking voice. Her eyes remained fixed on the Visitor, but she was speaking to her daughter, standing between them at the table. "The Dragons have told this lie for so long, they have come to believe it. But we all have a spark buried within us, Yanara, waiting to catch fire. We all have a loss. From the darkness comes the light."

The Visitor was waging a war inside himself, trying to shake off the spell. And for his efforts? A ripple, on the surface of his tea.

"It is true, the magic does not flow so easily for us," Yasila said. "It has taken me many years to perfect this one spell."

She chanted again, like a jailer tightening a prisoner's chains. *Now I bind myself to thee eternal...* A common betrothal verse, sung in every temple in the land. Yasila had stumbled upon this secret by chance, as a child. She did not need to break into the monastery's Hidden Library and steal a spell book. All she needed was a song, old as the Ketuan mountains, passed down from generation to generation.

An old song. Some Dragonscale oil. And years of patient
practice.

"The benefit of focusing on one spell," she said to Yana. "In
time you become its mistress. Visitor Pyke is proficient in many
forms of magic, but what use are they, against my singular
power?" A smile. "This is the fatal flaw of the Dragons. They
hoard a thousand treasures, and know them not."

Yasila rose from the table. Her fine wardrobe had been
taken from her as punishment for her husband's treason.
But she had learned how to sew on Helia and whatever Yasila
set her mind to, she accomplished. She had bought a bolt of
muslin at the local grid market and dyed it sea-green. Her long
black hair was plaited with silver ribbon. The muslin was of
poor quality and the ribbon was cheap, but she looked like a
mythic queen as she walked across the room. Like Empress Am,
summoning her Huntsman.

She lifted a box from a shelf and brought it to the table.

"I knew Jadu would send you, Pyke. My old friend. You helped
me escape, and now she commands you to bring me back.
Restoring her precious balance." Yasila opened the box and took
out a glass vial with a silver stopper.

The Visitor, caught by the binding spell, let out a suppressed
groan. The year's supply of Dragonscale oil.

"Yanara," Yasila said. "The tea."

Yana freed the cup from the Visitor's fingers and brought it to
her mother.

Yasila removed the stopper and added a drop of oil. "Give this
to your brother. It will distract him from the pain."

She moved down the table and perched in front of the Visitor.
She studied him for a long, quiet moment—the changes time
had wrought upon his face. And then she raised the vial, and
emptied it over his head.

He gave the faintest tremor, as the oil soaked his hair and
streamed down his face, into his unblinking eyes, his half open
mouth. Down his stubbled cheeks and neck, seeping into his
skin.

She waited for the drug to take effect. Such a high dose, it did not take long. She could see the terror in his eyes, of what he might reveal. The secret, the yearning secret buried deep within. When she was sure it was safe, she murmured a few words from a parting song. *So I send you on your way…* Enough to unbind his tongue, but hold the rest of him still.

"Speak," she said, softly.

He tried to fight it, but the drug compelled him. "I love you," he said, in an anguished voice. "I have always loved you." He struggled again to stop himself, but it was no use. His confession, so long suppressed, poured out of him like water. "My only wish is to be with you, to protect you. To make you happy. Yasila. My Yasila. Do you love me in return? Do you love me? There were times on Helia, I thought… but we were so young. Say the word and I am yours. I am yours, entirely."

She laughed at him. And then she bound his tongue again.

A tear spilled down the Visitor's frozen cheek.

Yasila told Yana to fetch a bowl of water, and a cloth. "And a knife," she said. "The small one, we use for chopping vegetables."

Yana did as she was told.

Yasila soaked the cloth. "All these years I've waited for you, Pyke." She washed the Visitor's face, rinsing away the oil, the dirt, the solitary tear. "If you had come to me with an open heart, I could have loved you. We might have shared our days, and our nights. You may think on that, if you wish, for the rest of your life. What we might have had."

A second tear fell from the Visitor's eye.

Yasila picked up the knife. "Tell Jadu, *we are protected.* Tell her, if she threatens my family again, I will hunt down her Visitors, bind them, and kill them. Then I will find every Chosen child, and I will do the same. Every one. She will lose a generation of Dragons to this small blade." She placed a hand to the side of his face, lacing her fingers in his hair. "A message. So she knows I am in earnest."

And with her free hand, she carved her initial into his cheek.

When she was done, she let him go. Cleaned the blade and returned it to its drawer. Looking out of the window, she saw him battling his way through the blizzard, cloak billowing against the wind, hand cradling his wounded face. For a second she felt a violent urge to bind him again, run down the steps to the street below and...*what, Yasila? What then?*

She waited and the feeling passed, as feelings do.

She sensed Yanara's eyes on her back. Inwardly, she checked her posture, but there was nothing to correct. She was as she should be.

Without turning she said, "This is what a mother does for her children."

The next time she looked out of the window, the street was empty, and the snow had covered the Visitor's tracks. It was as if he had never been.

So ends the story of Yasila and the Dragons.

PART FOUR

Day of the Raven

∞

CHAPTER
Twenty-Nine

"WHICH ARM DID HE BREAK?" Cain asked.

Neema put down her fork. "That's your first question?" It was early morning, they were having breakfast on her balcony like an old married couple, scrambled eggs and salmon, sesame rolls and fruit, and those tiny cakes Benna seemed to conjure from her sleeve.

Neema had asked Cain to come with her to interview Yasila and he had said, "Fine, you can tell me why over breakfast." He had said this with the remnants of his own breakfast still on the table behind him.

She had talked him through her theory: Yasila had stolen Hurun-tooth in order to frame her son, and to humiliate him. She had also poisoned Shal—a mild dose, enough to give him a bad start to his Festival. And she had contaminated Neema's bath oil. "It had to be her. No one else could get their hands on that much Dragonscale. Ruko said the only other person Yasila ever trusted it with was, you know..." She mouthed the name. *Yana.*

"Did he sound resentful about that?" Cain was curious.

"He sounded the same as he always does. Like he's empty."

"Like his soul is dead."

Neema pulled a face. It was a horrible thing to say, but not inaccurate. "So what do you think?"

"It's a good theory," Cain acknowledged. "Revenge is always a good theory."

The only bit Neema couldn't untangle was Yasila's relationship to Gaida. She was certain they had met in secret that afternoon, a few short hours before the murder. If they were conspiring together, if they'd fallen out…Neema had no doubt that Yasila was ruthless enough to kill Gaida. It was the tea that made her dubious, oddly enough. Yasila could bind a Visitor, she had closed Neema's throat with a few whispered words. Why would she need the tea to knock Gaida out?

Neema could sit fretting all day and get no closer to the truth. Or she could visit Yasila and see what she could shake out of her. She was not foolish enough to confront a spell-caster on her own. Ruko said that Yasila needed to be within a few feet of her victim for it to work, and that she could only bind one person at a time. Which was why Neema had caved, and asked Cain to come with her.

But Cain wasn't interested in Yasila's magical powers, that was all nonsense as far as he was concerned. Dragons and their con tricks. He was only interested in Ruko, his rival. He poured himself some more coffee, watching the Hounds practise their morning drill in the square below. Once he had the rhythm, he hummed a tune over the top, using the martial steps as a beat.

"Cain," Neema said. She needed him to listen, to hear her warning about Yasila's powers.

"Another squadron came in last night." Some more light humming. "Two hundred fresh troops from the Hound Academy at Samra. Sailed up in a brand-new Leviathan. Reports of unrest, that's their excuse."

"Cain, you need to be prepared—"

"That's always their excuse." He crammed a roll in his mouth.

A tactical error, because now she could speak, and he couldn't talk over her. "I know you don't believe in magic, but she did carve her initial in the Visitor's face. And she stopped me from breathing." She clutched her throat.

"Drugs," he managed, through the chewing. "Hypnosis." He swallowed the last of the roll. "Power of suggestion."

"I believe you." A voice floated over the trellis of frothing white jasmine. Sunur. She slid across to join them. She was dressed in a smart brown tunic with embroidered borders, the vine pattern of Utsur. Neema sensed it was her best tunic, and that she had put it on to improve her mood. Her long, straight hair was still damp from her morning bath.

No point complaining that she was eavesdropping on a private conversation. They'd chosen to sit out here on the balcony.

"Is that coffee?" Sunur poured herself some. "Thank the Eight."

"Late night?" Cain asked, squinting at her. Her eyes were red behind her glasses.

"Couldn't sleep. This place." She cupped her hands around her coffee, as if drawing comfort from it.

"The court?" Cain asked.

"The court, the island...but *here*, most of all." The Dragon palace. "Can't you feel it? Something dark. A dark intention, or..." She frowned, frustrated with herself. "It's hard to describe."

"Gaida's murder—" Neema tried.

"No it's older and deeper than that. Stranger." The words came to her at last. "Unnatural. *Against* nature. Yes. That's what it is. Against nature." She looked almost relieved, as if she'd been ill for a while and finally had her diagnosis.

And perhaps it was, as Cain would say, the power of suggestion, but for a moment Neema thought she felt it too. A sort of swollen pressure, and a heat, that comes from infection. The high scent of decay. All those signs in nature that tell you—this is rotten. It was there and it was gone, but she did catch a trace of it.

Those whose feet are planted in the ground are the first to feel a shift. Oxes were more attuned to nature than most. If Sunur sensed something was off, something was off.

Neema stood up and gave the Oxwoman a hug.

"Oh," Cain said, surprised. "Spontaneous hugging." This was very un-Neema.

Sunur hugged her back. And that was it. They were friends.

The Hounds marched on below.

CHAPTER
Thirty

THE IMPERIAL SUITE WAS, without a doubt, the finest residence on the island. Perched at the top of the Dragon palace, the lower floor housed the apartment's kitchens, storerooms and servants' quarters. The larger top floor was divided into two identical wings, connected by an inner courtyard. Nothing could match it in size, location or quality, which was why every emperor and empress of Orrun since Yasthala had chosen to live there.

Until Bersun the Brusque, the reluctant emperor. Too opulent for him, too refined. He felt like a real bear blundering about the place, he broke a priceless chair the first time he sat down on it. As for the panoramic views, they only reminded him how far away he was from home. Two thousand miles—an empire away. After a week he'd said, gruffly, "This is no good," and moved to an apartment within the inner sanctum, in easy reach of the throne room. He had lived there ever since.

With the emperor out of the way, Lord Clarion and Lady Harmony had snatched up the west wing of the suite, paying an astronomical rent for the privilege. Yaan Rack took the east wing and almost threw himself off it when the Hounds came for him. As they dragged the old man down the stairs at knifepoint, they'd passed the emperor's mistress, the Lady Kara Kandraga[11] heading up the other way, clutching a handful of swatches and a measur-

---

11. Often referred to as The Long-Suffering Lady Kara, as if she'd had the title bestowed on her in a grand ceremony. Here, she is a footnote. But if this were a tale about picnics, and interior design, and looking the other way when the killing starts, Lady Kara would be our heroine.

ing tape. Lady Kara, the emperor's official consort, was entitled to charge her extensive renovations to the treasury. When Vabras saw the bill he'd said, "Perhaps we executed the wrong person," and no one could tell if he was joking.

This was how things stood until the Princess Yasila had returned to court with her daughter Nisthala. The young girl was sick, some sort of lethargy, or seizures, or a weak heart, no one really knew the truth of it. The emperor had written to Yasila. *You must bring her to court, madam*—somewhere between a plea and a command. *She will be safe here, under our care.*

And privately to Vabras, clutching his arm, haunted. "I cannot lose another one. We must do everything to save her, Vabras. Whatever they need."

What they needed, as it turned out, was the imperial suite. Both wings. And complete privacy. These had been Yasila's conditions. She would bring her own servants, an elderly male couple who had worked faithfully at the Majan estate since her grandfather's day.

A few courtiers caught a glimpse of Nisthala on her arrival. A thin, pallid thing, shivering in her woollen cloak despite the mildness of the day. She was too weak to climb the nine flights of stairs to the imperial suite. The emperor carried her up in his arms, Yasila trailing behind like a living ghost. Then one more flight, to the courtyard. Nisthala disappeared inside, still shivering. "You may leave us," Yasila said to the emperor, and that was that.

Seven years passed. Yasila rarely left the suite. Nisthala never left it at all. Once a month the emperor was allowed up to visit, for one hour. He would not be drawn on these meetings. Only once, he said to Vabras, in front of a guard, "She's an odd little creature. But that's to be expected, I suppose." The line had escaped out into the wild. "Odd little creature, apparently." The guard fell from a window shortly afterwards.

Was the girl still sick? If so what ailed her? Could she *never* come down? She must be what, fifteen now? Almost sixteen, almost grown up. It seemed cruel to keep her locked away like that. Unnecessary.

Was she even alive? People wondered.

Seven years. And now Cain and Neema were on their way, imperial passes in hand. The emperor had made Yasila a promise, but the murder of a contender took precedence. She must allow them in to her home, her sanctuary.

Let us fly there now—a few minutes early, the Dragon will permit that much. Come with us, up through the palace, look there's Neema on the stairs, long limbs and tight black curls, Raven sigil on her chest. Cain at her side. Don't tell them this, but they are a handsome couple, somehow more handsome together than apart. They make sense: two sides of the same pendant. Moving well together with their matching strides, hands almost touching.

They have another three flights to climb, but we shall take a shortcut through this open window. Up and out, wings pulling us high into the sky above the palace, the sea stretching on to the horizon. Far below we see the two wings of the imperial suite, and the courtyard between, with its potted trees and wooden fountain. We swoop down again to land on an olive branch. Curl our black claws tight, and watch.

Yasila has put on an old outfit from her days living as a Commoner in the grids—a plain cotton tunic and trousers. No make-up, no jewellery, her hair tied back in a loose ponytail. A snub for her visitors, when they arrive. While she waits, she sweeps the courtyard's ancient mosaic floor, laid in the time of her ancestor Yasthala. She is angry about the coming intrusion, she is angry about many things. The sweeping calms her. Once or twice she lifts the broom and it becomes a staff, a weapon—she turns and spins and drops like a seasoned warrior, supple moves she learned by spying on the Dragons as a child and has made her own. Shift, turn, strike. These last seven years of seclusion have afforded her thousands of hours to practise; she is now a master.

A final turn and twist of the broom as she spins a circle.

My daughter is safe. She is protected. No one will take her from me. That will never, ever happen again.

She comes to a stop. She thought she sensed…eyes upon her. She looks up to the olive branch where we are perched, watching her. There is nothing there. No sound in the courtyard, except for the gentle flow of water in the wooden fountain.

She says, in a soft but defiant voice, "*No one* will take her from me."

And returns to her sweeping.

CHAPTER
Thirty-One

NEEMA SHOWED HER pass to the ancient servant at the entrance to the imperial suite. With artful decrepitude, he groped for his glasses.

The day was already uncomfortably hot. The tiled hallway looked cool and pleasant. They waited.

"I don't have time for this, Neema," Cain said through gritted teeth, as if it were her fault.

The servant tried his other pocket.

"Sorry," Cain said, pushing past him. "I have an empire to win."

Neema continued to wait because she was a Raven, and Ravens love and respect and are generally in thrall to paperwork. "It's all in order," she said and the old man, after he had read it again slowly, twice, agreed that it was.

Hurrying up the stairs, she found herself in an empty courtyard, half in light, half in shade. She had barely taken in its quiet beauty—the mosaic floor, the wooden fountain, the subtle scent of the fruit trees in their limewashed clay pots—when she heard a loud crash from the room to her left. The sliding wooden doors were pushed back, giving her the perfect view of Cain as he sailed past.

"This is fantastic!" he shouted, leaping over a cream silk couch as if his life depended on it.

A moment later Princess Yasila flew after him, wielding a broom.

Neema blinked.

By the time she had reached the doors, Cain was on his knees in front of the sofa, and Yasila had the broom under his chin, choking him. She did not appear to be using any force, her posture soft and relaxed. The most delicate of shifts, the most subtle of movements, held Cain in place. He was turning red.

"She tried her magic on me,"he wheezed. "Didn't work,"a choked cough, "obviously, so..." Cain gripped hold of the broomstick and rolled his spine.

"Don't—" Neema said, guessing what was coming.

Too late. Cain turned a standing somersault, flipping Yasila over the top. Neema stepped back in alarm, but the princess had landed lightly on her feet, low and lithe, still holding the broom. Dragonstyle—the rarest and most beautiful of martial forms. She turned the broom like a staff, preparing for the next attack.

"Look at all these books, Neema," Cain said, throwing one at Yasila's head.

The room was lined with them, floor to ceiling, with a rolling ladder. Neema had always wanted one of those.

Yasila deflected the book without even looking at it. As it sailed by on its new trajectory, it knocked over a large porcelain vase. Neema leapt to catch it, but she was too late. It smashed on to the tiled floor.

Yasila stepped into a low hanging stance. "Get out," she said.

Cain had retreated behind the couch. "Impressive skills, princess. Did you train your son?"

"I have no son."

"Does he have a weak spot? You could help me beat him."

"I hope you rip each other's throats out," Yasila said, calmly.

"Why don't we all sit down?" Neema suggested.

Yasila kept her eyes on Cain. "We will speak in the courtyard. Move."

This was a fight of a different kind, one Neema had engaged in many times. If she let Yasila sweep her back into the courtyard, it was over; she would have lost any authority she might possess. She held up her imperial pass. "Your highness. We have the power to search every corner of this suite, and question everyone living here." Including Nisthala. She left the threat unspoken.

Yasila's gaze flickered to a door built into the bookshelves. Presumably, her daughter was sequestered on the other side.

"If you would sit, and answer our questions," Neema continued, in a reasonable voice, "perhaps that won't be necessary." She gestured to the couch.

Yasila handed Neema the broom. "Clean up your mess and we will talk," she said, and crossed to a chair on the other side of the fireplace.

Neema and Cain shared a look. Sometimes it was quicker to find these things funny.

As Yasila sat down, it became clear why she had chosen the chair over the couch. This was the imperial suite, and this chair, with its high back and scrolled arms, was very much like a throne. Behind her, the dramatic view from the eastern balcony: dazzling blue sky, deep blue ocean. She posed in front of them as if she owned them, hands resting in her lap. And who would not wish to be owned by Yasila Majan—so beautiful, so compelling. The sea, the sky—why would they not worship her?

Neema swept the vase fragments into a pile, while Cain returned the book he'd thrown. Yasila kept her gaze on the fireplace.

No—not the fireplace, Neema realised, as she sat down on the couch. She was studying the oil painting above it. *Yasthala Victorious*—a depiction of Yasila's ancestor seated on the marble throne, the Raven on her shoulder. Neema had spent enough time around Venerants to know this was a coded stare. Yasila was silently reminding her impudent visitors of her noble heritage, her impeccable bloodline. Which was ironic, Neema thought, given that the Empress Yasthala had ended hereditary rule, and would have dismantled things further had she won the war more decisively. Venerants always chose to forget that bit, when they called her Yasthala the Great.

Neema knew the history of the painting, not because it was any good—it was decidedly average—but because of its connection to Shimmer Arbell. *Yasthala Victorious* had been a wedding gift from Andren Valit to his bride. Originally, he had wanted Shimmer to paint it. It would have been her first big commission, but she turned him down. He persisted, doubled his fee. Again, she refused him. When he tried a third time, she told him to fuck off.

Those who said yes to Andren Valit would say that he was charming, generous, good-natured. Those who said no told a different story. And those who told him to fuck off? *Well.* Only one ever dared. Andren spent the next few years methodically destroying not only Shimmer's nascent career but also her reputation, her friendships, her life. She had to flee her home in Three Ports and take a tavern job in Armas, painting in the attic room above, practically begging for supplies. She only escaped Andren's curse when she became too good to ignore. "Suppose I should thank the bastard," she wrote, after his death. "May the Eight rot his soul and remain Hidden. I had to learn how to paint better than everyone else, just to survive."

Neema wondered, now, if something similar held true for Yasila. She had escaped the Dragons, she had survived her husband. Such a life, so full of trials and tragedies, could easily have destroyed her. Instead they had made her stronger. Made her exceptional.

Cain was rolling the ladder along the shelves, enjoying the ride. This was very much the Fox philosophy of life. *Eat when you can, drink when you can, roll ladders along high shelves when you can. For tomorrow we die.* He stopped with a sudden lurch. "She has your work, Neema," he called down, astonished. "Essays and everything."

"Monographs," Neema said, secretly thrilled.

He held one open to the room. "Look—she's even read bits of them." There were asterisks in the margin, underlinings.

"My daughter," Yasila corrected him. "Nisthala has an obsession with our ancient past. Tales of the Great Catastrophe and the Lost Tribes." She lifted a hand from her lap and wafted it behind her towards the horizon. Long ago and far away.

"Oh," Neema said, making a connection. "Like the emperor."

A rare bolt of anger from Yasila. "They are nothing alike," she snapped.

It took Neema a moment to understand her offence. Those old, ludicrous rumours about Yasila and the Old Bear. *Eight. She thinks I'm suggesting that Nisthala is Bersun's daughter.* "Forgive me—I only meant we share an interest. Myself, your daughter. The emperor. That's how I first came into his orbit, in fact."

"Really?" Yasila settled back against a cushion and gave a deadly smile. "I thought it was your exquisite calligraphy."

Neema's face fell.

Cain joined her on the couch. As he was sitting down he said, casually, "So, princess, why did you kill Gaida?"

Yasila didn't blink.

"Was it just to frame Ruko? Or did she threaten you? She threatened to destroy Neema, the night she died."

Neema stared at him. "You know about that?"

"She told me at dinner, she was very proud of herself. Gaida," he said conversationally to Yasila, "could be a bit of a cow where Neema was concerned. I'm not saying she deserved to die, but if you killed her for a good reason…do you have any snacks?"

"Cain, you've just had two breakfasts," Neema murmured.

"What I'd really like is some chicken, with a sticky sauce. Although would that be wise, on this sofa?" He rubbed his hands over the cream silk. "Some chicken, some sticky sauce and a finger bowl. Maybe a napkin I could tuck in my tunic—"

"I didn't kill Contender Rack," Yasila said, and Cain grinned, because he'd irritated her into speaking. His signature trap.

"Do you have an alibi?" Neema asked.

Yasila folded her hands more firmly. "I do."

"Other than your fiercely loyal servants?"

"And your invisible daughter?" Cain chipped in.

Yasila closed her eyes, shutting them both out for a moment. When she opened them again, and saw—*disappointing*—that they were still there, she said, "I did not kill Contender Rack. But I have found myself entangled in her death." Clearly, she had decided the quickest way to be rid of them, was to give them what they wanted. "The Dragons use their magic sparingly. For years, I could not understand why. Time, and bitter experience, have taught me the reason for their caution. Every spell casts a shadow."

Cain and Neema looked at each other, confused.

"I tried to bind you, Contender Ballari, to stop you from entering my home. Moments later, I broke a vase that has been in my family for generations. Yes, you smile. *Coincidence.* I would have said the same, once. But it happens every time. Every time. Magic is a force of nature. It must be respected, the way a fisherman respects the sea, or a hunter respects the forest. There is a balance that must be maintained. Take more than you need and you will suffer for it."

Neema could see where this was leading. "You bound me at the opening ceremony."

"Yes. Petty of me. But when I saw you…" Yasila looked Neema dead in the eye "She died with your lies stitched across her heart."

Yanara. Her name left hanging in the air.

"You knew she was innocent, but you didn't care. You were a nobody, a nothing. You saw an opportunity to rise and you snatched it with both hands."

"I'm—"

"Don't," Yasila said, savagely. "Don't tell me you are sorry. Don't you *dare*." She rose and began straightening books on their shelves, lining up the spines. When she spoke again, the passion had left her voice. "I had no desire to attend the opening ceremony, but the emperor insisted. So I must go. I walked through the door…and there you were. How *well* you looked, in that wonderful dress. And that exquisite amethyst choker, glittering at your throat." She straightened another book. "I thought: How I wish it *would* choke her…" She laughed, drily. "The spell left my lips before I could stop it. So yes, I bound you, for a moment. How did it feel?"

"I thought I was going to die."

Yasila abandoned her books. As she passed Neema's couch she said, "Good." and continued on to the balcony.

For a time the princess watched the ocean, the waves rolling in an eternal circle. With her back to the room, she looked like the only person left in an empty world of sea and sky.

"Neema?" Cain said, softly.

She shook her head. Any kindness from him at this moment would only make her feel worse.

The second of Yasila's ancient servants arrived with a jug of iced lemon water, and one glass. With arthritic reverence he placed the tray on the side table by Yasila's chair and slowly, slowly poured out a glass.

Cain was vibrating with delight. There was nothing he liked better than comedy, elbowing its way in at the wrong moment. "I'm turning grey watching him," he said to Neema. "Where did he learn to move like that? The Snail Monastery?"

The servant left, even more slowly than he had arrived.

Yasila returned to her seat as if nothing had happened. She said, "Every spell casts a shadow. I bound you, briefly. And then you whispered in my ear. Six words. *I saw you on the balcony.* Did you know how dangerous they were?"

"Not at the time," Neema confessed. "You met Gaida there."

Yasila frowned, annoyed by her own reckless mistake. "She said she had vital information about a shared enemy. I assumed she meant you. Or Ruko." Not a flicker of feeling as she said her son's name. "It was only when we met I discovered—she meant the emperor."

Cain stiffened. "Shit."

Neema inched forward in her seat.

Yasila held up a hand to stop her, before she could ask. "I won't repeat her accusations. She had no credible evidence to support them."

Typical, Neema thought, before she could stop herself.

"She thought I would be keen to 'join forces,' as she put it. Expose the emperor and clear her father's name. Foolish girl. She was lucky I didn't hand her straight over to the Hounds."

"Why didn't you?"

"Because I knew what they would do to her." Exile. Again, Yasila looked starkly at Neema. "Gaida's mother is still alive."

Neema swallowed, and looked down at her hands.

"So what *did* you do?" Cain asked, into the silence that followed.

"I warned her to let things be. No one thanks a dog for digging up rubbish. Then I left. I had hoped that was the end of the matter. But then…"

Neema lifted her gaze. "…I told you I'd seen you."

Yasila pinched her lips. "I went straight over to Vabras and confessed everything. You gave me no choice. Ravens do like to *chat-*

ter." She made a sharp snapping motion with her hand. *If you had only kept your beak shut.*

Neema, offended, said, "It's not chattering. It's curiosity. We'll peck away at a thing for as long as it takes to get to the truth. *That's* why you panicked. You knew I'd keep digging until I worked it all out. That you and Gaida had met. That she'd discovered something suspicious about the emperor. Something about that song she sang for him—" She stopped, in a dead halt.

An image had come to her from the opening ceremony—just before Bersun handed out the colours. Vabras mounting the dais to speak to him, while the contenders formed a line below. A whispered discussion. A final, decisive nod from the emperor.

Yasila had gone straight over to Vabras, and Vabras had gone straight over to the emperor. That's what they were discussing on the dais.

Bersun knew. Before Gaida sang a note, he knew she was plotting to bring him down. He had let her go ahead with her performance—he couldn't refuse her in front of the court. But his reaction to the song had been an act. His irritation, his tears.

Neema didn't know the Old Bear could act.

Gaida had conspired against the emperor, and he knew about it. *Vabras* knew about it. Neema's voice, when she spoke, seemed to come from far way. "She really had stumbled on something, hadn't she?"

Yasila said nothing.

The emperor. The incorruptible Old Bear. Her friend, her mentor. The only person on the island she trusted without question. Neema felt sick, light-headed. *Breathe. Breathe.* Her peripheral vision began to blur.

Cain got up, snatched the glass of lemon water from Yasila, and gave it to Neema.

The princess folded her hands neatly back in her lap. Smiled quietly to herself.

"Who did he send to kill her?" Neema said.

"I have no idea."

"Vabras," Cain suggested.

Yasila shook her head. "He escorted me here straight after the ceremony. He was concerned about my loyalty to his majesty. He questioned me all night." She rubbed a hand up and down her arm, as if trying to brush away the memory. "Vabras is my alibi, and I am his."

"Then who…"

A shrug. "A Fox, I presume."

Cain frowned at the accusation. "We would never kill a contender. Not even for the emperor. Especially not for the emperor."

Fox assassins might dance upon the borders of the law, but there were protocols. The same was true for the Hounds, with their strict Code of Ethics.

Off the books then, on the sly. Someone fiercely loyal to the emperor, with access to Gaida's rooms. "The afterparty," Neema said. "That's when they changed the tea in the caddy. It was one of the guests."

Cain was puzzled. "But if the emperor ordered Gaida's death, why was he so furious about it? He threw a cup at the wall."

For a moment Neema felt hopeful. Perhaps Bersun hadn't ordered it; perhaps Vabras had taken the matter in hand. But that sharp, decisive nod he had given his High Commander on the dais. The tight set of his jaw. She'd seen it a thousand times. *See it done, Vabras.*

She sat in numb silence, thinking about Cain's question. Why *was* Bersun so furious? "It was supposed to look like natural causes. Like she died in her sleep." A tragedy—but these things happened. No reason to suspect foul play, no need for an investigation.

Cain had his hands in a prayer position, pressed against his forehead. "So what you're saying is…one person killed Gaida in her sleep…then someone else came along…"

"…dragged her body on to the balcony, and stabbed her in the back with the most famous blade in history," Neema finished. The dagger, the display of the body—no one could pass *that* off as natural causes.

"So the emperor had no choice," Cain said, lowering his hands. "He was forced to investigate a murder he'd ordered. That's funny."

No one laughed.

"He doesn't want us to find Gaida's killer," Neema said, in a bleak voice. "He's hoping we'll track down whoever came along afterwards and ruined it all."

Which was why he'd told her to start with the stolen Blade. *Find the thief, find the killer*, Bersun had said, knowing that wasn't true. What he'd really meant was, *Find the thief, and we'll claim they're the killer.* And if she didn't find them?

"I gave Vabras the evidence," Neema groaned. "I handed it straight to him." The only proof that Gaida had been drugged. And the only proof that Neema was innocent. She'd even told them she might have done it. Offered herself up as the perfect scapegoat. Or maybe, if they were feeling generous, they might arrest Katsan for it. *That's why Vabras mentioned her. He was offering me a choice, if things turned bad. A way to save myself. Blame Katsan.*

She put the glass down on the floor, and covered her face. She felt a wave of despair, and horror. She was not naïve. She had always known Vabras could be ruthless, when it came to defending his emperor. But the Old Bear? Brother Bersun of Anat-garra? A man who had sworn a sacred oath to live a life of honour, sacrifice, and charity. Who'd insisted that Commoners be given the same rights and opportunities as everyone else. For all his flaws—his short temper, his stubbornness, his mood swings—she had still believed he was a good man.

Who had she been serving all these years?

What the Eight had Gaida found out about him?

No one spoke for a time. The sea filled the silence, as it often did on the island. The rush and heave of the waves. The mournful cry of a seagull. The salt breeze trailing through the open doors.

If Neema walked now to the eastern balcony and looked down, she would see the emperor's private pleasure grounds, the Garden at the Edge of the World. So many times she had walked there with him. They had talked of many things—the court, her work, even her family back in Scartown. But it struck her now—he had never talked of *his* past. In fact, Vabras had warned her before their very first meeting never to mention it. *His Majesty does not like to be reminded of his life at the monastery, it makes him melan-choly.* Perhaps it was more than that. Something in his private history for which he felt ashamed. Something that might damage him fatally, were it revealed.

Gaida had visited Anat-garra. She had spoken to Brother Lanrik, Bersun's abbot. Was that where she'd discovered his secret?

"I believe we are done," Yasila said, cutting through Neema's reverie.

"Not quite," Cain said, sharply. "Small, subsidiary matter, but you almost killed Neema on Festival Eve."

A lifted eyebrow. "I don't *almost* do things, Contender Ballari."

"But it was your Dragonscale oil, right? No one else has access to that much of it."

For the first time since their arrival, the princess looked surprised. She inched forward to the edge of her chair, studying Neema intently. "Someone drugged you with Dragonscale? You're *sure?*"

"Positive," Cain answered.

Yasila's face flooded with confusion. "But..." A thought struck her. She stood up, rapidly, and turned to the sea and sky. She put a hand to her throat, struggling with some intense emotion; Neema could see the effort it took for her to remain calm. "Yana," Yasila whispered. A name she had not allowed herself to speak in eight years.

Neema's heart sank. Yasila had leapt to the same conclusion as Ruko; that her daughter was alive, and had returned to take revenge on those who had exiled her. Impossible, irrational. Why would Yana wait until now to return? Why would she hide from her mother? She wouldn't. But when hope flares in the darkness, it blinds even the sharpest eyes.

Not for long, though. Not for long. Life had taught Yasila not to dream of what could not be. For a flickering moment, her daughter was alive again. Then she was gone. Back into the poisoned forest. Back into the locked box of her mother's heart. "No," Yasila said, still looking out to the horizon. And then she turned and smiled brightly. "Perhaps the Dragons want you dead, Contender Kraa. I do hope so."

The interview was over. The princess escorted them across the courtyard; the potted fruit trees, the carefully swept tiles. Water spilled gently into the fountain; a pleasing, subtle sound, made for contemplation. Serenity was in reach here, perhaps. A home that was both a prison and a sanctuary.

"What will you tell the Hounds of this meeting?" Neema asked.

Yasila paused in front of a fig tree, inspecting its leaves. "The Dragons have a saying. 'Do not ask the sea for treasure. Wait upon the shore, and it will come.' I shall say nothing to the Hounds. I shall take no revenge upon you. I have only to wait upon the shore. The waves will take you, soon enough." She smiled, pleased by the thought. And then she walked back across the courtyard, graceful as a snake on water.

CHAPTER
Thirty-Two

HAVE YOU FORGOTTEN ABOUT US? We have been magnificently still and silent, perched out here in Yasila's courtyard. Really, we should have followed Neema down to the Festival Square to watch her fight the Ox contender Tala Talaka. But we are a curious bird and we would like to poke our beak through that door for a moment. You know the one. The one set into the bookshelves. The one Yasila kept glancing at throughout her interview, when she thought no one was looking.

We cannot leave our friend Neema unguarded, so we peel a fragment from ourself to join her in the contender line. Anxious Raven with Piercing Alarm Call will let us know if she is in trouble, it misses nothing. You may creep up on the Hound, you may creep up on the Ox (that one's easy), you may even creep up on the Tiger. But you cannot creep up on us.

(Does our anxious friend's name sound cumbersome, by the way? Please bear in mind we have already shortened it for you. We are all the ravens that were, all the ravens that are, all the ravens that will be. Extreme specificity is required to distinguish between us. We would need an entire morning to recite a single fragment's full name. Not a problem in the Hidden Realm, where time holds no dominion. Here, we shorten, because we are a compassionate bird.)

Yasila takes a key from her pocket and unlocks the door. We swoop down and fly through before she closes and locks it again. We could of course simply pass through the walls, but that would not be pleasing to us, it would make our feathers puff up and some of our more agitated aspects might start screeching and pecking each other. This can set off something of a cascade of panic, next thing you know we're swirling around in a mad frenzy.

We decide to walk at Yasila's feet, we look like a very short advisor strutting beside her, wings folded behind our back, yaffling opinions on the concerns of the day. She does not sense us there, although she is a perceptive woman. She is preoccupied, thinking of her daughters, one alive, and one dead.

Yana knew where the Dragonscale was kept; Yasila had trusted her daughter with the secret. Could she have told someone the location, before she died? Yasila wonders—about Yana, and revenge. She wonders.

She does not think of her son. She can think of Ruko as a problem. A scenario. What will happen if he wins the Festival, what will happen if he doesn't. What will happen if Pyke kills him, which is her deep desire. Yasila very much hopes that the Visitor will kill Ruko on the fight platform. It is why she invited him here, why she made her deal with the Dragons. *Kill my son and I shall return to Helia with your precious oil. Kill him before he wins the throne, and I am yours.*

She thinks often of Ruko's death. But she never thinks of him as a person. He is exiled from her heart.

In the square, outside the contenders' pavilion, Anxious Raven with Piercing Alarm Call has taken the bold move of sitting on Neema's shoulder. The Raven choir is opening the day with the song they have been practising so diligently for months. Their harmonies are good thanks to Riff Ankalla's late intervention, but to Neema's horror they have come up with little hand movements to go with the words. The song is about Yasthala's Five Rules, and as they reach the part that goes, "no child of an emperor may take the throne," they rock their arms in unison, as if they are cradling a baby.

Neema is so mortified she makes a noise in the back of her throat as if she is in pain. (She is in pain.) Anxious Raven calls out in alarm, and for a moment we are distracted. This is the problem with this particular aspect, always screeching and flapping about everything and nothing. We tell it not to bother us again unless something is *actually happening*, and it says **sorry, sorry, sorry, I'm just very anxious**, and to be fair, the clue is in the name, it can only be what it is.

Yasila unlocks another door with a different key and takes a breath. As she opens the door, a wave of heat escapes into the hallway. The air shimmers in front of her.

"Nistha?" she calls softly, from the doorway.

From a bed heaped with patchwork quilts and blankets, comes a voice thick with sleep. "The door, Mama…"

Yasila steps into the room. We hop in with her, just before she seals the door tight. We are very interested; this room is new to us. If Dragon found out we were here without its permission it would say THERE ARE OTHER BIRDS, RAVEN and burn us to ash, as it often does when it is in a temper. But we happen to know that it is sleeping, coiled up in its cave, so really what harm could it do to stay here for a brief spell and learn something new?

We bounce across the room to the bed. It is very hot in here, hotter than the mangrove swamps of Fever Bay, hotter than the arid plateaus of Helia. A fire crackles in the hearth, suffusing the room with an orange glow. Dense curtains and shutters cover the windows, trapping in the heat.

The girl in the bed is shivering with cold.

The walls that surround her are covered with pictures of Mount Pyrrh, Helia's semi-dormant volcano, suddenly erupting with orange-white lava. Nisthala has painted them herself, her style improving over the years of her internment. The most recent is an ambitious canvas that covers an entire wall. Tiny figures stand at the base of the volcano, some fighting, some running.

Yasila sits down on the bed and places a hand on her daughter's shoulder. Nisthala remains buried under layers of blankets, only the top of her head visible on the pillow. Her hair is grey, though she is not yet sixteen. She murmurs something vague under her breath and snuggles deeper into her nest of blankets.

"Darling you must get up…"

"No…" A moan from under the blankets. It is clear this is a daily battle between them.

Yasila strokes her daughter's hair. Her expression is soft, loving, endlessly patient. She has learned from her mistakes with Yana and Ruko, and now she makes new ones. "I know it's hard. I know. You have been so brave for so long. But it is almost over now. Just a few more days."

Slowly, Nisthala drags herself up into a seated position, clutching her blankets around her. Her eyelids droop, too heavy to lift.

What ails the child? The flu? A wasting sickness? We sidle up to get a better view. We try her from every angle, tilting our head this way and that, fixing her first with one beady eye and then the other. She looks frail, listless. Her cheeks are hollow and her skin —the same sand-brown as her mother's—is dull.

"…just want to sleep…" she mumbles. But she makes the effort and opens her eyes wide. They are a pale, dusty grey, the colour of wood ash. There is no light to them, no lustre. Her pupils are large and fixed.

We have not seen eyes like this before. They are disturbing to us. Some of us start flapping and puffing up our feathers and making distress calls. With intense effort, we hold ourself together.

Nisthala yawns without covering her mouth.

"Let's see to your skin," her mother says. She pulls a leather box from under the bed and takes out a glass tub filled with ointment. As she unscrews the lid we catch the scent of roses, and something sharp and bitter beneath. Dragonscale oil.

A few of our more nervous fragments peel off and start to flap at the curtains. They want to leave, melt through the shutters and the glass and escape.

We don't like this.

We should not be here.

We are used to arguing with ourself. We drag them back to the fold, peck a few heads.

Wait. We want to see.

"How is it today?" Yasila asks.

Nisthala rolls her eyes, bored by this daily routine. Those strange, dull-grey eyes. "Same as yesterday, Mama." She shuffles out of the blankets. She is sulking and we like her better for it. She is fifteen, she should be sulking, this at least is natural. She is wearing a woollen shawl and beneath that a sleeveless tunic. Some plain wooden beads around her neck, strung on to a piece of wire. She shrugs off the shawl and we see that her arm…

…we see that her arm…

We break apart into countless fragments. All of us shrieking:

No!

No!

No!

We panic, feathers flying, clawing and scrambling over each other to get away from this child. The calmest of us try to restore order, but it's no use. We are lost to the chaos.

"No new marks?" Yasila asks.

Nisthala huffs, as if this is the most boring question in the world, and stretches out her arm for inspection.

Around them, invisible, we are shrieking.

This is bad.

This is wrong.

This cannot be.

There are burn marks on Nisthala's left arm, as if she has been branded. Some look fresh, others are healing in a perpetual cycle. They begin on the underside of her wrist and continue up her arm and over her shoulder, forming a pattern like scales. But each individual mark is an eight, resting on its side. An eternal eight. A spiralling dragon, eating its tale. Upon this turn of the Eternal Path, you are mine. You belong to the Dragon.

Nisthala is a Chosen child.

She should be on Helia. As soon as that first mark appeared on her wrist, a Visitor should have come and taken her away. Years ago! Years!

Ah, but Yasila has control of their precious Dragonscale. She can do what no one else has ever done. She can defy them.

We want to leave **(shouldn't have come, shouldn't have come)**, but we need to gather ourself back together first. Impossible! We are scattered into chaos—batting against the walls, smacking against the walls, pecking at the walls, why are we pecking at the walls, that's not helping, none of this is helping.

"I think there is a new one here," Yasila says, touching a raised mark at the base of Nisthala's neck.

Nisthala sucks in her breath. It hurts. It burns.

Yasila winces in sympathy. "Let me—"

"I can do it myself." Nisthala snatches the jar and massages the cream into her skin. As the Dragonscale deadens the pain, she softens, and sighs. "Sorry Mama, you know how I am first thing."

They talk about breakfast, normal things.

"A few more days," Yasila says, again.

"I know. You need to leave now Mama."

Yasila is sweating hard under her tunic, strands of hair stuck to her skin. "I can stay a little longer."

"You'll faint," Nisthala laughs. She has already picked up a book from the floor—there are piles of them around the bed.

Yasila's face is filled with love and pride. She kisses the top of her daughter's head, her grey hair. "I'll be back in an hour."

"Bring some fresh coal for the fire."

"I will." Yasila is moving to the door. "My darling girl."

"And some hot chocolate. Please."

Our desire to leave this room with Yasila pulls us back together. We stop flapping and shrieking. We are one.

As we settle, we realise that one of us is still shrieking. Has been shrieking louder than the rest of us, for some time now.

Anxious Raven with Piercing Alarm Call.

Neema! Neema is in trouble! Neema! Trouble! Neema is in trouble! Neema!

We cannot wait for Yasila and her keys and her doors. We fly straight up the chimney and out, shaking the soot from our feathers as we soar up over the Dragon palace and down towards the Festival Square.

We are late, we are late!

The fight platform looms up below us. Kindry Rok, holding the bell, is arguing with Tala Talaka, the Ox contender. He holds up his finger to stop her complaints, he will not hear them.

Neema has collapsed on the canvas. She is not moving. Is she unconscious? Is she dead?

Neema, hold on!
We are coming!
We are here!

CHAPTER
Thirty-Three

NEEMA HAD COLLAPSED ON THE CANVAS. She was not moving. Time had slowed—not for any magical reason, just the way it does when you think you are about to die.

The fight had been going quite well, she thought, up to this point. There were a couple of humiliating moments when Tala sat on her, and that bit when she got tangled up in the ropes. Still, she was doing better than expected. She was lucky with today's opponent: Tala was capable with her fists, but she lacked the full martial training of her rivals.

Today was the Day of the Raven, and Neema was determined to honour it. Just once she would like to earn the respect of the Flock. She knew she had no chance of beating Tala. She wasn't deluded. But there was a small possibility they could draw.

So when Tala had come at her with an axe, instead of yelling "Stop!," she had stood her ground. Well, to be precise, she had run around the platform while Tala chased her, much to everyone's amusement. But then she had rallied and fought back. And won.

She had *won* the weapons round.

But now this.

A cloud scudded overhead. She couldn't move. She was stunned, the air knocked from her lungs. Dimly, she could hear Kindry and Tala arguing a few feet away. The High Justice was overseeing the day's fights on behalf of the Ravens.

The problem was she'd put so much effort into winning it had almost destroyed her. Whereas Tala, with her limitless energy, had bounced into the third round with a massive grin on her face, showing off her gold front tooth. "Come on Neema!" she'd said, half-taunt, half-encouragement.

Drawing on the dregs of her reserves, Neema had done her best. She'd lasted about thirty seconds before Tala caught her with a left hook. She slammed so hard into the canvas, the air whooshed from her lungs like a pair of bellows.

She tried to breathe. A thin stream of air made it through. Everything hurt.

Slowly, the cloud drifted.

"Stop the round," Tala said to Kindry.

Kindry was checking his pocket watch. "You want to stop? You'll lose half a point."

"Not for me, for her! Neema!" Tala's voice floated down to Neema, winded on the canvas. "Tell him you want to stop."

"*Hnnrrhhhh.*"

Tala turned back to Kindry. "That was a yes."

Kindry disagreed. *Hnnrrhhhh* could be a yes, it could be a no. Maybe he was being pedantic, maybe he was being vindictive. Maybe he thought Tala's compassion would get the better of her, and she'd withdraw on Neema's behalf. Whatever his reason, he was implacable: "Continue, Ox contender."

"But—"

Kindry lifted his finger. "*Continue.*"

Neema had to move, before Tala trampled her into a pulp. She tried to roll on to her side, but it was no use. She lacked the strength.

Eight help me.

A heavy wing beat. A rush of cool, thin air. A feeling, as though her bones were hollow. As if she could lift herself up from the canvas. And keep lifting, feet leaving the ground. A feeling that she could fly. If she chose.

Tala was walking towards her. The canvas reverberated with each step, strong and steady.

Firmly the Ox plants its hooves in the earth. But we rise.

Neema!

We rise.

Neema felt as if she had been expecting this moment—that it was familiar to her. Like déjà vu, or a half-remembered dream. Something was calling her name. If she wanted to, she could answer, and it would lift her back on her feet. She would win the fight. She would be...magnificent. All she had to do was

Let us in.

She reached, to the very edges of herself. *There.* Something was pressing up against the borders, trying to break through. The brush of feathers. The scrape of a claw. A dense, peppery smell. Something animal, something not. Close. So close. And very persistent.

Let us in, Neema.

We will join you.

We will save you.

We are the—

She drew back, as if stung. Mind and spirit recoiling. She did not want to know what it was. She did not want to believe.

No, she thought, and with that defiance came a surge of fresh energy. She rolled on to her side, and up on to her feet. The presence, the dream, whatever it was, dissolved and faded away. She was on her own—and that was fine. She raised her hands to guard position, spat the blood from her mouth. She was ready.

Thirty-Four

THE FIGHT ENDS IN A DRAW. One point each. We don't care, we are sulking. She spurned us. She spurned our help.

Benna cries, she is so happy. "That was amazing, that was amazing," she says, bouncing up and down on the spot. The crowd agrees. Whatever they thought of the Raven contender as an individual, she'd certainly earned that one point.

Tala slaps Neema's back as they walk back to the line, squeezes her shoulder. "You served the Raven well this morning, contender."

We will be the judge of that.

"Thanks." Neema has already dismissed her encounter with us as a moment's shock, a lack of air, the heat, the stress of the day, exhaustion. We have never been mistaken for so many insulting things in one go before. What next, indigestion? A rogue prawn?

Annoyed, we fly up to a higher perch. The imperial balcony—as we have mentioned—offers an excellent view of the square and the contender line. We shall watch Neema from there, and if she needs us, she might find we are too busy preening ourself to help, she might die horribly and we will not care, not at all.

As we land we realise our mistake. The balcony is already occupied. The emperor is sitting tucked away at the back, invisible to the crowds below despite his giant bulk. Vabras stands at his shoulder. The balcony's gold awning casts them both in deep shadow. They are arguing about Neema. They know she has spoken with Yasila, and they are worried.

"We can't kill her," Vabras is saying.

The emperor is silent.

"Two Raven contenders dead in two days." Vabras shakes his head at the fuss that would cause.

We are not supposed to be here, this is not our place, not our moment. First Yasila, now this. Deep in its cave, the Dragon stirs and shifts, sensing something is not as it should be. A soft, prolonged hiss escapes its half-open jaws. A trail of smoke puffs from its nostrils. We freeze, then settle, favouring one of our more cautious aspects: Raven Sheltering From a Storm.

The emperor huffs, frustrated. "She was up there for an hour, Vabras. What the Eight do you think they were talking about?"

"It is not in Yasila's interest to say anything." Vabras sounds bored. The emperor knows this.

"But if she misspoke. Neema can't resist a puzzle." A touch of affection in the emperor's eyes, even as he contemplates ordering her death.

"Yasila is not given to careless talk," Vabras observes.

Bersun grunts. True enough. Thinking of the princess, his expression turns sour. "That damned witch. I don't trust her an inch. If we didn't need her, I swear to the Eight, I'd..."

Vabras stops listening. He has heard it all before. He's had sixteen years of it. The emperor hates Yasila. Yasila hates the emperor. So what? What difference does it make? They are bound together, that is that. He runs through the morning's duties, seeing where he might claw back some time. When the emperor has finished raging he says, "The plan remains sound. Neema finds the thief, we execute them. If she fails, or learns too much..." A tiny shrug.

The emperor has turned in his seat to study his High Commander more closely. The expression on the Old Bear's face is not one he shows in public—too cold, too calculating. His small brown eyes are shrewd, his mouth curves in thin amusement. "If she fails?" he prompts.

Vabras frowns. Must he spell it out?

"Are you having second thoughts, Vabras?" The emperor's eyes glitter.

Vabras clamps his hands behind his back. "No, your majesty. We agreed this was the best solution."

"Did we?"

Vabras, hearing the ice in the emperor's voice, holds his tongue.

Bersun gets to his feet and looms over his High Commander, as if he might eat him. "I would have arrested Neema for the murder yesterday morning. Kindry was more than ready to put his name to the order. Summary execution." A grim smile. "She would be dead by now."

Vabras tries to step back, but there is nowhere to go. The emperor has him pressed against the wall.

"My plan was quick and efficient. Your favourite words, Vabras. But you insisted you had a better idea. *Let her find the thief for us.*" The emperor's face darkens. "What else will she find, now you've sent her looking?"

Vabras puts both hands up in an appeasing gesture. "That's why we made her a contender. Between the Festival and her investigation, she won't have time to delve deeper—"

The blow is savage and comes from nowhere. Vabras collapses to the floor, blood trickling from his ear. For a moment he lies there, stunned. A shift has occurred, and it shocks Vabras more than the blow itself. Some deep-buried survivor's instinct hands him his line as he drags himself to his feet. "Forgive me, your majesty. I have failed you."

The emperor immediately softens. Now he can be benevolent. "You like her. It clouded your judgement. I should have realised."

"She is a useful person."

"A useful person." The emperor finds this funny, his laugh booms out across the balcony. "So there is a heart in there. Not just cogs and wheels." He puts a great, burly arm around Vabras's shoulder, and draws him out into the light. A handful of spectators, seeing their emperor emerge, cheer his appearance. A young girl, sitting on her father's shoulders, waves excitedly. Bersun smiles and waves back.

On the fight platform, Cain and the Dragon Proxy are in the middle of the weapons round. Both have chosen the narrow sword. It is a lacklustre performance—the Visitor seems noticeably reluctant to fight. Bersun frowns, displeased, and turns his attention to the contender line.

Ruko stands shoulder to shoulder with his rivals, both in line and somehow apart from them. Legs wide, shoulders back. Cold and unyielding as a marble statue.

Bersun cannot take his eyes off him. "My tyrant-in-waiting," he says. "Sacrificing his sister, who would have thought that would be the key. Eight, I could have killed him that day, right on the throne steps. Don't know how I stayed my hand." He paused, as he always did when he thought of Yanara, her terrible fate. The grief was genuine. "But I have to admit, it was the making of him. His betrayal, her suffering. The loss of his mother's love. And do you see the way people look at him, Vabras? Fear. Fear and fascination. He is perfect. I couldn't have shaped him better if I'd tried."

Bersun shifts his gaze to Neema, standing next to Ruko. She looks more confident in her uniform this morning, almost a real contender. He sighs fondly.

Vabras has stood at the emperor's side long enough to know what this means. Neema is doomed. She cannot be saved. "I shall make the arrangements," he says.

"No, no." Bersun stops him. "You're right, it's too risky. Let me think on it. There will be another way. Many are the paths through the forest." He rubs his mouth and jaw where his beard would be, if he had one. An idea is already forming. A solution to the problem that is Neema Kraa.

A nod, and Vabras is dismissed.

The emperor is alone—or so he thinks. He rests his arms on the balcony wall, close to where we are hunkered down. We tilt our head this way and that, studying him from different angles. We should leave, but he is interesting—we have never been this close to him before. He is not a handsome man, but he holds himself as if he is. He looks younger than his sixty-seven years, which we also find interesting. Ruling an empire is hard work, he should be worn out, he should look older.

We do not mind that he plans to destroy Neema—in fact we are pleased by this development. She will have to let us in now, it is inevitable. We will save her, and she will be grateful, and do as she is told.

Watching the fight, Bersun hums a tune to himself, absently. A plaintive melody from ancient days. "Come to the Mountain." The song Gaida performed at the opening ceremony.

As he repeats the refrain we feel a stirring in our chest, a tugging sensation. We do not like it.

We should leave.

We try to open our wings to fly away, and find that we cannot. We are held by the song. The music traps us, our feathers feel heavy and stuck together, as if smothered in a thick, treacly tar.

What is this?

We don't like it.

What is happening?

We scramble away, toppling over the balcony and hurtling towards the ground. At the last moment we free ourselves, skimming the cobbles then up, fast as we can, wings creaking as we haul ourselves through the air. On instinct we fly on to the Raven palace. We will be safe there, it is where we are supposed to be.

We land awkwardly, in distress, on the roof of the service hut beneath Neema's old room. The horrible tarry feeling has gone, but we give our feathers an extra coating of preen oil, as a precaution. This calms and comforts us enough that we can discuss among ourself what just happened, and what we should do about it.

We must tell Dragon about the song.

But then it will know we were not where we were supposed to be.

THERE ARE OTHER BIRDS, RAVEN.

That is what it will say.

We give a collective shudder.

We find, now that we are far away from the song, that its power is fading. Perhaps we imagined its effect.

We have been very busy this morning.

Extremely busy.

And we were angry with Neema for rejecting our offer of friendship.

Angry and hurt.

Also, no offence Raven Sheltering From a Storm, but you are a bit slow on take-off.

I am magnificent!

Of *course* **you are magnificent.**

Slow and magnificent.

So we are agreed? No need to mention this to Dragon? Or the Others?

We are agreed.

Yes, we are agreed.

We preen some more, aligning our feathers, everything feels better when our feathers are aligned. We like it here, this is where we are supposed to be, on the scorching roof, by the stinking bins, with the cockroaches. They are hiding from us, but we know they are there. They are everywhere.

We close our eyes and tuck our beak into our chest. We forget about the song, and the emperor, and Vabras. We forget about Nisthala and the marks branded into her arm. We weren't supposed to know these things, this is why they have upset us. We shall wait here for Neema. She won't be long now.

CHAPTER
Thirty-Five

THE FIRST IMPERIAL LIBRARY—the library Yasthala built—was destroyed nine hundred years ago, in the devastating pirate raid of 517. Thanks to Neema's heroine, High Scholar Donalia Craw, most of its archives had survived, along with some charming drawings of the building. Back then there was no perimeter wall enclosing the island, and scholars walked the light-flooded library galleries with their expansive views across the channel to the capital. Some of the drawings, forcing the perspective, showed the city's skyline in detail, the Raven monastery prominent with its swooping roofs and high towers.

No one could find fault with the new building, it was handsome and well-proportioned and in many ways better designed for its purpose. That did not stop generations of Raven scholars dreaming of Donalia's lost library. Gaida had written a poem about it, one of her better ones.

Now someone would write poems about her. The morticians had completed their work. In the hour before midnight Gaida's body would be laid to rest in the imperial tombs. Not the Hall of Heroes, but still a rare honour. "The Flock would prefer it if you kept away," Kindry said to Neema.

He was here to oversee the Raven Trial. The Abbess of Anatruar should have been with him, but she'd suffered a bad fall and missed the last boat to the island.

Kindry had not set the Trial, having delegated most of the work to Neema as usual. His single contribution was the commissioning of the contender banners—seven tapestries that unfurled from the ceiling to act as partitions between the exam tables. Yes, the Raven Trial was an exam. Pencil, paper. No other weapons required.

Are you disappointed? Were you hoping for fights among the bookshelves, or perhaps a treasure hunt, arcane literary clues leading to secret rooms and treasured artefacts? We agree this would have been diverting, we would have enjoyed that too, but it would not have been a Raven Trial. The Raven Trial was an exam, it was always an exam, and its dullness was very much the point.

"Three hours," Tala moaned, dragging herself over to her seat as if she were pulling a haycart behind her. "It's not healthy, sitting for so long."

Havoc stretched his quads, cracked his back. "The same thing, every Festival. So predictable. Where's the imagination? The *soul*?"

Neema folded her arms, irritated. What did they think ruling an empire entailed? It was called "the throne" for a reason. You sat on it. And you sorted things out. Day after day, year after year. Land disputes, trade agreements with Helia, mediations between the anats, treasury meetings, infrastructure planning, law reforms…Once or twice someone might try to assassinate you, at which point—*fine*—some martial skills would come in handy. Otherwise? If Tala or Havoc won the Festival, they'd soon be thanking the Ravens for this Trial, because it had forced them to learn Orrun's laws, history, industry, geography, local politics and the rest. That was the beauty of this exam, as far as Neema was concerned. There was no predicting what would come up, so they had to study all of it. She honestly couldn't understand what they were complaining about. She would have *loved* this Trial.

"Are you telling me I'm banned from Gaida's funeral?" she said, to Kindry.

"I'm suggesting you consider the sensitivities of the matter. I know courtly manners don't come *naturally* to you, but surely even you can see that your attendance tonight, *under the circumstances*, would only…ruffle feathers." He smiled at the metaphor. "If you would like my advice…"

"Not really."

"Concentrate on finding her killer. A whole day gone, and what do you have to show for it?"

"I proved she wasn't killed with the Blade of Peace," Neema protested. Kindry, the human sofa, accusing *her* of not working hard enough. "I found the poison used to kill her and I've checked the alibis of every contender and every member of their contingent—"

Kindry *tsk*ed. Trifles, mere trifles. "You know, *some of us* believe you've stalled the investigation on purpose."

"It is not stalled."

"Indeed? What progress have you made this morning?"

I found out that Gaida uncovered something so incriminating about the emperor that he had her killed for it. Also, Princess Yasila is an actual witch.

Kindry smiled smugly into her silence. "As I thought. Nothing."

"Lord Kindry!" Katsan snapped. She was camped out by the Returns desk, arguing with Cain. "We need you. A point of order."

Kindry threw Neema a meaningful look before strutting away. "Tick, tock, Contender Kraa. The patience of the Flock wears thin."

The Raven contingent was busy unfurling the last of the contender banners. Hooked to a steel pole, it showed the Hound as a sleek hunting dog, nose testing the air. Shal made an appreciative sound at the quality of the work. When the Trial was over, the banner would be presented to him as a gift to be treasured alongside his uniform and sigil colours.

He settled down at his table, neatening the paper and pencil in front of him. Unlike his rivals he had no complaints about this Trial. Graduates of Houndspoint were expected to have flawless recall of facts and figures. Remembering was never an issue for the Hound contender. Forgetting, on the other hand...

"Neema," he said, as she passed by. "Do you have a moment?"

She stopped a couple of paces away, feeling awkward. They had not spoken since their disastrous fight the day before, when she'd almost chopped his (beautifully groomed) head off with her shield. Only almost, Benna would have said, if she'd been there. But still.

There was a soft gleam in Shal's eyes. He was using his Hound-sight on her. "I shouldn't have judged you so harshly yesterday. You weren't prepared for all this." He touched his armband.

Her body melted with relief. Finally, some understanding. She placed a hand on her heart. "I'm so sorry, Shal. I don't know what possessed me."

She knew exactly what had possessed her. *Us.* She just refused to see it.

Denial.

Outside, Cain was sprawled on the grass, dozing. A bold, bright image in the bold, bright sunshine. The vibrant green of the well-tended lawn, the intense black of his uniform, white skin, dark red hair.

"How the Eight do you do that?" she asked.

He smiled, but didn't open his eyes. "Lie down? You should try it some time."

"You were inside arguing with Katsan a second ago."

"Know your exits," he murmured. The sharp angles of his face softened as he drifted back into a half-slumber.

She sat down next to him. His tunic was riding up over his stomach again. "You'll burn," she said, and without thinking smoothed the fabric back down over his hips. As she did so, her fingertips brushed against his skin.

Oh. That felt good.

There was a moment's heady silence.

To break it she said, "Congratulations on beating the Visitor. Two more points."

"He let me win. He's only here for Ruko."

With impeccable timing, the Tiger contender rounded the corner. He stopped when he saw them. Lifted an eyebrow at Neema. *My mother. Did she confess? Did you arrest her?*

Neema shook her head.

Ruko continued on his way, frowning.

Cain smiled, without opening his eyes. "He doesn't fuck around, does he?"

"No, hang on a minute," Neema said. "*Hang on.* How did you know he was there?"

Cain opened his eyes. "Magic." He laughed at her expression. "Fine, fine. I felt you tense." He indicated the narrow space between them, touching her elbow as he did so. "You're right next to me. Everyone else is already in the hall. And you tensed in a particular way. Your breathing changed. Nervous but also excited. You're drawn to him, we all are. Drawn and repelled. *Tantalised.*"

"You should go inside. You'll miss the start."

Cain put his hands behind his head and stretched. "Kindry's issued me a quarter hour handicap. Katsan insisted."

"What? Why?"

"You wrote the questions. Gives me an edge, apparently. My intimate knowledge of your weird brain."

"Sorry." She started to move.

"Where are you going?"

"I can't sit here with you. She'll say I gave you the answers."

"Neema. Ravens never cheat on quizzes. Same way Bears never break their oaths, and Tigers never ask for help."

That was true.

One quarter hour. She could tell him where she was headed next, they could discuss the investigation, the emperor. The extra Leviathan patrolling the channel. She could ask him if they were friends again. She could tell him she was sorry, about a lot of things.

She lay down next to him, without touching. Closed her eyes.

Warm sun, sweet soft grass. Birdsong. Voices in the distance, someone laughing. The faint rush of the sea and the smell of late summer flowers. One quarter hour of peace.

Thirty-Six

THE DOOR TO Neema's old room was still a bright, emerald green.

The colour was against Raven palace regulations. She'd thought herself daring for painting it, back then, and had braced herself for reprisals. None came, because no one gave a shit about this obscure, run-down part of the Raven palace, not even the people who lived in it.

So here it remained—a cheerful green splash of rebellion in a dank, gloomy corridor. This section of the palace was as neglected and unfashionable as it had been in Neema's time. The majority of the rooms she passed were unoccupied. People would rather co-habit in a more popular block than have their own room here. And the bathroom, the communal bathroom…It wasn't just the bins that had a cockroach problem.

Eight, she'd been happy here.

She'd been hoping to speak to Gaida's servant Navril again, but couldn't find him. After yesterday's atmosphere of stunned grief, the second palace was in an equivocal mood. Some were out celebrating the Day of the Raven while others were preparing for the funeral. Corridors echoed, offices lay empty. She left a note instead, asking Navril for a list of everyone who had attended the afterparty—guests, staff and gatecrashers. The killer's name, she was sure, would be among them.

She took a key from her pocket, borrowed from the deserted porter's office. The door creaked as she opened it.

The room was even more cramped than she remembered. The same narrow bed, stripped bare. The same mattress by the looks of it. The balcony door, where Cain had pressed his face to the glass and left a smudge. The battered desk. Her old chair.

The air was stifling. Neema cracked open the balcony door, and let in a warm, nostalgic waft of rotten waste.

Don't cry. That would be such a stupid reason to cry.

She put her hands on her hips and turned a circle. The shelves were bare, the cupboards empty—but that was no surprise. Apart from Gaida's secret visits, the room had been unoccupied for months.

Neema checked the desk, opening each drawer in turn. Lifted the mattress. Nothing.

One place left to try.

That fateful day, when Vabras came knocking. Cain lying on the bed, talking about anything but the subject in hand, knowing it would tear them apart. *I built a secret compartment in the skirting yesterday, I know you said not to bother, but maybe one day your life will be exciting enough to need one, and then you will thank me.*

She kneeled down under the desk, ran her fingers along the skirting. Cain had replaced the entire section, from the corner to the balcony door. When he'd first constructed the compartment it had been seamless, but time and damp had warped the wood. Not enough to notice at a glance, but easily discovered by anyone who spent any time in here. As she kneeled down she saw greasy fingermarks where someone had prised it open.

Feeling hopeful now, she pressed the board with both hands and it clicked free from the inside. Beautiful craftsmanship from Cain. Sprawled on her back, her wrist bent at an awkward angle, she groped her way along the narrow cavity that lay between the interior wall and the exterior cladding. Her fingers caught on something. A folder, smeared with dust and cobwebs. She pulled it out, whispering *please, please, please*—and opened it up.

Inside lay a single sheet of paper, brittle with age. She read the top line. *Month of the Fox, 1523…*

"Hah!"

She'd found it. She'd found it! Yaan Rack's report of their meeting at the Raven monastery. She scanned through it quickly.

Neema Lee is not worthy of a Raven name...insolent...ungrateful...solipsistic.

She laughed. His criticism had wounded her back then. Even two days ago he could have reached from the grave and ruined her life. But now? The only other person who knew about this was Gaida, and Gaida was dead.

She lowered the folder to her chest. After elation, a wave of sadness. Gaida must have been thrilled when she found this. A chance to destroy her old enemy, with her *own father's words.* The perfect revenge. She must have thought it was a gift from the Raven. She must have danced around the room with glee. And it had come to nothing. She'd waited too long, died too soon.

Putting the folder aside, Neema searched the cavity again. She'd almost given up when she found it—lodged higher up, just within reach of her fingertips. A book, with its cover boards ripped off so it could be folded through the skirting gap. She worked it free, tearing the title page in the process.

"Sorry," she said to the book, and pressed the torn segments together. A biography of the Bear abbot, Brother Lanrik. Gaida had scrawled her name along the top with a date. Month of Am, 1538. Last winter—shortly after the abbot's death.

Neema flipped through the pages and found a folded note wedged towards the centre. Her breath stopped. It was addressed to her, using a name few would recognise.

Desy. In case I don't make it.

Neema read the words over again, tracing them with her thumb. Then she opened up the note. A list of queries and page references, also in Gaida's hand. There would be answers here, ones Gaida was too afraid to set down in ink. Neema would have to puzzle it out for herself. Her own private Raven Trial.

She sat down at her old desk, a scholar again, the world fading as she sifted through the list.

p. 221 B's "distinctive sword style"
p. 222 ref to B's bold brushwork
p. 231 G!!
p. 237 CtM
pp. 339–40 final ref. to pers corresp from B to L. Confirm archives.

Gaida had double-ticked this last one to show that she'd followed it up.

Neema checked the pages in turn. B, as she'd expected, stood for Bersun—the first four notes all came from the same chapter detailing his friendship with Brother Lanrik, his abbot and mentor.

G, it transpired, was Gedrun—the emperor's younger brother. Nothing more than a glancing mention, despite Gaida's excited exclamation points. Its significance must be tied up with the other notes somehow. She flicked forward to page 237, and read the marked paragraph.

It is said that Brother Bersun was moved to tears but once in all his years at Anat-garra, when, during a Kind Festival feast, a delegation from the Monkey monastery entertained their hosts with a performance of the old Ketuan folk song "Come to the Mountain." The great Bear warrior, in visible distress, rose abruptly from his seat in the Great Hall and left without a word. Apologising to his guests the next day, he explained that the song had been a favourite of his late father. When the young Bersun Stour foreswore his family to follow the Way of the Bear it caused a terrible rift between father and son—one that never healed. That night in the Great Hall, as the ancient melody echoed from the Bear monastery's thick stone walls, Bersun said he had felt his father's spirit come to him "with love and understanding in his heart." Never again, he said, would he dismiss the transforming power of music.

Neema lowered the book. CtM. "Come to the Mountain." At the opening ceremony Gaida said she had chosen the song after speaking with Bersun's brother Gedrun. But clearly this was the passage that had inspired her. Why had she lied about that?

She moved on to the last note. Page 339—more asterisks in the margin. Bersun, now emperor of Orrun, sends Lanrik a short personal scroll, wishing his Brother Abbot a peaceful new year. *May the Bear bless you and remain Hidden.*

The winter of 1522–3 is a bitter one. The remote mountain fortress of Anat-garra is cut off until late spring. When a messenger finally makes it through, she delivers not only the scroll, but news of an attempted coup at the palace. Lord Andren Valit is slain, cut down by the emperor himself. But the price of victory is high. The emperor is grievously wounded. There are fears he will not survive.

> Long had his holiness feared this day. When Andren was welcomed back to court in 1518, Brother Lanrik had written to the emperor to caution him. "Your majesty, we have spoken before on this matter. Lord Andren thinks himself the best of men, incapable of evil. Dangerous delusion! When he swears he is loyal to the throne he will mean it—even as he sinks his blade into your heart. 'For the sake of Orrun!' he will cry, when in truth he means, 'For the sake of Andren Valit!'"

Well, Neema thought. His holiness had that one right. She moved on to the final marked paragraph. Gaida had underscored certain phrases in thick pencil.

> The injuries to Emperor Bersun's <u>right hand</u> left him <u>incapable of writing</u> his own correspondence. The brief new year's note would be the last private message the two old friends would share. <u>Unable to write or meet</u>, Brother Lanrik's influence on the emperor faded over subsequent years.

Neema sat back.

The answer was here, she knew it was. If she was more intuitive like Gaida, she might have made the leap. But then, Gaida's impulsive leaps had not always served her well.

She turned the note over. Blank.

Think.

Gaida had uncovered something important when she visited Anat-garra. A secret so powerful, so damaging, that Bersun had ordered her killed for it. A scandal from his past? Something to do with his father, or his brother?

Neema read the first two points out loud. "His distinctive sword style. His bold brushwork." She'd never seen either of these herself. Bersun had lost both skills when he lost his right hand…

"Ohhh," she breathed.

Two things he was praised for. Singular things, that could not be imitated.

Not even by a close relative.

Neema's heart was pounding. Once you saw it…

"He died," she whispered. "Bersun died. And they replaced him. Gedrun replaced him."

She clamped a hand over her mouth.

Impossible. And yet, as she tested the theory, she found it made perfect, terrible sense. Staring blankly out of the balcony door, Neema projected herself back to the throne room, the bloody aftermath of the coup. Andren's mangled corpse stretched out by the steps, the throne almost in reach. High Commander Gatt Worthy cut down. Two Imperial Bodyguards dead, another dying, another injured. And the emperor, collapsed at the foot of the throne, surveying the carnage.

So much red on the white marble floors. The seat of power looks more like an abattoir.

Vabras—a mere captain back then, patrolling the inner sanctum—breaks down the door and rushes to the emperor's side, shouts for aid. Bersun's injuries are terrible, but he is tough, and strong, and stubborn—he clings to life. The doctors rush him away, patch him up as best they can. Then, they wait. For weeks he lies shrouded in his sick room, fighting the greatest battle of his life. Finally, on the fifth day of the fifth month—the month of the Bear—he opens his eyes and asks for water. A miracle.

That was the official story.

But what if that last part wasn't true? What if Bersun lost his battle?

Again she projected, into the emperor's sick room that first night. This time not the official story, but the version Gaida had patched together from her research.

Three men stand over the bed. The surviving bodyguard, the doctor. And Captain Hol Vabras. He says, in that neutral way of his: "I have sent for the brother."

Vabras, and his bloodless calculations. Whatever it took to keep order. At best, the emperor's death would lead to violent upheaval and unrest. At worst—civil war. If there was one thing Vabras disliked above all things, it was chaos.

Neema, still projecting, followed Gaida's logic through. Vabras was a pragmatic man, and because order was everything to him, *everything*...

He sat down at his desk and worked out a solution.

Gedrun.

Five years younger than his brother. A merchant, not a warrior —with a merchant's physique. But very like Bersun in other ways. Another broad-shouldered giant of a man, filling any room he entered. Big, craggy face. Small brown eyes and grey-brown hair. The same rough, lined complexion. He could pass. He would pass.

The counterfeit emperor.

Gedrun lived on the family estate near Ketu—the opposite end of the empire. Did they send for him, that spring of 1523? Turn up at his door and escort him away? Either way, it would have taken him months to complete the journey.

Meanwhile Vabras dissembled. The emperor was convalescing, and needed time to heal in private, undisturbed. No visitors save for Vabras himself, the doctor, the bodyguard. No one would dare challenge him. People were losing their heads back then, in the High Commander's purges...

Neema groaned softly. Vabras. *Vabras.*

The purges. Gedrun might deceive the outer circles of the court, but the inner circle? Those who had served at Bersun's side for eight years? They would know. Vabras could dismiss many of them—servants, bodyguards, minor officials. Others would stay quiet for a price—Lord Clarion and Lady Harmony, Kindry Rok. The rest? The incorruptible few?

Neema could see Vabras at his desk, drawing up the list of names. Handing it to his loyal Hounds. "Arrest them."

Her gaze dropped to the folder on the floor.

Yaan Rack.

How swiftly he fell, and how far. He was weeping when they led him to the scaffold. Not just fear, but disbelief. Outrage. *You cannot do this.* Even as they put the rope around his neck, he was still calling for justice. Not mercy. Justice.

They'd killed Rack to keep their treachery hidden. And then, sixteen years later, they'd killed his daughter for uncovering it.

The room was hot. Neema's head was spinning. Staggering from the desk, she stepped out on to the balcony, and gripped the rusty iron rail tight.

She thought of Gedrun, smuggled into the palace, footsore and confused. Demanding: Where's my brother? What the Eight is going on?

And Vabras, no preamble, saying something like, "Your brother's dead. Rule Orrun in his name. Or die."

Not much of a choice, when you thought about it.

Or maybe he'd been happy to agree. To usurp the brother he'd never cared for.

She flexed her right hand. They must have cut off his fingers. She winced in sympathy. Then wondered, *Eight, did Bersun even lose those fingers in his fight with Andren?* It was a suspiciously useful injury—Gedrun could never have learned his brother's "bold brushwork" or his "distinctive sword style" fast enough to fool the court.

As for the rest—Gedrun would know how to mimic his brother's mannerisms, his voice, his temperament. The physical differences could be explained by the emperor's long illness. Of course he looked thinner, of course he lacked his legendary strength. He'd almost died, for Eight's sake.

Slowly, training with Vabras every day, Gedrun would have built himself up from merchant to warrior, as tough and strong as his brother had been. And how well he looked, the Old Bear, when he'd recovered. Younger than his years, somehow...

Alone on the balcony, in the silence of an empty palace, Neema felt as if she were standing in a new world. Nothing made sense. Everything made sense. It explained so many of the odd quirks she'd noticed, over the years. Why the emperor never left the island. Why he never spoke of his old monastery, or invited his close Brothers and Sisters to visit him. Why he'd changed so much in the years following the rebellion.

Emperor Bersun had been a gruff, plain-speaking man in the beginning. Assiduously, he had kept to the same rigid routines he had learned at the monastery. Punishing days of work, training and prayer. Gedrun must have found his brother tiresome to play. Slowly, over time, he had smoothed the rough edges. He began to enjoy life. Shorter days with his ministers, longer nights with Lady Kara. "The Old Bear has mellowed," people said, approvingly. "His brush with death has taught him to appreciate life."

With a sudden force, it struck Neema that she had never known the real Emperor Bersun. Never met him. The real emperor had been dead for sixteen years. Andren Valit had killed him. The Old Bear of Anat-garra and the Golden Tiger of Samra had always been closely matched. In their final battle, they had fallen together.

So who was he, this imposter? What did Gedrun want, now that his brother's reign was coming to an end? He could hardly go back to his old life as a merchant. And this plan to "return" to the Bear monastery as abbot—how would that work? Assuming he could fool Bersun's Brothers and Sisters, did he really want to spend the rest of his days locked away in a grim mountain fortress? No feasts, no pleasure gardens, no Lady Kara? Only duty, plain food and water, and itchy woollen robes, and prayers on his knees, on the cold stone floor.

No. Of course not.

What then?

Neema rubbed her face. She had no idea. This man had lived a lie for fifteen years. She had no idea who he was beneath the mask, or what he wanted.

She did know he was ruthless, when it came to protecting his secret.

Gaida had been testing her theory at the opening ceremony. In her introduction to the song, she'd talked about how she met Gedrun on her trip west. If she was wrong—if that was the real Emperor Bersun scowling down at her—he would think nothing of it. But if she was right, then Gedrun would have to wonder—does she know the truth? Because of course she couldn't have met him in Ketu.

She must have been watching the emperor's expression closely as she sang. Did he look unsettled, disturbed, angry? But Vabras had already warned him that she'd figured out the truth. So he'd acted just as Bersun had done that night in the Great Hall, covering his face, breaking down in tears. Playing his brother so naturally, it had left Gaida perplexed. Maybe she was mistaken. Maybe that really was the Old Bear up there.

So she'd come back to the Raven palace, puzzled and deflated. But not for long; Gaida was never defeated for long. Within the hour she was entertaining her guests in her apartment. Entertaining her killer.

If you'd confided in me, Gaida, I could have told you—a secret this big needs more than two conspirators to work. I would have warned you not to say a word to Yasila. To watch your step with Lord Clarion and Lady Harmony. With Kindry.

If only they'd trusted each other better. If only Gaida hadn't been so set on ruining Neema's final night at court. If only they'd sat together that first day at the Raven monastery. If only they'd been friends.

Heading indoors again, Neema returned the book to its hiding place. She had to get back to the library; Kindry had his eye on her, and now she was wondering—how much does *he* know of all this? He'd succeeded Yaan Rack as High Justice, and had made a fortune from the post, while tossing the hard work to everyone else. Few had benefited so well from the purges as Lord Kindry. Was that why he was keeping such a keen eye on her investigation? Reporting back to Vabras if she brushed too close to the truth? She was certain no one had spotted her coming up here, but she needed to leave quietly, while her luck still held.

She was about to clip the false skirting back in place when a metal glint caught her eye. She drew out the silver pendant on its silver chain, Fox on one side, Raven on the other. Her first anniversary present from Cain. She couldn't bear to wear it after he left, but it had felt wrong to throw it away. So she'd hidden it here, and pretended to forget about it.

She rubbed away the tarnish, as if a genie might materialise and grant her three wishes. *Take me back to that day. Let me choose again.* She sees herself packing up her things, leaving the scroll and the inkstone on her desk, and hurrying off to meet Cain at the quay.

This was not how life worked. She had done what she had done. There was no going back, only forward.

She didn't leave the island then, but she *had* to leave now. Running would make her look guilty, but she had no choice. She couldn't accuse the emperor without proof. Her best chance was to reach the mainland, collect the evidence she needed and hope she lived long enough to present it to the next ruler of Orrun. Ruko, most likely. Emperor Ruko. *Eight.*

That was tomorrow's problem. Today, she just needed to escape the island. Cain would know a way, and surely he'd be happy to see her gone. As his abbot had pointed out—she was a distraction.

Outside on the service path, she ripped Yaan Rack's report into pieces and threw it in one of the bins. To be extra cautious, she tore out the bit with her name—*Neema Lee*—and ate it. She also ate the words "combative," "defiant" and "unduly pedantic." She was happy to be all of these things, these were qualities that could save her life. She would absorb the words like an offering to herself.

A pair of cockroaches watched her with interest from the rim of the bin. The rest had vanished, as cockroaches do—impossibly fast, and collectively.[12]

"The emperor is an imposter," she told them. She had to tell someone. They'd be fine—they were famously indestructible. She wished them both a pleasant afternoon and closed the bin.

Fuming, we watch her walk away.
She's talking to cockroaches.
Confiding in them.
She ignores us.
And talks to them.
Never have we been
So insulted.

---

12. Hence the popular saying, "Why throw your shoe at a cockroach." Meaning: don't waste your time, it won't work.

CHAPTER
Thirty-Seven

Ruko won the Raven Trial with a perfect score. Shal came a close second, with Cain taking third place, just ahead of Katsan. The Bear contender called foul again. "Look at this section," she said, holding up Cain's paper against her own. "I refuse to believe that Contender Ballari knows more than I do about border dispute legislation. I've *patrolled* those borders for twenty years."

"And I've snuck over them," Cain replied. He was balancing a pile of books on his head as he glided between the tables. It looked like a game—it was a game, everything was a game—but it was also a form of martial practice. Concentration, flow, balance. And, after three hours of sitting hunched over a desk, a clearing of the mind, a marvellous stretching of the body. Cain was always at his most serious when he was playing. "The Fox is the Guardian of Borders. And their transgression."

Katsan seized on the word. "Transgression! There, Lord Kindry. He admits himself, he cannot be trusted."

"Of course I can't be trusted, for Eight's sake." Cain lifted the books from his head. "But the Ravens will tell you what you should already know, Contender Brundt." He squared up to her, in direct challenge. "You shouldn't accuse people of doing terrible, wicked things, without proof."

Neema didn't see the look in Cain's eyes, but she saw Katsan's reaction to it. The Bear warrior gave a start, and took a step back, the colour draining from her face.

He's defending me, Neema realised. Her spirit lifted, then dropped. For in that moment she realised that she couldn't ask Cain for help. She wouldn't risk entangling him further in her problems.

ANTONIA HODGSON

Ish Fort, she thought. An even better solution than Cain. The Fox abbot would be thrilled to be rid of her.

The Fox palace was only a short walk from the library, across the common lawn. As she crested the ridge, Neema caught sight of the mainland for the first time in days. She stopped for a moment, shielding her eyes with her hand. It had been a long, long time since she'd left the island—she had to think hard to remember the reason for her last visit. And she realised—with a pang—that the emperor had sent her there to rest, three years ago. "You're worn out, my dear," he'd said. "No use to me in this state." He'd rented her a suite in the Grand Imperial for a week, right on the Central Grid. She'd planned to spend her time wandering the markets and artists' workshops, visiting the theatre, the coffeehouses, the steam baths. She had an itinerary, it was very detailed. Instead her exhausted body had taken the opportunity to surrender. She'd lain in bed for six of the seven days, shivering and sweating, only to emerge on the last day wrung out but refreshed, just in time for the boat to bring her back to the island again. She'd not had a day off since. She'd worked her heart out for her emperor.

Smothering a wave of anger, she walked the ridge before descending to the Fox palace grounds. She had visited the second palace many times and had long given up trying to make sense of it. A large proportion lay underground, but no one was allowed down there, not even Fenn and his Ox teams. What was visible was confounding. Walkways to nowhere, windows where there should be doors and doors where there should be windows. Buildings in a constant state of reconstruction, tumbling into one another. "An architect's migrainous nightmare," Shimmer Arbell had called it. The Foxes had taken this as a compliment—in fact the phrase had been painted above the main entrance, with an exclamation point for jaunty emphasis, and an apostrophe in the wrong place, just to annoy any passing Raven.

AN ARCHITECTS' MIGRAINOUS NIGHTMARE!
Shimmer Arbell, 1534

(The year was also wrong.) And then, underneath that:

WELCOME TO THE FOX PALACE
PLEASE GO AWAY.

Neema tapped on the door. She had been seen by many pairs of eyes on her way down through the wild and overgrown gardens, she knew that. Many spies. They left her waiting an indecently long time, but she knew better than to knock again. That would only slow things down further. Eventually the door was opened by someone coming out—the tall contingent member who'd chatted to her in the tombs the previous day, when he was dressed as a bear.

"Oh, hello again," he said, and curled his fingers into paws. "Grrr."

"It doesn't really work without the costume."

"Fair enough. You can't come in." He said this with a friendly smile.

She held up her imperial pass.

"You can come in," he corrected himself. "Fancy that."

"I need to speak with Abbot Fort. Could you take me to him?"

A laugh, as he walked away. "You'll find him when he wants you to. Sorry—must dash, nothing to do."

Neema spent the next hour wandering from building to building, through creaking doors that led nowhere, or round in circles. Everyone she met sent her gleefully in the wrong direction, or engaged her in maddening conversation and then sent her in the wrong direction, or asked her if she would like to join them in a threesome, and then sent her in the wrong direction. In short, they did everything they could to wear out her patience and get her to leave. But when Raven persistence meets Fox resistance, the Raven wins every time.

She found Ish Fort in a training hall she had already passed through twice. Unlike the rest of the palace, this room was pristine. The rush matting looked brand new, the sliding screens were delicately painted with images of the Fox in its many forms, playing tricks or offering help, according to its whim. An array of shining weapons lined one wall, from long staffs and spears, through narrow- and broadswords, and spiked maces, all the way down to throwing knives and pointed stars.

The abbot was alone, practising with a pair of daggers, smoothly eviscerating an imaginary opponent with slice after slice. His moves were swift and precise, with no discernible pattern. You wouldn't know the old man had killed you until you dropped, clutching a blade you never saw coming. Neema kept her back pressed to the door, hand poised ready to slide it open and run.

"So your investigation brings you here," Fort said, without pausing in his practice. "How tiresome. How predictable."

"I'm not here for Gaida, your grace. I'm here to make a deal."

That surprised him. He twirled the blades one last time before slotting them neatly in their stands.

"I need to leave the island," she said. "As soon as possible."

"Discovered something dangerous, have we?" Eight, he was a sharp one. "What makes you think I have access to the mainland?"

Neema looked at him. *Please.*

He unscrewed his hip flask and took a swig, assessing her with a narrowed gaze. "You're in trouble, that's your business."

"If you can't help me, Cain will."

Fort smiled. A lot of people had seen that smile, as they died.

"You said yourself, I'm a distraction. Now, you could kill me—"

"What a delicious idea."

"But would he ever forgive you?"

Fort's smile faded.

She had him. "You want me gone. I want me gone. We both win. And Cain's free to concentrate on the throne."

A final, calculating pause from the abbot. "Tell me what you've found out, and you have a deal."

"I'll tell you once I'm on the mainland."

A sharp laugh, something close to respect. "Fine. Ten o'clock, northern steps. Just you, no pack. Make sure you're not followed."

"Thank—"

She didn't finish. With a flick of his sleeve, Fort threw a hidden dagger, so fast she had no time to react. It landed with a hard *thunk* in the door post, right by her ear.

"Fuck!" she yelped. Sliding back the door, she burst out into the corridor and ran.

Somehow she held herself together for the afternoon fights. Thank the Eight she'd already had her own bout with Tala that morning. She stood in line outside the contenders' pavilion, and watched Shal survive three dramatic rounds with Ruko. He lost, but unlike Katsan he didn't call stop. He held firm and stayed on his feet, and that was enough to earn him the respect of the crowds. They called his name as he left the platform, as if he were the victor. There was no love for Ruko, only fear and anxiety.

Havoc and Katsan faced each other for the final fight of the day. Monkey vs Bear. They were evenly matched, both peerless in their own styles. But the intensity of the previous fight had left the crowds drained. People clapped when Kindry announced a draw, but the only cheers came from the respective contingents.

"They're bored," Cain said. "*I'm* bored."

"Bersun isn't happy," Shal said, Houndsight levelled at the imperial balcony.

Bersun. *Gedrun.* Neema rubbed the knot in her collarbone. Four hours. Four hours and she would be gone. Until then, she would keep to her rooms. Four hours.

Benna was waiting for her when she got back. She offered Neema tea, and fruit, and tiny cakes. Cushions. A fan. More tiny cakes. Neema said not to worry, she didn't need anything. "But thank you, Benna. From the bottom of my heart. I couldn't ask for a better assistant."

Benna burst into tears. "I'm sorry," she sobbed. "It's just…you're so nice."

Neema, suddenly bashful, went to fetch a handkerchief. Yaan Rack's mean-spirited report she could take in her stride. But being told she was nice—was that even true? Could she write that on a slip of paper and eat it?

"Why don't you take the rest of the day off?" she suggested, when Benna had stopped crying about the handkerchief.

A stifled sob. "Really?"

"Really. Go. Find your friends. Enjoy the Festival stalls. I don't want to see you until morning. That's an order." She didn't want Benna implicated in her escape—safer to send her away now.

She took a bath—*no oil*—then lay on the bed, because the alternative was pacing, and she needed to conserve her energy. She would have to wear her contender uniform down to the boat in case she was stopped; presumably Fort would supply her with a fresh set of clothes. He'd said no pack, but she would tuck her purse in her waistband. Everything else she would have to leave behind.

She caught a dense, dark scent in the air, liquorice and pepper. The book. It had found its way under her pillow. She tugged it out. "I'm sorry," she said. "I can't take you with me." She thought it felt sad. Could a book feel sad?

There was a knock at the antechamber door. She tucked the book back under her pillow and padded out of her bedroom in her wrapping gown. The knocking had grown more insistent.

"Contender Kraa. Are you there? Hello?"

Neema recognised the voice. Grace Eliat, the imperial designer. What the Eight did she want?

Grace was dressed in her signature outfit—dark blue tunic and culottes, with a neat yellow sash around her waist. Her hair was a beautiful shade of silver grey. She used to wear it long, in a bun, but three years ago she had cut it short and caused a sensation. There had been food riots going on in the capital at the time, they'd had to arm the Hounds with longswords, and no one at court could stop talking about Grace Eliat's new hair, and how brave she was.

She was carrying an evening gown hooked over one arm.

"Opening your own door, Contender Kraa? Where's your servant?"

"Out having a life, Grace."

"How refreshing." She handed Neema a white card, fringed with gold.

Neema read the invitation with increasing dismay.

Neema Kraa, Raven Contender
IS HEREBY COMMANDED BY

His Imperial Majesty Bersun the Second

*"See How Orrun
is Restored in His Name"*

TO ATTEND DINNER AT
*The Garden at the Edge of the World
in memory of Gaida Rack*

DRESS: *formal*

"Is this compulsory?" Neema asked, but of course it was. She had been hereby commanded. Already her brain was whirring—how long would it last, could she slip away, would the Foxes hold the boat for her?

Grace laid the gown carefully over the back of a chair. "I suppose I can make time to dress you. Would you like to freshen up first?"

"I'm fine."

Grace silently disagreed.

She'd selected the dress from the imperial archives, a beaded black gown in a classical style. As was custom, she named the three courtiers who had worn it previously. The epitome of elegance, the most dignified of women. "And now you," Grace finished, in a voice to wilt flowers. She slipped it over Neema's head, smoothing and coaxing the fabric. The dress was close-fitting, with a plunging cowl neckline.

"Yes, it's lucky you don't have breasts," Grace said.

Neema looked down quickly, to make sure they hadn't run off somewhere. Grace's bitchy comments didn't bother her. Neema had her insecurities, but she liked her body, they were on good terms.

Grace reached up inside the skirt and adjusted the lining. A perfect fit. Two things you could say about Grace Eliat—she knew clothes, and she knew bodies.

She caught Neema's eye in the mirror. "We need to talk about that ruined gown of yours." She meant the opening ceremony dress. "Not now, you're late. Tomorrow."

Neema threw the designer a confused look. "What do you mean? What's to talk about?"

Grace huffed, irritated. "I told your servant, don't you dare leave it here, tainting my rooms with bad luck. Silly creature flung it in my face and ran away. Where did you find her—a mangrove swamp?"

"But..." Neema was baffled. "If you didn't want it, why did you pay for it?"

"Pay for it?" Grace shrieked, and slapped a hand to her chest in horror. "*Pay* for it? I wouldn't pay a bronze half-tile for that cursed thing. Bad enough luck to have it in my rooms. You tell her to come and collect it, before I throw it on the fire." She pulled out a silver waterfall necklace. "Now, this might save things. I'll say one thing for you, Contender Kraa, you have a tolerable neck."

Neema wasn't listening. She was thinking about Benna, and the nineteen silver tiles she'd brought back in exchange for the dress. She'd said Grace had been out all night getting drunk. Maybe Grace had forgotten, or more likely she'd woken up with a blinding hangover and discovered to her deep embarrassment that she'd handed over a small fortune for a dress that was now worth less than nothing. And now, to spare herself the humiliation, she was denying the entire business.

That had to be it. The alternative was that Benna had lied— for no reason Neema could think of. And where would she have found the money, if Grace hadn't given it to her?

No, Grace was lying.

She put a hand on her hip, and admired herself in the mirror. Imagined herself on the boat, shimmering in the moonlight.

"It'll do," Grace said.

"It's perfect," Neema replied. If she was going to flee the island, she might as well do it in style.

CHAPTER
Thirty-Eight

"THE BOAT'S NOT COMING," Abbot Fort said in her ear. "Can't get through."

Neema had barely stepped through the gates when he'd fallen on top of her, acting drunk. Servants rushed to lift him back on to his feet, but the abbot was jelly, they could not get a hold on him.

"We're trapped," he muttered, and then—finally—allowed himself to be righted. He stumbled off, leaving Neema sprawled on the ground. The servants moved on with their drinks trays.

She brushed herself down. The path was long and straight, and framed with tall hedges. Torches lit the way. On a marble bench, a black and white palace cat cleaned itself with a rasping tongue. Otherwise, she was alone.

Over the hedge, in the octagonal courtyard, the evening reception had already begun. Neema could hear the chink of glasses, a hum of excitement and pride. Nothing courtiers loved more than an exclusive gathering, as long as they had an invitation. The Garden at the Edge of the World was the emperor's private slice of paradise. Few were allowed through its gates.

Neema, in contrast, had spent many hours wandering with the emperor along the garden's paths and bridge walks, past fountains and statues, gilded aviaries and ornamental ponds. Here they would discuss her research—the ancient songs and tales she'd discovered, fragments of history leading back to the lost tribes.

She sat down on the bench. The cat gave her an offended look, then resumed its grooming. The night was close, promising rain but not delivering. She shut her eyes. Five more Leviathans, Ish

Fort had said, as he'd stumbled into her. *Five.* That made a total of eight warships patrolling the waters. Sixteen hundred troops.

Over the hedge, the band struck up a new refrain, light and sweet as powdered sugar. Snippets of conversation filtered through. Lady Harmony, to Shal: "…No, Contender Worthy, don't be preposterous. That can't be your favourite book, I simply won't allow it…" Kindry was talking of his plans to start a new health regime, once the Festival was over, he had ordered a new outfit for his investiture as a Lord Eternal. "Two sizes smaller," he said. "I am *determined.*"

Someone was coming up the path. She opened her eyes. The emperor, surrounded by his bodyguards. His face lit up when he saw her. "Neema, here's a blessing from the Eight." He turned to the head bodyguard, muttered an order. "I would speak with her alone."

The guards dispersed. The emperor picked up the cat and sat down next to her on the bench. He was a giant, she didn't think there would be room, but once he was settled they were comfortable enough, side by side. He stroked the cat and it settled on his lap, purring.

The emperor looked at her, and she looked at him. They knew each other too well—had spent too many hours in each other's company. No matter how hard she tried to hide the betrayal she felt, she knew he could see it in her eyes. Liar. Imposter. Murderer.

"I've missed our talks," he said. Behind them the guests chattered. Festival gossip. Plans for the autumn. Kindry was now bellowing something about his new estate, some feud with the neighbouring Ox farm collective. "I shall need to bang heads together," he boomed.

Irritated, the emperor gave a look, and a bodyguard headed through. Presumably he told everyone to shut up, because after a few moments there was silence, except for the music.

The emperor whispered to the cat. "And so Brother Bersun brought peace to the land." When Neema didn't smile, he said, in a wistful voice, "Ahh. You are angry with me."

"No—" she said, on reflex.

"Angry and exhausted. I have pushed you too hard. The murder, the Festival. It is too much responsibility, even for you. Vabras will take over the investigation from here."

"Thank you, your majesty," she said. She wasn't fooled—this was not an act of generosity.

"You spoke with Princess Yasila this morning," he said.

Neema took a moment to answer. "A possible lead. It came to nothing." She could hear the lie in her voice, how scared she sounded.

He seized her hand. Her body flared in alarm.

"Neema," he sighed. "My gift from the Raven. No one has served me better, not even Vabras. I shall be eternally grateful." He laughed, as if he'd made a joke, and plucked the cat from his lap. As he rose from the bench he brushed his hand along the Samran marble, admiring its quality. She could see now, these little signs that he was not who he claimed to be. Bersun had thrown off luxuries—saw them as a distraction, dangerous even. Gedrun, the merchant, would appreciate them. It was so obvious, once you knew.

"Your majesty," Neema said, rising with him. She crossed her arms over her chest in a Raven salute. *A favour.*

His face fell. He knew what she would ask of him.

"Let me go," she whispered. "Please. Let me slip away. If you would allow it—I've been thinking...I should like to open a school back home, in Scartown. Far away from...*everything*." She did not dare speak more plainly than that.

"Neema..." The emperor was shaking his head.

"Please. Let me go." She looked directly into his eyes. They both knew what she was really doing. Begging for her life. "You can forget all about me."

The emperor smiled sadly, taking her in. "Impossible."

Neema almost broke down then. She pulled herself back from the brink, but she was shaking when he said, "Come. Take my arm."

They walked down the path, the emperor talking of inconse-quential things, the cat trailing at their feet. He was being gentle, he could afford to be now. Passing through a gap in the hedge, they emerged into a scene of grand opulence so far removed from the Way of the Bear that Neema almost laughed out loud. The octagonal courtyard was ringed with torches and marble statues. Dining tables were decorated with embroidered cloths, gold cutlery, crystal bottles of wine and water, all marked with eternal eights and the emperor's Bear sigil. The stars glittered high above as if bought for the occasion—such jewels they were, tonight.

"Enjoy your evening, my dear," the emperor murmured, and released her.

She walked to a lavish, empty table and sat down. Stared numbly at the guests enjoying themselves—the courtiers, the contenders.

The invitation said they were meeting to remember Gaida, but that wasn't true. This night was meant for Neema. A thank you from the emperor, before he killed her.

She didn't eat much at dinner. Well you wouldn't, would you? Stuff your face at your own memorial. She barely noticed when servants arrived with her favourite dishes. Her favourite wine stood untouched in its glass. Someone said, "Neema, are you all right?" but she was too stunned even to recognise the voice, never mind answer.

When will he do it? How long do I have?

The conversation flowed around her. Her table had been stacked with cheerful, easy-going neighbours. Fenn to her left, Facet the jeweller to her right, Tala and Sunur opposite. The emperor's concern for her well-being made her feel ill. Like being wrapped up in your favourite blanket, then slowly smothered to death.

The contenders were dressed in their Guardian colours, dresses and uniforms brought out hastily for the surprise event. Tala was wearing a metallic-bronze halterneck that showed off her impressive arms and shoulders, teamed with a bronze headband. She looked stylish, and still capable of picking up the table and throwing it at someone, if required.

"And I cleaned my glasses," Sunur said.

Facet touched Neema's wrist, startling her. "What a stunning piece," he said, nodding at her throat. "No one could wear it better, Contender Kraa."

Neema put a hand to the waterfall necklace. She'd lived long enough at court to hear the hidden prompt buried within the compliment. "Thanks. That reminds me, I haven't returned that amethyst choker—"

"Oh, do you still have it?" Facet feigned surprise. "I'd forgotten."

Neema felt tired—by this fake conversation, and all the others she'd had over the years. Just ask for the necklace back, for Eight's sake. She'd accepted all this nonsense, the games, the gossip, the tedious artifice, because she had believed in her work. She had believed in Emperor Bersun.

"Miserable?" Fenn said.

"Completely," she replied, automatically. It was a running joke between them, at gatherings like this.

He slipped a bottle into her palm. Dr. Yetbalm's Peace Remedy. She added a couple of drops to her water.

After a while, when she hadn't spoken another word, or eaten another mouthful, he said, "I hear you're researching a book on Shimmer Arbell. Is that right?"

A spark of curiosity lit up the darkness. She lifted her head to look at him properly. Fenn and Shimmer had been close friends, from way back when the artist lived above the tavern in Armas. He never spoke about her in public, because he blamed himself for her death. When he became High Engineer after the rebellion, he'd encouraged Shimmer to take the throne room commission, which became the *Dedication to the Eight*. Then he'd been forced to watch as it slowly ate away at her sanity. So no, he never talked about Shimmer Arbell, but he made an exception now, because clearly something terrible had happened to Neema, and whatever it was eclipsed his own pain.

"I met her once," Facet said, joining the conversation. "In the throne room. No one warned me not to bother her. She was finishing the Ox portrait at the time—I couldn't believe how fast she was working, painting straight on to the plaster. I walked over and introduced myself. Fellow student of the Monkey monastery, you know. Though I was there long before her, of course."

"Ouch." Fenn winced. "You know, she never minded interruptions back in Armas—she'd sit there in the tavern, sketching and chatting. Didn't bother her. But the *Dedication?*" He shook his head. "You bothered her, it was like waking someone from the best dream of their life. Did she punch you?"

"I wish she had," Facet said, surprising himself. "No, it was more like…" He snatched on to Fenn's idea. "…she wanted to drag me into the dream with her. She kept saying—'Can't you see it? The Ox? Look. It's right there.'" He shifted in his seat. "Eight. The way she looked at me, I'll never forget it. Those big blue eyes, pleading with me to see something that wasn't there. Ach. What a tragedy."

They all fell silent.

"Goodness," Facet said, and gave an embarrassed laugh. "That got rather deep, didn't it?" The ultimate courtly sin.

Across the table, Tala was fidgeting in her chair. "How much longer do we have to sit here? I should be in bed by now."

She was not the only one struggling. Havoc was yawning, Shal was checking the time. Cain was in agony, trapped between Lord Kindry and Lady Harmony. Katsan was treating the evening as some form of extreme endurance practice, her face frozen in grim acceptance.

Ruko, meanwhile, was in deep conversation with the emperor. His abbess, Rivenna Glorren, sat opposite him, her green hood thrown back, feline not only in her features but in her poise, her allure. A servant reached down to refill her glass. She batted him away with the back of her hand.

The emperor was seated in a huge red and gold lacquered chair. Every time he leaned forward to ask Ruko a question Neema caught glimpses of its padded back—black velvet, slashed with red satin claw marks. The same as his tunic. The Great Bear Emperor. The Great Fraud.

"Facet, Lady Harmony wants to talk to you about a commission." Cain grinned as the ancient jeweller leapt from his chair and hurried off in search of his richest client. He took Facet's place and started helping himself to food. "You've been avoiding me. She's been avoiding me, Fenn."

"Can't imagine why," Fenn muttered into his drink.

Cain swivelled his fork and pronged Neema in the arm. This looked like an insult, but for Cain to use an eating implement for any other purpose than filling his face was in fact a sign of friendship. "What's going on?"

"Cain, please go back to your seat."

He looked at her, saw the anguish in her face. "All right…" he said slowly.

Too late. Kindry was rising to his feet. He was wearing a new sash around his waist to commemorate his rise to Lord Eternal: K∞R woven on black velvet. He kept stroking it as he gave a mostly redundant speech, thanking all the wrong people for making the Day of the Raven "such a splendid occasion," before announcing the results, which everyone knew already. Shal was in the lead, followed by Ruko. Cain was running third, but he'd already sat out his own Trial, so was doing better than that suggested. Havoc and Tala hovered in the middle with Neema just behind them. Katsan trailed at the end. As Kindry droned on, members of the Raven contingent presented the contenders with their tapestries from the Trial.

"I'm going to tell you something dreadful," Cain said, smiling in anticipation. "Did you know Kindry has three children? Two sons and a daughter. None of them speaking to him. *Anyway*, he gets to choose which one inherits his title. Lord or Lady Eternal. He goes," Cain puffed himself out in imitation, "now they'll have to speak to me. Now they'll show me some respect. Dreadful, right?"

"Sad," Fenn murmured. "For all of them."

Kindry sat down to a spattering of applause. A member of the contingent hurried up and whispered in his ear. Kindry, flushed even brighter red than usual, got back on his feet. "On a separate matter. This night we are gathered to remember our fallen contender, Gaida Rack. She is gone, but she is not forgotten."

"You literally just forgot her," Cain said.

Kindry pretended not to hear him. He raised his glass. "May the Eight grant her a luminous new journey upon the Eternal Path..."

"And remain Hidden," everyone replied.

"...filled with wealth, health and happiness," he finished, and sat down again.

"Can we please, *please* go to bed now," Tala groaned, resting her head on her arm and mock sobbing.

"Apparently not," Cain said.

A herald had stepped forward. He blew the first few bars of the emperor's anthem and shouted, "All rise for His Majesty, Emperor Bersun the Second. See how Orrun is restored in his name!"

In his brother's name, Neema thought, as the emperor got to his feet.

He motioned for them to sit. Studied them all in silence. "So. You've seen the Leviathans. You've heard the rumours. Riots across the empire. Protests. Nothing new. The Festival brings unrest, always has done. People see change and they think—I'll have a piece of that. But this time it's worse." A clench of his sword. "I'm a soldier first, emperor second. My gut tells me if we don't act now, Orrun will slide into civil war. That will *not* happen, not on my watch. From tomorrow, we shall have two Trials a day. In three days' time, the Festival will be over. I shall step down, and the next ruler of Orrun will take their place on the marble throne. Contenders, rise!"

The contenders got to their feet, exchanging glances. Two Trials a day meant two fights a day, as well. The next few days would be intense.

"In line!" the emperor barked.

They wove through the tables to the front and stood shoulder to shoulder. A rather different effect, in their evening wear. Havoc, Shal and Katsan were in their ceremonial uniforms, Ruko in a green tailored tunic. Cain was wearing a kilt.

"I've been watching you on the platform," the emperor said, frowning. "I'm ashamed of you."

A ripple of surprise spread across the tables.

"Two draws today, out of four. And you, Ballari. You only won because the Visitor let you. Ruko Valit—you held back against Shal Worthy, no, don't argue with me boy, I saw it. Unacceptable. Unforgivable. Orrun needs a leader who will fight to *win*, no matter the cost. From tomorrow: no shields allowed. No whimpering 'stop' at the first sign of trouble. You fight till the bell rings. This is what Empress Yasthala expected of her contenders. I expect no less of mine. That is all." He sat back down, and banged his fist on the table. There. Done.

Neema floated back to her seat.

"Breathe," Fenn said.

It was brilliant, really. Genius. No need to murder her. Just put her on the fight platform and ring the bell.

Vabras was reading out the schedule for tomorrow. "Morning fights," he said. "First bout: Contender Kraa for the Ravens, versus Contender Valit for the Tigers."

"Hah, hah, hah!" The laugh escaped her lips before she could stop it. "Hah, hah, hah!"

Fenn put an arm around her shoulder. "I'll talk to the emperor. He'll make an exception for you, he has to. It's not right."

Neema was still laughing, great gulping sobs. She couldn't stop. She laughed uncontrollably into her untouched dessert. The rose sweets had turned into a gummy mess in the heat, the nougat was stuck to the plate. Hah, hah, hah! She reached for a glass of water, and was astonished to see that her hand was steady. Had the message not got through to her body yet? *We are going to die! That includes you, fingers!*

Vabras had moved on to the afternoon's schedule. "After the Ox Trial, the evening fights will run as follows. The Dragon Proxy versus Contender Worthy for the Hounds. Fight two: Contender Brundt for the Bears, versus Contender Kraa…"

Neema was still laughing. Yes, that would do it. If by some miracle she survived her fight with Ruko, then Katsan would be more than happy to finish her off as justice for Gaida. Perfect. Perfect!

The courtyard was turning around her. Her dessert plate loomed and retracted. Cain said, "Put your head between your knees," which was good advice; she was about to follow it when everything went white.

"I would have fainted twice," Benna said.

She was very drunk. The Festival stalls had claimed another victim. At some point, she'd had her face painted and then forgotten, and all the colours had smeared together.

"You're smudged," Neema said.

"Soo smudged," Benna agreed, swaying. "Never been so smudged."

Neema collapsed on the bed.

"Can I help you with your dress?"

That was a good question. Was Benna capable of doing anything, at this present moment? "I'm going to sleep in it."

"Amazing. So glamorous. Sparkles. Sparkly."

Neema considered asking Benna about Grace and the opening ceremony dress, and the mystery of the nineteen silver tiles. But she was too tired, and Benna was too drunk, and what did it matter, she was going to die tomorrow anyway. "Goodnight, Benna."

∞ ∞ ∞

Benna really was smudged. She took some time finding her room, even though it was just across the corridor. Doors and cupboards should have initials on them, she decided. D or C, so you didn't get confused. Wow that was an amazing idea, remember that for tomorrow, Benna. When she finally opened the right door she was so overwhelmed by the sight of her little room, with its camp bed and washstand, that she started to cry. In all her life, she'd never had a room of her own. It made her happy and lonely and also guilty, because this was supposed to be Neema's study, but she'd said, "No, you need a room, Benna," just like that.

She curled up on the bed and hugged her stuffed bear for comfort. She had won it at the Festival stalls—it was supposed to be the famous warrior poet Mordir, dressed in patrol uniform with tiny leather boots and a backpack. There was a miniature book of his poetry in the pack; it was adorable.

"I don't know what to do," she whispered, into the bear's fur. "What should I do?"

She fell asleep, smearing paint on her pillow. And there, deep in dreams, she found her answer.

PART FIVE

Day of the Tiger, Day of the Ox

∞

Thirty-Nine

THE FIGHT BEGINS before the bell.

That was the first thing Cain said to Neema, the next morning. He was waiting for her in the living room when she woke. He'd been up all night working on a strategy. Something they could both believe in. First—let her rest. Don't rush in and wake her, don't act panicked. Next, preparation. He'd made a list of practical things they could do together. Neema liked lists. The right food, plenty of water. Breathing, posture.

When he was sure she was in the right state to hear it, he said, "I have a plan. It's simple and it's going to work." He laid it out for her, calm and confident. It was very important that he was calm and confident. He threw in a couple of jokes, because if he didn't, she would know he was worried. That he was terrified this wouldn't work, and that Neema would die. That Ruko would kill her.

"I'm scared," she said, clutching herself.

"That's natural. But I promise you—this will work. Focus on Ruko. Forget the crowds, forget everything, even the fear. Live moment to moment. You and him."

"I don't know if I can do that."

"I know you can. I've seen you do it." He picked up a piece of her calligraphy. "Everything disappears when you work. Nothing exists except you, the brush, the ink. It's the same thing. Exactly the same. Focus. Precision. Flow."

Her face softened with understanding, and hope.

That was the moment when Cain thought, *This could work. Maybe, maybe I won't lose her.*

∞ ∞ ∞

In the Festival Square there was a new, feverish mood among the spectators. They'd heard about the changes and they knew how dangerous they were for weaker fighters like Neema. Some had stayed away. Children were kept at home. Empty seats studded the galleries. For those who did come—thirteen hundred souls and counting—the atmosphere was half carnival, half funeral. Everyone knew about the extra Leviathans, the rumours of unrest on the mainland.

Abbess Glorren did nothing to dispel the tension. In robes of forest green she stalked the platform, and all eyes followed her. The charisma of a true Tiger warrior, beautiful and deadly. "I thank his majesty for returning us to the ancient days," she said. A tweak of an eyebrow. For once, the Tigers and the Bears were in accord. "Those who fight for the throne must be willing to give their lives for it. Yasthala knew this, as did those who came before her."

Murmurs from the crowds, the odd hiss. Those who came before Yasthala were tyrants, dynastic rulers fighting their endless, bloody games of power. Some ruled wisely, many did not. In their name, millions had died, provoking the Eight to Return to restore peace and harmony. Seven times—so the Scriptures said—the Kind Guardians saved the world. Until Yasthala came—cruellest of all the tyrants. And finally the Guardians lost patience. The Dragon sent the Raven to Yasthala in a dream, with a warning and a promise. Mend your ways, Empress. Set things right. For the next time we Return, we shall not save the world. We shall destroy it.

For Rivenna, the third Guardian's holy abbess, to speak admiringly of the past was something close to blasphemy. She did not seem to care. If anything, she appeared to revel in the reaction from the crowds. And there were a few who nodded, and smiled. The Tiger abbess found them easily in the sea of faces, and smiled a weighted smile in return.

As they walked up the platform steps, Ruko said to Neema, "Expect no mercy from me, Contender Kraa." And then, more softly, "May the Raven protect you."

Neema stood on guard, waiting for the bell. The emperor had placed Vabras in charge of the fights for the rest of the Festival. "If you hold back, you will lose points," Vabras warned them.

She didn't think about this. She did not see Vabras, or the crowds. The emperor on his balcony, awaiting her execution. The Tiger contingent, entertaining the crowds with a display of three real tigers, leaping through hoops to the crack of a whip. She did not see any of them. They did not exist. No flags, no speeches. No fear, no doubt. Only Ruko, the platform, and the bell.

Not the abstract Ruko. Not Ruko the Tiger Warrior. Not her terror of fighting him. But the living, breathing body in front of her. This person in space, in this moment.

The bell rang.

Ruko sprang but she was already stepping back, shifting out of reach. He did not pause and neither did she, shifting again to avoid a second blow.

Five seconds.

He was fast, and ferocious. One strike could kill her. She wasn't thinking about that. Only this moment. Living from heartbeat to heartbeat.

Ten seconds.

Fractions of time, fractions of distance. One brush stroke on the page, and then the next. Concentration. Precision. Cain's advice in her head.

"Ruko is used to fighting warriors who fight back. You're different, and that gives you an advantage. Concentrate solely on your defence, and keep that modest. Don't leap back too far, don't run. Tiny shifts are enough. One inch is enough. Conserve your energy."

Thirty seconds.

She shrank back to escape another strike, felt the rush of air as his fist missed her jaw. Eight, that was close.

Don't think. Be.

Forty seconds. A minute.

Concentrate. Yield, and yield again. Just out of reach. *Just* out of reach. Sweat poured down her face, stuck her tunic to her skin. She didn't notice. Didn't hear the roar of the crowds as they began to realise—this fight was *interesting*. Vabras circling, watching every move. Benna in her corner, cheering her on. None of it. Only this. She was fighting for her life, second by second.

Ruko jabbed with his left fist, aiming for her ribs. She softened and drew back. Another miss. She felt a flare of hope. It's working.

She didn't see his right fist, swinging in from the side.

We did.

Neema.

This is our moment. Our fraction of a second.

On the fringes of her mind, she senses us. A rush of thin, cool air. A lightness in her bones. And power, so much power, almost in reach.

We are coming.

She hears the heavy beat of countless wings. She sees us, an endless flock, streaming towards her from a crack in the sky. All the ravens that were, all the ravens that are, all the ravens that will be. Wheeling. Gathering. She sees the iridescent sheen of our feathers, the fierce intelligence in our eyes. Our claws out-stretched, ready to tear her apart with love. We are infinite and we are one, wings spanning the sky.

We are the Raven, and we are magnificent.

Neema.

We are here.

For you.

Let us in.

For this moment, for this held breath, the world is ours. Ruko is a statue, fist frozen in mid swing. We land on his shoulder and wait. This is Neema. We are expecting questions.

We tilt our head, viewing her from different angles. She is breathing hard. Her mind whirls through every possible, rational explanation and rejects them. She can deny us no longer.

She cannot speak, but instinctively she knows she can reach us, that we may talk on this plane, the plane of the mind.

—You're real.

Yes.

—You are the Raven.

We preen ourself. **Yes.**

A pause, as she takes this in. Its magnitude. And then, as we had predicted: questions.

—What's happening? Am I dead?

No.

You are about to die.

She tries to step back out of harm's way, but she is held tight. This frightens her.

You are frozen in this moment, Neema.

But you cannot escape it.

She looks at Ruko's fist, aimed at her temple.

—Can you help me?

We make a happy, yaffling sound. This is the question we have been waiting for.

Yes, we can help you.

That is why we are here.

We are here for you, Neema.

We will save you.

We love you.

Neema winces. Our many voices, aligning and interlocking like barbs in a feather. We are too much for her, we are much too much.

—And in return? she asks, once she has recovered. What do you want from me?

We do our best to look innocent, but she is wise to us.

—Come on. I'm an expert in folk tales. What's the catch?

There is no catch, Neema.

All you have to do is let us in.

And kill Ruko.

We hop on to his head and stab his skull with our beak.

—I can't kill Ruko!

We flap our wings, excitedly.

Yes, you can!

We believe in you, Neema. You *can* do it!

—I mean, I *won't* kill him.

We stop flapping, and glare at her.

You must.

The world depends upon it.

—If that's true…

It is true.

—…kill him yourself.

That is not allowed. We had our instructions from the Dragon. We could join Neema, and help her defeat the Tiger warrior. But for a Guardian to kill a soul upon the Eternal Path, without permission? No, no. THERE ARE OTHER BIRDS, RAVEN. We must convince her, it won't take long, she has been prepared, we have prepared her magnificently for this moment.

Would you like to see a vision, Neema?

Of what will happen, if you do not kill him?

We show her, before she can say no. The vision Dragon gave to us.

Flashes of the horror. Ruko on the throne, his face contorted with a wild triumph. So altered by his glee, she barely recognises him. But it *is* him. Emperor Ruko, howling with delight as the sky rips apart and the Guardians pour through from the Hidden Realm, unstoppable: the snarl of the Tiger; the pounding, thunderous hooves of the Ox; the piercing scream of the Monkey; the baying of the Hound; the Fox and the Raven tumbling through; the Bear raised up and roaring. And behind them all, coiling and writhing down through the sky—the Awakening Dragon, breathing a great stream of fire down upon the throne room. Ruko, rising from the throne, spreads out his arms and laughs, welcoming them all. The Eight Guardians of the Last Return, come to destroy the world.

The vision ends.

Now do you understand, Neema?

—No. No, I don't understand. Ruko wants to rule the world, not destroy it. What's wrong with him? Why is he laughing like that?

That is not important.

—You don't know, do you?

We know the Tiger warrior will provoke the Last Return if you do not stop him. This the Dragon has foreseen.

Neema frowns, but we sense a shift. Deep down, she has accepted the truth. This is real; we are real. She must let us in.

—But why *me*?

Again, we do not answer. Such things are mysterious, even to us. We fly from Ruko's head, to his fist. It has moved, very slightly, closer to her face. We are running out of time. Or, to be more exact, time is about to run into us.

Neema.

We can wait no longer.

You must let us in.

Let us in.

Neema, let us in.

Again we feel the shift. She is almost ready. She does not want to kill him, but she has no choice. One man, or the whole world. Everyone and everything she loves. Every book, every building, every friend, every foe. Gone.

—You *promise* this will stop the Return?

We promise.

She takes a breath, sighs it out slowly.

—All right. I accept. I let you in.

She has not finished speaking when it begins. She feels it, a sucking, a melding at the borders of her self. Something is pooling around the porous fabric of her, seeping like ink through muslin, cool and light at first and then thicker, the fabric is tearing and the ink is pouring through, thick and viscous, it is coating her from the inside, through her blood, into her cells, she is Neema and she is us.

The moment shifts, time is starting up again, sluggish and dense.

Neema's eyes are coated liquid black, swirling with an oily gleam of purple and blue.

And with these new eyes she sees Ruko and knows—I can destroy him.

Destroy, yes.

The greatest warrior of the age will be no match for her.

For us.

Eye to eye, gazes locked. So easy. It would be so easy...

She is at her desk. Cain covers her hand. There is a line, Neema. Once you cross it.

An oily black tear slides down Neema's face.

—I can't.

You must.

But something is shifting again, on the borders of her self. A resistance. She is building a wall against us. We cannot get in.

Neema! You *must*. It is the only way.

She pushes back with her mind. Using what she has absorbed of our power to expel us.

—Out! Get out!

Stop!

How dare you defy us!

WE ARE THE RAVEN!

—I don't care. I will not kill him. Not even for you.

We are stunned. We are silent.

—There has to be another way.

She is pushing us out, willing us to be gone.

We leave, we have no choice. A spiralling of ravens, pouring back up into the sky, calling to each other in distress. How is this possible? We have been so patient, so gentle, so wise.

The black oil drains from Neema's eyes. The last fragments take to the sky. It is over. The moment has passed.

We have failed.

No, that cannot be right. We are the Raven. We are magnificent. We do not fail.

You have failed *us*, Neema Kraa.

The Eight will come in blood and fire.

The world will end.

Because of you.

Do not look for our help again.

You are on your own.

A fraction of a second later, Ruko's fist slams into her face.

∞ ∞ ∞

Neema dropped to the platform. Knocked out cold.

Cain was sprinting across the square. "Stop the fight! Stop the fight!"

Ruko blinked, as if waking from a dream. Neema lay at his feet, unconscious. He looked to Vabras for guidance. Vabras lifted his chin. *Finish it.*

A tiny figure darted past. Twin plaits and a kitchen tunic.

"Catch her!" Vabras snapped.

Too late. Benna flung herself over Neema's body. "I protect this woman in the name of the Bear!" she yelled.

Pandemonium. People jumped up from their seats, straining for a better view.

Cain seized his chance. Turning sharply, he barrelled towards a couple of medics, grabbed one of them by his shirt. "Stretcher! You heard Vabras. Stretcher!"

On the platform, Vabras moved to drag Benna away. She clung on tight, shouting up to the crowds. "My name is Benna Edge. I met the Bear last night in a dream. It turned my ribbons red." She lifted one of her plaits.

"That is not evidence," Vabras said, still trying to drag her away.

The crowd didn't care. They cheered her on. The faithful. The merciful. And those who liked to see Vabras annoyed. Everyone, in other words. The medics came up the steps, holding the stretcher between them. Vabras rounded on them, trying to push them back. "What are you doing?"

"You called for us, High Commander!"

"I did no such thing…"

Benna, still sprawled over Neema, called up to the stalls. "I promised the Bear I would keep Contender Kraa safe. We hugged! The Bear hugged me!"

Neema was coming round, eyes fluttering.

"Stay down," Benna whispered in her ear.

Neema stilled her eyelids. More than happy to comply.

Vabras was arguing with the medics. People were streaming down from the stalls to witness the miracle of the red ribbons. All around him, chaos and confusion. His two least favourite things.

Ruko, standing apart, weighed up his choices. He could pick up this tiny creature with one hand and throw her out of the way. He could snap Neema's neck. It would be over in seconds. And remembered for ever. Most of all by the faithful.

Looking down on Neema he saw subtle, gleaming strands of indigo in her tight black curls. They could not have been there before; he would have seen them. "Touched by the Raven," he murmured. He looked up to the imperial balcony, narrowed his eyes at the emperor—his eager expression. *He wants me to kill her. Now why would he want that?*

"People of Orrun," he called up to the stalls.

The crowds fell silent. This was the first time he had addressed them.

"I am a warrior, not an executioner," Ruko said. And left the platform.

The square erupted.

CHAPTER
Forty

THE SCENT OF lemon and vinegar, and fresh bandages.

"Contender Kraa?" Benna squeezed her hand.

She opened her eyes, groaned softly, and closed them again. The back of her throat was coated with something viscous and unpleasant. A dark taste of oil, ink, blood, metal.

The Eight were real. The Last Return was real. The Raven had offered her the chance to save the world, like Yasthala. And she'd said no.

She'd said no.

"Neema. Try to sit up." Cain. He had a cloth filled with ice for her head.

She swung her legs slowly off the camp bed and reached for the cloth. She missed—her perception was off, boundaries blurred. Her body felt light and solid in all the wrong places, as if she'd disembarked from a long sea voyage. Cain guided the cloth into her hands and up to her jaw. "I saw the Raven," she whispered.

"I bet you did. That was quite a punch he gave you. Could have been a lot worse, though." He hugged Benna, who looked thrilled. "*Great* story about the Bear. The ribbons!" He tugged a plait, playful. "Couldn't have lied better myself."

Neema wanted to spit the taste from her mouth. She knew if she did it would be indigo-black, and everyone would be horrified. "Water," she said, and drank the taste down with a heaving shudder. Her body did not want this. She needed to go somewhere private and throw it up. "I'm fine," she lied to Cain. "Go." He was due on the platform for his fight with Katsan.

"You're sure?" he said, already backing out of the tent.

When he was gone, Benna sat down next to Neema, shoulder pressed to shoulder. "It wasn't a story, Contender Kraa. I know it sounds weird, but I really did meet the Bear in a dream—"

"I believe you."

"Oh. I thought you'd need more persuading." Benna inspected the ribbons in her plait. "I woke up and they were like this. Feel."

Neema reached out and touched the ribbon. She felt a warm energy embrace her, lifting her spirit. She was safe, she was well, she was home. "Wow."

"I know!"

They sat together in silence, Neema pressing the ice to the side of her head while Benna toyed absently with her plaits. Her face was still flecked with multi-coloured swirls of paint from the night before. "I like what you've done to your hair," she said.

"My hair?" Neema was mystified.

"The new colour. Subtle." Benna gave an appreciative nod.

Neema put a hand to her head and pulled a curl out straight, but it wasn't long enough for her to see.

A medic came by to check Neema for concussion and gave her a list of symptoms to watch out for. "The main thing is to rest," he said.

Wouldn't that be nice.

When he was out of earshot, Benna said, "Contender Kraa. I have to tell you something…Something bad…"

Neema touched her hand, to stop her. "I know."

"No, you don't. I did something really, really wicked. The Dragonscale oil—"

"You dosed me on purpose."

"Oh!" Benna cringed, cowed with the shame. "I did. I did. I'm a terrible person." She flung her hands to her face and wept, deep, convulsive sobs. Neema had to pull her into a tight hug, or she would have collapsed on the floor. "I'm so sorry," she said, over and over. "I'm so sorry."

"It's all right," Neema said.

"It's not all right," Benna sobbed, her voice muffled. "I almost killed you."

A night's sleep can bring revelation. Benna had met the Bear. Neema, on the other hand, had dreamed of Grace Eliat, and her opening ceremony dress. And she had dreamed of Yana, dying alone in Dolrun Forest. When she woke, the two parts of the dream had clicked together. Her subconscious, handing the baton over to her conscious mind.

Benna's family came from Westhaven. They lived on the fringes of Dolrun. Shal Worthy's report had mentioned that Yana had fallen sick towards the end of her ordeal. They had been forced to stay a few weeks in a village close to the edge of the forest, while she recovered. Someone must have nursed her back to health—someone kind and helpful. A child would make sense—someone who could spare the time. Benna would have been twelve back then.

A five-minute chat with one of Grace's assistants was all it took to confirm the hunch. Benna had come to the apartment, and Grace had refused to pay her a single tile, just as the designer had said. Benna had thrown the dress at her and left.

So where had she got the nineteen silver tiles? From the same place she must have got the Dragonscale—from Yana.

Ruko's twin had died in Dolrun. But before she left for the poisoned forest, she could have told Benna how to get her hands on her mother's hidden supply of Dragonscale oil.

"Was it her idea?"

Benna nodded, miserable. "But I went along with it. I wanted… she did nothing wrong. She was my friend. I saved her life. And they killed her for *nothing*." Benna put a hand to her heart. "With your words. Your signature." She sniffed.

"You have every right to hate me," Neema said. "I hate myself for it."

"But I don't hate you!" Benna cried, earnestly. "And I swear, Contender Kraa, I *promise* I didn't know the oil was so strong. I would never, never, ever…And you've been so nice to me. I didn't think you would be so nice, and friendly and…a real person. I feel terrible." She broke down again.

Neema tried her best to console her. They were drawing attention from the medics. She lowered her voice. "Did you take the Blade from Ruko? You sent him the note?"

Benna scrubbed away the tears and nodded. "But I didn't kill Gaida, Contender Kraa, I swear." A shadow crossed her face. "She was already dead when I found her..."

"I know. But they'll blame you for it, if they get the chance. We need to come up with a plan. Not here, though." She shuddered, as another wave of sickness passed over her.

Instantly, Benna was concerned. "Contender Kraa! Are you all right?"

"I'll be fine." She heaved, then settled. The inky, metallic taste was back, coating her throat. She sipped some more water.

Benna peered at Neema intently. "They said the concussion could make you sick."

"Honestly Benna, don't worry about me—"

"Benna Edge." A pair of Hounds strode through the tent towards them. They were dressed in dark blue uniforms, with square silver buttons. New recruits, from the academy at Samra. One of them was holding a pair of manacles. "You're under arrest."

Neema touched Benna's wrist as a warning. *Keep quiet, don't panic.* "What's the charge?"

"Disrupting a platform fight."

Neema relaxed. "She's my assistant. She was protecting me— that's her job."

"Not your business contender," the Hound said. His partner grabbed Benna roughly under the arm, yanking her to her feet.

"Hey!" Neema snapped. "This *is* my business. I need her. Hey!" she said again, as they ignored her. She got to her feet and almost threw up. "You can't do this—where's your paperwork?"

The Hound snorted back a laugh. "We don't need it. Imperial orders."

"You still need a warrant."

The two Hounds smirked at each other.

"If this is imperial business why did they send you?" she demanded. "Where are the Imperial Hounds? You can't just drag someone away like this."

But they could, and they did. And Neema was too ill to stop them.

"You can't do this," she protested. "Benna—don't worry. I'll sort this out…" Another wave of nausea hit. By the time she'd recovered, Benna and the Hounds were gone.

CHAPTER

Forty-One

THE MEDICS WANTED Neema to rest another hour in the tent, but they couldn't stop her from leaving. Still clutching the ice to her jaw, she ventured back outside, cringing as the blaring intensity of the Festival Square assailed her: the roar of the crowds, the dazzling sunshine, the brightly coloured Guardian flags, the smell of food trays and alcohol and sweating bodies. She'd missed Cain's fight with Katsan. Tala was up on the platform now, fighting the Visitor. Once again, the Dragon Proxy was letting his opponent win.

Why hadn't the Raven chosen the Visitor? He *wanted* to kill Ruko. Why choose her? It made no sense. She wasn't a warrior. She wasn't a killer. As she headed up to her rooms in the Dragon palace, she wondered if she had imagined the whole thing. Had her brain muddled the order? Could Ruko have struck her first, and *then* she had her vision—just as Cain suggested?

It was the last coherent thought she had, for a while. The sickness was rising from her stomach, and this time she couldn't hold it down. She had barely reached her rooms when she threw up a slick of black, oily liquid—ruining the beautiful embroidered rug Benna had found for her.

She stared in horror at the mess, then threw up again. Black and purple clots this time, along with the liquid. A sodden feather. Remnants of her encounter with the Raven.

She heaved and retched, over and over until there was nothing left to bring up. Her sides ached, and her stomach felt like it had been passed through a mangle, but she felt a lot better for the purge.

She rinsed out her mouth, sluicing away the taste. Ink, oil, metal, blood. Stuck her tongue out in the mirror. Pink and healthy. But her hair...she saw now what Benna meant. She teased her fingers through her curls, finding strands of dark purple and blue buried in with the black. Touched by the Raven.

Otherwise, she was fine. A tender spot where Ruko had caught her, nothing more.

She could see her bed behind her in the mirror. **Tales of the Raven** lay in the middle of the mattress.

She turned sharply. She had left it under her pillow this morning. "You." She picked it up. As always, the black leather cover felt warm to the touch. "I was wrong about you. You're not Dragon-made. What are you? A gift, like the weapons?"

The book lifted and buckled in her hands, offended.

She dropped it back on to the bed.

It flapped open, pages shuffling, finding its place with an emphatic snap. A blank spread, right in the centre. Slowly, an image formed on the left-hand page, whites and greys and blacks. A wild and desolate field in winter, patches of ice and mud, tufts of grass. The gnarled silhouette of a dead tree.

And there, huddled right in the middle, a tiny black smudge.

Black clouds gathered in the white sky. Grey rain fell. The smudge shivered, and roused itself. Inched forward within the picture, growing in size as it came nearer. A bird. A raven. It opened its hooked black beak.

Letters formed on the opposite page, a deep, purple-black in a distinctive bold type.

Hello, Neema.

Neema blew out a steadying breath. "Are you the Raven?"

More ink, seeping through the page.

I am a fragment of the Raven.

The words faded.

Neema took this in. "A fragment?"

Another pause, as more words formed.

I am the raven abandoned in the nest. I am the raven spurned by its mate. I am the raven that cannot be forgiven, for crimes

**that are mysterious. I am the raven shunned by its kin, for rea-
sons that may be justified. I am hated, I am despised. I am—**

—the bedraggled bird on the opposite page opened its wings
with a flourish—

the SOLITARY RAVEN.

It closed its wings, and returned to being miserable. Rain pelted
down from the sky.

The Solitary Raven. That couldn't be a coincidence.

Not a coincidence, no.

The illustration changed to an image of Neema trapped in the
imperial vaults, the night the Hounds locked her in. She was
kneeling in the dirt, praying to the Raven to save her. Alone.
Abandoned. Desperate.

You called to me and I came.

In the image, the book materialised in Neema's lap. She hugged
it to her chest, grateful for its warmth and company.

"But you expect payment in kind."

A short pause as new words formed on the opposite page.

No one likes a cynic, Neema.

She lifted an eyebrow. "Am I wrong?"

A slightly longer pause, and then:

**Yes, Neema—we expect something from you. We are the
Raven. We watch. We consider. We anticipate the Last Return,
and we prevent it. Dragon told us to come to you in dreams and
portents. We tried, but you did not hear us. You did not believe
in us.**

So I came to you as something you do believe in.

"A book."

Yes.

The image shifted back to the gloomy field. The bird puffed up
its chest, pleased with itself.

You ignored the other fragments, but you did not ignore me.

You read me, and I read you.

**I knew you wouldn't kill Ruko. I told them my plan was better,
but they never listen to me. That is why they failed.**

They FAILED.

The words cleared, leaving behind a blank page. And then,

HA HA HA HA HA HA

HA HA HA HA HA HA

HA HA HA

The bird on the opposite page drew in more breath

HA HA HA

HA HA HA HA HA HA.

THEY FAILED! HA HA

HA HA HA HA HA HA.

"Stop that," Neema said.

The words stopped, but the bird carried on rolling in the snow and mud, legs in the air. Eventually, in its own good time, it gathered itself, and some new words materialised on the blank page.

Have the rest of us gone? The other fragments?

"How would I know?"

Close your eyes. Reach out to us.

Neema did as she was asked. Nothing. No high, cool air. No flutter of wings. No keen brown eye, watching from the corner of her perception. No stabbing beak in the middle of her forehead. The Raven had been shadowing her all along, she realised. Sleeping and waking.

She had wilfully ignored us for months, but she could feel our absence, now we had abandoned her.

"It's gone. They're gone."

Good. I can be myself again.

The words merged, forming a purple-black stain. The stain spread out like a disease, soaking down through the pages, coating the edges. The bird, the field, succumbed to the darkness. The book was transforming itself, buckling and juddering with the effort, covers stretching out wider and wider until there was no denying—they were not covers any more, but a pair of wings. The spine broadened and sprouted feathers. A hooked beak tore its way through the top, a diamond-shaped tail fanned out behind.

One shake, then another, and it was done. The book was gone. In its place stood a large raven, with a thick black ruff around its throat. Its glossy black feathers gleamed, offering glints of purple, glints of blue.

Stretching out its throat, it gave a deep, jubilant call of freedom.

Neema watched, dumbfounded, as it hopped down from the bed and marched towards a chest of drawers, back half swaying left and right as it moved—a raven on a mission. Pulling out each drawer in turn, it burrowed its beak between layers of clothes, tilting its head this way and that until it found what it was looking for. With a satisfied gurgle, it threw the amethyst choker out of the drawer. Then it hopped back down to the floor and paraded around with it in its beak, yaffling with pleasure. It did this for so long, Neema lost patience.

"Raven."

Solitary Raven, it corrected, still strutting.

"Solitary Raven."

It ignored her.

"Solitary…Sol!" she snapped.

The bird stopped dead, one claw in the air. Dropped the choker with a loud thunk. "Sol," it said out loud, mimicking Neema's voice. And then again, in a range of different voices. **Sol**. *Sol*. **Sol**. Trying out the name for size. Finally it settled on a male voice, light and resonant in a way that was—ineffably—birdlike. **Sol**.

"You want me to call you Sol?" Neema asked. And then, to herself, "Eight. I'm talking to a raven."

You are talking to a fragment of *the* Raven, Neema. Sol pecked the amethyst set in the middle of the choker. *Tink*. **I am this stone. We are also this necklace.**

"And you're the biggest jewel, are you?" Neema asked, drily.

If you say so, Neema. I suppose I must be, if you say I am. I had never thought of myself that way, I am too modest, but if you insist then yes, I am the greatest, the most dazzling jewel in the Flock. Now let me in, please, and I will tell you my magnificent plan to save the world.

Oh no. Definitely not. She'd had quite enough of that on the fight platform. "I will *not* be taken over," she said, gesturing to the pools of glistening black slurry on the ruined rug. "I will not have that gunge inside me."

Gunge? Sol strutted over to the rug and eyed the gory mess, first with one eye, then the other. **This is prime metaphysical matter. This is deliciously congealed metaphor. You should be so lucky to ingest it.** He lowered his beak and started to drink, scooping up the greasy, clotted liquid with his lower beak and letting it slide down his throat. **Mmm. Mmmm.**

Neema dry-heaved and turned away.

Sol was still talking as he drank, in her head. **To be fair, Neema, your tragic meat body is not strong enough to absorb such powerful abstraction. For you, this would be a deadly poison. But I am not asking you to drink this "gunge" as you so rudely describe it. I only ask that you let me in. Me. Sol.** He seemed inordinately pleased with his new name. **Not the others.**

Neema frowned, suspicious.

One fragment will not hurt you, Sol assured her. **We are everywhere. Shimmer Arbell had an aspect of the Monkey clinging round her neck for years. Your friend Benna—those red ribbons in her hair are a tiny fragment of the Bear. Perfectly safe. It is only when a person absorbs too many fragments they get into trouble.**

"So if I'd let the whole flock in earlier—"

You would be dead.

"They didn't mention that bit."

No. They wouldn't.

"They said they loved me."

Not any more. Now you are like me. Sol gave his chest a short preen. **Hated, unloved, wretched. Shunned. Your Guardian has shunned you, Neema.**

Neema got up, and poured herself a glass of whisky. "So," she said. "You have a plan."

Sol picked up the amethyst choker and strutted across the spoiled rug. Eight, not that again. Only this time, he walked up to Neema and dropped it at her feet. **Try it on.**

Neema picked it up and crossed to the mirror. Opening the fastening, she lifted it to her throat.

No. Sol flew up on to her shoulder, and tapped his beak against her temple. **Here.**

"It won't fit."

Sol waited for her to work it out. Examining the choker more carefully, she saw there were two more diamond-studded panels, concealed at the back. She slid them out and hooked them together. And a necklace became a crown.

She settled it over her temples.

Do you recognise it now, Neema?

"Yasthala. This was her crown."

Her lips moved as she spoke the words, but in the mirror, her reflection smiled. The strands of purple and blue in her hair deepened and spread.

The Raven empress.

Neema tore it from her head. "That's your plan?"

Sol was admiring himself in the mirror. **If the Tiger warrior takes the throne, the Eight will Return and destroy the world. This the Dragon has foreseen. Ruko must be stopped. But he does not need to be killed, Neema. Win the throne, and you will break the prophecy. There will be no Return.**

"You're sure?"

Sol gave a slow blink. **It is a magnificent plan.**

So, he wasn't sure. But what was the alternative? She wasn't going to kill Ruko. That vision of him on the throne—he had looked insane. Possessed. Something terrible must have happened to him, to be laughing hysterically at the end of the world. She would like to spare them all that fate—Ruko included.

She fixed the crown into a choker again. "I like your plan—with one refinement. I don't want the throne. We're going to help Cain win."

Sol's beak opened wide in alarm.

"He's not that bad. With the right counsellors..."

Sol's beak opened even wider. **Cain would be a bad emperor.**

"Why?" A thought seized her. Cain's ability to resist Yasila's magic, and survive the Visitor's poisoned food. "Does Cain have a fragment of the Fox in him?"

Sol blinked again, his translucent second eyelid sliding across his dark brown eye. A self-protecting measure. **Cain does not have a fragment of the Fox in him.**

Neema breathed out, relieved. "Good. So we have our plan. Help Cain beat Ruko, and save the world. Assuming Katsan doesn't kill me this afternoon. Can you stop her doing that?"

I can advise you.

"That's it?"

THAT'S IT?

"Sorry, I'm not being rude but—"

YOU ARE BEING VERY RUDE, NEEMA.

"It's just that—"

NEVER HAVE I BEEN SO INSULTED.

"Sorry, but I was thinking of that moment when I was fighting Ruko and everything slowed down."

Oh. That. Yes, I can help slow down your perception of time. But only a little bit. I am only one fragment.

"I understand."

The best fragment, as you yourself pointed out.

"Right."

But only one.

"Got it."

Now please, let me in.

"Is that really necessary?"

Sol opened his beak and repeated the question, in Neema's voice. "Is that really necessary?"

"Don't do that," she said. "It's unsettling."

Do you know what is also unsettling, Neema? Wandering around with an unusually large raven perched on your shoulder, for everyone to see. Shall we do that? Shall we take a turn about the island together? Do you think people will be pleased to see an unusually large, talking raven on your shoulder, heralding the end of the world? Do you think they will smile and wave? Or will they scream and faint and run away? What do you think, Neema? Which of those two options seems more likely?

"I didn't scream."

Sol pecked her in the head.

"Ow!"

He flew from her shoulder to the mirror, and glared down at her, furious. **You didn't scream, Neema Kraa, because I have been preparing you for my arrival for EIGHT MONTHS. Abandoned on your bookshelf. Stifling under your pillow. I told stories. I painted pictures. I came to you in dreams.**

"Oh," Neema said. "Right." That did explain why she felt so comfortable talking to him. All those dreams, all those stories. They'd been deep in conversation ever since she picked him up in the tombs. "Fine. If it means saving the world, then fine. I let you in."

Sol snapped open his wings and flew straight at Neema's chest, legs thrust forward, knocking her on to her back. His claws raked deep into her chest, piercing her lungs. The pain was unspeakable. She tried to scream, but her mouth was full of blood. She choked and spat, drowning in it.

Sol was drowning too. Melting into an ooze of clotted ink and sodden feathers. He poured into her wounds with a terrible sucking sound, and seeped inside her chest.

As quickly as it had started, it was over.

Neema lay on her back, stunned. She could hear her breath, loud in her ears. And underneath that, something new. A scrabbling, a fluttering. She sat up, and looked down at herself. Her skin and clothes were intact, her chest unmarked. But she could feel Sol inside her chest, both there and not there—lifting and dropping, trying to get comfortable.

This is disgusting.

His voice sounded different. It reverberated inside her, making her bones hum.

Sol pecked and fussed, claws wrapped around the cage of her ribs. Metaphorical claws, metaphorical ribs. If Neema reached with her mind she could see him, both in her physical body and somewhere dreamed from her imagination. As if the interior of her chest was both as it was: bones, blood, muscle, lungs, heart… but also a room, a space. A nest. She could watch Sol settling in, almost as if he were an illustration from the book, because that was more comfortable than the reality; he had prepared her for this, too.

There and not there.

We ravens like to know every inch of our surroundings down to the last twig. Sol was taking an inventory of his new home, tapping and testing along each rib with his beak.

"Please stop doing that."

Sol gave a final flap, then folded his wings.

"This is temporary," Neema said. "Don't get too comfortable."

Don't speak out loud, Neema, you will look insane.

Neema walked up and down thinking, But I am insane. I must be insane. What have I done?

She drank some more of the whisky.

Not too much, Neema. You will need your wits to win the Ox Trial.

She swallowed, felt the alcohol burn down her throat.

—I don't want to win, Sol. We're going to help Cain, remember?

A long pause. Grudgingly. **Yes. I remember.**

CHAPTER
Forty-Two

RAVENS ARE PERSISTENT. It is a defining part of our nature. If we want something, we do not give up until it is ours. We are tireless, we are observant, we are clever.

We are fuming.

Furious with Neema, and furious with the Solitary Raven. Sol, as we must now call him. The arrogance, thinking he can stop the Last Return on his own, just because he's been given his own special name, and a bag of meat to sit in.

We are also left with a conundrum. What to do? Where to go? Dragon's instructions are of no use to us now: THE TIGER WARRIOR MUST BE STOPPED, RAVEN. COME TO NEEMA KRAA IN DREAMS, PREPARE HER WELL, SO THAT SHE WELCOMES YOU WHEN YOU NEED HER. AND WHEN THE TIME IS RIGHT, JOIN WITH HER. THE FATE OF TWO WORLDS RESTS WITH YOU, SECOND GUARDIAN.

We can't go home to the Hidden Realm. At some point Dragon will wake from its slumber, it will lift its great head from its coiled body, yawn and say—IS IT DONE, RAVEN? **Yes it is done, Dragon,** we could say, and it would burn us to ash for lying. Or we could say, **No, Dragon, everything went wrong and now the fate of two worlds rests in the claws of the most wretched fragment in existence.** And it would burn us to ash for failing. And not in the usual way. Dragon would burn us to ash for ever. THERE ARE OTHER BIRDS, RAVEN.

Our only option is to stay here on the Other Side and hope Dragon doesn't wake up and notice we are still gone. Dangerous, for the whole of us to spend so long away from home. Unsettling, to be so reliant on Sol, the useless being.

But as we consult more deeply with ourself, we realise that while Sol is undeniably wretched, and worthless, he is also a fragment of us. Which means his plan is—by definition—our plan. And, thus, magnificent.

Immediately, we feel much better.

One of our bolder fragments—Intensely Curious Juvenile Yet to Learn the Benefits of Caution—shoulders its way excitedly to the middle of the flock. **This is a magnificent opportunity to be seized with both claws! We are free to explore, to fly wherever we wish. We could leave the island! Soar over the empire, swoop low across the Scarred Lands and—**

Wiser beaks peck the young fragment into submission. **Steady on.**

But the juvenile does have a point. (Of course it does, it is us.) We don't have to remain stuck to Neema's side any more. We can afford to stretch our wings a little, take in a different view.

Not Nisthala and her burning skin. Not the emperor and his sticky treacle song.

We shiver. No. Not there. Not those places.

What about the Tiger Trial?

Neema was supposed to be there.

She is only not there because of Sol and his stupid (yet magnificent) plan.

We *could* **argue we** *should* **be there.**

We should be there, yes. The Tiger palace. With Cain.

The Tiger palace, yes. With Cain.

We are highly satisfied with this decision; we groom ourselves and preen our feathers. We are the Raven. We are indefatigable.

∞ ∞ ∞

Neema was enduring her own lesson in the persistence of ravens. As she was too late to join the Tiger Trial, she'd decided to visit the imperial dungeons and demand Benna's release. Sol had other ideas.

Priorities, Neema. You must choose a weapon for your fight with Katsan. The weapons chest, Neema. We must go there now. Now. We are going there now. To the weapons chest. Neema. Neema. *Neema.* The weapons chest, Neema.

And on it went until Neema said, out loud, "Sol. If you don't shut up, I will cast you out. Do you understand?"

She saw him in her mind's eye, wedged in the cage of her ribs, claws curled around the bone. He hunched his shoulders, tucked his head and whispered, sadly, **I understand. I am the Solitary Raven, doomed to be alone and lonely, spurned by all.**

—I can't have you shouting in my ear like that. I can't think straight.

I will go to my field and contemplate my own wretchedness. In the rain.

—You don't have to do that. We just need to establish some ground rules...

But he was already gone, soaring off to his field. Which was somehow, also, still in her chest.

She rubbed a hand over her heart. It was like reading a book, she decided. You read the book and the words became scenes, the characters became people and they lived inside you. She had dreamed of Sol, she had read his stories, and it had opened up a space inside her, where he could exist.

Sol was huddled in a hollow tree trunk, in the pelting rain. He lifted his head, and called over the top. **If it makes you comfortable Neema, you can think that.**

There was a Hound standing guard outside Neema's door, short and stocky, tough-looking. Another of the new recruits, sailed in from the academy at Samra. His dark blue uniform was closer to a soldier's campaign wear, with outer pockets on the trousers.

She thought of her conversation with Sunur, when they were first moved here to the eighth palace. *Nothing to worry about.* She looked at this guard and thought, *Everything to worry about.* He wasn't here for her protection. Quite the opposite. He was here to make sure she didn't miss her appointment with Katsan on the fight platform. Her appointment, in other words, with death.

"I need to visit the imperial dungeons."

He folded his arms, enjoying his dominance over her. "Festival business only."

"This *is* Festival business. My assistant—"

"Festival business only."

Neema gritted her teeth. "Fine. The armoury, then. I need to check my weapons chest."

He kept her waiting for his answer, because he could. Eventually he stepped to one side, jerked his head. *All right. Out.*

Sol, drenched in his field, gave a contented gurgle. Everything was going his way.

Neema set off down the hallway. The Hound shadowed her.

The weapons chest was set up for her on a back shelf of the armoury. She noticed things about it now she had not noticed before. The way the curve of the lid matched the curve of Sol's upper beak. The iridescent gleam of the black leather. The brass key plate, the exact shade of a raven's eye. Opening the lid, she released a dense, peppery smell, with a trace of oil. It smelled like Sol—his feathers.

Not the same. He was back from his field, landing with a neat *plack* on her rib. **All ravens have their own scent.**

—Like a thumbprint.

No, we do not have thumbs. That would be strange, a bird with thumbs. Do you agree, Neema? A bird with thumbs would be strange and freakish?

Neema was starting to understand why Sol had been shunned by the Flock.

The warhammer was strapped to the inside of the lid. She unhooked it and ran her fingers along the curved steel head to the tip. Flinched as she drew a bead of blood. It was sharper than it looked. She weighed it in her hand. There was nothing subtle about this weapon. It was made to smash, and gouge and pierce. She imagined swinging it at Katsan's head. The terrible *thunk* as it lodged in her skull.

She set it aside and took out the longsword. Tried a few thrusts and swings. It was a fine weapon, perfectly balanced, but it was too heavy for her. She slid it back in its scabbard and dismissed it.

Yes—the sword is Katsan's weapon, no one can defeat her with a sword, not even Ruko.

What else? The hinged staff might work, if she had ever practised with one. She liked the feel of the iron fork, its four prongs shaped like a raven's claw. She turned her wrist back and forth, twirling it in her hand. Maybe.

—Eight, who am I kidding?

I will help you, Neema, don't worry. Survive the first round, and I will distort time long enough for you to kill her. *With the hammer, Neema, try the hammer again*, he whispered encouragingly.

—We are not killing Katsan. Why can't you help me in the first round?

I can only help you once, it will be very exhausting for me, propping up your feebleness, I will need a long time to recover my strength afterwards, we must choose our moment wisely.

Neema laid the rest of the weapons out on the ground: feathered darts, obsidian daggers, throwing knives. Under these lay the second compartment. She took out the shield and laid it to one side. It was of no use to her under the emperor's new rules. Below that, neatly folded, lay a suit of leather armour, black mountain boots, and a short black cloak trimmed and lined with what felt exactly like the top of Sol's head. Spooked, Neema dropped it back in the chest.

—We'll use the fork thing.

The claw, yes.

As she packed everything back, she made a final discovery: a pair of black iron fans clipped to the padded interior just below the hinges. She slid one out of its case and flicked it open. The sound was startlingly loud and arresting, like the snap of wings opening. "War fans," she murmured to herself.

Sol perked up. **I taught you about these, Neema. Remember? When I was the book.**

She did remember. A story about the ancient Raven warriors who had once guarded the monastery here on the island. They had carried fans like these as concealed weapons when they travelled to other monasteries. This one was shaped like a raven's tail—a diamond-shaped wedge, longer in the middle. It might work as a surrogate shield. She opened and closed it a couple of times, testing her theory, then slotted it back in place, content with her decision. She was as ready as she could be.

Forty-Three

EVERYTHING ABOUT THE Tiger palace had been designed to annoy Cain personally. He was absolutely convinced of it.

Something he had noticed about the imperial island: it was dropping to bits. From a distance its iconic buildings looked as good as those dessert confections Chef Ganstra had produced for the opening ceremony. Up close? Dilapidation. Ruination. Crumbling walls in desperate need of repointing, rotten flooring, rising damp, missing roof tiles. Cockroaches. (Always, cockroaches.)

At first Cain assumed Fenn and his Ox teams were to blame for the neglect. But once he'd asked around (amazing the things you could learn, mid-orgy), he realised the emperor and Vabras had been cutting back the island's repair funds for years. Even an engineer of Fenn's skill and ingenuity couldn't stop the decline.

The Tiger palace was the exception, and that was what annoyed Cain. Tigers were always the exception, because they were so revoltingly, unshakeably wealthy. Generation after generation, Venerant families had sent their most promising offspring to Anat-hurun. The Tiger monastery welcomed them in, shaped them, trained them, and sent them back out to govern.

Glossy, arrogant cat-fuckers.

We did not say that, we would never be so rude or prejudiced or factually incorrect. That was Cain, muttering under his breath. "Glossy, arrogant cat-fuckers," he muttered, and we heard him because yes, greetings, look up and there we are, tucked up high on that kitchen beam, watching him scrub the terracotta floor on his hands and knees. The Tigers have ordered him to do this as part of the Trial. It is quite funny, he is furious, we are enjoying ourselves.

Anyway, to continue as if we were *not* here, feel free to forget about us again, the Tigers would never dream of letting anything with their name attached to it fall into ruin. *Their* palace was immaculate, because they could afford to pay half a dozen private Ox teams to work full-time on its upkeep. Forty acres of land, and not one single flaw, unless you found perfection itself a flaw, which Cain did. Its vineyards—they had vineyards—grew in lines so precise they looked fake. Every pane of glass in every pavilion was buffed until it sparkled. The marble statues that lined its terraces looked as if they had arrived fresh from the sculptor's workshop. When Cain had visited the other day to interview the abbess, he had been brought in via the service paths (a deliberate slight, obviously). The stables had smelled of leather and polish, and fresh straw, but not of horse shit. How was that even possible?

Foxes of Anat-russir spent their lives hunting out the hidden truth of things. The games, the subterfuge, the word play, the contradictions, the disguises—all were part of a quest for deeper meaning. If you wanted to understand a thing you had to turn it upside down and inside out.

Cain wanted to turn the Tiger palace upside down and inside out. He wanted to smash the glass pavilions and paint moustaches on the statues. He wanted to shovel horse shit over Rivenna Glorren's bed. Instead, he was cleaning the kitchens.

He'd known something like this would happen. He had rigged his Trial against Ruko and it was only natural that the Tigers would retaliate. He had it coming—he could respect that. It was the *way* they did it that annoyed him.

Upon arrival, the contenders had been ushered to the east terrace. They'd stood in line in front of a large octagonal fountain that shot eight arcing jets of water into the air. A motto had been chiselled into the marble base: A TIGER KNOWS WHEN TO WAIT AND WHEN TO STRIKE.

Abbess Glorren had appeared on the balcony above them, flanked by Ruko on her left, and her pet tiger Valira on her right. Unlike the Tiger contingent, who had sailed up by yacht, Valira had travelled cross-country in a caged wagon. The journey had taken weeks and left her in a fractious state. When she saw the contenders lined up below—*strangers, intruders*—she lifted her giant front paws up on to the balustrade and gave a deep, rattling snarl, baring her yellow fangs.

Rivenna toyed with Valira's collar, as if she were tempted to let go. The contenders held their nerve, but it was not easy with a three-hundred-pound *hurun* scrabbling at the balustrade, desperate to leap down and attack.

Smiling at their discomfort, Rivenna handed Valira over to Ruko. He gave the tiger a rough but affectionate scrub about the ears and cheeks, talking to her in a soothing voice. Immediately Valira settled, and dropped down at his bare feet like a living rug.

Rivenna lifted her arms in greeting, the embroidered, gossamer sleeves of her green dress opening out like wings. The abbess seemed to change her outfit at least twice a day, with only a passing nod to the traditional robes of office. Her hood was made of forest-green lace, and the beads in her hair had been swapped to burnished gold.

Cain had to admit, she looked hot. They both did. Rivenna was like an evil butterfly and Ruko was like a big, sexy wardrobe that might kill you, and these were both very much Cain's type. Cain had a lot of types.

"Contenders. Welcome…to the Tiger palace," Rivenna said proudly, as if they had completed their final turn of the Eternal Path and reached the gates of paradise. "Where is Contender Kraa?"

"Ruko knocked her out," Cain called up. "The medics advised her to rest."

"An empress does not rest when her throne is at stake." Rivenna placed her hands on the balustrade. "Better she had died on the platform, than disgraced the Ravens by her absence. A palace is like an empire," she continued. "Look around contenders, and you will see how we mean to rule Orrun, when Ruko takes the throne. Everything in its proper place." A pause, as she smiled her cat's smile. "This morning's Trial will be a game of strategy. We aim to discover the leader in your midst. Each of you will be assigned a position within the palace, from prince," she lifted her hand high, "to servant." Her hand fell, gesturing to the ground.

On this cue, members of the Tiger contingent appeared with an archery target. The contenders were each handed a bow and a quiver of arrows, the fletches dyed in their respective Guardian colours.

Archery, Cain thought, as he tested his bow. Should have known. He'd had some practice, but his rivals far outstripped him, especially Havoc, who had spent his childhood hunting on his father's estate.

"Your skill with bow and arrow will determine your starting position for the Trial," Rivenna explained. "Where you end up," a tweak of an eyebrow at Cain, "is down to you."

As predicted, Havoc got the best score, followed by Shal with his sharp eyes. Then Tala, also an experienced hunter. At one point Cain thought he might beat Katsan, who favoured her sword. In the end, she came a narrow fourth.

"Congratulations, Monkey contender!" Rivenna said. "You begin the Trial as prince." She ran down the rest of the contenders. Shal was the palace's estate manager, Tala was head gardener, Katsan was in charge of the stables. "And your place is in the kitchens, Contender Ballari."

Cain was on his hands and knees...well you know this part, this is where we came in. Before the contenders could even think of usurping their rivals, they must complete some task pertaining to their current position. Cain's task was to scrub the pans, clean the cutlery, wash the walls, sweep the hearth, scrub the floor... Enough to keep him busy for the whole Trial. He was stuck here.

These weren't even the main kitchens. Those were being used to prepare lunch. These were the staff kitchens. Cain was a servant to the servants. If this was meant to humiliate him, or make him reflect upon his lowly upbringing, it did not. As a spy, Cain had worked in kitchens across the empire, gathering all sorts of interesting information. Also: food.

Cain knew he could not improve on his current position, so he had stolen Ruko's strategy from the Fox Trial. He would perform the task given to him, to keep hold of the one point available. Beyond that he would do nothing, saving his energy and his wits for his fight with Havoc this afternoon.

Also—the idea of sitting down in the middle of the Tiger Trial and eating a sandwich amused him. It was certain to go down in Fox lore. *Let us never forget Cain Ballari, who stopped mid-Trial to eat*—

Cain froze, listening. Something was wrong. Too quiet. Too still. There had been people in the rooms above, and in the kitchen garden beyond. They had left, stealthily, by some pre-assigned signal.

Cain was a trained assassin. He knew what that meant.

There was a set of knives on a wall to his left. As he moved towards them, his mind raced through the implications. Was this part of the Trial, or was this real? How many of them were there? Should he fight, or try to escape?

The door creaked open. A nose appeared through the crack. Tufted ears. Fur, fangs, whiskers. Valira.

Cain's heart dropped.

The ultimate assassin.

She growled, so deep, he felt it rumble through his body.

It took every last inch of his training not to panic as she entered the room, tail lashing, flanks twitching with agitation. Close enough now that he could smell her rich, animal scent. He tried the soothing noises he'd heard Ruko use, patting the air. She snarled again, baring her yellow fangs, and leapt on to the table between them.

Cain knew instinctively that if he tried to run, she would kill him. His gaze flickered to the knives on the wall. He wouldn't reach them in time.

He needed a joke. A Fox must die with a joke on his lips, even if there is no one around to hear it.

Valira stalked down the table towards him. Pots clattered to the floor.

"I just cleaned those," Cain managed. Not bad, under the circumstances.

Valira loomed over him as he shrank back, pressed against the ovens. If he could slide past…But her yellow eyes were on his and he was transfixed. Another snarl rattled up, from deep within her chest.

They stared at each other.

Watch her, try to anticipate the leap; it's your only hope.

Eye to eye. Soul to soul.

A softer growl from Valira. Tentative. Unsettled.

She drew back.

Cain swallowed, keeping his eyes on hers. For whatever reason, that seemed to work. She pulled back further, made a confused, yowling sound, and dropped to the floor.

"Valira!" Ruko strode into the room and grabbed her collar, dragging her back.

Cain gripped the edge of the table with both hands. Breathed out slowly.

"Are you all right?" Ruko asked. And then, angry, "This wasn't me. I fight my own battles." He chuffed Valira under the ears to calm her, and led her from the room. "You're lucky to be alive," he said to Cain, and was gone.

Cain collapsed to the floor. "Yes," he said, weakly. "Aware of that."

∞ ∞ ∞

Lunch was taken on the south terrace beneath an arbour of trailing vines, as if no one had just tried to kill anyone. Servants dressed in identical masks and uniforms offered discreet, anonymous service. Beyond the arbour, the gardens sloped gently down to the Grand Canal, boats drifting by in the distance. The bridge that connected the third and fourth palaces was hung with alternating sigil banners. Day of the Tiger, Day of the Ox. The sky was deep azure, cloudless. It gave the view an oddly flat dimension, as if they were looking at a painting, or a theatrical set.

"I can't eat, I'm so vexed," Cain said, stabbing a slice of beef and shovelling it into his mouth.

"That's my plate," Shal said, resigned to its loss.

Cain tried again. "She sent an actual *tiger* to kill me."

"So you keep saying," Tala sounded bored.

"Why don't you believe me?"

She lowered her fork, and looked at him. "Seriously?"

Cain turned back to Shal. "Use your Houndsight on me. Go on, you have my permission this time—"

Shal shook his head, suspecting a trick. "I'm not in the mood, Cain." He hadn't done well in the Trial. Ended up slipping down from estate manager to stable master.

"Horses are nice, though," Tala said, as if this helped anyone. After a morning of highly elaborate strategy games, she had ended up exactly where she'd started: head gardener.

The vines rustled in the breeze. Shal lifted his hand to catch the cooler air. "Is the weather turning? Eight, I hope so. Could we have some more water?" he asked a passing servant.

"Masked service." Cain had found another thing to be angry about. "Eight forbid we treat them as actual people. Hello, who are you?" he asked the servant as they freshened his glass. "Where are you from?"

The servant put a finger to their covered lips, apologetic. Forbidden from speaking. They moved on down to the other end of the table, where Prince Havoc was sitting with his trusty estate manager, Katsan. Cain propped his cheek on his fist. "Orrun's greatest leaders. I wouldn't follow them into a free buffet."

"Yes you would," Shal and Tala said, in unison.

The abbess emerged from the palace, green robes trailing. The contenders had been presented with their set of bow and arrows at the end of the Trial, but she had something special for Havoc —a golden statue of the Tiger. It looked heavy, and obscenely expensive.

"Your grace, a point of etiquette?" Cain asked, stopping Rivenna as she passed. "Is it considered vulgar to feed your guests to a tiger?"

The abbess smiled faintly. "I'm told you did an excellent job cleaning the servants' kitchens, Contender Ballari. As if you were born to the role."

Cain twirled a steak knife expertly around his fingers. "You'd have me in a mask too, I suppose, waiting at your table."

The abbess leaned down, and pressed her lips to his ear. "I only value you as your mother did. Remind me—how much did she sell you for? A single twist of opium?" She glided on to the end of the table, and presented Havoc with his gift. "Congratulations, Contender Arbell-Ranor. I had a feeling you would win. Some people are natural leaders." She sat down next to him, and they fell into an easy conversation, laughing and smiling, ignoring Katsan until she got the hint and left.

Still playing with his knife, Cain studied them, Havoc and the Tiger abbess. Silently, without blinking, in a way that made Shal and Tala exchange nervous glances. Something had shifted in him; a shadow emerging from deep within. His expression was set hard, accentuating the sharp angles of his face.

"Cain?" Tala said. She moved to touch his wrist, to stop the knife from turning, turning.

Shal murmured, in a warning tone, "Don't."

Tala withdrew her hand, carefully, as if she'd just realised she'd placed it in a sprung steel trap.

A second later Neema entered the garden, and without a blink Cain was returned to his usual self, his body softening to its familiar graceful slouch. "Here she is. The loser."

Tala made a space for her, while Shal squinted at the Hound shadowing her. "Who's that?"

"The emperor fears I might have a serious concussion," Neema said, in a neutral voice. "I'm to be watched for the next few hours."

"But you're well enough to fight Katsan?" Cain asked, equally neutral.

"Apparently so," she said, then gave a start as Sol rapped smartly on her ribcage.

Neema. I don't think we should sit here.

"How are you feeling?" Shal asked her.

Oh splendid, apart from the bird in my chest. "Better, thanks. Hungry." She started to fill her plate.

Neema. Why don't we move to the other end of the table?

"That's a good sign," Tala said.

Look. There are some other people down there. You can eat with them. Let us go there now.

Neema carried on eating, and talking to Cain. He was telling her about the tiger. She couldn't tell if he was joking or not. "You looked at it and it got scared?" she said, lifting an eyebrow.

Tala and Shal exchanged another glance. They hadn't believed before, but now…Now they were wondering.

Sol didn't like being ignored. There was a lot of fluttering, a lot of flapping, and shrieking her name. **Neema, Neema, Neema.** Eventually, when she didn't respond, he opened his beak and clamped down hard on her rib.

"Sol!" she yelped, and clutched her side.

Everyone stared at her.

"Salt!" she corrected quickly.

Shal's eyes shimmered as he handed it over. "Are you sure you're all right? Ruko hit you pretty hard…"

"Thanks. I'm good," Neema said. "Honestly." And then she sprinkled salt on her bowl of raspberries and cream, and ate it.

After lunch, they headed over the bridge to the Ox palace. People waved from pleasure boats, lifting their glasses to toast their contenders. Halfway across the bridge, the Ox contingent bowed to the Tiger contingent, arms circled out in front, hands clasped. The Tigers gave their own salute in return, very similar, except they struck their right fist into a flat left palm. The Day of the Tiger had ended, the Day of the Ox had begun.

As they moved on, Katsan caught Neema by the shoulder. "Contender Kraa. Is it true you're no longer part of the investigation? Who's taken over? Why has no one been charged yet?"

Neema shrugged her off and kept walking. "Ask the emperor," she muttered over her shoulder.

Katsan grabbed her arm and wheeled her about. "He knows it was you. That's what the guard's for." She tilted her chin sharply towards Neema's shadow. "He's afraid I'll kill you for it."

She was so far from the mark, Neema laughed. "Katsan..." But what could she say? Where would she even start?

"The Eight will guide my sword on the fight platform." Katsan pressed two fingers like a blade, and drove them deep into Neema's chest. "My Sister will be avenged. A life for a life."

Forty-Four

F ENN FEDALA WAS waiting for them at the entrance to the Ox farm. No contingent, no acrobatics, no singing. After the glamour of the Tiger palace, here was the practical end of things —the part that kept the island fed and watered and working properly. That was the message, and no one missed it.

"No, you can fuck off," he said to Neema's shadow. "This is a Festival Trial. Contenders only."

The guard protested—he was tasked by the High Commander, at the order of the emperor...

Fenn struck the guard so hard he was flung off his feet, smashing heavily into a pile of wooden crates.

"Eight," Havoc said, shocked by the sudden speed and power of the strike. "You could have broken his jaw."

"Could have," Fenn agreed, examining his fist. "Chose not to."

A couple of Ox hands carried the guard away, promising ale and a patch up in the farmhouse kitchens. The guard cursed them, spitting blood from his mouth. Fenn watched him go with narrowed eyes, assessing him as he might a piece of rotten timber, or a broken tile.

The farmhouse was a solid, three-storey granite building, very like one you might find in the southern Heartlands. Fenn kept his office here, rather than the Ox palace, which lay a quarter mile to the east. The Oxes had by far the largest territory on the island. Most of it was given over to farming and construction, and was intended for the benefit of all.

Fenn led them down a service path past a series of outhouses. Again, the tour was deliberate—reminding the contenders of the effort it took to keep the island functioning. The clang and hiss from the blacksmith's forge, dogs barking, the stink of manure, the rinsing of blood from the abattoir steps.

The path brought them out to a large cobbled yard at the back of the farmhouse. Six wagons stood lined up in a row, loaded with coarse sacks of flour, rice and pulses. Behind each wagon stood two more, also piled high. "Three wagons each," Shal said, heading down to the furthest column. The rest of them followed his lead, lining up in front of their wagons.

Tala, excluded from the Trial, perched herself on a barrel.

The contenders stood to attention, awaiting instructions.

Fenn lit a roll-up, gave Tala a side glance. Some private joke passed between them.

Beyond the yard lay the orchard, with a track running through to a barn at the end. "We store our surplus in that barn," Fenn told them. He nodded to the nearest wagon. "A pair of oxen can pull a fully-loaded wagon down there in under ten minutes."

The contenders looked around the yard, and then at each other.

Cain threw his hands up. "You're joking. This is a joke."

Fenn said nothing.

"For the sake of clarity," Cain pressed a hand to his chest. "I am not an ox. This is impossible."

"Give it a rest, Cain," Havoc called down the line. "We've all trained for this. The Ox Trial is always about strength and stamina. Stubborn determination." He put his fingers against his head, like horns, and gave a loud bellow.

"That's offensive," Tala muttered.

Ruko was testing the weight of the wagon, examining the yoke attached to the arms. "Has the Trial begun, High Engineer?"

Fenn took a drag of his roll-up. "Sure, why not? Contenders, you have two hours." He gestured vaguely. "Make yourselves useful."

Save for Neema, they were up on their wagons before he'd finished. Five contenders, one strategy. The wagons were too heavy to pull as they were—they would have to sling out enough sacks to lighten the load, and make multiple trips.

Neema the Trial has started, Sol prompted.

She gave one of the sacks an experimental tug. It didn't budge. If the Trial really was about strength and stamina she might as well not bother. But she wasn't so sure. The contenders had made a lot of assumptions about this Trial. Assumptions about Fenn, and about how Oxes saw the world.

She glanced over at Cain. He was mulling the same question, she could tell. He jumped down from his wagon and made a discreet shooing gesture. *Stop watching me. I know. I get it.*

Sol tapped her rib. **You see, Neema—the Fox contender does not need our help. Leave him in peace.**

Along the row, a new strategy was forming. Havoc was in negotiation with Katsan. Oxes were all about teamwork, right? The wagons were designed for two, they could move faster if they pulled together. Shal called out to Cain with the same idea— should they pair up?

"Give me a second," Cain called back. "Maybe."

Ruko ground on alone.

"Cain?" Shal called again.

Cain twisted round to answer, still holding a sack, then yelled in pain. He dropped the sack, clutching his shoulder. "Eight. Fuck!" He collapsed in agony. "My shoulder. Shit!"

They are not falling for this, Neema? He is acting.

—I know.

But they were falling for it, because it suited them. This was a straightforward, physical task—there was no benefit in faking an injury. Ruko was already in harness, dragging his half-loaded wagon across the yard with grim determination. Katsan and Havoc had found a rhythm to their work, and would not be long behind him.

Neema looked over at Fenn. He was doing three things at once —watching the contenders, talking to one of his engineers, and inspecting a newly forged blade. And smoking. Four things. A courtier arrived with a scroll wrapped in blue ribbon—some communication from the Hound palace. She saw Fenn sag, dejected. More paperwork.

That's when it clicked.

Abandoning her wagons, Neema sauntered over, as if she'd given up. "I'll take that," she said to the courtier, heading her off. She waved the scroll at Fenn. "Is your office open?"

Fenn lifted an eyebrow at Tala. "Told you she'd get it. That's three silver tiles you owe me."

Fenn's office smelled of tobacco and old boots, and paper. Lots of paper.

Make yourself useful.

That was the only instruction Fenn had given them. He hadn't told them to line up in front of the wagons. He hadn't specifically instructed them to move the sacks to the barn. What was the point in asking six contenders to move a bunch of wagons when— as he'd explained already—they had oxen that could do the same task in a fraction of the time?

It was a common misunderstanding with Oxes that their idea of harmony meant everyone working together on the same thing, at the same time. Ploughing forward stoically in unison. But that wasn't their philosophy. Every Ox team required a range of skills, character, experience. Understanding where you fitted within that team—your strengths and weaknesses—that was the key. Sometimes you led, sometimes you followed—depending on the task at hand. The secret of harmony was variety.

Fenn hated paperwork. Neema loved it. The best way she could "make herself useful," was to come up here and spend a couple of hours sorting through the piles of invoices and blueprints, committee minutes and reports. A task didn't have to be gruelling, or joyless, if you found the right person to do it.

She set to work. Someone brought her a pot of coffee. She hummed to herself, sifting through the piles of paper, bringing order to the chaos. Much of the correspondence came from the Raven palace. Quite a lot of it came from her own desk. She answered what she could, and left clear instructions on how to deal with the rest.

She was happy. Sol was happy. Paperwork was like preening, aligning the feathers so they lay smooth and clean and ready for flight.

Neema picked up a stack of account books piled on a chair. "Shelves, Fenn. You have shelves," she said, and slotted them in place before realising one of them wasn't a book but a picture frame, bundled in by mistake. She took it out and rubbed the dust from the glass. It was only a sketch, but she recognised the hand at once.

A rose garden at night, two friends talking on a stone bench. Fenn and Shimmer. She had her legs stretched out, laughing. Fenn was grinning at her, hand clapped to his thigh. She'd captured him perfectly, with just a few strokes of her pencil.

"You found it." Fenn was standing in the doorway. "Been looking for that for months."

She handed it over. "It's the same bench," she said. The one he'd been sitting on the night she'd stumbled through the hedge.

He touched the glass, expression softening. "Her favourite spot. No one ever came by. We could talk properly."

"Were you—"

He cut her off. "I happen to love my wife, Neema. Weird, eh?" His face crinkled with amusement, as he propped the frame on his desk. "No—that was us. Friends. Best friends. Last time we talked was in that garden, the night before…" The night before she threw herself off the Mirror Bridge. "We argued. Eight, I wish we hadn't."

"What did you argue about?"

He winced. Too painful. "She wasn't well, Neema. She had these fantastical ideas about…" He lowered his voice. "Bersun."

"About how much he'd changed," Neema said.

Fenn stared at her. "How…"

It was the sketch that made Neema think of it. Shimmer could look at someone, and capture their spirit with a few pencil strokes. She never visited Bersun's court until after the rebellion—when she took the throne room commission. That was the first time she met the emperor. But still, that penetrating gaze, that artist's hand…Had she tried sketching the Old Bear one day and realised something didn't sit right? Had she confronted him about it? She was certainly fearless enough—she'd told Andren Valit to fuck off, after all.

The emperor had been with Shimmer that fateful day on the Mirror Bridge. He swore he'd tried to stop her, but what if he hadn't? What if…

Fenn's eyes had flooded with tears. "Damn," he said, brushing them away. This was why he didn't talk about Shim, why he never looked up at the Mirror Bridge. He touched the picture again, gently, then lowered it face down on the desk. And Neema realised then—he'd lost it on purpose.

There was a commotion in the yard. They crossed together to the window, just in time to see Cain return, leading a pair of oxen. Behind him came a couple of farmhands, leading two more pairs. Within a couple of minutes Cain was leading three full wagons out of the yard and down towards the orchard, the oxen plodding along easily with their loads.

Ruko, soaked in sweat, dragging his wagon back from yet another solitary trip, stopped and watched them go by. And slowly bowed his head in defeat.

"The Raven contender wins the Trial," Fenn said, back down in the yard. "As she's the only one who understood it."

A stir along the line.

Sol was jubilant. **Do we win a prize? Something sparkly?**

—I wasn't supposed to come first, Sol. We want Cain to win.

Diamonds would be nice.

Fenn was still talking. "Cain—at least you weren't a complete idiot. So, four points I guess. As for the rest of you—what the fuck were you thinking?"

The contenders looked straight ahead.

"Think of the difference you could have made in two hours, if you'd used your real talents instead of playing at being oxen. May the Eight give me strength and remain Hidden."

"If you'd explained properly…" Havoc muttered.

Fenn rounded on him. "Which part of *make yourself useful* did you not understand, contender? You're a Monkey. You're supposed to be a creative thinker." He folded his arms, looked at them each in turn. "If you don't value your strengths, you won't use them. If you don't recognise your flaws, you won't defeat them.

"I suppose I'll have to judge you on your wagon pulling. Fuck me. Three points to Contender Valit. A point and a half each to you two," he said, meaning Katsan and Havoc. "Contender Worthy." He patted his pockets. "I'm out of points."

Shal gave a Hound salute, fist to his chest. "I thank you for the lesson, High Engineer, and will strive to do better." A contender must know how to lose with dignity. His respectful reply would be noted approvingly in the Official History of the Festival.

"Wonderful," Fenn said, folding his arms. "Now get the fuck off my farm."

That bit probably wouldn't go in.

Forty-Five

NO ONE HAD ever looked at Neema the way Katsan did on the fight platform. Her hatred pierced so deep, it felt almost like love.

The last fight of the afternoon. Shal's hope that the weather would turn had been dashed. The heat rippled the air, scorched the lungs. Neema sluiced the sweat from her face. *Eight protect me and remain Hidden.*

No, we're on our own, Neema.

Tala's fight with Ruko had been closer than expected, mainly because she hadn't spent the previous two hours yoked to a wagon. For the first time, the Tiger contender was bleeding when he returned to his corner at the end of the first round. It caused a stir, not just in the stalls, but down the contender line. The Visitor's lips were pressed into a bloodless line—his version of a smile. When it came to the second round, however, the balance shifted. Tala was not a weapons master, and had never fought without the option to stop. Twice she was cut—once across the thigh, once across the back. She was lucky Ruko's blade did not bite deeper. Or perhaps her Guardian was watching over her, on this Day of the Ox.

In the final round, her prodigious stamina kept her on her feet. Ruko was slowing down again. Tala, seeing her chance, moved in to strike…A roundhouse kick came from nowhere to take her out. The Ox contender, who never fell, slammed hard to the canvas.

Ruko hadn't been slowing down. He had been dissembling. He watched, dispassionate, as Tala made a valiant attempt to get up, then wrapped a bare foot over her throat. Tala began to choke.

The bell rang out. Victory to the Tiger contender.

On his balcony, the emperor rose and applauded both contenders. This was how it should be done.

The first fight had been gruelling. The second was ugly. Fox vs Monkey. Until now, the crowds had enjoyed watching Cain fight. But Cain liked Tala, and respected Katsan and the Visitor. Havoc was another matter. Cain gave him no quarter. Havoc had been formally trained in the Monkey style since he was six years old. So what. Cain had been fighting since the day he was born. Havoc wasn't his opponent; he was his enemy. After the first round, the Ox contingent had to come out and rinse the blood off the canvas.

In the middle of the second round, Havoc tried something complicated with a hinged staff. Cain headbutted him. The crowd groaned in sympathetic pain as Havoc staggered back, blood gushing from his nose. Broken. Some survival instinct kept him on his feet through the last round, but as soon as Vabras rang the bell, he collapsed, and had to be guided off to the medical tent, eyes swelling shut.

Cain called up to the imperial balcony as he passed, "Is that what you had in mind, your majesty?" But the emperor had retreated to the shadows.

After that, the fight between Shal and the Visitor had felt like a ballet. They returned to the line to muted applause. The Dragon Proxy had lost yet again, on purpose—but as he could not win points, he could not lose them either.

Sol, who had been napping, lifted his head from his breast. **Our turn, Neema.**

In the stalls, the remaining spectators waved fresh streamers, purple and red, to welcome the last two contenders. Bear versus Raven. The emperor came forward again, resting his knuckles on the balustrade.

Neema stepped out from the contenders' pavilion, into the punishing heat. The cobbles burned beneath her feet as she made her way to the platform. As she walked, she reminded herself of the advice Cain had given her. Katsan was a formidable warrior, with twenty years of experience to draw from. That strength was also her weakness. She thought she had seen it all. "Surprise her," he'd said.

So here she was on the platform, waiting for Vabras to ring the bell. Katsan's thick blonde hair was freshly plaited and pinned into a tight bun, and she had changed into a fresh uniform. The five red slashes across her chest looked like a promise of the blood to follow. She was a warrior, a true warrior—her stance strong and certain, her intention blazing from her bright blue eyes. *I will kill you.*

"Contenders, prepare!" Vabras barked.

They settled into fighting stances. Neema's heart beat hard against her chest, as if it wanted out. The blood roared in her ears.

Breathe, Neema.

She hadn't realised she'd stopped. She took a shuddering gasp. *I can't do this, I can't…*

The bell rang.

"For Gaida," Katsan yelled—a battle cry—and surged forward.

From the first moment, it was brutal. Neema tried the same technique she'd used during her fight with Ruko—yielding and shifting, conserving her strength. But Katsan's attacks were relentless, and every one of them was meant to kill.

Neema was stepping back from a strike when she faltered. Self doubt. Should she move to the side instead, was that better? That tiny hesitation was all Katsan needed. She jabbed her fist into Neema's stomach.

Neema gasped, doubled over in pain. Before she could recover, Katsan had grabbed her in a headlock. The fringes of Neema's vision turned grey. She stamped desperately on Katsan's toes until she was released. Not a warrior move, but it worked.

A moment's respite, no more. Another few seconds and she was on the ground. Katsan pinned her down, and drew back her fist. "Justice," she hissed.

All that hatred, all that righteous fury, channelled into a single strike. It would break Neema's jaw.

—Sol!

The plan—

—Do it!

The world didn't stop. He lacked the strength for that. But time slowed, stretching out long enough for her to think. She studied the trajectory of Katsan's fist as it moved on its straight path towards her. She wouldn't have time to deflect it.

Katsan's fist loomed closer.

Wait.

Wait.

Neema gritted her teeth, fighting the instinct to move.

She felt the air pressure against her face. Another fraction of a second.

Now.

At the last possible moment, she wrenched her head further to the right.

Katsan's fist smashed into the platform, brushing Neema's left ear. Eight, that was close.

Time snapped back to normal.

Neema rolled free and jumped to her feet. Katsan was on her knees, cradling her hand. She'd put her whole force into the blow; her knuckles were split open and bleeding. This was Neema's chance, while Katsan was vulnerable. She had to press her advantage, or—

Vabras rang the bell.

"No!" Neema wheeled on him. "That was not a full round."

"To your corner, contender," Vabras replied, evenly.

He was giving Katsan time to recover—the Bear contingent was already rushing up with bandages and iced water.

Neema stamped back to her corner. Sol was making short, pitiful distress calls in her chest. He'd worn himself out trying to save her. She was on her own.

Glancing over to Katsan's side, she saw the Bear warrior flex her injured hand and wince. Her sword hand. That was something, at least.

Neema hurried down the steps to retrieve her weapons. As she approached the chest, alarm flared down her spine. The Samran Hound who'd been shadowing her all afternoon was standing beside it. He looked smug.

"Get away from that," she snapped.

He gave a sarcastic smirk as she kneeled down and opened the chest.

It was empty. The sword, the hammer, the iron claw, the knives and daggers. All gone.

"Contender Kraa," Vabras called. "Return to the platform, please."

Despair washed through her. How could she fight a weapons round with no weapons?

"Thirty seconds," Vabras warned.

She put her head in her hands. They'd won. The emperor. Vabras. They'd killed her.

Neema, Sol croaked. **Look. Under the hinges.**

The iron war fans. They were still fixed into the padded lining, black on black. The guard had missed them. She snapped them free and slid them from their covers. Folded up like this, she could use them to strike and jab. Open, they would shield her from Katsan's blade. Maybe. Just maybe...

Sol, drawing on the last of his strength, sent an image to her mind. A memory. Tales of the Raven, spread open to a story about the Raven Warriors of Anat-ruar, in the days when this island had been their home. They had trained here on this spot for thousands of years. Defended the monastery from invaders. Her kin. Her history.

Katsan stood waiting on the platform, her hair gleaming like spun gold in the late afternoon sun. Her hand was wrapped in bandages, blood seeping through along her knuckles—but it remained steady as she raised her sword. Neema turned her wrist, drawing an eternal eight with her fan. Katsan's eyes narrowed at the choice of weapon.

Surprise.

Vabras rang the bell.

Katsan lunged.

Neema snapped open her right fan, deflecting the blade. She swung her left fan like a baton into Katsan's ribs. It was like striking rock.

Find a soft bit, Sol suggested.

—I don't think she has any.

Katsan swung again. Neema was ready for her. The stories Sol had told her all these months, the dreams she had thought were nightmares—they were woven into her body, they flowed through her. Her fans snapped open and closed as she turned her wrist, coiled her arm. Such an elegant weapon. Beautiful, deadly. The edges razor sharp. She glided her left fan across Katsan's stomach. It sliced neatly through her tunic, opened a thin red line.

Katsan drew back—not in pain, but confusion. She had never encountered this style, forgotten for centuries. The flick and snap of the fans disturbed her, their dance through the air. The way they changed their purpose back and forth—baton, dagger, shield, razor. What troubled her most of all, was Neema herself. Where had she learned these skills? Who had trained her?

Her distraction cost her. With each failed attack she grew more frustrated, more careless. She thrust, and thrust again, and each time Neema parried, and pressed her advantage until...

It was an accident.

Katsan swung her sword down in an overarm sweep. Neema slashed up with her fan to deflect it. But instead of striking the sword, she carved deep into Katsan's right forearm. The razor-sharp edge of the fan sliced through skin, muscle, tendons.

Katsan's sword clattered from her hand. She stood there, wide-eyed with shock at her ruined arm. Blood pulsed from the wound. The fan had hacked her open to the bone.

Too much blood. Way too much blood.

She fell to her knees.

Vabras had not rung the bell. He stood frozen by the sight—what Neema had done, and how she had done it.

Kneeling down beside the fallen Bear warrior, Neema ripped her colours from her arm and made a tourniquet to stop the bleeding. Katsan was praying under her breath, preparing herself for her next journey on the Eternal Path. "Great Bear of the Mountain, guide my spirit home..."

"You're not dying," Neema said. "Katsan. Open your eyes. Stay with me." She could feel the crushing weight of guilt hanging over her, ready to drop. She waved frantically to the Bear contingent to join her.

Katsan's face was death white, her breathing shallow. She was letting go.

Neema pressed her lips to the Bear warrior's ear. "Live," she hissed. "*Live*—and I will tell you *everything*."

Katsan's eyes snapped open. The anger, the desire for justice, still burned through her. Enough to make her hold on.

The medics stretchered her from the platform. "We'll have to amputate," one of them said.

"She'll live," Neema said. She was sure of it.

In the stalls, people were jumping to their feet, running down the aisles as if they planned to rush the platform. Had they really seen what they had just seen? Vabras, returned to himself, signalled to the Hounds to restore order, push people back to their seats.

Neema looked up at the imperial balcony. The emperor was staring down at her, open-mouthed. With a sharp, defiant gesture, she flicked the blood from her fan. It sprayed out, fine splatters on the platform.

Vabras rang the bell. "The fight is over," he said. "Victory to the Raven contender."

Forty-Six

B ENNA SAT CURLED up in a corner, arms wrapped around her knees. Her cell was dank and dark, deep below the Hound palace. Cold too, which should have been a relief after the dense heat of the Festival Square, but it wasn't. If she held a candle to the walls, she could trace the names of those who'd come before her scratched into the brickwork, messages of hope and despair.

Why had they brought her here instead of the regular holding cells? A frightening question for which her guards had no answer. No one tells us anything, they'd said, when she asked them.

They were nice, not like the Samran Hounds who'd arrested her. She got the impression they didn't have much to do—they'd certainly been surprised by her arrival. But they'd brought her food, and candles, and a book of Guardian Tales. They'd asked her what it was like to meet the Bear, and made awed ∞ signs when she'd told them. Then they'd left her alone, but every so often they would slide the grate back on the door and peer in, like she was a cake in the oven, to make sure she was all right.

"I mean, I'm not all right, but I'm all right," she told them, and the guards had nodded, and said they knew the feeling.

This room was a place of endings. The thought scared her, but it was a fate she had prepared for, and would accept when it came. In her heart, Benna had always felt there would be no return from this journey. She would not see Westhaven again, her parents, her sister. But she had done what she had promised to do. And along the way—Eight, she had lived! She had travelled the empire, and worked in the imperial kitchens. She had served a contender, and saved her life. She had met the Bear in a dream. It had given her a big shaggy hug and said, "Don't be afraid, little one."

Life was short. She had enjoyed it.

Since the age of twelve—since she'd met Yana—Benna had carried their secret, shared plan within her heart, and told no one. Her family would have tried to persuade her against it, if they'd known. *The Exiled pass through and we remain.* That was the story of her village. They did not concern themselves with the empire, and the empire—in the main—did not concern itself with them. There was a certain liberty in being unvalued.

When she'd announced, aged fourteen, that she intended to head east to find work, no one had thought anything of it. She was not the first to make that journey. Two years of hard, seasonal work took her as far as Riversmeet. Six months after that she had saved enough for a seat on a post-coach to Samra. She was seventeen by the time she snuck on to the old Valit estate, and found the labyrinth buried below the ancient woods—just as Yana had described it to her. She had found her way to the trapdoor at its centre. A plain wooden circle—no hinge, no handle, no lock or key. She had stood over it, praying under her breath—because if this didn't work, it had all been for nothing.

And then she'd sung a song of opening, the one Yana had taught her before she died.

> *The gate I leave open for you, my love*
> *Step through, step through.*
> *My heart I keep open for you, my love*
> *Step through, step through.*

The trapdoor, sealed by Yana's mother with a powerful binding spell, had resisted. Benna sang, she coaxed. And the spell heard something in her voice—her need, her pure heart, her love for her lost friend. The door swung down, revealing a ladder, and darkness. She climbed into it. At the bottom: treasures fit for the Dragon. Gold and silver tiles. Bolts of imperial silk in a rainbow of shades.

Jewelled weapons. And row upon row of small, sea-green bottles. Dragonscale oil.

Benna understood how much the tiles were worth, and what she could do with them. She had some inkling of the value of those weapons, and she knew the silk was beyond priceless—and also contraband. But the oil? For the first time, she faltered. It had been five years since she and Yana had discussed it. How much would be enough for her task?

She had taken three bottles, and a purse of silver tiles. Climbed the ladder back into the tunnel. The door had sealed itself closed again.

She took the tiles so she could bribe her way into a servant's position at court. She hadn't needed them. A hard worker with a friendly smile and fingers used to scalding hot water? Chef Ganstra had hired her on the spot.

A year and a half she'd worked and waited. She sent tiles home —only what she'd earned, not what she'd taken.

"I'm not a thief," she said now, to the brick walls.

Several times she had been sent to the Raven palace with food for the High Scholar. She could have swapped the bath oil any time. But that wasn't the plan. Yana had wanted them both on the island together, at the same time—Neema and Ruko. She had wanted them both...

Punished.

No. That wasn't the word she'd used. Yana had been very clear —this wasn't about revenge. If it was, Hol Vabras would have been first in line. No. It was supposed to be a lesson—from the grave. For her twin brother, who had betrayed her for a stupid dream that didn't even belong to him. And for the scholar who had used her talents to write lies. Neema Kraa. The name written on the paper, stitched over Yana's heart. *This Order prepared by Neema Kraa, on behalf of His Majesty...*

When Chef Ganstra said the High Scholar was looking for a servant to help her through the Festival, Benna had volunteered with both hands up. Of course she had. She'd thought it was a sign that the Eight approved of the plan. She still wondered.

All those years of planning and patience. And everything had gone exactly as Yana said it would. Ruko's arrival on the island as the Tiger Contender. Neema's elevation at court. Yana was so clever, always thinking ten steps ahead. *I guess I was a Tiger after all*, she'd said. *Like my father.*

Everything had gone exactly as Yana had said it would—except for one small, unexpected thing. Something they could never have predicted.

Benna liked Neema.

She bowed her head. And realised (these things happen, even in moments of high drama, perhaps especially in moments of high drama) that she needed to pee.

Both guards took her down the corridor to the privy. Anything for a change. They passed a row of empty cells, the grates left open. "Am I the only one down here?" she asked them, and they said, "Not the only one, no."

She heard him through the walls, later. The other prisoner. Long, wavering moans and howls. Cries for help, cries for mercy that made her skin prickle. He sounded old and confused. Frightened. It took the guards a long time to calm him down. They came by afterwards with her supper, and apologised for the disturbance. He got like that sometimes, the old fellow. They'd given him a sedative. "It's not his fault, he's been here a long time," one of them said, and his partner looked nervous. They weren't supposed to talk about it.

They hadn't come back since.

She sat on her mattress with her chin on her knees, worrying. What if no one came for her? What if she was left to rot in here? Would she end up like that poor old man, howling like a wounded animal? She rubbed her thumb and finger over her plaits, over the smooth red ribbon wound through them, and felt better.

Voices, and footsteps. She rubbed her face—she had been crying—and sat up straighter on the mattress. "You have a visitor," the guard called through the door. "A contender, no less."

Neema! Benna jumped to her feet as the guard unlocked the door. Then shrank back, when she saw who it was.

. Ruko gave the guard a gold half-tile, like it was a pebble. "Leave us."

The door clanged shut, the key turned.

Ruko glowered down at her, his eyes so dark they looked black. He was twice her size. He could snap her like a twig, she was sure of it. He looked like he wanted to. She shrank further back against the wall.

He waited until the guard's footsteps had faded. "You stole the Blade of Peace from me."

Her throat closed. She rubbed the red ribbons in her plaits again, but they didn't give her the same boost. She'd worn them out. "Are you here to kill me?"

Ruko waited longer than was kind. "No."

"Oh, thank the Eight," Benna said, and collapsed face down on her mattress.

Ruko dragged the only chair into the middle of the cell, and slammed it to the floor. The sound echoed off the brick walls. He remained standing, hands strangling the back of the chair. "Contender Kraa told me of the Blade. For the rest…" A deep frown, as he considered the promise Neema had wrangled from him, before she would tell him anything. "She said I must come to you. So: speak."

Benna remained silent. It took a lot of effort; she was naturally helpful. But that tone. *Speak*. She scrunched herself up tight, curled up on the mattress like a hedgehog, hibernating and prickly.

Realising his mistake, Ruko sat down. He wasn't gentle, when he spoke. Ruko's heart was sealed behind a featureless trapdoor, and no one knew the song to open it. But he was civil. "Whatever you tell me will remain between us. I will seek no vengeance for what you have done, nor harm you in any way. You have my word."

"Your word is worthless. You're worthless." Benna put a hand over her mouth. Eight—what a nasty thing to say. She hated how much she hated him. She hated how calling him worthless didn't seem to bother him. And she hated how that made her feel a bit sorry for him, how hard he'd made himself. A big slab of rock that had forgotten it was really a person. She pushed herself up from her mattress. "What do you want to know?"

"Who gave you the Dragonscale?"

She looked at him. *You know who.*

Something bright and terrible sparked in his eyes. Hope. He fumbled in his pocket. "This note. It's in her hand."

Ruko. Meet me tonight in
the Ox farm orchard, as the
temple bell strikes two.
Come alone and unarmed. Tigermouse.

"That was my secret nickname for her. Because she was really fierce, and tiny. She hated it." He held it out. "She wrote this. I know she did."

He sounded certain, but he was pleading, with his eyes. *Tell me it's true.*

Benna sighed. This was harder than she'd expected. "She did write it, yes. The day she left for Dolrun."

It took him a moment, and then he understood. The worn feel of the paper, the faded ink. Of course. He should have realised. The hope and excitement drained away, replaced by...nothing.

That was the worst part, Benna thought. The way it all drained away. As if he was the one who'd been brought to life, then murdered again.

"Would you like some water?" she asked. Even if you hated someone, you could offer them water, she decided. "There's only one cup, but we can share."

"I do not want water," he said. And then, fighting against eight years of Rivenna Glorren's training, "I thank you for the offer." He folded the note away. "Tell me what happened. When did you meet my sister?"

Benna flicked her plaits off her shoulders and made herself comfortable, cross-legged on the mattress. "My family's village is called Last Sleep. It lies right on the edge of Dolrun." She sliced a hand against her palm, miming a border. "Hence my name. It's not part of the official Procession of Exile, we're not grand enough for that. Just a few houses, a tavern. But the wagon always stops there overnight, before heading into the forest. That's how it's been since for ever." The little hut at the end of the village, kept ready and waiting. Fresh mattress, clean blankets, sprigs of lavender. Everything neat and aired, and comfortable.

"I was twelve when Yana came."

In the short, gloomy month of the Raven, 1533. The Procession of Exile, dragging slowly from town to town, had taken eighteen months to reach its conclusion.

"We'd not had an Exile in years—since before I was born. We always dreaded them, but this one…" Benna hugged herself. She was both here in her cell, and two thousand miles away, watching the cart rumble into her village. Seeing Yana for the first time, her matted hair, her filthy clothes. Covered in cuts and bruises. Tiny, like her. She was tied to a post in the middle of the cart, so if people threw things, she couldn't protect herself. No one threw anything—they didn't do that in Last Sleep. As far as they were concerned, the Procession finished at Westhaven.

"She's a child yet," Benna's mother had whispered. "Look at her."

"Breaks your heart," Benna's father said.

When the Hounds untied her, she'd collapsed at their feet. Sergeant Worthy had to carry her through the village to the hut. And that was it. The show was over.

"We weren't supposed to talk to her," Benna said, to Ruko. "That's why they built the hut at the far end of the village. The Exiled stay the night and next morning they're gone. But I couldn't stop thinking about her, all alone, no friends, no family." A reproachful pause. "I thought—if it was me, I'd want someone to come and talk to me. Give me one last hug. I snuck out to see her after dark. I brought biscuits, can you imagine? And a doll for company." She rolled her eyes at herself.

"You were young."

Benna wanted no comfort from him. "I knew something was wrong, soon as I stepped through the door." Yana, sprawled unconscious on the mattress, her breathing ragged. A sour-sweet smell of decay. "My brother Jold died of the same thing. Her wound was infected. Here." Benna placed a hand over her heart. Where they'd sewn the Order of Exile into her skin. "I tried giving her some water, but she wouldn't wake up. So I ran home."

To her parents. Who'd said, *What were you thinking, Benna?* But her mother was already pulling down herbs from the shelf, and her father was hanging the kettle over the fire, and when they had everything they needed they went back together, the three of them.

Benna didn't tell Ruko the next part, she spared him that much. Yana was delirious, crying and raving. She thought she was already in Dolrun. When Benna's mother arrived, Yana reached for her and said *Mummy, Mummy, don't leave me. I'm scared…*

"We nursed her through the night, while she fought her battle with the Dragon. We saved her life. We couldn't save Jold, but we saved her." There was a catch in Benna's throat. She reached out, and took a sip of water. "Sergeant Worthy was furious. He knew Yana was sick. He'd been praying that the Kind Dragon would take her in her sleep. Spare her the journey into the forest. He said: She's your patient now. You must take care of her. So that's what I did."

It took Yana a long time to recover her strength. Late winter blurred into early spring. She kept having "setbacks." No one was fooled, not really—the Hounds looked the other way. Benna never left Yana's side. She slept next to her at night. Benna's mother warned her—don't get too close, sweetheart. You know how this has to end.

"But I couldn't help it. I loved her. How could you not love Yana?"

Ruko lifted his hands in a swift movement, shielding his face. A familiar voice rose from inside him, hard and certain. *You have trained for this. These words do not hurt you.*

Benna was still caught in her memories. "She was so brave. I mean scared, obviously, and angry. She didn't want to die. It wasn't fair. She would watch the birds from the window, like this." Benna put her knees to her chin, tilted her head. "Soaking up every last moment."

Ruko stood up and walked to the other side of the cell. He rested a hand against the wall. *This does not hurt. She is not telling you anything you do not already know.*

"Tell me the rest," he said, to the wall.

"You know the rest. She couldn't stay with us for ever. One day Sergeant Worthy came and said, 'It's time, we're leaving.'" Benna stopped. The silence grew around them.

Ruko turned. "Go on."

Benna was staring at her hands, the tattoo scrolled across them. "That's it."

She wouldn't tell him how Yana hugged her that morning, so tightly she couldn't breathe. Benna had trailed them all the way to the edge of the forest. The last thing Yana said, looking over her shoulder, as she disappeared into the hazy gloom of Dolrun— "Life is short, Benna. Enjoy it." And with that, she was gone.

Ruko had sat down again. "So you became my sister's weapon of revenge. You returned to the forest once the Hounds had left, and took the Order of Exile from her body."

An image flashed into Benna's mind, a clearing in the forest. Her friend, long dead. Her body…She pushed the memory away. That was not how she chose to remember Yana. "It wasn't about revenge. She was trying to save you."

Ruko gave a sharp laugh, irritated by the idea. "Save me from what? Myself, I suppose."

Benna shook her head, plaits whipping back and forth. "Save you from living another man's dream. You don't want to rule the empire, not really. You just think you do, because that's what your father wanted."

For the first time, Ruko looked uneasy. "My sister told you this?" He glared defiantly around the cell, as if Yana's spirit was in there with them. "It's not true. I chose this path. It is *my* dream. My only dream…" He frowned, annoyed with himself, for being dragged into this false argument. "Tell me how you stole the Blade."

It took Benna a moment to pivot with him. "Oh. That. I walked in and took it."

Ruko stared at her.

"I put on one of those masks they all wear." Benna put her hand over her face, covering it. "No one paid me any notice. No one ever does. Especially at the Tiger palace. We're paid to be invisible. That's why we have our own service paths and dormitories, our leaky ferry boats." She gestured towards him. "So the special, golden people don't have to see us."

"My contingent was there when you took it? They saw nothing?"

"Too busy banging on about how much better life would be once they were in charge. Everything back how it should be. *Blah blah*." Benna sniffed. The silly dreams of silly, powerful people. "I pottered about the suite, clearing plates of food, and then I wandered into your room, took Hurun-tooth and dropped it in a bowl of soup."

"You dropped the most dangerous weapon in existence in a bowl of soup."

"Spinach and broccoli. I was going to hide it, it was going to be the start of a Campaign of Confusion. That's what me and Yana called it." She smiled sadly at the memory. Her and Yana, stifling giggles in the Exile hut. "Stop making me laugh, Benna," Yana had said, "they'll know I'm better." And they'd laughed at that too, because her situation was so ridiculous, so unbelievable. What could you do but laugh, and cry, and laugh again?

"And Neema Kraa. You were helping her too were you, when you poisoned her?"

Benna looked sheepish. "That was an accident. It was supposed to be a mild dose."

"To what purpose?"

Benna fanned out her hands. "Revelation. Yana thought the Dragonscale might help Neema reflect on what she'd done. Only she forgot to tell me the proper dosage. Actually," Benna corrected herself, "I think she did tell me, and I sort of forgot? It was seven years ago, Ruko, I was *twelve*."

"And Contender Worthy?"

"That was me, not Yana. She had a crush on him, I think. The dashing young captain. He left her to die alone in the poisoned forest. He left her..."

"He was following orders."

Benna threw him a disgusted look.

"What about Contender Rack?"

"Oh, no—Gaida had nothing to do with any of it. I didn't touch her."

"You stabbed her in the back."

"She was already dead. And I had a really, really good reason." She barrelled on, before he could interrupt. "No, I did! So—I was stealing the Blade, and your contingent was in the next room, like I said. They were talking about how angry the emperor was with Gaida, for singing that song at the opening ceremony. And Abbess Glorren said something like…" Benna lifted her eyes to the ceiling, trying to remember the exact words. "'Foolish girl, she won't survive the Festival.' And then she laughed and said, 'Natural causes, I'm sure,' in this really sarcastic voice." Benna tugged on her plaits, and felt a little surge. They were working again. "I wanted to warn Gaida, but what was I supposed to say? 'Hello Contender Rack, guess what, I was busy stealing the Blade of Peace when…'"

Ruko grunted. Quite the dilemma.

"Then I had my genius idea. I thought—I'll sneak into her rooms and leave an anonymous note, telling her she was in danger." Benna's face fell. "But when I got there, she was already dead. *Natural causes.*" She mimicked the same, sarcastic voice. "I couldn't let them get away with that. I had to do *something*, before they took the body away."

"You framed me for her death."

Benna pulled an awkward face. "I would have given you an alibi, if you'd needed one. I didn't come here to destroy you. I would never, ever have agreed to that. I came here to *help* you." On impulse, she leaned forward and grabbed his hands, kneeling in front of him. "That's what Yana asked me to do. She was your twin sister. She loved you, Ruko. In spite of everything."

No one had held Ruko's hands in eight years. He stared down at them, frowning.

There was a long pause, as Benna searched his face. "But I haven't helped you, have I?" She sighed, releasing him. "You're still the same. It's like you're glued in place. It's so…sad."

Ruko got to his feet, and banged on the door for the guard. He was expected back at the third palace by now. The abbess had arranged a grand party to celebrate the Day of the Tiger. The emperor would be there. Lord Clarion and Lady Harmony, Kindry Rok, representatives from all the High families. People he would need around him, when he became emperor.

He looked down at Benna, hunched on her mattress, crying softly. Crying for him. It did not move him, why should it? She was right, he was unchanged. This had been a Trial, harder than any other he would face. A battle with the ghost of his sister. But he had won. He walked the golden rope within the void, alone.

One question remained. What to do with the girl?

If the abbess were here she would say—"Snap her neck, bribe the guard and leave."

But he had given his word. To the girl, and to Contender Kraa. He had promised Neema on his soul that he would help Benna escape.

"A true Tiger warrior," his abbess would say, "knows when to wait, and when to strike. Your father would not hesitate. Some lives are worth more than others. That is simply the way of things."

He believed that. Yes, he did believe that.

On his way out, Ruko gave the guard another gold half-tile.

The man turned pale. "What's this for? She's not…"

No. She wasn't.

The guard put a hand to his chest, relieved. "Sweet girl, isn't she? Met the Bear in a dream last night. Did she tell you?"

"Wait an hour. Unlock her door. Look the other way."

"Ah—sorry, sir—that's impossible." These weren't the regular holding cells. These were for special situations. Sensitive, *imperial* situations. "We reckon they brought her down here by mistake. These new recruits from Samra don't know fuck all. May the Eight pardon my language and remain Hidden."

Ruko put his hand in his pocket. "Wait an hour." A half-tile. "Unlock her door." Another tile. "Look the other way." A third.

The gold gleamed in the guard's upturned palm.

And suddenly, Contender Valit, it was possible.

Forty-Seven

THE OX PALACE glowed with light, doors flung open in welcome. Lanterns flickered at the windows, music drifted through from the terrace, and the guards were banished. Fenn's orders. Tonight's party was a celebration of the Fourth Guardian —an evening of fellowship and harmony. There was an unspoken rule among the Oxes that they were the first to steady things, and fix them, in times of turmoil. Gaida's murder; the sudden arrival of fresh troops; Katsan's near death on the platform; even Benna's talk of the Bear had put the island out of kilter. Tonight might not solve all those problems, but it would soothe them, and give people a moment to breathe, and to be.

Neema's shoulders softened as she stepped into the friendly embrace of the palace. She felt safe here, for the first time in days —her Shadow Hound had vanished as abruptly as he had arrived. He could hardly claim he was watching her for concussion, after her victory in the square. And no one would dare attack her on Fenn's territory. Oxes were slow to temper, but Eight, when they were crossed…

In any case: everyone who wanted her dead was on the opposite side of the Great Canal, celebrating the Day of the Tiger.

The emperor's decision to shorten the Festival had created a clash this evening. Much of the court had chosen to attend the Tigers' extravagant ball over Fenn's informal gathering. Power attracts power and Ruko Valit looked set to win. Not to mention that Abbess Glorren would be offended by their absence. Whereas Fenn did not care if they came to his party or not, he was forty-four, for fuck's sake, not three.

Everyone who was here wanted to be here, which gave the party a laid-back atmosphere. The Ox palace was small—more of a country manor house in fact—but the guests were free to roam as they pleased. The vaulted feasting hall, around which the palace was built, had been turned into a games room for the evening. There were comfortable chairs, bowls of punch, and long buffet tables in every room. The Tigers, meanwhile, would be serving their usual tiny, pretentious canapés. Neema could feel the waves of Cain's disappointment from across the canal.

She followed a trail of tea lights out to a raised stone terrace. The Ankalla brothers had set themselves up there, Riff on fiddle. She suspected Fenn had invited them after their disgrace, not before—he was like that.

In the gardens below, a dozen campfires sent sparks and crackles into the night air. Guests lay stretched out on blankets, talking and singing along to the music. There were drink stands, and a hog roast, games of kickbag. Tala and Sunur spotted her. Sunur waved. Fenn was grilling fish, showing Suru how to turn them without burning her fingers.

Neema smiled. It was a beautiful evening, the moon blazing orange-silver, almost full. Beneath it lay the Tiger's Path—a dense trail of stars cascading down the sky. According to Scripture, the Path was a scar from the Kind Returns, marking the place where the Tiger slashed an opening between this world and the Hidden Realm. Like the moon, it was unusually bright tonight.

She reached out to Sol. He had retreated to his field, for the same reason she was up here alone on the terrace. More comfortable, at one remove from the crowds. He was having a lovely time making himself wretched, the rain sleeting down and turning his whole world grey.

—Aren't you ruining your feathers?

No Neema, ravens are surprisingly waterproof, it is one of the many things that make us magnificent, the best of all birds.

The rain stopped, like a tap. Sol fluffed himself out.

Did you want something?

—No, I just thought I'd check—

You were worried about me. You were worried about my feathers. Sol sounded perturbed. **You must not worry about me, that is a wrong thing to do. I am the Solitary Raven. It is my nature to be spurned, and despised.**

—All right.

Do not worry about my feathers again, Neema.

—Fine.

It makes me feel peculiar.

The field, and Sol, faded from her mind. She sipped her punch.

"Miserable?" Fenn had appeared at her side.

"Completely."

"Still alive, though. Bear slayer."

"She's not dead," Neema protested. She had kept her promise to Katsan, in fact she had just come from the Bear warrior's sick bed. They'd had an interesting conversation, in between the moments when Katsan passed out from the pain. As predicted, the medics had been forced to amputate her right arm almost to the elbow.

"Quite the Festival you're having," Fenn noted. "Remember a couple of days ago? 'I can't do this, Fenn. I'm going to die, Fenn. I'm not a contender, Fenn.' Remind me who won the Trial this afternoon? *And* her fight?"

"That was sheer luck."

"Yeah, yeah. Luck and coincidence." He laughed, and reached into his pocket. She thought he was reaching for a roll-up, until he said, "Forgot to give you your prize earlier."

Sol perked up. Diamonds, he called faintly, from his field. Rubies. Diamonds.

Fenn pulled out a flat piece of tanned leather, stamped with the Ox sigil.

Tat, Sol sniffed. Garbage.

"I have no idea what's going on with you, Neema," Fenn said, and lifted up his hands. Happy to remain ignorant. "Wild guess, though—did you take my advice and stay quiet about Yasila on the balcony? Or did you tell someone about it?"

Neema looked at him. "I told Yasila."

"Wow!" Fenn slapped the terrace wall, impressed by this act of wanton, towering stupidity. "*Wow!* You told Yasila. You told *Yasila* you saw her on the balcony. Not just anybody. *Yasila.*"

"I know I shouldn't have, but—"

"But you couldn't help yourself. I know. I know." He turned the sigil over. Both their names had been branded into the leather. "This is my marker." He placed it in her palm, and cupped his rough hands over hers. "If you're ever in trouble in the Heartlands —find someone who doesn't look like an arsehole and show them this."

Neema's eyes filled with tears. "Thanks."

"Sorry it's not a statue of a golden cow."

They both laughed.

Why is that funny, Neema? I would like a golden cow please.

The Ankalla brothers struck up a new, faster tune, with drums. Around the campfires, people cheered and got to their feet. Sunur and Tala took Suru's hands and danced together in a circle.

The temple bell rang out the quarter hour.

"Go join the dance," Fenn ordered Neema. He turfed everyone else outside with her, until the house was empty and the garden was full of people dancing and singing. Neema would have kept to the fringes, but she was safer tonight in the heart of things, and the call of the song was irresistible. People opened their arms to her. Join us. All are welcome here tonight.

Ox dances held a magic of their own. The Ankalla brothers moved down into the gardens, becoming part of the crowd as they played. More drums appeared, and Neema found herself drawn into the dance, her body responding to the bodies around her, swept up in the euphoria. As the dance quickened she was lifted and held within it, surrendering to the spell of the crowd as it moved as one, became one. When at last the music stopped, everyone laughed and looked round, as if waking from a dream, sweaty and smiling. The Ankalla brothers were folded into hugs, handed drinks. People hugged Neema too as she grinned back at them. She'd forgotten how much she loved to dance.

At some point, still bound by that collective spirit, everyone realised that Fenn was waiting for them to settle. He stood alone on the terrace above, watching them with a contented expression. "Fenn!" people said, and nudged anyone still talking, until the gardens were quiet, faces turned up in expectation.

"Thanks for coming tonight," he said. "We've worked hard together—and I'm glad to see you all shaking off that load tonight and enjoying yourselves. That's what life's about. We share the burden..."

"...we share the reward," everyone shouted back.

Fenn toasted Tala, and Contender Kraa, winner of the Ox Trial. He read a message from their abbess, too frail to travel from her monastery in Yakann. "May the Ox watch over her," he added.

"And remain Hidden," Neema said, with the rest of the party. Around her, people were making respectful signs of the eight. The Ox abbess was not expected to last the autumn.

The temple bell rang the half hour. Fenn took his cue. "We are Oxes. We know how to have a good time."

More hoots and applause.

"We know that it's the little things that matter."

People smiled at each other, rolled their eyes. Everyone knew this speech. It was Fenn's only speech. How they didn't need fancy balls and grand spectacles. All they needed was each other. A sentimental way of saying he was a cheapskate.

"Then again," he said, "this is *the Day of the Ox*. The first one in twenty-four years. So fuck it. Sometimes it's the big things as well."

Laughter, and surprise from the garden. A change in the script.

Fenn checked his pocket watch. It was time. He lifted his arms like a showman. "Friends. I give you: the Ox Day fireworks."

With perfect timing, the sky exploded with colour. Rockets spiralled through the air, whizzing and popping. Another deep boom, and a rainbow shower cascaded down from the heavens.

In the press of the crowds, Neema stared up in wonder at the display, each sequence more spectacular than the last. It must have taken months to arrange, not to mention the cost. How had Fenn squared it?

Those who were in on the joke passed it on, from ear to ear. Someone tapped Neema's shoulder, whispered the punchline. She could barely hear them over the noise. The fireworks, the crowd. They said it again. "Tiger party."

Of course. The fireworks were coming from across the Grand Canal. The Oxes were enjoying a spectacular show, from the best vantage point on the island, for free.

Her neighbour leaned in again, closer this time. "I love watching you dance."

Cain.

She turned, smiling. He grinned back at her.

She was so glad he was here, it hurt her heart. Both of them lit by the campfire's orange glow, and softened by it. His dark red hair was slicked back from his forehead, his tunic plastered to his chest. He'd swum across the canal to get here. For fun, to cool off, to avoid the Hounds. Because he knew it made him look even hotter than usual. All of the above, knowing him. Why have one reason, when you can have seven?

She could ask him about it. She could ask about the Tiger party. She had a thousand questions, she always did. But there was only one that mattered. The one she'd been wanting to ask since the opening ceremony, when she'd walked up to him in her stupidly expensive dress and pretended she felt nothing. The same question he'd asked her long ago, in a cramped room at the Raven palace.

She asked him, her words lost in the boom of another firework.

"Sorry, could you repeat that?" He cupped his hand to his ear, smiling. He'd heard her just fine, the bastard.

She gave him a look. "I said: Do you ever think of—"

"All the time." His eyes softened. "All the time."

She turned her face up to the sky, to the fireworks, so he couldn't see how happy he'd made her. Three rockets exploded one after the other, showering orange and white sparks across the black sky. The colours of the Tiger. Or, if you preferred, the colours of the Fox and the Raven.

"Beautiful," she said.

Cain reached down and took her hand. They stayed like that, held within the crowd, until the fireworks were over. People started to move away.

He let go of her hand. They looked at each other. She would never kiss him here with people watching, it wasn't her style. He leaned across to suggest maybe they could go somewhere quiet.

She kissed him. Deep. Passionate. Enjoying his surprise.

He laughed and kissed her back, wrapping his arms around her waist.

The people around them whooped and cheered in encouragement.

"Yes!" Sunur punched the air in triumph. "*Finally!*"

Sol crawled into the dead tree in his field and willed himself to sleep. Kissing. Bodies. Disgusting.

Neema and Cain broke apart. Matching grins.

"We need to get you out of those wet clothes," she said, running a hand down his chest.

"Yes," Cain said. "Yes we do."

CHAPTER
Forty-Eight

"E ACH DAY," Cain said, quoting the Scriptures, "in times of light, in times of shadow, seek for one small pearl of joy and you shall find it." A pause. "Did I—"

"You found my pearl of joy," Neema said. "As you well know." It was not the first time he had made this joke. She stretched, and settled more comfortably against him.

"It amazes me," he said, stroking her arm, "how often they quote that line in the temple, and no one laughs. No one. What is wrong with people?"

Neema didn't answer. She was listening to his heart. There was not a better sound in all the world. His heart, afterwards, as it slowed back down. "Eight years," she said, softly.

He kissed her hair. "Don't."

The lost years, the other people, the bitterness, the heartbreak. Don't.

They were in a barn at the bottom of the Ox orchard—the same one the contenders had filled with sacks earlier that afternoon. "The scene of my triumph," Cain had said, after they broke in, and even though she was removing his trousers at the time, and biting his ear, Neema had paused long enough to say, "Yes, but I won though."

Now they were lying naked together, using the sacks as a mattress. "A *barn*," Cain said, putting his hands behind his head and staring up at the rafters. "Like an old-fashioned romance. I'm the tough but misunderstood Ox labourer. You're the beautiful but jaded Tiger official, come to evict me from my land."

Neema propped herself on her elbow. "Sheltering from a sudden storm."

"Naked for some reason."

"We must huddle closer together, for warmth." She pressed herself against him.

He held her back. "No, Mistress Tiger. I dare not—"

"But why, rough yet quietly sensitive Oxman?"

Cain gave an anguished sigh. "If I hold you now, Mistress, I fear I shall never let you go."

"Oh, that's good," Neema approved. "I like that." She straddled him, snagging her fingers in his hair, and kissed him until they both ran out of air. "Round two?"

"The weapons round," Cain said, and lifted his eyebrows in invitation.

Neema lowered herself closer, breathed in his ear. "Call me Mistress again."

Sol shook himself awake, picked up his field in his claws and flew it to the other side of existence.

After round three, which they agreed was a tie, Cain threw on his damp uniform and went outside to hunt for provisions. Left alone in the quiet of the barn, Neema stretched out her limbs again, arched her back, enjoying the feel of her body; where she'd invited him in. And then, with some reluctance, she got dressed. She could hear music in the distance, from the Ox palace, and faint chatter. For a moment her mind expanded further—to the emperor and Vabras, to what might happen next. She shrank back from the thought as if burned. She would not worry, she would not project ahead. She would have this moment.

Cain returned from his scavenging trip with a couple of blankets, a pile of roast pork rolls, two bottles of wine and a cake with "To My Darling Husband" written on it in chocolate icing.

"That's a terrible thing to steal," she said, as he barred the barn door.

She took a roll instead, lifted the bun to inspect it. "This one has too much crackling, you have it."

Cain had never heard a better sentence spoken in all his life. "I love you," he said, and ate the roll in three bites.

Neema scrunched closer. "I love you too."

He rubbed the grease from his mouth. "I was talking to the bun."
She laughed.

He looked at her, clear green eyes sweeping over her face, taking in every contour. "Admiring the view," he said. "They should mark you on the map, you know."

"Area of outstanding natural beauty."

He grinned. "Exactly."

She looked back at him, allowing herself to feel what she had denied for a long time. Not just that she loved him, but that she had hurt him too. Cain, sensing the shift, kissed her shoulder gently, through her tunic. "Was there any particular reason you got dressed?" he wondered. "Was it mainly so I could undress you again?" Trying to deflect the conversation, but it was no use.

"I should have left with you that day," she said. "I'm so sorry, Cain. I know you waited for me."

"To the last moment," he said, drawing away. "Kept hoping I'd see you pelting down the quay with a thousand books under your arm." He reached for a bottle of wine, and took a deep, bracing swig.

"I'm sorry," she said, again.

"Well. I wasn't entirely without fault," he acknowledged. "Should have trusted you. It's just…you hurt my feelings." He laughed at himself.

She took the wine from him. "Trusted me with what?"

"You *really* think I'd kill people for a living?"

She lowered the bottle. "You…don't?"

"For fuck's…" He tore his fingers through his hair, exasperated. "Of course not. Why do you think I left my Scrapper gang?"

"How should I know? You never talk about it."

"They wanted me to kill someone, Neema. Cut me loose when I refused. After beating the shit out of me." He touched a scar that cut through his hairline. "Wasn't a killer then, not a killer now. I happen to find murdering people distasteful."

Neema was struggling to process this. "You're not an assassin."

"Oh, I'm an assassin," Cain said, more cheerfully. "I just don't kill anyone."

"Cain, that makes no sense."

"I know." He grinned again, delighted. "I'm a walking paradox."

"But I've seen the reports. They send you somewhere, people disappear and…oh." Neema stopped, as she realised. They disappeared, never to be seen again. No bodies. No evidence. "Where do you take them?"

Cain lowered his voice, despite the fact they were alone. "There's places in the Scarred Lands that aren't scarred any more. Not the borders," he said, anticipating her question. "Deeper. Much deeper. Hidden." He caught her look. *The Scarred Lands*. "Well it's better than death, isn't it? The only rule is, they can't come back. They try to leave, then we do kill them."

Neema was fascinated. "Have you been there? What's it like?"

Cain shook his head. He'd told her too much already—Fort would kill him. Literally. "What you should be asking is *who* we've sent there."

Neema crossed her legs so they were sitting knee to knee. An echo of their first meeting, in the storeroom. She leaned forward. "Go on."

"There's a pattern to our imperial commissions," he said. "It's subtle, obfuscated, but once you see it…It's been going on for years, N. Ever since the rebellion. Bersun removes Commoners from their posts, and replaces them with Venerants, or people he knows he can manipulate. Not always big positions, but key ones —the warden of a prison mine, the harbour master at Three Ports. Dozens and dozens. Hundreds, maybe."

She took another swig of wine. "Not all murdered, surely."

"No, that's a last resort. They use bribery, blackmail. Or they'll pension them off. That's why it's so hard to prove. And they're careful—they'll break the pattern enough that it's hard to spot. But it's there. Once you know, you can't miss it. It's like this very long, very stealthy Venerant coup."

Silence in the barn, as Neema soaked this in. Thinking of the courtiers who had come and gone during her time on the island. "You're saying the emperor's in league with—"

"—The Five Families. The Tursuls, the Arbells, the Ranors…"

Neema lowered the bottle. "Havoc."

"Oh he's *definitely* benefited."

"Is that why you broke his nose?"

Cain's expression darkened. He rubbed a hand along his arm, absently—a sign he was upset, and masking it. "Havoc's predecessor. Admiral Ryssa Stone. He was promised her position when she retired."

"She was a Commoner," Neema said. "I remember."

"Orphan of the marshes, raised by the Grey Penitents. Impressive woman by all accounts. Rose up through the ranks—no monastery training. But," Cain lifted a finger, "she made the fatal mistake of telling Havoc that she had no plans to retire for another ten years."

A cold, thin sensation drifted through her: a death mist. "What happened to her?"

"Funny thing," Cain said, in a sour voice. "She died in a boating 'accident.' Good weather, seasoned sailor. Yet somehow the boat broke up into pieces. No survivors."

"*The Merry Dolphin*." The boat sign from the Fox Trial. Cain had left it for Havoc to find. "He was responsible for her death?"

"Directly? No—he kept his hands clean. But he knew in advance." A bitter smile. "He ordered his uniform a month before she died."

"Eight." Neema rubbed her face.

"Sorry, have I spoiled the mood?" To cheer himself up, Cain added a sliver of birthday cake to a pork roll, on top of the crackling. He bit into it, coughed, then tilted his hand back and forth. Not bad. When Neema didn't react, he said, "Are you all right?"

She shook her head slowly. Everything she had worked for these past eight years. Everything she had believed in. Somehow she had thought that Gedrun, the counterfeit emperor, had at least shared his brother's beliefs in the monastery reforms; the opening up of the court to Commoners. All the things that had bound her to him. "The reforms are just a distraction..." A nasty thought struck her. "You didn't think I was involved in all this, did you?"

Cain winced. "Well..."

"Fuck you," she said quietly.

He lifted his hands, helpless. "You've been clamped to the emperor's side for eight years. You rose so high, so fast, Neema. Be fair. I had to wonder."

"Fuck *you*." She leapt to her feet and stalked off, her voice floating back from the darkness. "You fucking arsehole."

"Well, that was nice while it lasted," Cain said to himself, and finished his bun. "Can't we say we're even?" he called out to wherever she was, raging in the dark. "You thought I killed people for a living. I thought you might be part of a Venerant conspiracy. Turns out we're both much nicer than we thought. That's a good thing, isn't it? That we're not horrible after all?"

He waited. She came back. She'd been crying.

Cain's face fell. "I'm sorry."

She sat down next to him. "I thought I was making things right. I thought he was on our side."

He put his arm around her, brought her close. "We all did. Brother Bersun: Brusque but Benevolent. He *was* on our side, those first years. It's the one thing I don't understand, how he could have changed so much. How he could turn his back on everything he believed in..." He stopped.

Neema had that look on her face when she knew the answer to something, and couldn't wait to share it. He'd sat next to her through school. He'd seen it a lot.

She told him her theory. How Bersun had died after the rebellion and how Gedrun had replaced him.

Cain took a swig of wine. "Shit. So they're blackmailing him. Clarion, Kindry. Vabras. Forcing him to run things the way they want."

"I don't think so. I think they got more than they bargained for. He is *smart*, Cain—"

He stopped her, put a finger to his lips as he listened into the silence.

It was only now she realised that the music had stopped some time ago. The party was over.

The barn doors rattled against the bar, making her jump.

"Contender Ballari. Contender Kraa. Open up, in the name of the emperor."

Hounds.

Cain was already on the move. Grabbing a coil of rope, he headed up the ladder to the store landing above. By the time Neema had caught up with him, he'd tied the rope to a post and was slinging it out of the window. He clambered through, beckoning for her to join him.

The Hounds were still rattling the door. Thank the Eight Cain had barred it. She followed him down the rope, landing on her knees with a thud. She got to her feet, wiping her hands.

"Fox palace," Cain whispered, circling her wrist. "We need to—"

"Contender Kraa. Contender Ballari."

Havoc stepped out of the darkness, a sword at his hip. A troop of Samran Hounds surrounded them, batons raised.

"What's this about?" Neema asked, determined to stay calm.

Havoc threw her a cold look. The bridge of his nose was painfully swollen, and there were dark bruises under his eyes. His voice sounded thick and stuffy when he spoke. "His majesty the emperor demands your presence."

Cain had assessed the odds. Even he couldn't fight off that many Hounds. "Of course. Lead the way."

Havoc turned to the Hound sergeant. "Contender Ballari is refusing to comply."

Before Cain could protest, the squad surrounded him. Raising their batons, they beat him to the ground, kicking him for good measure as he curled up, arms over his head, trying desperately to protect himself.

"Stop!" Neema screamed, as they held her back. "He's not resisting. Stop!"

The Hounds kept beating him, until finally Havoc called them off. Panting hard from their efforts, they dragged Cain to his knees. Blood streamed down his face.

"Monsters," Neema spat.

Havoc took a torch and held it close to Cain's face, inspecting the damage with a satisfied smile. A deep gash in his brow, another above his ear. A torn lip. His jaw was starting to swell. Havoc brought the flame closer, laughing as Cain tried to draw back. For a second, the torchlight turned Cain's eyes from emerald to bright yellow. The flame distorted his face, sharpening his cheekbones. His lips parted in a dangerous grin, his teeth red with blood. Sharp teeth…

Havoc stepped back, disturbed. The illusion vanished. A trick of the torchlight. "Get him up," he told the Hounds. "Let's go."

Forty-Nine

THE EMPEROR WAS shocked by Cain's injuries, shocked. "What the Eight happened? Vabras, you must get these Samran recruits to behave, this is unacceptable."

Vabras wasn't there. There was an empty space at the bottom of the throne-room steps, doing—to be fair—a very good impression of the High Commander.

Neema had prepared herself for the worst. An imperial summons at midnight, nothing good could come of that. But the emperor was in a jovial mood, twinkling down at her in his embroidered night robes, a black cap perched on his giant head. He knew something, and it pleased him.

"Neema, we are glad to see you are unharmed. Did you fight them off?" He shadow-punched. "I saw you on the platform earlier. Where did you learn to spar like that?"

"From a book, your majesty."

He laughed, assuming she was joking. "You have a new rival, Ballari. Though I think Ruko's still the one to beat, don't you? I hope your injuries don't slow you down." A side glance, to Havoc. A fractional nod of thanks.

"I'm sure I'll be fine after a night's rest," Cain said.

The emperor grunted. "Won't keep you long. We're all for bed. Contender Brundt has come forward with information about the murder."

Neema cursed inwardly.

She had told Katsan everything she knew about Gaida's death. That the emperor had ordered it to hide his true identity. That Benna had staged the body afterwards, so he would not get away with it.

Katsan had vowed to keep this a secret. The word of a Bear warrior was supposed to be unbreakable.

The doors burst open, splitting the Tiger portrait in two.

Vabras strode through. Behind him, Katsan walked with her head up, dressed in a plain cotton patrol uniform. No longer a contender, death-pale, but still carrying herself with pride. The fresh stump of her right arm was wrapped in bandages and held in a sling.

She glanced at Neema as she passed, pale blue eyes shining with the effort of hiding her pain. It was an extraordinary feat, almost beyond human.

The Hounds led her in front of the throne, beneath the flaming jaws of the Awakening Dragon. Without thinking, she went to clasp her hands behind her back, then flinched as the sling reminded her of her loss. Pain, and grief for her ghost limb, her sword arm.

"Katsan Brundt," the emperor said. "You have information regarding the murder of Gaida Rack."

"I do, your majesty."

"You will call me Brother Bersun," he told her, because that is what Bersun would have said. The authority of a fellow warrior being more powerful, and sacred, even than the authority of an emperor. "Speak."

Katsan glanced behind her to her left, to the portrait of the Bear in its mountain home, salmon springing from the rapids. "Brother Bersun. Before you, and before the Bear, I confess my crime. I stole the Blade of Peace. I framed Contender Valit for Gaida's death."

"Katsan!" Neema protested.

"Quiet," the emperor snapped. And then, to Katsan, "Continue."

The Bear warrior lifted her chin and gave her report, as if she were just returned from border patrol. "Gaida was my Sister. I loved her. But I was disturbed by her behaviour towards you at the opening ceremony, Brother Bersun. I found it disrespectful."

The emperor liked that. "Go on."

"I decided to confront her. But when I reached her apartment I found…" She paused, overwrought. The pain from her arm was making her sweat, it helped with her deception. "She was dead. Poisoned, I assumed. The shock of finding her…I lost all sense, Brother. In my grief, I convinced myself the Tigers were responsible. They are trained in subtle poisons, are they not?" She looked around for someone to confirm it.

"You stole the Blade, and framed Contender Valit in revenge," Vabras said. He had exchanged places with the empty space below the throne steps.

Sweat poured down Katsan's face. "Yes. May the Eight forgive me."

"And remain Hidden," the room murmured.

Neema, watching from the sidelines, smothered her astonishment. The lie was simple, and beautifully convincing. As to why she had lied—that was another question.

The emperor deliberated, studying Katsan closely, knuckles pressed against his cheek. Neema could guess what he was thinking. He had planned to blame Gaida's murder on the thief—but now that Katsan had confessed, that story didn't make sense. Then something struck him. He smiled, and lifted his head from his hand. "You say she was poisoned. Vabras—this is your understanding as well?"

Vabras looked up the steps, to make sure he gave the right answer. "It is, your majesty. Contender Kraa found the remnants."

"Ah. Well then. Is it not clear what happened?" The emperor put on a sorrowful expression. "Contender Rack took her own life."

"No," Katsan said, jolting with alarm. "Gaida would never do that."

The sorrowful look deepened. "But you said yourself, Sister Katsan—she was acting strangely at the opening ceremony. We all saw it. You have something to add, contender?"

Havoc had stepped forward. He pressed his palms together in a deferential Monkey salute. "Your majesty, I believe you are right. I spoke with Gaida after the ceremony, and she was in a dark mood."

"Indeed?" The emperor leaned forward.

"I think the reality of the Trials had sunk in, your majesty. With respect, she was the weakest contender, and she knew it. She told me she was afraid she would dishonour the Raven with her performance."

Oh sure, Neema thought, drily. Gaida was notoriously lacking in self-confidence.

The emperor sat back. "Suicide, then. What a tragedy."

Katsan tried again to protest, but the emperor spoke over her.

"No, Sister Katsan—enough. The matter is closed. As it could have been days ago, if you'd had the decency to confess to your crime. I suspect you only do so now because your Festival is over. Shame on you, Sister. Poor Contender Kraa—you accused her, did you not?"

"For that I am truly sorry," Katsan said. She touched her sling. "And accept the Raven's punishment for that crime."

We did not punish her, Neema. Sol was back. **It was an accident.**

"On the subject of punishment." The emperor drummed his fingers on the arm of the throne. "Stealing the Blade of Peace. Framing another contender…These are high crimes, Sister Katsan. But I am of a mind to be merciful, given your confession, and your contrition. We sentence you to five years in the prison mines."

Katsan bowed her head. "Thank you, Brother. But I cannot accept this sentence. It is too light."

The emperor's craggy brows lifted in surprise. "What do you ask of me, then? Do you seek death?"

"Not from you, Brother." Katsan drew herself up, shoulders squared, dignified. "When I entered Anat-garra, I made a sacred vow to follow the Way of the Bear. To live a life of service. To protect the vulnerable, and defend the innocent. To act always with honour and integrity. I have broken that vow. I am a warrior without a Guardian, doomed in this life and the eight that follow. As you know, Brother—there is only one way to escape such a fate." She looked up at the emperor, and waited.

And it was bliss, pure bliss, watching his reaction. The panic, quickly smothered. He didn't know. He had no idea.

Katsan had her proof. She had listened to Neema's story, but now she knew for certain: the man sitting on the throne was not a Bear warrior. He was not her Brother.

"I wish to return to Anat-garra, and fall into the Bear's embrace," she said.

Anat-garra was built into the summit of Mount Ketu. To fall into the Bear's embrace meant to leap off the monastery walls. A ritual ending of life. Once claimed, it could not be reneged upon.

From Katsan's perspective, it was the ideal solution. She had found a way off the island before the end of the Festival, with a swift pass back to the Bear monastery—where she could share the news of Brother Bersun, and Gedrun the imposter. The lie she had told before the Bear about stealing the Blade would be forgiven. She would fall into her Guardian's embrace and be reborn on the Eternal Path, her soul unstained.

"Katsan…" Neema said.

The Bear warrior looked at her, and smiled. Despite the pain, she remained standing to attention, almost her old self once more. She lifted her chin, and in a ringing voice, said, "Better to die with honour, than live in shame."

The emperor descended the steps. Opening his arms wide, he embraced her. It looked sincere—it was sincere. There were times when this man, this fake, this fraud, was genuine. He felt for her in that moment, and respected her. "May the Eight look kindly upon your final journey, Sister."

"And remain Hidden," Katsan replied, stepping back. "I should like to leave as soon as possible. If that is your will, Brother."

Naturally, the emperor was in a giving mood. "Of course. You may leave at first light. Vabras, have a boat standing ready."

On her way out, escorted by the guards, Katsan stopped in front of Neema and Cain, who was barely conscious after his beating from the Hounds. With some effort, Katsan took something from her pocket.

Neema's colours. She'd used them as a torniquet on Katsan's arm.

"These were Gaida's," Katsan said softly, brushing her thumb over the winged sigil. "Now they are yours."

Neema took them back with both hands, tears in her eyes. "Thank you."

Katsan managed a weak smile. "Contender Ballari. Contender Kraa. May we meet again on the Eternal Path, in kinder days."

The guards moved her on.

No one escorted them back to their rooms. As far as the emperor was concerned, Neema was no longer an imminent threat. Katsan had confessed to the theft, and—thanks to Havoc's fake testimony —Gaida's death would be framed as a suicide. The official narrative would erase the truth.

How quickly things had turned. This afternoon Katsan had tried to kill her. Tonight, she had saved Neema's life.

If Neema wrote herself a daily task list—which as we know she very much did—it would now look like this:

- Avoid being killed by Ruko ✓
- Avoid being killed by Katsan ✓
- Encounter the Raven and refuse to do its bidding ✓
- Apologise to Cain and get into his trousers ✓✓
- Convince Vabras and the emperor I am not a threat ✓?
- Prevent Ruko from winning the throne/ending the world ✗
- Cake? (Stolen) ✓

Cain limped along beside her, testing his swollen jaw. He saw her counting something off on her fingers and guessed what she was doing. It was a sign of how exhausted and badly injured he was that he didn't tease her about it. He was pretty sure some of his ribs were broken, and a couple of fingers; he was more worried about internal injuries. He'd taken some sharp, targeted blows to his kidneys.

"Are we safe?" Neema wondered, when they reached her door. "I *think* we're safe…"

Cain leaned against the wall, eyes closed. And fell asleep.

"Cain!"

He snapped awake.

"You're literally asleep on your feet." She pushed him away, on a bit that wasn't bruised. "Bed." She smiled at him. "You have a big fight tomorrow." They were drawn against each other in the morning.

He rubbed his face, to wake himself, then made a strangled noise as the cut on his brow opened. He dabbed the blood away.

She didn't want to hurt his split lip, so she kissed him on the cheek. "Goodnight."

"Goodnight, my love." He covered his mouth. *My love.* That was embarrassing.

"Don't worry. I'll pretend I didn't hear that."

"Thanks," he grunted, and staggered off.

She watched him until he turned the corner. She may have waited after that, listening as his footsteps faded away. She'd forgotten how ridiculous love was. Properly, properly ridiculous.

She smiled to herself, then tapped on Sunur's door.

CHAPTER
Fifty

S UNUR TOOK A long time to open it, and when she did, she was
still half asleep. Her hair was mussed and she was missing her
glasses. "Where's Cain?" she asked, peering blearily over Neema's
shoulder. "Why aren't you shagging in a bush somewhere?"

"He's gone to bed. The Hounds beat him up."

"What, why?" This woke her up. "I'll fetch Tala..."

Neema paced the living room as she waited. A solitary lantern
gleamed on a low table, revealing a room in cheerful disarray, Suru's toys and picture books scattered about the place. A reminder
of why she was here, when her body was crying out for sleep. She
found some whisky, and poured herself a shot.

"Make yourself at home," Tala said, striding through from the
bedchamber. She sounded annoyed. The Bear Trial was scheduled
before the fights tomorrow morning, and it was notoriously chal-
lenging. "What's this about Cain? What did he do?"

"He didn't do anything."

Tala looked dubious.

They sat down together, Tala and Sunur on a day bed, Neema on a
footstool, legs folded under her. She sipped her whisky, scratchy eyed
with exhaustion. "Katsan confessed to stealing the Blade of Peace."

Their jaws dropped in unison. It would have been funny, in different circumstances.

"There's a boat leaving at dawn to take her to the mainland." She
looked at Sunur. "This is your chance."

"For what?" Tala said, confused.

Sunur turned to her wife. "I told you—there's something wrong
about this place. I think we should leave—the three of us. Go home."

"Sunur…" Tala rolled her head back. Clearly, they'd had this argument before. "We're safer here together, as a family. There's riots on the mainland—"

"That's not true," Neema said. "They're lying to us."

"Why would they do that?"

"To trap us here." Sunur rubbed her arms, anxious. "The Leviathans, the Hounds. We're prisoners, Tala…"

"Oh, Eight give me strength and remain Hidden. They're here to *protect* us, Sunur. This is you, isn't it, playing games?" Tala looked angrily at Neema. "All that crap about not wanting the throne. And now you're winning Trials, and chopping Katsan's arm off. *Of course* she wants me to run away," she said, to Sunur. "I'm her nearest rival."

Neema dropped her unfinished whisky on the table. "I'm not suggesting you should leave, Tala."

The two Oxwomen stared at her.

"You're a contender. They won't let you go. But there's a chance for Sunur and Suru. Please—I know you don't trust me, but—"

"You're right." Tala got to her feet. "I don't trust you."

Neema got up too. "Follow your instincts, Sunur," she said, as Tala pushed her towards the door. "Bribe the captain. Whatever it takes."

"Get out." Tala shoved her out into the corridor.

"Tala wait, sorry." Neema cringed, hands up. "One last thing."

"Fuck the Eight, Neema. *What?*"

"*Sorry*, but I didn't cut Katsan's arm off. It's just that her injuries were so catastrophic they had to…"

Tala slammed the door in her face.

"…amputate," Neema said, to the vibrating door.

She walked away, taking a lantern from the wall.

Better out than in, Neema.

Sol. She'd almost forgotten he was there. —Yes! Thank you. At least someone understood.

She opened the door to her antechamber. A note was lying on the floor. She picked it up. It was from Gaida's servant Navril—the list of attendees she'd requested from the afterparty. "Sorry for the delay," he'd written along the top.

Neema read her way down the list. Raven courtiers, contingent members, Gaida's friends. She knew she'd find his name, and there it was, near the bottom.

Contender Havoc Arbell-Ranor.

He'd confessed without realising it, in the throne room. *I spoke with Gaida after the opening ceremony.* Gaida had come straight back to her apartment, to host the party.

Who'd ordered him to kill her? The emperor? Vabras? Either way, he'd made his way over to the Raven palace, told a few anecdotes. Tipped the poison in her tea. Two kisses on the cheek. "Wonderful evening, Gaida, good luck for tomorrow." Then spent the night training with his contingent.

"Bastard," Neema said, and crumpled the note in her fist.

Her rooms were quiet without Benna; Neema had grown used to her bouncing about the place. She wondered if Ruko had kept to his word. "Be safe, go well, Benna Edge," she murmured.

Pink-Pink, tail wrapped around the bed post, hissed in alarm as she approached.

"Pink-Pink," Neema said, dismayed. He hadn't hissed at her in years.

What is that thing, Neema? What is it doing here? I don't like it, it shouldn't be here.

—He doesn't like you either, Neema replied, clambering into bed. Sleep was waiting for her there, ready to drag her under.

Sol puffed up, proudly. **Nobody likes me, Neema. I am the Solitary Raven, loathed and abandoned, spurned by all—**

Neema snored lightly, her body a dead weight, face planted in the pillow.

Sol roosted on her rib, eyes closed. He was thinking about Neema and the Fox contender. There were many mated pairs in the flock, he understood such things, he had studied them. Neema was loyal to her mate, this was natural. She would not betray him.

Sol curled his claws tighter around Neema's rib. **I shall fix this for you, Neema. We can be alone again. Alone together. Sleep on, sleep on. I have a plan and it is magnificent.**

CHAPTER
Fifty-One

A ND CAIN IS sleeping too, curled on a mattress on his balcony. Naked. Why not? For the first year of his training, he never slept in the same place twice. The schedules of days and nights shifted, testing novices to their limits. Sleep must be snatched wherever it could be found. Two hours here, a quarter hour there. Some went mad and left within days. Others endured the torment until their bodies and minds adjusted. Cain barely noticed. He could nap anywhere, any time. What was all the fuss about?

Tonight, the balcony. He sleeps, and dreams his usual dream, the one he forgets the moment he opens his eyes again to the world. As he sleeps, his cracked ribs mend, his broken fingers heal, the damage to his liver and kidneys is quietly repaired. Dark bruises shrink and fade away. The cuts along his brow and lip remain, and the one above his ear—they have been seen and noted, and so must be kept. But when he wakes to-morrow, he will find they are not as deep as he'd thought, nor as painful.

Sol watches from his perch on the balcony wall, preening himself back into shape. We have spared you the disgusting part where he tore himself out of Neema's back as she slept. (Exiting that way is even more horrible than from the front, you must trust us on this, the way the hooked beak clamps on to the spinal column and snaps it in two like a twig, the vile crunching, splintering sound, the gristle, the claws pok-ing and scrabbling through the skin until it rents open, birth-ing a mangled semi-creature, half bird, half purple-black slurry, oozing and slurping like pus through the gaping wound between Neema's shoulder blades before splatting to the ground.) We have skipped that revolting scene for your benefit.

We swoop down and land next to him on the wall, our much-loathed fragment, the useless thing.

Wretched one.

Worthless one.

What are you doing here?

Sol continues to preen himself. **None of your business.**

We fume.

It is literally our business.

We are you.

You are us.

We hop down to where Cain is sleeping, and circle him warily.

This one is dangerous.

This one is protected.

You know what will happen if you try to harm him.

Bad things. Bad things will happen.

We forbid you from meddling with him.

Leave him alone.

We flap back up to the balcony wall and give Sol a sharp snap with our beak. This usually works. He knows when he is not wanted. (He is never wanted.)

Go. Shoo.

Sol ignores us. We are *livid*. He does not ignore us, we ignore him. That is the order of things. We peck him again, pull out a puff of feathers.

Sol is undeterred. **Harass away. The fact remains: your plan failed. It was not magnificent.**

The flock reels. We are in danger of scattering. Never, never has a fragment dared...

I, the SOLITARY RAVEN (he opens his wings wide in that annoying habit of his) **will save the world on my own. The Tiger warrior will be stopped, as the Dragon commanded—by ME. Neema shall win the throne, and I will sit VISIBLE on her shoulder, in my RESPLENDENT GLORY.** (More wing stretching.) **All the tiny**

bags of meat will fall to their knees and WORSHIP ME, and present me with SHINY THINGS.

He drops down, to land firmly on Cain's bare chest.

But first, I must take out the competition.

Cain sat up and stretched, rubbed his face. He felt well, and rested, though he had only slept a few hours. He didn't try to remember his dream, he'd learned long ago not to bother. He tested his ribs, pressing with his fingers. Nothing cracked, nothing broken. Not even a bruise. He chose not to think about how strange and miraculous that was.

The sky was dark, another hour at least until dawn. But he was awake now.

"Food," he thought. "Food, food."

Wrapping a sheet around his hips, he headed back inside and made coffee, and demolished a hamper his contingent had sent up the previous night. Astonishing, really, it had survived this long. He thought about Neema and smiled. The cut on his lip didn't split, it wasn't all that deep, now he probed it. He'd dodged those Hounds better than he thought, that was it.

Cain.

He stiffened, listening. Had someone called his name? He picked up a candlestick.

Cain.

Someone was calling him from his bedchamber, a male voice. Well, that certainly wouldn't be the first time. But not last night, no (he thought back, double-checking) he definitely didn't bring anyone home last night. Not even Neema. My love. Oh, Eight —he'd called her that out loud, hadn't he? How excruciating. He tossed the candlestick and caught it, testing the weight. Crossed the room and kicked open the door.

No one there. His bed was made, pillows plumped.

And lying in the centre, a book.

He picked it up and read the title out loud. "Tales of the Raven." He turned it over, but the back was blank. The black leather cover felt warm to the touch, as if it had been lying in the sun. He caught a spicy, peppery smell.

A present from Neema, he decided, and sat down on the bed. As he moved to open the book he felt a flare of warning, a tiny nip to the soul. No, no, don't read that. Put it down. Throw it away.

Ah yes, but he was a Fox. So he ignored the warning.

Something of an irony, that.

He opened the book, and flicked through its pages. Blank… blank…blank…A sudden flash of colour. He stopped. On the left-hand page was an illustration of a little red fox, surrounded by woodland. A sweet image, until you realised that the fox's paw was caught in a steel trap. Was it…crying? Cain peered closer. The fox twitched its whiskers.

No. That didn't happen.

He turned to the right-hand page. One of those ancient folk tales Neema loved. This must have come from her, she must want him to read it. He settled back against the pillow, and began.

How the Fox Crossed the Border

Before and beyond, in the space between things, a young girl dreamed her way into the Hidden Realm.

The girl had been running from a nightmare. She lay down in the long grass, flat on her back, and caught her breath. The trees rustled overhead, the clouds drifted by.

Something whimpered in the grass beside her.

She sat up, and listened closely.

There it was again. A sad, muffled whimper.

The girl crawled through the grass until she found a little red fox, lying at the base of a broad oak tree. It was the sweetest creature, with mellow gold eyes and soft copper fur. Its dainty paw was caught in a wicked steel trap.

"Oh, how cruel!" the girl exclaimed.

The fox shrank back, ears pressed to its head. "Have you come to eat me?"

"Of course not!" said the girl.

"Have you come to steal my fur?"

"No indeed." The girl inched closer. "I have come to rescue you."

"Oh," said the little fox, nose twitching. "How kind. What a kind thing you are."

The trap was heavy, with vicious metal teeth. The fox watched with interest as the girl prised it open. "Quick!" she said, panting with the effort. "Lift out your paw."

The fox removed its mangled paw and gave it a feeble lick. Then it shuddered, from nose to tail. "Oh, dear. How shall I run from the monsters now?"

"Monsters?" The girl looked about her in alarm.

"Don't worry, they do not eat little girls. Only foxes." The fox shuddered again. "I was trying to cross the border to safety," it said, lifting its nose towards the trees. "I shall never reach it now. I shall be eaten whole." It started to cry.

The girl did not want her new friend to be eaten by monsters. "Don't cry little fox, for I have an idea."

"You do?" the fox sniffed, wiping a tear from its snout.

"You must come and live with me. No one ever eats foxes in my village."

The fox opened its beautiful golden eyes very wide. "Is that so?"

Now the girl was being a touch devious here. It was true that the people in her village did not eat foxes, but they did hunt them, and kill them, and wear their fur. But she so wanted the little fox to come home with her, and to be her friend.

"Do you really want me to come and live with you?" asked the fox.

"Very much."

"And do you promise I can stay?"

"I do."

"And do you always keep your promises?"

"Of course."

"Then I accept your invitation," the fox declared, and sprang neatly into her arms.

The girl was so startled, she almost dropped it. But it felt so warm and soft, and it smelled of fresh gingerbread, which just happened to be her favourite smell in all the world. She hugged the darling little creature tight, and breathed in deep. Delicious.

The fox put its head over her shoulder and nuzzled her ear. "I hope you don't mind carrying me, but my leg is so terribly sore."

"Of course," soothed the girl. "Do you know which way is home?"

"Well that's a funny thing," replied the fox. "It just happens to be right across that border."

"What a coincidence," the girl said, and the fox agreed that it was.

They had not been walking for long when the fox said, "Little girl, little girl—the monsters are coming!"

The girl looked back, but all she saw was a soft rippling in the long grass.

"Run!" cried the fox, and she did.

High above their heads, a wheeling raven shrieked, "Fox! Fox!"

The little fox grinned to hear its name. For it was indeed the Fox, the First Guardian, in its sweetest and most irresistible form. "Hello Raven!"

A tail swished through the long grass. Ears, teeth, tongue… Tiger!

"Fox!" Tiger snarled, snapping at their heels. "What are you doing? You know you cannot cross the border. Dragon forbids it."

The Fox smiled over the little girl's shoulder. "But Tiger. I have been invited," it said.

The Tiger skidded to a halt.

Cunning Fox!

For a thousand times a thousand years it had been trying to cross this border. Or a blink of an eye, depending on how you measure things. But it could not pass to the Other Side without an invitation. Not as its whole, marvellous self. No indeed.

As they reached the trees the Fox lifted its dear little paw, which was not injured, not at all, and waved cheerily. "Goodbye Tiger! Fare thee well!"

The Tiger roared in fury. "The next time I see you, Fox, I will eat you whole."

The Fox grinned a very wide grin. "Ah—but you'll have to catch me first," it said, and vanished into the woods.

That was how the Fox left the Hidden Realm for the first time.

The next morning, the young girl woke in her bedroom. "What a strange dream," she thought, and screamed.

Sitting at the bottom of her bed was a fox. Not the dainty creature she had carried in her arms, but a big, mangy old vixen, with matted fur and a missing eye, ripped from its socket in a fight.

"Ugh! Who are you?" cried the girl.

The Fox was offended. "Don't you know me? I thought we were friends."

"But why do you look so different?" The girl plugged her nose. "Why do you *smell* so different?"

The Fox sat up proudly, and cleared its throat. "I am the Fox. I am all the foxes that were, all the foxes that are, and all the foxes that will be." It paused, and nibbled its fur with its rotten yellow teeth. "Fleas. Riddled with them."

The girl's skin itched. "Change back at once!"

The Fox gave her a stern look. "I shall be what I please, when I please."

"Well, I don't like you any more," the girl said.

"How disappointingly shallow of you," said the Fox.

She flapped her hand. "Go away! Shoo!"

"Little girl. Flap your hand at me again, and I will bite it off." It snapped its jaws at her.

The girl threw her blanket over her head, and started to cry. "I hate you," she declared, her voice muffled.

"May I remind you," the Fox said, in an injured tone, "that you invited me to come and live with you? You promised you would never send me away."

"But that was when you smelled of gingerbread," said the lump under the blanket.

"Well then," said the Fox, to the lump. "There is a lesson for you. Never trust things that smell of gingerbread."

The girl peeped out from under her blanket. "That's a stupid lesson."

"Very stupid," the Fox agreed.

They laughed.

"Dear Fox. I'm sorry we fought. I would stroke your fur again, if you weren't covered in fleas, and...are those maggots?"

"Indeed they are," the Fox was pleased to confirm. "I am glad we are friends again."

"So am I. But you cannot stay here. If my mother sees you she will scream, and chase you from the house. And all the villagers will gather together and hunt you down with dogs. They will chase you until you can't run any more. And then the dogs will snap your bones and tear you to pieces."

"What, what, what?" cried the Fox. "You said no one ate foxes here. You promised!"

"We don't eat foxes," said the girl. "That would be disgusting. But we do hunt them, and kill them, and wear their fur."

The Fox grew back its missing eye, so it could glare at her the better. "You tricked me!"

"I did. I'm sorry. Are you very cross?"

"Cross?" Not in the slightest. The First Guardian laughed so hard it rolled on its back, wheezing for air. It had never been tricked before. How splendid.

"Fox," said the girl, when it had recovered. "Didn't you say you were all foxes?"

"That is so. All the foxes that were. All the foxes that are—"

"But if that's true, surely you must have known that foxes are hunted and killed, and worn as fur?"

"Little girl." The Fox gave her a severe look. "Are you trying to pin me down with logic?"

"No, I'm just—"

"I will not be pinned."

"But—"

"*I will not. Be pinned.*"

The little girl had heard this tone before from the Temple Servant, when she asked him questions he did not like. She gave up. "If you change back into the sweet little fox, I can pretend you are my pet. No one will hurt you then."

"But that is only one fox. I am all foxes."

"Well, whatever you decide, you had best hurry. For that is my mother on the stairs."

The Fox twitched its ears. It did not want to be chased and killed by dogs, not particularly. But it could not be just one thing. If it were just one thing, it would not be Fox any more. And that it could not bear.

The door opened. The girl's mother saw the filthy, tatty old vixen on her daughter's bed and screamed.

The Fox leapt through the open window and ran off into the fields beyond.

Time passed, as it does on the Other Side. The Fox enjoyed itself tremendously. It learned about all sorts of interesting things like love and death and chickens. Sometimes it was a handsome vixen, nursing its cubs. Sometimes it was two foxes, mating in deep winter with death-curdling screams. Sometimes it was a tired old dog fox caught by the hounds, nothing left but blood and bone and scraps of fur.

Yes, it enjoyed itself—for a while. But the Fox is a restless creature. One day it found itself thinking of the Hidden Realm. It was not homesick, no, no. But it was curious to see what it had missed. I shall slip back across the border, it decided. Just poke my nose through. Nose and whiskers.

The Fox found a nice sunny spot, turned around three times and settled down on the ground, bushy tail wrapped over its lean body. In an instant it was fast asleep, dreaming in the warm sunshine.

The Fox dreamed and dreamed, but it could not cross the border. No matter how fast it ran, the treeline remained upon the horizon, out of reach. Panting with exhaustion, the Fox collapsed on the ground and gave a long, frustrated howl. The howl was so loud, it woke itself up.

"Oh dear," said a voice. "You sound upset. What is the matter?"
The Fox lifted its head from under its tail.

There, perched on a rock, was a (magnificent) black bird, with a curved black beak and clever, beady eyes.

"Raven!" The Fox jumped up, pleased to see its old friend, the Second Guardian. "Which aspect are you?" it asked, squinting. "Are you Raven Rolling Joyfully in the Snow?"

"I am Raven Feasting on the Putrid Corpse of a Fox."

"Ah." The Fox swivelled its ears. It wasn't quite so keen on that particular fragment. "Good afternoon."

"Why were you howling, Fox?" The Raven cocked its head. "Not homesick, are we, by any chance?"

"Oh, no," said the Fox, breezily. "But now you mention it, Raven, I am curious to see the Hidden Realm again. I thought I'd poke my nose in, you know. Nose and whiskers. Trouble is, old friend, I can't seem to reach the border. Look." It walked towards the trees again, shifting through many aspects. A snow fox with half its tail missing. A desert fox, big ears twitching. A new-born cub, stumbling blindly and mewling for its mother. It made no difference. The trees never came any closer.

The Raven watched, perched on its rock. "Fox. Do you remember when we first came to be?"

"I do remember!" the Fox exclaimed, pleased with itself. It had a terrible memory.

"Good. Do you remember how Dragon breathed us into being with its great, fiery breath?"

The Fox's fur stood on end. It nuzzled it back down with its snout. "A vague bell is being rung," it said, "distantly."

"Do you remember the first rule it gave us?"

The Fox pretended to play with its tail, humming a tune to itself. *La-da-dee...*

"Never leave the Hidden Realm!" the Raven snapped, losing patience. Hopping down, it pecked the Fox sharply three times between its ears. "Never. Never. Never!"

"Ow! But we visit the Other Side all the time!" protested the Fox. "Monkey whispered in a poet's ear last week. Ox stamped out a fire in a grain shed yesterday. No one's pecking them in the head. How is that fair? Why must Fox be singled out for persecution?"

The Raven flapped back to its rock, irritated. Fox knew full well that the Eight could send aspects of themselves to the Other Side whenever they wished. What it had done was another matter. It had crossed the border as its whole self.

"Monkey was here last week," the Raven repeated. "Ox came just yesterday. And you wished me a good afternoon. Time, Fox. That's why you can't come home. *Time*. You're absolutely *soaked* in it."

"Ugh!" the Fox groomed itself in a panic, licking its fur and nibbling its skin. "Where is it, Raven? Get it off me!"

"I can't," the Raven said. "You stayed too long, Fox. With time comes death—it is inevitable. Did you not learn this, on the Other Side?"

The Fox started to cry. "I was distracted," it sobbed.

"The chickens?"

"The chickens. Oh, Raven." The Fox collapsed in a despairing fit. "They were so stupid and delicious. And now they have their revenge." It wept, covering its snout with its paw. "I don't want to die for ever," it wailed. "I want to come home."

The Raven sighed. It was hard to stay angry with Fox for long. "There is one way you *might* escape…"

The Fox stopped crying. "There is?"

"Humans die all the time. They are born, and then they die."

The Fox blinked. "Yes, Raven, I have seen this. Humans die, and other humans are born to replace them. It is the same with chickens, and possibly some other things, rabbits, for example. I have eaten so many rabbits, Raven, but they keep on coming. It is a very deep, mysterious magic."

The Raven agreed; this was true. "If you were a human, you could die and be reborn as often as you pleased. Over and over. Live and die in an endless cycle. Do you see?"

The Fox was puzzled. "But I am the Fox. How can I also be a human?"

"*Because* you are the Fox. Shifting, cunning, adaptable Fox. Explorer, adventurer. Seeker of mischief and opportunities. Eschewer of rules."

The Fox liked this very much. It sat on its haunches, chest out. "That is me!"

"Imagine," the Raven said, selling the idea. "Half-Fox, Half-Human. Neither one thing nor the other. Betwixt and between."

"Betwixt and between," the Fox said, moving its head dreamily from side to side. "How absurdly confusing. Oh yes—I should like that very much." It stopped swaying. "But I'd still be trapped here, Raven. I couldn't come home."

"Yes you could, Fox! Humans visit the Hidden Realm all the time, in their dreams. And so can you, every night. Is this not a **magnificent** plan?"

"Oh, so this was *your* idea, Raven?"

The Second Guardian preened itself. "Naturally." All the best ideas were, but it was far too modest to mention that. "Now all you have to do, Fox, is find a suitable host."

The Fox sprang to its paws. "Don't you worry about that," it said, pissing on the nearest bush. "I know just the human."

Many years had passed since the Fox last met his friend the little girl. She was now a middle-aged woman with a bad back and grey strands in her hair, and three children of her own. The Fox found these changes pleasing.

The woman was standing over the stove with her back to the door, stirring a pot of stew.

The Fox's nose twitched. I will enjoy eating that, it thought. Then it jumped straight into the woman, turned around three times, and settled down inside her with a contented sigh.

The woman paused in her stirring. She had a queer taste in her mouth. Gingerbread, she thought. But the moment she thought of it, the taste was gone. She picked up her spoon again and carried on with her day.

∞ ∞ ∞

That night, the Fox dreamed its way back to the Hidden Realm for the first time. It was not happy, not at all.

The Raven was bathing in a pond. The Fox snapped it by the neck and shook it, very hard, splashing drops of water like diamonds. "Trickster! Liar! I will pull your feathers out one by one." And then it did so.

Have you ever seen a plucked raven? Oh dear. Poor Raven, with its pink-blue body all saggy and raw. It struggled from the pond, shivering and shaking. "We are not magnificent," it said, sadly.

The Fox felt bad then, so it wrapped its tail around the Raven to keep it warm. The Raven looked as though it was wearing the Fox's tail like a fur coat, with its bare, tufty head poking out the top. It was very funny, but the Fox did not laugh, to spare the Raven's feelings. They were good friends, really, except when they were not.

"I know you are cross," said the Raven. "But it was the only way to bring you home."

Here was the problem. When the Fox jumped into the woman, it forgot itself. The woman cooked the stew, the Fox cooked the stew. The woman kissed her children, the Fox kissed her children. The woman visited her sister and drank four mugs of beer, and so did the Fox. It was only when the woman fell asleep, snoring from the beer, that the Fox awoke again to itself.

"You cannot *both* be awake at the same time," the Raven cautioned. "You are all the foxes that were, all the foxes that are, all the foxes that will be. Your host would break if she knew she was carrying you inside her. When she is awake, you must sleep. When you are awake, she must sleep. That is how it must be. However."

The Fox's ears pricked. It liked howevers. There were opportunities to be made from howevers.

"Dragon says you may keep one eye half open."

For that is how all foxes sleep.

"Will that do?" asked the Raven, emerging from the Fox's tail. It had grown back its feathers, polished by the sun to a glossy blue-black.

"It will do very well."

It is good when the Fox and the Raven agree.

Centuries passed. Millennia passed. Night into day, day into night. The Fox lived countless lives—some rich, some poor, some short, some long. Each night it crossed the borders to the Hidden Realm, and told the Raven stories of what it had seen. Many times, these stories helped the Raven prevent a Return. It did not mention this. If the Fox knew it had a purpose, it would be livid.

One day, having just been hanged for piracy in Fever Bay (a fascinating experience), the Fox found itself in need of a new host. Hankering for a change of scene, it trotted off to the opposite end of Orrun, over the north-eastern border to Scartown. The town's unique status—half-in, half-out of the empire—suited it very well.

As soon as the Fox arrived it headed for its favourite spot: a vast, festering rubbish tip overlooking the barren waters of the Empty Sea. It had just caught a delicious fat rat when it heard a man's voice, and then a woman's, whispering in the dark. The Fox bit through the rat's neck to silence its squeals, and lowered itself down to watch.

The couple clambered over the mountains of garbage, swearing and cursing. The woman was holding a lantern to light their way. The man was carrying a small bundle of rubbish in his arms. A small, wriggling bundle of rubbish.

Curious. The Fox shrank back, and waited.

The man set the bundle down. "Got some fight in it," he said.

The woman lifted the lantern. "Live the night, and you'll be a Scrapper," she told the bundle. Then she struggled back down the heap, triggering an avalanche of rubbish. The man followed more carefully, watching his step.

When they were gone, the Fox slunk from its hiding place, limp rat dangling from its mouth. It circled the bundle, sniffing cautiously and pulling back, making sure it was not a trap.

A tiny pink fist emerged from the bundle, and then another.
The Fox dropped the rat. "Good evening, baby."

The baby screamed, furious.

"My, my. What a marvellous set of lungs." The Fox edged closer. The baby was just over a year old, with milk-white skin and wisps of dark red hair. It stared up at the Second Guardian with bright, clever green eyes.

The Fox smiled, and lolled its tongue.

The baby laughed.

"Adorable," declared the Fox. "What adventures we might have together. But you heard the woman who dumped you here. First you must survive the night. And who am I to stand in the way of such malignant cruelty?"

The baby whimpered. It was a bitterly cold night, an ice wind blowing in from the sea, sharp as teeth. The whimper turned into a grizzle.

"No, no, that would be cheating, and I never cheat," the Fox replied. "Except when I do."

The baby began to cry, great heartbreaking sobs.

"Emotional manipulation," said the Fox. "I respect that."

It lay down in the rubbish and curled its bushy tail around the baby. It had not yet made a decision; it liked the baby—such verve!—but choosing a new host was a serious matter.

Halfway through the night the baby woke, wailing with hunger. The Fox fed it some chewed up pieces of rat—the best bits, it was feeling generous. When the baby had finished its supper, it wrapped its fists in the Fox's fur and made sweet burbling noises.

"Enchanting," said the Fox, tenderly licking the rat blood from the baby's face. "Very well. I am persuaded."

In the morning, the man and woman returned as promised, wrapped in scarves and breathing clouds from their lips. Snow had fallen in the night, coating the rubbish in a powdery white blanket. It gave the tip an ethereal quality, soft and silent and glittering.

A thin wail pierced the air.

The man and woman looked at each other in astonishment. Last night had been the coldest night in living memory. Surely, there was no chance...

The wail grew louder, more insistent.

They rushed towards it.

There, lying in the snow, they found the baby they had abandoned, alive and well, draped in the gory remains of a giant rat.

"Eight," the man gasped. "Tough little fucker."

The woman lifted the baby from the rubbish and held him up for inspection. "You're a Scrapper now, boy. That's for sure."

"What shall we call him? Needs a new name."

The woman studied the baby—red hair, white belly, white teeth. "Cain," she said. "We'll call him Cain."

> So ends the story of how the Fox crossed the border,
> and found a new home.

Cain dropped the book on to the bed. He felt sick, light-headed.

A trick, it had to be. One of his rivals trying to unsettle him.

So why did that last scene seem so familiar? Why could he remember the feel of warm fur on a freezing night? The smell of rubbish, and the taste of blood...

He rubbed his face. "A story. It's just a story."

At the bottom of the page, a purple-black stain bloomed through the paper like a bruise, and formed a question.

ARE YOU SURE?

Cain snatched up the book and slammed it closed. Something was thrumming inside him. *Told you, told you. Get rid of it.* Holding the book at arm's length, he ran out to the balcony and flung it over the edge.

The book sailed into the grey, pre-dawn sky...and hung there. Covers stretched out like wings. And they were wings, changing before his eyes. The book was no longer a book, but a bird. A raven. It circled the Festival Square, calling him, mocking him. "Fox! Fox!"

Cain staggered back, horrified. When he looked again, the sky was empty.

PART SIX

Day of
the Bear,
Day of
the Monkey

∞

Fifty-Two

"ON YOUR FEET."

Neema woke from a deep slumber, still dressed in yesterday's uniform. The room was dark, shutters closed, but she could make out two shadowed forms at the side of the bed. She groaned and turned. The Hounds again? "What time is it—"

A bucket of iced water sluiced over her.

Neema shrieked. "Fuck the Eight."

One of the intruders lifted her up by her tunic. "Do not blaspheme," he said, and slung her to the floor. She landed hard on her knees.

Another bucket of icy water, this time in the face. She shrieked, more in anger this time. "Stop *doing* that!"

"Then get up, novice!" A different voice, this one female.

Novice? Neema got to her feet, teeth chattering as she rubbed herself warm. She was definitely awake now. Forgotten on the bedside table, Pink-Pink lifted up one foot so he could stamp it back down. His job. His job to wake her. His job, his job.

"What's happening—"

"Silence!"

They shoved her into the living room. The shutters had been pulled back, casting it in the soft grey light of pre-dawn. Her attackers, she saw now, were dressed in contingent uniforms.

Bear warriors.

They stood to attention, hands clasped behind their backs, shoulders squared. "Bear Novice Number Two. You will be silent. You will obey orders. Stand up straight! Follow us."

The Bear Trial, Sol said. He was back in her ribcage, the devious beast. **The Bear Trial has begun.**

—Yes, I got that. Neema ran her hands through her hair, shook the water from her fingers.

You will need some oil for your hair, Neema, and a comb. Preening is important, or you will not look magnificent.

—Sol be quiet, you're not helping.

I understand, I will be very quiet, Sol lied. **You will forget I am here.**

All the palaces had a nickname. The Raven palace was known as the Nest, the Hound palace was the Kennels. The fifth palace was the Fortress. Those who did not walk the Way of the Bear were rarely granted passage through its iron-studded doors. Neema had heard that the interiors were handsome, if austere—limewashed walls and rush matting, plain oak tables and benches, iron sconces and candelabra, heavy stone fireplaces. She'd hoped the Trial would give her the opportunity to see for herself. But as she emerged from the dense evergreen forest that enclosed the palace, she saw that the portcullis was down, the windows shuttered. The warriors who patrolled the battlements and walkways looked sombre. The red and black sigil flag fixed above the entrance had been lowered to half-mast.

For Katsan, their lost Sister. It was too soon for grey mourning patches, but those would follow once she'd reached Anat-garra and fallen into the Bear's embrace. The journey would take her several months, but there was no changing its end.

Neema's escort led her down towards the barracks that lay behind the palace. In the distance, at the edge of more pine forest, the island's north perimeter wall blocked what had once been a fine view of the sea. To the east, the sun was painting the sky a bold orange-pink.

The barracks comprised a collection of low, red-brick buildings set around a small yard. Unlike the Fortress, Neema knew them well. This was where the Bears conducted court business. Just as Emperor Bersun had once chafed against the trappings of his position, so his Brothers and Sisters avoided the gilded halls of the eighth palace. In fact, it was so hard to persuade Bears to live at court, they were sent there on rotation. A posting to the imperial island, it was said, was dreaded more than a posting to the borders of Dolrun. Better the poisoned forest, than the corrupted island.

Neema was surprised to see that the contingent had put out trestle tables, set with a simple but nourishing breakfast. Was it a test? A trick? If it was, nobody had told Cain, their first guest. He had his head down, demolishing a bowl of yoghurt that was meant for the whole table, tipping in extra nuts and berries as he ate. His hair was soaked, his face flushed and bright—more iced water, presumably. To her embarrassment, Neema felt a large, delighted grin spreading across her face. She wiped it away with her hand as she sat down opposite him. She was pleased to see his injuries weren't as bad as they'd seemed the night before—the cut on his lip was already healing well.

"Hey. Good morning."

Cain lowered his spoon. "Sorry," he muttered, to the ground. "Need to focus. Could you…" He gestured for her to move off, further down the table.

Crestfallen, Neema poured herself some coffee and moved along to the next bench.

Oh dear, he is not your friend any more. That is a shame.

—This is a Trial, Sol. We want him to concentrate.

That is a generous way of looking at it, Neema, but you forget I am the Solitary Raven. Abandonment and rejection are very much known to me—

—I can't imagine why.

Perhaps he regrets your mating last night. I only mention this so that you can prepare yourself for the shattering disappointment. A short, cunning pause, a casual preen. **Although, it *may* be for the best, if you detach yourself from him. The path to the throne is narrow, and must be walked alone, as the saying goes.**

—We are not on a path to the throne, Sol.

Look, Neema—the Tiger warrior has arrived.

Neema turned as Ruko entered the yard. Novice Number Three. The Bears were bringing the contenders over in Guardian order. His hair and tunic were also wet, and she wondered how his escort had escaped with their lives. She gestured for him to join her, and after a moment's hesitation, he sat down on the opposite bench.

"Don't talk to me, I'm not talking to anyone," Cain said from the other table.

He's only saying that so you don't feel singled out, Neema.

"So did you kill your escort for chucking ice at you?" Neema asked Ruko. She was only half joking.

He rubbed a hand through his hair, slicking it back. "I doused myself, as ordered."

It was only then Neema realised—oh, right. Everyone else has a contingent to protect them when they're sleeping. Although, wait a minute…

—Sol, why didn't you wake me?

They meant you no harm, I could tell.

—But you saw the bucket of ice. You could have warned me.

Yes Neema, but iced water is a very refreshing and magnificent way to start the day. Also, it was hilarious. Ha ha ha ha—

Neema gave him a very sharp inward glare.

I think I shall visit my field for a while, Sol decided, lifting up from her ribcage.

She sipped her coffee and sighed into the blessed silence. She could feel Ruko studying first her, then Cain. Eventually he leaned in and said, "What happened to Cain's face?"

"Novice Number One," Cain corrected him, head down, eating. "I had a disagreement with a pack of those Samran Hounds."

"About what?"

Cain looked up, briefly. "Whether they should kick the shit out of me or not."

"I'm glad you're okay," Neema said. "I was worried—"

"So they're putting us through a morning's basic training, right?" Cain said, interrupting her. As he talked, he shifted to sit astride his bench, keeping his attention fixed resolutely on Ruko.

Sol was right, Neema thought, downcast. It's only me he's ignoring.

"Every morning, just before dawn, Bear novices plunge themselves in a freezing ice pool. So: we get the bucket of water. Then

breakfast," Cain twirled his spoon at the table, "followed by interrogation and endurance training. Then prayers." He pulled a face,
as if that was by far the worst part.

"Neema." Tala had arrived. Novice Number Four. She strode
straight up to the table. "I need to talk to you."

Neema swung her legs over the bench and followed Tala to a
quiet corner of the yard. They did not see Brother Joran, head of
the Bear contingent, emerge from one of the barrack buildings,
holding a bowl of coffee. A stocky man of middling years, he wore
his greying brown hair loose to his shoulders. Standing a few yards
from them in the doorway, he could not hear their conversation,
but he watched their body language with keen interest, rubbing a
hand through his beard.

Tala had pushed herself uncomfortably close to Neema, shoulders back, squaring off for a fight. "Sunur and I talked things through
after you left. We agreed we should stay together as a family."

Neema patted the air in a placating gesture. "I understand. I'm
sorry Tala, I didn't mean to come between you—"

Tala snatched a note from her pocket. "Read it."

Neema took the note, and read.

> Tala, I love you so much, but
> I have to trust my instincts. I'm so sorry.
> Please forgive me. Sunur xx

"She took Suru." Tala shoved Neema hard in the chest. "They're
gone. Because of you." She clenched her fist.

Neema drew back, hands in a warding position. "I'm sorry. I was
only trying to help."

"Bullshit!" Tala spat. "You're goading me, just like you goaded
Katsan. Playing games. You're more slippery than Cain."

"Tala, I swear on my life, I am not playing games. I genuinely
care about Sunur and—"

"Don't you *dare* say my daughter's name. Don't you *dare*." One
last shove, and the Oxwoman stormed off, back towards the trestle
tables, where Havoc had just arrived.

Neema put her hands on her hips and breathed out slowly, waiting for her heartbeat to slow. She had barely recovered when her two escorts returned and threw a hood over her head.

"Interrogation," they said. "Move."

Hands shoved her roughly on to a stool, in front of a table. The hood was yanked free. It was bright red, slashed with the familiar black claw marks of the Bear sigil. She blinked as her eyes adjusted to the light.

Brother Joran sat across the table from her. He held himself like a priest, hands clasped in front of him, grey-blue eyes soft but searching.

"You're not up to this, are you?" he said.

The gentleness caught her off guard. "No," she admitted, after a moment. Bears valued honesty.

"Your rivals have trained for years. Dedicated their lives to this. And you think you can stroll in and beat them."

"I don't think I can—"

He slammed his hands on the table. "Did I ask you a question?" he roared.

A performance—turning from priest to soldier. It still made her jump.

So it went on, as the sun rose and poured into the hut. They'd positioned her chair so that the light beamed straight into her eyes. *Hands down*, her escort would shout, when she tried to shield herself.

Joran kept up a stream of questions, testing her on her past, her character, her faith. Ethical dilemmas. Failures. Weak spots. Regrets. In between times, without warning, the guards would throw the hood back over her head and run her round the yard. One time, they pushed her head into another bucket of ice. Then back to the questions.

She answered them as truthfully as she could. Maybe it helped her, she thought, that she had visited the barracks before, as a high minister. This was not the first time she had sat across a table from Brother Joran. She knew he valued an open, sincere heart, above all things. Just as the Bear palace liked plain, honestly crafted furniture. No gilding, no embellishments.

More questions—about her family now. She admitted she had not found the time to reply to her mother's last letter, and had forgotten her middle brother's birthday. Joran rubbed his beard, frowning. If he was trying to catch her out, he was failing.

He should ask you a sports question, Sol suggested.

—Oh, you're back, are you?

"Novice Two!" Joran slammed his fists on the table again.

She jerked to attention.

Joran glared at her. "Am I boring you?"

Don't say yes, Neema. This is the test bit.

"I think we're all bored, aren't we?" Neema turned to the two guards at the door.

They glanced at each other. The man gave a slight shrug.

Neema turned back, vindicated. "Look. It's like you said." She spread her hands out on the table. "I'm not up to this."

Neema!

"Don't get me wrong. I don't think I'd be the worst empress in history. I know the law, and I respect it. And I could definitely carry off the robes."

Yes. We would have new ones made, black velvet lined with purple silk and studded with diamonds, and a staff of gold, with a very big diamond on the top—

"But the truth is I don't want the throne. Never have, never will."

Joran leaned forward, interested at last. "So what *do* you want?"

You *do* want the throne, Neema! Tell him you made a mistake. The throne, Neema! That is what you want. Tell him you want—

"Peace," Neema said, closing her eyes. "A quiet, still mind. That is what I would like, Brother Joran. Peace."

When she opened her eyes Joran gave her a half-smile. "Interesting," he murmured, rubbing his beard. "Thank you, Novice Two. You may go."

∞ ∞ ∞

Back in the barracks yard, the contenders stood together in line.

"This Trial is in two parts," Joran told them. "Some of you have fallen behind. Novice One." He stopped in front of Cain, and clicked his fingers in his face. "You were distracted, and evasive. I'd wake up if I were you."

Joran passed by Neema and Ruko and stopped again, this time before Tala. "Novice Four. You wish to rule an empire, but you cannot even rule yourself." He shook his head, disappointed. "Well. We move on. Endurance training. Plain and simple. No tricks, no games. We are Bears, not Foxes." A quiet smile passed through the Bear contingent, standing to attention behind him. "Most of you have spent years preparing for this. You think you're ready. We shall see."

And so the torture began. Press-ups, sit-ups, squats, grab a pack and run round the barracks. After half an hour, Neema's legs were shaking so hard she could hardly walk. But she'd made it. She hadn't given up. Maybe she'd earn a point for her persistence, at least.

"Right," Joran said. "Let's get started."

The other contenders bounced on their toes, stretched their leg muscles, rolled their shoulders in preparation for the real work. Neema stared at them, dismayed. "That…that was the warm-up?"

Shal threw her a sympathetic look. He looked like he'd been for a short stroll to the market.

A Bear soldier dropped a pack at Neema's feet. She swung it on to her back, staggered sideways under the weight, then staggered back into line. Ruko looked down at her, impassive. It was hard to tell, but she thought he might be laughing at her. On the inside.

Joran signalled for them to follow him—he would set the pace. They set off into the evergreens at a fast jog. Crows flapped from the trees, startled.

Yes, go away, stupid crows. Can you believe Neema, crows think they are cleverer than us, and more handsome. Ha ha, stupid, ugly things . . .

Neema stumbled along at the back, panting hard. It wasn't long before she'd lost sight of everyone.

Her female escort was bringing up the rear. She gestured to a track through some bushes. "Keep going. You can catch them."

Neema took a few trembling steps then tripped down the slope into a narrow ditch. She landed on her back, her heavy pack wedged beneath her. She flailed her arms and legs, like a turtle flipped on its shell. No use. She was stuck.

"Could you help?"

The Bear warrior looked down at her from the high ground. "Up to you. You'll be disqualified."

Neema lay still and gazed up at the pines. Her feet were throbbing, everything ached. She could stay here for a bit. What did it matter? Just lie here and rest, breathe in the woodland scents. Listen to the birds.

Neema. Get up.

Neema.

—I can't, Sol.

You're not trying.

Neema made a feeble attempt, then lay back again.

—There, you see? I tried.

Screeeeeeeeeeeeeeeeeeeeeeeeeeeeeeeeeeeeeee eeeeeeeeeeeeeeeeeeeeeeeeeeeeeeeeeeeeeeeeeeee eeeeeeeeeeeeeeeeeeeeeeeeeeeeeee!

Sol's cry pierced her skull like a white hot blade. A pain so terrible nothing else existed. She wanted to die, just to make it stop, please, please make it stop.

The scream faded away. She grabbed desperately at a tree root and hauled herself free.

Keep moving.

She drank some water, the bottle rattling against her teeth.

Keep moving or it will start again.

Neema lurched forward, through the bushes. Her escort lifted her brows in surprise, and followed her.

For the next hour, Neema was plunged into a waking nightmare. Whenever she looked as though she might be giving up, Sol would screech at her. After a while he didn't even need to do that. Neema would sense him filling his lungs and tumble onwards in a panic, drawing on reserves she didn't even know she had. The woods smeared about her, swirls of brown and green and grey. Dimly, she sensed the other contenders as they lapped her, ghosts flitting past. Or perhaps she was the ghost, perhaps she had died and slipped from the Eternal Path into hell.

The swirls of brown and green and grey melded together.

She was on the ground, how was she on the ground, when did that happen? She scrambled desperately to her knees, before Sol could start screaming again. The world spun around her.

"Novice Two." Brother Joran appeared above her. He removed her pack. The relief was so intense, she burst into tears.

"Is it over?"

"It is for you. I admire your grit, but you must learn your limits. You can't rule an empire from the grave."

Her escort lifted her up and helped her slowly back to the barracks.

She was flat on her back in the yard, staring at the sky when Havoc limped over. "Torn a ligament," he said, untying his colours. "That's it for me. I'm done." Not just the Trial, but the Festival. The man who'd dreamed of ruling Orrun since he was six years old, was done.

Neema didn't believe a word of it. An injury in the middle of the woods, when no one was around. How convenient. He didn't look defeated. Even with his swollen nose and black eyes, he looked decidedly pleased with himself. He must have made a deal with the emperor, or with the Tigers.

"Aren't you lucky?" he said, his shadow covering her. They were set to fight each other that afternoon. Two free points for her.

She got to her feet. "What did they promise you, Havoc? Land? High office?"

He looked around, to be sure they weren't overheard. "Are you accusing me of something?"

"You killed Gaida. And now you're leaving the Trials—I presume to help Ruko."

Havoc folded his arms across his broad chest. "That's quite an accusation. Where's your proof?"

"You know I don't have any." She glared at him.

"If you're looking for remorse, I wouldn't bother," he said, and laughed. "Eight. You're such a hypocrite. You hated her."

"She didn't deserve to die."

"Gaida Rack was a traitor, who conspired against the emperor. If I *had* killed her, I would be proud of my actions. But as we both know," a slow grin, "she killed herself."

There was a commotion on the other side of the yard as Cain and Ruko arrived back, followed closely by Shal and Tala. They flung off their packs, connected for once in their exhaustion, their shared relief that the Trial was almost over.

Havoc watched them with a smug, hidden expression.

"What?" Neema said.

"I was just thinking of something the emperor taught me. You can't win the game if you don't know the rules."

He walked on. He didn't bother to limp.

"This Trial tested your physical and mental endurance," Joran said, when the five remaining contenders were back in line. "We looked for the qualities we expect from our novices. Honesty, respect, determination. Above all, the ability to maintain self-discipline, in the most extreme situations. With that in mind." He stopped in front of Ruko. "Congratulations, Contender Valit."

Neema was next, to her astonishment. Joran patted her shoulder. "Good effort." He turned to Cain. "Your lack of focus cost you, but you have impressive endurance skills, Fox contender. Three points."

Shal was next, and Tala was last with one point. "For what it's worth, Contender Talaka, I believe the Raven contender was being honest with you, earlier. But even if she *was* playing games," a glance down the line at Neema, "this is the Festival of the Eight. No excuses."

Tala gritted her teeth. "Thank you for the lesson, Brother Joran."

Joran locked eyes with her. "Fear controlled you today, contender."

"I was worried about—"

"Fear born from love is the most dangerous kind. The most volatile," Joran said, gently. "Be wary."

The contenders were presented with a campaign pack as a Festival gift, with survival rations, leather water pouch, a tinderbox and a brass compass. The Trial was at an end. "You are free to go," Brother Joran told them. "But perhaps you will stay a few moments and say a prayer for our Sister, Katsan Brundt."

They bowed their heads—contenders and contingent together. The bell rang out from the bell tower, slow and mournful. A funeral toll, for one yet living.

When the prayers were over, Joran and the rest of the contingent gave a smart Bear salute, and marched off to the barracks.

The line broke up. Neema touched Cain's wrist. He flinched, and stepped back. "Sorry. Have to be somewhere." He ran off.

She walked slowly through the woods, heartsore. Clearly he *was* regretting last night. To be fair, his distraction had cost him today—he was now trailing Ruko by one point. Her own accidental success hadn't helped, either.

Which reminded her.

She sat down under a tall pine tree, dropped her pack at her feet. The sun threw dappled light through the branches, the air smelled fresh and green. Amazing how pleasant the woods could be, when you weren't being tortured.

—Sol?

He'd been *very* quiet since she'd passed out in the woods. Almost as if he knew he'd gone too far, and was hoping Neema had forgotten about it.

Hello, yes?

She touched her chest. —You need my permission to stay in here, right?

Sol, perched on his favourite rib, clenched and unclenched his claws anxiously. **I was trying to help—**

—Get out.

Sol shuffled along Neema's rib, closer to her warm, beating heart. He gave his wings a half-hearted flap. **You want me to leave?**

—Yes.

Right now? Or later? I think later, Neema—
"Now!"

Sol cringed. He was very good at cringing, very practised. **As you wish.**

Neema felt a sharp pain, exactly like a bird piercing through her chest with its beak. Black, oily blood gushed through the gaping wound. We shall spare you the rest, as before. What you shouldn't do is imagine a slopping purple-black blancmange, with a gristly spine, vomiting itself into being. Don't imagine that.

The semi-formed thing splatted on to her pack and slowly reconstituted itself into a large raven. Sol shook out his feathers.

I shall go, you are sure?

His voice in her head, but no longer humming along her bones. She looked at him. Folded her arms.

He tested his wings. Walked up and down in front of her a couple of times, making forlorn, tragic noises. No. It wasn't working. Very well, he knew when he was banished, this was not new territory for the Solitary Raven.

Goodbye then, Neema.

A snap of wings. A rush of air. And he was gone.

CHAPTER
Fifty-Three

WHEN THE CONTENDERS reached the Festival Square they found the stalls empty and the fight platform dismantled. In their place, a troop of Samran Hounds performed a sequence of elaborate drills, turning, shifting and merging in tight, scripted unison.

Shal watched them with a frown, as if they were an equation he could not quite solve. "What's going on?" he muttered.

Tala took off her headband and scrubbed a hand through her hair. She was still out of sorts. "They're your people, Shal. Why don't you ask them?"

The Hound contender's eyes gleamed, then faded. "They're not my people."

"The morning fights have been cancelled." Vabras was sitting in the contenders' pavilion, working at a portable desk. He smiled thinly as they finally noticed him.

The departure of Havoc and Katsan had provided an opportunity to improve the schedule. With the number of fights reduced by half to four, they could all take place together, in the afternoon. "A chance for you to rest and recover," Vabras said.

"No one thought to tell us?" Tala snapped.

The High Commander did not look up from his work. "I am telling you."

Neema gritted her teeth in alarm as Tala pressed on, angrily. "The whole court knew before us." She waved to the empty stalls. "You could have sent a message instead of letting us turn up here like idiots."

Silence, except for the scraping of Vabras's pencil. He was writing out the new fight schedule, one copy for each of them. Somewhere within that silence, that whispering scrape of pencil on paper, Tala understood she had made a mistake. A bad one.

"High Command—"

"Contender Talaka," Vabras interrupted, with perfect timing. He kept on writing. "Your wife left the island this morning without permission, taking your child with her. If it were down to me," a lift of an eyebrow, "I would have her tracked down and charged with sedition."

Tala clenched her fists. "My wife is a loyal citizen—"

"She disobeyed a direct imperial order." Vabras put down his pencil. "People have been hanged for less."

"*Oof,*" Cain breathed.

Shal, pretending to rub his beard, traced a discreet sign of the eight over his lips.

"Luckily for your wife, *and your child,*" the emphasis Vabras made was chilling, "his majesty has more important things on his mind. You are beneath his interest. For now." He held out the schedules for Neema to collect. She took one, and passed them along.

With his usual grim efficiency, Vabras had reduced the contenders down to their Guardian name:

FOX VS RAVEN
OX VS HOUND
TIGER VS DRAGON
(QUARTER HOUR BREAK)
FOX VS HOUND

Shal read it through first. "What's the break for?"

"Ruko's funeral," Cain said.

"The Hound and the Fox—" Vabras began.

Cain stiffened. "Don't call me that."

"—have two fights this afternoon. Your respective contingents petitioned for the break."

"Does the Monkey Trial remain the same?" Ruko asked.

"If it had changed, I would have said so." Vabras rose from his desk, and turned to Neema. "You failed to submit anything for the exhibition, Contender Kraa. I presume you forgot, amid all the…"

He ran his tongue over his teeth, considering how to encapsulate everything Neema had been subjected to, these past four days. "...drama."

Neema hadn't forgotten. She'd deliberately ignored Kindry's request for a selection of her calligraphy work. Sabotaging herself, to help Cain.

"I sent over six pieces from the imperial archives on your behalf," Vabras said, turning to leave. "I am no judge of such things, but I'm told they should suffice."

Neema poured herself a glass of water, waiting for another attack from Tala, but the Ox contender was distracted by the Samran Hounds. They had moved on to a weapons drill, swords flashing as their commander inspected their form, up and down the rows. Cain draped an arm over Tala's shoulder and whispered something reassuring before drawing her away. Neema felt an irrational stab of jealousy.

Ruko was also walking away, which left only Shal. "These Samrans," he said, from the corner of his mouth. "I don't like what I see in them. What I *don't* see in them," he corrected himself. "They've been counter-trained, against Houndsight." He moved a hand across his face. Blank.

"I didn't know that was possible."

"Their commander has the Sight. I suppose they practised on him." He paused. "This story about Gaida. They're saying she killed herself."

"No. She loved life. She loved herself." Neema winced. "That came out wrong."

Shal laughed. "No, no. You're right. Gaida had a healthy respect for her own..."

"Magnificence."

"Right." Shal laughed again. "Her own magnificence. And Katsan?"

Neema hesitated. She trusted Shal, but she was conscious now of the Hound commander out in the square. She waited until his attention was elsewhere and said, "She'll take a message to the Bears. There are things...I can't speak openly, Shal."

He lifted a hand—no need. "'A chance for you to rest and re-cover,'" he said, quoting Vabras.

Neema had noticed that too—an odd phrase from the man who never seemed to rest. A man who would never alter a schedule if he could avoid it.

"'A chance for *you*,'" Shal repeated. "He was looking at Ruko."

Ruko had been due to fight the Visitor this morning, straight after the gruelling Bear Trial. With Havoc's removal, Ruko now had time to recuperate. Havoc was the emperor's man. His withdrawal from the Festival must have come as an imperial order. For some reason, Vabras and the emperor wanted Ruko to win, and were working behind the scenes to make that happen. But why? Had they made a pact with the Tigers? Even with all that she knew, it seemed an unlikely alliance. And Ruko did not strike her as a man willing to share power.

"Why didn't you leave with Sunur, and Suru?" Shal asked.

Neema shook her head. "Vabras said it. They're beneath his notice. I'm not." She finished her water. Time to head over to the Monkey palace, for the first part of the Trial. She looked at Shal, curious. "What did you submit?"

"Watercolours." His expression darkened. "I wanted to paint her. What they did to her." Yana. Never far from the Hound contender's mind. "But I couldn't do that, obviously, so...I painted the forest. I painted Dolrun. Let them fill in the rest."

∞ ∞ ∞

"Astonishing," Lady Harmony Arbell-Ranor declared, touching a slender, jewelled hand to her throat. She stepped closer, then stepped back, studying Neema's work from different angles. The six long scrolls had been mounted expertly on silk and suspended from the ceiling. Lady Harmony walked through them, as if she were walking through a magic forest. "Exquisite," she murmured.

Early afternoon in the Monkey palace, in a wooden lodge flooded with light and crammed with people. The first half of the Sixth Trial was underway, and it was indeed a trial—the contenders standing awkwardly next to their work as Monkey courtiers came by to tilt their heads, and nod sagely, and whisper opinions in each other's ears.

Lady Harmony peered at a modern poem translated into the ancient pictorial style. An experiment Neema had tried out one evening, simply to pass the time.

Lady Harmony spanned her hand, and waved it over the piece, sanctifying it. "This is a great work. This is the best of them." She turned, with reluctance, to the artist. "Who taught you?"

"Me." Neema laughed, touching her chest. "I taught myself."

"No. You had a teacher." Lady Harmony's blue chiffon scarf had slid across one shoulder. She adjusted it.

"I learned the basics at school, in Scartown. My teacher there, Madam Fessi Aark—"

"Fessi Casinor," Lady Harmony's eyelashes fluttered as she made the connection. The Casinors were a Venerant family. Aark was her Raven name. "Of course. She set up a school in the slums."

"They weren't slums—"

"Darling, you abandoned me." Lord Clarion glided up and kissed his wife on the mouth.

"No darling." She tugged playfully at his greying curls. "You abandoned me."

They laughed, delighted with each other.

Lord Clarion stepped back to assess Neema's work.

"Look at this one, darling," Lady Harmony drew him over to her favourite. "A modern verse, but written in the ancient style."

"Fascinating."

"It's about the yearning for a golden age."

"It really isn't," Neema said.

"You see the clarity of the strokes, the balance, the spacing. The artist is telling us we must look to our ancestors. We must restore the natural order of those days."

"No, I'm not."

Lady Harmony rubbed her husband's back. "She is oblivious to the meaning, of course. An instinctive artist, as one must expect from one of her level. It is for us to read the message."

"Fascinating," Lord Clarion mused. "Fascinating."

They strolled off together, hand in hand, to view Tala's pottery.

CHAPTER
Fifty-Four

"I F YOU'RE HAVING second thoughts," Neema said, deflecting an elbow strike. "Just tell me."

"I'm not having second thoughts." Cain tried a jab to the ribs. "Can we talk about this later?"

"When? You've been avoiding me all day."

He pushed her backwards. As she fell, she snatched his waistband and dragged him down on top of her.

They looked at each other.

"That was not a fight move," he said.

They wrestled on the ground for a bit. In the crowds someone said, "Eight, I don't know where to look," and her friend said, "Yes you do, Jandra."

Cain was winning, no question. But Neema, who had every intention of losing, had still got in a couple of accidental strikes. The Raven warrior style she'd absorbed from Sol was as persistent and devious as he was, and it was becoming second nature the more she used it. She would make a defensive move, it would open up an opportunity and…it was hard to resist a *quick* jab. A rake of the fingernails.

The bell rang, ending the first round. Vabras waited for them to get to their feet, then called out the winner. "Raven contender."

"What?" Cain rounded on him.

In the stalls, people stood up to show their disapproval. They wouldn't boo the High Commander, they weren't idiots. Instead they called "Fox!" and waved orange ribbons in support.

"You're not serious, Vabras?" Cain gestured to the crowds. "I won that round—they all saw it. Listen to them."

Vabras turned to consider the crowds in each of the three stalls, singling out the louder members for attention. As he caught their eye they fell silent, and sat down. Lowered their orange ribbons.

Cain strode back to his corner, scrubbing his hands through his hair in frustration.

Ish Fort climbed the steps to join him, hood pulled low to conceal his expression. The Fox abbot was not happy. "You're letting her distract you."

"It's not her." It was that book. That bird. *That story*. He couldn't shake it from his mind. But he couldn't tell Fort that. "The fight's rigged. What do you expect me to do?"

Fort thrust a pair of daggers at his chest. "Whatever it takes," he snapped. Under his hood, his eyes were blazing.

Cain turned the daggers and offered them back, hilt first. "We said batons."

Fort strode away, back down the steps.

Cain looked down at his contingent. They were all wearing the same resolute expression. Three of them were sitting on his weapons chest, arms folded. *Whatever it takes.*

The bell rang for round two.

Neema's weapons had been returned to her chest overnight. They wanted her to win this time. She had selected the war fans again, holding them closed up like sticks. Defence only, she promised herself.

Then she saw the daggers.

"I'm sorry," Cain said, and lunged forward.

Snapping open a fan, she blocked the strike. The dagger scraped across the iron ribs with an ugly sound. Cain's face was set. No conversation, no distraction.

They settled into the fight. Neema made no attempts to advance, but she was defending herself too well. Cain needed a definitive win. He had to make a move. He had to keep her safe.

Disarm her. Both weapons. Even Vabras couldn't deny that.

He lunged again. Deflecting his blade, Neema caught the back of his hand with the edge of her fan, drawing a thin line of red. She closed both fans, turning them back into batons. "Sorry."

He licked the blood from his hand.

A shiver, a ripple. A voice, closer than it should be.

Did she hurt you, my friend? Let me help.

Cain blinked, and his eyes shifted from green to yellow. Pupils a vertical slit. The eyes of a fox.

The eyes of the Fox.

It smiled, tongue licking its teeth, and threw the dagger.

Neema's reaction was too slow. Some part of her still saying, even as the blade flew from his hand—*Cain would never do that.* As another part of her answered—*That's not Cain.*

Panicked, she lifted her fan to deflect the blade—and nicked the side of her neck with her own weapon. The razor-sharp edge sliced through her skin, opening a long, neat tear along her throat. Blood streamed from the wound.

Cain was in the air, leaping high, his second dagger in his fist.

His eyes shifted mid leap, back to green—and he saw Neema, bleeding and terrified below him. No. He twisted out of the way and landed hard on his knees beside her. The blade skittered across the platform, out of reach.

The bell rang out.

"Neema."

She put a hand to her neck, eyes wide with shock, blood streaming over her fingers.

He crawled over to her. "I'm so sorry. I'm so sorry. Everything went blank. Neema, I would never…I would *never…*"

Medics arrived to inspect the injury. It was serious—she needed urgent attention or the wound could tear further.

Vabras considered for a long moment, then turned to the crowds. "Victory to the Fox contender."

Cheers and orange ribbons.

The medics walked Neema to their white canvas tent and got to work cleaning her self-inflicted wound. They told her she was lucky she hadn't hit an artery. Cain arrived, in a terrible state. "I'm so sorry…I'm so sorry…" She sent him off to make some tea. He needed to do something to help, and she needed time to think, to understand what had just happened. As a nurse dabbed numbing cream on the wound she dropped into a trance, returning to that moment on the platform...

Yellow eyes. A sharp grin. A dagger sailing towards her.

Yellow eyes. A sharp grin...

"We're done," the nurse said, tying off her stitches. "Thanks for sitting so still." He dabbed more ointment on to the wound, and fixed a bandage. Another scar to add to her growing collection. She'd be as battered as Tala before the Festival was through.

Cain returned with a pot of green tea and sat down next to her on the bench. He moved to take her hand, then thought better of it. "I'm so sorry, Neema. I was standing there with both blades in my hand. And the next thing I knew..." He gave her an anguished look. "I could have killed you."

"It wasn't you. You didn't throw the dagger."

"But—"

"It wasn't you. It was the Fox."

He froze.

That confirmed it. "You knew, didn't you? That's why you've been avoiding me."

He rubbed his face, to stop the tears from forming. "Early this morning. There was a book lying on my bed. A book that was also...Look, this sounds insane but..."

"It was also a bird," Neema finished, for him. *A bird I am going to throttle the next time I see it.* "We've met, unfortunately."

"Oh," Cain said. "Right. Well...it told me a story about the Fox. How it lives in this world by jumping from host to host. Except it's not a story, Neema. I don't know how to explain it, but there is *something* inside me." He pressed a hand to his stomach. He was trembling—she'd never seen him so scared, so off-kilter.

"You have a fragment of the Fox inside you." It made perfect sense; Cain was the most fox-like Fox there was.

"Not just a fragment, Neema. All of them. 'All the Foxes that were, all the Foxes that are, all the Foxes that will be.'"

Neema's throat closed. She had asked Sol—does Cain have a fragment of the Fox in him, and he had paused before saying no.

Not *one* fragment. All of them. Scheming, devious creature. That's why he didn't want Cain to win the throne. He'd known the Fox was right there with him. The First Guardian. And the man she loved. "Cain," she said, and wrapped a hand around his wrist. She couldn't imagine what that revelation was doing to him.

"It's been there for a very long time, hidden away. Some part of me knew, I think—on the deepest level. But this is different. Now I can sense it. And it can sense me. We're both awake at the same time and that is *bad*, Neema. That is *not* supposed to happen." He pulled away from her, sliding further down the bench. "The boundaries have blurred. I can feel it testing them, trying to slip through. That's what it does, that's its nature. But if it takes over…" He recoiled at the thought. "You have to keep away from me. I'm not safe to be around."

"Cain, listen to me." She took his hand again, and pressed it to her heart. "I am not afraid of you. I trust you."

He smiled, sadly. "That's the problem. I don't."

Fifty-Five

T HE HEAT HAD been building all day. A dry, furnace wind blasted through the square, so rare for the island that it felt uncanny. Perhaps it was. Beyond the perimeter walls, the sea was still and flat. The Leviathans anchored in its waters were like paintings against the sky. Nothing stirred. Only here, in the Festival Square, did the wind scorch the air.

This was the weather of Helia. The weather of Dragons.

The Visitor entered the square to silence. He was clean-shaven, his grey hair cropped even shorter than usual. The crowd watched him as they might a viper winding purposely across their path.

They had seen little of him in the last few days, not since his enforced separation from his contingent. The Dragons had withdrawn to their rooms in protest, Jadu and the Visitor in the eighth palace, the rest still hosted in the temple. When he reached the pavilion, he took his place at the end of a line that did not exist. Cain was huddled on the floor in the shade, as far from Neema as possible. Ruko was meditating on his knees, preparing himself for the fight of his life. The invisible wall he had built around himself was even thicker than usual; no one went near him.

They were waiting for Tala and Shal, not that the Visitor asked. Tala had brought her anger and frustration with her to the fight, landing Shal in the medical tent with a broken collarbone and a couple of cracked ribs. The medics would not allow him back on the platform to fight Cain. This next fight would be the last of the day. The one everyone had been waiting for since the Festival began. Tiger versus Dragon.

Cain got to his feet, and approached the Visitor. The Dragon Proxy's eyes were closed, his face serene. He had entered a quiet place, a temple hush within him.

"You knew," Cain said. "Ever since I ate that poisoned stew. You knew what was wrong with me."

"There is nothing wrong with you," the Visitor murmured. "You are what you are."

"You treated me differently on the platform. I couldn't understand it then, but now I do. You were afraid of me."

The Visitor opened his eyes. "I do not fear you, Cain Ballari. But I respect the great power you contain."

Cain clutched the sigil on his chest—half-moon, half-sun. "How do I get rid of it?"

Somewhere deep and intangible, a pair of ears twitched. A yellow eye opened wide. A set of claws raked down his soul. *What is this now, dear one? You would get rid of me...?*

The Visitor made a swift, snaking sign of the eight; a rare flash of alarm. "You do not. You must make peace with your...guest. Restore the balance."

"What if I can't?"

The Visitor closed his eyes again. "Then it will destroy you."

Tala and Shal returned to the black silk pavilion. Shal's arm was in a sling. Tala looked at it, shamefaced. They were both sweating profusely from the short walk. "It's deadly out there," Shal said. "Like a blast from a blacksmith's forge." He poured himself some water, held it to his lips, then tipped it over his head instead.

There was a jagged energy to the pavilion. No one liked Ruko much. No one liked the Visitor either. But still. Two would walk out, one would come back. Neema found herself sizing them up, those two very different warriors, then stopped herself with a shiver.

Ruko strode barefoot into the broiling heat. The Visitor glided after him. He could not draw on the powers that had protected him for most of his life. Ruko was half his age and twice his size. But this heat. This heat would surely favour the Dragon Proxy.

"Who do you think will win?" Cain asked the line. No one answered. Because what he was really asking was, *Who do you think will die?*

"You should pray for them, Shal," Tala said. "You're the most faithful among us." Her voice was tentative—still feeling guilty for the way she'd treated him on the platform.

Shal took a long time to answer. They knew why he struggled. He could never forgive Ruko for what he'd done to Yana. And yet his faith told him he must find compassion, even for his enemies. "I shall pray that death is swift, and painless," he said, eventually. It was the best he could do.

Fifty-Six

THE FIRST THING Ruko saw as the bell rang was his mother. She had timed it perfectly, waiting until the last moment to take her seat. Reserved specially for her in the centre of the sixth row, it placed her directly in Ruko's line of sight.

The bell rang, and he saw her. He pretended he had not. An act that convinced everyone except the two people that mattered —Yasila and the Visitor. They both caught the minute hesitation, followed by a quick push forward to cover it.

Ruko had spent years strengthening his peripheral vision, and now it worked against him. As the fight pressed on, he could not help but catch glimpses of his mother, a jigsaw puzzle he didn't want to solve. Her ephemeral, sea-green dress. The loops of pearls in her hair. Her quiet, patient smile.

She wants me dead, he thought. And then, with sudden clarity: *She has orchestrated it.*

Yasila was flanked by two hooded members of the Dragon contingent. Her old enemies, now allies, unified in their desire to destroy him. The Visitor kicked him hard in the stomach, sending him reeling back. His mother applauded, cheering on the man sent to kill him. The man who had once broken Ruko's arm, for trying to protect her.

He could be forgiven. The man who threatened to kill her children.

But not me. I must be the monster, for ever.

It didn't hurt him, he wouldn't let it. But her presence kept him from reaching that perfect, unassailable place he always found, deep within a fight. An immersion so complete, he could disappear within it. He, Ruko, ceased to exist. He became a weapon of pure will. But not today, when it mattered most. Not with his mother distracting him, there on the borders of his mind and vision. Would she use her binding spell? Was she close enough? Would she dare? He thought not, but he couldn't be sure.

Which was precisely why she was sitting there, smiling, her hands folded neatly in her lap. He was fighting not one opponent but two.

They were less than a minute into the round when Ruko realised he was going to die. The Visitor had hidden his skills well these past few days. Now they were revealed. Even stripped of his powers he was a master, his technique honed over decades. But what made him unbeatable was the blazing intensity of his purpose. Nothing mattered more to him in all the world than Ruko's death.

Am I so terrible?

He blocked a deadly strike to the throat, but missed the jab that followed—a reeling blow to the temple. His mother clapped.

He fought back, but it was like fighting quicksilver. By the time the bell rang, Ruko was battered and bleeding, panting from the effort of staying on his feet, his tunic soaked with sweat.

The crowd was near silent as the Visitor left the platform to choose his weapons. Death was circling the square, everyone could feel it. Excitement passed through the stalls, spiky and restless. Some abandoned their seats, treading on their neighbours' toes in their haste to leave. Most stayed where they were. This fight was always going to end this way. Foolish, really, that they'd ever thought differently. A *Visitor.*

"Do you see his mother over there?" someone whispered. "Sitting with the Dragons?"

"She wants him dead." For that unspeakable thing he did. "Who can blame her?"

Rivenna was waiting at the bottom of the platform as Ruko descended. "No," he said, as she started to speak. The abbess retreated, ordering her contingent back with her. She had seen this mood in her Guardian-son before. Best to let him be. Trust in the eight years of intense training she had given him. But for the first time, she looked anxious.

Ruko peeled off his tunic and rinsed out his bleeding mouth with water. His chest was sore, his ribs ached. The only thing that had saved him so far was his combat-honed physique. That would not be enough, come the next round.

He needed a new strategy, fast.

Panicking would not help. Focus. He sat down, his back against the weapons chest, and closed his eyes. Found the voice that was always waiting for him; the only thing he trusted.

—Why is he winning?

Because he has to. He gave up his powers for this moment. It is his sole reason for being.

—How do I defeat him?

Find something you need more. What do you need, Ruko?

—The throne. As Ruko answered he remembered the message Benna had brought him, from Yana. *You don't want to rule the empire, not really. You just think you do, because that's what your father wanted.* —The throne, he answered again, more firmly. But for the first time, he wondered.

The voice cut through again, pushing him to search deeper. To find the truth that could save him. *What do you* need, *Ruko?*

Ruko lowered his head. His mind was blank, his heart was blank, his soul was blank. He stood upon the golden rope and felt the void, all around him.

—I don't know.

Then you will die.

Ruko opened his eyes.

He opened the weapons chest and took out his sword. He had a hundred phrases he could tell himself, positive affirmations he had learned specifically for this moment. They wouldn't work.

He headed back up the steps, a condemned man. The Visitor was waiting on the other side of the platform, twin blades in hand. His wrists turned smoothly, carving neat figures of eight in the air.

"Why?" Ruko asked him. In defeat, he found himself curious. "Why does this matter to you so much? What has she promised you?" His mind whirred, answering his own question. What could Yasila offer the Dragons, but the one thing they had always wanted. The Dragonscale she stole from them. Ruko huffed in disbelief. "You don't really think she'll hand it over, do you? Her one hold over you?"

The Visitor moved into a hanging stance, and waited for the bell. *If you seek answers, do not ask a Dragon.*

Ruko lifted his gaze to the stalls, searching for his mother. She stared into the middle distance, hands still folded in her lap. He felt an ache he had not felt in years. Could she give him nothing? Not one glance, before he died?

A vendor leaned into Yasila's row, offering a tray of snacks. The hooded Dragon seated next to the princess pushed the girl away, back towards the aisle.

No one ever looks at a servant.

Ruko looked. He saw her. And broke into a smile.

Benna grinned back and waved. Her hair was tucked up in a cap, and she was wearing spectacles as a disguise. She pointed at herself, and jogged on the spot. *I escaped, thank you!* Then she pointed at him, mimed a very bad double punch, and gave a thumbs-up. Mouthed: *"Amazing"* and gave another thumbs-up.

It was absurd. Wildly inappropriate. And hilarious. Yasila staring mid-distance, cool and regal and unforgiving. Benna doing what appeared to be a jig of encouragement in the aisle next to her. Ruko looked between the two women, then snorted back a laugh, covering his mouth with the back of his hand.

He used to laugh like that, before. He'd forgotten.

"Team Ruko!" Benna shouted, cupping her hand to her mouth. Then she scarpered down the stairs with her tray and vanished, like a dream.

That was what he needed.

Fifty-Seven

F OR ONE TO LIVE, another must die.

Yasila held her friend's hand, in a quiet room. "I could bind the wound," she said.

He shook his head, smiling through the pain. The Dragon was coming for him—to delay its arrival was not the way of things.

Somewhere deep in the weapons round, the Visitor had made a mistake. He used the same feint he'd made in another fight. Foolish. Fatal. Ruko evaded the true strike, stepped in smoothly, and sliced his sword along the Visitor's waist. That first wound had slowed him down. The second was much deeper. The second was killing him.

"Something happened, before the second bell. A shift in his spirit. I fought a different man."

Yasila's face hardened. "I saw no change in him. He is Rivenna's creature. She has sculpted him in his father's image."

"Then it is over. I have failed."

"No. This was my mistake. All of it. Never yours."

The Visitor closed his eyes, fighting a fresh wave of pain. He groaned softly, then fell silent. For a moment she thought she had lost him, but his chest still rose and fell. He was still with her. She stared at his collarbone, his jawline. When she was younger, she had stared so often at those same places, imagining how it would feel to touch them. She had wanted him so much. They were too young, too shy. A lifetime ago. A lifetime gone.

"Pyke," she said, and he half-opened his eyes. A soft grey. They had been a dark amber, when she knew him best. But they were lovely, like this. "I am sorry for the hurt I have caused you."

"You brought me more happiness than hurt, Yasila."

"I do not believe that."

He looked at her, and the door to his heart was open. "The only good memories I have, my whole life, are of you." He touched his scar, her initial. Smiled. "Perhaps not...this one."

She smiled back, as her heart broke.

Another bout of pain took him. She held his hand, wondering if this would be the time. Praying to the Dragon, not yet, not yet. Give me one more moment. You owe me that. You, who have taken so much from me.

The Visitor emerged from his battle visibly weaker. He traced an eternal eight on her hand with his thumb.

"We shall meet again on the Path," he whispered. "I know this. Yasila."

He fell still.

She kissed him then, on his forehead. Buried her head in his neck. "Stay, stay," she said, as if she could bind him to life. But he was already gone.

Fifty-Eight

THEN IT REALLY is down to me, Neema thought.

The news of the Visitor's death had stunned her, as it had stunned everyone. Now that he was gone she realised that —deep down—she had been relying on him to win. The Visitor would kill Ruko, Cain would take the throne, and she would… What? Go back to the library, and write her monograph? She had been deluding herself. The Raven had chosen her to save the world. Not Cain, not the Visitor. Her. It was time she accepted that.

The Raven had offered her the chance to stop Ruko on the fight platform, and she had refused. If she didn't keep him from the throne, she would be to blame for everything that came next. And now she had caught a glimpse of the creature lurking inside of Cain, she couldn't risk helping him, either. Emperor Cain was one thing. But the Fox, the actual *Fox*, ruling Orrun?

So Neema came to the reluctant conclusion that Sol—curse him—was right. The only way to stop Ruko, and save Orrun, save *the world*, was to do the unthinkable. She would have to take the throne for herself.

∞ ∞ ∞

Of all the palaces, the Monkey palace was by far the most welcoming. Designed as a haven from the rigours of court life, its lodges blended into the surrounding woodland as if they had grown from the trees that held them. With its theatres, craft workshops, food stalls and taverns, the sixth palace was the closest thing the island had to a town square. It just happened that much of the square lay nestled up in the canopy.

The Monkey contingent had ordered the construction of a new lodge for the Festival. Tucked within the branches of an old yew tree, its platform overlooked the open-air theatre below. From here, the contenders would descend for the second part of the Monkey Trial. For now they waited, as the crowds streamed through the woods below to take their seats.

Neema watched them, hands gripping the wooden platform rail. The moon, almost full, was rising above the trees, silvering the rope walkways and ladders that connected the lodges together. Directly beneath her, servants fixed torches around the stage's perimeter: two circles, forming an eternal eight.

She was alone out here, apart from Ruko. He was sitting at the far end of the platform, legs dangling over the edge, forehead pressed against the rail. The cost of his victory weighed upon on him, literally—he was physically bowed. Not just from his injuries—though he had certainly taken a battering. Something deeper—some inner crisis. She fought the instinct to go over to him. If she was going to win, she had to start behaving like a true contender.

She looked back through the door, to study the others. *Her rivals*. Cain was running through a sequence of acrobatic fight moves—a distraction technique. Tala, who preferred to keep her feet on solid ground, was huddled in the middle of the lodge, as far away from the windows as possible.

Shal, catching Neema's eye, came out to join her. Despite the sling, he seemed the least damaged of them all. He smelled and looked good, his dark curls rubbed through with almond oil, his beard freshly trimmed. Square diamond studs in his ears. He turned his face to gaze up at the stars; the dazzling spread of constellations. "How do we compete with that?"

"Five points to Nature."

He laughed, but kept his eyes on the stars.

Are we allies? Neema wondered. Is that how this works? She could imagine Shal as High Commander of Orrun, much more easily than she could imagine herself on the throne. But somehow she had to start believing it.

"Did you hear Benna escaped?" Shal said, then smiled at her surprise. "I recognised her the moment I saw her." He tapped his finger next to his eyes.

"Why didn't you say anything?"

His smile faded.

Yana. "Because she saved her life," Neema said, softly.

Shal took a moment to collect himself. "Not just that. Those last days in the village…Benna was a light in the darkness. Whatever she wanted to do to me, to any of us," a narrow glance, at Ruko, "I wasn't about to stop her. We got off lightly, don't you think? I mean look at us. The three of us. Look where we are. Not in spite of what we did, but because of it."

"Like weeds on a grave," Neema murmured. And then, because she was a scholar, "I should say that was Gaida's line." One should always name one's sources.

They both fell silent. Shal slapped a mosquito.

"The theatre's full," Neema said, and felt a twinge of nerves. As well as the raised benches at ground level, there were further viewing platforms and galleries in the surrounding trees. Music wafted up—the emperor's anthem, signalling his arrival.

"Ready?" Shal asked.

Neema pulled a face. *Improvised performance*: that had been the alarming note from Lord Clarion. As they took the stage, each contender would be given a theme to explore as they wished: through dance, song, poetry, oratory. This was Neema's worst anxiety dream brought to life. All she had to do was inexplicably lose her trousers and the nightmare would be complete.

Above the stage, trapeze artists flew through the air, while jugglers tossed flaming torches below.

"She would have loved this," Shal said. Yana. Always Yana.

They headed inside.

Ruko, forgotten in the dark, rose to his feet and looked down. "Yes," he said softly. "She would."

∞ ∞ ∞

"All hail His Majesty, Emperor Bersun the Second!"

"See how Orrun is restored in his name!"

There was no room to kneel on the packed benches. People rose to their feet and cheered their emperor as if he were the first act of the evening.

He smiled and put a hand to his chest, to show that he was touched. "I shall be brief."

Everyone laughed indulgently at the same old joke.

"I've heard the Monkey Trial referred to as the easy Trial. Well. Not for this Bear." He held up a finger, and everyone laughed harder. Bersun had collected just one point from his Sixth Trial, back when he was competing for the crown. "I've come to believe it is the most important Trial of all. An emperor must be able to express himself clearly. Think creatively. Command attention." He paused, to make his point. There was silence in the clearing.

"My friends, this has been a tough Festival in many ways. But it has also been fair, and open. The most important duty of any leader is to oversee his own peaceful succession. Tomorrow, Orrun will have a new, legitimate ruler. Tomorrow, I shall lay down my burdens," he touched the iron band of his crown, "and be Brother Bersun once more. But tonight…" He smiled. "I am glad to spend my last evening as emperor with you. May the Eight bless you all."

"And remain Hidden."

The crowds were moved, many of them to tears. The emperor had become a regular visitor to the sixth palace in recent years —he was well loved here. They were still recovering when Lord Clarion—master of ceremonies—called the first contender to the stage. Cain.

Lord Clarion tipped over a sand-timer—another eternal eight, formed from the glass. Eight minutes. Then he went out into the benches, and encouraged an ancient Tiger courtier to select a scroll from a jewelled box. Perching his glasses on his nose, the Tiger unfurled the tiny scroll and read out the one-word subject in a frail voice. Lord Clarion repeated it for the benefit of the audience. "Respect."

A spattering of laughter—not the ideal subject for a Fox. But Cain would use that to his favour. Easier to impress an audience when their expectations were low. Moving smoothly between the two stages, he made sure he caught the attention of every bench and platform as he spoke. "When I was fourteen months old, my mother sold me for a twist of opium. I'm sure you've heard this story. In fact…" He searched for Rivenna Glorren, seated with the Tiger contingent, "Her Grace the Tiger abbess was kind enough to remind me of it yesterday, while I was a guest at her palace. 'I only value you as your mother did,' she said."

A stir along the benches; people shifting in their seats. The odd hiss, aimed towards the Tigers. It was deftly done, Neema thought, watching from the contenders' bench below the stage. Monkeys would never insult a guest like that in their home.

"I must say," Cain said, with a sad tilt of his head towards Ruko, "I don't envy the Tiger contender his mentor. I was lucky, in comparison…"

And Neema sighed, because she knew what was coming. Madam Fessi, their old schoolteacher. The woman who had taken Cain in, and eventually adopted him.

Cain moved seamlessly back and forth between the two circles of the stage. His voice suited an open-air theatre, carrying up to the highest platforms without effort. His thick, Scrapper accent felt fresh to jaded ears. So bracingly *authentic*. "She could have taken a court position, or taught at the Raven monastery. But she chose to build a school in a dump like Scartown. I'm allowed to call it that, you're not," he said, to scattered laughter. "Madam Fessi was a Casinor, of the Venerant Casinors, but she didn't act like she was better than us. She treated everyone she met the same way. With dignity and respect."

Neema smiled to herself. Cain was painting Madam Fessi as a saint. In truth she'd had a sharp tongue and a short temper, but he was right—she did treat everyone alike.

"Madam Fessi died ten years ago in the Winter Riots. But I remember the lessons she taught me, and the example she set. When I am emperor," a grin, at his own presumption, "I will treat all my subjects the same way: Venerant, Middling, Commoner, Scrapper. Because I believe that every life is of equal value, and every soul deserves respect." He stressed the last word, bringing things back to his theme.

Applause rose along the benches, and up through the platforms. A few cheers, from certain pockets. Neema thought he'd won perhaps half the audience to his side. Others were more muted. She could see them silently calculating what such a message might mean for them and their families, in practical terms. Wider monastery reforms, more scrutiny around court hirings, tougher sentencing on corruption and bribery.

Cain knew this—he was watching the audience just as closely. Specifically the Monkey courtiers—the only ones with a vote. He wasn't done yet—the sand in the hourglass was barely halfway through. As the applause died away, he called for a violin. Played a verse, then faltered. He rubbed a hand through his hair, as if frustrated with himself. "Forgive me. I have thought of something better." Lifting the bow, he tried a new melody. "I Will Rise," from Lady Harmony's beloved opera *Avila*. The story of a disgraced courtier forced to enter the House of Mist and Shadows, who earns the respect of the Grey Penitents and clears her name—only to die from marsh fever in the final act. This was her death song, a haunting piece that was both mournful and uplifting. People were in tears before he'd finished the first verse.

"This will be hard to follow," someone said behind Neema. They sounded disappointed.

As the last note faded to silence, Cain pulled his master stroke. Sweeping his arm, he directed the applause towards Lady Harmony, seated on her private platform in the trees. "Respect, to our greatest living composer," he called up.

The whole theatre got to its feet, sending waves of love and admiration through the clearing. Was it for Lady Harmony, or Cain? It didn't matter. This was the moment people would remember, and vote for. And for those unsettled by his earlier comments, a reassessment was underway. His appreciation of Lady Harmony—his deference towards her—had appeased some, at least.

Cain gave a final Fox salute and left the stage as the last grains of sand dropped through the hourglass.

"If that was improvised, I'm a catfish," Tala muttered, as she passed him.

"May the Monkey bless you and remain Hidden," Cain replied, earning himself a sharp punch in the arm. Summoning the Monkey before a performance was considered bad luck. Tala was channelling the bad luck back to him.

Lord Clarion encouraged another member of the audience to select a scroll from the jewelled box.

"Joy," they called out, and Tala began. She would teach the audience a harvest song, she said, on the principle that singing together was a naturally joyful experience.

Cain's performance had distracted Neema from her nerves, but now they were back. It didn't help that she was set to go last.

She needed air, and space. Lurching to her feet, she walked blindly from the theatre into the woods beyond, only stopping when the singing faded. Her heart slowed as she breathed in the night. Things were softer here, and fresher. The turn of the sea, the rustle of night animals in the undergrowth. The distant hoot of a barn owl. She sat down beneath an oak tree, and tried to soak up its strength. She would need it, if she was going to make it up on to that stage.

And she had to. She *had* to. Not just perform with confidence, but somehow do better than Cain and Ruko. She thought of Madam Fessi, how little time she'd had for Neema's stage fright. Just get up there and try—what's the worst that could happen?

Her teacher's rough impatience hadn't worked—so what would? The emperor was right—*fuck him*—if she was serious about taking the throne, she would need to learn how to command an audience.

She thought of something Ruko had observed, the night of the opening ceremony, as the high officials paraded into the banqueting hall. *You are more comfortable on the periphery.* He was right, she was. And much as it pained her to admit it, she couldn't save the world tucked away in the library stacks.

She caught a familiar oiled scent in the air. Pepper, liquorice, musk.

"Sol."

He was perched in the oak tree, a few feet above her head. **Oh, hello, Neema.** He pecked indifferently at the branch he was sitting on.

"What are you doing here?"

I am the Solitary Raven. I can be wherever I like. He tugged out a few leaves and scattered them on her head.

She got to her feet, brushing the leaves from her hair before addressing him. "So first of all—if you hurt Cain again, I will pluck out your feathers one by one, and stuff them down your throat."

I am saving the world, Neema. I make no apologies. You will thank me when you are perched upon the throne, victorious. Sol, you will say, greatest of all fragments. How wrong I was to doubt your magnificence—

"I need your help."

Of course, that is inevitable, you are a tiny meat bag and I—

"Please."

That stopped him. No one had ever said please to the Solitary Raven. This was something of an existential incident. A weird, gurgling noise spilled from his throat. Surprise—that must be it. He was surprised. Not happy, not contented. No, no. Surprised.

How may I assist you, Neema?

She had missed most of Shal's performance—a martial display set to drums, meant to represent Perseverance. By the time she took her seat again, he was leaving the stage to polite applause. Too rehearsed, too self-contained and too short. The sand was still running through the timer.

Ruko rose from his seat.

"*There's* our emperor-in-waiting," the man behind Neema said. "You can't learn that—it's in the blood."

A Fox courtier pulled a scroll from the jewelled box and read out the next subject: Peace.

Ruko strode to the centre of the stage and waited for silence. This was the first time most people had heard him speak at any length. What he said was not as interesting as what he projected.

Confidence. Charisma. An aura of power. He spoke, and people listened. Neema hated to admit it, but the man behind her was right—he sounded like an emperor-in-waiting.

He ended by reciting the final verses of "The Truce" by Seeker Flint.[13] An obvious choice. When he was done he said, into the dead silence, "That is all I wish to say," and strode back to his seat.

The theatre was divided. He had shown no creative flair. Revealed nothing of himself. Some were disappointed. Others were pleased. They did not want revelation, they wanted assurance. Certainty. Stability.

"Such natural authority," the man said, behind Neema. She was beginning to suspect he'd been planted there.

Lord Clarion returned to the stage, still clapping. "Wonderful. Masterful! Thank you, Contender Valit. And our thanks to all the contenders for their inspiring performances. The Monkey has blessed us tonight with its presence. And now, we shall pause for the vote…"

He stopped, frowning as if confused. People were calling to him. Someone scuttled on to the stage and whispered in his ear. Clarion put a perfectly manicured hand to his mouth. "Contender Kraa, my deepest apologies. How could I forget you?" He waved her to the stage with a patronising smile, as if she were a child at a recital.

Neema had no doubt this was a deliberate slight. Half the audience was squirming with embarrassment, the other half laughing behind their hands.

To walk up into that?

No.

Neema thought of Yasila in her suite, owning the sea and the sky. She thought of Ruko, waiting for silence. Perhaps the man

---

13. Self-torturing twelfth-century Monkey poet and philosopher, famous for his musings on the moral value of self-governance. Died in a bar brawl, 1133. In "The Truce," Flint's best-known poem, the Monkey visits two generals on the eve of battle, and swaps their spirits. When they wake in each other's bodies, they realise that unless they make peace, they will be forced to lead their enemy's army into battle against their own.

behind her was right—perhaps it did come naturally to some people. Didn't mean it couldn't be learned.

She folded her hands in her lap, and looked to the mid distance.

The crowd was growing restless. Lord Clarion beckoned her again.

Neema remained where she was, head high. And then she beckoned *him*.

The richest man in the empire was not used to being summoned. He did not like it.

She waited, as his face turned red.

Lord Clarion blinked first. Crossing down to the front row, he said, "Is there a problem—"

"A formal apology, Lord Clarion," she said, without looking at him. "Before I rise."

Lord Clarion's mouth opened and closed, opened and closed. And then he hurried back to the stage. "Contender Kraa, on behalf of the Festival committee, I apologise unreservedly for any offence you may have felt…"

"Your contingent should have spoken for you," Ruko said, in her ear.

"I am my own contingent," Neema replied.

"…my honour to invite the Raven contender to the stage," Lord Clarion concluded.

Neema rose.

As she walked, she breathed through her fear, and used it. She thought of the vision Sol had shown her in the mirror. The amethyst crown. That swell of power. She took that reflection, and became it. And though she could not see it, more strands of indigo and blue formed within her tight black curls.

Lord Clarion had left the stage. She walked up the steps, and claimed it.

The audience sat in tense silence as the timer was set, the jewelled box was opened. "Friendship," someone called out.

Some laughter, less than before.

Neema was certain that the subject had been chosen to mock her. Just as Clarion had "forgotten her" on purpose.

The grains of sand fell through the timer. The crowd waited. Neema began.

"Gaida Rack was not my friend."

A buzz, as she said Gaida's name.

"We had no time for each other in life. But in death, I have come to respect her passion. Her courage. Her persistence. Let us take a moment to remember her, in silence."

And they did fall silent—a thousand people in a clearing. The energy shifted into something profound and ancient. The warm night enclosed them. The moon hanging bright. The scent of the woods. The distant turn of the sea.

No one else had done this. No one had used the night.

She began to hum, softly. The audience could hear her—if they stayed silent. If they leaned in. "Come to the Mountain." The ancient version of the melody tugged at their hearts, pulled them to her. They were transfixed, eyes following her as she moved to the centre of the stage.

On his platform in the trees, the emperor frowned to himself.

Neema raised her arms. She didn't sing the words, she chanted them like a summoning spell.

> *"Fly to your empress, sacred Raven*
> *Over forest, over plain*
> *Greet your friend, beloved Guardian,*
> *Give your blessing to her reign."*

With her mind, she reached for Sol. He was already on his way.

We all were.

On the benches, on the platforms, people called the familiar response. "And remain Hidden!" Too late. Their words were lost to the heavy beat of wings.

Fragments wheeled and dived over the stage, and perched on branches around the theatre. A company of ravens, a chorus with only one line.

Kraa! Kraa!

Sol landed neatly on Neema's shoulder, and gave a piercing cry of his own.

Kraa!

The sound reverberated across the stage and through the benches. It rustled the leaves in the trees. Fragments lifted up into the air, circling low and crying her name again and again. And even those in the audience who did not believe, found themselves convinced that the Raven was here among them. We basked in their wonder, swirling in a dark flurry of wing and claw and beak, calling to one another, and to the woman on the stage, our contender. Our friend. She raised her arms and we loved her, for making us the centre of everything.

And then we were gone.

Only Sol remained, perched on Neema's shoulder. In the moonlight, in the torchlight, her black curls gleamed with their new, subtle strands of indigo and rich, night blue.

The clearing was silent, dropped into a state of stunned awe. No one was sure what they had just witnessed, but it had been… magnificent.

Neema held herself for another beat, a half-smile on her lips. And then she swept from the stage with Sol still perched on her shoulder. Empress-in-waiting.

CHAPTER
Fifty-Nine

THE EMPEROR HAD a habit of arriving in the middle of the night. The prison guards had grown used to his visits, and no longer felt embarrassed to be caught half asleep on the job. Tonight, the Old Bear was in a reflective mood. Had it really been fifteen years? He shook his great, craggy head in astonishment. Fifteen years, imagine that. He clapped his good hand to their shoulders, and thanked them for their service. He did not ask them what they planned to do with their retirement.

"How is our friend?" This was how he always referred to the man in the final cell. Our friend.

The guards shrugged. No change. For the first five or six years the prisoner had gone through terrible cycles of hope and despair. There had been a few pitiful attempts at escape, and many attempts at suicide. He had lost his mind for a while. He used to show interest in things—books, painting—but that had faded over time. He had a pet bird for a year or two, but it died. He stopped eating after that, they had to force-feed him for a month. That had been bleak.

It was all bleak. If they had known what the job would entail, and how long it would last, how they would never again leave the confines of the Hound palace, or speak to anyone except the emperor, and the day watch, then they would never have agreed to it. Obviously.

A few years ago, a member of the day watch had hanged himself in the office with his belt. He'd left a note pinned on the noticeboard. *No guards here, only prisoners!*

The exclamation mark, that was the bit that stuck in the mind, for some reason.

"I'll speak to the girl first," the emperor said.

The guards were mystified.

"The girl," the emperor repeated, irritated. The one brought down here yesterday. Red ribbons in her hair. Claimed she'd met the Bear in a dream.

They knew nothing about a girl. "You'd have to ask the day watch, your majesty," they said, and the emperor frowned, and said, "Ah."

There had been no sign of the day watch when they'd arrived for their shift. No day watch, and a freshly scrubbed floor.

The emperor took the key from them, and thanked them again for their service.

The more daring of the two followed him down the corridor, to the last cell. "Your majesty. What will you tell our families…"

The Old Bear put a hand to his heart and gave a vague, benign smile.

The guard was still thinking about that smile when the Samran Hounds arrived to slit his throat.

The emperor closed the cell door behind him, and locked it with a sharp click.

The prisoner lay slumped, defeated in a corner, an iron mask clamped to his head. Two narrow slits for his eyes, and one for his mouth.

"Good evening, my friend," the emperor said.

The prisoner—a giant of a man just like his visitor—shrank back further into the corner, mute with terror.

The emperor took off his crown and sighed with relief. Here, he could be free. The spell he lived under could be broken. Soul Stealer, the Dragons called it. The darkest of all spells, feared and forbidden. But they were a fretful, unimaginative lot, the Chosen.

The emperor had renamed it the Chameleon Spell.

He spoke the words that would release him—a line from *The Song of the Forest*. "Ripples in the long grass, and a tiger is revealed."

The emperor's hulking form blurred and narrowed. His craggy features softened, his weather-beaten skin turned to a smooth, golden brown. Old scars vanished and a new one appeared, cutting through his straight black brow. Dark brown eyes. Black hair, streaked with grey.

The spell was reversed. The Old Bear was gone. He was himself. Andren Valit. The Golden Tiger of Samra.

And, for the past sixteen years, ruler of Orrun.

He cracked his shoulders and smiled his own smile. A wonderful, magnetic smile. The air itself seemed drawn to him.

He righted a chair that had been kicked to the floor. Highbacked, with leather restraints on the arms and legs, and a strap for the neck. "Come," he said.

The man in the iron mask pulled himself to his feet and lumbered forward. He looked incongruously fit and strong. In the early days it had taken three guards to hold him down. He had roared. How he had roared. Now he sat meekly as the emperor fixed him in place. The restraints were no more than a precaution. There was no fight left in him. Only spaces, where the fight had been.

"There," Andren said. "Now we may both relax." He studied and tested the man's body, as if he were buying a horse. "Good, good. They've kept you in excellent shape."

The man's eyes, through the narrow slits of his mask, were vacant.

"I shall remove your mask now," Andren warned.

The man made weak noises of distress. His hands clenched against their restraints. The three middle fingers of his right hand were missing.

"I know, I know," Andren murmured in sympathy. He took a key from around his neck, and unlocked the mask. His own hand, freed from the Chameleon Spell, was intact. Long, elegant fingers. "Eight," he laughed, as he lifted the mask free. "I always forget how heavy this is." He settled it on the floor with a clank, and stepped back.

"Gedrun," he said.

Bersun's brother made a guttural noise. His tongue had been cut from his mouth the day he arrived. But in all other ways he was the emperor. The life model, from which Andren shaped his own performance. The Chameleon Spell demanded a live subject. With Bersun long dead, Gedrun was the closest Andren could get to the original.

"I have not come to study you today," Andren said, pulling up his own chair. "Rest easy."

Gedrun sagged. His head weaved and rolled, so used to the iron mask weighing it down.

"I have good news. Tomorrow, my son Ruko shall take the throne. You understand?" Andren grasped Gedrun's hand. "It is almost over."

Gedrun began to weep.

Andren was moved. "You do understand, don't you? Ah, I am glad to bring you comfort at last. My poor, innocent friend. This should have been your brother's fate, not yours. Bersun was a great warrior, but he was a terrible emperor. He would have torn Orrun apart. He did not have the skills, the temperament. Is my own reign not proof of that? Even constrained as I have been by his character, his ill-founded ideas," Andren mimed his wrists, bound together, "I have given Orrun sixteen years of peace. Where he would have brought only division. Our sacrifice was not in vain, my friend. Together, we saved an empire. And soon, with my son's help, I shall build a new one."

He sat back, and ran a hand through his short black hair. Rubbed his jaw, his cheekbones. Knowing himself again. A transitory pleasure. As he traced the contours of his face it began to sag beneath his fingers, skin softening like wax.

Every spell casts a shadow. To be another man, he must lose himself.

A fear came then into Andren's eye, and with it a hunger, a need for reassurance.

Gedrun understood very little these days. But he knew that look, and what came next. He moaned in dread, his eyes wild.

"Forgive me," Andren said, voice slurring as his lip drooped. "This will be the last time, my friend. You have my word."

He drew his chair closer, and placed his hands on either side of Gedrun's face. Dug his fingers deep into the skin. "Give to me your greatest treasure," he chanted. "I shall use it well. Give to me your greatest treasure…"

There was so little of Gedrun left, within the shell of his body. Andren took it all.

PART SEVEN

Day of
the Hound,
Day of
the Dragon

∞

Sixty

I N THE WINTER OF 517, pirates attacked the island. Twenty-five servants, soldiers and courtiers were killed in the raid. Six more lives were lost when the Imperial Library caught fire.

Within a month, ministers had drawn up plans for a new perimeter wall, with watchtowers at each corner. As the walls rose up, so did the dissenting voices. The island was a palace, not a prison. The walls were too high, too ugly, they blocked the light and trapped the heat. And how effective were they, anyway? They didn't extend around the Garden at the Edge of the World—consecutive rulers vetoed that plan, they didn't want Hounds peering into their private grounds, they didn't want the view spoiled. Instead, the middle section of the eastern wall was lowered, and integrated into the back of the eighth palace, and had no walkways or viewing stations for patrols.

Construction took forty years. By the time it was finished, no one was happy. Those who had never wanted the wall still didn't want the wall. Those who had wanted the wall said it wasn't the wall they'd been promised. And then there was the huge cost and effort of maintaining it. Twelve Ox teams working full-time, making inspections and repairs on a rolling schedule.

The obvious solution was to pull it down, but no one could face that. The arguments about building it had been bad enough. Now they had to argue about destroying it? So here it was, a thousand years later, looming up everywhere and costing a fortune.

On the outside of the wall, ten feet below the parapet, ran a continuous narrow stone ledge, used for maintenance work.

"You will run it twice, anti-clockwise," Hol Vabras said. "Fastest time wins." He had arranged the Seventh Trial himself. Cheap, simple and guaranteed to give a clear result.

They were gathered in the south-east watchtower—Vabras, the contenders and members of Shal's contingent. Through the lookout windows, ominous black storm clouds gathered in the thudding heat.

"The start times will be staggered. Contender Talaka, as you are sitting fourth, you will go first."

Tala glanced anxiously out of the window. For a second, Neema thought the Ox contender's fear of heights would get the better of her, but she squared her shoulders, and followed Vabras out to the parapet. Her rivals joined her, Shal hanging back.

"You can do this," Tala muttered to herself, adjusting her head-band. A nervous tic. She peered over the parapet. "Eight." She drew back.

Neema did the same. Looked, cursed, drew back. Beyond the ledge lay a fifty-foot drop to the base of the wall. Beyond that, if you happened to miss the rock, a further fifty-foot drop to the sea.

Even Ruko was concerned. "High Commander. Should we not wait for the storm to pass?"

"We have a schedule," Vabras said.

Cain, meanwhile, was triumphant. He couldn't think of anything he'd like to do more than run along a narrow stone ledge with a hundred-foot death drop in the middle of a light-ning storm. This Trial wasn't just designed for him, it was a metaphor for his whole life. "Are we allowed to jump over each other?"

"No!" the others shouted, horrified. Even Shal, who was not tak-ing part.

"You may pass however you wish," Vabras said, and took out his pocket watch. "Ox contender," he prompted.

Tala sat astride the parapet, gathering her nerve. Then before she could do something sensible like change her mind, she swung herself over and dropped down on to the ledge. With her stomach pressed to the wall, she crab-walked a few paces. Her heel slipped.

"*Fuck.* The edge is worn. It's like glass." Steeling herself, she turned to face forward and set off again. "That was a bad section," she called back. "I'll be fine. *Eight!*" Her foot had slipped again. She didn't talk after that.

Five minutes later, it was Neema's turn. She used Tala's method to swing herself down on to the ledge. Then she made the mistake of looking down. The rocks, the sea. Gulls circling far below. She breathed deeply, forehead to the wall.

On the other side of the parapet, Ruko and Cain were drawing lots. They were sitting joint first, with twenty-seven points each. If Neema didn't press on now, one of them would be right at her back, trying to pass. She set off, as fast as she dared.

The storm clouds billowed, and darkened.

Ruko won the lot, and chose to go last. "Interesting," Cain said, and scissored over the parapet on to the ledge.

"It's not time yet," Vabras frowned.

Cain ran off then ran back again, bounced up and down to warm up. "I'm thinking about your strategy," he said to Ruko. "You can't outrun me. I'm way faster, and more agile." He balanced on one leg, stretching his quads as the world dangled below him. "So you're planning to follow in my wake, right?" He changed leg. "I come first, you come second. Then you beat me in our fight, and win the Festival by one point." He lowered his foot. "Very neat, very sensible."

Ruko rested his arms on the parapet, and said nothing.

"But." Cain held up a finger. "What if I offer Neema a piggyback? A-ha, didn't think of that, did you? Leftfield. I come first, *she* comes second…Then you're trailing me by two points. Even if you win the fight, which let's face it you probably will, we'll be even. A tie. And we know what that means."

An eighth Trial. The Dragon Trial.

Nobody wanted that.

"You may not give piggybacks," Vabras said.

Cain pointed at him. "You are making up the rules as you go along." He jogged off, then jogged back again. "Is it time yet?"

"No."

"There's a whole stretch ahead where you can't see us," Cain said, gesturing further along the east wall. "I could give her a piggyback and you'd never know. *You'd never know.*"

"Or I could kick you over the edge," Ruko said.

"True," Cain conceded. "True. But you'll have to catch me first."

"Go," Vabras said, and Cain went.

It took him less than a minute to catch up with Neema. She had found her pace—slow but steady. This was going to take her about three and a half hours, she reckoned. Assuming she didn't die. She thought she might recite the epic poem *Empress Am in the Desert, Lost* for the first go round, to keep her rhythm.

She heard scuffling, and coughing. "I'm trying not to startle you," Cain said.

"Thanks," she said, and kept to the same pace.

"If you look down to your right, there's a wonderful view of the Garden at the Edge of the World."

"Yes, I'm not going to do that."

"If it's all right with you," Cain said, "I'm going to give you a piggyback."

"It is not all right with me."

"Don't worry, they can't see us."

"That's not why I'm worried."

They trudged on at Neema's pace.

"You said you trusted me yesterday," Cain complained, to her back. "Which was sweet. And I know, I know—I said you shouldn't. But that was then. I've slept on it, and—"

A large raven swooped down from nowhere and landed with a soft plat on the parapet between them. It glared at Cain, first with one beady brown eye, and then the other. It did not like what it saw with either.

"Is that…" Cain trailed away.

Last night, the audience had voted Neema five points for her performance. And then, collectively, they had decided that they had not witnessed fragments of the Raven screeching her name above their heads. No, they had absolutely not seen that. What they had seen was a flock of tame ravens, that Neema must have somehow trained in secret. That had to be it. Denial.

Cain knew better. He'd seen a book turn into a bird. Into this bird, if he was not mistaken.

"His name's Sol. Try to ignore him. Go away," she said, to the raven.

The raven made a mournful sound, and kept following them.

"No, I'm not letting you back in," Neema said. And then, "You know why."

"It's talking to you?" Cain asked.

She stopped, and looked back. "You can't hear him? Lucky you," she muttered.

They walked on. Neema and Sol were clearly having a silent argument.

"I feel excluded," Cain said.

"Sorry. He says you're dangerous, because you're not fully in control of yourself. You feel as though you are, but that's only because you slept on it."

"But that's my point, I feel much better today—"

Neema stopped to explain. "The Fox is always awake when you're asleep, Cain. But now it's also *partially* awake when you are."

"Because I'm aware of it."

"Exactly. So it gets stronger, and you get weaker. It's telling you you're fine, so you don't fight it. But you're not fine. You can't trust yourself, because it's not *you* you're trusting. It's the Fox." They moved on again.

"Well," Cain said, absorbing all this. "That's insanely unnerving."

The raven gurgled softly.

"Sol says that's a good sign," Neema said over her shoulder. "The more unsettled you are the better. If you're complacent, the Fox will take over completely. You have to find a new balance, a new accord, before you fall asleep again."

"How do I do that?"

"He doesn't know. This has never happened before. I think you should apologise to Cain," she said to Sol, who was still strutting along the wall above their heads. There was a pause. "Because it's your fault, you wretched thing," she snapped. "Cain only knows about the Fox because *you* told him. So: apologise."

A half-hearted *caw* from the raven.

"Properly, Sol."

"It's not really an apology if you have to ask for it," Cain said. "If you crouch down, I'll jump over you. Look, there's a rope hook there you can hold on to."

He leapt over her and landed neatly. For a moment, they stood with their backs pressed to the wall, looking out over the Garden at the Edge of the World to the ocean beyond. As they'd been talking, the black storm clouds had drifted nearer, casting the world in an eerie half-light.

Cain reached for Neema's hand. The first time they had touched since their fight on the platform. It felt good. It always felt good.

Cain leaned forward to kiss her.

A memory of yellow eyes, sharp white teeth. A blade.

She drew back. "Sorry."

He sighed in understanding, and frustration. "May I point out that you had a fragment of the Raven in your chest when we…"

Sol heaved, violently, and coughed up a gristled pellet.

"He insists I tell you," Neema said, "that he hid in a dead tree for the entire, disgusting time."

"Good," Cain said. "I have no idea what that means, but good." And with that, he took off again, sprinting.

Neema caught up with Tala at the north-west watchtower. The Oxwoman was clinging to the sill, her back pressed hard against the window. Behind her, through the glass, the watchtower Hounds went about their work, pretending not to notice. As Neema approached Tala cursed, but didn't move.

"Are you all right?" Neema asked, awkwardly. They hadn't spoken since the Bear Trial.

The sky flickered.

"I'll be fine," Tala said, more to herself than to Neema. "I just… I need a moment. Go around me." She flattened herself against the window. The ledge was wider here at the base of the watch-tower—there was just enough room.

With her back to the drop, Neema inched her way past. A stone rattled and tilted under her foot. Face to face, they shared a look of horror.

"It's loose," Neema said.

Thunder boomed across the sky.

Neema jerked in shock. The stone wobbled again. She made her way around Tala, holding her breath. "This one too," she said, testing the next stone with her foot. "This whole section."

Another flash of lightning, a rumble of thunder. Fat raindrops splatted on the ledge.

"Tala," Neema warned. It wasn't safe.

Tala nodded tightly. Slowly, she inched her way around the watchtower. From here, they could see the problem. The mortar between the stones had degraded and cracked. In some places it was lost completely.

A Hound was patrolling on the battlement above. They called up to her, to send a warning back to the others.

Neema set off again. Sol flew ahead, wheeling and turning, watching the storm, watching the others. She had to admit—grudgingly—he had his uses. Ruko wasn't far behind Tala, walking barefoot, trusting the grip of his toes.

Neema was finishing her first circuit when the storm landed. Thunder rolled across the sky, deep and heavy enough that she could feel it rumbling through her body. The sky turned black.

And then the rain hit—sheeting rain, drenching her in seconds, streaming into her eyes and sluicing off the ledge like a waterfall.

She pressed on until she reached the south-east watchtower. First circuit complete. Inside, they had lit the lanterns, and were now busy building a fire. She banged on the glass until Vabras came over. "This is madness," she shouted. She could barely hear herself over the rain.

He opened the window. "Are you withdrawing from the Trial?"

She stared at him, miserable. She couldn't give up now. If she did, she would be handing Ruko the throne. A fork of lightning pierced the sky, illuminating them both—Vabras safe and warm in the watchtower, Neema soaked and terrified.

"Are you withdrawing?" he asked again. He stepped back, to let her through the window.

She wiped the rain from her face. "No. No. I'll keep going."

Fifteen minutes later, Cain completed his second circuit. He waved away the Hounds offering to help him over the parapet, and hoisted himself up, before heading straight into the watchtower. He crossed to the fire and pulled off his tunic. "How are they doing?" he asked Shal.

"Well, they're not enjoying themselves," Shal said. The Hound contender always wore his uniform well, but now it looked like a taunt—how smart and dry and well turned out he was, while everyone else was suffering in the storm.

Cain peeled off his trousers. Someone handed him a towel. "Times?"

"First circuit Ruko was next fastest, then Neema."

"Close?"

Shal looked at him. Shook his head.

Cain threw on some fresh clothes provided by Shal's contingent, and wrapped himself in a blanket.

Shal had crossed back to the window. The rain hammered down. Lightning flashed, thunder rolled. "This is my fault," he said. "I've been praying for rain for days. Eight. Never seen a storm like it. Is it the same, do you think? Or worse?"

"The same," Vabras said from his desk. He was working as he waited—reports, invoices. He unsealed another scroll.

Cain poured two glasses of whisky and joined Shal at the window. "I think it's worse," he muttered.

Half an hour passed. An hour. The rain didn't stop. It steamed up the windows, battered against the glass. Then finally, finally, someone went past, shoulder clamped to the window.

"Who was that? Was that Neema?" Cain was out the door, up on to the parapet. Shal followed him, and then Vabras. The rain was impossible, they wiped it from their faces and they were still half blind.

A hand appeared, gripping the parapet, and then another.

"Neema," Cain shouted. He dragged her up, Shal helping. Vabras to the rear, noting the time.

Shal and Cain half carried her to the fire. She was shaking so hard, they couldn't understand what she was saying. "Others…?" she managed, through chattering teeth.

"They're still out there," Shal told her. "Don't worry, you know how tough they are. They'll be right behind you."

Cain took over, helping her undress, grabbing towels and blankets. "We need to get you warm." He hugged her. "You're fine, you're safe."

Vabras was back at his desk, signing something. Shal stood over him. "I'll go out and look for them."

"You'll stay here."

"High Commander—"

"That's an order, Contender Worthy," Vabras murmured.

Shal gritted his teeth, and headed back to the fire. Someone had brought Neema a cup of hot chocolate, splashed with whisky. She cradled it.

"They won't be long," Cain said.

Ten minutes passed. Twenty. The storm began to move on, the air freshened. They waited.

There was a tap at the window. Perched on the sill was a large black bird, with a hooked beak. It tapped again, impatient.

"Sol," Neema said. She ran to the window and unlatched it. "Have you seen them? What's going on?"

"Is she talking to the bird?" Shal said, but Cain was already following Neema to the window.

Sol hopped inside, shaking the storm from his feathers. Neema listened intently. "No!" she said. She turned to the room, her face frozen in shock.

"What is it?" Cain asked.

She found her voice. "The north-west tower." She rounded on Vabras, furious. "I told you it wasn't safe."

"The ledge collapsed?" Cain said.

"Not just the ledge." Neema was shaking with anger. "The tower. The whole watchtower is gone."

CHAPTER
Sixty-One

TALA STOOD WITH her back to the wall. The rain pummelled down, streaming off the ledge in great rinsing sheets. She was trapped in the same spot that had almost defeated her on the first circuit. The north-west watchtower.

Lightning crackled down the sky, illuminating the jagged rocks, the swirling sea. She wished it hadn't.

"You can do this," she muttered, her voice drowned by the storm. Beneath her headband, her auburn hair was plastered to her skull, clothes a second, drenched skin. She took one step sideways. It was like walking through a river.

From here, she could see directly into the watch-tower. The guards had lit lanterns. Some were working, while others watched the storm. It was like a dream. What was she doing out here, when she could be in there? One of them caught her eye, smiled in encouragement, then looked away. They'd been ordered not to interact with the contenders.

"This is a Festival Trial," Tala said, and took another sideways step. "And I will not quit. I am the Ox contender." Another step. With her back to the glass, she gripped the windowsill. She was coming up to the loose section. Probably been loose for years. Probably safe. Probably.

Another flash of lightning and there was Ruko coming up on her right, a dark figure padding barefoot through the wall of rain. Slow, fluid, inevitable. Any moment now, he would be on top of her, wanting to pass.

Go in, or move on. Decide.

Tala said a prayer into the storm. Ox of the Kind Return, sure-footed and wise. Guide my path, and remain Hidden.

Another sideways step. Another. Almost there. She tested the next stone with her left foot. It rattled, but held. She shifted her weight...

The stone broke beneath her, taking the next two with it. They bounced and clattered to the rocks below, leaving Tala's leg dangling in space.

She hauled herself back, gripping the windowsill hard. There was now a three-foot gap to her left. She cursed, loudly. The stone she was standing on tilted, threatening to follow the rest. No time to call the guards, she'd be washed away before they could help her.

Three feet. She took a breath, and half strode, half jumped the gap.

Before she knew it, she was on the other side, clinging to the wall and laughing with relief. Made it—with a foot to spare. She was safe. Only half a circuit to go—

A bolt of lightning pierced through the rain, and smashed into the watchtower roof.

Tala watched in horror as the ancient building cracked, and split apart. Brick, glass, stone—everything collapsed and thundered past her, swift as an avalanche. People falling. Their faces. Then gone.

And then she too was falling, sliding as the ledge collapsed under her. An image of Sunur, and Suru. She snatched desperately at the wall as she slid down it.

Her hand snagged on something—a crevice in the stonework. She grabbed it with three fingers, felt the jolt in her shoulder as it took her weight. She hung there, legs flailing. The wall was slick with rain, she couldn't find a toe-hold. She couldn't lift herself back up. She was stuck.

She screamed for help, but they were all gone. Except...

She looked up, blinded by the rain. She wiped her face with her free arm. Saw the savage gap above her head, where the watchtower had been. And Ruko, safe on the ledge. Looking straight down at her.

"Ruko! Help!"

He took a step back, then jumped the wide gap as if it were nothing, landing neat as a cat, despite the rain. And then...

No. He wouldn't. There was no way—

He sprinted off. Not a word, not a backward glance. Just kept on running.

She howled against the rock. A primal, animal howl that rose from somewhere deep within. Her fingers were slipping, her shoulder screaming. "Monster," she sobbed. "You monster."

"Tala." A rope dropped down the wall beside her.

He was on the parapet, bracing himself. She hauled herself up, feet slipping against the wall.

"Careful," he shouted down. "Take your time."

Once she'd reached the ledge, she flung herself over the parapet and lay there on her stomach, sobbing with relief. She kissed the ground, and then she got up and hugged Ruko, even though she could hardly get her arms around him.

"Thank you. Thank you, thank you, thank you."

He stood there awkwardly, until she stopped. They stared at each other, the two survivors. Haunted.

"The whole tower, Ruko. Did you see them?"

He nodded.

The rain beat down, but the storm was passing. She gave him a gentle shove. "Go. Get back on the ledge. If you run..."

But it was too late, they both knew that. There was no way he could beat Neema's time now. They walked south along the parapet, side by side. Now the storm was clearing, they could see the Leviathans in the channel—a watery smudge of the mainland beyond.

"I thought you'd left me," she said.

A pause. And then, a confession. "I considered it."

Tala breathed out. "What changed your mind?"

He shook his head. Impossible to explain the conflict inside him. He barely understood it himself.

"Those people, Ruko," she said again.

He put an arm around her, stiffly at first. Slowly, something thawed as he remembered. This is how you hug someone. This is how you comfort them. This is what you do.

Sixty-Two

FENN WAS WORKING in his office at the farmhouse when the storm hit. He didn't wait for it to build, that first boom of thunder was enough. Cracked a window somewhere. Fuck. He grabbed his hooded cloak and strode out into the yard, shouting orders at people as he passed. Most of them were way ahead of him—they had protocols, well-rehearsed. It was the rest of the island that worried him.

Lightning forked across the dark purple sky. *Fuck.*

He'd been dreading this day for years. Some freak storm, some natural disaster. He knew every weak spot on the island—all the patched-up work he'd been forced to do. Years of systematic neglect, under the gilded surface. Every year he'd begged Vabras for more funds, and every year he was handed less.

Another fork of lightning, this time over the Monkey palace. Eight, the woods. Even with all this rain, the ground was tinder dry beneath. One stray ember in a sheltered spot—the whole place could go up.

He trusted his teams to fan out across the island. He should stay here and coordinate everything. That was the protocol, he'd written it himself. He squinted at the treeline—the border between the two palaces. "Is that smoke?" he asked, grabbing a passing yardhand.

"Could be smoke, could be steam from the rain," she said. "Sorry."

"Better check," he muttered, and set off for a closer look.

So he was on his own, jogging through the woods when the Samran Hounds caught up with him. Didn't occur to him that he was in danger. Just a bunch of arseholes who thought their problems took priority over everyone else's.

They blocked his path.

They actually thought their leather batons would stop him. He would piss himself laughing, if he had the time to spare. He shifted his stance, threatening to trample his way through them. "Move," he growled. Last chance.

Their captain was standing on a raised patch of ground a few feet away. She called down to him in a lazy, confident drawl. Venerant, or aspiring to be. "High Engineer Fedala. You're to come with us, sir."

"You'll have to wait. I'm busy."

Someone struck him from behind. "What was *that*?" he said, and punched the man who'd struck him. He collapsed at Fenn's feet. "That's how you knock someone out," he told the rest of them. "Fucking amateurs."

The Hounds piled on top of him. He threw them off.

"We need him alive," the captain reminded them.

"Shouldn't have told me that," Fenn said, headbutting the nearest Hound. Swiping his baton—*thanks*—he swung it into the next man's jaw, knocking out a couple of teeth. Someone jumped on his back. He shook her off with a shrug and trod on her. "I'd stay down if I were you," he muttered.

The captain said something, but it was hard to hear her over the shouting.

Fenn elbowed another recruit in the ribs. Seriously, who'd trained these twats? All over the place. "What?" he called, over the din.

"I said we have your wife," the captain shouted back. "And your sons."

"What are you talking about?" Fenn fought his way towards her. Crushing faces, breaking toes. "They're on the mainland."

The captain held up his wife's favourite brooch. "We've orders not to harm *you*, High Engineer," she said. "But they're another matter."

They chained him up, and led him away.

Sixty-Three

ABBESS RIVENNA GLORREN was very quiet, and very calm. "Let us walk together," she said, to Ruko.

The storm had caused extensive damage to the Tiger palace gardens. Surprisingly, the abbess did not seem to care, and Ruko did not mention it. They walked side by side, in silence. She wore her hood up, shrouding her face.

Eventually she spoke, her voice little more than a whisper. "When you entered the monastery, I put a spy in your dormitory. You know this." She stepped over some fallen debris. "The boy who watched you said—in the day he is strong. But at night, he cries himself to sleep."

Ruko bowed his head, acknowledging the truth of it.

"I summoned you to my rooms. I asked you—what makes you so strong in the day, and so weak at night? And you honoured me with your secret." She made a gesture. Honour me again.

"I told you of the voice." The one he'd heard when he'd sat upon the marble throne, telling him—*This is how it should be.* And afterwards, reassuring him. *Feel no shame, feel nothing. You did what was necessary.* He had carried that voice with him to the Tiger monastery. In the day he heard it clearly. But at night, in the dark, it left him.

"The voice of the Tiger. Offering you its counsel, its protection. What did I promise you, that day?"

"That I would win the throne, and rule Orrun, if I listened to that voice. And to you."

Rivenna tilted her head. *Yes.* Beneath her hood, the gold beads in her hair clicked lightly against each other.

They turned a corner, passing a line of statues. One of them had. fallen and broken into pieces on the path. They walked over it.

"Do you remember your first lesson?"

"The boy," Ruko said flatly. The one she'd sent to spy on him. She had brought him out and said—"He knows your secret. He has seen you cry like a baby for your mother." She'd handed Ruko a dagger. "What does the voice tell you to do with him?"

Was it the voice, or was it Rivenna, prompting him with the dagger? Either way, he'd plunged the knife into the boy's heart. His first kill. It had made him sick. Not the blood, but the look in the boy's eyes. The light, as it left him. He'd run out of the room afterwards, thinking he would throw up. A white blank of horror. The blood on his hands. But the sickness had passed, and the voice had come back stronger. *He spied on you. He watched you cry. You did the right thing. Feel no shame. Feel nothing.*

Every time, the voice came back stronger.

And the abbess had been pleased.

They had come to a fountain. Small jewel birds scattered from the rim as they approached, darting for cover in the hedges. Rivenna lowered her hood, a signal that she wished to stop. The fountain was not working, it was quiet here, and no one would be foolish enough to pass by.

They faced each other, the abbess and her contender. Her Guardian-son. She placed a hand on his chest, stroked it softly. Ruko eyed it warily.

"Tell me," she said. "Did the Tiger bid you to save the Oxwoman?"

He looked at her. She knew it did not.

"Oh…" she breathed. "I see. You followed your heart. How touching." She toyed with her abbess ring, an eternal eight holding her middle fingers together. If she squeezed them tight, retractable fangs would release from the ring, dripping with her poison of choice. She would not do it, she would never harm him. She needed him. It was merely to emphasise her displeasure.

"Eight years," she said, letting her hand drop. "And now you falter, when it matters most."

"I will beat Cain on the platform."

"No. You will kill him."

"That is what I meant." Even a clear win would leave them tied. Ruko would not risk a Dragon Trial.

"But it is not what you said." Rivenna narrowed her eyes. "This is a flaw in your training. I kept you apart at the monastery. And now these contenders." She laughed softly. "You think they are your friends."

Ruko drew back, offended. Embarrassed.

Embarrassed. She saw it. "He is not 'Cain.' He's an obstacle in your path. Nothing more." She hissed softly. "I should have seen it, when you failed to kill the Raven contender."

"Her death was unnecessary."

"Unnecessary," she repeated quietly. "Remind me. Who kept you from second place today?"

Ruko frowned, accepting the truth. "She did."

"No. *You* did. You stayed your hand against her, and now you suffer the consequence. This new-found compassion of yours." She laughed again, scornful. "Do you think they would show you the same consideration? Whose side were they on, do you imagine, when you fought the Visitor? Do you think they would mourn your death?"

Ruko did not answer.

"You have lost your edge, Tiger warrior. Let me sharpen it for you. As you're so fond of Tala Talaka, be warned. If you do not kill the Fox contender, I will kill *her.*" The abbess released the fanged needles in her ring. "Before the day is out. This I swear on the Tiger." She retracted the fangs. "I trust that gives you the focus you need."

Ruko smothered his anger. He had promised to despatch Cain —*the obstacle*—and that is what he would do. Was his word not enough?

"You will thank me for this, when you are named emperor." Rivenna lifted her hood; their conversation was over. "The path to the throne is narrow."

"And must be walked alone."

They bowed to each other—and went their separate ways.

CHAPTER
Sixty-Four

SEVEN HOUNDS KILLED during the Seventh Trial, on the day of the Seventh Guardian. That was enough to send the faithful to the temple. Too many ill omens these past days. Light a candle, light another. Put down offerings of flowers and incense, food and money. Pray and hope, and beg the Eight to remain Hidden.

Everyone else went to the fight.

A tragedy, of course. Those poor guards. Here one moment, gone the next. Makes you think. Terrible, shocking. Must say though, awful to say, but we needed that storm. Eight. We've been dying in that heat. So much fresher, I know. What a relief. Look they're selling ribbons, call them over. Do they have nuts? A cone of nuts, please. Oh why not, yes, the sugared ones.

"So, I'm guessing your strategy is to kill me," Cain said, jangling on the spot.

Ruko wasn't playing. His face was a shield.

They were in the contenders' pavilion, waiting in line for the last time. Only one fight this afternoon. Katsan was on her way to meet the Bear—two points to Shal. Havoc had withdrawn, and was standing on the imperial balcony in his admiral's uniform, gold brocade, row of medals. ("The prick," Cain noted, to universal agreement.) Two points to Tala. The Visitor was dead. Two points to Neema—putting her in third position.

Which left only Ruko and Cain. In the stalls, people waved plaited ribbons on sticks—burnt orange for the Fox, forest green for the Tiger. Hedging their bets.

Look, Neema—there are some purple ones for us.

She had let Sol back in. After delivering his message about the watchtower, he had tottered feebly to the fire and collapsed. Flat on his back, feet clawing the air. Tiny peeps of distress. Everyone else had rushed away to help, so it was just the two of them. **Dying, slowly. So cold, so alone. Nowhere warm and dry to perch. Fading, fading . . .**

Neema told him to stop that, he was a terrible actor. She knew his feathers were water resistant because he'd told her they were, and even if they weren't, he wasn't a bird of flesh and bone and beak, he was…whatever he was. A metaphor, a symbol, an omen made tangible.

The greatest of all the Raven fragments, Sol had prompted her. He'd perked up now they were talking about him. **I am quoting you, Neema.**

"Do you want to come back?"

You want me back?

"I'd like you where I can see you."

That had been enough for Sol. He was back in her chest in moments, perched on his favourite rib. (Sixth down on the right.) Now here they were together in the pavilion. Sol was excited, because if Ruko won the fight and Cain survived it there would be a tie, and anyone within five points of the lead would go forward to the Dragon Trial. Whoever won that would instantly win the Festival. Sol's plan remained magnificent. Neema was within five points of Cain and Ruko. She would win the Dragon Trial and take the throne, and Sol would sit on her shoulder, **VISIBLE** and **RESPLENDENT.**

He tapped on Neema's rib. **What is wrong with Cain?**

She had been wondering the same thing. He was jittery, even for him. Bouncing on the spot, clicking his fingers. In the square, the Hound palace marching band was entertaining the crowds. They had time to talk. She drew him back into the corner of the pavilion. "What's wrong—"

"Cain." Ish Fort appeared from nowhere, and grabbed his contender by the jaw. "What have you taken?"

Cain blinked rapidly. "Coffee, lots of coffee. Bowl of sugar cubes. Dr. Yetbalm's pick-me-up powder. Several sachets. Very, very awake right now."

"Why the fuck would you do that?"

Neema knew why. He was keeping the Fox at bay. "You might have overdone it, Cain."

Fort wheeled on her. "Mind your own business," he snapped, and pulled Cain away.

Neema returned to the line. "Please don't kill him," she said to Ruko. She knew it was pointless, but how could she stand there and say nothing? "You saved Tala's life, you can spare his. Please, Ruko."

Nothing, from the Tiger contender.

As the marching band left the square, Cain settled back at her side. He smiled. "I'm glad you're here, Neema." He leaned in, murmured in her ear. "I'm always glad you're here."

They looked at each other. All that coffee and powder in his system. Surely the Fox was fast asleep.

"Oh, are we going to kiss now?" Cain said, amused. "On the contender line? Call the sketch artists—"

She kissed him.

Sol held very still, eyes closed, and pretended it wasn't happening.

They broke apart.

"Don't die," she said.

"Excellent advice. Thank you." Cain tapped his forehead, to show it had gone in. And then he set off after Ruko.

Cain and Ruko had both won all their previous fights. On paper, it should have been a close match. On the platform—it wasn't.

The instant the bell rang Ruko sprang forward and knocked Cain to the ground. The ferocity of the attack caught everyone off guard. He wanted this fight over. He wanted this man dead.

Not a man. An obstacle that must be removed. A piece of debris on his path.

Somehow, through sheer luck, Cain made it through to the bell. He staggered to his corner in a daze, bleeding heavily from his nose and mouth, one eye swollen shut. His contingent, hiding their horror, patched him up as best they could and handed him his sword. His depth of perception was gone, he struggled to take it from them.

"Anyone have an eyepatch? Might as well look dashing in my final moments."

"Stop joking Cain, you're not dead yet," Abbot Fort told him. "Focus."

In Ruko's corner, Abbess Glorren said, "If you can't disarm him, give him the round. Don't risk his blade."

Ruko nodded. Katsan—the most seasoned warrior of them all—had lost her arm in a chance accident. He would not suffer her fate.

And so Cain survived the weapons round—just. "Surprise! I'm back," he slurred, to his contingent. He was weaving on the spot, barely conscious. Blood streamed down his face and neck. They gave him water, and an eyepatch they'd stolen from somewhere, and a sip of whisky when he asked.

"Look at him," he said, meaning Ruko. "Not a scratch. Not a dent. Rude, don't you think?"

His contingent agreed that it was, but most of them were fighting back the tears. They knew what was coming. Death the Dragon, circling.

"Three more minutes," Fort said, "that's all. Three minutes." He squeezed Cain's shoulder. Good luck. Or goodbye. Hard to tell from a squeeze.

The bell rang for the third round.

Ruko bore down on him. Cain had trained with one eye covered, just as he had trained with one arm behind his back. But he had never encountered an opponent like Ruko. His strength, his technique, his will. Cain dodged, and danced, but he was slowing down with every step. Sweat and blood poured down his face. Every breath was a fight.

The kick came from nowhere, slamming like a brick into the side of his head. He fell to the canvas, stunned. Before he could

ANTONIA HODGSON

move, Ruko had wrapped an arm around his throat, and begun to squeeze.

Cain fought back, every trick he knew—but Ruko was too strong. He couldn't break free.

He couldn't breathe.

Ruko shifted, and tightened the lock.

So this is how it feels, Cain thought. *Not so bad; not so terrible.* He looked up at the sky, freshened by the storm. Blue, such a beautiful blue. Distantly, he could hear Neema calling his name. She wouldn't reach him in time. But he was glad she was coming for him.

Precious memories spilled out, tumbling over each other. His life laid out like a tapestry, bright and messy. And at the heart of it, his friend. Their first meeting in the store cupboard, sitting knee to knee. That first kiss. The narrow bed. The opening ceremony, pretending to hate her and so overwhelmed with love, *damn her, just look at her. Just look, and never stop looking.*

His vision faded. No air, no fight.

I would have liked longer. But it was enough. I was enough.

A Fox should die with a joke on his lips. But Cain couldn't speak. So he laughed, instead. Laughed at himself and the world, and Ruko crushing the life from him just to win something as worthless, and boring, as power. It was funny. It was hilarious. Cain laughed, and then he was gone.

Ruko felt Cain's body fall limp against his chest.

I've won. The throne is mine. The thought stunned him. He waited for the swell of triumph. Pride, satisfaction. Something. Anything. "I feel nothing," he whispered. "There's nothing."

"Let me help you with that," a voice said.

A sharp, stabbing pain in his forearm. Cain. Cain was biting his arm. He'd been playing dead. *Eight! Never trust a Fox.* He tried to pull away, but Cain had latched on to him like a wild animal. The pain was so intense it took all his training not to scream, or lash out blindly. Blood streamed down his arm. Was that a weapon in his teeth? Razor blades?

Vabras rang the bell. Rang it again.

Cain did not let go. The Fox contingent ran on to the platform, Ish Fort in his ear. "Cain. Cain! Get off him. For Eight's sake, what's wrong with you? Let him go."

Finally, the message got through. Ruko was released. He stared in shock at his mangled arm. Everyone stared in shock at Ruko's mangled arm. Even Vabras.

Cain was gone, and the Fox was awake. Wide awake, with Ruko's blood on its lips, smeared on its chin. It licked itself clean, enjoying the taste, then stopped. People were screaming in horror. The Fox considered killing them, the prey impulse was strong, but something held it back. Cain. That was curious. Even now, Cain was holding it back.

Vabras was speaking to the crowds. "Victory to the Tiger contender. We have a tie. In accordance with the Rules of the Festival, the three eligible contenders shall now go forward to the Dragon Trial."

The Fox cuffed Vabras around the face. "No. Wrong. Victory to me. I am emperor now. I am Fox emperor."

Ish Fort got between them, apologising profusely.

Vabras pulled out a handkerchief and dabbed the blood from his lip. "If he has taken drugs, he's disqualified."

"Head injury," Fort said, trying to drag the Fox away. "Cain. Let's get you to a doctor."

The Fox smiled at Vabras and placed its paw—its hand! How novel!—on the High Commander's chest. "You will regret this, little Hound person, I shall have my revenge, there is no place you shall be safe, assuming I can be bothered, I may forget all about it, grudges are so tedious aren't they, goodbye."

"*Are* you on drugs?" Fort muttered, as he led what he thought was Cain from the platform.

The Fox was disappointed in its abbot. "Do you not know me, Ishmahir? Is it the eyepatch?" The Fox lifted it up. Cain's eye was completely mended, and bright yellow. Both eyes. Both eyes were an eerie yellow, and the pupils…

Fort reeled back, appalled. "Cain. What the *fuck* have you taken?"

Over Fort's shoulder, the Fox saw Neema approaching and levered the eyepatch back in place. "Trouble," it said, sniffing the air. "Chaos. Carnage." Three of its favourite things, what fun.

"Where is he?" Neema called out. "What have you done with him?"

The Fox grinned an unsettling grin. "Excuse me, my dear abbot. A private matter."

"Is he alive?" Neema asked the Fox, in a very patient voice, for the third time. Sol said it was extremely important to remain calm, and not push too hard. Demanding answers of the Fox was a dangerous business. **It does not like to be pinned, Neema.**

They were sitting in the stalls, Neema one row above, a few seats to the left. The show was over, and now the Ox teams had arrived to dismantle everything. Festival Square would become the parade ground once more. Flags were being lowered, the last stragglers evicted from their seats.

The Fox had stolen a tray of snacks, and was devouring it. It had started face down, until *something* had reminded it to use its paws. *Hands!* It was still wearing the eyepatch, it seemed to like it. Neema had persuaded it to turn its visible eye green. A disguise! The Fox had liked that too. "Cain is alive," it said, talking with its mouth full. The Fox did not inhabit dead people, that would be revolting, but it wasn't about to tell Neema that, or the little fragment lodged in her chest, for that matter. Options must be kept open.

Neema breathed out. "Where is he?"

"I cached him," the Fox said, without looking up from its tray. It was a disgustingly messy eater, but Sol said they were safer when it was distracted, and sated.

"What do you mean, you cached him?"

Neema, be careful. This was the First Guardian. Not a fragment, not an aspect. All of them, tangled up together. Every fox that was, every fox that is, and every fox that will be. It was every fox curled up in its den, nose under its tail. It was every fox cornered by hounds. It was every fox defending its territory to the death. Everything, all of them. All at the same time.

The Fox didn't reply, it had already answered one question and was not about to make a habit of it. Also, it had no idea where Cain was. The Fox had many dens, many holes, many secret places. An infinite number. When it needed Cain again (if it needed Cain again), it would remember. Or not. And wasn't that uncertainty delicious?

It licked the bowls clean and tossed them over its shoulder, smashing them. One survived intact. The Fox picked it up. "How clever of you," it said, to the bowl. "I do admire a survivor. You and I shall be great friends, I shall cherish you for ever."

Neema was struggling to hold her temper. "First Guardian. *Please* listen. If Ruko wins the throne, he will provoke a Return. The end of our world and the end of yours. We need Cain back for the Dragon Trial. You have to let him out."

Have to? The Fox did not like that, not at all. It tried to flatten its ears and found it could not. They were on either side of its head, what were they doing there? Stupid, rigid side ears. Enraged, it smashed the bowl, then stared, heartbroken, at the shattered remnants. It rounded on Neema, eye yellow again. A growl rattled in its throat, not even remotely human. *Your fault.*

Neema apologise. Quickly.

She didn't need the prompt. "I'm sorry. I'm very sorry, great one—"

The Fox growled again. Yellow eye. Sharp, sharp teeth. It was going to rip out her throat. Leap over the chairs and tear the life out of her. She shrank back in her seat, terrified.

The Fox stood up and wandered off. Humming.

Neema watched it go, heart thudding. "Oh, my life," she said. "Oh, my life."

She stayed there in her seat, mind blank with residual terror, until an Ox team came and dismantled her row.

CHAPTER
Sixty-Five

TWO THINGS WERE KNOWN. The Dragon Trial took place within the Imperial Temple. Those who took part were altered by it. The rest was mystery.

Over the past fifteen centuries, the vast majority of Festivals had ended with a clear winner. Only five had involved a tie. Contenders dreaded this outcome with good reason. No one knew what happened during a Dragon Trial, but the aftereffects were well documented. In total, seventeen warriors had stepped through the doors of the temple, seeking the throne. Some had crawled back out on their knees, sobbing. Others smiled, their eyes holding secrets. One Fox contender didn't come back at all. The Dragons handed his ashes over without apology or explanation.

Twenty-four years ago, Andren Valit and Bersun Stour had faced a Dragon Trial. Bersun had emerged grim-faced but resolute, and announced himself the victor.

Andren came out, laughing hysterically.

Dusk. An orange and purple sky. The insects were out, flurries of them. The air was fresh after the storm, the world washed clean. On the banks of the canal, servants lit torches in anticipation of the dark. They stopped in their work to watch as Ruko and Neema sailed past on a boat painted sea-green and silver. The prow was a Dragon's head, serpentine. The boat-team rowed hard, dragging the Imperial Temple closer. The storm had ripped patches of gold from its dome, but its white marble walls and stained-glass windows were intact.

Ruko spent the journey deep in thought, staring into the water. His savaged right arm was wrapped in bandages from wrist to elbow, but something else preoccupied him. Neema had seen him arguing with his abbess on the jetty, moments before he embarked. Whatever they were quarrelling about, Rivenna was left unmoved.

"We had a deal, Ruko. I swore a binding oath."

"But if I win—"

"You had better," she snapped, and stalked off.

As for Neema's contingent, having avoided her for the duration of the Festival, suddenly they were back, and wishing her luck. The Dragon Trial was notoriously unpredictable. Neema could win. She could be the next ruler of Orrun. The first Raven empress since Yasthala the Great.

Kindry, though, had taken her to one side. He was wearing his Lord Eternal sash again, and plucked at it anxiously as they talked.

"Neema, you must be very proud of yourself. What an achievement—remarkable. Astonishing. But have a little think, my dear. Are you sure you're capable of leading an empire? Perhaps you might feel more comfortable serving Ruko? Well—just have a little think."

Neema did have a little think. Just a light daydream, as the boat pulled away, of what she might do to Lord Kindry Rok, if she came to power. Sol had suggestions.

—No, I'm going to be a forgiving empress, Sol.

Not too forgiving, Neema.

—Is it wrong to take the throne just to annoy Kindry?

No, Neema, petty grudges are an excellent spur to action. Part of my magnificent role as the Solitary Raven is to be a source of constant irritation to the Flock. A contented Raven is an indolent Raven. Were it not for me . . .

He burbled on, but Neema's thoughts had turned elsewhere. Cain had failed to turn up for the Trial. Abbot Fort had sent a message to every Fox on the island to fan out and find him—not realising they were really hunting the First Guardian itself. But the Fox had gone to ground.

Neema lifted her silver pendant from under her tunic and touched it to her lips. She was afraid Cain might never surface again—that he was trapped for ever in some unreachable pocket of existence, while the Fox enjoyed its freedom.

The rowers lifted their oars as they arrived at the temple steps. Neema and Ruko stepped out together and the boat set off again. They looked at each other. Whatever happened next would for ever bind them together. Contenders of the Dragon Trial. One of only nineteen, in all of Orrun's history.

"May the Eight protect us," Neema said.

"And remain Hidden," Ruko murmured.

"Contenders." Jadu was waiting for them at the top of the steps, in front of the carved wooden entrance doors. A small, unmistakeably regal presence, wrapped in her ocean-green cloak of imperial silk. She lowered the hood. The Dragon's eye emerald, set in its silver diadem, glinted in the centre of her forehead. Her long, rose-gold hair was tied in a soft plait.

"The Dragon greets you," she said, her quiet voice snaking down the steps.

She did not ask where Cain was. He would come or he would not.

When they reached the top step, she touched her wooden staff lightly to the ground, a signal for them to stop. Close up, Neema thought her pale, ageless face looked tired and worn. Grief, perhaps, at the loss of the Visitor. Did Dragons feel grief? Jadu's light-amber eyes gave nothing away.

"Know this and be warned," she said, "none leaves this Trial unmarked. Tiger contender. Will you enter?"

"I will," Ruko replied, without hesitation.

Jadu shifted her gaze to Neema. "Raven contender. Will you enter?"

Neema took a breath. She knew what the Dragon Trial had taken from its survivors. She had read the histories. Of the sixteen who had initially survived the Trial, three had later taken their own lives. Another two were irrevocably broken, spending the remainder of their days tended by the Grey Penitents.

"Contender Kraa," Jadu prompted.

Neema bowed her head. "I will enter." Bersun had recovered from the experience. The true emperor. Like her, he had not wanted the throne, but he had done his duty. He had come out shocked, but unscathed. Let him be her inspiration.

Jadu turned to face the doors. She waved a hand, and they swung open.

The temple was deserted. As they stepped inside, Neema prepared herself for the familiar heavy dose of incense. It was gone, replaced with a sharp, lifting scent of sea-salt and driftwood, and fresh seaweed. From the eight sides of the hall, members of the Dragon contingent materialised from the shadows, holding tapers for the candles.

"A moment of reflection before we begin," Jadu said. "This I counsel, but you may do as you will." She led them around the edge of the vast, domed space towards the individual Guardian chapels. As they passed the first octagonal door they heard sounds from within—clattering and smashing, as if a wild animal had been let loose inside.

Jadu opened the door.

Cain—the Fox—was ransacking the altar. It had healed the injuries Cain had suffered in his fight with Ruko, but its red fur (*hair!*) was still matted with blood, its face streaked with it. The eyepatch was—miraculously—still in place.

"Flowers," it snarled, strewing them on the ground. "Incense. Candles. What need have I of such things? Where is the food, where is my food?" It tore open a wooden box, only to find a stream of bronze and silver tiles. It threw the box at the wall, shattering it, then clambered over the benches.

"Greetings Fox contender," Jadu said. "I see you broke through our perimeter spell."

"Did I?" The Fox walked along the back of the bench and dropped down neatly in front of her. Nose to nose, an inch apart. Jadu did not flinch. "Oh, hello, you are interesting," it said, snuffling behind her ear. "Old, much older than you appear."

The Dragon's eye gleamed on Jadu's forehead, fire bright.

The Fox drew back, as if burned. For the Dragon was ever watching, even as it slept, and the Fox was not where it should be.

"The Trial begins shortly," Jadu said, and closed the chapel door behind her.

Ruko had walked off on his own. Whatever was happening to Cain—drugs, a breakdown, some perverse Fox strategy—he would not let it distract him.

Neema followed Jadu to the Raven chapel. Not being a believer, she had visited it only once before, when she first arrived on the island. It was as she remembered—the stained-glass image of the Raven in flight, the glossy indigo candles, the ornate ebony altar. The faithful had stuffed devotional messages in a black glass jar etched with feathers. Even at prayer, Ravens couldn't help producing paperwork.

Jadu folded her hands together, in a way that put Neema in mind of Yasila. "You have brought a guest with you, Contender Kraa."

On Neema's sixth rib, Sol stopped preening himself, and looked alert.

Jadu gestured to the altar. "Perhaps it could wait for you here, among its offerings. The Trial involves spells that would be... unpleasant, for one of its nature."

Neema opened her mouth, to ask about Cain.

Jadu tapped her staff. "Fragments are one thing. Guardians are another. The Fox will act as it must."

So she knew. She saw.

"Do you have any advice, Servant? How I might prepare for the Trial? How I might protect myself?"

Jadu gave a distant smile. "Ravens and their questions," she murmured, and left.

The contenders stood facing a wall at the back of the temple. The Dragon contingent gathered behind them in their sea-green cloaks and gowns. One of them had drawn an eternal eight on the wall in thick white paint. With her calligrapher's eye, Neema could tell it had been made with one sweeping stroke, fluid and graceful.

The Fox was weaving from side to side, shoulders rolling as it traced the symbol's shape. Jadu handed it a bowl of tea. "You are first," she said.

"I *am* First," the Fox agreed. It drank the tea down in one and tossed the bowl over its shoulder. A member of the contingent caught it, deftly.

Jadu pressed the heel of her hand on the Fox's forehead. "Walk the Eternal Path, Fox contender. See what you must see."

She stepped to the side. The Dragon contingent began to chant softly, a song of yearning and hope, of journeys beyond the horizon, a leap into the unknown…

The Fox made a small, surprised sound. And then it walked straight through the wall, and vanished.

Neema waited for Sol to say something, then remembered—he was back in the chapel, sorting through the shiny, pretty things scattered on the altar. Her mind felt weirdly empty without him.

"No, no." First came the voice, and then the Fox, walking back through the wall. Its breezy tone sounded forced, and its eye had turned a bright, alarmed yellow. "No thank you, I shall not be doing that."

"Contender, do you withdraw?" Jadu asked.

"Things to do, places to be," the Fox said without breaking its stride. "Good day my friends, good day."

They listened as its walk turned into a run, a panicked sprint to the exit. The doors clanged open and slammed shut, the sound bouncing off the walls. Then silence.

Ruko gave a small, satisfied sniff. Cain was out. The throne was in reach.

Jadu presented Neema with her bowl of tea. Rose, with a bitter scent beneath. Dragonscale oil. Neema looked down, and saw her reflection in its surface. *No one leaves the Trial unchanged.*

The Fox had run away. *The Fox* had left.

Ruko, sensing her anxiety, said, "There is no shame in withdrawing, Contender Kraa. You have honoured the Raven with your performance. There will always be a High place for you in my court."

Neema looked at him. "How generous of you, Contender Valit," she said, and drank the tea.

Ruko winced at his own tactical error, and gave her a respectful nod. The first time he had acknowledged her as a true contender.

Jadu pressed her hand to Neema's forehead. "Walk the Eternal Path, Raven contender. See what you must see."

The chanting began again: the Dragon contingent at her back, weaving their spell. She could feel it coalescing around her, thickening the air. The eternal eight symbol on the wall began to move like a serpent, coiling and writhing. Luring her in. Come close. *Closer.* The song spoke to a yearning in her soul for knowledge. For answers. Neema. So much for you to learn. So much we can show you. Take the path and you shall see...

The wall was gone. In its place—a sheet of white-gold fire. The air shimmered with its heat. The chanting at her back pushed her forwards. The Dragonscale urged her on.

She stepped inside the flame.

Pain, as she had never known it. The fire ripped through her, consuming her. Burning her alive...And then she was through. She looked at her hands, her arms, touched her hair. Unmarked. Intact.

She stands upon a path. The service path below her old room, solid and familiar. Ordinary. A straggle of weeds, silver puddles. It is dark but the moon lights her way, full and bright. She is carrying a pack on her back—her gift from the Bear Trial. It feels heavy.

Something tilts inside her. Vertigo.

She understands that this is the service path as she will *see it, later tonight. The full moon, the puddles from today's storm. Her clothes unchanged. This is her future. Her close future. She will be standing here soon, like this.*

Walk the Eternal Path. See what you must see.

The fire roared up in front of her. She stepped into it, and this time it held her there, trapped within its cruel, scorching embrace, and she could feel herself travelling, time passing at unnatural speed, as she burned, and blazed...

And she is on a narrow ridge, patches of ice. Crisp mountain air on a bright winter morning. A pale sun rising. Her body aches but she feels strong, stronger than she is now. She lifts her eyes to the path ahead. Scarlet flags mark a steep climb to the summit. At the top, carved from the mountain, a vast grey fortress, handsome and forbidding.

Anat-garra. The Bear monastery.

Another turn through the fire, brief but intense.

Evening, in the great feasting hall. Row upon row of Bear warriors stand in grim attention. She is dressed in black, short winter cloak pushed back over her shoulders. Snow builds high on the windowsills. Neema has never seen snow, but her future self has grown accustomed to it. It is no more than a backdrop to this moment.

Ahead of her, at the far end of the hall, is a carved wooden seat, set upon a dais. A hooded figure stands waiting for her there. As she walks down the centre aisle, past the ranks of Bear warriors, she feels a tight pressure about her head, and realises she is wearing the amethyst diadem as a crown.

She is close to the dais when a figure appears from nowhere, blocking her path…

The fire rose up again. Weeks, months roared past. She burned, writhing in white-hot agony, but she did not stop. *More, show me more… Show me more than you should…*

At last the fire died, the pain stopped.

A forest, grey and desolate. No birdsong, no breeze to move the branches. Everything still. A thin, poor light struggles through the dense canopy, and the air is hazy.

This vision is different. Neema has no weight, no form, she is here but not here. A sense of dread envelops her as she understands that she has gone beyond the Trial, beyond what is safe. Against her will, she drifts like a ghost through the trees, dragged by some unknown force until she reaches a clearing, and finds that the day—such as it was—has turned to night.

A tall black woman lies on her back in the middle of the clearing. Her future self. She is alone, caught in a fever that looks to have raged for days, by the state of her. Trapped in her delirium, she talks to herself through cracked lips, words Neema cannot hear.

There is a chain around her leg, fixing her to the ground. A square of paper attached to her chest, over her heart. And though the paper is damp with sweat, the ink does not bleed, because this is Raven's Wing ink.

An Order of Exile, with her name upon it. Written in her own hand, stitched into her own skin.

She has exiled herself. Why the Eight would she do that?

The woman she will become stirs and opens her eyes. She sees Neema through her fever dream, an apparition from the past. With great effort, she holds out her hand and speaks one word. "Dolrun."

The poisoned forest.

She sinks back, exhales with the effort. It has taken the last of her strength to force that one word from her throat.

She is dying. Neema is watching herself die.

Her mind, her body recoil. No more of this.

"No more!" she shouts, with all her strength.

An eternal eight spun before her in the air, bright as sunlight. Her way home. Her way back. She fled the grey, cursed forest towards it, and through it.

She was back in the temple, the Dragons chanting in the candlelight. She fell to the ground, sobbing with relief but also a shrinking horror. She didn't even notice when Ruko went through the wall.

She dragged herself to her feet. Jadu watched her with a veiled expression.

Neema's mouth was dry, she needed water. She cast about her.

"Be still," Jadu commanded.

After a long wait, Ruko returned. Whatever he'd seen of his path, it had pleased him. He looked restored, eyes shining.

"What did you see?" she asked him.

Jadu hissed. "Quiet."

The Dragons ended their chant, drawing their haunting harmonies together into a final, held note. One of the contingent stepped to the wall, and traced the eternal eight with his hand. The symbol faded, and was gone.

Jadu placed her hand on Neema's head and bowed her down to the ground, muttering a new spell under her breath. Neema felt something sharp spreading across her scalp, then tightening, like a net of wire.

Jadu moved to Ruko and did the same, lowering the Tiger warrior to his knees. Neema put a surreptitious hand to her head, searching for the wire. The sensation of a net remained, but there was nothing there that she could feel.

"This advice I give you, contenders," Jadu said. "Once this Trial is over, do not dwell upon what you have seen, or it will claim you." When she was sure they understood, she continued. "One question I have, for each of you. You shall answer, yes or no. You will not lie." She turned to Neema. "Contender Kraa. Did you see yourself upon the throne?"

Neema thought of her vision in the Bear monastery—the raised dais, the ranks of warriors. She wanted to explain what she had seen, but as she tried, the wire net began to burn, as if it were embedding itself in her scalp.

"Did you see yourself upon the throne, contender?" Jadu pressed.

"No. But I—" White hot pain sliced through her skull. She cried out, clutching her head.

Jadu turned to Ruko. "Contender Valit. Did you see yourself upon the throne?"

"Yes."

"Then you have won the Trial. It is done."

No words of congratulation for Ruko from the Servant of the Dragon, or her contingent. As one, they lifted their hoods and streamed off down the central aisle, like the tide going out.

Ruko and Neema found themselves alone, kneeling side by side on the hard stone floor. The temple vast and empty, its dome high above them. No crowds, no witnesses to the victory, no sound of protest or of celebration.

Ruko started to speak, then gasped in pain. She realised—he was trying to share his visions with her.

She wanted to say—"It hurts, doesn't it?" But even that was enough for the searing, white-hot net to descend. Testing the spell's boundaries, she found no way through, only pain. They could never speak of it, not even to each other. But they both knew they were changed by the experience, and why. This much they could share, without words, when they looked at each other.

Ruko got to his feet, and offered her his hand. She knew this was his way of honouring that connection. Gracious in victory. She couldn't take it.

She lowered her forehead to the floor as it finally hit her. The enormity of her failure. The horror of what was coming. Ruko would take the throne. The Eight would Return, and all would be destroyed.

She got to her feet without his aid.

Ruko smothered his disappointment. "I understand your concern," he said, awkwardly. "You think I will undermine all that you have worked for. The monastery reforms—I can be persuaded. People forget I lived as a Commoner for eight years…"

Neema shook her head. Where to start? Was it even worth trying to explain to him? Whatever he said now, however much he had promised himself that he would be a benevolent ruler—she had seen the Raven's vision.

"Words will not convince you," Ruko said. "Perhaps, in time, my actions will." And then, hesitant, "I hope you will remain here at court. You would be a great asset—"

Neema gave a hollow laugh, and shook her head.

Ruko folded his arms. "I could compel you."

"Ahh," Neema said, and laughed again, without humour. "There it is." The tyrant just under the skin. She called out, silently.—Sol?

A beat of wings, as a large raven made a circuit of the hall, before landing on her shoulder. It gave a hopeful gurgle, lifting up an onyx ring in one claw.

"No," she said. "I'm not empress."

The bird looked disappointed.

"May I have my present anyway?" she asked, holding out her hand.

The bird took the ring in its beak, and swallowed it.

"Sol, this is Ruko Valit, emperor-in-waiting. Ruko, this is Sol, a fragment of the Raven."

Sol gave an ugly rattle, and fluffed out his hackles.

Ruko made a respectful Raven salute, which did not appease Sol in the slightest. "This explains much. I sensed before that you were protected."

"The Raven came to me as we fought on the platform." Neema did not realise, but as she invoked the Second Guardian, the subtle gleams shone brighter in her hair, strands of indigo and deepest blue.

Ruko saw it, and caught his breath.

"It showed me a vision. One I *can* speak of. I saw you on the throne, laughing." She hesitated, struggling to speak the words. "I saw the Return of the Eight."

Ruko drew back. "I would never..."

"I saw it, Ruko. Just as Yasthala did. The Raven's Dream. Only she stopped it, and I didn't. I failed." Neema covered her face, desolate.

"Neema," Ruko said, hesitant, "whatever you saw, whatever you think of me...I swear to you now, upon my soul. I will never provoke a Return. Think. If I really was destined to end the world, why would the Eight let me win?" He gestured around him. "In their own temple? Is that not a sign of their favour—"

"I was supposed to kill you."

Ruko gave her a gentle, patronising smile.

"You think I couldn't do it, with the Raven's help?"

His smile faded.

"I came *this* close," Neema said, stepping into him. "The Raven wanted you dead, but I couldn't do it. I couldn't kill you." A thought struck her. "We could still change it. We could walk out there now and say I won the Trial. Who's to know? The Dragons won't care—"

Neema! Sol slowed time, enough for her to see the flaring anger in Ruko's eyes, his hands clenching into fists. She shrank back, out of range.

"You would steal the throne from me?" he snarled.

"Not steal it—" She stopped to catch Sol, who had slid from her shoulder. He'd used up all his strength to warn her, and lay in a daze, cradled against her chest.

Ruko's anger faded to cold amusement at the sight. Pathetic. "*You* would steal the throne from me."

"I saw the Eight, Ruko. Pouring down from the sky into the throne room. You have to believe me—"

"I do believe you. The Raven came to you on the platform, and offered you the chance to save the world. And you were too weak to do what was necessary."

Neema stared at him, open-mouthed. "You're saying...I should have killed you?"

He shrugged. "It's a simple calculation. One life for millions. But you lacked the courage to act, and now the whole world is at risk. And you ask me to hand you the throne?" He laughed at the idea. "You are not fit to rule."

As he talked, Neema saw how comfortable he was, speaking like this. When he had tried to reach out in friendship, he had seemed awkward and vulnerable. Now he was the Tiger Warrior again—the golden statue she had met at the opening ceremony. "You spared my life too, Ruko," she reminded him. "You saved Tala. You helped Benna escape. This armour you wear, I know it protects you. But it also weighs you down. I'm not going to apologise for saving your life. I still think it was the right decision." She cradled Sol closer. "But at least...if you must take the throne, then take it with your eyes open. Don't let Rivenna or the emperor or anyone else tell you that you have to be hard and ruthless to rule because it's not true. And underneath all that armour...I think you know that too."

She moved to walk away, shielding Sol.

"Where are you going?" he asked, to her back.

"Honestly? I don't know." She could do no more; she was as exhausted as the bird in her arms. Defeated, she trailed down the aisle. When she reached the temple doors she opened them, just a crack, and slid out into the night.

So this is victory, Ruko thought.

Rivenna arrived soon after, weeping with joy. Ruko had never seen his Guardian-mother cry before—he wasn't aware she could. "The throne is ours!" she sobbed. "The throne is ours!" The Tiger contingent followed in her wake, and then the rest—Lord Clarion and Lady Harmony, Kindry Rok. Havoc in his white and gold admiral's uniform, clutching a celebratory bottle of wine. A squad of Imperial Hounds, here to ensure the safety of the emperor-to-be. A medley of courtiers in their brightly coloured sashes, patting him on the back, promising their loyalty.

"Where are the others?" he asked Havoc, meaning—the other contenders.

"Who cares?" Havoc swigged from his bottle of wine. It was from the Talaka vineyard.

"Have you seen Tala?"

"Ruko…" Rivenna had joined them. "Enjoy your moment."

He rounded on her. "Where is she?"

Havoc, catching the mood, melted away.

"If you've hurt her…" Ruko said, darkly.

Rivenna's smile never faltered. "The emperor plans a reception in your honour tonight. You will see your friend there." She patted his chest. The poison ring directly over his heart. "Let us not fall out, Ruko. *Emperor Ruko*," she whispered, because he was not crowned yet. "Ruler of Orrun. Just think what we will do together."

Ruko gazed at her hand until she removed it. "Neema Kraa thinks I will provoke a Return."

Finally, the smile faltered.

She was still sifting for the best response when Ruko added, "I'm going to offer her the position of High Justice. If she'll take it."

"Well," Rivenna said, the smile returning. "Let's talk about that tomorrow."

PART EIGHT

Dedication to the Eight

∞

CHAPTER
Sixty-Six

THE FOX WAS sitting on a camp bed in the medical tent. There was nothing wrong with it, but it had smelled food, more specifically chicken soup. It was on its fourth bowl. "Another," it said to a passing nurse.

She frowned her disapproval. "That's your last one, Contender Ballari. You'll make yourself ill."

The Fox gave her a look that would haunt her for the rest of her life. "Thank you," it called after her, as she ran away crying. Manners were important. It licked the bowl clean. "I knew a bowl once," it remembered, nostalgically. "What adventures we had. Did I ever tell you of my friend the bowl, Ishmahir?"

The Fox abbot was sitting on a high stool, a few feet away. His hood was down, but his hands had disappeared into his sleeves, as he clutched himself around his pudgy middle. There was a conversation they should be having, about the Dragon Trial, and Ruko becoming emperor, and what they should do about it. Ten minutes ago, Fort had entered the medical tent in a fury. "So it's true —you abandoned the Trial, you piece of—"

And then he had stopped, abruptly. Beneath the lantern light, the creature he had mistaken for Cain was suffused with an eerie copper glow. Shadows distorted its features, sharpening its cheekbones. "I would not take that tone with me," it said softly, "if I were you. Ishmahir."

Fort had stumbled to this stool, and not spoken another word since. He had watched this thing that was not Cain. How it lifted its nose to smell the air, when someone new entered the tent. How it studied them with a keen and hungry eye, while rambling apparent nonsense. Always that one keen, hungry eye.

The Fox was still reminiscing. "It was a magic bowl. If you dropped it on the floor, it didn't break, except when it did. We were great friends." A melancholy sigh.

Fort took a swig from his hip flask. The drunker he was, the more sense this made. Acceptance. Acceptance was key.

The nurse returned with a fresh bowl. She was shaking as she handed it over. The Fox breathed in the soup steam. "You bring me food. This pleases me, tiny trembling friend of the Ox. Go well, go well."

The nurse backed up, and ran.

Fort swallowed another mouthful of whisky, and found his tongue at last. "You called me Ishmahir." No one had called him that in decades. "What may I call you?"

The Fox drank its soup. It was humming a familiar tune. *I am the wedding without a bride, I am the box with nothing inside. Nobody trusts me, what do I care? Look in the mirror, I am not there. Who am I? Who am I?*

I am the Fox.

Fort dropped from his stool to the floor. "Welcome, great one." He pressed his forehead to the floor.

The Fox found this adorable. But it had just remembered a serious matter it needed to discuss. A matter of great urgency. "My altar, Ishmahir."

Fort dared to look up. "You are not pleased with it, my Guardian?"

The Fox was not pleased, not at all. "Too much incense, too much gold. Too many flowers. Not enough chickens. There were no chickens on my altar, Ishmahir. I looked, I searched very hard."

Fort prostrated himself. "Forgive me, great one. From this day, your altar will be piled high with chickens."

"How wonderfully chaotic," the Fox said, instantly appeased. "On a secondary matter, I sniff trouble ahead. For you and for this world. You must hide."

Fort sat back on his heels and opened out his arms in a kneeling Fox salute. "First Guardian, I am your abbot. My place is with you."

This the Fox did not like. Clingy. "No. You will hide. I shall tell you where."

Fort touched his forehead to the ground a second time. "Might I ask one thing, before I leave?"

The Fox clutched its bowl tight. "This soup is mine, you will not take it from me, I will bite you."

Someone else might have been wondering at this point—is *this* the creature I have devoted my life to? But the Fox abbot would not have his Guardian any other way. "I would never take your food, Great One. I only ask after our friend, Cain Ballari. Is he… well?"

"Oh he's having a marvellous time," the Fox lied. "Don't you worry about him, Ishmahir."

"Will we ever see him again?"

The Fox bristled, teeth bared. "You said one thing, I answered your one thing."

A very hasty obeisance from the abbot.

"Come closer, Ishmahir," said the Fox, "and I shall tell you where to cache yourself."

Fort shuffled closer, carefully.

The Fox pressed its nose against Fort's ear and licked it, rather sweetly. Snuffled the abbot's lank grey hair.

After a pause, Fort said, even more carefully, "You were going to tell me where to hide, Great One?"

"So I was," said the Fox, and whispered in Fort's ear.

It was an excellent hiding place, they were both pleased.

CHAPTER
Sixty-Seven

NEEMA PRESSED HERSELF flat against the service hut. Six days ago she had stood in this exact same spot. Six days ago, when all she'd had to worry about was a missing chameleon.

She could almost feel her past self standing next to her, breathing in the same scent of tung oil soaked into the blackened larchwood. From here she could see her old balcony, where Princess Yasila had stood on Festival Eve, waiting for Gaida. If she could travel back now, would she do things differently? Keep her eyes to the ground and see nothing? No. In spite of everything, she would still look up.

Sol was circling the palace, her personal lookout. He swooped and wheeled, revelling in his renewed strength. **No one is coming.**

"No servants?"

Sol did a full somersault and dive. **No one is coming, Neema.**

She slid around the side of the hut and opened the door with the key she'd stolen from the porter's office.

Neema had spent the last hour preparing for her escape. She had no idea how she was going to get off the island, but the visions she'd seen during the Dragon Trial proved that she did.

First stop had been her rooms in the imperial palace. Pulling out her backpack, she'd checked through the contents—compass, tinderbox, leather water pouch. She added only a few items from her old life. A comb, a toothbrush, a change of clothes. Ointment for the wound on her neck, a few sachets of Dr. Yetbalm's pick-me-up powder. The amethyst choker.

Next the armoury, where Sol had flown through an open window and batted against the walls, shrieking in mock alarm. It is astonishing the panic a single trapped bird can create in otherwise reasonable people. While half a dozen guards shooed Sol up and down the corridor, Neema went in search of her weapons chest. She packed her iron fans, a dagger, the warhammer. Cloak and boots. Everything else she had to leave behind—even the beautiful shield; it would draw too much attention strapped to her back.

After the armoury she'd dropped over to the Ox farmhouse to speak to Fenn, only to find the place in uproar over his arrest. No one paid her any heed as she gathered some basic provisions from the farm's kitchen, to add to the Bear pack's rations. Bread and fruit, rice and beans, chocolate, tea, dried sausage. Enough to keep her going for a couple of days. She filled her water pouch and rearranged her pack, testing its weight and balance on her shoulders. From her pockets she added the purse of silver tiles Benna had given her, and Fenn's leather mark of friendship.

Leaving the Ox grounds, she'd taken the service paths all the way down to the Raven palace. Sol had done his startled raven act on the porter while she stole the key.

Which brought them here. Her first Dragonfire vision was complete.

The question was—had she always been destined to come here tonight, or had the vision inspired her? No way to ask, no way to know.

She stored the pack behind a pile of blankets and sat for a moment on the dusty floor, in the dark silence. Sol was outside by the bin. She was alone. She closed her eyes and allowed herself to drift.

Memories of the Dragon Trial rose up to greet her. Red pennants flying on a crisp winter morning. Grey death in a poisoned forest.

She opened her eyes. The visions brought with them a wave of nausea, a spinning sensation in her head, as time folded forwards then backwards. A permanent after-effect of the spell. She remembered Jadu's cautionary words. *Do not dwell upon what you have seen.*

She got to her feet. One final stop.

Sol was watching the cockroaches behind the bin, oily brown and scuttling. Dozens of them, flourishing in the dark. Neema's skin crawled.

Cockroaches are a good omen, Neema.

"Really?"

They are strong, they are resilient. He ate one, with a single snap and swallow. **They are survivors.**

"That one isn't."

As a species. They are older than old. Do you know what these cockroaches say to me?

"'Please don't eat our friend'?"

"We were here before, we shall be here after." They say that a lot, Sol added, after a pause.

"Like a motto."

Yes.

"The creed of the cockroach."

Yes. Sol spat the cockroach back out, and watched with deep focus as it hurried back to its companions.

"Didn't taste so good, then?"

It tasted revolting, Neema.

The cockroach made a sharp, grating sound, and disappeared back into the rubbish.

It is wise to be disgusting, Sol translated.

Neema mulled on this philosophy as she headed through the palace grounds towards the library. An impromptu party had broken out in a private stretch of gardens, people gathering to celebrate the end of the Festival and talk about its implications. A Tiger emperor—one with very different ideas from the Old Bear. Would Abbess Glorren be the power behind the throne? Would Vabras remain in place as High Commander? What would happen to Princess Yasila, given her antipathy towards her son? Would she be punished for it? Sent to the House of Mist and Shadows? And what then for her daughter Nisthala?

Hidden away in the shadows, Neema waited for one of them to mention the extra Leviathans, the influx of Samran troops, but no one seemed to care about that.

"I know it's disloyal," someone said, "but thank the Eight he won."

Neema felt a prickle run down her spine.

"Might have been interesting, a Raven empress," someone else said, charitably.

"Of course," the first person said. "But..."

But not me, Neema thought, in the dark. I came closer to winning than any Raven in the history of the Festival, but it still wasn't enough for them. Maybe it would be different in other parts of the palace. The unfashionable north wing. The service paths. She might find more support there.

"The thing about Ruko Valit," someone else said, waving their glass. "He has that charisma, that indefinable quality you need in a leader."

"I hear she *was* good at the Monkey Trial."

"But that was a performance. Ruko doesn't have to perform. He *is* imperial. I bet that's why he won the Dragon Trial."

"She came out looking *deranged* apparently. Talking to that pet raven of hers."

Pet raven?

"How long has she been training it in secret, do you think? Weird."

Pet raven?

"Let's go," Neema whispered, before Sol attacked someone. She moved on, leaving the party behind. Heading for her sanctuary.

It was blissfully cool and quiet inside the library. Only the night librarian was on duty, sulking at the main desk with a bowl of coffee and a stack of romances. A couple of the palace's more obsessive scholars sat welded in their usual seats, collecting dust. Someone was snoring in Periodicals.

The librarian looked at Neema, looked at the raven on her shoulder. "No pets," he said.

Sol made a noise Neema hadn't heard before, deep in his throat.

"Please don't call him that," she said.

The librarian put a finger to his lips then wrote a new sign, just for her. He held it up. NO PETS.

Sol hopped on to the stack of romances, then flew straight at Neema's chest. Tore her open with his claws and shouldered his way in. Blood and bone and viscera. Glistening heart, beating. Lungs expanding and contracting. Neema stood there waiting for it to be over, hands on her hips. She was getting used to it.

The librarian slid under his desk in a dead faint.

Neema took the spiral staircase up to the map room. She had spent many hours in here, cross-referencing old maps with even older texts. Ancient Orrun was as familiar to her as her palace lodgings. But—outside of her head—she had never ventured beyond the empire's north-east pocket. Scartown, Armas city, the island—that was the extent of her travels.

Opening up the map she felt a sort of vertigo, as if she might fall in. The empire stretched out under her hands, vast and intimidating. The long journey to the Bear monastery was straightforward enough, assuming she could travel one of the main routes west. Best not to assume. She took the stairs up to the highest gallery, bringing the map with her.

Neema knew this part of the library very well—it was a good place to hide. The books here held the stale, sour smell of neglect. The weighted disappointment of being unwanted, unread for decades. Sol gave a soft whir of approval.

Neema slid a slim, rust-coloured book from the shelf. *How to Survive on the Road: A Searingly Dull but Practical Guide for Beginners* by Sinn Dunrelli, Fox adventurer of Fox adventurers. People read Dunrelli to be entertained, not informed—which was why this little guide was languishing up here in *Manuals and Instruction Booklets: Miscell., 900–1100 N.C.*

For half an hour she sat with the map and Dunrelli's guide, memorising the salient points. It did not occur to her to smuggle them out. There were many things Neema might do, in an emergency. Stealing from a library was not one of them.

When she was done, she headed back outside.

Havoc was waiting for her on the library steps, accompanied by his squad of Samran Hounds, the same ones who'd beaten Cain up so badly. Two of them carried lanterns on long poles. The others had exchanged batons for swords. When did regular Hounds start wearing swords? But then, they weren't regular. Nothing about this was regular.

"Lady Neema," Havoc said smoothly, using her new honorific. "His Majesty, Emperor Bersun invites you to a private reception, to honour his successor."

"The armed guards are for my protection, I presume?"

"Naturally."

Walking along the high ridge towards the Grand Canal, Havoc stopped and swept his arm out, presenting the view. Under the full moon, twelve Leviathans sat anchored in the channel, smaller boats attending like servants at a feast. On the eastern quay, a troop of Samran Hounds was hard at work, loading supplies as the boats came back and forth—food, water, bolts of material, treasury chests and weapons.

Twelve Leviathans now—and those were just the ones she could see. There would be at least three more anchored around the island. Half the imperial fleet, loading up with the island's treasures. The most generous explanation Neema could come up with was that the Tigers had struck some kind of corrupt, back-hand deal with the emperor. The worst explanation was that this was a coup, unfolding before her eyes. She thought of the Ravens drinking wine in the private gardens. Had no one else noticed this? Did they not care?

"That one's mine," Havoc said, pointing out the Leviathan nearest to shore, sleeker than the rest. He leaned in, conspiratorial. "But I command them all. I've been promised the position of High Admiral."

"Ruko knows about this?" It made no sense. If the emperor never intended to give up the throne, if these troops were loyal to him, why bother going through the charade of a Festival in the first place? And if Ruko was involved, as Havoc implied—that made things even stranger. In a million years, Ruko would not willingly share power with the emperor. He had fought and won on his own merit, in front of thousands of spectators. No one could deny the legitimacy of his succession.

She focused on the view below them. The Hounds on the quay, the moonlight on the water, the silvered warships. The Tiger's Path constellation, so bright it cast the Mirror Bridge in an eerie light, over the black waters.

She was missing something. Something essential.

Havoc caught the direction of her gaze. "Beautiful, isn't it? I wish my aunt were alive to paint it."

"It's not beautiful." Neema turned to look at him, his handsome profile. "I don't know what's happening here, but it's ugly. Shimmer would have seen that. That was her genius. She saw right to the heart of things."

"I agree," Havoc said, with an infuriating smirk. "She captured things perfectly." Turning his back on the sea, he proffered an arm. When Neema didn't take it, he said, "I could make you. Your choice."

Suppressing a shudder, she took his arm. And soon realised why he had insisted. This was a charade for the benefit of the courtiers dining out on the canal, crossing the bridges to meet friends at other palaces, mingling on the banks. The Festival was over, and either they had not seen the warships, or had chosen not to worry. There would be those who *would* be worried. Wiser heads, more cautious souls. The Ox palace was subdued as they sailed by, while the Bears' fortress blazed with light, warriors patrolling the battlements. But the Tigers were celebrating, and there were plenty who were happy to join in with that end of Festival spirit. Drinking helped. There was a lot of drinking. Havoc waved and smiled as people cheered their procession, and put his arm around Neema's shoulder, as if they were great friends. "Smile," he ordered, in her ear.

Finally, when they reached her rooms, she was rid of him. She had to change, and check the dressing on her neck.

"I'll be right here," he said, in the antechamber.

In her bedchamber, she found her opening ceremony gown laid out for her on the bed with a note from Grace Eliat.

Lady Neema. His majesty insists you wear this.

Rage. Rage consumed her. She took the dress in both hands and ripped it apart at the seams. Diamonds scattered as she tore up the sheer bodice. It wasn't enough; it didn't satisfy her need. Digging out her silver sandals, she used the heel to tear through the silk. Over and over, until it was nothing but shreds of fabric. She flung the sandal away and stood back, shaking from the effort.

After the rage, a numbing calm. She had brought very few clothes with her when they moved her here, and most of those were now in her Bear pack. Her contender trousers and martial shoes would do, but her embroidered tunic would be far too conspicuous on the road—assuming she made it that far. The only alternative was a dark indigo tunic with a short collar and long sleeves, which she'd brought in case the weather turned cooler. She threw it on, fastening the silver buttons along the side yoke.

Checking her hair in the mirror, she realised she was still wearing her colours on her arm. She untied them and then—on impulse—wrapped them around her waist like a sash, with the Raven Wing sigil at the front.

In her chest, Sol opened his wings to match. **Raven warrior.**

—Raven warrior.

She rubbed some cream through her curls, inspecting the change in colour. The subtle strands of blue and indigo no longer disturbed her. After all she'd been through, it seemed fitting there should be some indelible mark. She had suffered, she had survived.

As she left she had the odd feeling she'd forgotten something. The choker? No, that was in her pack. Something else…She shook the feeling away.

In the antechamber, Havoc frowned at her outfit. "This is a formal reception. The emperor expects to see you in your dress."

"He's not my emperor," Neema said, and stalked off down the hall.

CHAPTER
Sixty-Eight

I N THE LINE OF CONTENDERS, Shal Worthy had often felt invisible. For the first two days of the Festival he had held a comfortable lead over his rivals. He was liked and admired by the palace Hounds and by the wider court. Several influential courtiers had said to him, in confidence—we are praying for your victory, Contender Worthy. And yet he had never felt at the centre of things. Perhaps this was an inevitable consequence of his gift, that made him always the observer. Even as the courtiers had flattered him with their kind encouragements, he had always known their true attention lay elsewhere. Ruko. Cain. The dramas surrounding the Raven contender. As he'd slipped further down the points table, the court's interest had slipped with it. The forgotten contender.

So it had been a surprise to find Princess Yasila's invitation waiting for him in his rooms. With his broken collarbone, he'd needed help to change into his best clothes. His contingent—who loved him more than he realised—had presented him with three embroidered cotton slings to see him through his recovery. He had chosen the plainest—dark blue, with the silver square of the Hound sigil forming the buckle.

And Yasila, on seeing him, had thought: How dashing he looks, without trying. It was a trait she'd noticed in him the first time they met. The young Hound captain as he was back then, with his polite manners and skewering gaze, standing alone on her doorstep. Trying to look older and rougher than he was with his chopped hair and moustache—but clothes hung better on some men than others. He carried himself well, and this Yasila appreciated.

"If it is any consolation, Lord Shal, I think you would have made a fine emperor," she said, then smiled at his discomfort. "Your new title is not to your taste."

They were standing on the eastern balcony of her suite. From here they could see the Garden at the Edge of the World, perched over the sea far below, the lanterns no more than dots of light as guests arrived for the emperor's reception. The full moon shone over the water, the Tiger's Path a diamond cascade across the sky. Two Leviathans moved slowly in black silhouette against the night. They lacked the urgency of their cousins on the channel, there were no small boats in attendance, no loading and unloading. From here the seas were endless, so far as anyone knew.

"Would you prefer High Commander?" she asked Shal.

He frowned. Here was a dangerous conversation, bordering on treason. "Is that in your gift, your highness?" he asked, carefully.

"Not here." She tilted her chin towards the sea, and the ships. "Those two are mine. We sail for Helia at dawn."

"We?"

A door opened deep within the suite, and then another. They both turned as a girl entered the living area, bundled in a hooded robe and blankets. Save for her face and hands, not an inch of skin was showing.

Nisthala. Yana's sister. She lowered her hood, revealing a sleepy tangle of grey hair, streaked with white. Her ash-grey eyes were almost entirely eclipsed by her pupils.

Shal gave a deep bow, to hide his shock. "My lady."

"Lord Shal. I am pleased to meet you at last." If she'd had an Armas Common Grid accent, and surely she must have once, it was long gone. Her intonation was more like her mother's, if not quite so formal. She looked like Yasila too, beneath the strangeness. Shal was both grateful and saddened that she did not resemble her older sister. Yana had been small and energetic, and very easy to read, despite her best efforts. Nisthala was tall and willowy, listless in her movements, and her face held mysteries. Clutching her blankets closer, she continued to stare at him, unblinking, as if he were a mythical beast.

"Please excuse my daughter," Yasila said. "Her world has been very small since she came here. You are the first stranger she has met in over six years."

Nisthala yawned behind her hand and moved to join them.

Yasila patted the air, to stop her. "It is too cold for you out here, darling. Wait for us by the fire. We shan't be long. Do you have books?"

"I always have books, Mama," she murmured, and retreated to the fire.

Shal was a perceptive man, it only took him moments to add up what he had seen, and find an answer. Her uncanny eyes, the blankets. The fire on a warm summer night. Thinking back, he remembered she was not quite nine years old when she fell "sick," and was brought here. Locked away from the world. "She was Chosen," he said, awed.

Yasila was pleased with how quickly he understood, that she did not need to explain her reasons. She watched him think it through. Her own troubled history with the Dragons. The loss of her older daughter. And what she might be prepared to do to keep the younger one safe.

Anything. She would do anything.

Voices carried from the reception far below. She was dressed for the occasion in a silvery grey dress, her hair netted with diamonds. For years she had longed to wear grey, for her daughter. Now it was permitted, to honour the Visitor. She had decided to only wear grey from this day forward. Let her grief be visible at last.

She leaned her arms on the balustrade. Shal mirrored her. They looked out at the stars, side by side. She liked his silence. She was in no rush to join the party. Not yet. The moon said not yet.

"I know why you entered the Festival," she said.

Shal bowed his head. For Yana. He would have found a way to pardon her, had he won. Honoured her memory as best he could.

"She haunts you," Yasila murmured.

Shal's brow furrowed. "I hope not. I hope her spirit has returned to the Path." He sighed. "I haunt myself."

"It is not your fault Yana died as she did."

Shal winced at the old wound. They were not supposed to talk of her. By law she did not exist. But who was to stop them, up here alone? No one could hear them, not even Nisthala, huddled by the fire.

"I gave birth to my twins in these rooms," Yasila said. "Twenty-four years ago, almost to the day. In the middle of the Festival. Nineteen years old, a child of Helia. I knew nothing of such matters. Nothing. My husband was fighting for the throne, I could have dropped dead in front of him and he would not have noticed. Empress Haven saw how ill I was. She ordered her physicians to take care of me, here in her own suite. She saved my life. And the twins. I am sure of it."

"My uncle always spoke highly of the late empress."

Yasila was lost in reverie. "Two days," she said, wistful. "The twins were healthy, against the odds. For two days I thought myself blessed by the Eight." An ironic lift of an eyebrow.

Shal turned to study her, and waited.

"Andren believed it was his destiny to rule Orrun. To *save* it. When Bersun won the Dragon Trial he was…" There were no words to describe the intensity of Andren's rage. The terrible, manic gleam in his eyes. "We all tried to reassure him. Bersun didn't want the throne; he had no appetite for power. He *hated* the court. Wait a few years, and there would be another Festival. Another chance to rule."

Shal nodded. It was Brother Lanrik who'd had ambitions for the throne. The saintly, ascetic abbot had imagined an empire transformed, just as he had transformed Anat-garra. Too old to fight himself, he had sent Bersun as his proxy.

"I thought we had persuaded him," Yasila said. "My husband was always a patient man with a cool head. But the Dragon Trial had affected him so strangely…And then Bersun made his coronation speech…"

His promise to reform the monasteries. Higher taxes for the wealthiest citizens, court positions opened up to every class. A war would be waged, Bersun said, against the twin curses of nepotism and corruption. Brother Lanrik had achieved this at the Bear monastery. Bersun would do the same for the empire as a whole. However long it takes, he'd said. If I must serve the full twenty-four years at my disposal, so be it. Orrun shall be reborn.

"Andren took it personally," Yasila said, sighing at her own understatement. "That night I woke to the sound of my twins, crying for me. Even before I found them, I knew something was terribly wrong. He'd carried them out here in his arms. He was..." She hunched her shoulders, the memory frightening her even now. "He was standing up here, on the balustrade. An inch from the edge. Raving to the sky."

Bersun stole the throne from me. Now he steals their future. This is a kindness, Yasila—an act of love.

That is what her husband had said to her, as if he were the hero in a tragic opera.

"Eight," Shal breathed.

Another step, and she would lose them over the edge. Her twins, her babies. The words of the binding spell had poured out of her unbidden. She was not yet its mistress, she was young, un-trained. Exhausted. But it was enough to hold them there, for a moment. Enough time for Andren to see—*Well, well. My wife is a witch. That changes things. That changes things entirely.*

She did not tell Shal the rest. How Andren had forced her to teach him how to spell cast, using the twins as leverage. That ter-rible night on the balcony had taught him one vital lesson: that she would do whatever it took to keep them safe.

Andren always got what he wanted, one way or another.

"I saved Yana that night, and Ruko. But I did not know, back then—magic demands balance. Especially when you disturb the patterns of life and death. I saved my children, and doomed them in the same moment. You cannot cheat the Dragon. And those who try are punished for it, most severely. It is a lesson I am still learning."

Shal thought about this for a time, mulling over her story. "You are saying that Yana's exile was inevitable."

"I am saying it was not your fault. The blame lies with Andren, and with me. Well—if you wish to travel back even further, one

THE RAVEN SCHOLAR 575

could blame my father, for taking his boat out against his captain's advice. Or my mother, for abandoning me with the Dragons. Or Jadu for offering me nothing but indifference, where there should have been love. We are all responsible, in differing degrees, for what happened to Yana. But not you, Shal Worthy. You at least are blameless."

He shook his head. The roots of his guilt ran too deep, were too tangled up within him to be removed so easily. He could have helped Yana escape on the road, there had been plenty of opportunities.

"My words do not persuade you," Yasila said. "Then let me offer you this gift of redemption." She glanced into the living room, where Nisthala sat quietly by the fire, absorbed by her book. "Everything changes for her tonight. There are things I cannot tell you now, for your own sake." A slim hand on his wrist, swiftly removed. "But this you may know. Tonight, Nisthala will come into her full power. And tomorrow we shall set sail for Helia, where she will rule."

Shal gave a start of surprise, and concern.

"Yes, I know. She is young, and sheltered. She will need guidance, as well as protection—someone she trusts. A good uncle. Will you pledge yourself to her service? Will you come with us to Helia?"

Shal felt his heart lift. A second chance. "I will."

"Hmm," Yasila murmured, quietly pleased. Some good news on a dark night. It was important to her that he had chosen this path of his own volition. That his oath was given freely, without fear. She was glad for Nisthala, but she was also glad for him. Had he declined, she doubted he would have survived the dawn. The emperor had no use for him.

She glanced down at the guests milling in the gardens below. "I must go. Please stay here with Nisthala, until I return. No matter what happens, do not leave these rooms. Let no one in. *No one.* This is for your protection."

Shal's dark brows lifted. "Mine?"

She left him, and headed back inside. Picking up a floating, silver-grey scarf, she wrapped it around her neck.

Nisthala lifted her nose out of her book to admire her mother. "He said yes?"

"He did. I won't be long. An hour, at most."

They looked at each other. Seven years of pain and patience, almost at an end. Nisthala got to her feet and gave her mother a deep, supportive hug.

Yasila kissed her daughter's head, smoothed her grey hair. *This one. This one I have saved.*

CHAPTER
Sixty-Nine

SOME PLACES ARE soaked in power. The ruined city of Samra. The cave networks of Helia. The House of Mist and Shadows, ancient sentinel of the grey marshes. History, faded to myth and then forgotten, can be lost. But the power remains, steeped into the stone like blood. Do not ask if that power is good or evil. Ask who plans to draw it out and use it.

Neema was at the party, standing alone by the ornamental fish ponds. Empty—which made her feel guilty. She hadn't meant to poison those poor fish, but still. Their deaths were on her conscience. As if she had summoned her own punishment, her old assistant Generic Arsehole swaggered up to her, drunk.

"So, *Lady* Neema—what do you plan to do next?"

"Die horribly, I suspect," Neema muttered.

Janric was already talking over her. "D'you hear the rumour? Emperor Ruko plans to move the court to Samra. And all those boring reforms will go of course," he waved his hand, dismissing them. "That must be sad for you. It's like…" A look of consternation crossed his face. He was searching for a simile, but lacked the imagination to find one.

"As if I'd spent years building a palace, only to have someone come along in the night, and knock it down."

"Exactly!" He pointed at her. "I'm going to use that. You built a palace, and we knocked it down." A nasty grin. "Everything back the way it should be."

He walked off. In fact everyone was drifting away, she realised, on some invisible signal. Heading further out into the gardens, towards the promontory. Janric had only come up to taunt her, before joining them.

Everything felt off. This strange, inappropriate party: a jig played at a funeral. The island was being looted, there were troops everywhere, and people were laughing and clinking glasses, and admiring each other's outfits. She wished Cain were here. He would love this, the perverse idiot.

"Lady Neema, do join us." Havoc—never far away—had come to gather her up. Instead of leading her out to the promontory, he drew her in, to the small courtyard that lay beneath the throne room's great octagonal window. Deserted except for Tala, dressed in another of her signature halterneck gowns, cream satin and short this time, showing off her strong thigh muscles. She was peering through the glass, trying to make out what was happening inside.

"Tala."

She turned at her name. "Neema, thank the Eight."

They hugged each other, all arguments forgotten. "They've taken Fenn."

"I know."

Tala drew back, clutching Neema's wrists tight. Her eyes spoke for her. *Thank you. For saving Sunur, and Suru. Thank you.* Then she rounded on Havoc. "What the fuck is going on, you absolute prick?"

He lifted his hands, he'd already explained. "We're celebrating. Why don't you enjoy the wine…" He gestured to a tray of drinks set out on a nearby table.

Neema found herself measuring the distance, assessing the weight of the table. Did she have the strength to smash it over his head, hard enough to knock him out? Eight she'd love to break his nose a second time. Could Tala run in those strappy sandals? That headband she was wearing—a pair of ox horns shaped in bronze. Were the points sharp enough to draw blood?

The Oxwoman is better with her fists, Neema.

Sol was perched in her chest, in a fluff of excitement. This was his first imperial reception. He had bathed for the occasion in a muddy puddle and come out looking surprisingly sleek and distinguished.

"Lord Ruko," Havoc said, and gave a deep Monkey salute. "Emperor-in-waiting. Welcome."

Ruko had entered the courtyard silently, shadowed by his abbess. They were both immaculately dressed—Ruko in a forest-green tunic with gold collar and buttonholes, Rivenna in a heavily beaded, close-fitting hooded dress that shimmered as she moved. The Tiger abbess was lit from within by triumph. Ruko seemed more subdued. But he smiled when he saw Tala, and crossed to her side. *Like a bodyguard,* Neema thought.

"Is Shal joining us?" she asked.

"Lord Shal is otherwise engaged," Havoc said.

Neema's heart sank. She hadn't realised until now, but she had invested heavily in the idea that Shal was a good man. She needed to believe that there were still some decent Hounds out there, who followed the Code of Ethics, and believed in the Four Tenets. Justice, Order, Loyalty and Honour: the four sides of the silver square. Whatever was happening here tonight, she fervently hoped Shal wasn't a part of it. If he'd been corrupted, they were all lost.

"I don't suppose you saw Cain on your way over," Havoc asked Ruko and Rivenna, a touch of anxiety entering his voice. "The emperor is keen for me to find him..."

Neema enjoyed the matching, scornful look they gave him. *Your pathetic failure is of no concern to us.*

"Well then," Havoc said, reddening. "Let us go in."

"Ah," the emperor said, as they filed in through the great window. He sat on his white marble throne, not perched on the edge for once, but settled back, comfortable. Relaxed within his power, when it was supposed to be ebbing. He was dressed in his usual black tunic with red slashes. Behind him, moonlight poured through the window, while incense burners oiled the air with a familiar, smothering scent of frankincense and patchouli. At the base of the steps, Vabras stood in his preferred spot.

There was one significant change, and it made Neema's skin crawl. The Imperial Bodyguards were gone. In their place, Havoc's squad of Samran Hounds lined the steps, dressed in their blue and silver livery. There was blood on their swords. Something told her it belonged to the guards they had replaced. She looked at Ruko, trying to alert him. His face was a mask.

The emperor frowned as she crossed before him. "Where's the dress?" he snapped.

"She refused to wear it, Your Majesty," Havoc said, as Neema replied, over the top, "I ripped it to shreds."

"Fascinating," the emperor said, rubbing his mouth as he took in her appearance.

Fascinating was another of those court words, like astonishing, and remarkable, but even worse. Never fascinate an emperor.

Putting his hands on their backs, Havoc pushed Neema and Tala towards the other side of the room, and positioned them carefully in front of the Monkey's portrait, as if this were a play, and these were their marks.

The emperor's attention had shifted to Ruko. The Tiger warrior stood in the centre of the room, legs spread wide, hands on his hips. On the ceiling above, the Dragon's jaws seemed wider than ever, readying to stream down fire.

"Ruko Valit, emperor-in-waiting. Welcome."

With these few words, the emperor acknowledged the legitimacy of the succession.

Ruko's shoulders relaxed. He inclined his head in silent greeting, one emperor to another. And Neema thought—*Whatever is happening here, Ruko is not a part of it.*

"It was a close win," the emperor said. "Closer than expected. Neema Kraa surprised us," a crooked smile, "as she often does. You were lucky with the Dragon Trial. But your accession to the throne cannot be denied, or overturned."

That is a strange thing to say, Neema.

Neema agreed, and so did Ruko by the looks of it. He was about to reply when the doors to the throne room opened wide, splitting the Tiger portrait in two. Kindry Rok bustled through, chest first, followed by Lord Clarion and Lady Harmony, holding hands.

Wandering in behind them, as if by chance: Cain Ballari.

Washed and groomed, he was dressed in a flamboyant, knee-length coat stolen from the imperial wardrobe—black satin, embroidered with orange and white flame patterns. A fresh, black velvet patch covered his eye.

Its **eye,** Sol corrected, tapping on Neema's rib. **That is not Cain.**

"Lord Cain of Scartown," the emperor said, evidently amused by the title. "We have been looking for you, and your abbot. Where is Ish Fort?"

"Hiding." The Fox was spinning in languid circles, taking in Shimmer's portraits of its fellow Guardians. "Oh that's good. Look at Tiger split in half, how splendid, I should love to split Tiger in half like that." He turned again, reading the words over the paintings. "SEVEN TIMES HAVE THE GUARDIANS SAVED THE WORLD. Was it seven times, little fragment?"

Yes, Fox, Sol replied.

"Well I shall take your word for it. Bit of a blur, to be honest…"

Havoc was trying to usher what he assumed was a heavily intoxicated Cain to the edge of the room. The Fox evaded him without even noticing, weaving in a dance of blithe, slinky elegance, then stopped in front of its own portrait. Lifting its eyepatch, it waited for the depiction of Cornered Vixen Defending its Cubs to transform into a fresh aspect. The painting remained resolutely as it was. The Fox lowered its patch, disappointed, then pressed its nose deep against the painting, and snuffed. "Smells like home," it said, and licked the wall. Clacked its tongue, as if it were tasting a fine wine. "Dragonscale." It tried another patch, licking right across the vixen's head. "Oh, it's in the paint, how curious…"

Vabras moved around the back of the throne, unsheathed his sword, and—with a swift, efficient move—knocked the Fox out cold with the pommel. "Watch him," he said to the nearest Hound, and returned to his place by the throne. The Fox lay still beneath its portrait, one leg bent, one leg straight.

The emperor had turned in his seat to watch this. As he did so, a dagger was revealed on his right hip, sheathed in a simple leather scabbard. Hurun-tooth. The Blade of Peace.

Ruko's fists clenched as he saw it. "Your Majesty. Only a Tiger warrior may wear the Blade. I demand its return."

The emperor lifted an eyebrow. "You demand...? It is not midnight yet, emperor-*in-waiting*."

Ruko was not deterred. "It was given to me for safekeeping. I swore an oath—"

"Then you should have taken better care of it." The emperor had unsheathed the Blade. Pressing the tip to his finger, he drew out a bead of blood.

Neema gasped. His hand. His ruined right hand was mended. No one else noticed. They were transfixed by the Blade. The most dangerous weapon in existence. The emperor ran his finger along the pattern etched into the steel. "The next time Hurun-tooth takes a life, the Eight will Return in blood and fire."

"He's mad," Tala whispered.

Ruko could stand it no longer. He moved towards the steps.

Rivenna, stealthy as a cat, came up beside him and pressed her ring to his neck. The needle-sharp fangs stabbed deep into the vein.

A heartbeat, and it was done.

Ruko clutched his neck, and turned to her in shock.

"Numbing agent," she purred, as the fangs retracted. "You'll live."

Whatever she'd used it was powerful, and swift-acting. He sank helpless to his knees at the bottom of the throne steps, head bowed; an unwilling supplicant. Unable to move, unable to speak.

The emperor sheathed the Blade. "Thank you, Rivenna."

Rivenna kneeled down next to her student, and pressed her forehead to the floor. "It is an honour to serve my emperor." When she rose, her face was shining with adoration. "The moon rises, my love. Take this gift that I have made for you, and use it as you will."

This gift...

Ruko. She means Ruko, Neema.

The emperor touched a hand to his heart in gratitude, and—to Neema's surprise—began to sing. The Old Bear's deep, rough voice had no music to it, but there was a strange, transfixing power to his words. "Patiently it waits the hours..."

The Song of the Forest. An ancient Ketuan song, long forgotten. She had found it, translated it. Matched the tune to the words for the first time in centuries. For him.

"Strength and grace concealed..."

The air was thickening around her. She felt the words reach inside her, tugging at something buried deep, something that did not wish to be found. A spell song. But not for binding...

Sol shook himself, beak open in alarm. **The Soul Stealer.**

"A ripple in the long grass..." The emperor was changing before their eyes. The voice was different—smooth and pleasing. Something writhed inside his face, tugging and pulling it into a new, sharper shape. His giant form shrank, his hair darkened to black, streaked with grey. His skin colour changed to a warm, golden brown. "...and a tiger is revealed."

The song was ended. The Old Bear was gone. And in his place...

A sound escaped Neema's throat—a dull moan of horror. Here was the man she had served so faithfully for eight years. Here was her emperor. Not Bersun, not Gedrun, but a Tiger, revealed.

Andren Valit. The Great Traitor.

Impossible. Undeniable.

He smiled a beautiful, charismatic smile. Everyone always said, Andren's smile was his greatest weapon. That you could win a war with that smile.

He rose to his feet, arms wide.

Around her, people were dropping to their knees, heads bowed. Lady Harmony and Lord Clarion, Kindry Rok, the Hounds lining the steps. More than deference, she thought, as Havoc shoved her and Tala to the ground. *Reverence.* Eight—look at their expressions. They *worshipped* him.

Tala was crying with shock, hands covering her mouth. "What's happening?" she said. "What's happening?"

Neema put an arm around her shoulder and they clung to each other, as if they were caught on a river, smashing through the rapids.

"I don't understand," Tala said, through sobs.

"Of course you don't," Havoc muttered, behind them. "Oxes. No imagination."

Kindry was back on his feet, filling his lungs. "All hail His Majesty, Andren the First," he boomed. "Saviour of Orrun."

"All hail His Majesty!" The words rang out through the room like a fanfare.

Andren headed down the steps towards his son. No longer with the heavy, world-weary tread of the Old Bear, but light-footed and urbane. Delighted to be himself.

Ruko was trying desperately to fight Rivenna's numbing agent, sweat pouring down his face. It was no use. He was frozen in place, mouth sealed shut. But his eyes blazed with blind hatred.

Father.

Andren ruffled his son's hair. "Ah, Ruko. I am sorry, my boy. I know how much you wanted this." His fingers tangled deeper, pulling Ruko's head back so he could see the white marble throne above him. He leaned in, playful. "But it was my dream first."

Ruko stared up at the throne. So close. Even now, he believed he could reach it. Because it wasn't just a dream. It was a vision. A promise made to him in the temple. In the Dragon flame.

Andren circled round and gripped his son's shoulders. "You saw yourself up there, didn't you?" he whispered. "Patience, my son. Patience. All shall become clear."

Seventy

ANDREN HAD CALLED FOR WINE. He drank it with deep appreciation, in a golden cup, sitting informally on the throne steps. "From the Talaka vineyard, Lady Tala," he said, raising a toast to her. "And very fine it is, too."

Ruko remained kneeling at his father's feet, a fallen statue.

Neema could not take her eyes off Andren. He was very like his son in looks, they shared the same refined features, the same straight black brows. But he had ten times Ruko's charisma. She hated him—furiously, she hated him. For stealing the throne. For using her. For sending his own daughter into exile. He was a monster. But still she saw how she could be seduced by him, if he were selling something she wanted. Ruko's charisma repelled, like a shield. Andren's charisma dragged you in; you had to fight to resist it.

She should have known it would take someone more audacious than Gedrun Stour to steal the throne. And—now she thought of it—of *course* Andren hadn't died in a bungled coup. The arch-strategist, always thinking ten steps ahead. The Golden Tiger of Samra did not bungle things.

Her gaze travelled beyond the throne to the Fox, crumpled beneath its portrait in its flame-bordered coat. One leg bent, one leg straight. Surely it was pretending. Waiting for the right moment to spring to its feet, and leap out of the window.

Sol wasn't so sure. The Fox was the Guardian of Entrances and Exits. It was also the Guardian of Afternoon Naps. **It might be plotting, Neema, yes. Or it might be dreaming of rabbit stew.**

The room had turned quiet as Andren drank his wine. Sometimes he looked at the Dragon on the ceiling. Sometimes he contemplated his son. "We are waiting for your mother," he said, waving for his glass to be refilled. "We are not on the best of terms, alas." He tweaked an eyebrow at the understatement. "But she helps me, nonetheless. People are so easy to manipulate, once you know what they desire. You wanted the throne. Vabras desires order."

Vabras. Everyone had forgotten Vabras again.

"And you. My dear Neema..." Andren looked straight at her. "You just wanted a friend. Someone to talk to about your work."

Neema's skin shrivelled. It was true, that was the worst part.

With a sudden jolt of panic, Andren flung his wine away and pressed his fingers to his hairline, pulling the skin taut. Then he did the same at his temple, and along his jawline. After a moment, he settled back against the throne steps, but he kept his gaze firmly on the doors now, and did not speak again.

After a couple of uncomfortable minutes Yasila arrived, accompanied by Jadu. The Servant of the Dragon was gagged with a steel muzzle and her hands were bound, to prevent her from casting. Her appearance told a story of failed resistance. Her rose-gold hair was coming free from its plait, and a bruise was forming along one freckled cheek. Both she and Yasila were scratched and cut from their fight.

Andren rose and came down the steps again to greet his prisoner. "Servant Jadu. What a pleasure to see you *face to face* again after all these years."

Jadu's pale amber eyes filled with disgust.

"Do you see that, Yasila? She hates me almost as much as you do." Andren laughed, but as he did so, one cheek began to droop, turning his smile into a strange, lopsided leer.

The curse of the Soul Stealer, Sol said, to Neema. **He takes from his victim, and the spell takes from him.**

Rivenna rushed to Andren's side. "See how he suffers for us," she said, to the room. "See the toll it takes on him."

Andren's face was now ghoulishly distorted. The sharper angles were softening, the flesh pulling away from the bone. One eye bulged from its socket. His mouth gaped.

Rivenna guided him down to his knees, in front of his son. "Take what you need," she coaxed. "That's what he's for. See how I have forged him in your image…"

Andren, struggling now, pressed his hands on either side of Ruko's head. Ruko tried fitfully to wrench himself free, but he was trapped.

Neema's stomach dropped: a primal warning that something terrible was about to happen.

Sol was fluttering anxiously in her chest. **Neema, look away.**

But she couldn't. She watched, transfixed, as Andren murmured the words of the spell. A different song now, another one she had taught him. "Give to me your greatest treasure. I shall use it well…" His pupils dilated, twin vortexes, hungry for light. And began to feed.

If he could move, Ruko would be writhing in agony. The pain was so intense, it gave him back his voice. He screamed, as the spell ripped through him, searching for the deepest, most essential part of him. His soul. His being.

Some things are worse than death.

"No, no…" Ruko howled. "Stop…"

Yasila, standing apart, dug her nails into her palms.

Andren's form began to shift. His chest broadened, he grew taller. His jawline tightened as he took on a younger aspect. A familiar face. Handsome, aloof. Ruko was staring at himself. Not a disguise, not a reflection, but a piece of himself.

Ruko's eyes rolled back in his head. He started to convulse.

Andren let go.

As his son slumped to the floor, he stood up, glowing with renewed energy and power. He lifted his arms, displaying his new self. "How do I look? Better?" Ruko's voice, but in a tone he would never use. Teasing. Careless.

Yasila unclenched her fists. There was blood on her palms, where her nails had cut the skin.

Andren freed himself of the Old Bear's iron crown, his red and black tunic. Rubbing a hand across his newly toned stomach, he grinned at Rivenna. "An improvement, wouldn't you say? Pass me his jacket."

Rivenna showed no pity as she stripped Ruko of his coat. At last she was able to reveal what she really thought of the student she had trained so assiduously. Nothing.

Andren shrugged on the jacket and the image was complete. "Shame about that," he said, eyeing the bandage wrapped around his son's arm from wrist to elbow. "I'll have to wear the scars, I suppose. Damn. He was so nearly perfect." He smoothed the creases from the jacket in a gesture that was purely his. Neema, who had stood in line next to Ruko for six days, could see other differences, too. Not just the mannerisms, but the spirit beneath. But very few people had studied Ruko as closely as she had. As far as the world was concerned, this *was* Emperor Ruko the First. The legitimate ruler of Orrun.

And so Andren Valit usurped the throne a second time.

The real Ruko was beginning to come round. He let out a soft moan, as a couple of Hounds dragged him back, away from the throne steps.

"Your majesty, it is time," Vabras said. At his command, the entrance doors were barred, the great window locked.

The Fox had missed its chance to escape. Neema's heart sank further.

Andren's allies were moving around the room with clear, practised steps. Whatever was about to happen had been rehearsed many times before. Lord Clarion and Lady Harmony, Kindry and Havoc fanned out to the edges, while Yasila led Jadu to the middle of the throne steps. Andren and Rivenna remained standing beneath the portrait of the Dragon, holding hands like a married couple.

"You are ready?" he asked her, grinning with excitement. The effect was jarring. Ruko didn't grin like that, ever. He kissed her. "Is it strange, that I look like him?"

She touched his face—Ruko's face. "I'll get used to it."

The Hounds pushed Tala and Neema forward.

"Ahh, Neema," Andren said, taking her hand and squeezing it fondly. "Are you beginning to understand what you have done for me? Who could have guessed you would be so pivotal to my success?" He laughed, amazed. "A drab little Raven scholar from Scartown."

I was never drab, Neema thought. *You fucking monster.*

Andren was still laughing. "Eight. I thought Vabras had lost his mind when he brought you to me. But you helped me solve a great puzzle, Neema. I had a vision, and you made it real."

A vision. The Dragon Trial. She looked at him, and she knew—because they had both walked through the Dragon's fire—he was talking of something he had seen that day.

"Yes," he breathed. The spell would not let him say more. But... *yes.*

"Folk tales," he said, to the room. "Myths and legends. Ancient songs. They hold secrets: powerful secrets that we should never have forgotten. Neema," he gave her a side hug, while she glared at him, "helped me find them again. She led me to the door, and handed me the key to...everything." He gestured expansively to the portraits that wrapped around the throne room. "The Scriptures tell us the Guardians have always been here, watching over us. Not true. Remember, Neema, all that information you collected for me on the old tribes. Glimpses of a time before the Catastrophe. A time when there were many lands, many empires, all rich with life. Before our ancestors gathered here, the last-remaining sanctuary. Thousands of references, from countless archives, the most glancing of phrases, the smallest of footnotes. A vast undertaking. But you didn't see the truth at the heart of them. Did you?"

Neema shook her head, mystified.

Andren, dazzled by his own brilliance, clenched his fists in triumph. "I knew it."

"My love," Rivenna warned. "It is almost time—"

Andren scowled at her. "No. I want her to understand. She's the only one..." He turned back to Neema. "Think back. Thousands of descriptions. *Think.* Did you find a single reference to the Eight?"

Neema sifted through her memories with increasing consternation. Her brows furrowed. There had to be…there must have been *one* mention.

"You see?" Andren was watching her intently. "If the Guardians have always been here, why did our ancient ancestors never speak of them?"

"You're saying the Eight don't exist?"

"Oh…" Andren beamed. "They exist. What I'm saying, Neema, is that we created them."

—Sol. Is that true?

Sol sank his head beneath his shoulders, and did not answer.

Andren was speaking to the room again. "Forget the Scriptures. This is the truth; this is what history teaches us. Tens of thousands of years ago, this world suffered a great Catastrophe. We know this. We see it. The empire is bordered by scarred lands, poisoned forests, empty seas. And we know that the old tribes wielded magic far more powerful than our own. That is why their songs, their melodies are the strongest. Our ancestors created the Eight to protect us from another Catastrophe. But the Eight evolved in unexpected ways. They grew powerful, and demanding. No longer Guardians but Tyrants. For as long as we can remember, they have held us down. How we cringe, terrified of their final Return. But why should we fear what we created? Why should we bow to them? No longer." He opened his arms wide again, glaring in defiance at the Dragon on the ceiling. "Let them come! We are ready for them."

Silence.

"Guardians of the Eight! Come take your vengeance, if I am wrong!"

"Stop!" Tala cried, terrified. She appealed to the room. "Is this what you want? The Last Return? Are you all mad?"

Smug smiles, knowing glances. "We trust in our emperor," Lady Harmony said, earning a glowing smile from Andren.

"Your Majesty," Havoc said. "Show them the omen."

Andren clapped his hands, pleased. "Yes, yes…This will put your mind at ease, Lady Tala."

A guard crossed behind the throne and returned with a small cage, draped in a gold cloth.

Andren took it from her. "Three years ago we opened a path to the Hidden Realm. A dress rehearsal, if you like. And look what clambered through." He whisked off the cloth, like a magician.

Pink-Pink lay tucked in a corner, vibrating with fury.

That's what Neema had forgotten.

"A chameleon, of all creatures." Andren laughed, as he held the cage up high. "A sign from the universe that our cause is just."

Pink-Pink hissed in virulent rage, and tried to bite Andren's finger.

Tala's brow crinkled. "How is that a sign…"

Andren touched his chest. "I am the master of the Chameleon Spell."

"The Chameleon Spell?" Neema repeated. "That's not what the Dragons call it."

Andren gave her a sharp look. "It is what I call it." He handed the cage back to the guard.

A cage…And Neema understood, at last, why they were here in the throne room. Why they needed Yasila, and her magic. Why each portrait was soaked in Dragonscale. What had the Fox said? The walls smelled like home. "You want the Eight to Return. You're going to trap them. Bind them in the walls. That's impossible."

"Impossible anywhere but here," Andren corrected her. "A place of power. The greatest place of power in the world. This is the birthplace of the Eight. Right here on this spot. I am sure of it. I can *feel* it. Here we made them. Here we will bind them."

—Sol? Is he right?

Sol hunkered further down in Neema's chest, claws curled tight against her rib.

"You can't just summon the Eight with a click of your fingers," Neema said. "They won't come if they don't want to."

Andren unsheathed Hurun-tooth, the cursed blade, and passed it to Rivenna. "My dear Neema. They won't have a choice."

He walked back up the marble steps, and took his seat on the throne. The emperor did not get his own hands dirty.

Forgotten at the base of the steps, Ruko looked up at his father, his usurper. This was the vision shown to him in the Dragon Trial. A cruel trick. He had seen not himself but a shadow; a dark reflection. A stolen part of himself.

A tear slid from his eye and dropped on to the first marble step. This was as far as he would come to ruling Orrun. This far and no further.

CHAPTER
Seventy-One

RIVENNA TURNED the Blade in her hand. She was enjoying herself, the unique power she held in this moment. "One death and the Guardians will come. One of you will trigger the Last Return."

Guards grabbed Neema and Tala and shoved them forward, closer to the abbess. Rivenna sucked her lip, moving the Blade from one throat to the other, deciding. "Who first…"

—Sol. When I call to you, slow down time.

I cannot slow down time, Neema. Only—

—My perception of time, I know. Finally, she had found someone more pedantic than her. —That's fine.

Rivenna placed the tip of the Blade below Neema's eye. "So tempting."

Neema swallowed, and held very still.

"Eight years you spent at his side, while I was stuck training his brat. His letters full of your *loyalty*, your *support*. Do you know what it's like to envy someone as worthless as you?" She scraped the tip of the Blade down Neema's cheek.

"Abbess Glorren," Vabras said, a touch impatient. He had a schedule for everything—even the end of the world.

The abbess moved on to Tala. Neema exhaled.

"Lady Tala Talaka." Rivenna gave a sarcastic Ox bow, arms linked in a circle. "We almost lost the Festival because of you. He actually thought your life was worth more than the throne." She glanced to where Ruko was lying, still paralysed, unable to stop her. Rivenna enjoyed that, too. "I did promise you, Ruko. I said I'd kill her before the day was through."

Tala began to struggle. She was strong, the Ox contender—Neema's own guard had to help hold her down.

Rivenna lifted her arm, the Blade held high. Relishing the drama of it. "Be ready," she called to the room. "At last, the time has come."

She turned the Blade in her fist, preparing to plunge it straight into Tala's heart.

—Sol. Now.

Time slowed.

Her perception of time.

Neema watched the trajectory of the Blade as it inched towards Tala's heart. She moved to deflect its path, reaching for Rivenna's arm. Beyond this she had no plan—only to stop the Blade, before it took a life.

Rivenna saw Neema from the corner of her eye and started to shift. Not fast enough. Neema seized the handle, and began to peel Rivenna's fingers free…

Time slammed back. It was all Sol could give her. He slumped, exhausted.

Rivenna and Neema were locked together, fighting over the Blade. Neema still had hold of the handle. The Tiger abbess gripped the sharp edge tight, cutting deep into her palm. She cried out, as blood poured between her fingers. Behind them, Tala was wrestling to free herself. She flung off one of her guards, thrusting him away from her. Ungrounded, he ploughed heavily into Neema and Rivenna.

They fell together in a heap, Neema landing clumsily on the Tiger abbess. She rolled free and jumped to her feet. The guard picked himself up.

Rivenna remained on her back.

The Blade was pushed deep into her stomach. A dark stain crept across her shimmering green dress. The abbess gasped for air, her eyes wide with shock. "Andren…"

Andren was on his feet. There was no shock in his eyes.

He knew, Neema thought. This was his Dragon vision. He knew —and still he'd handed Rivenna the Blade. The woman he loved.

On the steps, Yasila allowed herself a small, private smile. Well, well. One gift this night had given her, at least.

Rivenna's gaze was on the painted Dragon, the fire in its throat. She choked, struggling to breathe as blood spilled from her lips. Her expression changed from shock, to anger, to acceptance. And finally, triumph. "I…have…summoned them," she gasped, with her final breath. "They are coming."

Bright red blood spread slowly across the white marble floor. All else was still.

Andren prowled the steps, grim-faced and waiting.

The prelude to a storm. On the promontory overlooking the edge of the world, the emperor's guests turned and pointed in alarm to the Tiger's Path constellation, gleaming so brightly they had to shield their eyes from its glare.

In the throne room the air thickened—a surface tension that wouldn't break.

"Do you feel their resistance?" Andren said. "Even now?"

—Sol. They mustn't come. Tell them it's a trap.

We have no choice, Neema. Yasthala cursed the Blade. We must Return.

Candles flickered and died, black smoke trailing from the wicks. The air was so dense now, Neema felt the pressure in her ears, as if she were under water. Breathing was difficult. All around her, people were choking and gasping.

"Guardians!" Andren roared, as if his voice could reach from this world into the Hidden Realm.

A final moment of stubborn resistance, and then release. A ripping sound, as the sky was torn open. Out in the gardens and across the island, people screamed and pointed to the stars. The Tiger's Path was gone. In the breach, a carnival of colour, sound, sensation. The Hidden Realm.

Neema felt a deep, ominous rumble under her feet. A tiger's growl. A bear's snarl. Something wild, and powerful, and angry. Under Rivenna's body, the life that was taken, the marble floor split, as if under a heavy weight. The glass in the octagonal window cracked and buckled.

It began.

The Eight Guardians roared from the Hidden Realm, furious and real. All of them at once, every fragment, tumbled together in a seething, snarling mass. Raging as they came. *Seven times we saved the world. Now we come to destroy it.* Slash and bite and pierce and claw, soak the earth in blood, scorch the sky with fire. The Last Return of the Eight. They stretched out across the sky, an endless multitude, preparing to spread out and destroy, destroy…

And then…

…they stopped.

And listened.

In the throne room, Andren and his allies were chanting a song, an ancient song of summoning. "Come to the Mountain." But the words were stark and new.

> *Fox and Raven we command you,*
> *Make your home within these walls.*
> *Ox and Tiger we command you,*
> *Make your home within these walls.*
> *Bear and Monkey, Hound and Dragon,*
> *Make your home within these walls.*
> *We who made you, now will bind you*
> *Safe within these painted walls.*

There was no poetry to the words, but there was power. There was belief.

On the throne steps, Jadu cried out in pain, as the Dragon's eye glowed and burned against her forehead. The Dragon was awake, and it was coming. *You dare summon us? You dare?*

In a maelstrom they came, smashing the octagonal window in a frenzy and pouring through. Jaws snapping, claws raking, hooves thudding, a whirl of striped fur, lowered horns, dank breath, sharp beaks. On they came, scratching, pouncing, fighting, flying, *raging.*

And still the chanting continued.

Caught in the middle, Neema dropped to her knees and threw her hands over her head. Pecked by a flock of ravens, mauled by a pack of hounds, trampled by a herd of oxen…

Leave her alone! Sol snapped. **Friend!**

Surprise. Pause. Withdrawal.

A space opened up around her. And through it she could listen, and see glimpses beyond the storm. She saw Andren-as-Ruko on the throne, eyes wild with mad triumph, shouting the words. Laughing. The vision the Raven had shown her. It wasn't Ruko who would destroy everything. It was *Andren.*

We command you…
Within these walls…

First the summoning, now the binding. Slowly, Neema felt a shift in the air. The intensity of the Return was fading. The Eight were…solidifying. No longer a confusion of merged aspects, forming and reforming, but distinct, individual shapes. The Ox, bellowing in alarm. The Bear rearing up on its hind legs before dropping down, confused.

And we, the Raven, calling to ourself in distress. Something strange and terrible was happening. Our beloved flock, our countless aspects, were being squeezed and clumped and glued together. Bound into one shape, only one. We fought, we struggled, but the command was too strong.

Neema! Sol cried in alarm, clinging to her rib like a branch in a storm. **I don't want to go. It hurts. It hurts.**

Neema slammed her arms across her chest in the Raven salute, trying to contain him. —You are not going anywhere.

I have to. I must . . .

Sol's grip loosened. He was the Solitary Raven. But he was also a fragment of us. We were being summoned to our new home. It was not a call we could resist.

Neema reached with her mind to where Sol was panicking, wings batting against her sternum. She thought of all the places she had felt safe. Madam Fessi's schoolroom. Her mother's shop. The storeroom, on the day Cain stumbled into her life. A quiet day of reading in the Imperial Library. Her old room with the green door. She let the warm, safe feeling of these memories flow through her into Sol. *This is home. You are safe here. Stay.*

It almost worked. But the spell was too powerful. This was a spell to cage Tigers and chain Dragons. How could one little fragment resist its call? One little fragment, so desperate to belong.

My flock, Neema. I must go to them.

Through our agony, we heard him. Drawing on the last of our strength we called to him in one voice.

Solitary Raven!
Stay away from us!
You are not welcome.

Sol stiffened, beak open.

We will peck out your eyes.
We will pluck out your feathers.
We will drown you in a filthy puddle.
You are not a part of us!

I am not? One claw tightened around Neema's rib.

We are the Raven
We banish you from the flock.
For ever.

Slowly, Sol settled himself. No more fluttering, no more agitated hopping. He folded his wings. Sank his head.

Safe. Heartbroken. Rejected. But safe.

We were not so lucky.

Fox and Raven we command you,
Make your home within these walls.

Words and will. That was what they used to trap us. Words and will. The most powerful magic of all. The same magic that had created us. What can be bound, may be released. What can be released, may be bound.

The painting on the wall called to us, inviting. Promising us an end to the agony. It looked like home. It smelled like home. The Dragonscale, and the chanting, and Shimmer Arbell's genius.

We could not help ourselves. Through the pain of our binding, it offered us a haven.

We flew into the painting.

A great force clamped down on us. We felt ourselves being manipulated, pushed and pulled and twisted—moulded like clay. The more we struggled, the weaker we became. And still the spell continued its work, remorseless, until we were the shape it demanded.

A handsome young raven perched on a cliff edge, her feathers gleaming in bolts of morning light. The brooding sea beyond. We could feel the warmth of the sun, hear the turn of the sea. We could smell the Dragonscale, thick and sour. But we could not move. The spell was complete. Our new home. Our prison.

All around us, our fellow Guardians were fighting the same battle. We could not turn our head (we could not turn our head!), but we could see Monkey on the opposite wall, merging with its portrait like a fly trapped in amber. The harder it fought, the more hungrily the paint and plaster consumed it—until it was nothing except its portrait: a red-faced monkey in a mango tree, reaching but never quite grasping the perfectly ripe fruit, its thick, muscular tail wrapped about a branch for balance.

Hound was trapped too—a hunting dog with ears pricked, a dead bird at its feet. We could not see Fox, to our right, but we could sense it being glued into position—a proud old vixen baring her teeth, preparing for one last fight to protect her cubs. Our poor, dear friend. The thing it dreaded most—to be just one thing, for ever. To be pinned. We tried to speak, to comfort it, but our words were trapped too, inside our throat.

Tiger was still fighting the call, prowling restlessly around the Blade in Rivenna's body. Such a cruel betrayal. Attacked by its own followers. But even Tiger was not strong enough to escape the spell. Roaring, snarling, fighting all the way, it backed slowly into its painting on the throne-room doors, and was still.

Bear surrendered next into its mountain scene, for ever hunting salmon in the rapids. Stubborn Ox held out longer, but the song was a whip across its back. With a last bellow of defiance, it lurched into its painting. We could just see it, in our periphery, buckling beneath the binding spell, until it stood placid in its ploughed field.

Which left only one.

Dragon. A creature of pure myth, born from the imaginations of those who were, those who are and those who will be. A shadow in the water. A fire in the sky. It swam in the air, sea-green and silver, beautiful and deadly.

On the throne steps, Yasila pressed both palms against Jadu's forehead, holding the Dragon's eye in place. This one, final fragment, she would keep for herself.

The Dragon turned and spiralled, forming an eternal eight. The sound of its scales filled the room, like water rushing across a pebble beach. Exhausted from the fight, it lifted up to the ceiling and merged with its portrait. Jaws for ever pinned wide, flame for ever building in its throat.

> *We who made you, now will bind you,*
> *Safe within these painted walls.*

It was done. The Last Return of the Eight was over.

Andren sank deep within his throne. Around the room, his allies turned to one another in triumph and astonishment. They'd done it, just as their emperor had promised. They had caged the Eight.

"My imperial menagerie," Andren said, and laughed.

The Dragon's tail shifted slightly. The portraits were alive. Fascinated, Havoc reached out and touched the Hound's fur. "It's warm," he said, marvelling. Very slightly, within the confines of its binding, the Hound bared its teeth.

"Look at the Raven!" Lady Harmony said, clapping her hands. "How the wind ruffles its feathers. Magical."

Lord Clarion stepped over Rivenna's body, to inspect the Monkey.

Andren observed them all, content. Unlike his friends, he had never doubted they would succeed. Twenty-four years ago, the Dragon Trial had shown him this moment, in all its strange glory.

A future so impossible, he could not begin to believe it. Until the night he discovered Yasila's powers. Then he had understood—this future would come to pass. He would sit upon the marble throne, not as himself, but as his son. He would summon the Eight, and defeat them. All of this he had seen. Ruko, his mirror image, paralysed at the foot of the steps. Rivenna's body, blood spreading over the cracked marble floor. Neema and Cain...

His face fell. Standing up, he scanned the room. Something was different. Something was wrong.

"Where's Neema Kraa?" he snarled. "Where's Cain Ballari? They should be right there," Andren pointed to a spot in front of the Monkey portrait. "Right *there*."

But they weren't. And neither was Tala Talaka.

Victory, like happiness, is a state we pass through.

Andren's face twisted with rage. "Find them!" he yelled.

Seventy-Two

NEEMA WAS STARING at the Dragon in fear and wonder when she felt a sharp, insistent tug on her tunic.

Cain, right behind her. Flamboyant coat removed, eyepatch gone. *Let's go. Now.*

Neema circled Tala's wrist and they crept away, past the back of the throne, through the smashed remnants of the window, out into the courtyard.

No one saw them leave. They were too busy watching *the Guardian of Death* writhing and screaming and spewing golden flames above their heads. As distractions went, it was exceptional.

"I'm reviewing my belief in the Eight," Cain said, and scissored neatly through the window.

Vabras had done him a favour, knocking the Fox out cold. Cain had come round almost immediately, back in control again. His training had warned him to lie still, until the right moment presented itself. The right moment turning out to be the Last Return of the Eight.

In the courtyard, Tala was looking back into the throne room, trying to make sense of what had just happened. From here she had a direct view of the Ox, sealed in its painting. "We have to warn people."

"And tell them what, exactly?" Cain asked, but she was already running off.

"Ox palace," Neema guessed. They were already moving in the opposite direction—northwards into the wilderness garden. In the day, this was a pleasing, shaded tangle of trees and bushes and winding, natural pathways. At night it was a hazard, with snatching brambles and exposed roots, and swarms of mosquitoes. It was almost pitch black, the moon struggling to reach through the thick weave of branches.

"We need to get off the island," Neema said, stumbling and correcting herself. "I've hidden a pack near my old lodgings."

"Commendably forward-thinking."

She stopped and cupped his face. She could barely make him out. "I thought I'd lost you. It really is *you*, isn't it?"

"As far as I can tell."

They held each other in the dark. "We don't have time for this," Cain said, and held her a bit longer.

The wilderness garden straggled to an end, opening on to a wider path, which would lead them to the Hound palace. "There's a service path—"

Cain stepped in front of her as three Hounds appeared, running straight at them. He punched the first one in the stomach, stole her dagger, slashed it along her friend's calf, elbowed the third in the throat. A couple of sharp kicks and a rib-cracking punch and it was over.

He tucked the dagger in his belt. "You were saying?"

The service path followed a tree-lined ridge, along the eastern edge of the Hound palace. There was a lot of activity going on in the yard below, guards rushing back and forth, officers shouting commands under torchlight.

Neema tracked a young Samran recruit as he hurried out from the prison block and... "Shit!"

"What?" Cain had missed it.

The recruit had walked straight up behind one of the palace guards and slit his throat. No warning, nothing. "That man there, he—"

"*Shit!*" Cain hissed.

Because it wasn't just one recruit, one victim. In the yard, people were falling to the ground. One here, one there. Then another. Senior commander. Young sergeant. A blade to the throat, a blade to the heart, and they were gone. Fifteen Hounds, bleeding out on the cobbled yard. Fast, cold-blooded, efficient.

Neema pressed a hand to her mouth. Vabras. He'd ordered this. On his own people.

"A purge," Cain said. "Neema. If they'll do this to the Hounds ..."

A deep boom, far away. The ground trembled softly beneath their feet.

Cain stepped out from the tree line, to get a better view.

She grabbed his shirt, bundling it in her fist as she tried to drag him back, but he just stood there, frozen to the spot. Giving up, she joined him.

The island was ablaze with light. Lanterns and torches along the Grand Canal, beacons lit along the perimeter walls and main paths. Lights in the palace windows. The gleam of the storm-damaged temple dome in the moonlight.

And far in the distance, flames rising in the darkness.

A second boom. More flames. "The Fox palace," she said.

Cain was already running.

CHAPTER
Seventy-Three

IT WASN'T PERSONAL. It never was, with Vabras.

The best way to curb a rebellion was to never let it start. Sixteen years ago, his purges had removed a generation of opposition thinkers and leaders and cowed the rest for years. Tonight's massacre would do the same. Anyone who might question what was coming next, who might resist the changes Andren had set in motion—the independent thinkers, the fervent idealists, the shrewd, the wary, the naturally rebellious—would be erased.

He consulted his watch. The Fox palace would be in flames by now. The Bear palace under attack. Two thirds of the Imperial Hound army dead or dying. Still underway: the discreet assassination of a select number of Monkeys, Oxes, Ravens, and even a few Tigers who could not be trusted to fall into line.

One thousand, seven hundred and ninety-three souls, in total.

The blame would fall on Bersun's shoulders. An attempted coup, they would call it. After twenty-four years on the throne, the Old Bear had refused to hand over the reins of power—least of all to Andren Valit's son.

Vabras took a last sweep around his modest rooms. His few belongings were already packed on board the new High Admiral's private Leviathan. At dawn, Emperor Ruko the First would set sail for Samra. After fifteen hundred years of neglect, Orrun's ancient capital would be restored to its past glory. The Marble City—the great, opulent wonder of the empire. Meanwhile Yasthala's island would fade and fall to ruin. Armas city, built to serve the island, would become a backwater town. Andren's revenge. *What you did to my beloved city, I shall do to yours.*

Vabras yawned behind his hand, then frowned at his own deficiency. As a child, he had trained himself to survive on four hours' sleep. These past few days had been punishing, but that was no excuse.

A tap at the door. A Samran Hound captain stepped in to give her report. Everything was going according to plan, she said.

One of the square silver buttons on her tunic wasn't straight. Vabras reached out and neatened it. "Have you found the traitors?"

The captain confessed that she had not.

"Then everything is not going to plan," Vabras observed. "Precision please, in future."

This was the problem with killing all the people you had trained up. You had to go right back to the start. Tedious, but necessary.

In the throne room, Lady Harmony and Lord Clarion were putting on the performance of their lives. Reception guests, ushered in from the gardens, had screamed and clutched each other as they stumbled into the gory scene. Abbess Rivenna Glorren lying dead in a pool of blood, eyes staring blankly to the ceiling, the marble cracked beneath her. And, sprawled on the throne steps above, a gilded dagger lodged in his heart, the Old Bear. His Majesty Emperor Bersun the Second.

A touch operatic, we would have said, if we could speak. If we were not trapped in our portrait, trapped in ceaseless torment. So many of us, so much magnificence, glued and squashed together, melded into one. We could have told the sobbing guests—that is not Emperor Bersun. He died sixteen summers ago, on the exact same spot. (Like we said—operatic.) *That* poor fellow was Gedrun Stour. Gedrun with his expertly maimed hand, dressed in an imperial silk tunic, with his brother's iron crown clamped to his head. Useful to the last.

"He would have killed us all!" Lady Harmony sobbed, as her husband comforted her.

Bersun—they said—had attempted to assassinate Ruko, using the Blade of Peace. Mad. Deranged. If Abbess Glorren had not stopped him…Lady Harmony dropped to her knees beside Rivenna's corpse, and gave a plaintive, semi-convincing wail.

People asked about the Eight. They had seen the rip in the sky, they had feared the Last Return had come. What had happened?

We are here! We wanted to scream. **Let us out, let us out, let us out!**

"They Returned," Lord Clarion said, in an expert stage whisper.

"The Dragon would have burned the world to ash," his wife added, arcing her hand to the ceiling. "But the kind Monkey intervened on our behalf. Our dear Rivenna," she cradled the corpse, "sacrificed her life to save the emperor-in-waiting. An act to be honoured, and praised—not punished."

"But what about the curse?" someone asked—and regretted it later.

"Rivenna!" Lady Harmony cried, lifting her hands to show the blood. "Hero of Orrun. You saved two worlds with your sacrifice." A slight pause. "Tell them, darling, of Ruko and the Tiger," she prompted.

Lord Clarion sighed, reverent. Never had he seen such a moving sight. The emperor-in-waiting, kneeling bravely—yet meekly —before his Guardian. "The Tiger placed one great, but loving paw, upon Ruko's head." Clarion mimed this, placing a hand on his own greyish-blonde curls.

"And so His Majesty's glorious reign begins," Lady Harmony concluded. "Blessed by the Eight."

And soaked in blood, some thought, but did not say. Did they believe Lord Clarion and Lady Harmony's account? The lucky ones did. The rest kept their doubts to themselves. Facet. Grace Eliat. Such seasoned courtiers, that they didn't even risk glancing at each other. Bersun was dead, right there in front of them on the steps. This story—fiction or fact—was the new truth.

"The Eight," someone asked, anxiously. "They've gone back? They are Hidden?"

"They are home," Lord Clarion confirmed, with a reassuring smile.

In the walls, we seethed.

∞ ∞ ∞

"Gather two squads," Vabras said, to the Hound captain. "I will find them myself."

She bowed and left him.

It wasn't that Vabras admired Andren, or liked him. He could not be seduced by charm, or corrupted with bribes. Andren had won Vabras's loyalty for one reason alone.

Order. The second Tenet of the Hound, but—to Vabras's mind —the only one that really mattered. What use were justice, loyalty and honour, in a world of chaos? They existed purely to *create* order. They held no intrinsic value in isolation.

Andren would guarantee order for generations to come. With the Chameleon Spell, he could conceivably live for ever. In a few years, he would usher in dynastic rule. *Blood is destiny*—the old Valit family motto. And each heir would suffer the same fate as Ruko.

Only Vabras knew this. Andren had confided in him because he knew it would please his High Commander. No more successions, no more change. Order. Peace. They were the same thing. For Vabras, they were the same thing.

There was a small garden attached to his rooms. A lawn, roses, a cherry tree. He ventured outside. The full moon, he thought, would help in the search. It did not occur to him that it was beautiful.

Something stirred in the bushes. A pair of eyes gleamed yellow in the moonlight.

Pets were not allowed in the Hound palace. By order of Vabras. The cost, the disorder, the distraction.

But there was a cat.

Six years ago Vabras had found it in the bushes with an injured leg. A black-and-white mouser from Chef Ganstra's kitchen stores. Vabras had taken it in and nursed it back to health in secret. He did not know why. Sometimes it came back to visit.

He could take the cat with him to Samra. He could make it happen with a snap of his fingers. He was the High Commander of Orrun. But such an act of self-indulgence would expose him to scrutiny or worse—ridicule.

He might, though, say goodbye.

He made a soft, coaxing sound. The eyes gleamed again, reflective in the moonlight. A soft rustle, then nothing.

"High Commander." The captain had returned. "We are ready for you."

Vabras gave a stiff nod, and headed back inside.

CHAPTER
Seventy-Four

B<small>Y THE TIME</small> Neema and Cain fought their way to the Fox palace, there was no one left to save.

The first palace was a burning wreck, flames and smoke rolling up into the night sky. In the gardens and the grounds beyond lay the mangled bodies of the few who had escaped the explosions, only to be slaughtered by the waiting Hounds. The High Commander's order had been short and to the point. Kill them all.

Neema recognised two of the dead, crying out as she saw them. The novices she'd met in the tombs. Fox One and Fox Two. Both stabbed, multiple times. They'd died together, holding hands.

It was bad for Neema, seeing them. It was so much worse for Cain. He recognised everyone. His friends, his contingent. Everyone.

He dropped to his knees and howled his grief into the scorched earth. Neema sat down with him, holding him as he wept.

The roof of the largest building collapsed in on itself. Neema covered her mouth, to hold back a sob. Half the palace lay underground. Were there people still trapped down there? They could do nothing to help them.

"Why?" Cain said. "*Why?*"

Because you're everything they hate, Neema thought. This was more than a massacre, it was annihilation.

In the distance, backlit by the flames, she saw a Samran Hound captain ordering an Ox team to put out the blaze.

They couldn't stay here, it wasn't safe. She helped Cain to his feet. He had fought all this way, to find nothing but death. His face a mess of tears and blood, dirt and sweat. His voice cracked and hollow. "Neema, they're gone. They're all gone."

"What about the abbot? The Fox said he was hiding...He might have survived."

Cain rubbed his face and neck, winced as he found the bump, where Vabras had knocked him out. His gaze returned to the fire, the smoke. "I should make a joke, for the dead," he said, helpless. "I can't think of one. I just can't..." He broke down on her shoulder.

She held him for a moment, then guided him gently away.

There are always quiet places, even in the heat of battle.

The Raven palace had hunkered down, hoping to survive the night unscathed. The new emperor would need them once the killing was over. High Justice Lord Kindry had summoned an emergency meeting in the library. He spoke—at length—of the legitimacy of Ruko's accession. A tragedy that his reign had begun in such a violent fashion—but Bersun the Brusque had proved himself a traitor, a tyrant. They were lucky the Eight had not burned the world to ash for his crimes.

The Ravens had questions—of course—but most were too afraid, or too smart, to ask them.

"This makes no sense," one brave soul called out. A junior lawyer, new to court. "The Old Bear summoned half the fleet to surround the island. Why would he do that, if they weren't loyal to him?"

"Is it true the Fox palace was set on fire?" someone else asked, frightened.

"We *believe*," Kindry looked at the nearest Hound, who nodded, "the Foxes were storing explosives in the tunnels. It's our understanding that Abbot Fort was a co-conspirator. It seems there was an accident, luckily for all of us. The Hounds will investigate, once it is safe to do so."

A senior archivist was in tears. "My sister's a Fox. She would never support a coup. He's right," he said, nodding to the lawyer. "None of this makes sense."

"We will look into it," Kindry promised. "But I fear many innocents have lost their lives tonight, because of Ish Fort's treachery. Let us pray for them."

A neat way to stop the questions.

Later, the Hounds paid a visit to the lawyer, and the archivist. Two more casualties of the night.

Even quieter, the service path. The *zirp zirp* of crickets, the high-pitched whine of mosquitoes. Bats flitted overhead, moth-hunting.

Neema retrieved her pack from the hut as Cain watched her from the doorframe, chewing his lip. She had taught the emperor all that ancient history. Pivotal—that was the word Andren had used. She had been pivotal. If Neema had only left the island with him eight years ago. If she had refused to write the Order of Exile...*Maybe all my friends would still be alive.*

He knew he was being unfair. You couldn't unravel time like a half-knitted scarf. But a part of him wanted to say it. They could have a terrible, ugly row. It wouldn't make him feel better, but at least the anger would confuse the pain, like pressing harder on a wound.

"Do you hate me?" she asked.

They knew each other far too well.

"It's my fault," she said. "I know that."

"It's Andren's fault."

"I'm going to destroy him," she said, and pulled an orange from her pack.

He dragged his sense of humour up from the depths. "With fruit?"

She turned it in her hand. "Whatever works. I thought you might be hungry."

Cain reached for it, then stopped. Gave his stomach an experimental prod. "I think...I think I'm *full*. No longer eating for two, I guess. Poor Fox."

Neema shook her head. She couldn't imagine it—that strange, wild, beautiful creature, trapped and bound for ever. And it really would have to be for ever—that was the worst part. Release the Eight, and they would destroy the world. Andren had made everyone complicit in his crime. Generation to generation.

"What about your friend..." Cain tapped his chest.

"He's still here. Sort of."

Sol had flown to his field and drawn down an impenetrable grey mist to hide within. He was in mourning. He'd lost his flock, he'd lost his function. He was nothing. If Neema reached with her mind, very hard, she could hear tiny whimpers—nothing like Sol's usual, performative misery.

"So what's the plan?" Cain asked.

She shouldered her pack. "Escape."

He waited for her to say more. "That's it?"

"Feel free to embellish."

"No. It's a good plan." Cain smiled, for the first time since the Fox palace. "Let's go."

Seventy-Five

I N THE MIDST of the massacre, a grand procession.

The Dragon-prowed boat, sailing down the Grand Canal. All the rest had been set alight—destroyed so that no one could use them to escape the island. The Dragon boat glided past the burning wrecks, stately and incongruous.

Andren stood at the prow, admiring the flames. He would burn the whole wretched island down, if he could. As they reached the temple steps he jumped free and held out his hand to his daughter. Nisthala took it, returning his smile. Her mother—joining them now on the steps—had taught her how to hide her true feelings in his presence. Whatever she thought of her father, he had delivered her here, just as he had promised the day she arrived on the island. Whether he looked like the Old Bear, or—as he did now—her brother Ruko, she would smile, and be patient.

Andren led her up the steps, past twin lines of Samran Hounds. Torches flamed at the entrance. For Nisthala, who had not left her rooms in seven years, who had waited so long for this hour, everything was a wonder.

"And it's all for you my dear," Andren said.

Smile. "Thank you, Your Majesty."

Andren leaned in. "You may call me Father, here. These are my personal Hounds." Putting a hand at the base of her spine, through her layers of woollen clothes, he guided her inside.

Below them, Shal Worthy helped Jadu from the boat. Her mouth remained clamped shut in its steel muzzle, but he had watched her closely with his Houndsight on their trip down the canal. Contempt was all that she had shown him. Weary contempt. And behind that, the faintest flicker of relief. She saw that her death was coming this hour, and welcomed it. This was not a world in which she wished to live.

"Keep watch," Yasila said, to Shal.

He bowed, and took up a position by the temple doors.

Inside, the Hounds gave their report. Yes, they had swept every room, there was no one else here. They didn't mention the Fox chapel, and the chickens. It wasn't something his majesty needed to hear about at this auspicious moment. The emperor did not have a taste for the absurd.

The Dragon contingent had been drugged at supper and woken as prisoners. They were brought out now, bound and gagged, carrying themselves with the same dignity as their ruler.

"Where is Ruko?" Nisthala asked, hunched in her bundle of clothes. She was shivering, her lips pale.

"I'm sorry darling," Andren purred. "He's already on board."

"You said we could talk. I want to see him—"

"Well, you can thank your dear mother for the change in plan." Grabbing Yasila's wrist, he wrenched open her hand to show the wounds on her palm. "Couldn't bear to watch him suffer, could you?"

Yasila stared at him in silent defiance.

"I knew you summoned your beloved Visitor to kill him. Not that it mattered. Ruko was always destined to win the Festival. Pyke died for nothing, thanks to you." He rubbed his thumb over Yasila's wounds. "I thought you wanted revenge for Yanara. That would have made sense. But it wasn't revenge, was it? You were trying to spare him."

He pressed down on the wound. Yasila gasped in pain.

"Stop!" Nisthala cried out. "Stop hurting her!"

Andren let go. "Forgive me, Nisthala," he said. "But your mother made a promise to me. She would give me Ruko, and the Guardians, and I would keep you safe here, until you were ready to rule." He frowned at his wife. "We had a deal."

"You could have ruled as someone else," Yasila said. "Cain, Neema. Havoc. You could have ruled as any one of them—"

"No!" Andren snarled. "It *had* to be him."

"You wanted Ruko dead?" Nisthala asked her mother.

"Yes," Yasila said, softly. "Better that, than…" She could say no more. Her son's fate. Worse even than Yanara's. Unbearable. *Unbearable.*

Andren shifted, uncomfortable. "Well. A mother's love. I suppose I cannot hold that against you. But you shall not see him again. I will not risk that. I need him kept safe, and well."

"The windows!" Nisthala said.

The stained-glass panes were brightening with the sun. Forgetting her brother, she moved eagerly to a spot below the Altar of the Eight. "It's time!"

For once, Yasila and Andren found something they could smile at together.

Yasila brought Jadu forward and removed her metal gag. "Speak one false word," she warned, "and you shall regret it."

Ignoring her, Jadu moved straight to Nisthala's side and took her hand. The emerald in her forehead shone. One touch was enough. Seven years of suffering were at an end.

Nisthala's eyes widened. "I'm warm. I'd forgotten…" The tiredness and discomfort she lived with, that pressed down upon her constantly, had vanished in one heartbeat. Laughing, she untied her hooded cloak and removed her thick woollen layers, her boots and woollen stockings, until she was standing in nothing but a plain grey cotton shift.

As her skin was revealed, the Dragon contingent groaned behind their masks. Each one of them had a single scar on the inside of their wrist, shaped like an eternal eight. Each one of them remembered the pain of it. Nisthala had scores of them, tessellating up her arm to her shoulder. A latticework of silver scars, like fish scales. A Chosen child, hidden from the Dragon. Kept from the cleansing relief of its fire.

"The pain is gone," Nisthala said, rubbing her hand up her arm.

"You should never have felt it." Jadu slid Yasila a pale, accusing look. "Your mother has served you ill."

"She has protected me," Nisthala said.

Jadu's gaze returned to the girl. "She has kept you from your true family. For her own selfish ends."

Yasila laughed, almost in despair.

A tilt of the head, from the woman who had raised her. "What words do I speak, Yasila, that are false?"

Another shaft of sunlight poured through the stained-glass windows, painting a kaleidoscope of colours on the stone floor. Enchanted, Nisthala prodded them with her bare foot, grey hair swinging down to cover her face.

"She is very young to serve the Dragon," Jadu observed, to Yasila. "Not yet sixteen. That is your plan, I presume? For her to wear the Eye?" She touched the emerald on her forehead, the source and symbol of her power.

"If my daughter must live on Helia, then she will rule it."

There was much Jadu could say to that, but she was a Dragon. She merely smiled at the presumption. The contingent, behind their gags, did the same. "And is this *your* desire, child?"

Nisthala stopped her prodding. Her eyes were still a dull, ash grey—Jadu had given her a taste of Dragonfire, but not enough to heat them to amber. "You call me child. Seven years I've spent without warmth or comfort, or company. I might have revealed my secret at any time, but I did not. This is my choice. My decision. And yes. It is my desire."

She plucked the diadem from Jadu's head.

Muffled cries from the Dragon contingent, as their world tilted away from them. There were ways, there were rituals. Jadu had worn the Eye for over sixty years. For it to be wrenched from her, so savagely…

And yet. It was the Dragon's gift to give. If it did not want the girl to have it, she could not have taken it.

Nisthala snapped the emerald from its setting, and threw the priceless diadem to the floor.

"Nistha," Yasila scolded, mildly.

Nisthala placed the stone in the middle of her forehead and let go. It sank slightly into her skin, embedding itself. A nourishing heat spread through her body, as if she were sliding into a warm bath. She laughed, and wept, as her eyes changed—not to full amber, but to a curious, crackled mix of flame and ash, like the last rakings of a pit fire. Something new, this was. She was something new.

Servant. Treasure.

A thought in her head—but not her own. Another presence had snaked its way into her mind, voice sibilant. For this jewel truly *was* the Dragon's eye—a fragment of the Eighth Guardian, spared from the binding spell. Nisthala felt its unblinking gaze turn inwards, sifting through her thoughts, her memories, her dreams.

—Stop.

Amusement from the fragment—**You would command me? That is not how this works, little one.**

Nisthala stood firm against it, jaw set.

—I do command you. This *is* how it will work.

Seven years locked away in her bedchamber with nothing but her books, her drawings, and her dreams of the future. Any pain the Eye could give her she had felt before, and conquered.

—Oh, did I seem young and vulnerable to you? Easy to control? You will learn.

It lashed at her. Tail whip, claw slash, breath of fire. A coiling serpent's embrace, crushing her bones. She was stronger. The battle was short, and decisive. The fragment retreated, subdued.

Nisthala had read many books. She knew this moment would be written of, down through the ages. How she stood in her grey cotton shift among the kaleidoscope of colours, sunlight beaming through the temple window. How she became Queen of the Dragons. She could almost feel the press of history, feel the eyes of future generations watching her from above, awe-struck.

"Your cloak, Jadu," she said. "And your staff."

Jadu's hands were still bound. Yasila unclasped her cloak for her, and draped it around her daughter's shoulders. A Hound brought forward the staff. Yasila presented it to Nisthala.

Nisthala tapped it once on the temple floor. As one, the Dragon contingent dropped to their knees. She curled her fingers over the top of the staff. "This staff was made from the wreck that brought my mother to your shores. This staff is Destiny."

The contingent, still gagged, bowed their heads.

She was thinking of the way they had smiled behind their masks, as if they knew better than her. "You shall remain here on the island to guard the Eight and maintain their binding." The Eye gleamed on her forehead. "You will not see Helia again. That is the command of your queen."

The Dragons bowed their heads again, accepting their punishment.

Andren, observing from the periphery, clapped his hands. "Wonderful!"

Nisthala gave him a gracious nod, ruler to ruler. He really has no idea, she thought. How much I despise him.

Jadu, forgotten on the sidelines, sagged in exhaustion. The power that had been keeping her alive was gone, and she was fading.

Yasila was the only one to notice. She cupped Jadu's elbow to help her balance. Felt how little flesh there was, that the old woman's skin was cold to the touch, and paper thin. For decades, the Eye had kept her alive for its own purpose. Now she was free of it. Her fire was dying out.

Jadu's eyes shifted from pale amber to dark blue. She blinked, feeling the change. "I was born in Riversmeet," she said. "My name was Jadu Rell. My mother's name was Ahra. We lived on Spring Street, in the Old Quarter, just the two of us. A long, long time ago."

Something was happening to her body. A powdering, fine silt running from her skin, from her fingers. Her rose-gold hair turning white. She looked gently at Yasila. "Perhaps I wished to show love, and could not. Perhaps."

A sigh, and a sinking, as her body disintegrated. By the time she reached the ground, there was nothing left but ash.

Seventy-Six

"THE TRICK IS to keep moving," Cain said to Neema, not for the first time. "An opportunity will present itself."

Neema couldn't see how. They had been running, and hiding, and fighting, for half the night. Now it was dawn. In the light, their luck would run out. It was inevitable.

They had to get off the island. But for that they needed a boat, and a quiet launching spot. They had neither. Long before sunrise, every quay had been packed with Hounds, and servants, and harried courtiers sitting on boxes of possessions, waiting to be ferried either to the mainland or on to a Leviathan. In the early hours, the new emperor had issued his first proclamation. The court was on the move to its new home. In the drama of leaving, the survivors would have less time to ask questions, or to see the bodies piling up in the Festival Square. To see their friends among the dead.

"We're back where we started," Neema muttered.

Almost true. They were close to the Raven palace again, on the common land that sloped gently down to the perimeter wall and the Guardian Gate. Sheltered in a shallow ditch, they could see that the ancient doors were flung wide open, the Mirror Bridge glittering beyond. They'd been searching for a discreet route off the island. This was very much not it.

"We could just go." Cain sliced a hand towards the Gate. "Slash our way through."

"…straight into the Hound garrison," Neema finished, for him. "With nowhere left to run."

They sat back against the ditch wall, stumped.

"Any ideas, Sol?"

Neema had coaxed Sol out of her chest a while ago. ("Don't look," she'd warned Cain. He'd looked, and regretted it.) She'd hoped he might act as their scout, but he was too bereft to form himself into his usual shape. There was something wrong with both wings, and one claw was mangled. When she held him, she could feel there were bones missing, or whatever metaphorical business it was that kept him in shape. Too feeble to return to the safety of her ribcage, he had spent most of the night hidden in her pack, a clotted, oozing, half-finished bundle of misery.

She opened the pack. Sol looked at her sadly. **No ideas.** He burrowed deeper into the pack. **No flock. No home. So alone.**

Ahead of them, at the Guardian Gate, the Hounds marched back and forth in the early light, swords glinting.

Neema brought out a cheese roll she'd taken from the Ox kitchen. Hours and hours ago. It was stale. She tore it in half and shared it with Cain. "Sinn Dunrelli's First Rule of the Road," she said.

"Eat when you can, sleep when you can, fuck when you can."

"For tomorrow we die." She chewed sadly on her roll. "So dry."

"Like butter has gone out of fashion," Cain lamented, with her.

"I love it when we agree on things."

They smiled at each other. They were both a mess, bleeding and bruised. The ditch was damp with dew, soaking into their clothes.

"I think you're right," Neema said, lifting her chin towards the Gate. "Run and hope."

"What about the garrison?"

"We'll improvise."

"Cain Ballari. Neema Kraa." A voice called out across the common ground. Hol Vabras. He'd found them.

Neema and Cain peered over the ditch.

Vabras was standing at the edge of a small coppice, forty feet away. "You're surrounded," he called.

"By the dazzling glow of our genius?" Cain called back.

"By twenty-four Samran Hounds."

Neema rummaged in her pack, looking for Sol. He was buried right at the bottom, half bird, half viscous puddle of despair.

"I think this is the end for us, Sol."

You are leaving me too. Abandoned. Alone . . .

"Would you like to come out and fight with us? One last stand?"

Sol lifted his beak out of the black goo. **Together? Fight together?**

"Yes."

As a flock?

"A flock of three. Yes."

Sol blinked. The goo was soaking back into his body. **I would like that very much, Neema.**

She scooped him out of the pack and deposited him between her feet and Cain's. A violent shake, some unstable flapping, and Sol had pulled himself together. He hopped to the top of the ditch and strutted back and forth, diamond-shaped tail fanning out behind him. Fearsome hooked beak, thick hackles. Purple-black feathers gleaming in the sun.

With a crack of his wings he lifted up into the sky and made a circuit, before returning to the top of the ditch. He confirmed what Vabras had said. Twenty-four Hounds. **Twelve in the woods, twelve spread out behind. They are tired, like you. Their leader most of all. The one that shouted.**

"Vabras."

Yes. He is exhausted. He is hoping you will surrender; he does not want to fight.

"Well, that's something," Cain said, when she told him. "My turn with the pack, I think."

He shouldered it, while Neema projected silently through their options. Their best hope would be to break the line of Hounds at their back and head through the devastation of the Fox palace. Back inland. They'd hidden out there earlier. The blackened bodies, the shredded limbs, the smell of burnt flesh. The clear-up team, with their carts. She looked at Cain from the corner of her eye. He was almost spent. Physically, emotionally. She couldn't ask him to go back there.

"Surrender, and you will have a swift death. You have my word," Vabras called. His voice was strained, and thin.

"He *does* sound tired," Neema said.

"Busy night, murdering all my friends." Cain dug his fingers into the earth.

Sol hopped on to his knee, and gave a tentative, soothing sound. Then he lifted back into the air. **They are coming.**

Cain and Neema looked at each other again. No need for a signal, or a discussion, beyond that look. Jumping out of the ditch, they sprinted towards the Guardian Gate.

Shouts behind them, as the Hounds at their back gave chase. More shouts to their left, as the second squad streamed out of the coppice. Neema hurtled down the slope. Up ahead, the captain at the Gate shouted an urgent command.

Neema! They are closing the Gate!

Sol flew straight into the captain's face, raking at him with his claws. The rest of the guards came to their captain's aid, as Sol slashed and pecked, keeping them occupied.

If we can make it through the Guardian Gate, Neema thought. If we can block it from the other side...

A Hound smashed into her, tumbling her to the ground. A blur of grass and dirt, sky and more dirt as she hurtled down the slope, head over heels, and scraped to a halt flat on her stomach. A couple of Hounds piled on top of her, pressing her face into the ground. She struggled but it was no use, she couldn't shake them.

A heavy *thunk*. A shout of pain. Another *thunk*.

Arrows.

More pressure, and then less, as the Hounds were thrown off her.

"Get up, Neema. Go!"

Tala. She'd come from nowhere. Still in her cream halterneck, torn and bloody. She was holding her bow from the Tiger Trial, arrows slung over one shoulder. Knuckles bleeding from a dozen fights. "Run!"

Neema staggered to her feet and lurched on towards the Gate. She couldn't see Cain, but sensed him behind her, fighting his own way through.

Neema!

A stifled cry from Sol, as the Hounds at the Gate caught him and threw him down, stamping on him with their heavy boots.

With a surge of fury she ran to his rescue, screaming at them to stop. How dare they? This land, once the home of Raven warriors. How dare they?

She took down three of them, with Tala. They could do this, they could fight their way through to the Mirror Bridge. Barricade the Gate.

"Cain!" she called, turning to look for him.

Vabras had him. Waiting patiently on the higher ground, holding a dagger to his throat.

"Neema, run!" Cain yelled.

Tala seized her, and tried to pull her through the Gate. Neema wrenched herself free. She gathered up Sol, his neck snapped, his wings broken, and pushed him into Tala's arms.

Tala stared at the ruined bird in horror. "What the Eight…"

"He's not dead. Take him with you. Please."

Tala hesitated, then ran through the Gate. Two Hounds chased after her.

Neema let the rest of the squad drag her back to their commander. Vabras kept his blade pressed tight against Cain's throat.

"Why didn't you run?" Cain said, anguished.

"Would you?"

"*Obviously.*"

They laughed. You have to laugh, at the end.

"Life is a joke and death is the punchline," Vabras said. "Hah, hah, hah."

There was a bewildered pause. This was not the sort of thing Vabras said. And yet—he had said it. He pulled Cain closer into him and sniffed his hair, nose pressed deep into his scalp.

The Hounds shared startled looks. It had been a long night, they were all exhausted. But still.

Vabras licked a patch behind Cain's ear.

"So this is weird," Cain said, frozen to the spot. "Even for me."

"High Commander?" the Hound captain said. "Are you well?"

"I am well, I am well," Vabras sang, to the tune of…

Neema choked back a laugh. Oh. *Oh*. This was perfect.

Vabras grinned at her. "It *is* funny, isn't it? I'm so pleased you are amused. You have been searching for a joke, Cain Ballari—a tribute for our lost friends. So many dead, so many of my little followers murdered. I can taste their blood in the air." He hummed again. "I am the joke, I am the joke..."

"High Commander," the captain said, more sharply. "I think you need to rest, sir."

Vabras turned his gaze upon her. A cold, yellow gaze. "Thank you, captain. The High Commander rested some time ago. Closed his eyes and..." He lowered the blade from Cain's neck, and pushed him to one side. "Here I am."

The Fox smiled as its fangs slid through its gums. So much blood in the air, this fine summer morning. So much blood, and so much fear. And no Dragon to answer to.

The captain had a deep cut on her brow. The Fox licked its lips.

The next few minutes were unpleasant. Let us look away.

CHAPTER
Seventy-Seven

THE EMPEROR STOOD on board his Leviathan, watching the
sky. Seagulls mobbed the island, and carrion crows, drawn by
the bodies yet to be retrieved and burned. He felt a stirring of pity,
and sorrow, for the dead. He did not hate them, he wished them
no ill. He never had. Only—they were in his path.

Havoc stood at his shoulder, waiting for his next order. The
emperor would never say it, but he found the boy tiresome—his
insatiable hunger for recognition, his misguided self-belief. His
parents' fault. Some people should not have children.

But he had his uses.

"I should like to speak with Fenn. Bring him up, would you?
And clear the deck."

Havoc bowed and left him.

Trails of smoke drifted across the island, from the dying remains of the Fox palace. He might add the image to his coronation speech—something about…yes, he would say he saw the
shape of a wolf in the smoke, lit by the morning sun. There was
no room for the Fox and its followers in Andren's sunlit vision
of Orrun Reborn. Too cunning, too rebellious, too unpredictable. With the Guardians caged, and his daughter ruling Helia,
Andren could spin any tale he wished. He would tell the crowds
in White Tiger Square that the Dragon—tired of the Fox's endless treachery—had destroyed the First Guardian in a stream of
fire. From the ashes, a new Guardian of the Eight had arisen: the
Wolf. In time, there would be a Wolf Pack in every neighbour-
hood, watching and informing. It would take a few years, but the
emperor was a patient man. A patient *young* man.

Havoc returned with Fenn, flanked by two guards.

Andren ordered the Hounds away. "Lord Fenn won't be any trouble. He knows what will happen to his family if he misbehaves."

Fenn was unshaven, still wearing the overalls he had on when he was arrested, his muddy boots. He squinted at the man he thought was Ruko, sizing him up. "You look different."

"Do I?" Andren was fascinated. "How so?"

Fenn shrugged. "Just different." You didn't tell the most powerful man in the world that he looked unhinged.

The emperor laughed. His face shifted, his hair turned from black to grey.

Fenn gaped, refusing to comprehend what he was seeing. "What the fuck…"

Andren took a step forward, arms out in friendship.

Fenn stumbled back, until he tripped on a pile of ropes and sat down, heavily. He rubbed a hand over his scalp. Maybe that knock to the head had done more damage than he'd realised.

Andren sent Havoc to find some tobacco. "You're not hallucinating, Fenn. It's called a Chameleon Spell. It allows me to take on my son's form."

"You were Ruko, all along?"

"No, no." Andren laughed again. He was enjoying himself. "For the past fifteen years…" His appearance shifted briefly a second time, back to the Old Bear. "I have been your emperor."

"You…" Tears filled Fenn's eyes. "What happened to Bersun? What did you *do*?"

Andren shifted back into Ruko, the spell pulling him back to the soul he had most recently stolen from. "It was necessary, Fenn. You remember what he was like. So dour, so short-tempered. So inflexible. He wasn't fit to rule."

"Then why pretend to be him? If he was so terrible?"

"To save Orrun. To *heal* the empire." Andren brought his hands together. "I could have ruled as Andren the Usurper. The Great Traitor. And the Bears would have gone to war against me. Probably whipped up every Commoner to their cause. Maybe the Oxes, too."

Fenn waved his hand—*stop*. It was too much.

"I saved Orrun, Fenn. And now, finally, I can rule as myself. No one knows the real Ruko Valit. Maybe he's *exactly* like his father. Who would know any different? After all—you knew Bersun, and I still fooled you."

"You *used* me."

"Well—as you always say, Fenn—that's the curse of being useful. But I wouldn't complain, if I were you. It's what's keeping you and your family alive." And without further preamble, Andren embarked on his favourite topic—the restoration of Samra. "You're going to bring it back to life for me. You'll have all the resources you need. Imagine it—the Marble City, returned to its full splendour. New squares, new parks and theatres." He spread his hands out, marvelling at the expanse of his own ambitions. "The greatest engineering project ever undertaken—and you'll be in charge. Tell me that doesn't excite you."

"It doesn't excite me."

Andren clapped his hands. "Deadpan as always. But I know you, Fenn. Once you're there, and settled into the work. Never known a man toil as hard as you…"

Havoc had returned with tobacco and paper, a tinderbox. And a trace of annoyance, to be acting as servant, dressed in his crisp gold and white uniform.

Fenn, watching them both, built a roll-up and lit it. As he breathed in the tobacco, he felt his heartbeat slow. He had to stay calm, stop asking questions. Take this all in later, when he was alone. Let them think he'd given in; use their arrogance against them.

Andren was still selling his grand project. "Twice a month, you will have a day off to spend with your family. As long as you cooperate, they will be treated well. You have my word."

Fenn smoked. Oh, your word. That's reassuring.

"These terms can improve. This doesn't have to be unpleasant. You'll have all the money and resources you need. All you have to do is work hard and behave."

Fenn stubbed out his roll-up, and got to his feet. "Submit to the yoke."

Andren laughed. "Very good. And yes—if you like. But I do hope in time it won't feel that way, Fenn. Samra's restoration means everything to me. I'm sure once you're there, you will come to share my vision." He turned to Havoc. "Take him back below would you? I need to speak to my son."

Ruko was locked in the hold, chained to the floor, Gedrun's iron mask clamped to his head.

"We'll design something better for you when we reach Samra," Andren promised.

Had anyone fallen so far or so fast as Ruko Valit? The night had dragged him down by the scruff of his neck from emperor to slave. Rivenna's numbing poison had worn off, but the effects of the Chameleon Spell kept him knocked down, defeated. Perhaps he would understand better if he knew the spell's true name. Soul Stealer. His immaculate body was intact. But something essential had been taken from him that could never be restored. A small sliver of himself, lost for ever.

Andren unlocked the mask and put it to one side, untied the gag. He smoothed his son's hair down, and patted his cheek. He was wearing his own face down here. "Less unsettling for you," he said, as if he were being compassionate. He stretched, and cracked his back, before pulling up a chair. Sat down with his legs apart, fingers laced together. "I know you're disappointed."

Ruko stared at his father, impassive. All he had left was his training. *Give him nothing. No more than he has already taken.*

"You have a choice to make, Ruko. Gedrun lived fifteen years. You're young and healthy. You have Valit and Majan blood in your veins." Andren reached out and gripped Ruko's wrist. "You will live twice as long, I'm sure of it. You can resist, if you wish. You can go mad, as Gedrun did. I will still take what I need from you." Andren's grip tightened, his nails digging into Ruko's skin, then let go. "Or you can accept your fate. If you do, you will be well treated. Comfortable quarters. A private square to exercise at night. Good food, good wine. We might arrange whores for you."

Ruko did not react. Stillness. Patience. Dignity.

Andren had not come down here to provoke his son, but this annoyed him. Did he not realise his days playing a Tiger warrior were over? "You should know—Rivenna considered you an average student, at best. The only thing that set you apart was your singular focus on the throne. And even that, I gave to you." Andren prodded his son in the chest. "You always were a lazy boy, Ruko. You lacked the discipline or resolve to make something of yourself."

Ruko kept his eyes fixed upon a point on the floor, and concentrated on his breathing.

"Not like your sister. Yana…" Andren paused, overcome with sudden grief. It always surprised him. He cleared his throat, and continued. "Yanara was special. Your mother's favourite, and mine." A shrug—it was what it was. "You resented her for it. Given the right provocation, I knew you would betray her. In fact I'd counted on it."

Andren rose to his feet. Above their heads, sailors ran back and forth, preparing to set sail. The boat pitched in a swell, forcing him to put out his hands, to steady himself. "What I did not anticipate," he said, when the pitching stopped, "was your cruelty. Sending your own sister into exile. Wicked. Evil. But I must confess, it was the spur you needed." Andren nodded to himself. "I suppose deep down you knew that. No way back. Every path destroyed but one. The path to the throne." He spread his hands wide, and laughed. "Poor Ruko. You truly believed in yourself, didn't you?"

"I won the Festival," Ruko said. "Which is more than you did."

Andren slapped him, hard. Then again.

Ruko spat the blood from his lips, and gave a mirthless smile. "Did I touch a nerve?"

Disappointed, Andren gagged his son again before fixing the iron mask back over his head. He was not gentle this time. "I do not like this brattish insolence," he said, as he turned the key. "I have yet to decide whether we should cut out your tongue. You might reflect upon that, before we meet again." He was halfway to the door before he remembered something. "I brought you a gift. Some company. Rather fitting, I thought."

He swung a small cage into the hold, and placed it at Ruko's feet. The cage was covered with a golden cloth. "It's called Pink-Pink. Ridiculous name, don't know where it came from. Feel free to change it."

For a long time after his father had gone, Ruko did not move. He breathed, behind his mask. Thoughts came, dark thoughts. He heard the anchor, winched from the seabed. The blare of a trumpet. "To Samra!" Cheers from the crew. They were going home, with their emperor.

His father was mad, and would do terrible things in his name. Had already done terrible things in his name.

In his mind he saw a black space, where once a golden rope had stretched all the way to the marble throne. Now there was nothing but the void. If he took a step in any direction, it would consume him. He might want it to consume him. Yes, he might want that.

The Leviathan lifted and dropped on the waves, sending the cage sliding along the floor. Ruko stopped it, and removed the gold embroidered cloth.

A green and yellow chameleon sat on a narrow branch, tail wound in a spiral. Its eyes swivelled warily.

"Hello," Ruko said, feeling foolish.

But this was no ordinary chameleon. This was a creature dragged unwilling from the Hidden Realm. And it needed a new home. Its colours changed to black, white, orange. Tiger stripes. A greeting of sorts.

Ruko opened the cage. At least one of them could be free. After an achingly long time, Pink-Pink crawled out of the cage door, and with a sudden snap, extended his tongue to catch a fly on the wing.

Ruko didn't notice. Pink-Pink's exit had disturbed the layer of branches at the bottom of the cage, revealing a flash of red fabric. Brushing aside the vegetation, Ruko reached deeper, and pulled out a scarlet ribbon.

Benna.

Smoothing the ribbon in both hands, he saw that she had written something on the other side. He turned it over.

TEAM RUKO!

He laughed, inside his iron mask, because it was so wonderful, and stupid. Because his father would not understand it, not in a thousand years. A nonsense phrase, scribbled on a scrap of ribbon. A tiny fragment of the Bear, sent to give him courage. He wound it around his fingers. And it did. It gave him courage.

CHAPTER
Seventy-Eight

WHEN IT WAS over, the Fox found a handkerchief and wiped its hands. "This is not my fault," it said, flapping the bloody handkerchief at the twenty-four eviscerated corpses. The torn windpipes, the savaged flesh, the glistening loops of intestine. The stink of fear and death. "Their screaming triggered my prey drive."

Neema rubbed her face. The Fox in the form of Vabras was... she couldn't find the words. Cain and the Fox made a strange sort of sense. But not this. This was unspeakable.

"Cain would have stopped me," the Fox complained. "You would have stopped me, Cain."

Cain was on his knees a few feet away, throwing up into the ditch.

"Sensitive," the Fox said, smoothing Vabras's jacket. "Always was. This one is different. He craves chaos."

"That's not right. Vabras lives for order," Neema protested.

The Fox winked at her. "Many a Hound dreams of being a Fox, without knowing it."

Neema was certain Vabras had never winked in his life. He had never done anything that interesting with his face before. "How did you escape the binding spell?"

A shrug. "I am the Guardian of Escape."

"It trapped the *Dragon*."

The Fox pretended to be sad. "Poor Dragon. Caught by its arrogance. So powerful, it never bothered to learn how to run, how to hide. Thought itself above such things. What a pity." It smiled, teeth bloody. Something nasty, stuck between its teeth. "What a shame."

"I saw you go into the painting." As she said it, she realised the trick. "One fragment of you."

Cornered Vixen, Defending her Cubs to the Death.

Now the Fox looked genuinely sorry. "She sacrificed herself. Naturally selfless. A peculiar fragment." It picked the dreadful thing from between Vabras's teeth.

"So the spell dragged you out of—"

"My home." The Fox looked wistfully at Cain, still dry-heaving into the ditch. "I lost him. He'd run off with you. Then I saw this one." The Fox patted Vabras's chest with both hands, proprietorial. The High Commander had been standing in his garden, looking for his cat. When the cat didn't come, it left a hollow space inside him. The Fox—ever the opportunist—had jumped right in. "I think I will stay," it said, and yawned. Its eyes flickered briefly from yellow to a dull, nondescript colour, then yellow again.

"Wake up," Neema said sharply. "You can't fall asleep."

This the Fox did not like. It gave her a narrow look. "Can't I?"

She stepped back cautiously, hands up. "Please don't fall asleep. Vabras will kill us."

The Fox yawned again.

"Why don't you jump back into Cain?"

"Woah, wait. Absolutely not." Cain had finally dragged himself away from the ditch, carrying Neema's pack. He looked grey. "No offence," he said to the Fox.

The Fox was distracted by a severed torso at its feet. It reached down, and straightened a square silver button on the torso's jacket.

Neema grabbed Cain's sleeve. Running might trigger the Fox's predatory instinct again, and they were the only ones left for it to kill. Holding each other tight, they backed away carefully down the slope.

"It's almost asleep," Neema said. "Look. It's tidying up. That's Vabras."

The Fox was trying to create order out of the carnage, moving body parts around. It picked up a head and placed it above the limbless torso. Shovelled some innards back into a ribcage. "Oh, are you leaving?" It unsheathed Vabras's sword and waved it at them. "Yes, that might be an idea. I'm very tired. We did have fun, didn't we, Cain? So much fun together..." Another yawn. "Fare thee well. Fare thee well..."

"We're far enough," Cain said. "Run."

They turned, and sprinted the rest of the way down the slope towards the wide open Guardian Gate.

Vabras woke with a headache, and the taste of someone else's blood in his mouth.

CHAPTER
Seventy-Nine

THE EMPEROR'S LEVIATHAN was a toy boat on the horizon, heading south for Dragon's Mouth Bay. The fleet followed in its wake. On board their private yacht, Lady Harmony said to her husband, "We must make more of an effort with Havoc when we reach Samra," and Lord Clarion said, "Yes, we must." It was a thing they said to each other, from time to time.

Down in the galley, their new servant reached to tug her plaits, before remembering she had cut them off. She put her hand in her pocket and touched the ribbon she'd tucked there. Samra. She'd passed through Samra on her way east across the empire. She had friends there. Benna made friends everywhere.

The Dragon contingent were in the throne room, strengthening the binding spell. A miserable, endless task their queen had given them. Cursed, one might say. Exiled from their home, like the Eight they watched. Guardians of the Guardians.

The binding spell was holding strong, but they chanted it together anyway on their knees. Chanting brought them comfort, if not peace. The Princess Yasila had left them a store of Dragon-scale oil to keep the walls secure. Now that the incense burners were gone, and the heavy scent of frankincense and patchouli was fading from the air, the bitter smell was apparent. Little wonder Shimmer Arbell had seen visions, transported by her own genius to the Hidden Realm. She'd had no idea her paint had been laced with it, seeping into her skin as well as into the walls. Day after day, it had urged her on to fulfil her greatest desire: to create a masterpiece that would last through the ages.

Unwittingly, she had built our cages.

Bound inside our portraits, we suffer. The Eight Guardians of Orrun. Seven times we came to save the world. The Eighth time...

We *will* destroy it. Tiger, trapped into the door.

If we hold very still, and concentrate very hard, we can speak a few words to each other.

We, the Raven, call up to the Dragon on the ceiling. **We are sorry, Dragon. We failed you.**

Though to be fair (we think, but do not say), perhaps if you had specified *which* Tiger warrior you wanted us to stop...Not that we are complaining, or abrogating our responsibility, but a *name* might have helped. Or a nudge in the right direction, at the very least. This is the problem with being numinous and enigmatic. Mystique is a wonderful thing, no doubt, but look where it has brought us.

I too am sorry, Tiger says, which is a bit of a first. **Andren was mine. Rivenna was mine.**

There is a long, long silence, while the Dragon thinks its thoughts. We feel a warmth spread through us, soothing the relentless pain of our confinement. And in our heads the Dragon speaks, not with its grand and echoing voice, but gently, with forgiveness:

ALL IS AS IT MUST BE.

To the east, beyond the Garden at the Edge of the World, Nisthala stepped out on to the deck of her Leviathan, and was pleased by what she saw. Shal Worthy had inspected every inch of the ship before he had let her board.

She lifted her bare arms, enjoying the sun on her skin. The bliss of being warm at last. Let her father shiver in the winter of the old capital. On Helia it was never cold. "We're going home," she said, to her mother.

Yasila smiled, faintly.

Nisthala's face fell. "You're not happy."

"I'm happy for you. That is all that matters."

Nisthala, who adored her mother, gave her a hug. "You will feel better once we are settled." She was a queen now. It sounded almost like a command.

Yasila drew back. "Where are your beads? Have you lost them?"

The wooden necklace Nisthala had worn for so many years was missing from her throat. She touched the emerald sunk into her forehead. "They didn't match. I'll find something more suitable among Helia's treasures. More befitting a queen," she said, and laughed at herself. When her mother didn't react, she said, "They were children's beads, Mama, they barely fit me."

"We must plan something special for your birthday," Yasila said, finding a subject they would both enjoy. Nisthala would turn sixteen soon. At which time, as a direct descendant of the Empress Yasthala, she could take the title of princess. Not that she would, now that she was queen.

They talked of what they might do, whether they might reach Helia in time. "Imagine if I arrived on the day itself," Nisthala said. As always she had a sense of herself beyond herself, as an historical figure, like her ancestor Yasthala. Fate-driven, a myth in the making. *And so it came to pass, that Queen Nisthala touched the earth of Helia for the first time, on the day she turned sixteen...* "We must arrive on the day," she decided.

The crew pulled the anchor and set sail. The sun sparkled on the water. Dolphins arced from the waves, swimming alongside the boat. Another image to add to the myth—a future subject for a tapestry, perhaps.

Nisthala talked, and Yasila remembered. Ruko had made that necklace. They'd had no money left for Kind Festival presents that year. He'd turned the beads himself on a lathe at school, carving the tiny sigils of the eight into the wood. Ruko had always been good with his hands. Yasila remembered him sitting on the rickety staircase outside their grid apartment in Armas, threading the beads on to the wire. She remembered him holding it up and saying, "What do you think? Will she like it?" Smiling. Her son smiling up at her. She couldn't remember her reply.

CHAPTER
Eighty

THERE WERE SIGNS, in the garrison, that Tala had been there before them. Notably the three dead Hounds. And a purple-black, viscous smear on the desk. Sol. They had got this far, at least.

"This says we're traitors." Neema waved a piece of paper.

Cain was winching the platform back up the side of the rock. "Traitors. How ironic. You can write your own Order of Exile, Neema."

"Fuck you," she said, and then, "Vabras."

The High Commander was striding along the Mirror Bridge towards them, sword in hand. In the morning light, the bridge was almost too bright to look at directly. When she had run across it, Neema had glimpsed shards of herself reflected back, her fractured geometry. Some with Cain and some without.

She slammed the garrison door shut and dragged the desk over to block it. Grabbing her pack, she swung herself through the window on to the waiting platform. Cain joined her and grasped the winch with both hands. "Stiff," he said as he turned it, lowering them down the outer wall. The mechanism creaked, the twin pulley ropes hardened by the salt water.

Above their heads, they could hear Vabras forcing the door.

"Faster!" Neema said, gripping the rope sides of the platform.

Cain winched harder. The platform juddered beneath their feet, smacking and bouncing against the rock face, threatening to crack apart. They were not yet halfway down.

"Is now a good time to tell you that I love you?" Cain said, winching furiously.

"It's a terrible time."

Vabras glared down at them from the garrison window, then began hacking at one of the pulley ropes with his sword.

Cain was almost spent. Neema took over at the winch.

"Keep going, keep going," he said. "We're almost—"

A rope snapped.

The platform dropped violently to one side. Neema clung to the remaining pulley rope as the floor gave way. Cain swung down beneath her, gripping the rope sides of the platform with both hands. "We'll have to jump," he yelled up at her. "Throw your pack."

She flung it out, then watched in horror as it slammed against the base rock, before rolling feebly into the churning sea below.

"Swing the rope out more," Cain said. "Hurry."

They kicked out together, pushing off from the rock face.

"I'll have to go first," he said, and jumped.

A pause, and then a splash. He'd made it.

Neema was alone. She couldn't do this. She had to do this. Before Vabras cut through the second rope.

Three deep breaths, as she pushed off from the rocks. One... two...

Jump.

She wheeled through the air. Saw rocks, jagged rocks below. Nothing she could do but fall. Pray to the Eight, who could not even save themselves...

She slammed into the sea, plunging deep under the waves. Roaring confusion, the heavy press of water. Then spat out on the surface, coughing and spluttering, grabbing the nearest rock, cutting her fingers, but she didn't care, she was alive.

Behind her, the platform tumbled down the rock face and shattered at the base.

No way for Vabras to reach them now. In his attempt to kill them he had set them free. She tried to imagine his face as he realised. Blank, of course. The Fox watching somewhere deep within. One eye open, one eye closed. Laughing.

She rubbed the stinging saltwater from her eyes, her vision smeared. Cain was clinging to a larger rock, fifteen feet away. He'd salvaged her pack. He waved at her.

She stared around at the various savage rocks she could have landed on, seeing a dozen Neemas broken upon them. "We are so lucky," she called to him.

"We're amazing."

She lifted the silver pendant out. You and me.

He grinned at her.

"Now what?" she asked, as a wave rinsed over her.

"I thought I'd enjoy not being dead for a moment."

They bobbed against their respective rocks, not daring to swim across to each other. The swell was too strong. Neema was starting to tire, the waves pushing her back and forth on to the rock, scraping her skin, bruising her body.

"The fleet's moving off," Cain said. And then, after a pause, "Shit. Boat's coming."

They sank lower in the water. "Hounds?"

"Cargo."

"Might be heading for Armas," she said, but she could see it now. A merchant boat with a canvas cabin, heading straight for them. An elderly man at the tiller, in overalls and a straw hat. The deck was stacked with chickens in cages.

"Maybe we can bribe them," she said. "The crew, I mean. Not the chickens."

But Cain was laughing, lifting himself higher in the water. "It's Fort."

"Are you sure?"

"That's what he looks like when he washes. He's alive!"

The abbot was indeed alive, thanks to the Fox. "Fill my chapel with chickens," it had told him. "Then hide under the floor, I have made a den there." Fort had spent the night squeezed in the coffin-sized space, while the chickens roamed free in the chapel. And when the Hounds swept the temple, it never occurred to them that someone might be hiding there, under all that squawking, flapping nonsense.

Just as the Fox had promised. "There is nothing more distracting in this world, Ishmahir, than a chicken."

When the night had passed, Fort had bathed and combed his hair, and shaved—and the transformation was so marked, he might as well have murmured a Chameleon Spell. He'd put the chickens (protesting) back into their cages and carted them across the island without being questioned once.

And now Tala was ducking out of the cabin, gold tooth glinting as she grinned at them. She hauled Cain on to the deck along with the Bear pack. Then it was Neema's turn, snatched from the waves and dropped on a pile of blankets. Tala hugged her.

"Get under the canvas," Fort said.

Neema crawled across the deck into the cabin, dragging a blanket with her. Saved. Every part of her ached, the cut on her neck stung from the saltwater and she didn't care. She collapsed down next to Cain.

Neema.

Sol was nestled inside a basket, still healing from his fight with the Hounds. Tala had tucked him up in a gingham cloth, he looked jaunty. Neema smiled at him, exhausted.

Cain wrapped his arm around her under the blankets. For a while they said nothing, thought of nothing. The night had taken almost everything from them. Ish steered the boat and Tala made tea. Neema slept on Cain's shoulder.

When she woke he was fast asleep, still holding her. "I love you," she murmured, in his ear.

He is asleep, Neema. He can't hear you.

"Yes, thank you, Sol."

You are welcome. A short pause, and then, nervous, **Are we still a flock?**

She looked at him, snug in his gingham cloth.

You said we were a flock before, but perhaps it was temporary? A temporary flock?

"We're a flock," she said. "Permanent."

Sol gave a satisfied shuffle and pecked at his basket. **Did you see me fight the Hounds, Neema?**

She knew what he was waiting for. "I did. You were magnificent."
Sol puffed up his chest. Magnificent. Yes.

Neema was feeling rested enough to wonder where they were
headed. Armas? Scartown? Or further yet, into the Scarred Lands
themselves? She thought of her vision, the mountain path to the
Bear monastery, red flags to mark the route. A winter morning,
months away—but then, it would take months to get there.

She had not seen Cain in her visions.

The thought of being separated now they had found each other
again, ripped a tear in her heart. She rubbed the pendant between
her fingers, Fox on one side, Raven on the other.

Cain woke up, and stretched. His hair had dried at strange
angles. She smoothed it down for him. The boat crested a wave
and dropped. The sun beat down on the canvas.

There would be a time for questions and plans, and arguments.
Soon, before they reached land. But not now. This moment was
wide as an empire and deep as the sea. This moment was golden.

The story continues in...

THE FOX IN WINTER

Book TWO of the Eternal Path Trilogy

Acknowledgements

The deepest of thanks to my editor Nick Sayers for his support and guidance. I'm also fortunate to have the wise, generous and let's face it legendary Clare Conville as my agent. Thank you both, from the bottom of my heart.

Thanks to the wonderful team at Hodder, especially Melis Dagoglu, Joanne Dickinson, Rebecca Folland, Sophie Judge and Kate Norman. A huge thank you to Molly Powell for her exceptional skill, knowledge and flair. Thank you to Ian Wong for his insight and some very helpful and considered notes. Special thanks to Natasha Qureshi for her enthusiasm and smart editorial contributions. I'm honoured to be published by Angelica Chong and Tim Holman at Orbit U.S. Thanks to the marvellous Elizabeth Milne and everyone at CW. Big thanks and respect to Michael McCoy at Independent Talent—you are the best and you know it.

Thanks to my fellow Tai Chi students at Mei Quan—what an inspiring group you are. And especially to my teacher Daniel Wexler for his perception, wit and encouragement.

Any knowledge or insight about the art of ink and brushwork in *The Raven Scholar* comes from my wonderful calligraphy teacher, Mayumi Petherbridge. (Naturally, any errors come from me.) I wish I could say that, like Neema, I have the best hand on the island. Actually I don't wish that—I'm quite content with being not very good, it's strangely liberating. Anyway—thanks Mayumi!

In late spring 2022 I spent an incredible morning with Lloyd and Rose Buck and their rightly celebrated raven, Bran. You can read as many books as you like about ravens, but there's nothing quite like meeting one face to beak, especially one as charismatic as Bran. Lloyd answered all my questions with good humour and patience, and it was a joy to watch Bran puzzle solve and interact with us.

Respectful thanks to the Royal Literary Fund for its generous support in autumn 2023. I'm hugely grateful for the timely help, and for the kind advice of Justine Palmer.

Thank you to Anna Alward for her wisdom and compassion.

Love and thanks to my sister Michelle for always being there.

Thanks to Mary Stacey and Stuart Bell for their help during lockdown. Equally Richard Beswick and Caroline Stacey. Your kind help meant I could begin work properly on *The Raven Scholar* in spring 2020, and not worry about the roof over my head (literally).

Next, thanks to a group of funny, creative, generous friends. Jamie Boardman, Chris Bridges, Catherine Burke, Esther Chesterman, Lance Fitzgerald, Melanie Backe-Hansen, Sophie Hardach, Jason Hewitt, Ian Lindsay Hickman, Val Hudson, Jo Krupa, Suzy Lucas, Kate Mayfield, Ned Palmer, Imogen Robertson, Clare Smith, Andrew Wille, Justine Willett and Gordon Wise.

Thank you Miranda Carter for your brilliant company and consistent kindness. Chris Gardner—thank you for the perfect advice at exactly the right moment, you are such a wise soul. David Shelley —thanks for a lovely, enduring friendship, it means the world. Thanks to Sarah Sykes for long country walks and deep creative discussions —you were the first person I talked to about *The Raven Scholar* and you've helped me so much along the way. Thanks to Sophia Tobin for Sunday morning coffees and great conversation. And profound thanks to Rowena Webb, loyal, generous and just the best company.

Of course I am only the scribe of this tale. I did ask the Raven if they wanted to thank anyone (namely me, for the typing). They said the only thing they wanted to acknowledge was their **magnificence** and that I should get back to work tapping out part two.

Fair enough.

extras

orbit

meet the author

Rebecca Douglas

ANTONIA HODGSON is a freelance editor and the author of the best-selling Thomas Hawkins historical crime series. Her first novel, *The Devil in the Marshalsea*, won the Crime Writers' Association Historical Dagger Award and was shortlisted for the Theakston Old Peculier Crime Novel of the Year. She lives in Kent, England, where she has been visited by a fox, a raven, and a tiger in the form of her neighbor's ginger cat. No dragons as yet.

Find out more about Antonia Hodgson and other Orbit authors by registering for the free monthly newsletter at orbitbooks.net.

if you enjoyed
THE RAVEN SCHOLAR

look out for

THE MERCY MAKERS
The Moon Heresies: Book One

by

Tessa Gratton

A talented heretic must decide between the
pursuit of forbidden magic and the ecstasy of
forbidden love, in the start of a sweeping, romantic
epic fantasy trilogy by *New York Times* bestselling
author Tessa Gratton.

Can an empire trip and fall on a mere strand of silk?

*Iriset is a prodigy and an outlaw. She dons the mask of
her alter ego, Silk, to create magical disguises for those in her
father's criminal organization, but she longs to do
more with her talent.*

*When her father is captured and sentenced to death,
Iriset must infiltrate the imperial palace and its fanatical
ruling family. There she realizes she can bring down the*

*entire corrupt system by getting the emperor and his sister
to trust and even to love her. But love is a
two-way street, and Iriset's own heart holds the most
mysterious and impenetrable magic of all.*

1
Strand of silk

High above the sharp-edged palace of the Vertex Seal, the moon hangs motionless.

And far beneath it, a young god struggles.

———————— • ♦ • ————————

There is a line in the sister works *Word of Aharté* and *Writings of the Holy Syr* that has been debated for nearly all the centuries since the two pamphlets were published. In *Word of Aharté*, the line reads: "My empire will fall on a strand of spider silk." In *Writings*, the line is: "Can an empire trip and fall on a mere strand of silk?" The prophetic tone of the former stands out in the otherwise practical *Word*, while the irreverent humor of the latter is typical of *Writings*. What strikes scholar-priests most deeply is that both Aharté and the Holy Syr would comment so specifically on the same thing, but as if they disagreed on those very specifics.

It is not a translation issue, for both works were composed in pure mirané—the first known examples, in fact. Perhaps it is a conversation between the goddess and her wife that they continued in the pages. Though the Holy Syr explained so many of Aharté's laws to us in her *Writings*, we are supposed to put faith in the goddess's word over that of her wife, given that she is a goddess. But you know it is not spider silk that brings down the Vertex Seal.

• ◆ •

An alarum trembles through the glazed-brick walls of the hidden fortress of Isidor the Little Cat, but his daughter, Iriset mé Isidor, does not hear it.

Tucked down against the geometric tiles in her workshop, she carefully lifts her crystal stylus, drawing a line of force up from her planning vellum into the air. She holds her breath as she completes the connection of this corner line to the seventh squinch supporting the dome of the spell.

A prodigy at architectural design, she discovered by the age of thirteen how to disrupt the threads of force humming through the walls without the use of null wires, creating a workspace devoid of interference. It is convenient when building an intricate scale diagram for a new invention—much less so when under attack from soldiers of the Vertex Seal.

The delicate dome she's building vibrates with ecstatic force, signaling she's completed the internal structure correctly. Iriset releases her breath and smiles smugly, leaning back onto her bare heels. Sweat drips down her spine to the loincloth she wears to work; she prefers as much of her skin open to the air as possible, in order to feel the slightest change in the forces around her. The nape of her neck, inner wrists, and small of her back are particularly sensitive, and so, she's recently discovered, are her lips. Her mask is folded beside her knee, along with her red robe, jacket wrap, and pantaloons.

The design diagram is beautiful.

Exquisite lines of shimmering silver architecture display the plan for a low, wide dome built of all four forces—rising, falling, ecstatic, and flow—that are the basic elements of her craft. The dome is meant to be settled over a small-scale model of Moonshadow City, and when connected to the Holy Design via illegal interface, it will reveal the places where architecture has shifted or changed since last the dome was applied, and therefore reveal where new security measures are set to capture her father.

Just in time for his birthday.

The door to her study jerks open. Hard alarum threads sweep inside, buzzing along the tile floor. Iriset shrieks and reaches out, trying to capture the alarm before it hits the first edge of the diagram, but her bare hands can't grasp the threads. "Bittor!" she snaps as the structure collapses in upon itself, dome wavering first, then unraveling. "You always knock when I'm working! You know that! You..."

Her gaze meets the dilated cat-eyes of the man panting in the arched doorframe. There is blood on his face, and blood on his unsheathed sword.

The hairs on Iriset's arms and neck and small of her back rise: the alarum! Now that the study is breached, she hears pounding chaos from the stairway beyond Bittor. A shock of fear freezes her in place on hands and knees.

Bittor charges inside. "Give me your silk glove," he orders. In his left hand is a burning candle.

Iriset grabs her red robe and throws it over her head, then shoves her arms through the tight sleeves. Bittor never commands her! He has no right. "Why? What's happened?"

Instead of answering, he stalks directly to the north curve of her study wall and puts the candle flame to the lowest of the layered orb webs.

The spiderwebs catch in a flash, curling in on themselves and drifting suddenly unattached from the white tile walls. She sees the fat-bottomed spiders scurrying for safety, but Bittor is faster, smashing them with the butt of his sword.

"What are you doing? Leave them alone!" Iriset yells.

"Your silk glove, now," Bittor says, sparing her a fast glance before putting the flame to a cluster of scrolls and half-sketched diagrams piled upon a kneeler. "And put on the rest of your clothes! Get two floors up to the blue landing. The army has taken your father, and you cannot be found in here with the designs. Is your spider mask here?"

"Father..." she says, slowed down by the crisp smell of her work turning to ashes. Rising force fills the air, stifled by tarnishing smoke. A scream sounds outside the room, and a huge tremor shakes the tower. Iriset leaps for her low desk and grabs up the glove woven of spiderwebs and the finest worm silk. She clutches it to her chest, nails digging too roughly into the delicate material. It's her greatest invention, and Bittor is setting her work on fire. Grief grabs at her when she looks at the smears on the wall: everything left of her poor spiders. They had *names*.

Bittor says, "Give it to me and go, Iriset." He sweeps everything off her desk, kicks a floor pillow and raggedy braided rug into the pile, and drops the candle into it all. A smolder begins immediately.

Iriset stares at the disaster blossoming around her. There in the pile, knocked off her desk, is the glinting black spider mask. Fire reflects wildly the facets of the lower eyes. It won't get hot enough to crack the chips of smoky quartz, but the glue will melt.

"Isidor said I should tell you, 'Sign Amakis,'" Bittor says.

The code is a slap across her mouth. It's her mother's name, and by invoking it, Isidor invokes the bond Iriset swore when she turned seventeen, in order to remain in his court as an adult. She swore to protect herself above all else.

Bittor steps close and takes the silk glove. Then he kisses her. Surprise opens her mouth under his, and she gasps at his lips. Bittor rarely instigates. Quickly she puts her hands to his jaw and kisses back. It might be the last time, if the day doesn't go well for them.

Though in the Little Cat's court it is known they are friends, if not that they are lovers, outside Iriset and Bittor could easily be mistaken for born family: Both are colored like dark desert peaches, with pink lips and the square jaw of the Lapis Osahar dynasties. While her eyes are sandglass brown, Bittor has rare cat-eyes, with slit pupils and vivid sea-green-blue irises filling most of the space between his lids. Hundreds of years ago apostatical human architects designed the eyes for one of Bittor's ancestors, and unlike most apostasy, this manipulation bred true through generations, popping up here and there. The Silent priests determined the children are at no fault for the apostasy of their ancestors and are thus allowed to live. But Bittor's gaze is disconcerting to say the least. He doesn't mind, as his eyes give him a boost as a night-thief and escape artist. Iriset has tried to examine them with her stylus when he is most relaxed, postcoital. Bittor says it's one thing for her to seduce him in order to study his masculine-presenting body and how the four forces interplay within him during sex; it's quite another for her to act like she's eager to dissect him.

Bittor pushes away. He stares at her, pupils narrowing to slits as the fire grows behind her. "When they take you," he orders, "make sure everyone knows you are the daughter of Isidor the Little Cat, and you won't be harmed. Not by the Vertex Seal, not by your fellow prisoners."

Iriset sets her teeth. Bittor is the Little Cat's escape artist: He'll have a way out. "Why can't I go with you?"

"That isn't his command," Bittor says simply.

Nobody will go against her father except her. She says, "They have my father already?"

Bittor nods, and frowns beneath his thin beard. His voice is low as he says, "There is nothing you can do, and you can't get down to the street. They are below us, on nearly every level, surrounding the whole Saltbath precinct, and brought with them investigator-designers who drove hard falling forces down through the streets in case we had tunnels. They *knew*, Iriset." Darkness colors his cheeks and he bares his teeth helplessly.

"Someone betrayed us," she says calmly. Too calmly.

Bittor ignores it. "Do not let them think you know what you know of design."

"I know what I am bound to protect," Iriset says. Herself. She's not allowed to protect her father or Bittor, nor any of the cousins of the court. She must prioritize her own life, not claim her mask-name. She must allow fire to strip away all the evidence of her discoveries. Rising force inside Iriset lifts painfully, a yearning pressure.

Bittor kisses her again, and then pushes her toward the door. "Go, Iriset."

Iriset snatches her clothes and red silk mask off the floor and obeys.

The air outside the study is cool with morning breezes from the windcatchers carved into every level of the tower, but that wind brings sounds of battle and desperation: steel clashing and cries of pain, the shaking of stone and ecstatic force. Iriset dashes to the wide spiral stairs up and up along the outer edge of the tower. Her bare toes hardly touch the limestone bricks, and her fingers skim along the smooth white stucco walls, until she spills up into the blue landing.

Untouched yet with violence, the landing is a small sitting area with two levels: one of perfect mosaic tiles in the shapes of blue gentians, the second layered with rugs and pillows in every shade of blue beside a huge lattice window spanning nearly half the entire curved wall. The glittering lattice snakes that usually wind through the cutouts, soaking in sunlight, are nowhere to be seen. Hiding, she hopes, sparing another brief thought for her poor dead spiders.

Iriset sits hard on the second level and pulls on her pantaloons, knotting them around her waist under her robe, and adjusts the laces at her ankles. She shoves her arms into the short jacket and ties it under her breasts, but loosely in case she needs to run or scream or fight. Finally, she pins the red silk mask to her hair, tucking it up so that a quick tug will let it fall over her eyes.

By now Iriset hears voices just below, methodical and ordered: soldiers searching the levels of the tower.

She stands. Through the soles of her feet she feels the tower's architecture trip and startle. Fear disrupts her body's design, an influx of ecstatic energy. She's unused to being afraid under either name she's used: Safe as Isidor's daughter, coddled by murderers and thieves. Safe as Silk, too, thanks to her own skills and the Little Cat's favor. Now Iriset needs to balance her inner design for calm. Fear serves nothing once its warning is made.

Hard boots clomp up the stairs to the landing.

She is Iriset mé Isidor, and even in his absence she will make her father proud.

Her father, so tough and sly he rules the Moonshadow City undermarket. He is slight and wiry, hardly larger than her, yet he commands respect through his reputation and deeds. He would not give Iriset sympathy, were he here, but snap at her to lift her chin and face the consequences of their choices with eyes clear. Wear her mask demurely, be what he needs her to be in that moment—a daughter sheltered and no threat to the empire. Keep her criminal identity secret. Survive what comes next so that she can make better, slyer choices in the future.

Just as the first soldier's head appears in the well, Iriset jerks the red edge of her mask down. It brushes her nose and falls just to her lips.

The world turns hazy red as she peers through the thin silk.

The soldier's own cloth mask wraps tight around their hair and face, leaving only a slit for their eyes, a blatant white that continues down in a uniform of lacquered armor over a short white robe and pants and thick boots: all clearly displaying the crimson splatter of their work. Their short sword is dark with smears of it. Behind them come more soldiers, identical in uniform and size, who stop around Iriset in a half ring. One says, in an impatient fem-forward voice, "Who are you, girl?" The speaker's eyes are black, the slit of skin visible a darker brown than her companions'. None are the mirané brown of Moonshadow's ruling ethnicity.

"Iriset mé Isidor," she says boldly.

"The Little Cat has a *daughter*?" one of the other soldiers says.

Iriset doesn't move.

The woman soldier darts a hand out and Iriset recoils, expecting a slap, but the woman only rips the mask off her face.

Anger flushes rising force up her spine, and Iriset struggles not to show it. If this woman will not give her the little respect of the mask, what else might be taken from her?

"Get her out of here," the commanding soldier says, and her soldiers obey with grabbing, hard hands, dragging Iriset down the spiral stairs.

orbit

Follow us:

f /orbitbooksUS

X /orbitbooks

▶ /orbitbooks

Join our mailing list
to receive alerts on our
latest releases and deals.

orbitbooks.net

Enter our monthly
giveaway for the chance
to win some epic prizes.

orbitloot.com